FAERIES
CANDACE ROBINSON
OF
AMBER R. DUELL
OZ
the complete series

FAERIES OF OZ

LION

TIN

CROW

OZMA

TIK-TOK

For anyone who ever wanted to visit Oz

LION

PREQUEL SHORT STORY

CHAPTER ONE

LION

Green light coated everything in the Emerald City twice a day—once at dawn and again at dusk. Lion avoided stepping out during those times if he could help it. He hated that it made everything look sickly, but a summons from the Wizard of Oz was never optional. Though, if Lion were being honest, a gnarled troll banging on his door when it was nearly dark was intriguing. He rarely had visitors, and if he did, they were *never* from Oz's personal guard. Things had become far too monotonous since the Wizard marred Tin's face with iron— even the cursed pixies that tortured the residents calmed down after that stunt—but perhaps that was about to change.

Lion had his courage.

What he needed was something to do with it.

The troll led him through freezing green glass corridors. His footsteps echoed through the dim hall, then again off the impossibly high ceiling, as they made straight for Oz's private chambers. Two expressionless elves guarded a massive, scrolled doorway. When the troll approached, the elves swung the doors open without a word. The moment Lion was inside—they slammed the entrance shut again. With a scowl, Lion tucked his long blond hair behind his ears and scanned the seemingly empty bedroom. His top lip lifted in disgust as the putrid smell hit him like a stone wall.

The bed was bare, a single blanket and stained pillow tossed haphazardly onto the mattress. Feathers spilled from a few holes and garbage littered the floor. The room itself was opulent—hanging crystal lighting, floor-to-ceiling windows, hand-crafted furniture. The emeralds and diamonds embedded in the headboard had to cost more than Lion's entire home. Dark curtains hung crookedly from their rods. The embroidery was stitched with mermaid hair and embellished with crystallized nixie tears, but the sparkle of both was hidden beneath a thick layer of dust.

Lion's boot crunched over a slice of moldy, stale bread, but that was the least of the food problems. Rotting fruit cores were scattered around the room, the sickly scent permeating the air. *What the hell happened in here?* Surely there was a mistake. Oz couldn't have gotten this bad with his faerie fruit addiction without someone interfering on his behalf...

"Wizard?" Lion called, his tail flicking nervously behind him.

Something banged on the other side of the bed followed by a soft *oof.* "Lion!" Oz's head popped up over the far side of the bed, scratching his scabbed scalp. The unmistakable gleam of red faerie fruit juice glistened on his lips when he gave a smile full of blackened teeth. His thinning white hair stuck up at different angles as if he hadn't brushed it in days, and his wrinkled skin had taken on a yellow hue. "You made good time getting here."

Lion ventured farther into the room with a cocked eyebrow. "Is everything okay?"

"Of course. Why wouldn't it be?"

"Have you fired the maids?" Lion asked carefully.

"Those spies! Good riddance. Always poking through my things." He flung a small suitcase onto his mattress. "Hand me that map, would you?"

Lion glanced at the partially unfolded paper Oz pointed at on the end table. Circles with symbols he didn't know how to read dotted the fae countries north of the Land of Oz. "Are you going to a diplomatic meeting?"

Oz snapped his fingers anxiously until Lion handed the map to him. "Just a trip. Nothing to worry about."

Lion shifted suspiciously. "Am I to come along?"

"What? No. I'm going on my own. Guards would only get in the way." Oz shot him a withering look. "Why would I bring you with me, of all people?"

"Why would you summon me?" Lion asked. Oz hadn't bothered him since Dorothy returned to Kansas. Lion was gifted a cozy cottage inside the city and a small stipend for his part in killing the Wicked Witch, Reva, but that was the last personal interaction they had. "It's been years since we've seen each other."

Oz's hands shook as he stared into his closet where his clothes were stuffed haphazardly. He murmured under his breath about foreign weather and something called *galoshes*. Lion scowled. How much fruit had he eaten today?

"Wizard," he said in a stern voice. "Why am I here?"

Oz blinked and looked at Lion as if he'd forgotten he had company. "Right. Yes. I have a quest for you, but the walls have ears."

Lion looked around at the glimmering green wallpaper with its swirling pattern of leaves. That was either another strange human saying—because there were no ears—or Oz's addiction to faerie fruit was worse than anyone feared.

"Go to Langwidere. Tell her I'll legitimize her rule of the West now that Reva's dead, if she…" Oz jerked into a crouch as if something had flown at his head. "I've written it all down. Names and locations. Everything you'll need, it's there … in the top drawer."

Lion moved slowly as he tugged on the round knob and picked up an envelope with his name on it. Part of him wanted to put it back and leave, but he couldn't help being curious. If the letter contained the ramblings of a madman, perhaps he could use it to blackmail the Wizard into taking him on the trip. An adventure would do him some good and Oz clearly needed someone to go with him for his own safety.

"It's vital you finish this before I return," Oz said.

Lion cracked the wax seal and scanned the letter with a pounding heart. "You're not serious?"

"Completely."

Lion licked his lips. Tin was the killer—not him. Not to mention that the people Tin assassinated were much less important than the name on this paper, and their deaths had earned the woodsman an iron scar. "You're not thinking clearly."

"I am!" Spittle rained from Oz's mouth. "Oz is changing. If we don't remold it to our advantage then our enemies will."

Our. Lion bristled. There was no *our.* Oz had no use for him before today, and now he wanted him to act as a hired gun. Lion hadn't worked so hard for his courage to waste it on a good for nothing addict. If he was going to kill an important figure, it would be because he got something out of it. Something he'd been searching for since Dorothy, Tin, and Crow left him alone in the Emerald City: a person to need him. And not only because he was convenient at the moment, but really and truly *needed* him. The only way for Lion to secure that kind of devotion was to give something no one else could give.

Lion smiled to himself as he slipped the envelope into the back pocket of his tan pants. "Consider it taken care of."

CHAPTER TWO

LANGWIDERE

Langwidere cherished her heads more than anything. Heads. Heads. *Heads*. She loved them blonde, loved them even more brunette, loved them red, loved them with perky noses, rosebud lips, arched eyebrows. She switched them out like she did her frilly white dresses. And when she grew tired and bored of them, Langwidere buried the heads beneath the dirt, burned them to ashes, or sank them to the bottom of the ocean.

The Wicked Witch of the West—Reva—was dead. The Wicked Witch of the East—Inora—was dead. Both had died at the hands of the same human girl—one melted by magic, the other crushed by the girl's house. The witches got what they'd deserved because neither one was ever fit to rule, just as Glinda—the Good Witch of the South—wasn't. She'd loathed Glinda and her insufferably deluded optimism for as long as she could remember.

Langwidere had made a visit to see Locasta, the "Good" Witch of the North, to make a deal to divide the territories between the two of them once she'd discovered the intruder—Dorothy—had melted Reva. The truth was, Locasta was never good—she had secrets of her own locked and buried away.

Locasta was just as bad as Langwidere, and if Langwidere didn't respect the witch for her secretly wicked ways, she would've swiped her head. But Locasta's head didn't have the sort of beauty that Langwidere yearned for.

Now, her fingers twitched at the thought of collecting even more faces. She craved the feel of cleaning them up, wiping the blood away from their delicate skin, twisting their features into an expression that she wanted them to hold as they sat in their boxes and waited their turn to be worn.

As Langwidere gazed at her blonde wavy hair and pouty lips in the golden full-length mirror, she imagined the crown that would be atop her different hairstyles each day. But there was one problem still to solve. A nuisance. Glinda. Langwidere would need to get rid of the dopey witch so she could take over the South territory. And to achieve this, what she needed was a helper… Someone who would follow her lead…

She tapped several times at her dimpled chin then ran her hands down the lace of her dress. Oz would've been a good tool, but his body had grown too old and frail over the years. Besides, who knew how much longer he had to live. His mind was growing too forgetful from his addiction to faerie fruit, along with age. But alas, he was human after all—they all died in the end. Oz had been the perfect lover for a time—brainless, a follower, one who would eat the faerie fruit right out of her hand, lapping up each speck of juice from her palm, as she moved her naked hips against his.

Dropping her fingers from the front button of her dress, Langwidere focused on what needed to be done, and she removed her head from atop her neck. Holding it in between her fingers, she could still see by maintaining skin contact. She gazed up at the row of silver and ivory cabinets with clear glass displaying her collection. Even without her head attached, she was still beautiful with a willowy body, luscious breasts, a narrow waist, and soft pale skin. Every single inch of her was perfect in every single way—she knew this because she explored it with her hands each chance she got.

Opening an empty glass case in the middle, Langwidere placed her spent head inside, the world growing dark as she released her touch on it. She shut the glass and felt around for the case beside it, turning the bumpy knob. Langwidere pressed her palms inside and as soon as her fingertips brushed the fluffy curls of one of her beauties, sight came barreling back. Smiling, she brought the head toward her after shutting the case.

With a soft click, she adjusted the new head atop her neck. Each head contained a silver rounded disc at its base, as did her neck, so the attachment was flawless. She then wrapped a black ribbon around her throat to hide the thin line.

"There," she murmured as her new emerald eyes met her image. In the glass sat a beautiful heart-shaped face with freckles, a button of a nose, and thick obsidian curls, falling just past her shoulders.

A heavy knock came at her front door, making her jump a fraction, interrupting *her* moment. Letting out an irritated sigh, Langwidere sauntered out of the room and down the hall as the skirts of her dress swished. All she could think about was how several of her cases were empty, and how she needed more heads to fill them. Ones that she could watch with pleasure, that she wouldn't grow bored of. She would find the missing silver slippers, and she *would* take all the territories.

Her heels clicked across the hard-emerald floor before coming to a stop in front of the jewel-covered oval door. She pulled it open. To her astonishment, there stood a male—bare-chested, with long, wavy blond hair and wearing a fur-lined cloak resembling a lion's mane. She knew who this was right away— she knew what he did to help a little girl take care of Reva—she knew how gullible he could be. He would be the perfect specimen, the one she now didn't have to look for, the one who would do what she wanted in her bed as well as out of it.

"And what brings you to my home, Lion?"

CHAPTER THREE

LION

Lion's smile oozed charm and confidence. The Wizard had told him that Langwidere was a fae of many faces, but he neglected to mention how attractive the rest of her was. He didn't bother to hide his examination of her body before meeting her eyes again. The old Lion wouldn't have known what to do with himself.

"The tales of your beauty hold true, Lady Langwidere," Lion said with honesty.

She folded her arms. "Don't tell me something I know full well. I asked what brought you here."

"Oz ordered me to come and I owed him a favor." Lion stepped closer to the threshold and attempted to touch Langwidere's curls. She flicked his hand away. "Let me in so we can chat."

"Your newfound courage has made you foolish, Lion. Why would I let an enemy into my home?"

Lion looked up at her from beneath his lashes. "Are you so sure I'm your enemy?"

Langwidere's full lips turned into a frown. "You helped the mortal girl. It was very difficult to deal with Locasta after the human killed Reva, and it almost cost me the West."

"Sorry about that." Lion wasn't sorry. Not even a little bit. Lion was glad to leave his cowardly ways behind, no matter the cost, and he'd do the same to *keep* his valor. "Oz may have a solution to your territory problems, if it would please you to listen…?"

Langwidere scoffed but stepped aside. "This better be good."

Lion grinned and turned to maintain eye contact as he sauntered inside. "All of my ideas are good," he told her and licked his lower lip.

"I thought this was Oz's idea?" She glared at Lion, unamused, then stepped forward and picked up a lock of his hair. Her face softened. "Such a lovely color."

"I—"

"Shh." Langwidere's index finger landed on Lion's lips. It stayed only a moment before she traced each angle of his face with exaggerated slowness. Her eyes glazed over as she examined every inch of skin, from his neck up.

"Do you like what you see?" Lion inquired as she lightly skimmed his long eyelashes.

"Tsk." Langwidere dropped her hand to her side and her eyes cleared. "It's too bad I only wear female heads. Yours would do quite nicely."

Lion smirked at the compliment. "Then you'll just need to keep me around to appreciate my beauty."

Langwidere narrowed her eyes at his confidence and spun on her heel to lead the way into a large room with high ceilings. A plush white carpet was settled over emerald flooring and gold filigree coated the walls. Between the molded leaves, faces stared out. There were elves and fauns and centaurs—every kind of fae was represented at least once, with one thing in common: open-mouthed, wide-eyed terror. The hair on Lion's arms lifted and he tore his eyes away to take in the rest of the room.

The only piece of furniture was a gold high-backed chair with a white velvet cushion. With a snap of Langwidere's fingers, bright orange flames sparked to life in a pit set in the center of the room. The faces on the wall seemed to glow as the flames danced across the filigree, but Lion forced himself not to look.

"A throne," Lion commented.

Langwidere circled the fire once before sitting down. She crossed her legs and propped her elbows on the arms of the chair. "As any queen would have."

Lion approached the fire and held his hands out to warm himself after traveling from the Emerald City. Early spring had left him with a deep chill. "Queen of what, my lady? You may have taken control of the West after Dorothy killed Reva, but Glinda still rules the South. That's what you *really* want, isn't it? Without the South, how will you ever have enough power to take the rest of Oz from Locasta?"

Langwidere wrapped her fingers around the ends of the chair. "Is that what Oz told you?"

"No." Lion looked across the flames at her, sitting so regally with someone else's head on her shoulders. "I wasn't the fae without a brain, dearest Langwidere. It's easy enough to see your intentions and you can be sure that I'm not the only one. Which is why I think you should take the Wizard up on his proposal."

Her eyes narrowed. "You tread on thin ice."

"That's half the fun."

"Out with it before I toss you from my home," she warned.

Lion let his arms drop back to his sides. "Oz is succumbing to his love of faerie fruit—which I'm not to tell you but I'm sure you know as you're rumored to be the one who got him addicted to it. He's losing his grip on the capital right along with his mind. Without the Emerald City, he holds no sway over the territories or their leaders."

A small smirk graced her lips. "I fail to see the problem with this."

"Nor do I. We never should've allowed a mortal to rule over fae lands, which is why you should accept his offer."

"You make no sense, Lion."

He grinned widely, proud of his plan. "He wants you to acquire a new head. A specific *powerful* head that belongs to someone who won't fall in line. In exchange, he will legitimize your claim to the West."

"Will he?" Langwidere's laugh bounced off the walls. "It's already mine with or without his acceptance."

"Yes." Lion's wicked grin grew, showing his perfectly white teeth. "But if you appear to fail the job Oz gave you, with the simple change of a head, you could take a territory without anyone being the wiser."

Langwidere leaned forward. "And what would you get out of this?"

"You, obviously." When Langwidere opened her mouth, outrage written on her face, he held up a hand to stop her. "I want to be valued for my service. Use me, my lady. Make yourself a queen and me your knight."

The crackle of the fire was the only sound in the room. Lion knew this was a long shot. Langwidere's loyalties were largely unknown, other than to herself. There was an equal chance she'd tell Oz of his betrayal as there was of her accepting his help. He was banking on her seeing the genius of his plan. Fail in appearance only and gain both a territory and a new head.

With a sharp clap, Langwidere summoned a servant. A young female on all fours rolled into the room with wheels fused to her hands and feet. Her limbs were long and slender, her spine curved to accommodate her posture. A white ribbon, stained red with blood where it pierced her skin, sealed her mouth shut. How did she eat? Lion's stomach twisted as the female's pink irises focused on her master. She was no servant—she was a slave. And he'd just offered himself into Langwidere's control.

"Show Lion to a guest chamber. Make sure he feels at home until I decide what to do with him."

Lion tore his gaze away from the slave and gave Langwidere a playful smile. This would be a test of wills. He didn't want power for himself—that was too much responsibility—he simply wanted to be close to power. To be needed and important now that he had the courage to become someone of note. He only hoped it would be worth it.

CHAPTER FOUR

LANGWIDERE

So Lion wanted to be her knight... This was making everything so much easier. It was as though all the heads were falling into place.

Langwidere would not only have the West but the South as well. And one day, not soon, she planned to take Locasta's territories, too. But for now, she would need to build little by little, and take it slowly.

She gazed at the male before her, wondering if he could truly pass her test. Lion's beauty could spin tales, but she'd also heard of his cowardice. Had he truly gained the courage that would be required?

"I'm tired of wearing this," Langwidere said in a bored tone. *New day, new head.* "Come, Lion. We must prove your worth."

He nodded, shifting his stance, his golden eyes seeming to dance beneath the light. "Of course we must."

Pivoting on her heels, Langwidere walked down the hallway, her ivory dress swishing against her legs. Lion followed behind her, too close, almost predatory. He was lucky he wasn't female because his face was one of the most beautiful she'd ever seen. But there were plenty of other ways he'd be beneficial—instead of wearing him one way, she could wear him another. His skin pressed against hers.

The rows of curio cabinets slipped into view, all the heads at the same angle and position. Their expressions were all the same, frozen, lifeless, until their flesh connected with Langwidere's.

Langwidere whirled to face Lion, pressing her hand to his cheek. "Choose one you like." She was curious as to what his type was. Would he select one that had raven-colored hair like she originally used to have, or something the color of wheat? Perhaps one with a button nose or freckles? Did he prefer full or thin lips?

She thought about her original head, the one she'd burned to ash once she'd collected her first prize to replace the old. The kill had come from a fae before the female was to be married, already dressed in a white gown. On Langwidere's body, the head appeared much better—as did the white dress. After that, Langwidere no longer had to think about her disfigurements of her original face—the uneven eyes, the missing nose, the crooked mouth.

He cocked his head and scanned the cabinets. "I like them all."

"If you could have only one for a night, whose lips would you want yours pressed against." She tapped her fingers against her thigh, waiting for him to choose wrong.

Lion sauntered around the room, his tail swinging back and forth. He looked at each face before lifting his index finger and pointing to the glass to his left. "That one." It was a female with porcelain skin, ruby red lips, and thick black curls. Hair like she used to have. He'd made the right choice.

"If you are to be my knight," Langwidere said, inching toward the glass, "next time you answer me right away."

"I will."

"Zo!" Langwidere called as she opened the glass, then she turned to Lion's confused face. "The Wheeler who was in here earlier. I took her and the others from the border near the Deadly Desert, and now they're mine."

"Such extravagant … creatures."

Zo rolled to a stop, silent forever by the string in her mouth. The string was sewn in by Langwidere of course. But the Wheelers willingly volunteered.

"Zo, can you bring Lion a white robe?"

She nodded and pushed away on her oversized arms and legs.

Lion arched a perfect blond brow. "A robe?"

"You'll see." Langwidere opened the cabinet to her right and took off her head with a click. As she set it in its place, everything fell to darkness when her hands left the head. She felt her way back to the other open cabinet until her fingers brushed the thick curls.

Her sight came back to her as she cradled the head and set it in its proper place atop her neck. She blinked and blinked again as she focused on Lion who watched her in what looked to be awe. "How do I look?"

"Even more beautiful." And that was the sort of honesty that she yearned for.

The sound of Zo's wheels echoed down the hallway, growing closer and closer. She came to a halt in front of Lion, the robe draped across her back. As soon as he plucked it up, the Wheeler zoomed right off.

"Now"—Langwidere grinned—"I want you to get dressed … or undressed, then meet me in the back of my home." Without another word, Langwidere turned on her heels and left the room. She wandered down the long winding hallway to the very back room where she'd left the door shut.

She didn't have to wait long before Lion sauntered down the hallway, as though there was something new in his step.

"Ready?" Langwidere asked.

"Yes."

With a smile, she opened the door and slipped inside. Emerald fire lit up the entirety of the room, making it appear as though flames were dancing atop the walls.

A rustling came from the corner and Lion's gaze moved in that direction, catching sight of what Langwidere wanted him to see.

"What is this?" He continued to study the trembling female dressed in a thin white gown.

"A female fae I took from the Emerald City." Langwidere shrugged. "I saw her dancing and spinning, such lithe movements, such a unique face. Her freckles are like their own constellation. I *need* her. Or rather, I need her head."

"For your collection?" Lion nodded. "I understand."

Langwidere remembered how she'd first heard about Lion—it was because he'd helped the human girl—Dorothy—on a quest. That girl had been the one to defeat two powerful witches of Oz.

"So you were friends with Dorothy, part of the party who defeated Reva?"

"More like acquaintances. We helped each other get what we needed and then said goodbye. Nothing more." He paused. "Besides, our world has gotten worse because of her."

"Perhaps if she ever returns, I shall wear her head."

"Perhaps. Dorothy did desert Oz, after all."

Langwidere would never do that. She would conquer and she would stay, for as long as her immortality allowed her to.

"When was the last time you were with another, my courageous Lion?" She brought her hand to his cheek and stroked his flawless skin with her thumb.

Straightening his spine, his eyes met hers and gleamed with pride. "Never."

Lion's answer surprised and intrigued her. She felt pity for him, because he'd been so cowardly that he couldn't even bring himself to lay with another. "Perhaps I'll give you a reward if you finish this task."

His brows drew closer together as he studied her face. "What task?"

"If you're to be my knight, then you're going to have to prove your loyalty." Langwidere grabbed the sword from against the wall and pressed it into Lion's strong hands, then turned him to face the fae. "Now, show me just how brave you are."

CHAPTER FIVE

LION

Lion didn't need to be told twice. He'd been waiting for a chance to prove himself since Oz gave him courage. Sword gripped tightly in hand, his lips curled in disgust, Lion approached the cowering female fae. Death was inevitable—she should accept it with dignity.

"You'll look better on her body," he said with venom.

Then he swung.

The female's scream was cut short as the blade passed cleanly through her neck. Hot blood splattered onto Lion's chest. Red splashed across the corner of the room like a macabre painting, while the body slumped on the tiled floor.

Langwidere stepped around him and knelt beside the blood-slicked head. "It's a clean cut." She lifted the head by the hair and studied the wide nose and strong jawline. "Perhaps there's hope for you after all."

Lion's chest swelled with pride. "I'm happy to be of service."

Langwidere smiled wickedly at him before setting the head into a waiting box with a wet thump. She took a moment to lovingly brush the hair off the dead fae's forehead then settled the top over it. When she turned, flicking blood from her fingertips, a wild look flashed in her eyes.

"Take off the robe," she told Lion.

He obeyed instantly and stood tall as she drank in his naked body from a few feet away. This time, he wouldn't shy away from a good fuck. "Am I pleasing enough for you?"

"Don't be cocky," she chided. Her gaze fell to his crotch at the last word.

Lion grinned, smug. "And your gown, my queen?"

"Not yet." She spoke slowly as she sauntered up to him. "You have to earn the sight of my body."

Lion stared at Langwidere's white dress as if he could see through it if he tried hard enough. His cock swelled as he caught the hint of her curves. His eyes traveled up to hers and held her lusty gaze, daring her to look lower with an arched brow.

Langwidere moved closer until there was only an inch between their bodies. Her hand, still covered in blood, landed on his chest. She dragged it slowly over Lion's firm muscles, exploring, and his tail twitched in anticipation. The lower her hand dipped, the more his body shook, but Langwidere was careful not to touch the one thing he now desperately needed her to.

Perhaps she was waiting for him to make a move. To take charge and show her that he could be brave in more than one arena. He gripped her wrist as her hand slid up his side, then back down. Just as he was about to place her fingers on his hard cock, she snatched her wrist away and swatted the back of his hand.

"Presumptuous, aren't we?" She looked down for the first time then back up through her lashes. "Sit down."

Lion tilted his head, caught between amusement, confusion, and growing need, but he would play along. Give her what she wanted. *Control.* He would let her command him as any good knight would do.

So he sat down on top of his discarded robe, legs stretched out before him, and propped himself up with his palms. He stared up at Langwidere, waiting, as his cock throbbed in anticipation.

Langwidere moved slowly, purposely, showcasing her power

without lifting a finger. Her hands gripped the front of her dress and gradually hitched the fabric up. Lion stared hungrily as, inch by agonizing inch, her smooth legs appeared, and he licked his lips.

When Langwidere's hem reached her knees, she stopped and stood over Lion's legs. It felt like ages to Lion before she lowered herself. Longer still until she took his length inside her. His head fell back with a moan as she rode him without touching him anywhere else. *Good fucking lord.* Nothing had *ever* felt as good as this.

Lion wanted to bury his hands in her hair, his tongue in her mouth, but somehow he knew she wouldn't allow it. And he couldn't risk her stopping. He needed this—needed *her.* His breath came faster and faster. His pulse thundered. His hips shifted up so she took him at a deeper angle.

"Look at me," Langwidere commanded.

Lion obeyed. The way she stared at him made him groan again, his breath increasingly uneven. He wasn't going to last much longer. His release was building, building, building, and he clenched his jaw to hold it back. A moment later Langwidere cried out, her movements slowing as she climaxed, and he let himself go, too.

They both sat there, chests heaving, for a long minute. Then Langwidere stood, threw her skirts back down, and stalked back to the closed box. "I have to prepare my new head before it gets too old."

Lion glared at her in disbelief. "And me?"

"What about you?" She lifted the box and cradled it in her arms. "You've served your purpose today."

"Does this mean—"

"I'm still considering your offer," she said.

"But..."

Langwidere stalked to the door and paused. "I'm pleased with you so far. Don't ruin it."

Lion laughed quietly. She was going to agree—he could sense it—but she had to make a show of it. Had to be the one in charge. That was fine with him, as long as he was needed and important. With his plan, that wouldn't be a problem. "Yes, my queen," he replied.

CHAPTER SIX

LANGWIDERE

Langwidere continued to teach Lion her lessons. Each day, she had him remove another's head. It was more than usual, but he needed to learn the proper technique to make sure her new heads remained undamaged. She'd have him discard the old ones she didn't feel the need to wear anymore—usually in the ocean or beneath the dirt. Then she'd reward him with another fuck.

For someone new to the art of pleasure, he excelled at it, more than she'd expected. Before him, Oz had been an exceptional lover, but that was because the faerie fruit enhanced the urge for humans to obey *her* better, but not Lion. He didn't need to be under influence, because she was naturally his drug, and he was a generous and obedient lover.

Langwidere straightened her dress as her eyes roamed Lion's glorious body drenched in sweat. This time she let him be behind her, plowing into her over and over until she couldn't control herself from shouting his name.

"Now, get dressed." She ran the tip of her finger slowly from his clavicle bone to right under his belly button, his cock already hardening again. "We'll be leaving after you and the others place everything into the carriage." Leaning forward, she purred at his ear, "Be extra careful loading the new case. It's large enough to hold a head with a crown."

Langwidere was tempted to take him for another round, or this time have his head between her legs again, but they could do that while traveling in the carriage. She had more important things to do right then.

Lion pulled on his trousers and boots, leaving his shirt off as she liked. His golden eyes met hers and she touched the side of his cheek. "You've pleased me more than I could've wished for. Now, gather the trunks into the carriage. Then we'll load the heads." All the trunks were filled with her ivory dresses. Langwidere wouldn't dare to leave them behind unless she grew tired of her need for them individually. Ivory brought out her complexion better than any other one, and the color represented perfection.

As Lion obeyed and lifted the trunks near the front door, Langwidere wandered to her now-empty cabinets of heads. It was strange seeing them this way. They had never *not* had anything inside, except for when she'd first started.

A squeak of wheels came barreling up behind her. Zo picked up her wheels, softly batting them at the floor, wanting to know if Langwidere needed her for anything. "You will gather the others and follow us to the new place. There, you will be first guard and in charge of the rest of the Wheelers. I'm going to put you and the others to good use."

Zo nodded, her nostrils flaring, eyes wide. She was silently thanking her. Zo and the others appreciated what Langwidere had done to them—they had to, or she would've thrown them all into the Deadly Desert, then watched them turn to sand.

As Zo wheeled out of the room, Lion turned the corner and came to a halt in front of Langwidere, his muscular chest glistening under the light.

Damn him, she couldn't help herself. "Take it out."

In answer, he slid his cock from his pants, already hard. His golden eyes appeared thrilled by what was to come next.

"Pump it for me," she demanded.

"As you wish." He obeyed thoroughly, stroking slowly at

first.

"Now"—she stepped closer—"have you told me all your secrets?"

"Every last one."

"Since Oz only wanted me as a tool, is there anything about that bastard you're leaving out?" Did Oz truly believe that he could pick someone to use her? Langwidere was the master at control, and he just so happened to pick someone who would fit perfectly with her. Oz was nothing but a halfwit.

Lion's hand increased its pace as he remained watching her. "Before I left, there was a map."

"What kind of map?" What was the imbecile planning now? He was fine with giving up his hold on the Emerald City for some reason. And perhaps this map had to do with it.

"I don't know," he groaned. "It was a drawing of the Land of Oz, all the deserts surrounding it, and the outer layers of Oz. But there were several strange markings on the outer layers, and the territory of Ev was circled in red."

Langwidere tapped at her chin and noticed there was crimson staining her gown from the head she'd collected earlier. "That old dolt is up to something."

"I'll kill him for you," Lion gasped.

"Perhaps one day." She watched Lion's hand move faster. "Now stop."

His hand immediately halted, and he didn't even beg for release. He truly was learning well.

"You'll come when I say you can." Since he'd played all the cards right, it was time for her to reward him. The blood staining her dress couldn't have come at a better time. She pressed her hand near the first button at her clavicle bone and unclasped. Lion licked his lips. Then she did the next and the next, exposing her plump breasts, her nipples pebbling. Finally, she let her dress drift to the floor. It would need to be buried since the blood would never come out.

"Say it," she said as she sauntered toward him, swaying her naked hips, knowing she was as beautiful as he. Lion was permanent, she could already tell. Her executioner and her lover.

"Please," he begged, voice rough, desperate.

She lowered herself to her knees, something she never did for anyone. But he was unlike anyone she'd ever had control of. Gripping his firmness tightly in her hand, she could feel the throb against her palm.

"I love you," he rasped.

"Of course you do. I can be what, and whoever, anyone wants." Langwidere then slipped his length inside her mouth to provide him the pleasure that would satisfy them both before they started their journey. Together, they would take over the South, and one day, she would be queen of *all* of Oz.

TIN

BOOK 1

CHAPTER ONE

TIN

Tin picked absently at the dried blood on his iron-tipped gloves. Day had turned to night with no sign of his target. Lord save the ugly bastard if he was off killing the brownie who'd hired him. She still owed Tin half his money, payable only when the dwarf's head was delivered. The dwarf was as good as dead either way, if only because Tin was stuck perched in the damn tree for so long, but he was a professional.

And professionals got paid.

With an exaggerated huff, Tin pried his iron axe from where it was imbedded in the tree near his head. An unusual weapon for a faerie, but he had long ago embraced the pain of iron. He had no choice, really—it was that or go mad. Almost as mad as this dwarf was making him. It was no wonder someone wanted the miner dead.

A light-skinned sprite landed on the branch just above him, all spindly limbs and unkempt hair. She seemed oblivious to Tin's presence as she plucked delicate white leaves from the otherwise-green foliage and tucked them into a little basket on her arm. Her wings shook, golden pollen raining down.

Tin jerked away from the shimmering powder before it landed in his long silver hair, and snatched the sprite in a blindingly fast motion. The tiny creature shrieked inside his closed fist, then fell silent as he tightened his grip until bones crunched.

"Nasty creature," he spat, though sprites weren't particularly bothersome, and unfurled his fingers. Bits of sprite coated his gloved hand. He brushed it off the best he could, wiping the remnants on his pants.

The sprite's innards weren't the only relic of a kill to adorn his clothing. Kelpie scales were artfully sewn into his dark clothing for extra protection, and the small rings holding the right side of his hair back were whittled from their blackened bones.

A low whistle sounded in the distance, the tune cheerful and carefree. Tin gripped his axe tighter and leapt lithely from the tree, landing silently in the grass. He edged around the wide trunk and peered in the direction of the lighthearted song.

The dwarf he'd been waiting for crested the hill with a massive pack strapped to his back. Over his shoulder, a pickaxe was visible in the moonlight, the handle tucked safely away. His hands were empty. Good. It was annoying when they fought back.

Tin held his breath and watched his mark close the distance between them. The dwarf had a gnarled beard, ratty, knotted black hair, and a bulbous nose, all of which were coated in dark powder from the mineral mines. Suddenly, Tin regretted not bringing a bag to carry the head in. Mineral powder was even harder to wash from around the kelpie scales than pixie dust. Alas…

The dwarf was still whistling his merry tune when Tin leapt from his hiding place, axe swinging. His mark flailed and his heavy pack pulled him backward where he landed in a heap. "Wait! I—"

His eyes went wide and he sucked in a breath as the moonlight flashed over Tin's face. The mark of shame—or as Tin thought of it, his badge of honor—was known in every corner of Oz. The Wizard had taken *pity* on him after Tin's heart turned back into stone. Instead of being sentenced to death for assassinating eleven fae lords, he'd been branded. Shackled and bound, he'd been unable to escape as liquid iron was dripped slowly onto the side of his face. Each drop had landed at the edge of his cheekbone where it scalded a path across his skin. By the time it was finished and the iron cooled, Tin had been left with a design of wild, twisting silver lines that covered nearly half his right cheek.

"Have mercy," the dwarf begged.

Tin grinned savagely. The Wizard should've killed him. "There is no mercy in this world."

"Why?" the dwarf asked in a cracking voice. "I've done nothing!"

"Everyone has done *something*."

Tin swung his axe, severing the target's head before he could scream. He bent, fisting the dingy hair. Bright red blood gushed from the neck as he lifted the proof of his work. As he sauntered back toward the brownie's house to collect the rest of his fee, leaving a red trail in his wake, he whistled the end of the dwarf's song.

Firelight and music reached the brownie's cave from the nearby village. When Tin arrived, he found the old female atop a rock outside the opening, swaying to the song as she waited for him. Thin wisps of white hair floated around her molting head. Toenails curled over the ends of her feet. Age spots marked her olive skin, just as red stripes decorated her loose dress.

"You're late," she snapped.

"What do you care? He's dead." Tin threw the bloody head at the brownie, nearly knocking the portly faerie off the rock. This job was too far below his skill-set—and his pay grade—for him to put up with snide comments.

"I hired you to kill him *before* sundown."

Tin cracked his neck. It would be more profitable to kill the brownie and take whatever valuables she owned. She was ancient and barely came to his knee—it would be easy—but if he began killing his clientele, no one would seek him out. It was already hard enough finding work outside of the Emerald City. Country folk weren't much in the way of intrigue like those in the capital, but they made up for it with their ruthlessness. If the fae here didn't take care of their own problems, no one would.

The brownie must've sensed the shift in Tin's thoughts because she made a show of checking the validity of the head. "Fine. It's done." She reached down the front of her dress for a small bag. She pretended to weigh it in her hands before tossing it at his feet. "This concludes our business, assassin."

He caught the bag with the toe of his boot just before it landed in the dirt. It took every ounce of his meager self-control not to lunge for her throat. Tin opened the bag to be sure it was full of diamonds and not pebbles, though he was confident the brownie wasn't stupid enough to swindle him. The last person who'd tried that ended up impaled.

Satisfied, he turned on his heel and walked toward the town for a well-deserved drink. If he could find a room for the night, and someone to buy the gemstones off him before he moved to the next town, all the better.

Glimpses of fae flashed through the trees as he neared the edge of the clearing. Vivid, gem-colored fabric swirled around their lithe bodies. The firelight caressed exposed skin, some pale, some dark, some flecked with scales and others with feathers. Ribbons tied to posts lifted and fell in time with their flawless movements.

It seemed a nightly ritual in this part of Oz to greet the dawn with dance, which meant they would be at it all night. He'd never stepped foot in this particular town and wasn't sure what their reaction to him might be. Sometimes they called for his head, other times they hid inside and bolted the doors. Often it was a mixture of both. Whatever the response to his iron scars, Tin didn't much care unless it created extra work for himself.

Tin touched the rings in his hair without meaning to. He refused to hide his face, even if it made things easier, so he dropped his hand and strode straight into the town and through the party. The dancers faltered as they noticed him. Hooves ceased stomping, wings stilled, and soon the music sputtered out as well.

Tin made an exaggerated bow and held his breath. When no one screamed or made to attack, Tin dodged the decorative floating balls of light on his way to the tavern. It was better to hurry before they made up their minds on how to respond. The sign for the Peppered Pike hung crooked over the door in elvish writing. He steeled himself for the owner to give him the boot the moment he stepped inside, but he could really do with a night in an actual bed. Right after a drink.

Inside, the tavern was empty save for a female wiping down the bar. Two ribbed horns circled the sides of her head and her dark hair was styled to run parallel with them. "Welco—" Her words cut off as her gaze met his, recognizing him immediately.

Tin did his best to give her a reassuring smile but the iron distorted half of it. "Do you have any rooms?"

The girl shifted back warily. "We're … closed … during the…"

He didn't mention that she'd started to welcome him before she looked up. Instead, he pulled out one of the larger diamonds and held it in the center of his palm. Her eyes grew impossibly wide at the sight of all the fresh blood on his glove.

Shit. Diamond or no diamond, he knew she was five seconds away from bolting.

"Give the man a room, sweetmeat."

Tin froze at the familiar voice—one he blissfully hadn't heard in years—and eyed the alcohol behind the bar. "What are you doing here, Lion?"

"Good. You remember who I am," he said with a chuckle. "Join me."

The last time Tin saw the bastard was at his hearing, when

Lion was called as a witness against him. For all the courage Lion gained, it had only made him a fool. Tin ground his teeth together and turned to face the other fae. Lion was exactly as he remembered: coarse golden hair tied in a low ponytail, bronze skin, and piercing golden eyes. The tuft at the end of his tawny tail skimmed the floor beside his boots. A fur cloak wrapping around Lion's broad shoulders made him appear even larger.

But, no matter how much bigger Lion was, Tin was certain he wasn't a threat. Lion had a heart, after all, even if it was darker than most, and that bloody organ made all creatures weak.

"What are you doing out of the South?" Tin growled.

Lion smirked arrogantly and flicked a look at the tavern girl, who let out a sharp gasp from behind the bar. "Another drink, if you wouldn't mind, and one for my friend."

"I asked you a question."

Lion rolled his eyes. "Stop being an ass and sit down."

Tin drew a slow, steady breath and reached for the axe at his hip.

"You're going to scare the lady," Lion warned coolly.

The hell if he cared. "I warned you. If I ever saw you again—"

"We're immortal, Tin. There's plenty of time to kill me. I have a job for you, so you may as well make your fortune first."

Fortune. Tin kept his hand on his axe but didn't wield it. He didn't kill people because he needed money—he *liked* killing—but that wasn't to say that he didn't recognize its usefulness.

The horned female sat the drinks down on the table with shaking hands. Some of the foam splashed over the sides, landing on Lion's sleeve. He growled at her and she hurtled out the back door.

Once they were alone, Lion continued. "You remember Dorothy, don't you?"

Tin narrowed his eyes, his grip tightening on his weapon. It was rather hard to forget the little human girl who'd crashed into his life and set him on the path to self-destruction.

"Of course you remember the little bitch." Lion took a long

gulp of his drink, studying Tin over the rim of the glass. He nudged the empty chair across from him with his boot. Another invitation to sit.

This time, Tin accepted.

CHAPTER TWO

DOROTHY

Dorothy gripped the handle of the garden fork so hard that her palm would most likely bleed. With the tool and gritted teeth, she ripped a carrot from the dirt— then another and another and another. Her fierce actions were scarring the flesh of the vegetables, but she didn't care because she needed as many as possible.

Blowing out an exhausted breath, she stared at her aching hands—red and rubbed raw. She didn't mind the aches and pains. This farm had to survive, not only for her, but for Aunt Em and Uncle Henry. It had to.

Tears ran down her filthy cheeks, landing against her striped overalls as she thought about her aunt and uncle. Uncle Henry had been gone for five years now, and Aunt Em nine months. After Uncle Henry died from scarlet fever, most of the workers had left, and the farm's profits took a nose dive. The remaining workers had stopped showing up when Aunt Em passed from a heart attack. There was no way to make the business thrive with only Dorothy. Nobody in town wanted to work for Crazy Dorothy Gale. No one.

She fisted a carrot, fingernails digging into the vegetable as she thought of the place that everyone had told her didn't exist—

no matter how many times she screamed and yelled that it did. At times, she wasn't so sure what to believe anymore. A flash of emerald crawled into her thoughts and she closed her eyes, shutting out what Aunt Em had beaten into her head—it wasn't true.

"There's no place like home," she said through clenched teeth. "There's no place like home, Dorothy. Because this is the only place that's real. Oz never existed." She breathed heavily, remembering the needles, the pokes, the prods, the medicines, the shock therapy—all of it.

And still, the place lingered in her mind when she opened her eyes.

As Dorothy leaned back down to grab her shovel and return to the task she'd set for herself, a line of dust, farther out from the farm along the dirt road, filled the air with brown smoky clouds. She froze.

Dorothy recognized the black two-seater Roadster, and knew right away it was Jimmy. Time wasn't on her side anymore. Jimmy was a friend she'd known for years, but more importantly, he was the messenger for his father. His father, Glenn, had been trying to take the farm from under her feet for months. Dorothy had made the decision two weeks ago that the last way to possibly prevent the farm from being taken was to sleep with Jimmy. She liked him well enough, and she was desperate, but it was a terrible action on her part. A terrible action she'd repeated multiple times since then.

Brushing a dirt-covered hand across her forehead, Dorothy wiped away the beads of sweat that had collected, as best she could, and removed her sun hat. The hot ball of fire in the sky beat down against her tan skin as she watched Jimmy's car approaching from afar. In that moment, she wished so badly that Aunt Em was here. She had always been better at prolonging things than Dorothy.

The car came sputtering across the pebbled drive, past the wheat fields, and stopped in front of the foundation of the old porch. After the tornado had torn across everything with its windy paws, the rebuild hadn't gone easily, especially with the cost of supplies and labor. That had been the start of the farm's downfall.

As Jimmy stepped out from the car, she waited for her heart to speed up at the sight of him, wished she could make it thump harder. But she just couldn't fall in love with him, no matter how much he dreamed of her doing so, no matter how much she wanted to. He was nice and it would save her farm but the convenience would never be enough.

He took off his hat—displaying his neatly side-swept blond hair—and placed it at his chest while he moved toward her, as though he was prepared for a funeral. Dressed in an all-black suit, he seemed calm, but she noticed the rhythmic motions of his fingertips against his hat. She knew right then and there the news wasn't going to be good. It was a funeral, one for her home—a home she would have to leave, and never return to. She didn't know where she would go next. Back to the institution? That was where the town would try to send her anyway, even if Jimmy tried to stop them.

"Hello, Dorothy." Jimmy smiled, his pearly teeth shining under the sun.

"Hello, Jimmy." Dorothy tried to smile back, but she couldn't. Her heart did start pounding then, because she needed him to just spill the beans instead of hoarding them in his pocket.

Jimmy craned his neck and studied the pile of vegetables on the ground behind her. "You know you can't pluck all those carrots and save the farm." He wasn't being mean about it, only speaking the truth.

"I know." She sighed, taking a step closer to him so he could unharness the news.

"Then come with me." He dropped his hat on the grass and grasped her hands with his warm fingers, his sky-blue eyes catching hers. "Marry me."

Dorothy hesitated, thought about saying yes, since that would make things better. But it wouldn't be fair to Jimmy because she didn't love him like that. She had never loved him in the way that two hearts should be drawn together. Instead she'd made mistakes in her desperation and done things she shouldn't have. With all her being, she didn't mean to hurt him. "You know I can't..."

"Who else are you going to find to take care of you?" His hand skimmed the side of her face, cradling it.

"Why?" Dorothy tore herself away from him. "Because everyone in town thinks of me as Crazy Dorothy?" She pressed her finger to his chest, jabbing it in as deeply as she could, not caring that it was un-lady like. It may have been the 1920s, but sometimes this town felt as if it was trapped in centuries past. "You think I'm crazy, don't you? Besides, I can handle myself just fine."

"I don't think you're crazy, Dorothy." He looked defeated while worry lines etched into his forehead. "I just think you've had a hard time. When we were kids, after the tornado, and you said you'd come back from a faerie world called Oz, you changed. But just because you think something is real, and it isn't, that doesn't make you crazy."

Perhaps the missing piece of why her heart could never be his was because he'd never once believed that maybe her story was true. "I still can't marry you. The right girl is waiting out there for you. I know it."

Jimmy didn't say a single word as he studied the ground.

She couldn't handle the silence any longer. "Now just break it to me. What's to become of the farm? Is there any saving it?"

He scooped up his hat from the ground and placed it gingerly back on, then silently pursed his lips and shook his head. "No. My father isn't keeping it or I could have tried harder. It's worth more to auction off to a buyer." Glenn was lead at the bank, and Jimmy worked for him. But even with Jimmy pushing his father to help her out, it was no use. The farm was just in too much debt.

Reaching into his jacket pocket, he pulled out an off-white envelope and handed it to her. "I'm sorry, Dorothy. All it says is that the house will be claimed in two days. I really do wish my father would have listened to me." His hand pressed softly against her cheek again. "If you ever need a door open for you, mine will always be." He turned and walked away, his shoulders slumping a bit more than when he'd originally arrived.

"I'm sorry, too," she whispered to herself. Sorry he'd believed she would have loved him. Even then, she hated Glenn and wouldn't have wanted to see the man's face as her father-in-law. She silently hoped Jimmy would never turn out like his father, but something told her he'd always be a proper gentleman.

She watched the car back out and drive off, kicking up the dust of the road once more. She plummeted to her knees when she knew he could no longer see her. Dorothy should have asked Jimmy to stay with her a little longer, not as a lover, but a friend, the one who had always defended her in front of everyone. Yet Dorothy truly believed that deep, deep down in his heart, he thought her to be crazy, too. She wished *someone* believed her about her past.

Wicked Witch. Glinda. Slippers. Scarecrow. Lion. Tin Man. Emerald City. Home. She pressed her palms to her head and pushed as hard as she could, trying to shove away the thoughts of creatures that everyone told her weren't real. She screamed across the wheat and corn fields again and again until her voice cracked and her throat felt rough.

"It isn't real. It isn't real."

"It is real. It is real."

The silver slippers that had taken her back home hadn't been on her feet when she'd awoken ten years ago in the wheat field. If it was real, then where were they?

"Stop it!" But she couldn't control her spinning thoughts.

Leaving everything sprawled out across the ground, except for the shovel, she ran toward the house. Once she crossed the threshold, she stomped to the living room and smashed the shovel across the family portraits resting on the work bench, the paintings from the walls, the knickknacks on the shelves, then slammed the tool against the wooden table where no one ate but her. Fighting back her tears, Dorothy struck the wall, creating a large dent before tossing the shovel to the wood floor with a clang. "Why couldn't you two believe me?" she screamed to the ghosts of her aunt and uncle, wherever they were. "If you two loved me so much, then why couldn't you just listen to me!"

Dorothy didn't feel like eating, even though she'd slaughtered the last remaining pig that morning to prepare one final stew. Now, there were no animals left to worry about either. She'd sold all the chickens and cows in an attempt to save the farm. There was nothing left to sell anymore.

With heavy eyelids, she walked over broken glass and prepared a bath. She stripped herself of her dirty clothing and slumped down into the warm water. Closing her eyes, she repeated the words *there's no place like home*, until she drifted away, praying she would wake in the Land of Oz.

Something sounded, jolting Dorothy out of her deep dreamless world she'd entered. She'd fallen asleep in the bath—the water was no longer warm but freezing, her skin covered in gooseflesh.

The sound came again, a light tinkling of metal against metal. Snatching up a towel from the sink, she wrapped it around her wet body and hurried into her room. She tossed on a sleeveless white button-up shirt with a collar, paired with a clean set of striped overalls and black flats.

Remaining as quiet as possible, Dorothy fished out her uncle's rifle from beneath her bed. Numerous wolves had come on to the farm that she'd had to shoot so they wouldn't harm the other animals or destroy the crops. But this disturbance sounded different. There was always the chance of an intruder, too. Everyone in town knew "Crazy Dorothy" lived by herself out on the farm with no nearby neighbors. It would be so easy for someone to break into her house and take what little she had.

But she had her rifle prepared, and because of Uncle Henry, she knew how to use it well.

The noise came again, out the window, somewhere in the wheat field. She scrambled to light a lantern as she opened the front door while holding the rifle awkwardly in the other hand. A sharp thrash echoed directly in the middle of the wheat, the tall stalks swaying with the wind under the silvery glow of the moon. This time, the noise was accompanied by a trickle of emerald green light, illuminating the wheat stalks. Flashing once, twice, and continuing as though it were signaling her to draw closer. She inhaled sharply, setting down the lantern. That brilliant green was something she knew all too well, despite the ten years that had passed since she'd been eleven.

"Oz," she whispered, almost dropping the rifle. "No, no. That can't be it." Aunt Em would be ashamed if Dorothy chose to believe, if she slipped down that yellow brick road of insanity again. After all the work Aunt Em had put in to reversing Dorothy's delusions.

Aunt Em was no longer there to make Dorothy think she could be wrong.

I could be right. I could have always been right.

Heart galloping in her chest, she took off toward the field, skirting around stalks of wheat, like she was eleven years old once again. Except the last time there was emerald illumination, she'd been inside of her house within a tornado. But that light had been there, too.

Right then, she would do anything for the yellow brick road to lead her anywhere else but here—instead of remaining in a world with nothing. She was supposed to be out of the house in two days' time, but if she could find a way back to Oz—a place where no one thought of her as Crazy Dorothy—she would take the opportunity and not look back.

Pushing away tall and thin stalks of wheat, while avoiding the scurrying of mice feet, Dorothy followed the flickering light until, in front of her, there stood a green outline shimmering in the air, resembling a doorway.

"Dorothy," a male's deep voice called—one that was all-too familiar. "Dorothy, you need to come back. *Now.*"

It was real. It was real. It was real. She wished Aunt Em and Uncle Henry were alive to see this, to believe her. And she *wished* Toto was by her side, as he'd been the last time. But even her little dog had passed on to a new life.

Breathing in the night air and the heavy scent of her farm, she pressed her hand into the doorway and wiggled her fingers. She tugged her arm back and peered down at her palm. To see the land of Oz in all its glory, all she had to do was step through. With a smile she couldn't contain, Dorothy pressed her hand into the flickering green once more. Something roughly grasped her palm and yanked her within the portal, not leaving her enough time to scream or even yelp as she dropped her rifle in the dirt.

CHAPTER THREE

TIN

The moment a delicate hand came through the portal, Tin snatched the wrist and hauled the rest of the human into Oz. A human that was *supposed* to be Dorothy. Had he gotten the location wrong? He'd traveled far to reach the same dwarf-infested village she'd dropped into ten years ago, but this was distinctly *not* a little girl.

This was … a woman. Wearing tight striped overalls that accentuated her curves and a white collared shirt that barely contained what was underneath. Her hair was dreadfully tousled and sopping wet from the shoulders down, but the wonder filling her eyes made something crack deep inside him. Tin threw her arm from his grasp, his lip curling in disgust at the thought.

"Oz." Her voice was barely audible as she slowly turned away from him, taking in the dwarf village.

He followed the mortal woman's eyes as they took in the decrepit town. Dozens of fire-lit posts highlighted the short, white buildings with round straw roofs. All the color in town came from the broken shutters, paint-chipped doors, and crooked flowerboxes, though it was difficult to see any of it at night. Stone paths led from each doorstep to the main square, which butted against the swirled end of the yellow and red brick roads. Where Dorothy's house had fallen on the Wicked Witch of the East stood a golden statue of the girl with a braid over each shoulder and, beside her, that wiry, four-legged creature she was so attached to.

"This is *Oz*," Dorothy said a bit louder.

"Where the hell else would it be?" Tin stepped in front of her, jaw clenched. "Who are you?"

"My name's—" Her eyes fell on his face for the first time and she gasped.

Tin grabbed the woman by the upper arms before she could run, screaming, and alert every fae in town. The iron tips of his gloves pricked her skin when he squeezed. "Who. Are. You?"

"Dorothy." She struggled to free herself but he held firm. "It's *me*, Tin. Dorothy. Now let go."

He scowled at her, and she scowled right back. There was no way this was the same human who'd destroyed the Wicked Witch of the West—Reva. The real Dorothy was at least a foot shorter with a rounder face and an overall naivety about her. The statue directly behind this fraud was a perfect likeness, from the ribbons holding her braided hair, right down to the ruffled socks on her feet.

"Imposter," Tin snarled.

"Of course it's me!" She fought against his grip again but only managed to dig the iron tips on his gloves deeper into her arms.

Tin glared menacingly. Mortals aged faster than the fae, but this progression seemed extreme. "That's Dorothy." He spun her around to face the dulled statue and pointed. "See the difference?"

She wrinkled her nose. "They made me into a monument?"

"Stop lying!" he roared.

"It's been ten years, you oaf!" she snapped. "I *grew up*. And speaking of looking differently, what happened to your face?" Her lips parted as she studied him, seeming to grow concerned.

Tin released her as fast as one would drop a red-hot ember. Everyone knew what happened to his face—he had become a story parents told offspring to make them behave. *Do as I say or the Tin Man will snatch you from your bed.* It made sense this woman didn't know specifics, but she wouldn't ask what happened if she hadn't seen him before the branding.

"If you're Dorothy," he said carefully, "Where's your little rat, Tutu?"

Her eyes narrowed. "*Toto.*"

"That's what I said."

"My *dog* died, not that it's any of your business." She crossed her arms, the movement pushing up her cleavage. Tin couldn't stop his eyes from flicking downward. "You *are* Tin, aren't you?"

He held out his arms as if to say *who else would I be?* They were both quiet for a long moment before Dorothy broke the silence.

"That's impossible. The Tin I knew wasn't a self-righteous prick."

A surprised laugh burst from his chest. Tin leaned in closer, smelling the light scent of her soap, and cocked an eyebrow. "The fae you knew ten years ago wanted to be good."

"Which is why the Wizard broke the curse on your heart."

"An entirely useless organ. I'm glad it turned back to stone." He took in the statue of Dorothy again and considered the drastic change. Lion better not try to weasel out of payment, especially if Tin had to put up with her shit for very long. Lion's macabre lover wanted to wear Dorothy's head? Well, this was the only one Dorothy had. His gaze flicked back to the grown woman to find her staring, lips parted in horror at his revelation—an expression he was used to—and sighed.

"Your heart is stone again?" She gripped her chest as though he would rip her heart from beneath her ribcage to replace it with his.

There was nothing for her to worry about. He wouldn't touch her fragile mortal organ. The Gnome King had done him a favor when he'd cursed Tin's parents—the Heartless Curse had turned his heart to stone in retaliation for the lack of mercy they'd shown the Gnome Queen. The queen had begged for their help to hide her from gremlin marauders but, understandably, his parents bolted their door shut instead. When the queen was cut down on the doorstep of Tin's childhood home, the king had needed someone to punish. Perhaps the avenging king wouldn't have cursed Tin's mother if he'd known Tin grew in her womb—damning an innocent child to the same fate—or if he'd found the gremlins responsible. He was grateful the Gnome King hadn't known because if the few short years with a beating heart had taught Tin anything, it was that emotions made a mess of everything. It was a welcomed event when Oz's magic wore off and his heart solidified again. Dorothy could keep her wretched thing thumping in her chest.

At least until Lion got ahold of her.

"And this fae doesn't give a fuck." Tin ground his teeth. "We have to get off the road before we're seen, unless you want to be ripped apart by the night beasts tonight."

Dorothy grew rigid and stayed silent. Finally, an action from her that pleased him.

She shifted her concerned gaze to the dwarves' lantern-lit homes. Each door was painted a different pastel color and the inn where Tin had already secured a room was no different. He gave her a small push toward the pink door at the edge of town. Unfortunately, he hadn't factored his strength—or her mortal body—into the motion, and Dorothy stumbled forward.

"What the hell?"

He winced at the volume of her voice. The last thing they needed was to wake the dwarves this time of night. There was no telling whether they would get cranky miners, peppy singers, or, gods forbid, someone who recognized the woman beside him.

"Apologies," he mumbled to quiet her. There was nothing to be sorry for.

It seemed to pacify her despite the insincerity in his tone. "Where are the munchkins?"

"The mun—oh. Right. The dwarves." He'd forgotten Dorothy called them that.

She looked at him skeptically. "Glinda said they were munchkins."

"Glinda is an idiot," he snapped and tucked Dorothy into his side. She shifted away from him as he hid her beneath his cloak. Was she going to make everything difficult? This was why he preferred jobs that ended in blood. Heads didn't talk once they were removed. "Stop fussing. Oz isn't how you remember it."

Some residual trust must've lingered inside Dorothy because she relaxed into Tin and allowed him to lead her into the inn. They hurried through the closed tavern with the long liquid-stained tables, worn stools, and wooden steins hanging from hooks behind the bar. Small barrels rested on shelves, ready to be cracked when the tavern opened again the next night. The sound of shuffling feet in a back room had Tin hauling Dorothy upstairs to their room. Every squeak of the planked floor had him wincing, and he nearly had to bend in half to fit through the doorframes, but they made it all the way to the room without seeing anyone else. Langwidere expected Tin to deliver Dorothy within the next week, *alive*, so her head could be properly removed, but he needed to rest first. Not flee in the middle of the night.

The click of the lock seemed to mean something completely different to Dorothy, however. "Where's Glinda?" Without waiting for an answer, she asked, "Why isn't Oz how I remember it? And what happened to your heart?"

Gods. Will this girl shut the hell up already?

Once his cloak was folded on the chair, he lifted his axe from his waist and tucked the head of the weapon beneath his pillow. The room was almost too warm, the bed too soft, and the ceiling too low, but it was more comfortable than the forest floor. Tin pulled his shirt off next, along with his gloves, and tossed the black fabric over the painted statue of a young Dorothy that sat on the nightstand. A vase of red flowers tipped, spilling water all over the floor, but that was fine with him. There were more on the windowsill, dresser, and round table anyway. He flopped down on top of the bed covers without sparing Dorothy a word.

The weight of Dorothy's stare on his abdomen made his muscles flex involuntarily. If she asked about the handful of scars decorating his skin, he wouldn't lie. The jagged one on his side came from an ogre, and the puckered circle on his shoulder from a poisoned spear. He couldn't remember where he got other smaller ones, but the important thing was that every wound ended with a big, fat payday. Something told Tin that Dorothy wouldn't appreciate hearing how his new profession was murder.

"See something you like?" he asked with a lazy grin. She blushed bright red. Tin yawned, satisfied with her reaction, and shut his eyes. The silver key to their shared room was securely in his right pants' pocket, which meant Dorothy was securely in his grasp. They would leave at dawn, after the dwarves settled into their routines for the day, to avoid unnecessary attention.

"Tin!"

He cracked one eye to find Dorothy flushed with anger. "Are you really not going to tell me anything?"

"I don't see why any of it matters," he grumbled. She made a choked noise. "Fine. If it will get you to shut up. Glinda hasn't come out of the South in years. She's too busy doing whatever it is she does. My heart is my business. Oz isn't the same because the Wizard is a faerie fruit addicted fool who left the Emerald City, which is now in chaos. And you're back because I opened a portal and *brought you here*. The last bit was rather exhausting though, so do me a favor and stop talking."

"But—"

"At the very least, try not to draw attention to us by gawking out the window or stomping around like an angry troll."

His cloak landed hard on his face. "Call me a troll again," Dorothy snarled.

Tin blinked in surprise at her audacity before using the cloak as a blanket. "An *angry* troll. And you just proved my point."

"We haven't seen each other in ten years, you pull me back to Oz, and then want to take a nap?" she asked, indignant.

"Let's get one thing clear, shall we?" His piercing silver eyes latched onto her brown ones. "I don't care. Not about old times, not about you. This is a job."

"Job?"

"Lion hired me to bring you to him." If he left out the part about Lion's courage driving him into darkness, and into the bed of that crazy bitch Langwidere, Dorothy wouldn't know to be wary of her old friend. She would follow Tin straight to Langwidere's door for the tradeoff. "He needs your help." *To keep his lover happy and swimming in new heads.*

"Is he okay? What does he need help with?"

"Dorothy," Tin warned.

"What about Crow?"

He rolled over and gave Dorothy his back. The truth was, Tin had no idea what had happened to Crow after the Wizard got his brain working properly, but if he had to guess, it wasn't good. Nothing was anymore.

CHAPTER FOUR

DOROTHY

Dorothy stood in the darkened night of a strange, utterly small room with a low ceiling that her head almost brushed against, that Tin's *had* touched. While the sun had already set in her world, it had also found its hiding place here.

Her breathing increased with growing annoyance as she watched the fae in front of her, the moonlight highlighting the silver of his long hair.

When she'd first realized that Tin was the one who'd pulled her through the portal, she couldn't help being overjoyed. But that had quickly slipped away when it had become apparent that he wasn't the same person.

And now, he thought he could just roll over and turn his back on her? Wearing a cloak like a blanket? That she would be fine and dandy about it? Outrageous. She stomped to the other side of the bed, not bothering to placate him with silence. But as soon as her gaze took in the markings on his cheek again, her anger left her. Where had the silver lines come from? And how was he already asleep? Her feet clomping the wood hadn't disrupted him in the slightest, as his breaths came out slow and even.

She'd noted as she'd peered under the tall fiery posts, at the houses with chipped paint and broken pieces, that this wasn't the Oz she remembered. This wasn't the Tin she remembered either. Everyone had been happy-go-lucky before, besides the witch and her minion monkeys. But she hadn't come across anyone else yet either, so perhaps the rest of Oz wasn't as gloomy as this outer layer.

When she'd last been in Oz with Tin and the others, he'd been quiet and sulky, but nothing like this. It was as though he was jaded now. And when his stone heart had become a live, beating organ, he'd even cracked a smile at her before she'd left. That perfect smile had remained with her while back in Kansas, the one she'd always sworn to herself that she'd see again. There were no smiles now.

He'd told her Lion needed her. If she couldn't get answers from Tin tonight, well, she'd leave him behind and go find her other friend. She wasn't going to waste her time here. And maybe once she found Lion, he could tell her where Crow was.

"Sorry, Tin, you can catch up with me if you so desire," she whispered to herself, and made way for the door, this time keeping her feet silent.

Only, she found the door locked when she tried to turn the knob. She narrowed her eyes with the discovery that it needed a key to exit from inside. Her gaze drifted back to the sleeping fae.

She'd seen him stow his axe—his prized possession— beneath the pillow, but nothing else. Her one chance of leaving had to be on his body, and she had a feeling he wouldn't hand it over to her willingly.

Dorothy tiptoed back to the bed, her eyes lingering on the rise of his naked chest where a portion of his cloak had slipped away. No key would be found there. In fact, she didn't know how he wasn't getting chilly with all that exposed skin in the cold room.

Reaching forward, she softly padded her hands down the sides of his cloak, finding only emptiness. As her eyes drifted to his pants, her face heated at where her hands would have to venture next.

Taking a deep swallow that felt too loud in her ears, she slipped her fingertips inside his right pocket. *Ah-ha.* Something metal brushed along her digits. Just as she was about to pull it out, two firm and warm hands grasped both her wrists, preventing her escape.

"I don't think so," Tin growled in a low whisper.

Before she could respond, her fingers were ripped from his pocket—key long gone from her grasp—and her body shoved up against his with an arm planted at her waist. All 'snug and cozy,' except she knew his intentions were anything but.

"Apparently," he murmured by her ear, his breath warm and tickling her nape, "you're not to be trusted. Goodnight."

There was no goodnight.

Grunting, she wiggled and tried to roll over to face him, but he was too strong. So she settled on talking to the grimy windowpane instead of his face. "Before, you mentioned that Lion needs me. I think we should go now. No need to sleep."

He didn't answer. If anything, he seemed to hold onto her tighter.

Huffing, she turned her head over her shoulder, unable to see anything in the dark now that the moonlight had shifted. "Can you at least answer why we need to stay here?"

He exhaled with agitation, and even without seeing him, she knew he was scowling. "I don't think you want to venture out into Oz at this time of night. As I said, things aren't as they once were."

She'd traveled through the night before. The last time she was here, she remembered holding on to Crow's hand for a good bit of the journey. He may not have been able to talk very clearly most of the time, but she'd felt closest to him, like he was her protector. As for Tin, there'd been a different feeling about him, one she hadn't been able to name back then, one she was no longer feeling now. And Lion, while being a big baby, had done the best he could.

Dorothy wished she hadn't dropped her shotgun on the way into the portal. She wished she had Toto who would bark and scare the things of this world. But now it was only her and this man who wasn't really a man at all.

"Tell me why then," she said. "Why can't we leave now?"

He didn't answer.

"Tin." She hated that his name came out more of a plea.

"Stop saying that."

"What?" Her brows lowered in confusion. "Your name?"

"Calling me by name would mean we're friends, and we're not that. Not anymore."

"But—"

He let out a grumble as if he was warring with himself before he finally added, "If we left now, you'd have wished you stayed, so trust me on this. I told you earlier, there are night beasts here."

Dorothy couldn't help wanting to spew out more questions about what kind of night beasts, but he was already asleep again. Something told her to listen to him, especially when crackling sounds outside stirred. She lifted her head an inch and listened. It wasn't the chanting of the munchkins in song—*dwarves*—it was something far more sinister. Low growls and gurgles seemed to swarm the town. *It must be the night beasts Tin mentioned.*

A shiver ran up her spine and she closed her eyes, curling closer into Tin, even though she should have moved farther away. As the sounds grew louder and louder, she was grateful the bed was far too narrow for him to push her away. He may not consider her a friend anymore, but she still considered him one as she remembered his smile to her, from long ago, once more.

Her farm was no longer hers, and regardless of the changes to this place, she wanted to stay in Oz. Same as the last time she was here, she would make things better again. How bad could it truly be?

A yawn escaped her and her eyes fluttered before she drifted off to sleep, pressed tightly against Tin's arm.

Something hard nudged Dorothy's shoulder. "Sleeping," she said, knowing it was Tin. He'd had his terms last night on when to sleep. This time, things would be on *her* terms of when to wake up.

The nudge came again, harder than before. She flicked open her eyes, meeting that of a bare chest with a few pale scars running up it. Tin's chest was firm and ripped, and nothing like Jimmy's flat chest and stomach. She quickly tore her gaze away and focused on the wooden handle of the axe poking at her arm.

Narrowing her eyes, she drifted her gaze up to Tin's face, catching on his silver irises. He was scowling at her, and she found herself unsurprised by his expression.

"You could have just said, 'Dorothy, it's time to leave.' You know, like a gentleman would do."

"I'm no gentleman." Tin tugged his shirt on and placed his cloak around his shoulders.

"That you aren't," she muttered and sat on the edge of the bed, reaching her hands up, and arching her back forward to pop it. The farm work the day before had done a number on her body. The sky out the window appeared bright, and whatever beastly noises had erupted through the night were gone now.

"What are you doing?" Tin asked, observing her as if she was a species he'd never seen before.

"Can I not stretch for a moment?"

"No," he grunted, turning around and heading for the door.

Rolling her eyes, she hurried after him as he unlocked it with a silver key.

"What's for breakfast?" she asked as she followed him down the narrow hallway with its bare, sickly-green walls, to the stairs on the first floor. The room stood empty except for a dwarf with spiraled gray hair, seated at the front desk.

"Whatever you find on the way." Tin didn't look back at her as he slammed the key down in front of the dwarf.

"Hi, I'm—"

Tin wrapped a hand over her mouth. "Leaving. She's

leaving." He pushed her through the door and out toward the yellow brick road. Tired of his coldness already, she bit his hand and he cursed, quickly removing it.

"What was that about?" she asked.

"Don't mention your name to anyone, understand?" He shook his hand out then balled it into a fist. "It's dangerous."

"I'm not fae. People can call me Dorothy Gale all they want, and I can't be controlled." She wondered what Tin's full name was, but she knew he would never tell her. And if he did, she'd control him right then.

He sighed. "Everyone knows what you did before, and while a lot are happy about it, some aren't. You'll eventually understand why."

Dorothy took a deep swallow, as she peered at the unkempt village, wondering how defeating the Wicked Witch of the West would make people unhappy. "But—"

"That's enough."

She could tell he was in no mood to say anything else on that matter. "Fine, but I really do need something to eat." Her stomach twisted and turned—it had been without anything since early the day before.

With a frustrated shake of the head, he pointed to a fruit tree up the road.

She narrowed her eyes. "I can't eat faerie fruit." Crow had warned her what it did to mortals, and apparently, the Wizard was addicted to it. Even when she'd met him, he hadn't seemed completely sane, so perhaps he was back then too.

"Mmm, too bad then."

She scowled.

He pointed again toward the trees. "There are some past those with various nuts."

"Thank you."

"Don't thank me."

Dorothy stepped onto the yellow brick road and stared at the withering houses as she passed. Her heart beat rapidly as she gathered nuts into the pockets of her overalls while stepping on several to crack them open.

Tin ate a few, then bit into a luscious-looking piece of fruit before they started back down the yellow path toward the South. The breeze held a tinge of coolness as it blew around them. The trees shuffled and swayed as Dorothy watched brownies and faeries swarm around the yellow and orange fruit.

As they trekked farther and farther away from Dwarf Country, where only forestry surrounded them, something wobbled beneath her feet, catching her off balance.

She peered down and gasped at the cracked, shifted rectangular pieces. "What happened to the yellow brick road?"

Tin only shook his head and continued walking past her.

"What happened?" Dorothy asked again. The road was not only a faded yellow now but there were cracks, some broken bricks, others missing, as though a tornado had run itself across the once beautiful path.

"Most of the Emerald City and outlying areas have been destroyed." He shrugged with nonchalance. "None of the territories are what they used to be."

"But not Glinda's, right? The South is okay, isn't it?" It couldn't be that bad if that was where they were headed, could it?

He paused. "You ask too many questions. That's where we're headed because that's where Lion is."

"I defeated the Wicked Witch of the West. My house landed on the Wicked Witch of the East. Things should be better." There was Locasta of the North and Glinda of the South. Both were good and both had planned to share the territories that the wicked had held.

"Once a villain dies, another always rises. Good doesn't always conquer evil. Besides, why do you care? You left Oz and never looked back."

She grasped his arm and spun him around, her anger boiling. "I never stopped looking back! I went home, Tin. But that didn't mean I didn't ever want to return! I couldn't! No one ever came to me, I never found another portal, and the people in my world didn't believe me. I was locked away for months at a time. People hurt me, physically and emotionally. Do you even know what that's like?"

His expression slipped for a moment, only briefly, but it was there. He'd looked as though he wanted to give a full answer, but then he simply said, "No."

"That's right, because you have a heart of stone." Her nostrils flared.

"And you are but a lowly mortal." He shrugged and walked away.

Her anger rose, and she clenched her fists. She would head to the South by herself, but not before she forced him to show some emotion.

She lunged forward, yanked the axe from his grip, and took off with a heavy sprint. It may have been childish to steal his weapon, but she didn't care. He was irritating her to no end.

Behind her, the pound of his feet reverberated, but she was quickly gaining space between them. Then a body slammed into her from the side, knocking her to the ground. She released hold of the axe and shouted in Tin's face, "You're the new coward! Somehow since I've been gone, you've inherited Lion's old ways."

But it wasn't Tin's silver irises she was looking at; it was something else, with reddened eyes and saliva dripping from its mouth. A man with rotting skin and clumps of hair missing—mortal—one who had eaten too much faerie fruit.

As the man snapped his teeth down toward her face, the slice of a weapon came across his neck. The head vanished and hot blood sprayed Dorothy.

All that remained was a headless body slumped on her chest, warm blood pooling out from the dead man's neck.

Strong hands yanked Dorothy up by her arms, the still body falling from her. Two silver eyes met hers, blazing with fury.

"I told you Oz isn't the same," Tin said through gritted teeth. "Now, are you going to listen to me?"

She quickly nodded, even though it wasn't entirely true, but right then she would.

CHAPTER FIVE

TIN

Humans and fae didn't have much in common, but neither seemed to listen to sense. Apparently, Dorothy was one of them—even if she had just agreed to start. With a snarl on his lips, Tin stared down at the blood-soaked woman. The faerie fruit addict's body sprawled at their feet, his head tossed aside, and his blood coating Dorothy's face. He had expected her to cry or scream. It was good she hadn't. Little was worse than getting a mouthful of blood, especially that of a mortal addicted to faerie fruit. Something about the fruit made it disgustingly bitter. He'd found that out the hard way, completely by accident, when he'd assassinated a human at the beginning of his career in exchange for a week of room and board. He should've expected a good amount of blood to spurt from the thing's neck and stood to the side, but live and learn… More dangerous for Dorothy, the blood carried a scant trace of the fruit's addictive properties.

"Are you sure you're going to listen now?" Tin growled at Dorothy. "Because it will make saving you repeatedly a real hassle if you don't have any coin."

Dorothy shook in his grip, undoubtedly from the shock settling in, mixed with fury. "You'd charge me to save my life?"

"I charge per kill." It was double the price if a client charged headfirst into trouble and made things more difficult. Tin released her to settle his bloody axe back on his hip. They would stop at the first body of water to wash off the weapon and their filth before the scent attracted fae beasts. "Since you didn't know that, and given our history, there's no charge for this one."

She had to be delivered to Lion and Langwidere *alive* for him to cash in—a payment he deserved ten times over already—but Dorothy didn't need to know that. A good dose of fear had the potential to keep her in line.

When Dorothy simply stood there, staring at the decapitated body, Tin scraped moss off a nearby tree. "Here. Use this before any of the blood gets in your mouth."

She snatched the moss from his palm and lowered her brows. "How is this supposed to help?"

"Wipe your face with it," he instructed. Dorothy dropped the moss to the ground and used her hands instead, which only smeared the blood more. Tin shook his head in disdain. "Use the moss like a cloth."

"This is fine for now." She wiped her hands on her thighs.

"You'd rather risk a faerie fruit high than use the moss?" he asked in disbelief.

Her eyes flicked up to his for a moment, almost as if she was gauging whether he was serious, before scooping the moss up from the ground. "Thanks."

He hadn't given it to her for thanks. He gave her the moss to cut down on the smell and risk of contamination. Though, if he was being honest with himself, the contamination didn't matter much. He was delivering her to Langwidere, after all.

"Did I get it all?" Dorothy asked after scrubbing her face. The blood stained her skin light pink, but the moss had effectively collected a majority of the mess.

"Mostly."

She reached for the same tree Tin had taken the moss from. He watched her struggle to scrape more than tiny bits and pieces off, amused at her effort, before using his iron-tipped gloves to rip a larger patch free. "Allow me."

Dorothy stretched for the fresh moss, but Tin swung his arm out of reach. The worried gleam in her eyes made Tin smirk. Without another word, he had the moss to Dorothy's jaw line where a large streak of blood remained. She gasped as he pulled it slowly from her ear toward her chin and the sound caused a crumbling sensation behind his ribs.

For a mortal woman, she wasn't unattractive. Langwidere would be pleased with her delicate features. Though, admittedly, in a different way than it pleased him. He'd taken pleasure from a few masochistic thrill-seekers over the years, but he never knew their names. Dorothy was different. Wondering what expression she would wear in the throes of passion wasn't an idea Tin should entertain. Ever. And yet, the desire to touch her burned sudden and deep. Having her firmly against him in such a small bed all night didn't help either. She was so warm, so trusting, as she pressed her soft body against him, filling his senses with her feminine aroma. It lingered even now, and Tin's cock stiffened. Would she taste as good as she smelled?

He jerked away from Dorothy in frustration. "Good enough to keep us alive until we hit the river."

"Excuse me?" she asked, slightly breathless but recovering quickly. "What do you mean, keep us alive?"

Tin held his arms out to signal the forest. "I mean, all the pixies, kobolds, and leprechauns who call these woods home. If you thought the addict was bad…"

He let the threat linger in hopes of further ensuring her obedience, but they weren't likely to be attacked by any of those fae. Others would, but occasionally his reputation worked in his favor. It was the trolls they had to avoid. The kelpies at the river still had it out for him after he'd butchered one to use the scales for his clothes. Both were manageable threats though, and he *did* need Dorothy to walk through the forest. He had no intention of carrying her if she became too frightened, and there wasn't time to walk around the forest before Lion's deadline.

"Shall we try this again?" Tin asked.

Dorothy nodded, then quickly shook her head. "One minute," she mumbled as she ran back to the headless body. She bent over him and carefully plucked a small knife from where it was tucked inside one of his boots. Blade clutched to her chest, Dorothy hurried back to Tin's side.

"You don't need that," he told her. He would protect her until she was with Lion.

Dorothy pointed to the bloody scene behind her. "I disagree."

"Fine." He drew a deep breath and pushed it out sharply. "Let's get moving."

He didn't wait for her to respond before turning on his heel and marching forward. For a moment he worried she wouldn't follow and he would be forced to drag her the entire way south. His fingers curled into fists, his ears straining to hear her. Maybe it *would* be faster—carrying her. An annoyed grunt left Tin's throat and the soft padding of Dorothy's footsteps sounded behind him.

By the time Tin and Dorothy arrived at the river bank, he was ready to toss her to the kelpies himself. She hadn't said a word since they began their journey a second time, but Tin was acutely aware of all the things she wasn't saying. He felt the unspoken words squeezing him like a vise.

Something was holding her back from saying whatever it was she had on her mind and Tin didn't care what that thing was. He was glad she wasn't asking the hard questions, glad he didn't have to explain. Gladder still that he didn't have to lie to her about Lion's intentions. His meeting with Lion a few nights ago was surprising, even to Tin. He had thought he'd heard it all from his clients, but procuring a former friend for decapitation as a *gift*? Lion's lover, Langwidere, would wear Dorothy's head well, just as she wore the dozens already in her possession. The head of a mortal child had seemed a strange choice when Lion had asked Tin to bring Dorothy back to Oz and lead her to Langwidere's doorstep alive, but it made sense now. Dorothy was already aging so rapidly. Her life wouldn't be cut short too prematurely. Besides, the pay was undeniably good.

Tin bent at the water's edge and dunked his hands beneath the liquid. After scanning the surface of the river for signs of life, he looked over his shoulder at the silent woman. Her cheeks were flushed and her chest rose and fell a little too quickly. He stood and studied her.

"Are you ill?"

"What?" she asked breathlessly.

He narrowed his eyes as if it would help him see what ailed her. Would it change things? Could Langwidere still utilize the head if she was sick? If not, they would have to treat the sickness themselves. Alive was alive—Lion never mentioned her health. "You look ill."

"I'm *tired*. Do you know what tired is?"

"We've only been traveling a few hours, and I've kept a slow pace for your mortal legs."

She scowled at him. "My *mortal legs* are significantly shorter than yours. I've practically had to sprint to keep up with you."

Tin blinked in surprise as his gaze fell to her legs. They were shorter, yes, but seemed perfectly capable of matching his pace. "What would you have me do? Crawl to Lion?"

"Yes. Crawl. It might give you back some of the humility you lost when your heart turned back into stone," she snapped.

"Clean yourself," he spat before he could dignify that with a response. It wouldn't be long until he never had to deal with her or her smart mouth again. He tugged the axe from his hip and Dorothy scrambled back a step. "Relax. I'm not going to hurt you."

Dorothy stood until Tin turned away from her and began cleaning the blood from his weapon, then joined him. He watched her splash water on her face from the corner of his eyes.

It soaked the hair around her face, the strands clinging to her cheeks and forehead. Beads of water ran down her neck. Tin's gaze inadvertently fixed on the liquid drops as they raced further down into her cleavage, as he continued to shine the same spot on his axe, though it was no longer dirty. She moved on to her clothes—scrubbing at the stains with a rock and splashing water onto the fabric until the bright red faded to a muted pink. The white shirt Dorothy had on beneath her overalls hid *nothing* when wet. All he needed was to glimpse something he shouldn't when his malehood was already in revolt, so he turned his attention to his weapon.

When he looked up again, it was to find Dorothy staring at him and, for the first time in years, he wished he could hide his face. The blackened rings of bone held his silver locks tightly in place, however, showcasing his iron mutilation. Heavens above, what was he doing? Clearly, he'd gone too long without a female. When this job was finished, he needed a good fuck. It might take a while to find a brothel willing to serve him, but he'd pay an exorbitant price for their worst girl if that was what it took.

"I know it's none of my business, but will you tell me what happened to your face, Tin?" Dorothy asked in a quiet, thoughtful voice.

Tin sighed. "What does it matter?"

"It matters a lot." The tacky mud along the riverbank squished when she stood and came closer to him. "Tell me who *I* need to kill, because I don't think you did this to yourself."

He stiffened at her words. The thought of Dorothy killing anyone made him irrationally protective of her and her still-pure heart. He didn't understand why. Besides, his truth would change her opinion of him, and he wasn't sure he wanted that. It wasn't that Tin was ashamed of the events leading up to the Wizard's punishment. He rarely felt anything more than anger and resignation since his heart hardened again, but if Dorothy knew what he was… If she knew he was an assassin—the *best* assassin in Oz—she would look at him like everyone else did. It would also lead to suspicions he couldn't afford. Lion could've hired anyone with knowledge of portals to bring Dorothy back if it was a friendly visit.

But he didn't. He'd hired Tin.

Tin, whose resume boasted thousands of kills and a distinct lack of morals, was once Dorothy's friend. They'd bonded as they traveled the yellow brick road together with Lion and Crow. If Oz had managed to truly break the Heartless Curse placed on Tin by the Gnome King, Lion's coin wouldn't weigh down his pocket now. But it *hadn't* worked. Lion knew that—all of Oz knew—which was likely why Lion hired Tin specifically.

If Lion's lover lopped off Dorothy's pretty little head and wore it as if it was her own, what was it to Tin? Nothing. So what if Langwidere continued terrorizing the South while pretending to be the savior of Oz?

"The Wizard did it," he said before he could stop himself. What did it matter if he told Dorothy how he was branded? She wouldn't be around long enough for it to make a difference and he could leave out certain details. So, he took a cloth from his bag to dry his axe and continued, "I was convicted of murder after the curse returned. Before that, I was one of the Wizard's bodyguards, so he let me off easy. Instead of having me publicly executed, he poured a single drop of molten iron upon me for each life I took."

Dorothy's eyes grew impossibly wide. "How many fae did you kill?"

Tin finished drying his axe, stood, and put the sharp blade back at his hip. "I didn't stick around to count. Dozens by then, I suppose. The eleven lords were what got me caught, though."

"But…" She paused, and Tin tried to read the mixture of horrified emotions on her face. It was impossible. "Oz would never do something so horrible to anyone!"

He scoffed. Dorothy had to be the only person in Oz—in *all* the fae lands—who would doubt the Wizard punished Tin. There had nearly been a riot when he wasn't sentenced to death. "Do you really want those answers, Dorothy? You won't like them."

"Of course I want the answers!"

Tin stepped closer and leaned down, perhaps too close, to give her a good look at the shining metal on his cheek. Past the blood still coating her clothing, a lingering scent of her soap mixed with his own scent from the night before struck his nostrils. Dorothy's eyes seemed to trace over each twisting path of iron. His skin had burned around the iron, and had never stopped. Burned and burned and burned until his only option was to embrace the pain. It was the ever-present ember that kept his rage smoldering even on his best day.

"One night, I left a gaming hall in the capital slightly inebriated and found the owner's son harassing a female outside. It didn't seem wrong to snap his neck—it still doesn't seem wrong. He deserved his fate. The female, less so, but she refused to stop screaming."

He stopped then. Stopped and waited for Dorothy to do the same. After hearing that story, the only sane response would be to run. Instead, she looked at him with pity, and there was nothing worse than that.

"I burned down the entire gambling hall afterward," he said to erase her expression. "If anyone tried to escape the inferno, I took them down with my axe. And that was only the beginning."

Tin had no idea what had come over him that night. The two deaths outside had been warranted, but not the rest. The Wizard should've had him killed for that first act—it would've saved a lot of lives. Since Oz had granted *mercy* though, Tin had schooled himself. He may not have a heart anymore, but that didn't mean he wanted to die. Murderous rampages were only tolerated if the coin purse was heavy enough now.

"Terrified of me yet?" he asked with a sneer. "Don't worry. You're safe as long as you're with me. Lion is paying me to deliver you alive and well. Finish getting cleaned up. I'll be just a few trees away."

Dorothy bit down on her bottom lip and met his gaze. Instead of fear, Tin found sorrow. Pity, as it turned out, wasn't the worst look he could receive.

CHAPTER SIX

DOROTHY

Exhaustion had taken over Dorothy's whole body from traveling—her slip-on shoes had done nothing except cause her feet to hurt. What she needed were boots like Tin wore, but it wasn't as if there was a store right around the corner in the middle of nowhere. Only fruit trees and a broken brick road surrounded them.

After washing the remainder of the blood and grime from herself as best she could at the river, she and Tin kept heading south, only stopping when he slayed something for them to eat. He remained quiet—she remained inquisitive. The world around her was broken … like Tin … like her, even the trees appeared melancholic, with their drooping branches. Tin wasn't the same fae she'd once known. He was a murderer, but he was what he was because this place had turned him that way.

Should she hate him? Yes. Was she frustrated with him? Yes. Did she feel pity for him? Yes…

Dorothy knew Tin wanted to take her to Lion, and the fae had been desperate enough to pay another to bring her to him. Perhaps Lion was cowardly once more, or he would have come for her himself. This was all the Wizard's fault for making them believe that happiness could be permanent, that by her returning home everything would be perfect—it wasn't.

After she reunited with Lion, how would she even be able to help him? Dorothy no longer had the sparkling silver slippers to provide her with magic.

In the distance, something achingly familiar caught her attention, making her heart thump wildly: a city—the Emerald City. Lion… Tin… What she needed was someone else, someone who was braver than anyone she knew. *Crow.* He'd said he would remain in the city, that he'd needed to think about things.

Dorothy whirled to the side at the thought of Crow, almost gripping one of Tin's strong arms, absently wondering how firm it would feel beneath her fingertips… She shook away the thought and kept her minimal distance.

"I think I have an idea for our next step," Dorothy said with a wide smile, knowing that somewhere in the city her good friend waited.

Slowly, his demeanor dangerous, Tin halted and turned to face her, his silver eyes hard, his brows becoming one. "What are you talking about now?"

"I think instead of us going straight to the South, we should head to the Emerald City first." As Dorothy gazed in the distance, her smile dropped as the dying light highlighted the city. Like everything else she'd encountered, a sky-scraping tower appeared, crumbled in half. "What happened to the capital?" she whispered. Tin had told her everything was a mess, but she hadn't expected this.

"We aren't going anywhere else." He stepped toward her, close, closer, incredibly close. "The same thing happened there that's happened everywhere. A measly knife won't save you either. Oz left the Emerald City for who knows where, and Locasta and her beasts have claimed the eastern and northern territories. She's battling for the Emerald City to be hers, too."

"Locasta? But she's good." Lion and Tin had both told her Locasta was good, like Glinda.

"Sometimes things change." He shrugged as though he didn't

care, as if he didn't have a heart. Which, she supposed, he didn't since it had hardened back up.

"What about the West? Who has it since the Wicked Witch of the West is dead?"

He shrugged again. "Another fae like Locasta."

Dorothy remembered what Oz had done to Tin—she now knew he'd given Tin a heart that wasn't permanent. Lion didn't have his courage any longer. But what about Crow? What if he'd lost his brain, too? Unless their curses were different and his was really broken. But what if it wasn't? He was wiser than any of them when he was at full capacity. Even when he'd spoken in nonsensical riddles, Crow had somehow known how to keep her safe when she was just a young girl.

Not one to back down, Dorothy stepped as close as she could get and peered up at Tin. "I'm still going to leave and search for Crow there. Maybe someone has answers. If you don't want to come, then once I find him, we can meet you and Lion in the South. Then we'll head straight to Glinda. I know she can help us." Glinda might have been bubbly at times, but she knew fae magic better than anyone. And perhaps Glinda could also help Tin … help him to restore his heart. As Dorothy stared at his face, at the hard silver ripples on his left cheek, she knew the scar still hurt. It didn't bother her to look at him. He was still beautiful, just as he was when he'd smiled at her before she'd left. But there was no smile now, hadn't been for a long time.

"No." Tin's answer sounded final.

Dorothy drew in a sharp breath and narrowed her eyes. "What do you mean *no*?"

"No." And there that word was again…

"Is this because of the payment?" she asked. "Lion will understand."

"No."

"Then I'm sorry, but we'll have to part ways for now. I promise I'll meet you in the South as soon as I can." She'd traveled by herself here before, then she'd stumbled upon Crow first. Perhaps she hadn't been alone because she'd had Toto, but she'd been by herself on her farm for quite some time. She may not have been able to save that, but she could try and help Tin by locating the silver slippers.

Dorothy knew what was about to come out of his mouth would be argumentative, but his eyes turned to the darkening sky and he released a string of curses. "I don't have time for this."

"I don't care—"

"The Emerald City is a wreck—I doubt Crow's even still there. So shut your mouth." Tin lifted her up from the ground. She gasped when he threw her over his shoulder as if she weighed nothing.

"I swear to God, I'm going to scream if you don't put me down right this instant!" She beat her fists against his hard back, but he didn't even seem fazed.

"Be quiet!" he growled in a low and deadly voice. "The sun is going down."

"And?" She wiggled her hips, trying to slip from his grasp. It didn't work.

"Like last night, the night beasts are going to come out soon." He moved off the broken yellow bricks toward the edge of the forest. "We don't have time to make it to another inn. Do you know whose fault that is? Yours. For traveling at a glacial pace and then starting this ridiculous discussion about searching for Crow, a fae who has been absent for years."

What she needed was her rifle. All she had was the small blade she'd swiped from the now-headless man who'd became addicted to faerie fruit. It was better for him to be dead than what he'd become.

"I don't care what you say," Dorothy seethed. "In the morning, I'm going to find Crow. He can shift—he'd be more help to Lion than I'd ever be."

"No."

When she was here last, she'd led the way, been the one in charge, but she'd taken everyone's thoughts into consideration. When had he decided to not listen to anyone but himself?

In the distance, a stirring sounded, a loud beating of wings.

Then came the hooting, the growling, the ear-piercing screams, all from the Emerald City. While being outdoors this time, the noises clearer, she was able to recognize the sounds of the beasts. The minions had once belonged to the Wicked Witch, but they were now here. Why hadn't they chosen to rule themselves after the Wicked Witch died instead of flock to another? Dorothy lifted her head from Tin's back and watched in horror as the little bit of shining light filtered across a dull sparkle of green building wrapped in dead vines.

Before she could see the beasts clearly, Tin tossed them both to the ground. He threw his cloak around them. "Cradle your legs around my hips and hold me as close as you can."

"*What?*" Dorothy asked, horrified at the thought. She hadn't even had her legs that tightly around Jimmy the times they'd been together.

"Damn it, just do it—we're not fucking," he spat. "If you don't want to die out here, listen. If we stay hidden, they won't find us."

Getting ripped apart by flying monkeys with long talons, fangs, and thorned tails wasn't something she would wish for. Chest heaving, Dorothy heard the noisy rustling of the beasts drawing closer. Thankfully, she wasn't wearing a dress this time as she folded her legs around Tin's narrow waist and her arms around his warm neck.

He hurriedly adjusted his cloak and unlatched secret panels to make the cloth larger, then stretched it to fully cover them both. His arms seemed to hesitate for a split-second before they took hold around her. She could feel his soft breaths at her scalp just as he probably felt her rapid ones at his throat. An earthy scent enveloped her.

Dorothy's heart pounded as the growling and heavy flapping of wings boomed above them. The crashing of the monstrous things swarmed between branches, through leaves, colliding with the wind. Her grip on Tin tightened, even though she was still frustrated with him, even though she wanted to leave him behind and search for Crow. But he was keeping her safe. No matter what, she knew he was keeping her safe because he was still her friend—even a stone-hearted one. Just as she would keep him safe—once she broke his curse with Glinda and Crow's help.

The sounds faded, lighter and lighter, until they'd completely died down. Dorothy tried to inch backward, but Tin only held her tighter.

"It's fine now," she whispered at his ear.

"It's *not* fine." His voice came out raspy. "The beasts have watchers everywhere at night. There could even be one in the tree right above us."

She shuddered at the thought. "But can't they hear us?"

"No, that's why we need to stay put. The fae magic of my cloak will protect us."

"How did you come across such a thing? You didn't have it before." When she'd first found him, all he'd had was a rusted axe, a stone in his chest, and worn clothing. He'd even been without boots. The thought of that poor, once-optimistic fae made her chest tighten.

"You ask too many questions," he grumbled against her hair.

"And I'll ask more. Where did you get it?"

"I stole it from Oz. He'd stolen it from a witch."

"I'd say I think he deserved it." Oz had pretended to be a wizard, and he'd only been a man. She should have known to never trust him.

Tin chuckled, but then he interrupted it with a light cough as though he didn't want to laugh. "Go to sleep."

"I'm still going to search for Crow in the morning."

"No."

She would.

It didn't take long for Tin's heavy breaths to come out even—it seemed he could easily fall asleep at any time. A numbing tingle rippled up her left leg where Tin's side was starting to crush her. Dorothy could barely feel her limb and couldn't stay like this all night, so she tried to adjust her position while maneuvering her right leg a bit.

All that did was press her lower half to Tin. She stilled when she felt *him* against her—something hard. Tin's breaths were still even. But as she twisted a little more to drag her leg out, Tin's body froze, his breaths no longer steady.

"Sorry, that was my fault," she said, embarrassed. "I couldn't get comfortable."

"You keep making things more complicated, don't you?" He sighed. "Just. Hold on. I'm going to roll over but, for once, listen, and stay still the rest of the night." Releasing his grip on her, he carefully rolled over while she stayed on her side, planted to the dirt. The cloak continued to keep them hidden. Tin's back was now to her chest with his legs pulled up like an infant's. He wrapped one of her legs around to his stomach while the other was tucked directly under his buttocks.

"There," he muttered and went straight back to sleep.

She closed her eyes, noticing Tin's breaths didn't sound even—they were almost ragged, as though he were thinking about something else. Steadily, she brought her fingertips to his cheek where the ridges lay, and lightly brushed them across, hoping to ease him into sleep. The heat from the iron tingled and nipped at her digits. He inhaled a sharp breath, but didn't say a word. Not even his favorite word of the day—*no.*

Lowering her palm, Dorothy cradled the spot on his chest, where his stone heart rested, and remembered the young fae he'd once been. She couldn't help but imagine what his skin, beneath his shirt, would feel like against her fingertips.

Stop it, Dorothy. You're at the edge of a forest with monstrous beasts who could be watching your every move, and all you can think about is touching someone's skin? Someone who has been nothing but intolerable? But she understood why he was the way he was.

The stirring of wings rumbled again—she couldn't control her body from trembling a bit as she pressed her face into Tin's warm neck. Even if she'd still had her rifle, there wouldn't have been enough bullets to slaughter them all.

CHAPTER SEVEN

TIN

If one night with Dorothy pressed against Tin wasn't enough to drive him mad, the second was. Damn whoever'd cursed those pixies who forced Tin and Dorothy beneath his cloak. *Flying monkeys*, Dorothy had called them. No doubt it was another term she'd learned from Glinda. Why Dorothy wanted to journey to that dimwitted witch was beyond him. Crow was different—they had traveled through Oz together—but Glinda hadn't done much outside of giving Dorothy the silver slippers. She had probably floated away in her fucking bubble and got distracted by will-o-wisps on her way home. She should be defending the South more, instead of letting Langwidere attempt to conquer it. Tin had kept silent on Langwidere having the western territory because he hadn't wanted to bring her name up.

"Please tell me that's a town." Dorothy hurried to Tin's side, slightly out of breath and pointing through the trees where the edge of a large village peeked through. They'd seen nothing but foliage all day so he couldn't blame her sudden burst of excitement. Their tense, silent journey was almost over for another day. "It's not a trick, is it?"

The sight of thatched roofs and old, worn buildings was far from welcome. Towns meant fae. Fae meant a hassle. But the yellow brick road ran straight down the center of it. Tin had traveled across most of Oz over the years, but he'd never been to Langwidere's place before. Even if he had, he needed the brick road to navigate the South in general and they weren't too far from the border.

"It's a town," Tin grumbled.

They just weren't stepping foot in it. They needed the road, but that was easy enough to find again if they walked around this little pocket of civilization. If they kept moving, they could be in the South by nightfall. A quick break at the southern border if Dorothy needed it, and they would arrive at Langwidere's a day ahead of schedule. Resting in town would get them there on the last day of Lion's deadline, and he *wasn't* taking an entire night to rest. Dorothy, on the other hand, stumbled with each step and appeared ready to blow over with the slightest breeze.

"I can't wait to take a bath and eat something other than nuts." She let her head fall back and closed her eyes.

Tin bit his tongue to keep from reminding her that he'd hunted for their lunch hours ago. The meat was tough and clung to the bone, but it was filling enough. He hadn't *needed* to kill a second bird for her.

"And sleep in a bed … *alone.*"

The last addition to her list set Tin on edge. It wasn't *that* bad sleeping against him, was it? He'd kept his hands to himself. Though there'd been no stopping his very obvious attraction to her when the softest part of her had been pressed against him. He *knew* she'd felt his erection last night, but his cloak wasn't big enough for them to sleep safely apart. The enchanted fabric saved them from the monstrous pixies and his body heat kept her from freezing when the temperatures had dropped. As much as he hated to admit it, Tin's hardened heart had felt something when she hadn't flinched away. Her fingers had traced his scar without any sign of disgust and her hand had rested on his chest as if it were the most natural thing in the world. Even the whores that took his coin hadn't touched him that warmly—they hadn't even *looked* at his face. But Dorothy… Her heat, her compassion, sent humming vibrations through him even now.

"We aren't staying," he said before he could stop himself.

Dorothy glared at him. "Excuse me?"

"We're continuing south."

"I told you, I'm going to find Crow. I only stayed with you another day because you promised we would find a town, and I need supplies." He should have known she hadn't let go of searching for Crow.

Tin snorted. Even with supplies, she wouldn't last a day on the yellow brick road without him. The Emerald City was even more hazardous with the continued fighting. Why Dorothy assumed Crow would still be there was beyond him. Whatever condition Crow's brain was in now, he had to be smart enough not to get involved in that power struggle.

"We did find a town." He motioned to the sleepy village. Smoke rose from chimneys, but the streets were empty as the fae settled into their homes for the evening. The rich scent of roasting meat filled the air, even this far away. It would be a lie to say it didn't make Tin's mouth water, though he knew it wasn't worth the trouble. "And now we walk around it."

Dorothy pursed her lips, a defiant gleam in her eyes, and sprinted toward the buildings.

Tin stood immobile. Never had he met someone so insolent… No one had been this utterly unafraid of his wrath in years.

Dorothy was nearly at the edge of town when he bolted after her. He snatched her wrist and spun her to his chest. A small gasp escaped her as he pressed her into a wide tree trunk, trapping her there with his weight. "No sane fae goes to the Emerald City."

"I'm not a fae, and I've been called insane on numerous occasions," Dorothy said, her eyes becoming glassy. "If your heart is stone again, maybe Crow's brain isn't intact either. He could still be there."

Tin cursed under his breath. "Even before he got his brain unscrambled, Crow wasn't *that* stupid, so behave. You're not leaving my side until we get to Lion."

She shoved at his chest, but he didn't budge against the feeble attempt. "I'm not your prisoner, Tin. You can't force me to stay with you."

"I was paid to do a job, and I always follow through."

"Is that all I am to you?" Dorothy lifted her chin, her eyes no longer glassy. "A job?"

Was it? A muscle ticked in his jaw. She was a job but was that *all?* Dorothy wasn't like anyone else he knew—she'd grown into a fearless, determined woman. She was naïve, compassionate, bold… His gaze fell to her mouth and he leaned in. Another inch and he would be kissing her. How he wanted to close that gap. To see what she tasted like. He suppressed a groan at the thought.

She *was* a job. Soon her face—this flawless face—would no longer belong to Dorothy. It would sit in a glass case or, worse, on Langwidere's shoulders. Would Lion be with his lover while she looked like Dorothy? Would he part her lips with his tongue and explore? Stare into these warm brown eyes as he entered her? An intense wave of anger washed over Tin and he leaned in, running his nose along the soft skin of her neck.

"What are you doing?" Dorothy whispered, but didn't try to shove him away again.

What was he doing? What *the fuck* was he doing? He lifted his head just enough to meet her eyes. "We'll stay until tomorrow morning."

If they missed Lion's deadline, he wouldn't get paid, and then leading Dorothy to her death would be pointless. He could send her back to Kansas instead… Or keep her for himself… He pushed away from Dorothy, as well as his thoughts, and rubbed a hand over the smooth side of his face.

"Good. You need some sleep to get rid of this attitude." Dorothy made a show of brushing off her dirty, stained clothes and stepped away from the tree.

"Dorothy?" he croaked.

She paused and looked over her shoulder at him, waiting.

"I… Townsfolk don't usually welcome me with open arms,"

he admitted. A small sense of shame rose inside him. The emotion startled him almost as much as the trepidation he felt at being run out of town in front of her. He didn't care about the townsfolk or their opinions. *He didn't.* Dorothy was … different.

She backtracked to him and wove her fingers between his, squeezing. "You're not the monster you think you are."

Wasn't that a nice notion? That he somehow deserved to have her holding his hand as if he hadn't used it to kill countless fae? The warmth of her skin crept through his gloves, making him want to squeeze her hand in return, but the blood of his prey had heated his hand too. Tin swallowed hard. "I'm every bit the monster and they know it."

She opened her mouth, likely to deny it again, but Tin freed his hand from hers and strode into town. All the way, he flexed his hand as he walked, still feeling her warm fingers entwined with his. The town was another full of dwarves, as most in the East were, but being closer to the southern border attracted different fae, too. Brownies, gnomes, pixies of the non-cursed variety, and even a few banshees were known in these parts. He knew because he'd been hired to kill at least one of each.

They headed down a handful of paths before seeing another soul. Tin quickly turned the marred side of his face away from the female nymph and folded his hands behind his back to hide his iron-tipped gloves. For whatever reason, he didn't want Dorothy to witness the female running away screaming.

"Hello!" Dorothy called cheerfully and waved to the nymph.

Tin sighed inwardly. *What the hell is she doing now?*

The female blinked her large green eyes in surprise. She wore a bright yellow dress made of spider silk with matching ribbons woven through her black hair and cheaply made jewelry draped around her neck. A prostitute, given her rumpled state and how her hand rested on the door to the brothel.

"Don't draw attention," Tin whispered.

Dorothy ignored the warning and approached with her hand out. "It's nice to see a friendly face."

The girl sized Dorothy up, looking strangely at her hand, as fae didn't shake, and then scanned Tin. He watched her ring-laden fingers skim down the front of her dress and tensed. If she went for a weapon, she'd be dead before she drew another breath and they'd be on their way to Lion.

"Thirty silver for both of you," she said in a sultry voice.

"For both of us?" Dorothy asked.

"Thirty silver?" Tin quickly flung his arm around Dorothy's shoulders. If she didn't want to do what she was told, he'd teach her a lesson. "That seems a bit steep."

The nymph parted her ruby lips. "It would be for you alone, but not many fae here will take a human to bed. Or rather, none of the clean ones will anyway."

Dorothy tried to jump away from Tin, but he held her to his side, without letting the iron on his face be seen. *Oh, yes,* he thought. Judging by the red creeping into her face, this was going to be more fun than he'd anticipated.

"There's been a misunderstanding," Dorothy squeaked.

"Darling, it's okay," he said in a soothing voice. "We can have fun on our own."

"We won't be doing any such thing!"

"It's disappointing, I know." He sighed loudly enough for the nymph to hear. Then Tin chuckled into Dorothy's hair and led her away from the brothel before they created a scene. "You promised to listen," he mumbled in her ear.

"All I did was say hello. There was no reason for you to…"

Tin grinned at her deepening blush. "To what?"

"Look. There's an inn," she blurted instead of answering.

She was right. An inn sat at the crossroads, but not the kind where she would want to stay. Definitely the only kind that would accept his coin, however. He let go of her and fished his money out as she hurried across the brick street. The excitement in her expression only made him worry more about the innkeeper chasing him out of town. He stretched his jaw, feeling the iron pull against his skin. An actual bed would do them both some good—after a night in the dirt—though she would need to sleep beside him again. There was no chance he was letting

Dorothy have her own room when she was so adamant about going their separate ways to look for Crow.

Dorothy barely waited for him to catch up before she pushed her way through the door with another pleasant *hello*. Tin eased in after her, allowing her to steal the attention from him. Maybe he should have given her the coin to secure a room on their behalf—the innkeeper would have rented to her just to make her stop acting as if they were lifelong friends.

A beady-eyed brownie sat on a worn velvet chair with a guest book before her. Wrinkles covered her dark face and the skin on her hands was so tight it looked as if it was about to burst. She wore a high-necked black dress covered in some sort of animal fur and too much brown powder to cover her graying hair.

The brownie licked her fingertip and turned the page, pen in hand. "One room or two?"

"One," Tin said at the same time Dorothy said, "two".

The brownie paused and Tin felt her gaze sink into him. He kept his face tilted again and arranged his cloak to hide the axe at his hip. Curse his notoriety. "The Tin Man," the brownie finally squeaked, yellow eyes bulging with fear. "Not in here. No, no, no. Even I have my limits!"

Tin released a breath and faced her fully. "My companion needs to rest."

"The Knoll House has plenty of rooms available."

"But we aren't *at* the Knoll House," Tin said through his teeth. For Dorothy's sake, he tried to remain calm. He wasn't sure how long he could keep it up because he, too, had limits.

"He won't hurt anyone," Dorothy promised. He wished she hadn't. "We have enough money."

How would she know how much he carried? And how stupid of her to announce it in a place that catered to criminals and cutthroats. If someone tried to rob them, there went his promise of no killing. Tin cleared his throat.

Dorothy shot him a stern look. "Don't even try to deny it. We're staying here."

The brownie shut her book and inched closer to Dorothy.

"Dearest human." She eyed Tin warily and shifted to use Dorothy's leg as a shield for her short, plump body. "Do you not know who you travel with?"

"Of course I know him."

The brownie blanched. "I can't allow it. I'll have no customers left."

Tin huffed and snatched one of the keys hanging on the wall. With a quick glance at the tag, he informed her, "We'll be in room eleven. Send food up—*no faerie fruit*. Knock and leave it outside the door."

"You can't do that!" The brownie cowered as she spoke. "Give it back!"

"You won't even know we're here," Dorothy vowed with a pleading smile.

"Leave her. She won't give us any trouble," Tin said, moving away from the frightened fae. Once again, he had to bend to keep from hitting his head as he climbed the stairs. Next time he splurged on an inn, it would be one built for someone of his height. The rooms were clearly marked with large gouges in the wooden doors, and Tin wasted no time locking them both inside theirs.

A lumpy mattress and round wooden tub took up most of the room, leaving only enough space for a one-person table and another two people to stand. It smelled awful, like mildew, wet dirt, and sex, but at least the bedding appeared fresh.

"You couldn't have grabbed two keys?" Dorothy cocked her head, then took in the room.

"Sorry, *princess*. Do the accommodations not suit you? We could continue on like I wanted—the brownie would be thrilled."

"I'm not continuing on with you," she said. "I'm just staying the one night and then getting supplies so I can find Crow."

"Good luck with that." Tin stuck the key in his pocket with purpose, noticing Dorothy's eyes glued to the metal. "Remember how things ended last time."

She flopped down on the bed and stretched. "I won't argue

with you."

Neither would he, but he let the subject drop. She wouldn't be going anywhere. With a sigh, he sat, using the table as a chair. His fingers moved unconsciously to his face. If it wasn't for the iron snaking across his cheek, maybe he would have been able to blend in enough to secure a better room for her. A woman on the path to death deserved that much—at least *this* woman did.

"Tin, it's not so bad," Dorothy whispered. "The marks—I know you worry about them, even if you don't want to admit it. They make you look almost fierce, a beautiful sort of untamed." She cleared her throat, her face turning red. "Anyway, my point is, there's nothing wrong with them."

He snorted. "Nothing except making me look like a fierce, untamed beast, you mean."

"No. I meant that as a compliment."

Tin moved his hand to the small pieces of bone holding his hair away from his face. Maybe he should remove them. His hair would cover the worst of it. "It's not a compliment."

"You don't seem like the type to care about what other people think." She propped herself up on her elbows. "You certainly don't care what *I* think, and we were friends."

"You're right. I *don't* care," he lied. "Hiding my face just might make getting you to Lion easier on us both. Quicker money, less hassle."

She rolled her eyes and fell back onto the bed. "If believing that makes you feel better…"

The brownie left them cold stew and stale bread for a late dinner like he'd instructed, but despite the innkeeper's passive aggressive meal choices, it was the best food they'd had in days. Dorothy ate it slowly, like she was savoring each taste. Tin watched her mouth and wondered what her lips would feel like on his. On his neck, his stomach. Lower.

Right at dusk, Dorothy fell into a blissful sleep, unaware of his thoughts. But time passed and Tin couldn't make the lewd ideas disappear. How would her hair feel if he buried his fingers into it? What sounds would she make? He grazed her cheek with his knuckles as she slumbered. Even with his gloves on, it sent a thrill through him. His balls ached from denying his release day after day and he shifted uncomfortably. The problem could be solved rather quickly if he wasn't afraid Dorothy would wake up to the sight of him stroking himself. *Ah, hell.* He shouldn't have even let the thought surface because now his cock was rising to the occasion.

The thin blanket did nothing to hide Dorothy's curves. Beneath her clothes, he wondered what her naked body looked like, how heavy her breasts would feel in his hands, how her legs would feel wrapped around his waist as he thrust inside her. A sweat broke on the back of his neck.

The brothel.

It was right across the street and Dorothy was fast asleep. The innkeeper wouldn't come knocking if she didn't see Tin leave so Dorothy would be safe here alone. He could be quick about it. Who was he kidding? It *would* be quick after suffering temptation for so long.

That settled it.

Tin carefully got up from the edge of the bed, slipped from the room, and locked Dorothy in again without making a sound. He used his cloak to move through the hallway and lobby unseen and entered the brothel across the street without drawing any attention.

Half-naked fae worked the opulent room, leaning over males as they played cards and perching on their laps in the sitting area. Pillows were strewn on couches and in corners. A deep purple rug padded the center of a gleaming crystal floor. Faerie lights floated near the ceiling, casting a soft glow down onto the room and its inhabitants. Wall murals depicted a variety of sexual scenes, some subtle, others perverse, in deep, sensual colors. The artist was so skilled that it looked to Tin as if he could feel the faes' satiny skin if he grazed the wall.

The workers were a menu of endless variety. If one preferred horns or wings or pointed teeth, they could be found under this roof, but Tin wasn't picky. He couldn't afford to be. The gems of any brothel, however, were the nymphs, because they actually enjoyed the profession. Each of the nymphs in this establishment wore a different jewel colored gown with stone or ribbons in their hair and the perfect blend of color painted on their delicate faces. Tin's breath grew ragged knowing one of them would be beneath him soon.

"Can I help you, my lord?" a female asked. Tin turned to see the nymph in the yellow dress from earlier. She was put together now, hair brushed to a shine and dress smoothed of its wrinkles. "Oh, it's you. Where's your human friend?"

Tin suppressed a snarl. "Forget you saw her."

She ran a hand down his arm, making his cock grow even harder as he thought about Dorothy stroking his skin instead. *Damn it.* Why did she have to bring Dorothy up? She was the last person he wanted to think about right now.

"In that case, what's your pleasure?" the female asked.

A nymph in a blue dress caught his eye on the other side of the room. Wavy brown hair fell to her hips with strands of pearls worked into a circlet of braids. Deep brown eyes met his. He adjusted his pants as he stepped away from the female in yellow. "She is."

Tin tried not to think about how much she resembled Dorothy as he approached. He would need to pay her an exorbitant amount to have him, he knew, but he would gladly do so.

"Good evening, my lord," she said in a sweet voice. "Are you here for a game of cards?"

Tin didn't even spare a look at the gaming table beside her. "I'm here for company."

"Wonderful." Her smile was only slightly believable as she scanned him up and down. He knew he appeared unnerving—

partially hidden beneath a cloak—but he didn't care. As long as she didn't scream when she saw his face without the hood, recognizing him as the Tin Man. "Follow me upstairs, won't you?"

Moans of other patrons' pleasure, mixed with the creaking of beds, filled the second floor. Incense floated through the air and Tin nearly moaned himself. It was no surprise the brothel was infused with the scent of an aphrodisiac. They wanted customers in and out to make more money. Tin had nearly been mad with need before, but now, he was worried about making it to the room without taking the nymph against the wall right there in the hallway.

"After you, my lord," the female in blue said and held back a thick red curtain to her room. A large bed covered in silks and furs waited inside but the room was otherwise empty.

He took one step toward the room and froze when he heard his name from the room next door.

"The Tin Man, yes," said a male. The curtain was closed so he couldn't see who the voice belonged to. "Have you seen him?"

"I think I would remember a beast like that," the female replied.

"And the human girl? Brown hair, about this tall…"

"Forgive me, my lord, but we don't see many humans in these parts. Are you sure I can't—"

A hand touched Tin's and he jerked back to find the nymph staring at him. "Is everything all right?" she asked.

Shit. Shit, shit, shit.

His cock throbbed painfully, but if someone had tracked them here, Dorothy could be in danger. And he'd left her alone for *this.*

"No need," the mystery male said. "If you do see them, please leave word for Crow with your madam and I'll check back before I head south."

Crow.

No. It couldn't be him. What would he be doing here? And

why? There was no reason he should even know Dorothy had returned to Oz. If Dorothy found out he was looking for her, Tin would have to drag her to Lion unconscious. And Crow... If he discovered why Tin was taking Dorothy south, Crow would do everything in his power to stop him.

Shit!

Tin turned on his heel and bolted back to the inn. He'd never moved so fast in his life. Everything and everyone in his peripheral vision became a blur, while his rapid breath echoed in his ears.

The door to his inn room was suddenly in front of him, the key in his fingertips. He fumbled to fit it into the lock with shaking hands. On the third attempt, it slid in and Tin shoved his way inside to find Dorothy exactly where he'd left her. Breath filled his tight, burning lungs. Every muscle relaxed at once and he leaned against the door, sliding to the floor.

It wasn't until he wiped the sweat from his forehead that he realized he was worried—not because he wanted Lion's money, but because he wasn't ready to *not* see her again. Whatever that meant. If the bed had been empty, he wasn't sure what his reaction would've been.

But she *was* there. Her lips were parted, her chest rising and falling with each steady breath. He wanted to touch her flawless skin like she had touched his iron mark, to give her the same warm feeling her touch had given to him.

Tin gripped the fabric over his chest. Something behind his breastbone cracked, shattered, exploded and a painful pounding suddenly assaulted him from the inside out. He gasped, his wide gaze locking onto Dorothy's sleeping form. The raging pulse in his ears, the heavy *thump thump thump* beneath his ribs. His heart. It was back.

Fuck!

CHAPTER EIGHT

DOROTHY

The heavy thud of booted footsteps against the wooden floor drew Dorothy out from her dreamless sleep. Her eyes flicked open, but she didn't move as Tin reentered the inn bedroom. His body slumped to the floor. Where had he gone? Had he left her here to go and get inebriated? She hadn't even heard him leave. It must have been the journey, making her more exhausted than usual, even though her endurance was typically steady because of the farm work.

What is he doing? Dorothy thought as he stood back up and came her way.

As Tin crept closer to the bed, slower than usual, Dorothy kept her breathing even, in and out, out and in, because she had a plan. She was no longer tired, but wide awake.

She and Tin weren't near the flying monkey beasts who howled through the night. There were only the sounds of the normal night world—bugs chirping. Beside her, the mattress dipped, slightly shaking her body. Tin seemed to hesitate before lying beside her, close, smelling of incense, his warmth practically cocooning her. It was that same feeling as when his body had been pressed against her at that tree, his nose brushing her neck, the feel of *him* against her the other night. And even then, he'd been mostly insufferable. But…

Steady. Keep breathing steady. Tin was once her friend, even if he believed he wasn't now, he could be again—once she cracked open his stone heart. His arm slipped around her, almost hesitantly, but she knew it was most likely so she wouldn't try and run off. After what seemed like forever, finally, Tin's breaths came slow and even.

Dorothy gave it a few extra moments before, ever so slowly, she rolled to face him. Even in the dark, she wasn't afraid of him, whether he wielded an axe or not. What she wondered was how anyone could ever be afraid of his soulful face.

She'd read such macabre books as *The Phantom of the Opera, Grimms' Fairy Tales, Dr. Jekyll and Mr. Hyde,* and the creatures in those books were ones to be feared, not Tin, not his face.

Staying silent as snowflakes falling in winter, Dorothy once again shifted her hand toward Tin's pocket of his pants. He'd woken the last time she'd done this at the previous inn—this time she'd be more careful. Her movements remained quiet, feather-light, like a true pickpocket as she pressed her fingers inside the place where the key to her escape lay hidden. An unexpected image came to her then, one of her slipping her hand elsewhere, into the waistband of Tin's pants. She froze as certain parts of her tingled at the thought—she hurried and pushed it away. *How un-lady-like, Dorothy.* It wasn't as if she was a virginal woman anyway—she'd lain with Jimmy before.

Holding her breath and a shiver back at the same time, Dorothy pushed her fingers farther in, then felt the brass against her digits. With caution, she dragged the key out, inch by daunting inch. Until it was fully in her grasp.

Dorothy couldn't help but grin, yet the tricky part would be getting out of the bed and then the room. She rolled over and scooted to the edge of the mattress before placing her shoes on. Tightening her grip on the key, she tiptoed her way across the wood floor to the door. The room was too dark to see clearly, and she strained her eyes as she lifted the key to press into the lock. When she turned the key to the right, there was a soft click.

She stilled before glancing over her shoulder, prepared for Tin to rip away the key and hold her in his arms once more. He didn't—he still lay in bed, fast asleep.

Turning the knob, Dorothy took a step out into the dimly-lit hallway and locked the door behind her with the key. She tossed the brass key into the air and caught it with a smile on her face. *Now who is the one locked in the room? Not me, that's who.*

She wished she could see Tin's face when he woke to discover he'd been outwitted. With quick footsteps, Dorothy hurried down the stairs to the front desk, passing a brownie who was paying no mind to her as he wrote on a sheet of paper with a quill. He grunted as she bid him a goodbye, still keeping his nose buried in whatever he was writing.

The Emerald City had become a place that was no longer alluring. Battle for control raged inside, and she knew she couldn't go in there with only a measly knife. She should have also taken Tin's axe for this little bit of her journey—too late for that. Tin had warned her that the night wasn't safe, but it wasn't a haven the last time she was here either.

Where could she find something better to use? Then Dorothy remembered the nymph in the yellow dress at the brothel that she and Tin had run into earlier. Perhaps the nymph would help her, but there might be a price. Dorothy was sure she could barter something. If not, maybe the nymph could at least point her in another direction.

She rushed across the yellow brick road and through tufts of grass toward the brothel. The grimy windows of the building were lit by dozens and dozens of candles, and the thatched roof appeared as though it might cave in at any moment.

As she opened the door and walked inside, the air struck her nose, reeking of sex, ale, and perfume. To her left rested a cluster of tables filled with patrons, touching their hired fae for the night while playing cards. At a table in the corner, a fae sat with flowing blonde hair and goat horns sprouting from her forehead, while a male with his shirt unbuttoned painted her. Against the opposite wall stood another couple—a faerie with long lilac wings draping the floor as her hands ran up her client's chest. Dorothy didn't want to watch all of this, but she couldn't fight the allure of it all. She finally tore her gaze away and took a step forward when an arm dropped down around her shoulders.

"Hello, beautiful, I think I've been bewitched," a voice slurred at her ear. "I didn't know mortals worked in this part of Oz."

Dorothy could barely move as her eyes met a fae male with sleek black hair, eyes the color of tree bark, faun ears, and curving horns. "I'm sorry, I won't be here long."

"It would only take a moment to slip inside you, and I've never been in a mortal before. I'll pay whatever you wish," he purred at her ear as her eyes widened in surprise.

Before she could say no and move away, a voice spoke up from behind her, "She doesn't work here. Now drop your arm from her, because she's mine."

"Sorry, Falyn," the faun said in a sullen voice, "I didn't realize she was already taken." He pried his arm from Dorothy's shoulders, turned on his hoofed feet, and headed to a velvet settee where a group of nymphs wearing see-through scarves were feeding each other green faerie fruit.

Dorothy focused on the fae she'd been looking for, still wearing her canary-yellow dress made of spider silk and matching ribbon in her obsidian hair. The nymph—Falyn— wrapped her hand around Dorothy's wrist and tugged her to the very back of the room, to two high-backed chairs in a darkened corner.

Falyn pushed Dorothy into one of the chairs and hovered over her. The nymph's moss-colored eyes open wide. "What's your name?" Her words came out in a rush.

Dorothy's brows lowered in confusion. She'd come here to find Falyn and now it seemed as though the nymph had been looking for her. "Why?"

"Just, what is it?"

Tin would have told her to be quiet and not answer, but he wasn't there, and she wasn't going to listen to anyone except herself. Besides, Dorothy believed that Falyn might be willing to help after ridding her of the faun. "Dorothy."

Lips parting, the nymph's hand flew to her mouth and her green eyes lit up with glee. "As in Dorothy Gale? It is, isn't it? He's looking for you."

Dorothy stilled, scanning the room, prepared to find Tin already there with his axe in hand. But he wasn't anywhere in sight. "What do you mean exactly? Who?"

"Crow," Falyn whispered. "He was here earlier, asking about you. I didn't know he was here, but Chara came and told me Crow had come, sniffing around for the Tin Man and a human woman. Chara hadn't seen you two, but then it clicked that I had."

Dorothy perked up, leaning forward while growing anxious. "I need to find him. That's actually why I came back here, because I was going to see about getting supplies to retrieve him from the Emerald City. Where is he?" She searched the room, not seeing a single sign of him. Perhaps he was in one of the other rooms.

"He already left." Falyn shrugged. "But he did mention something to Chara about heading south."

Dorothy stood from her chair. "I'd better hurry so I can get to him." The sooner she left, the sooner she could catch up and find him.

Falyn placed a hand on Dorothy's shoulder. "You may not be heading to the Emerald City any longer, but you can't go empty-handed, either. The South is dangerous, too."

"I don't have any money." She patted the pockets of her overalls, knowing nothing but lint rested inside. "Perhaps I could barter by bringing you back something?"

"You're Dorothy Gale." Falyn smiled. "You destroyed the Wicked Witch of the West, and even with our world in shambles at the moment, I believe now that you're back, all can be righted once again."

What the fae of Oz didn't realize was that Dorothy had always been just a girl. It was all because of the silver slippers—

that was what had given her the magic to defeat the Wicked Witch. And anyone who put on those slippers could have done the same, but for some reason no one seemed to care about that fact. She thought back to when she'd reentered Oz and there had been a statue built of her. If she did get the slippers again, maybe she could help like she had before.

"Follow me," Falyn continued and waved her down a narrow hallway with walls covered in gold leaves and copper branches. Dorothy could only focus on the moans and groans coming from behind the closed curtains.

Falyn opened the curtain to a room smelling of rose petals, with only a bed, a vanity, and a wardrobe. From beneath the bed, Falyn pulled out a sheathed machete. She handed it, along with the strap, to Dorothy. "You can wear it."

"Are you sure?" Dorothy asked, tightening it on her back. She was used to a rifle, but this would be perfect. No bullets to run out of.

"Yes."

She peered up at Falyn and slid the knife from her pocket. "I know it's not an even trade, but keep this."

Falyn rolled the small blade in her hand. "I like this better. No one will see it coming if I need to use it."

Dorothy hoped Falyn wouldn't have to use it. "If Tin comes, please don't tell him I was here."

"He was actually here not too long ago," Falyn said, studying her with what might have been sympathy.

"He was?" But then she recognized the smell of incense, the one that had come from Tin when he'd slipped into bed.

"Yes." She nodded. "He went to see one of the other nymphs."

Tin hadn't been drunk off of wine—he'd been delirious from sex, or perhaps both. "Oh." Dorothy couldn't stop to wonder about why it felt like a punch to the chest. She also couldn't help but imagine what it would be like to have Tin's naked body, slick with sweat, moving against hers while her unclothed form was heated head to toe from his touch.

Dorothy shook away the thought. She needed to make herself focus only on getting to Crow. Now that she knew she wouldn't have to fight her way through the Emerald City to find him, it would hopefully make things much easier. "Thank you, Falyn."

"Never thank a fae." Falyn shot her a glare. "But in this case, you're welcome. Be sure to keep your head on your shoulders. Even with Glinda there, the South isn't a good place to be anymore. Most have fled."

The East hadn't been too terribly bad. How much worse could the South be? "Tin told me it's not like it used to be."

Falyn nodded and looked like she wanted to say more, but Dorothy needed to leave.

With a goodbye, Dorothy headed out of the brothel and back into the starry night. She stepped onto the yellow brick road, feeling every crack and broken piece beneath her feet.

While she should be shifting all her attention to Crow, Dorothy could only think about Tin entwined with another female. An anger came then, one she didn't understand, but she let that emotion fuel her as she took off at a fast sprint. There was no time to dally and walk when she could reach Crow much quicker if she just ran. Together, they would get to Glinda. But a fear nagged at her... What if Crow was changed like Tin?

CHAPTER NINE

TIN

*T*hump-thump. *Thump-thump.*

The pace of Tin's now-beating heart tugged him slowly from a deep sleep. His chest was raw and vulnerable over the unfamiliar organ. He hadn't expected to regain a real heart—hadn't *wanted* to—but he felt more alive than ever now. It returned to stone so long ago that he forgot how the steady rhythm flowed from head-to-toe.

Tin thought once his heart was encased in stone again, it would remain that way. That the Wizard had pulled a horrible trick on him. The strength of his pulse had lessened so subtly over the first two years with the beating organ that he hadn't noticed he was in trouble until the day he'd woken up to find it had changed back to a solid stone in his chest, but now he knew the truth. His heart had never truly been lost to the curse. It was waiting. Waiting for Dorothy to return and break it open again. All it took was her touch, genuine and unafraid.

Tin stretched across the too-small mattress with a faint smile and cracked a few aching joints. The pillow smelled vaguely of piss, but it wasn't the worst place he'd laid his head. He was just relieved to have finally gotten a good night's rest after having had Dorothy pressed—

Holy shit.

Dorothy.

Tin jerked forward and ran his hands frantically over the empty bed as if it would somehow summon her. When it didn't, he flew to his feet and spun, hoping she was anywhere else in the tiny room. His breaths became labored. This was impossible. How? Unless that good for nothing brownie had another key and a severe death wish. He would kill everything under three feet tall until one of them produced Dorothy. *Unbelievable!* Oh, the ways he was going to punish the devious little innkeeper for this. He swept his axe up and attempted to wrench the door open. The wood shuddered but the locked door held fast. Tin growled angrily and dug into his pocket for the key.

The world seemed to still for a long moment. It was gone. The key was *gone!* He *knew* he'd locked the door before he got back in bed with Dorothy—his resurrected heart beat like a caged bird. Thinking the key fell out while he slept, Tin ripped the sheets away and shook the blankets. He knelt to look beneath the bed. Nothing. The key was nowhere to be seen.

The truth trickled in slowly. Tin wanted to deny that Dorothy could've gotten the key off him while he slept, but couldn't. The relief at seeing her in the room, not stolen away by Crow, and the shock of his heart returning, had pulled him into a deep sleep. Too deep, considering the danger lurking in every direction. The breaking of his curse seemed to have worn him out in every sense of the word. Not only had Dorothy put her hand in his pocket and extracted the key, but also climbed out from beneath his arm to get off the bed, opened the door, *and* locked it again.

"Damn it!" Tin's blood boiled at his negligence. At Dorothy's utter disregard for her own safety.

Tin gripped his axe tighter and slammed it into the door. Again and again he swung. Splinters flew all around him as he demolished the wood. When it was nothing more than a frame with hinges and a knob, he stormed through the jagged hole.

Two beady-eyed brownies stared in horror as he strode down the stairs, then he impaled the axe into the record book. The young, pale-skinned female sitting at the entrance leapt back, knocking over her tall chair. Tin took two heaving breaths before regaining his ability to speak. "What have you done with her?"

The brownie squeaked unintelligibly.

It took every ounce of Tin's self-control not to kill her then and there, but he needed her answer first. Returned heart be damned. "Where. Is. The. Girl?"

"She left shortly after you returned," the bearded male yelped from the top of the staircase. "Walked right out the door, she did."

Tin straightened his back, shoulders stiff. Fucking Dorothy and her fucking determination to find Crow. And that piece of shit witch, Glinda. Dorothy *knew* Tin wouldn't let her out of his sight if she waited until morning. Knew he wouldn't allow her to find supplies and waltz off. So instead, Dorothy had decided to get herself killed because, apparently, Crow was more important than her own life.

"Was she alone?" Tin demanded.

The brownie nodded.

Of course she was. Because she was *fucking stupid*. What more proof did she need that Oz was dangerous? The yellow brick road was destroyed, the Emerald City a battle ground, and cursed pixies trolled the land every night. If anything harmed her, it would be her own fault. Not that he wouldn't track and kill whatever dared touch her.

Hypocrite, Tin chided himself. Hadn't he originally been leading Dorothy to two fae who would commit the worst kind of violence against her? Maybe Dorothy wasn't so stupid after all. Maybe she *should* be running away from him. It didn't hurt any less that she'd fled in the middle of the night. *Damn his heart for coming back* now. This would be so much easier if he didn't have feelings to contend with.

Tin tore through the front door of the inn and froze. Where would she have gone? Back toward the Emerald City? Even though he told her there was no way Crow was still there…

Fuck.

He covered his face with his free hand, ignoring the burn

from the iron tipped glove, and tried to piece together what Dorothy might do. She wasn't a little girl anymore and he'd only known *this* Dorothy for a few days. He didn't know how she thought. Fae were easier to read, easier to predict. Money and power fueled them while something else fueled Dorothy.

Money and power.

The brothel. Crow had told the nymph he would be back to check with the madam before he left town. If he hadn't returned, that meant he was still nearby. Unless he didn't have to check because he found someone else who'd seen Dorothy…

Tin shook the thought from his mind and raced back to the brothel. The door slammed against the inner wall, startling dazed patrons and workers alike. The madam could've been any of them or none of them, but Crow, Tin knew, wouldn't go unnoticed.

"Did Crow come back?" he boomed, drawing every eye in the room.

The fae shifted, filling the air with tension, as Tin's identity finally broke through their drugged haze. A lanky elf shoved a naked, horned female from her lap and screamed. Pandemonium followed. Chairs fell as their occupants scrambled to their feet—a smaller fae tripped over the displaced furniture, before a hoofed creature trampled it. Males shoved their prostitutes in Tin's direction and raced for the back exit. The females cried. One fainted. It was an overly-dramatic scene that Tin didn't want to deal with.

"Damn useless pieces of shit!" he roared.

There would be no answers here. He turned on his heel and tried to remember what he knew of Crow from before, when the fae's brain had still been a mess. A loner. Quiet. Enjoyed working with his hands. But then he got his brain fixed and damned if Tin knew what his personality was like now.

Think, Tin, think.

Crow wouldn't want to stay in town, even one as quiet as this. He preferred nature to an actual shelter, and that much couldn't have changed. To the woods, then. Somewhere close, but not too close… Tin grumbled a string of curses and set off for the edge of town.

Two perimeter sweeps of the woods later, one farther out from town than the first, Tin finally came across his first clue to Crow's whereabouts. An elvish song carried through the trees, deep and gentle. Tin scanned the branches above in search of the cursed pixies and found them blissfully empty. Only Crow would be stupid enough to camp in these woods and purposely draw attention to himself.

Tin's heart thundered in his chest as he tracked the somber song through the woods. He shoved down all traces of emotion that tried to barrel into his thoughts. Dorothy was about to regret running. Almost as much as Crow was about to regret luring her to a place as dangerous as these woods. If Dorothy had told Crow they were heading to Lion, they would both regret it because then Tin would have to fight for Dorothy. When Tin fought, he won, and he didn't particularly want to slaughter Crow. At least not in front of Dorothy, when she clearly cared for him. But why should he care how Dorothy felt? She clearly didn't care how *he* felt. Even if she did care, Crow was nothing but a nuisance to Tin. So what if Dorothy hated him for the last day or two of her life? He'd leave her to Langwidere and walk away a richer fae. His heart would harden again soon enough if history was any indication, and any reservations he had would die along with it.

The thought soured his stomach. *No.* Whatever Dorothy did, however she hurt him, he wouldn't give her to Lion or Langwidere. Any thought of doing so now was as silent as his chest had been yesterday morning.

The trees thinned and Tin paused. This was where the song originated, but there was no Crow. He stared at the dead leaves scattered over exposed dirt and listened harder as his hand drifted to the head of his axe. The song ended abruptly and Tin ground his teeth together in annoyance.

"You could simply ask me to come down," Crow said from above. "No need to chop down any trees, Woodsman."

Tin's gaze snapped up to find a dark canvas stretched between two thick branches. Dark blue leaves camouflaged the hammock in thick foliage, the fabric swinging slightly when a pointed black boot appeared over the side. The movement sent a few brittle, dying leaves floating gently toward Tin's head.

Relief at finding Crow faded almost instantly when he remembered that it meant actually having to *deal* with Crow. Ten years apart wasn't nearly enough. Once Dorothy left, Crow did too, taking off on his own without so much as a goodbye to anyone in the Emerald City. *Selfish bastard.* "There's no need to take your name seriously either, and yet you've nested twenty feet off the ground."

"Says the fae with metal burned into his face."

Iron wasn't tin, but he had bigger things to worry about. "Get your ass down here."

There was a brief moment of silence before Crow exhaled loudly. A dark figure dropped from the hammock, landing in a crouched position, like he was a fucking bird. Crow rose slowly, straightening his spine, looking every bit like a shadow of death when he'd probably never killed a thing in his miserable life.

Dark feathers were braided into Crow's long black hair. His locks cascaded over his shoulders from beneath a sleek black mask shaped like a beak. The slope came to a point near his chin while the back flared up in an elegant curve. Thin, hand-knotted ropes draped down his bare, muscular chest in varying lengths, ending just above his belt.

"I've been looking for you," Crow admitted. He pulled the mask from his face to reveal light brown eyes, high cheek bones, and a faint horizontal scar over the bridge of his nose.

"Not just me," Tin accused. "Where's Dorothy?"

Crow's eyes widened. "Isn't she with you? Word came to me

from the dwarves that you brought her back and were traveling together."

Damn dwarves. One of them must've seen him drag Dorothy through the portal. "Do you see her?" he growled, stepping forward.

Crow glanced into the woods behind Tin. "She isn't hidden somewhere safe?"

"Don't play games with me." Tin advanced on Crow and grabbed him by the throat. "She snuck out of the inn after insisting we find *you.* Do you really expect me to believe you *just happened* to be in town the same night she disappears?"

Crow stared Tin in the eye, unfazed by the violence. "If Dorothy isn't with you and she isn't with me, it seems we share a problem."

Tin released Crow and roared. He didn't care if a swarm of cursed pixies descended on him—killing them might release some of the anger and fear swirling through Tin's body. His heart was beating fast, urging him to calm down, and he wanted to rip it out and slam the bloody thing against a tree. He ignored it once more and instead slammed his axe into the nearest trunk. "Damn, stubborn woman!"

CHAPTER TEN

DOROTHY

Dorothy hadn't stopped much throughout the night, only when strange howling sounds had erupted close to the path. She'd hid behind a bush for a long while until the thumping of feet and growls took off in another direction. The road before her had then slipped into complete darkness the further she got away from the village. While she continued alone, her determination to get to the South and find Crow had left her fearless. If she'd slept or turned around, then she could have missed Crow. But she hadn't encountered him. Where was he? What if she was wasting her time coming this way?

As the sun fully plopped itself into the deep blue sky, Dorothy ate a few nuts. Her stomach wanted more than that—she yearned to taste a bright green piece of fruit from the trees just ahead, but she couldn't.

A wooden board—painted bright pink and gold was centered on tall posts, with cursive words etched in—caught her attention. *The South.* She'd made it.

Her chest sank—if Crow had already made it to the South, he could be anywhere. Dorothy took a few steps farther, past a curve and trees with yellow-flowered branches surrounding the path. As she pushed a limb aside and stepped through, her breath caught. The architecture was so different than that of the East and the Emerald City. Beneath her feet, the yellow brick road was no longer broken. She wondered what the North and the West looked like.

All the buildings around were boxy and painted in bright hues. Some in multicolor. It was a territory fit for a queen, and couldn't have been more fitting for Glinda. Tin had mentioned that all the territories had problems, but there were no dilapidated buildings here, no sounds of battle taking place. The world was perfectly quiet.

"Take a deep breath, Dorothy. You've always started tasks alone, or mostly alone. This is just a new task." She rotated her exhausted shoulders, feeling the machete's protection snuggly against her back.

Dorothy trekked down a small hill. At its base rested several pink and purple buildings. *Po's Bakery, Saya's Meats, June's Tricks.*

Perhaps Crow stopped at one of the shops. He always loved indulging in food.

The South stayed utterly quiet as she continued forward to one of the shops. It seemed almost strange after dodging flying monkeys and seeing other villagers for days.

She gripped the doorknob, shaped like a carrot, and pulled open the entrance to June's Tricks. Inside the building rested four small tables with stools surrounding them. Cups for tea or coffee were set in each of the customers' spots, but the place sat empty. An odor assaulted her nose—something rotten.

"Hello?" Dorothy called, approaching the stone counter. Three wicker baskets rested on top with balls of yarn and knitting hooks.

No reply.

When she reached the counter, Dorothy touched a ball of pink yarn. She leaned her head over the counter and gasped. With her hands flying up to cover her mouth, she stumbled back, knocking a basket to the floor, a ball of yarn unraveling as it rolled near a table. "No," she whispered.

It wasn't as though she'd never seen a dead body with no

head attached before. Tin had cut off the head of the addict who'd attacked her on the yellow brick road. But this was different, much different.

She took the machete from her back and moved around the counter to see if she'd been mistaken. She wasn't. There was indeed no head. Only a body in a flowy pale-blue dress speckled with dried blood. A dark crimson stain covered the floor where the head should have been. The flesh had grown gray and shriveled, and she didn't want to think about how long the body had been laying here.

There was nothing Dorothy could do, so she flew out the door of the shop and hurried in to the pink building next door. No one. Her gaze drifted from the paintings of fae on the wall, to the empty yellow settees, then fell to the corner of the room. She'd been wrong—the place wasn't empty. Resting in the dark corner lay a body sprawled in an awkward position, wearing a crimson dress. The body was skeletal, with no head attached, like the one from the other shop. Dark stains were splattered on the wall and across the floor. Tin was telling the truth—Lion really needed her. Something sinister was lurking within the quiet of the South.

Dorothy was hesitant to go into the last building, but she crept slowly, gripping her machete. If someone was in there, alive, she could question them, but considering what she'd seen, she didn't hold much hope.

As soon as she opened the door to the bakery, a loud scream echoed off the walls. Dorothy straightened, meeting the stares of two fae females. One wore her hair in two ropey braids and the other had short, wild locks and an upturned nose.

"Sorry," Dorothy rushed the words out. "I didn't mean to frighten you, but I went to the other buildings…"

The two faes' eyes shifted from wooden benches to the corner of the room and Dorothy's gaze followed. And then she noticed the smell. Another body, this one laying in what once may have been a pool of crimson blood around a headless form.

Dorothy tightened her fingers around the machete, not

taking her eyes off the two fae. Could they have done this? None of the bodies appeared fresh with the exception of this one. "What happened?"

The fae with the two ropey braids took a step forward. Dorothy noticed a raised pink scar running down her left cheek. "She wanted her head..."

Dorothy froze, her brows drawing together. "Who did?"

A soft whimper came. The fae with short hair stood trembling, her face also marred by a thick scar. "Langwidere. Our older sister—Natal—had sent us away, promised to meet up with us, and when she didn't come, we returned. And this is all that was left of her."

"Who's Langwidere?" Dorothy tried to recall hearing the name when she was here last, or even when she was with Tin. It wasn't familiar in the slightest.

Dorothy remembered something Falyn had said. *Be sure to keep your head on your shoulders.* She shuddered at what she now knew to be a warning.

The braided-haired fae clasped her mouth as she began to cry, tears sliding down her cheeks. "I can say no more. But me and the one sister I have left are leaving. We won't be coming back. I'll tell you now, if you stay here, with a face like that, then you're as good as dead. I suggest marring your flesh, too." With that, she grabbed the other fae's hand and scrambled out from the building, leaving Dorothy once again alone. This time, a heavy chill raced through her bones.

A loud noise came from outside and Dorothy stilled. Her fingers dug into the machete, her knuckles turning white. She didn't believe for a second that the two fae had come back, so she scurried behind the counter, peeking her head forward at the glass display case. Behind her, the scent of bread lingered in the area. The door creaked open with a loud thud and in walked a fae male.

"I can smell you," he said.

"Not a step further," Dorothy warned, rising from her position. She'd used a machete plenty of times in the corn field.

Swiping one measly male fae if she had to wouldn't be a problem.

But then she caught sight of the male's cloak, with fur stitched in at the top like a lion's mane from her world. Her gaze settled on his fur-lined boots, his long blond hair, golden irises, the tail swinging behind his back.

Her eyes widened. "Lion," she whispered. On instinct, she wanted to run toward him and wrap him in a hug, but she remembered what had happened with Tin. He'd changed, seen her differently. What if it was the same with Lion?

He straightened, his face appearing almost regal, confidence wafting off him. In her world, any woman would swoon over him. His face held a certain androgynous beauty. Yet he didn't have a face like Tin. Why was she thinking about Tin's face now?

"Who are you?" he cooed, inching closer, ever the animal.

"It's me. Dorothy." She couldn't have been that unrecognizable to him too. Her *face* was the same, even if her body wasn't.

Lion's expression appeared stunned for a moment before his eyes narrowed as he searched around the small area. "Where's Tin?"

"I…" She bit her lip. "It's not his fault. I left while he slept to come here and search for Crow."

"It really is you, then?" Lion smiled. It was the same smile he'd worn when she'd found him in the forest, where she'd offered to save him and bring him with her, Crow, and Tin to the Emerald City.

He held out his arms and she rushed forward, folding herself around him. "I've missed you." She sighed, inhaling the fur scent of his cloak.

"I've missed you more, Dorothy," he said, stroking her hair.

"What is going on here?" she mumbled into his chest. "There are decapitated bodies in all the shops! I ran into two fae who wanted me to cut my face and mentioned someone named Langwidere. This fae named Langwidere has been taking heads!" She didn't cry, only held onto her friend tighter.

Lion rotated his shoulders, pulled back, and held her upper

arms gently. "Let me take you to Glinda. She'll be able to explain everything."

"Glinda's all right?" Dorothy exclaimed, a new sense of hope filling her chest. Glinda had given her advice about how to defeat the Wicked Witch. She knew how to get around, be sneaky, and get things done.

"She is," Lion murmured, bowing his head, "but for how long? She needs your help, just like the last time you were here. Langwidere's tactics have gotten more savage."

"I'll go with you, but what about Crow?" Dorothy couldn't forget about him. He'd already been without a working brain once. What if this Langwidere had already taken his head after he'd gotten here? She held the nausea stirring inside her back.

"He's already there."

CHAPTER ELEVEN

TIN

Returning to town was the furthest thing from safe. For the residents—not Tin. He couldn't care less if anyone tried to flee the moment they saw him, or tried to attack him. In fact, he would welcome it. Maybe spilling a bit of blood would help calm him down so he could focus on a plan. His brain was dizzy with thoughts of where Dorothy might be, what danger could've befallen her, if she was hungry, hurt, lost…

There his heart was, kicking in again.

"Wait here," Crow said outside the brothel.

Tin jerked at the sound of his voice. Crow hadn't spoken a word since collecting his hammock, placing his mask back over his face, and telling Tin to save his energy for the cursed pixies when this was all over.

What if they'd decided to venture closer to the South to hunt Dorothy?

He felt the blood drain from his face at the thought. It wasn't rational—there was countless prey in the woods for the pixies to hunt near the capital—but it was possible. That was enough to make him worry. "We don't have time for this. How many more businesses did you ask to rat us out?"

"All of them," Crow said casually. "But if you think I hadn't heard of your late night visit to a lovely nymph, you're wrong.

Go on. Applaud me for my restraint."

Tin fought the heat rising in his cheeks. He wasn't proud of what he'd almost done at the brothel. Maybe if he admitted it was Dorothy he wanted, admitted he *felt* something when he was around her, she would have accepted him. Then her ass wouldn't have run off in the middle of the night. Because it would have been rocking beneath him, her body and his both covered in sweat.

"Your restraint?" Tin mocked.

"I had half a mind to bust through your inn room door but didn't want to jeopardize Dorothy's safety."

So he knew where they were staying, yet waited. *The fool.* If he'd come after Dorothy last night, she wouldn't be lost right now and the whole situation with Crow would've already concluded. With Dorothy at his side and Crow far, far away, even if Tin had to tie him to a tree to accomplish it.

"I wouldn't hurt her," he snarled.

"No?" Crow's masked face tilted. "Why don't I believe that?"

Tin opened his mouth to argue but Crow swept into the building. The door shut in Tin's face with a quiet thunk. Did Crow really think he would've hurt Dorothy? She was infuriating, but he wouldn't have raised a hand to her. The worst he'd done was intimidate her, but she deserved that for refusing to listen. It was her safety at risk when she ignored him. *Shit.* Why was he wasting time worrying about her safety instead of worrying about his bounty? Her head was practically in one of Langwidere's infamous glass cases already because *he'd* brought her through the portal, because *he'd* dragged her south. Getting paid was the least he could expect, but he would rather keep Dorothy. He would rather *save* Dorothy, even if it meant losing her to the mortal world again.

Fuck. His. Heart.

"She went south," Crow said as he emerged again, chest heaving.

Tin rubbed his chest where his heart throbbed painfully. "Are you sure? Is your source reliable?"

"Don't worry your pretty face. I want to find Dorothy as much as you do. She and I have too much to discuss for us to follow false leads."

Any lead could be false. Tin had followed many when tracking his targets and that was when things usually ended in death for his informants. The prostitutes weren't afraid of Crow and had no reason to tell the truth, just as they had no reason to know where Dorothy went. He turned his glare to the brothel and narrowed his eyes. Were they harboring her?

"Coming?" Crow called.

Tin spun to find Crow striding down the street and hurried after him. "You can't believe them without investigating."

"Ah, Tin. Ever the trusting one."

"It's better than trusting everyone."

"Is it?" Crow stared at him with disdain, his brown eyes blazing within his perfectly fitted mask. "Would you like to waste time patting down the nymphs … again, or would you like to find Dorothy before she crosses the border into the South?"

While the East was dangerous, the South was worse, and he had no idea how much of a head start Dorothy had. "You'd better not be wrong about this," Tin growled.

Crow's face grew concerned. "You did warn Dorothy about Langwidere, didn't you?"

"Of course I did," Tin lied, his heart thumping with guilt.

Crossing into southern territory was almost like stepping into another world. A better world, like it used to be the first year after Dorothy returned to Kansas. The yellow brick road wasn't crumbling, and the trees had a bit more life than the ones in the East and West. Even with the violence going on in the South, Glinda had still managed to keep her land from withering as the rest of Oz had. Although it appeared safe, Tin knew Langwidere was still a problem here.

This land harbored the worst kind of danger. The kind that hid and lurked and stalked its prey. Dorothy had no idea of the creatures that prowled here. With her habit of rushing up to any stranger, she was bound to get herself eaten. Or worse. Tin shook the thought from his head.

"If you were Dorothy," Crow began as they passed the pink and gold southern signpost, "where would you go from here?"

"How should I know?"

"You spent the last few days with her, which is more than I have. What's she like?" Crow scratched his head. "Will she wander into the woods or stay to the path?"

Tin dug his knuckles into his eyes and swore under his breath. If Dorothy had veered off the road, there was no telling where she was. She could still be in the East for all they knew. Her sense of direction seemed average for a human, but that wasn't saying much. Tin wanted to tell Crow she would've realized that and stayed on the direct path to the South, but there was every possibility she hadn't. With her being in such a hurry to find Crow, she could've decided to try what she thought was a shortcut, or been led astray by a fae who lied about knowing where Crow was. The sky was the limit with her ignorance. This was partly his fault—he hadn't warned her about Langwidere taking heads in the South.

"I don't know," he finally snapped. His hands fell back to his sides and he huffed, annoyed. "She doesn't seem to have fully grasped how different Oz is now. Being as fearless as she is, she probably walked right up to a goblin to ask for directions."

Crow whipped around to stare at him. "She wouldn't dare approach something so vile. It's suicide."

Tin swung out his arms as if to say: *she would and that's exactly the problem*. "Why don't you shift into your bird form and take a gander from the sky?"

Crow bristled. "Listen, asshole. If I could've had a bird's eye view this whole time, don't you think I would have? Especially if Dorothy's inherited a brain as bad as mine used to be."

"She's a mortal—they're all too dimwitted for their own good," Tin grumbled. They needed to pick up their pace. Scouring the woods in any random direction wasn't going to do them any favors. "Let's just stick to the road for now. Maybe we'll find another town and you can question the locals."

Crow grabbed his elbow and squeezed it. "Dorothy is *not* a mortal."

Tin ripped himself free and laughed. "I see your mind is starting to fade after all. Good on you for keeping some of it this long."

"She's *not* a mortal. And, for the record, my brain is perfectly intact because I took the time to nurture it. You let your heart harden, just as Lion let his courage deprive him of a real connection with anyone."

Crow's words stung. His heart solidified because the world wasn't worth loving, not because he hadn't tended to it. The doors had snapped shut on their own and he hadn't bothered trying to open them again. It hadn't done him any good the first time, and now here the organ was again. Screwing everything up.

But… what if Crow was right? What if the curse returned because he hadn't taken care of his heart? It made sense that it would return now. Someone cared for him for the first time in years. Dorothy thought he was worth something, that he was good and redeemable. She wasn't afraid—she had touched him without hesitation. Ran her fingers gently over his scar.

Tin had heard how love was made of magic—perhaps Dorothy's love broke through the stone walls of his heart. His breath caught. *Love?* What was he thinking? Dorothy didn't *love* him, did she? No. How could she? He wasn't worth something so pure and good. But there were different kinds of love, weren't there? The love of friendship. Which sometimes turned into more over time.

"Fuck my heart. Why the hell is everyone so worried about that?" Tin snarled.

"Perhaps because of all the trouble you went through to *get it?*" Crow waved a dismissive hand through the air. "But you're right. Fuck it. I see the way you're worried about Dorothy, and my daughter deserves better than you."

Tin froze. His daughter? That was impossible. Dorothy grew up in the human world with a human family and an oversized pet rat. Crow wasn't smart enough or strong enough to open a portal and visit Kansas. Maybe his brain was completely gone after all. He didn't remember Crow being delusional before, but then again, Tin hadn't always been a murderer.

"Okay," Tin said slowly. He'd play along until they found Dorothy, then he'd get her as far away from Crow as possible. "Dorothy's half fae… Got it. Can we go now?"

"She's not *half* anything." Crow stormed past Tin.

No, they weren't done yet. Tin followed on his heels. Dorothy looked *nothing* like a fae. Her ears were round, her cheekbones low, though he supposed that could be from her mother's side. But even if it was true—which he doubted—how would Dorothy have made it to Kansas? And why? Crow seemed the type to adore children. He was patient and kind, protective. Fatherly. It didn't make sense for him to give his daughter away, and to mortals no less.

"Who's her mother?" Tin asked slowly, not taking his eyes off Crow.

Crow stumbled again and, instead of answering, pointed ahead. "There's a small settlement over there."

Tin didn't need to hear another word. He broke into a sprint, his heart thundering in his chest. She was there. She had to be. He was too frantic to care that he had feelings for Dorothy—too frantic to know what those feelings were—but he needed to see her. Touch her to confirm she was still all right—safe. It felt like he would combust if he wasted another moment.

A row of pink and purple buildings seemed to scream at him as he stormed into the small town. His limbs shook as he kicked in the door to a bakery. The metallic scent of blood greeted him and he froze. Time seemed to slow as he took in the headless body on the floor.

"No," he whispered to himself.

Not Langwidere. Not here. If Dorothy had come this way, then that meant… Tin's stomach twisted painfully. He bent over, pressing a fist into his abdomen. What was he doing? Bringing Dorothy here? Taking Lion's money for a job like this? He was every bit the monster everyone thought he was. *No.* He was *worse.*

"The town's been abandoned," Crow said from behind him.

"Not everyone left," he rasped. Even though he'd personally decapitated hundreds of fae, Tin couldn't look at the headless body another second. He knew where Dorothy was. In his gut, *he knew.* "Langwidere was here."

Crow peeked inside the bakery and jerked back. "That's not Langwidere's work."

"Who else do you know that steals heads?" Tin shouted.

Crow's brown eyes met Tin's silver ones with a heavy gaze. They both knew the answer. Langwidere had paraded her prized lover around every chance she got, and Lion seemed to pride himself on helping with Langwidere's unnatural hobby. If anyone knew that, Tin did. He'd sat across the table from Lion and watched the anticipation of getting Dorothy's head spark through his eyes.

"Fuck." Tin's mind swirled with thoughts again. Thoughts he shouldn't have… *Couldn't* have because he didn't care. About anything. Least of all Dorothy. But he realized that was quickly becoming a lie. "*Fuck!*"

"If he harms one hair on my daughter's head, I'll cut his off and shove it down Langwidere's throat," Crow vowed.

The steadiness of his threat made Tin pause. Crow meant that—every word. Whether he was capable of it was another thing, but Tin didn't care. He would cut Lion's head off for Crow if it came down to that. Hell, even if they found Dorothy unscathed, he would swing his axe.

And he wouldn't miss.

CHAPTER TWELVE

DOROTHY

Dorothy couldn't stop thinking about the headless bodies in the shops. The two decaying ones, the skeleton, the dried blood, so much blood. Even the smell lingered in her nostrils, on her clothing. A fae named Langwidere was the cause of this, and she needed to be stopped. Dorothy had a machete, but was that enough? Nothing would compare to the power she'd once possessed when wearing the silver slippers, but those were still gone, lost. Or perhaps … taken.

A machete could decapitate someone as cleanly as Langwidere's victims, and Dorothy would hack away with it until her dying breath, to save the South.

"Do you know what happened to the silver slippers?" Dorothy turned to Lion, who walked close beside her on the yellow brick road, studying her face as though she might vanish at any moment, or lose her head. She rubbed her neck at the side.

"Slippers?" Lion asked, focusing his attention straight ahead.

"Yes, don't act coy. The slippers that helped me defeat the Wicked Witch, that helped us get our wishes from Oz, the—"

"They no longer exist." He shrugged. "Used up all their power."

Was that even possible? Perhaps it could be since they were

only enchanted material. "What about Crow? How's he doing?" He'd been looking for her, and she'd been searching for him. Their paths would hopefully cross soon.

"He's fine. No need to worry." Lion curled a hand around her shoulder, his palm staying there until she pulled out from his grasp.

She hurried in front of him and pressed a hand to his chest, stopping him. "And you? You seem like something's bothering you."

"I'm fine. But of course things are bothering me. You left, remember? The world here has changed … for the worse."

Dorothy frowned. Was everyone mad at her for leaving? She had only been a little girl who'd wanted to go home to her aunt and uncle. Did they not understand that? When the tornado took her, she hadn't gotten to tell Aunt Em or Uncle Henry goodbye. Fear had driven her back home, but that was also the place where she'd felt she needed to be at the time.

"I'm sorry. I always meant to come back, but couldn't find a way. Until now, so I'm here. And I'm here to stay," Dorothy promised. This wasn't the Land of Oz she remembered, but that didn't mean it couldn't be again.

"And stay, you shall." He smiled, but it wasn't a smile she knew from Lion.

Together they continued down the yellow brick road, the sky above them a muted gray, the wind picking up. Ahead sat rows and rows of small pink, green, and blue cottages with thatched roofs. All looked spherical, as though they were bubbles coated in glitter. But there was no sign of anyone outside. A few of the clothing lines were empty—others held garments that appeared to be faded and possibly frayed from weather exposure.

"Where is everyone?" she asked, not taking her eyes from the tiny buildings.

"Most left, some are hiding, others ended up like what you saw at the shops."

Falyn had mentioned that most had fled. Couldn't they have tried fighting back? "But why would Langwidere want to take people's heads. Isn't one good enough?"

Lion chuckled. "She changes them every morning. Sometimes again after dinner, or so they say. When she wears them, she gains the power that those fae once held."

That didn't sound intriguing to Dorothy. It seemed evil, wrong. Aunt Em would have said that the devil himself was upon them, and perhaps she would have been right. As the breeze kicked up even faster, everything else remained quiet. She couldn't hear any sign of life, not even a single bird's chirp or the buzz of insects' wings.

The silence between her and Lion grew more and more uncomfortable. Even with Tin and his broodiness, it had never felt like this. Her shoulders tightened at the strangeness of her surroundings. She found herself missing the Lion from her past. "Why aren't you talking? You always talked. Are you like Tin? Lost a piece of yourself?"

He stopped in his tracks and narrowed his eyes. "Are you implying I'm a coward again?"

"No." She held up her hands. "That's not what I'm saying. I never thought you were a coward to begin with. I mean, you just don't seem yourself." Perhaps she should just stop talking for a while. She was making everything worse.

"You know, I didn't want to have to tell you"—Lion bit his lip and toyed with the end of his tail—"but you shouldn't trust Tin."

Dorothy furrowed her brow—the world seemed to close around her, as if she knew something bad was coming. Like when she'd found out the news about the farm foreclosing. "And why's that? Just because his heart is stone, that doesn't make him malicious—he didn't have a beating one the last time I was here. The Gnome King is to blame for that." He'd kept her safe from the faerie fruit addict on the yellow brick road and the flying fae at night.

"Because he was going to give your head to Langwidere," Lion pursed his lips. He looked as though it haunted him to say the words.

"*What?*" That couldn't be true. There was no way that was possible. "I think you're mistaken, Lion."

"No, Dorothy, I'm not. I can't hide it from you any longer. When I saw him last, he told me his plan and asked me to join in on it. I tried to stop him then, but before my blade could slice his throat, he took off. Even Glinda and Crow want him dead."

"Why would he do that?" Dorothy asked, still in disbelief. But then it truly hit home. Her heart beat rapidly, with the hurt coursing through her veins. "He said you were paying him to bring me to you to help the South."

"Lies. All lies." He waved his hand in the air, a scowl on his face. "You can't trust someone without a beating heart."

She should have known that. Tin had mentioned payment on the journey and how he wouldn't do anything for free. How he'd been paid to kill before. He had been so desperate to bring her to the South. Too desperate. And what was she? Gullible. Naïve. Stupid. It all felt like a kick to the gut. But she wasn't going to let sadness linger—she was growing angrier by the second. If—no, *when*, she ran into Tin again, he would lose something else to go along with his stone heart.

Dorothy peered out toward a small stream trickling in the woods. The exhaustion hit her then. Physically. Emotionally. She'd been up all night traveling, and she needed a break, and something to eat and drink.

"Let's stop here and rest for a bit before we move on," she suggested, heading in the direction of the water.

"No!" Lion shouted from behind her.

She whirled around, scanning the area for any sign of danger. The trees still appeared empty, quiet. "Why not?"

He sauntered up beside her, hand on the blade at his hip. "Because I need to get you to the palace as soon as possible."

"I need to eat. All I've had were nuts, and I need water. There's a stream right there."

"You'll be fine."

Gripping his arm, she tugged him to the side. "Lion, I need water or I won't be making it to the palace. And even then, I have no power to help the South. The slippers are what helped me before, and now that I don't have them, I'm nothing. Only a woman with a machete, who wouldn't be able to hold her own against a true warrior. So everyone here needs to stop believing that I'm some miracle saint, because I'm not. I'm Dorothy Gale, a farm girl, and that's all I'll ever be. Even then, I may have been stronger as a child when I held hope and believed nothing bad could happen in the world. Your world may have gotten worse, Lion, but so did mine." She tapped a finger fiercely at her chest.

He frowned, but nodded. "I understand."

Tin had been moodier, but he hadn't objected when she'd needed to drink water or relieve herself. Dorothy walked off the yellow brick road and sat at the edge of the narrow stream. She splashed her face with the water and brought handful after handful of cool liquid to her lips.

All along the stream's edge were patches of clovers and tiny colorful orange and yellow flowers. Red and gold fish swam within the stream's depths. Lion pushed his hand in and captured three fish. It took her several tries, but Dorothy grasped a scaly body and tossed it onto the grass. She watched it flip and wiggle before slicing off its head with her machete.

Dorothy and Lion gathered twigs and leaves to build a fire to cook the fish. She ran her hands up and down a stick over the pile. It bit into her flesh as the smoke rose, before the crackling flames took shape. Lion and Dorothy both held their sticks with the fish over the fire, letting it char the meat. Dorothy's came away black, and she blew onto it to cool it down.

"We need to get moving as soon as we finish," Lion said. "I got us these while collecting the sticks." He handed her something yellow and round.

"What is this?" Dorothy asked, inspecting the ridged surface.

"They're a nut that only blooms here in the South. You bite right into it." He rolled the object between his fingertips. "They have a lot of protein, so it will keep your energy up."

"Thanks." Since she'd been here, this was the best meal she'd had. She bit into the fish, and ate all the meat until only bones were left. The bones reminded her of the skeleton inside the shop, and she thrust the remains away from her.

Dorothy remembered when she, Crow, and Tin had stumbled upon Lion for the first time in the woods. Winged beasts had been out, swarming the trees, attacking something with their sharp talons.

Lion had been curled up on his side, filthy, disheveled, not even fighting back. Toto had stood brave and ran toward Lion, barking at everyone, scaring them away. Dorothy had grabbed the male's hand and helped him up, and he'd smiled. For the rest of the journey, Lion held on to Toto and stayed behind Dorothy, as though she was his protector.

"Why haven't you asked about Toto?" Dorothy asked, resting her back against the tree, and bringing the nut in between her lips.

"Who?" He tossed a fishbone to the side. "Oh, the dog. I forgot about him."

Yet Lion still didn't ask about him. Dorothy kept to herself that Toto was dead, because this Lion seemed as if he wouldn't have cared. She took a bite of the nut, but it wasn't hardness she felt. It was soft, juicy. A thin line ran down her chin. Dorothy jerked the nut from her mouth and tossed it to the ground. Her eyes widened and met Lion's golden irises as she spat out the chunk of faerie fruit. "That's not a nut," she breathed. "That's fruit."

Lion rose from the ground, standing above her, his shadow enveloping her. "Oh, my mistake. They may also contain a numbing aid."

Why would you give me a numbing aid? The words came in her head, but her lips wouldn't move for her to speak them aloud. Dorothy's arms grew heavy when she tried to raise them, and her body slumped to the side. Lion scooped her up and held her close. The new smile he'd given her earlier had returned, only this time it became wider, sharper, a smile she didn't know Lion could ever have. As though he were a true lion and she was his prey.

Lion leaned forward, his golden irises flashing. "You once told me fairy tales to build my courage. Remember Snow White? She was never the hero, only a damsel in distress. The witch had truly won, because Snow White did indeed eat the apple. There's no prince here to save you. From your story, I wanted to be more like the Evil Queen, so thank you for that. And thank you for making my job easier after Tin failed. Now, you'll stay silent as I bring you to Langwidere."

Dorothy tried to scream, to reach for her machete, to do *something*, but she couldn't do anything besides watch as Lion started walking her back toward the yellow brick road.

"Close your eyes and rest a bit." He paused then purred, "Oh, you can't close them, can you?" He pressed two fingers to her eyelids and shut them. The only thing left for her to see was darkness.

CHAPTER THIRTEEN

TIN

Langwidere's residence was a monstrosity. This was where he was supposed to deliver Dorothy to Lion? It kept with the southern architecture but was made entirely of delicately wrought metal. Layers and layers of intricate details formed a globe of tarnished vines with small discolored flowers flowing over the curves. It was every bit as feminine as the rumors of Langwidere herself, and upon closer inspection, nearly as dangerous. Jagged thorns covered the vines and the flower petals were filed to serrated edges.

"Hold on," Crow warned quietly, throwing an arm in front of Tin before he could storm the door. "It's too quiet."

"I think what you mean is *blissfully empty of Dorothy's screams.*" Which meant they needed to hurry, because Tin refused to believe they were too late. Lion only wanted Dorothy for one reason and Tin didn't imagine he would wait long to collect his prize. Crow uttered a soft *shh* and lowered into a crouch just inside the tree line. Tin stared down at him as if seeing him for the first time. "Did … you just *shush* me?"

"Of course I did." He gripped Tin's wrist and yanked him down beside him. The lawn around Langwidere's palace was cut through with gravel pathways, but was otherwise barren. "It would be more expedient to sneak in unnoticed than to fight whatever Langwidere has guarding this place. She has spies everywhere and probably knows we're coming already."

Tin grunted. He didn't particularly care if he had to slaughter a handful of lesser fae to gain entrance. In fact, he longed for the chance to spill blood, but if the ruckus alerted Langwidere, it could hasten Dorothy's decapitation. Tin grunted again, but this time from the painful coil of dread twisting his stomach.

"Wheelers." Crow bobbed his masked face toward the short stone staircase leading to the front doors. Something glinted beneath the steps.

Tin's hand found his axe. "Screw this."

"Tin, wait!" Crow hissed, but it was too late.

Tin rushed straight for the staircase, ready to swing. The air filled with the high-pitched squeak of rusting wheels. Dozens of Wheelers zoomed toward him, seemingly out of nowhere. The disfigured fae were bent like dogs, their backs arched, a sharp wheel attached to the end of each limb, their mouths stitched shut with bloody white ribbon. Their eyes were bloodshot. Haunted. Crazed. Just as the ones captured and interrogated in the Emerald City were before all hell broke loose.

It wasn't clear who swung first—Tin or one of them—but he was the first to draw blood. A Wheeler's arm came clean off in a spray of ruby blood, and his other wheels wobbled out from under him. Tin was already onto the next before the first hit the ground.

On and on he swung his axe while dodging their blows. One female sped by him and kicked out a razor-sharp wheel as she passed. Tin rolled over the back of another wheeled creature while slicing her leg from knee to ankle. They were no match for him—their strength was in their numbers, but even those were dwindling within the first minute.

It wasn't until Tin had dispatched the first round of them, and spun in search of his next target and came up empty, that he realized Crow had helped. How much he had helped was unclear, as he was relatively clean everywhere but his hands. Four silver blades extended from the back of his wrist, previously hidden beneath his bracers, and curved over his hands like talons. When the fuck had he learned how to fight? His best efforts used to be flailing his limbs around.

"I didn't need help." Tin wiped his chin with the back of his hand, smearing the splatter of blood.

Crow stepped over a Wheeler still twitching on the ground. With a heavy sigh, Crow turned around and dealt a final blow through his neck, then headed straight for the front door. "I wasn't helping *you*, you ignoramus."

Shit. Tin took the steps three at a time, his blood-soaked boots slipping slightly against the stone. The door flew open and the stench of decay blasted both Tin and Crow back a step.

"Holy shit," Crow said around a cough.

Tin narrowed his watering eyes and charged inside. "Dorothy! Dorothy, where are you?"

He took in the green and gold interior of the house, putting the layout together, puzzling out where Langwidere might bring someone to kill. Not in her foyer, surely. Carrying her victims upstairs and their bodies back down would be too much work. The heads would be on a higher level—that made the most sense for security. Two massive rooms off the entrance were completely empty of furniture, though one had a large firepit filled with charred crystals. Beyond it, the green floor tiles were broken, as if something had been ripped from the floor. A dark hallway extended further into the dwelling.

"Damn," Crow wheezed through his mask. "It doesn't look like anyone's been here in years."

Tin scowled as the state of the interior sunk in. Cobwebs hung from the ceiling in large sheets. The candles were burnt to nubs, the wax having dripped from the candelabras on the wall to the floor, where a thick layer of dust coated everything.

"I was supposed to bring Dorothy here," Tin said in a rushed breath. There were no footprints on the dusty floor, the cobwebs intact. Something wasn't right. "Langwidere was supposed to be *here*. Lion said… But… I don't understand. They should be here."

The heads. Langwidere wouldn't leave without them. Tin bolted up the staircase and began kicking in ornate doors until he found one filled with glass cases. Empty. Empty. *Empty.* From floor to ceiling, corner to corner, the cases held nothing but dust. His axe fell from his hand with a heavy thump. This couldn't be happening. He gripped the fabric over his beating heart, his iron nails digging into his skin as he fought to breathe.

Dorothy. I'm sorry, Doro—

Crow tackled Tin from behind. They both flew headfirst through a pane of glass. The jagged pieces tore into the scarred side of Tin's face and crunched beneath his boots as he struggled to right himself. Crow's weight held him in place.

"What the hell?" Tin demanded.

One of Crow's hands dug into his hair, grinding Tin's cheek into the rough edge of the broken glass. The iron prevented it from gouging his face in half while the kelpie scales on his clothing stopped the sharp points of Crow's talons from digging into his ribs.

"Give me one reason I shouldn't gut you right here," Crow growled.

Tin gripped the edge of the case and attempted to throw himself backward to gain the upper hand. Crow's talons only shifted higher. "What are you doing?" Tin roared. The movement scratched his bottom lip on a jagged edge. "Let me up, jackass."

Crow's breath was hot on his ear. "Lion hired you to bring my daughter to Langwidere?"

Shit. Tin stilled, letting the pain of his wounds sink in. He deserved this. *More* than this. "If it means anything, I changed my mind the night I overheard you in the brothel."

"You fucked a nymph and decided not to *murder my daughter?* How is that helping your case?"

"I didn't. Fuck the nymph, I mean. I was going to, but then I heard you…" The words tumbled out of Tin before he could stop them. When his mind finally caught up to his mouth, he decided to keep going. If this was it and Crow killed him, at least he would've died with someone knowing the truth. "I didn't want you or anyone else to take her from me. When she woke up, I planned on sending her home. Or letting her stay and protecting her. I don't know, Crow. We didn't get to discuss it because the next morning she was gone. But Langwidere wasn't going to touch her, I swear it."

Tin stopped short of saying he cared for Dorothy. It had to be clear to Crow regardless, and he was still working out exactly what *feelings* meant. He'd never managed to get the hang of them the first time.

"Dorothy's the only one in Oz who would dare to show you compassion after you've killed a friend or relative of damn near everyone here," Crow said in a low, guttural voice. He dragged his talons to Tin's chest and pressed them where Tin's heart was beating. "I see your heart has returned. But it doesn't matter, Tin, because you've broken hers as much as you've broken my trust."

"Dorothy's kindness broke my curse." Tin sighed miserably. "She doesn't know what Lion hired me for."

Crow shoved Tin deeper onto the broken glass as he released him. Tin sagged to the floor, defeated, and Crow kicked his axe toward him. "She *will* know."

"You're not going to kill me?" Tin wiped the blood trickling from his cut lip. "I deserve it."

"Oh, you will die," Crow promised. "But first you're going to fix this. You're going to use that cruelty of yours and thirst for blood to save my daughter, then you're going to tell her the truth. After, Dorothy will decide your fate."

With that, Crow spun on his heel and stormed from the abandoned building. Tin climbed slowly to his feet, dragging his axe up behind him.

Ah, he thought. *There's an emotion I remember.*

The shattering pain in his chest could be nothing other than heartbreak.

When they found Dorothy, when Lion and Langwidere were dead and Dorothy heard of his betrayal, he hoped she would be the one to end his suffering. Though perhaps letting him live would be the harsher punishment.

125

CHAPTER FOURTEEN

DOROTHY

*D*orothy stood in the center of a silver garden. A rocky circular path enveloped her, blooming tall with flowers of the same sparkling sheen. This world was completely gray. From behind a looming tree of iron came a shadow, a cloaked figure. He removed his dark hood from his head, his silver hair flapping in the wind. The purest eyes of silver she'd ever seen connected with hers. Tin.

He sauntered toward her, smiling that smile he'd worn before she'd returned to Kansas. The branch-like scars running down his cheek glistened beneath the sun and her heart sped up. He was the most beautiful thing she'd ever seen.

Dorothy inched closer, closer, until his hand came to her lower lip in a soft brush.

Tin's head leaned down to kiss her but before his mouth touched hers, his lips moved close to her ear, to where she'd felt his warm breath. "Sorry, Dorothy."

There wasn't enough time for her to think as he stepped back. Lion shifted out from behind a tree, nodding at Tin. Her eyes widened as Tin's hands arched up, swinging his axe. Her feet stayed planted in the dirt of the garden, unable to move as the blade bit into her neck and sailed through, spraying the silver garden in a sea of scarlet.

Dorothy woke up screaming—screaming so terribly loud.

But only in her head. Even inside there, it splintered her eardrums. She couldn't bring her lips to part. She couldn't move anything.

Two fingers drew her eyelids open. Her pupils took a moment to adjust to the new lighting. All Dorothy could do was watch the parts of the world above her move—the blue sky, the fluffy clouds, tops of colorful trees, and part of a fur cloak. *Lion.* The bastard.

How could he do this? *Why* would he do this? She shouldn't have been this stupid. It was because she'd known him before, had trusted him.

"I can tell you're awake now." Lion's voice boomed from above her, but she couldn't see his face. "I can see your eyes twitching." He adjusted her body so that his golden irises appeared in front of her. "I'm not doing this because I don't like you, Dorothy. Although, I don't care for you anymore, not since you left. I'm doing this for Langwidere. Your head will look much better on her body, anyway. Until we get there, I'll tell you stories, like you used to tell me to keep me calm."

Dorothy tried to scream again, but nothing came out.

The stories Lion started to tell her weren't ones as she'd told him from *Grimms' Fairy Tales*. These were stories that truly sickened her, because they were real.

"I began collecting heads for Langwidere years ago. She tested me the first time in her old home, where I was given the opportunity to decapitate a female she had tied up in another room. I completed the task, and you know what? It felt good— more than good—especially when she fucked me for the first time right afterward. It became a ritual for us. I'd kill a female, then she'd reward me with a fuck."

Lion didn't stop there. He continued on and on, about each of his kills, about the different heads Langwidere wore while he bedded her, and how sometimes there was blood in between their naked bodies while he slid inside her. Dorothy had never wanted to have her ears cut off, or her eardrums removed, more in her life than in that moment. She didn't want to hear about how Lion pleased Langwidere sexually or how he relished hearing the victims beg and plead before slicing off their heads. Some of the females they left tied up for days, others weeks, and some they let run so he could play a game of cat and mouse.

As Lion continued, Dorothy didn't understand why the faerie fruit wasn't affecting her the way it should have been. There should have been hallucinations, which would have been better than listening to Lion. But she wasn't feeling a high and she wasn't going crazy. There was only the numbing sensation, holding her body still.

Something thrummed in Dorothy's veins then. It was familiar, achingly familiar, but it couldn't be. It was the same inner strength she'd dredged up when she'd worn the silver slippers and used their power, except she wasn't wearing the shoes now. Dorothy's veins pulsed harder, almost like they were stirring up a tinge of magic. And now the hallucinations were starting—of that she was certain.

The rapture was coming, and she feared there would be no turning back. She was going to become a faerie fruit addict—deranged like the man who'd attacked her on the yellow brick road, or insane like Oz. Yearning and yearning for each precious bite of fruit while it blackened her teeth and tickled her insides. She would never be able to think clearly again—she'd be positively mad like the Mad Hatter from her favorite childhood story.

For a moment, Dorothy gave in to the hallucination, tried reaching into herself with invisible hands, pretended as though she was wearing the silver slippers. Her invisible fingers brushed against something not quite tangible. Clearer and clearer it became. Inside her shell of a body, she tightened her grip on a flexible surface, and before her, the bright glow of silver flared to life, like that of the slippers.

Dorothy's body stopped moving. Lion had halted, staring down at her, his voice appearing far away as he shouted, "What the fuck?"

Deeper and deeper she tapped into the silver, as deep as she could go. Like a shooting star, something within her—perhaps magic—exploded outward. Lion was shot backward and Dorothy fell on her back against the hard ground. Pain radiated up her spine.

A roar slipped out from her throat, echoing throughout the forest beside the yellow brick road.

Lion came to a crouch and slowly stood, staring at her in horror. A silvery glow expanded around her.

"Locasta wasn't lying. She spoke the truth about you," And instead of coming after her with his sword, the coward took off running in the opposite direction.

Dorothy's eyes fluttered as she reached for her machete, her body tingling with needle-like pricks. A sharp pain tore at the tips of her ears—she touched them and gasped. They weren't rounded any longer, but sharpened points, like those of elves. Her trembling hands automatically crawled to her face, skimming her cheekbones. They'd shifted higher.

What is happening?

With wide eyes, Dorothy peered around, needing to flee. She didn't know where in the South she was exactly. But she did know Lion wasn't with Glinda or Crow now. He was with Langwidere. She couldn't go back to Tin because he was trying to bring her to this bitch who took heads for her own sick pleasure. And she didn't know which path to follow on the yellow brick road to get to Glinda.

Farther back stood a cluster of tiny yellow and orange homes, resembling lemons and oranges with stacks of large brown leaves forming the roofs. She hurried in that direction, toward a short green fence enclosing all the houses.

When she entered the gate, multiple mounds in the earth caught her attention. Dorothy slowed her pace. In a grassy area filled with clovers, and tiny white flowers, rested cemetery markers. Written across each one was a female's name—there wasn't a single male's name. A sinking feeling washed over Dorothy. A few of the graves appeared fresh with exposed dirt but others were already grown over with grass. Whirling around, she took off toward the first house and banged on the door.

"You shouldn't be out here like this," a male voice called from a few cottages down. She turned in that direction and moved toward the satyr, until she came face to face with him. The top of his head came to her chest, and he appeared mostly goat-like, with horns, a tail, and hooves. Bright violet irises shone beneath the sun.

"I need your help," Dorothy said, trying not to sound desperate or look crazed as she gripped her machete.

The satyr waved her hurriedly inside his home. She didn't move toward it.

"I'm not going to hurt you." He sighed. "You shouldn't be out here like this. It's safe for us males but not the females, especially ones who look like you."

"What's wrong with me?" she asked, deciding it was better to go inside in case Lion did choose to return and search for her.

"There's nothing wrong with you. Langwidere simply favors elves with pretty faces. I'm sure you've already passed the grave markers. They all lost their heads because of her."

This Langwidere was starting to sound like the Headless Horseman from the Sleepy Hollow story, except she actually wore the heads. Dorothy shuddered at the thought.

As she stepped inside the satyr's home, she entered a small dining room area with a wooden kitchen table and two chairs. Two empty vases sat on the counter in the corner as if they'd once contained flowers. She took a seat in a chair and he sank down in the other.

Dorothy's eyes met the satyr's bright violet ones. She thought about his previous words and they struck her right then. "You mentioned Langwidere favors pretty elves, but I'm human."

His brow furrowed and his nose wrinkled. "You're not human. You're fae."

Dorothy froze, a cold feeling washing over her, spreading through her entire body. "Listen, I'm Dorothy Gale. I came here once before, and I'm human. Lion did something to me." Her chest heaved up and down as her heart raced. "What did that fruit do to me?”

“Um, let me get you some tea.” He stood from the table, picked up a tea kettle off the stove, and poured them both a cup. “I know who you are, but I don’t have the answers you’re searching for.”

As he handed her the cup of steaming tea, she tipped it back and took a sip, wishing she had something stronger. The liquid burned her throat as it slid down, but the burn felt good, nonetheless. “Do you have a mirror?”

“Yes, let me see what I can do.” The satyr left her sitting there, nervously tapping her fingers on the table. Right as she was about to go searching for a mirror herself, he slipped back into the kitchen area holding a small oval one with intricate vine engravings around the glass.

Despite wanting to rip the mirror from his grasp, she gently took it from the satyr’s fingers and held it up to her face. As she observed herself, her hands shook more. The tips of her ears were indeed pointed, eyes larger, cheekbones higher. She calmly set the mirror face down, as if nothing about her had changed. She didn’t want to look at herself anymore.

“Can you please tell me how to get to Glinda’s from here?” she asked, taking another sip of the herbal tea, the drink sloshing in the cup as her hands vibrated.

“By foot, it’s a few days’ journey from here—at the very bottom of the South in front of the mountains.” He paused, his expression grim. “However, I suggest going to one of the other territories instead. Glinda is a great leader and has been doing all she can to save the South, but Langwidere is growing stronger, more powerful.”

“I still have to go. Glinda is a friend.” Dorothy needed to warn her about Lion and Tin, that they were traitors.

“Let me at least feed you first.” Before she could reply, the satyr plopped down a plate in front of her with a meat pie on top. Her stomach rumbled as she peered down at the golden layers of the delicacy. Whatever she’d done to Lion had taken a lot of her energy. She dug in like a ravenous beast.

"Thank you… I'm sorry, I didn't ask your name," she said.

"Tigue." He smiled. "I've believed this entire time that Glinda would defeat Langwidere, but maybe she just needs your help. You are Dorothy Gale, after all, the one who took down the wickedest of them all."

Dorothy's chest sank, but she smiled in return. She thought about the fae and how, if someone spoke their full name, they could be controlled. When he'd just said her full name, she didn't feel a tug or buzz of anything. She couldn't be fae. There was no way possible. So, whatever was going on with her had to be temporary—it *had* to be.

After she finished eating, Tigue walked Dorothy outside and pointed her in the direction of a cluster of tall mountains far in the distance. "Be safe, Dorothy Gale."

To be extra careful, she stayed off the yellow brick road, near the outskirts of the forest. If she lingered on the road, she would have stood out like a beacon. She didn't know if Lion would be prowling about or if he'd continue to be a coward and run back to Langwidere.

Rows and rows of bright red apples hung from the leafy tree limbs. Even though she'd just eaten, they looked delicious. However, as she trekked down the bumpy path, she left them alone, in case none of this was truly real.

Near a fork in the road, voices came spiraling from her left. She scrambled and ducked behind a wide trunk covered in thick moss. As she peeked her head slowly around the side, the voices drew closer—male. Two of them. What if Lion had come back with a friend to help him collect her? Craning her neck, she listened closely. The travelers seemed to be arguing, and neither one had the soft voice of Lion.

As two cloaked figures came around a curve, Dorothy identified one immediately. She knew his broad shoulders, his steady gait, and the silver shining out from his hood. *Tin.* Her traitorous heart sped up at the sight of him until she remembered that he was a betraying bastard. But her lips parted when her gaze focused on his companion. She recognized the beaked mask, the sway of his cloak, the thin ropes draped across his bare chest, and his long dark hair braided with feathers. Crow. Tin was with *Crow.*

Did this mean that Tin was tricking Crow, or that Crow was helping Tin and Lion?

The pads of Dorothy's fingers rapidly beat against the moss. She didn't know what to do. Should she make herself known, or just let them pass and hurry to find Glinda?

"You'll be dead after we find Dorothy," Crow seethed. "I can't believe you would try to do something so foul to her."

At Crow's words, Dorothy sighed in relief because, for once, someone was on her side. Her attention went back to Tin, and her blood started to boil, because she'd liked him, really liked him. Had even felt something for him, despite him having a stone heart. *Well, not anymore.*

Ripping her machete free at her back, Dorothy jumped out from behind the tree and barreled for Tin. Before he could whirl around, she leapt onto his back and pushed him roughly to the bricked road. He quickly rolled over beneath her, but she shoved him down, his face full of surprise. Dorothy got in position, straddling his hips, her blade to his throat. "It looks as though you'll be the one losing your head," she spat. "Not me."

CHAPTER FIFTEEN

TIN

Tin's breath caught in his throat. *Dorothy?* It couldn't be. She looked so different … so *fae.* If she was beautiful before, she was strikingly gorgeous now. Her new fae features practically glowed with radiance. Even her body felt different as she straddled him—more lithe. But how? What caused these changes?

The prick of her machete against his neck sent Tin careening back to reality, and he met her haughty gaze. Hatred swirled in her eyes, the sentiment echoing on her snarling lips, and he fell utterly limp beneath her. Lion must've told her the truth. There was no doubt she'd met with him—Lion's earthy scent still lingered on her. But where was he now? The machete bit harder into his skin, painfully refocusing his attention on the deadly situation.

"If it's my head you want," he rasped, "it's yours. I won't fight you."

Confusion flickered through Dorothy's expression. "What?"

"It's no less than I deserve." Tin lifted his chin to give her better access. When she didn't move to strike, he closed a hand around hers, on the handle of the machete, pressing the blade deeper into his skin. A trickle of warm blood leaked down his throat. "Go on."

Dorothy launched herself off him with heavy breaths. "What is *wrong with you?*"

Tin sat up slowly, every muscle aching, and exhaled. *Fuck.* The infamous Tin Man was *not* going to be taken out by Crow. One way or another, Dorothy had to do it.

Dorothy paced away from him, then back, three times before turning her gaze to Crow. "He was going to kill me," she told him as if to justify her actions. "Lion paid him to bring me to Langwidere so she could wear my head."

Crow nodded. "I recently became aware."

Tin shifted onto his knees. "I can explain."

"*Explain?*" she shouted. "What is there to explain? You were going to let them cut off my head! My *head*, Tin!" She tapped at her skull several times as though to prove it was still there. "You're as stone-hearted as you told me you were."

Tin wanted to tell her that he wasn't—not anymore. That he could feel his heart beating in his chest again, and all the emotions that went along with it, but it didn't matter. He'd messed up. "I wasn't going to let Lion take you, not anymore," he said quietly. "Please believe me."

"Believe you?" Dorothy laughed bitterly. "I was the only one who *trusted* you, but I see now it was foolish of me to do so."

Tin climbed to his feet and moved toward her, but Crow stepped between them. "I told you that she would decide who ended your life. If she won't do it—" Crow flicked his wrist and his talons shot out over his hand, the metal glistening under the sun.

Dorothy's eyes widened. "This isn't your battle, Crow. Have you lost your mind?" Her hands flew to her mouth. "Oh no. You have, haven't you?"

Crow removed the mask from his face. "I haven't lost my brain. In fact, I've expanded it with years of study. Something I've come to learn is that a little violence to save lives is better than pacifism that leads to hundreds of deaths."

"He's not going to kill hundreds of people," Dorothy

grumbled, seemingly against her will. "Just me, apparently, and whoever got in the way of his payday."

Tin swallowed hard at her defense. He didn't deserve it, even if she was wrong about him killing her. That was never the plan—Lion asked for her to be brought alive. He or Langwidere were going to do the killing, but he would've facilitated it, which was almost the same thing.

"He's already killed hundreds," Crow said. "If not more."

It was definitely more, but he didn't dare say as much. Each death weighed on him now. It was a crushing force, one that almost made him wish for the oblivion Crow wanted to give him. Almost. But, while he deserved it, while he knew it was the fastest way to stop feeling this pain, he also knew there was no going back from death. Tin wasn't sure he could change. Bloodlust was ingrained in him now, but he could continue fighting it. And if Dorothy could find it in herself to forgive him, maybe he wasn't a lost cause.

Or maybe he had been right all along: his heart was never a gift from the Wizard. It was a curse.

"I don't care, Crow," Dorothy said. "We aren't killing him, because that would make us as bad as him."

"We aren't being conniving about it," Crow reasoned. "It would be a practical kill."

Conniving was a strong word. Appropriate this once, but Tin didn't feel it accurately described him in general. There wasn't much scheming that went into assassinations. The customer paid, his axe swung. The targets always knew what was about to happen if they saw him.

"No," Dorothy insisted.

Crow pressed his lips into a tight line and retracted his talons. "As you wish."

Her shoulders slumped with exhaustion, the immediate danger gone. A smile broke across her face and she lunged at Crow. She wrapped her arms around his neck in the biggest hug. "It's so good to see you."

"And you." Crow returned the hug without hesitation. "I

missed you."

Tin rolled his eyes as Crow spun her around, her feet lifting off the ground. "As touching as this reunion is, there seems to be a rather glaring issue to discuss."

The smile slipped from Dorothy's lips in an instant and she stepped away from the embrace. "You mean my face?"

Crow studied her, taking in each feature as if he'd never see them again. A peaceful expression fell over his features each time his eyes returned to Dorothy's new, high cheekbones. "Your glamour's gone. You look like—" He quickly cleared his throat. "What happened?"

"I don't know… I had a glamour?" Her fingers skimmed the lines of her new face, then the tips of her pointed ears. "Lion found me. He said you were with Glinda, and Tin had told me we were going to Lion's to help him, so I followed him. He tricked me into eating faerie fruit with numbing properties. When I regained use of my body, it had changed. Is … this an effect of the fruit?"

"No, sweetheart." Crow paused and fidgeted with the ropes hanging down his chest. "You're fae. A changeling who was glamoured to live among humans."

Tin exhaled impatiently. "If we're having this conversation here, let's cut straight to the point so we can get somewhere safe. Crow's your father." Both Crow and Dorothy's eyes widened in shock. Tin ignored the jolt of guilt their expressions sparked. "Now that we've got it out in the open, we need to get the hell out of the South."

"You're my *father*?" Dorothy asked in a hoarse whisper.

Crow nodded, his throat bobbing. Had the bastard been planning on keeping it a secret? Too bad. "You were taken from your mother and I. Once the Wizard corrected my brain and I remembered, it felt wrong to keep you here. You were safer there with the family you'd been given to."

Tin shuffled down the yellow brick road, hoping they would take the hint and talk as they walked. Neither moved. *Fine.* They could stand there and let Lion track them down, but Dorothy had better not ask Tin to let him live.

"Taken? Who is my mother?" Dorothy whispered. "I was always told my parents were dead. Is she… Is she dead? She must not be if you're here."

Crow swallowed hard. "Forgive me, but I'm not ready to tell you yet."

Tin rapped his fingers on the head of his axe, the iron tips clicking loudly, but no one seemed to notice. "We're running out of daylight," he called, agitated. Dorothy would *unquestionably* ask him not to kill Lion, and he wasn't ready to let her down again so soon.

"Let's find somewhere to camp then. You look exhausted." Crow spoke to Dorothy but shot Tin a scathing look. "After you rest, I'll be happy to answer all your questions."

Dorothy nodded, appearing in shock, then jumped away from Crow. "We can't go back to the East. We need to help Glinda. What if Lion tries to do something to her after tricking her?"

"Glinda has been holding her own," Crow soothed.

"And she has guards. Lion won't stand a chance on his own," Tin agreed. "Our priority is keeping you safe."

Dorothy adjusted the machete on her back. She hadn't once looked at Tin—it was as though he wasn't even there. "If that's true—"

The way she spoke was an accusation of a lie, and Tin dropped his gaze.

"—then you'll follow me to Glinda's, because I'm going."

Tin's head fell back with a groan. *Not this again.* She couldn't be this eager to die. Not after how angry she'd gotten at him for working with Lion. Why wouldn't she just *listen*? He ran his hands through his hair, the bone rings on one side catching on his iron-tipped gloves. How had his life become … this?

"Coming?" she called, heading farther south on the brick road.

Suddenly feeling as tired as Dorothy looked, Tin pulled his hood high over his head, hiding his shame. He would make this up to Dorothy. First by killing Lion and Langwidere; then, he suspected, by exiting her life forever.

They had only walked twenty minutes before stumbling upon an abandoned house. Pastel green paint peeled away and what was once a barn off to one side had collapsed, but the house offered shelter. Shelter that they might not find again if they continued traveling, so after some careful urging on Crow's part, they barricaded themselves inside with old furniture. Tables and chairs went against the door while large pieces such as the hutch cupboard covered the windows.

Tin sat quietly at the edge of the former sitting room, cleaning dried blood from his axe, while Crow continued answering Dorothy's questions on what it meant to be fae. She was now able to hear and see better. Move faster. Her body was more in tune with the world around them—something that Crow claimed might be overwhelming until she got used to it. She would age differently now. Immortality and all benefits. Maybe she inherited Crow's gift of shifting, but it was too soon to try.

Tin wasn't sure how many times Dorothy needed to hear the same thing in different words for them to sink in, but they had more pressing things to discuss. But, by some miracle, he held his tongue.

Eventually they moved away from the changes to Dorothy's body to the current state of Oz and what they'd both been doing for the last decade. Dorothy lost her mortal family, her dog, her farm, while gaining a reputation for being insane. Crow had studied every book at the library and looked for fae he'd forgotten about while cursed, though most had completely disappeared. It seemed to Tin that they were equally lost and lonely.

Maybe all of them were, Lion included. Was that what led to

their individual demises? The *need* for a sense of belonging like the four of them had while traveling together? None of them appeared to have found it again until, perhaps, now.

Tin waited and waited for them to run out of things to talk about. Or, even better, for them to circle back around to their biggest threat. It wasn't until Dorothy began talking about flying monkeys that he lost any semblance of patience.

"They aren't flying monkeys! The night beasts are cursed pixies." Tin slammed his axe down. "Are we going to talk about Langwidere?"

"Tin," Crow warned, extending his talons. Tin didn't give two shits about those blades. He'd chop them off with his axe if Crow tried anything.

Dorothy placed a hand on Crow's arm. "No. He's right. It's not enough to warn Glinda about the threat. We have to do more and help her fight."

"She's going to have more Wheelers." Crow leaned toward Dorothy. "Wheelers are fae that Langwidere rescued from the Deadly Desert in exchange for their servitude. She replaced their hands and feet with wheels and sewed their mouths shut. We had to dispatch some while searching Langwidere's for you."

Dorothy paled. "Was Langwidere home?"

"No one's been there in years, judging by the state of it," Crow said.

"If Langwidere isn't living there, where *is* she living?" Dorothy looked over her shoulder toward the table they'd placed in front of the door.

"Good question," Tin said. If they made it to Glinda's palace in one piece, maybe they would find out. Glinda was a simpleton, but the fae around her weren't. Someone had to know where Langwidere was, especially if she was still actively collecting heads.

When Dorothy yawned, Crow stood and offered her his hand. "None of us will be any good if we don't sleep."

Dorothy let him help her to her feet and guide her to one of the bedrooms. He opened the door for her and entered first, doing yet another sweep for danger. He'd never seen Crow act like this. Kind, always, pompous, yes, but this mother hen act was new. Was this what happened when one became a parent? Thank goodness he'd never procreated. Crow shook the massive wardrobe in front of the window, testing its strength, and Tin's upper lip lifted. What is she? An infant? Crow didn't need to check for monsters under the bed—they'd already made sure the house was clear. Let the girl sleep. No, not a girl, a *female*. A fae.

When Crow was finally satisfied, he ushered Dorothy farther into the room. "Do you need anything? I can go out to scavenge for some food and fill our canteens. Oh! There's bound to be extra blankets somewhere."

"Stars above, Crow. Leave her alone!" Tin put the axe back on his hip and paced the room.

"Goodnight," Dorothy said gently to Crow, then shot Tin a stern look.

"Sleep well," Crow replied. "Don't worry about Lion or Tin. I'll make sure you're safe."

Tin looked away to keep from snarling in Crow's direction. He wouldn't hurt Dorothy, but if he was planning to escape with her, there wasn't much Crow could do to stop him. With his weapon clean, Tin settled down on the floor to one side of Dorothy's door for the night and stared up at the ceiling.

"You can take one of the other bedrooms," Crow grumbled.

Tin closed his eyes and tucked his hands beneath his head as a pillow. "It's all yours."

Dorothy sighed heavily and slammed the door, shutting them both out. Crow stepped over Tin, kicking him in the process, and sprawled out on the moth-eaten couch. It didn't take long for his breath to even out.

Some guard you are.

From the other side of the door, Dorothy sniffled. Tin leaned up on his elbows and listened harder. Was she … crying? *Shit.* He'd had his heart back for all of one day. The instinct to cheer her up warred with his usual response to emotions: ignoring them. Easing to his feet, eyes glued on Crow, he cursed himself.

It seemed he couldn't help trying, but he braced himself for her instant rejection.

And then there was the fight he would have with Crow when her screams woke him.

With a sigh, he slipped quietly into the room. "Dorothy?"

"What do *you* want?" The soft light of dusk filtered through the windows of the small room, a glow sneaking around their barricades.

Tin eased down on the foot of the bed while she sat at the other end with her knees pressed against her chest. "Are you okay?"

"What do you think?" she snapped.

"I think, with your glamour gone, you can do anything you want—*be* anyone you want." She could make an entirely new life for herself if she chose.

"I could be Langwidere," she hissed. "Or I suppose she could be *me*."

Tin winced at the anger in her words. "I wasn't going to give you to Lion."

"*Liar.*"

He *was* a liar. When he'd opened that portal and dragged Dorothy back to Oz, he'd had every intention of delivering her for a huge sum. "I *was* but I changed my mind once I spent time with you."

Dorothy grunted. "I don't trust you."

"I know," he said softly. When Dorothy sniffled again, burying her face in her knees, Tin laid down on the bed. He stretched out with false confidence. His shoulder brushed her hip and he soaked in that small touch. "This is more comfortable than the floor."

"There's a perfectly good couch," she deadpanned.

"Ah, yes. But your father happens to be out cold on it."

Dorothy shifted to glare at him. "There's another bedroom."

"It's too cold," he lied. He hadn't even looked inside while Crow secured it.

Dorothy pushed his chest with her foot. "You can't stay in

here."

"Why not?" He caught her ankle gently. "We've slept next to each other every night since you came back."

"Because you *were going to have me decapitated, you bastard!*" She was angry, but she didn't reach for her weapon, didn't try to shove him again.

Tin tugged her down beside him, suppressing the fear that she would scream for Crow, and wrapped an arm around her waist. When she did nothing but tense against him, he shivered. He wanted to pull her closer but knew not to push his luck. "I'm sorry, Dorothy. But I'm different now."

Dorothy laughed bitterly. "You're so full of shit."

Tin took her hand and pressed it over his heart. Then he waited. Waited for her to *feel* it, to understand what it meant.

"Your heart," she whispered, her eyes full of wonder. "It's beating. How?"

He exhaled a laugh. "It seems you've broken my curse."

"What?" she asked, almost as if she hadn't heard.

"You still believed in me when no one else in this wretched land would. Because you cared about me, because you didn't give up despite everything, your compassion helped to break my heart from its stone prison."

Dorothy's eyes glistened. "I—"

"It's yours," he vowed. "You resurrected my heart when I thought it was gone forever, so its fate is yours. Rip it out and burn it to ash if that makes you happy. But know this: no matter how long you allow me to keep it, I will cherish this gift and use it to protect you."

"Wow." Dorothy scrunched her nose. "So dramatic, Tin. Who knew hearts came with a heaping side of valor?"

Tin gave her a small grin. "Enough of that, then. No more tears and no more talking. We both need to sleep."

Instead of pushing him away as he expected, Dorothy set her head on his chest and snuggled against his side with a contented sigh. She tucked a hand beneath her chin, right over the powerful *thump, thump, thump* of his heart. "Don't think this means I forgive you."

Tin's eyes drifted shut as he inhaled the light feminine scent wafting up from her. It was one of the things about her that had stayed the same. With her hand over his chest, a thirst began to spread through him, igniting everywhere. "I wouldn't dare think that."

But he knew she hadn't heard him. Her head had already gone heavy against his chest as she gave in to her exhaustion. Tin smiled against her hair and held her even closer as he followed suit.

CHAPTER SIXTEEN

DOROTHY

Squeak. Squeak. Squeal. Dorothy's eyes flew open when she heard another loud squeak, her heart thumping in her chest too fast for its own good. In her arms, she gripped something hard, firm—Tin. He was holding on to her just as tight. Before she could say anything, his hand came up and wrapped around her mouth. And at that moment, she knew she shouldn't have trusted him. Once a liar always a liar—heart or not.

He inched his mouth right beside her ear and whispered, "Shh, they'll hear."

She shouldn't have jumped to conclusions, but how could she not have after everything? Dorothy slowly nodded, and Tin released his calloused palm from her lips. In a quiet, yet deadly way, he stood from the bed and grabbed his axe, carefully creeping to the window. He held out a palm for her to remain there. She wasn't going to listen to him.

Silently rising from the bed, she pressed her bare feet to the cool floor and picked up her machete.

When he heard her steps, he shot her a hard glare, but didn't say anything as she sidled up beside him. Peering around his wide form, and between the slit of the barricade they'd put up, she

145

caught glimpses of shadowy figures passing quickly by their shelter. Clusters and clusters of them as though they'd never end. All she could make out clearly under the moon's yellow light were silvery wheels. *Wheelers.*

Dorothy had never encountered one before. In the dark, she was unable to see the ribbons that sewed their mouths shut. What kind of person sewed mouths shut and took heads? Langwidere and Lion might not be difficult to kill since there were only two of them, but an entire clan of Wheelers was a different story.

"What are they doing?" Dorothy asked softly, shifting back so she was pressed against the wall.

"Your guess is as good as mine, but I assume searching for more heads."

"Or searching for *my* head." Her grip tightened against the handle of the machete. "There are too many for us to fight if they come in here." Tin might be good with an axe, but how long would he last? And Crow's finger blades could take down a few, but not all. Then there was Dorothy's experience, taking down ... *corn*...

"They don't know we're here." Tin stepped away from the wall and tugged Dorothy back by her sleeve.

Instead of laying back down in bed, Dorothy headed into the sitting room to check on Crow. On the couch, he rested curled up on his side, arm hanging over the edge, and still passed out like a baby. *Her father.* He was her father...

She was still confused, with too many questions and not enough answers. But even when he hadn't remembered her, when she'd just met him, there had been something between them. He'd held her hand when she'd missed her family. She'd felt closer to him than anyone. And now she understood why.

Someone had taken her from her parents, and she hadn't pushed him about it, but she would have to soon.

Dorothy shrugged off whatever she was feeling, set down her machete, and slid back into bed, unable to return to sleep. Tin climbed in beside her, and neither of them spoke. After everything, she was still angry, and he wasn't forgiven. But, perhaps he eventually could be. Dorothy was good with forgiveness—Aunt Em had taught her that. Aunt Em… Uncle Henry… Neither one was real family, but they still felt like it, would always be. And she'd forgiven them, after they'd hurt her, too. Instead of believing her, they'd had her poked and prodded. Too many memories of needles and experiments. Perhaps there was a reason why she wasn't permanently damaged by it all, because she was fae. Not human.

Crow said he hadn't come back for her once he remembered because he thought she was better off. But had she been? She had no doubt that Aunt Em and Uncle Henry had both loved her, but they should have tried to believe her.

"You look like you're thinking too hard," Tin said, interrupting Dorothy's thoughts.

"Because I am." Her frown deepened as she thought about something else. She remembered the short chat she'd had with the satyr. "I don't even think Dorothy Gale is my true name."

"You would feel it if it was. Fae know."

Her head turned in his direction, but she couldn't make out his expression in the dark. "What is it?"

"I wouldn't know. Crow or your mother will know your first name. Your true full name is something you're born with and have to tap into."

Closing her eyes, Dorothy tried to tap into that bit of silver she'd been able to get to with Lion when she'd broken out from her glamour. Digging and digging, she couldn't feel it, couldn't see it. "I can't."

"Don't worry about it." Tin shifted closer, his arm almost brushing hers. "If you don't know your true name, then no one else can know it either. You wouldn't want to be controlled by another."

Something struck her then, and her heart dropped into her stomach. "Have you been controlled before?"

He shook his head. "No one knows my true name except for me, but I've seen it happen to others."

Relaxing her shoulders, she leaned back into her pillow. "It's a good secret to keep."

Tin blew out a huff of air and groaned, as if he was struggling with himself whether to speak or not. "When you went back to Kansas, I truly smiled for the first time. Not because I was given my heart, but because I knew you would go on to do great things. Your heart was always good, selfless and kind. It still is. And now that you're back, you're someone new, different. It's like we're meeting for the first time, you know?"

"I guess?" Dorothy did know, because she was seeing him through a woman's eyes now, not a girl's. Even though she wasn't technically a 'woman' anymore, she still felt like one.

"I know I'm getting too fucking deep here," he said. "But if I tell you my name, would you forgive me?"

The edges of Dorothy's lips tilted up. "Are you trying to barter with me?"

"No. It's just, if you can control me, then you can order me not to harm you. You'll never have to worry about—"

Dorothy's eyes widened and she flung her body forward, pressing her hand to his lips and straddling his hips. "I trust you." She threw the words out and smiled. "I forgive you. But if you betray my trust again, my machete will be put to use, just as your axe has been."

As she removed her palm from his mouth, her cheeks reddened because she was still cradling his hips … again. Why did she keep finding herself in this predicament with him? Before she could remove herself from him, Tin wrapped his strong arms around her and leaned forward. The words came out in a rush as he whispered them at her ear, his breath tickling her flesh. "Tarragontin Aodh Greenbriar."

Realizing what he'd just done, Dorothy inhaled sharply and lifted her hands to shove him for being so stupid. But he was fast, and he gripped her wrists, smiling. *Smiling.* And even in the dark, she could see that frustrating smile, the same one he'd given her before she'd left the Land of Oz.

He'd believed in her then, and he believed in her now.

Her shoulders relaxed and she leaned forward. Tin released her wrists, allowing her to wrap her arms around him. At his ear, she murmured, "I promise I won't ever tell anyone or use it against you."

He embraced her back, and mumbled beautiful words at the crook of her neck, "You may use me however you wish."

The sentence sank in, leaving Dorothy to focus on just how close their bodies were. Her chest heaved up and down, up and down. His breaths sounded hard, ragged. Reclining backward, she should have removed her legs from his hips—she didn't. Instead, she let her forehead kiss his in a warming touch. Lips. His lips were so close, his breath now mingling with hers, kissing there too. Everything was kissing except for their lips, and she wanted them to kiss, needed them to. As if under a spell, she angled her head to the side, and her lips finally pressed against his soft mouth.

Dorothy brought her hand to his iron scar, her fingers lightly touching the raised ridges. The warmth tingled her skin, and she wondered how often he felt pain from the scar, but she didn't ask and she didn't pull away from him. He inhaled and moved his lips against hers, as she traveled a slow journey across his. Tin's mouth caressed hers, his tongue parting her lips. Her tongue met his in a wicked dance, deepening and deepening.

Gripping her waist, he pulled her closer, and she could *feel* him, like she had that first night beneath his cloak. But this time, she wanted to continue to let him press into her. She yearned to explore what lay beneath all his layers. His heart beat hard against his chest, her hand, and that caused her to stop. Moments ago she'd hated him, and now what was she doing? Aunt Em would have told her she was being a trollop, and she wouldn't have cared. Dorothy was becoming too warm in places that needed to be touched, and she desperately wanted it to be by Tin's hand. But then she remembered they weren't alone in the house. Crow was in the other room—*her father.*

She pulled back as though she'd been scalded, peeling her legs from his waist. "That shows I forgive you, but it won't happen again."

"We both know it will," Tin rasped and tugged her to him.

In the morning Dorothy woke to an empty bed, remembering the kiss. *God, the kiss.* She would go on as though it hadn't happened, as if her lips still didn't tingle from it.

Voices came from outside her room—arguing.

"You think you can protect her?" Tin's voice boomed. "You didn't even stir when a clan of Wheelers rolled past last night."

"I would have woken up if they'd come in here," Crow spat.

Dorothy slipped on her shoes, grabbed her machete, and stumbled into the next room. Tin stood, gripping his axe while Crow's finger blades were out.

"Good morning," Crow said, retracting his blades and stepping toward her. "I was about to wake you so we could get started."

Dorothy bit her lip, not looking at Tin. "Crow, do you know what my real name is?" She didn't think she would ever call him "Father," because Crow was more comfortable, familiar.

Crow shook his head. "No, I didn't have time to learn it. Because of Locasta…"

"Locasta? What does she have to do with anything? Lion mentioned her name before he ran away, like the coward he is."

He rubbed a hand down the bottom portion of his face. "Just give me a moment. I said I would tell you, but this, this isn't going to be good."

With those words, he stepped outside, leaving Dorothy and Tin exchanging a confused glance.

Dorothy opened the door and she and Tin followed Crow outside, then came to a halt. A gasp escaped her lips as she scanned the yellow brick road. It wasn't yellow any longer—the strip appeared as if it had been painted in crimson. Blood coated it. Fresh blood from the night before, but most was drying already from the heat of the morning sun.

As she scanned the area, there wasn't just blood, but bodies. Several male and female fae with large white wings and obsidian horns lay torn and broken with heads still attached. They looked as though they'd been beaten and run over with wheels. The Wheelers...

"They didn't take the heads this time." Crow sighed. "And it looks as though the males aren't safe anymore either."

"This is because of me, isn't it?" Dorothy said, wondering if something was going to abduct her right then. "We need to bury these bodies."

"I think you—"

"No, we're doing it," Dorothy interrupted Tin. She knew he was going to tell her to leave the South, and that wasn't something she could do.

She didn't meet Tin's gaze, even though she could feel him silently watching, brooding again. Because of her.

The night before he'd told her his true name, she'd kissed him, and then told him it could never happen again. And yet, she wanted to do it again, even while surrounded by blood. What kind of person did that make her?

CHAPTER SEVENTEEN

TIN

Just as Tin thought that the world had thrown him everything there was to throw, he found himself in a six-foot hole. Sweat rolled down his face and back. Dirt clung to the moisture and somehow managed to work its way through his hair to his scalp. He dug the rusted shovel into the ground and sat down to catch his breath.

Dorothy had better appreciate this. If he was going to work up this much of a sweat, there were a dozen other activities he could think of that would be more enjoyable than digging a mass grave. Not that he should be thinking about what had happened between them. She hadn't spoken a single word to him all day and *clearly* regretted kissing him. He couldn't say the same. In fact, he felt the exact opposite. What he wouldn't give to have her straddle him again, preferably with less clothing next time. He hardened at the thought.

"The grave won't dig itself," Crow called from above.

"Fuck you," Tin yelled back, his cock shriveling at the sound of the nuisance's voice. "If you're in such a rush, help."

"If only we could find more than one shovel."

Tin bared his teeth. "Use your fucking claws."

Crow flicked his wrist and the talons shot out. "They're not very useful when it comes to digging, but if it makes you feel better, I can demonstrate what they *are* good for."

Tin ripped the shovel from the ground and chucked it at Crow's face without getting up. "It's your turn."

"What a surprise," he said sarcastically, catching the wooden handle before it hit him in the face. "The Tin Man would rather pick up bits and pieces of dead fae than dig a hole."

Tin held his breath and motioned toward the ten-by-ten square Dorothy had marked out. It was nearly complete with just one corner to finish, but was already more than enough to bury what was left outside the abandoned house. "We both know this size hole is overkill."

"Fine." Crow disappeared from the opening.

The next thing Tin knew, a bloody arm came sailing toward him. He ducked to avoid being hit in the head. A leg followed, then a wet pile of organs squished to the ground, barely missing his boots. His breath hitched as anger swelled. "Damn it, Crow! What the fuck?"

"Hey!" Dorothy shouted. "What do you two think you're doing? These are *innocent fae* you're throwing around."

Well, they used to be. Tin winced—he was supposed to be working on his conscience—and grabbed a root to pull himself from the grave. By the time he emerged, Crow was silently, almost repentantly, carrying a torso.

Dorothy *tsked* when he let it fall into the hole. "No respect."

Tin wasn't going to speak his thoughts out loud. Telling Dorothy that they had already done more than enough for the murdered fae would only earn him further resentment. She felt guilty enough that the Wheelers killed them as they hunted for her. If this kept happening like he suspected it would, either he or Crow would have to speak up. There was no way he was doing this again tomorrow. Dorothy would have to decide between reaching Glinda in time to stop Langwidere or burying half the population of Oz. Even Tin knew she would choose stopping Langwidere.

Crow continued placing body parts in the grave as gently as he could, and when he was finished, he begrudgingly took up the shovel again to complete the job. By the time everything was done, there was only an hour or two of sunlight left.

"We'll stay here another night," Tin announced, stretching his aching back. "No one would expect us to stay put after finding all that carnage."

Also he really, *really* needed to wash the day off and, though it wasn't exactly clean, there was a tub inside.

Dorothy nodded without looking at him. When she spoke, she directed it at Crow. "I'll run water for a bath. You both need it."

With narrowed eyes, Tin watched her walk back into the house. So she *was* paying attention to him.

"Tin," Crow said in a low voice.

Tin jerked his head to the side to find Crow much too close and eased back a step. "If this is about the bath, I'm going first."

"I need to tell Dorothy who her mother is. Just in case anything happens, she needs to know." He wrung his hands. "How do I tell her?"

Tin's brows shot up. "You're asking *me* for advice? Have you gone mad?"

"Pretend to be a decent male for a minute, would you?"

Tin bristled, but he was too tired to fight. He was also really damn curious about who Crow had knocked up all those years ago. Poor female… "Why not just tell her? Start with a name and how you met. Dorothy will ask a thousand questions after that and you won't have to worry about what to say. Just answer her."

"That's the problem." Crow grimaced. "Her mother is Reva."

Tin stared at Crow, the name processing as slow as molasses. He couldn't mean… No. That was impossible. Dorothy's mother couldn't be the Wicked Witch of the West. There had to be some sort of mistake—a mix-up in Crow's memories. Maybe Oz had scrambled things around in his brain a bit when he broke the Curse of Unknowing.

Tin hadn't known much about Reva. He only knew that Reva

was once the name of the Wicked Witch of the West, but she had put an end to anyone who dared use it. The name had faded from memory for most fae while she reigned because the Wicked Witch was so much more fitting.

"Reva," Tin repeated when he found his tongue again. "Of the West, Reva? That Dorothy killed? *That* Reva? Not some lonely barmaid with the same name?"

Crow's face contorted with pain. "So you see the problem then. If I tell Dorothy who her mother is, she'll have to live with the fact that she killed her."

Fuck.

"Fuck." Tin lightly scratched his head with his iron tipped gloves, loosening some of the dirt. This was going to gut Dorothy, even if her mother was a psychopath. "You're just as screwed as I am."

"Water's ready," came Dorothy's voice from inside.

Tin's whole body cringed at the mention of water—or as it was about to become known, the weapon she'd used to murder her mother. It almost made him want to skip bathing. *Almost.* It was more of a need than a want, and there was no way in hell he wanted to be there when Crow told her the truth. He bolted inside before Crow could try to trap him into assisting with their looming father-daughter conversation. It was the cowardly thing to do but Tin didn't give a shit. Dorothy already seemed to feel uncomfortable around him—being there to watch her break down wouldn't help any of them, despite his heart trying to tell him otherwise.

Once inside the dingy blue and yellow bathroom, Tin shucked his clothes off. Maybe he should've gone out to find a river instead. He'd washed in them countless times since he was a young fae. That was before his stone-hearted coldness pushed all his childhood friends away, despite his best efforts. He should've known better than to say his friend's mother dying wasn't a big deal because everyone died. And he shouldn't have eaten an entire loaf of bread in front of near-starving toddlers. Tin had wanted to say and do the right things then—he'd watched everyone else in the village and copied their mannerisms—but he was never shown compassion. He couldn't understand when he needed to pretend and when he didn't. It became easier as he got older, but by then it was too late. It was only during those two years with his heart that he realized what sympathy really meant and how much the world lacked it.

Tin stood naked, staring at his pile of dirty clothes. After his bath, he would need to give them a good shake, but ridding himself of filth wouldn't be so easy. One day Dorothy would realize he wasn't good, and she would leave him. No amount of time could take away the blood already staining his hands.

With a heavy sigh, he ignored the film floating on the water and stepped into the tepid bath. The previous owners had thankfully left a bar of soap behind. Once the dust was blown away from the soap, it would clean him well enough.

A quiet knock came on the door. "Tin?"

He jerked upright, sloshing water over the edge of the tub. His heart pounded at the sweet sound of Dorothy's voice addressing him. It had only been less than a day since she'd spoken directly to Tin, but it felt like an eternity. "Yes?"

"Thank you," she whispered through the door. "For digging the grave."

He hesitated to reply because that gave her the chance to end the conversation, but he couldn't stay silent forever. "You're welcome."

"Dorothy?" Crow asked from farther away. He sounded dejected, even to Tin. "We should talk about your mother."

Tin immediately sunk under the water to avoid overhearing the conversation, only allowing enough of his face to surface so he could breathe. He scrubbed his hair furiously until his scalp ached, then picked away the dirt that somehow made its way under his fingernails, despite the gloves. Soapy bubbles floated around him, mixing with the filth. Still, he washed a second time, and a third.

When a heart-wrenching cry—muffled by the water—hit his ears, Tin felt it as a blow to his chest. He sunk completely under and held his breath until his lungs ached. His heart thundered inside him, and he tried to make it stop.

Dorothy had killed her mother.

But only after her mother had tried to kill her.

Fuck, fuck, fuck!

CHAPTER EIGHTEEN

DOROTHY

"I need you to sit down, Dorothy," Crow said, clenching his teeth while his hands shook. "I'm going to tell you the story of your mother. I know you need to know who she is, especially now that you're here and in danger."

Dorothy's shoulders stiffened as she lowered herself on the couch beside Crow. She was nervous yet eager to hear the story of how Crow and her mother had met. And she wasn't alone anymore, like she'd been in Kansas. She had Crow and there was Tin, but now she also had someone who was a mother… She'd never had one of those before.

"I'm going to begin with you, Dorothy, and how you came about." Crow bit his lip and turned to face her. "I've been in love twice in my life. First with Locasta."

"Holy hell, is she my mother?" Dorothy had already heard not so good things about the Northern Witch.

"No!" he said hurriedly. "What I had with Locasta wasn't real, though. I fell in love with someone who didn't truly exist. Locasta pretended to be good, and like Langwidere, she wasn't."

Why was he talking about Langwidere? If she was the second person he was in love with, Dorothy would collapse right there.

"I know when you first came to Oz when you were younger,

you were led to believe that the two good witches were from the North and the South," Crow continued. "That isn't true for one of them. Eventually, when I found out Locasta had secretly been murdering and plotting to rule territories, I went to the West to start warning people there. What I didn't expect to find was a certain female—one who was strong, challenging, and found my witty charm to be … charmless." He chuckled sadly and rubbed at his lower lip. "Yet somehow through our fights, our arguing, we fell in love with each other, even though we were completely opposite in every way. I loved her, truly loved her … I still do. Then you came along, and Locasta showed up at your birth. She'd been planning her actions for some time. We didn't know, yet we should have been prepared anyway. Locasta first cursed your mother, then took you into her arms. She told me she was turning you into a changeling before she cursed me to the cornfield—the place where you eventually found me—with a scrambled brain."

Dorothy covered her mouth, her breath coming out uneven. "Oh, Crow…"

"That's not all. When I got my memory back, I remembered *everything*, and I chose not to reveal certain things. I didn't go searching for you later because I knew you already had a family, and you would have been happier there without knowing the truth."

"That's not true." Dorothy wrapped her hand around Crow's. "Where is my mother now? Did you break her curse? Or do we still need to break it?"

"No, her curse was never broken." Crow inhaled sharply. "Her name was Reva."

Reva… Reva… Dorothy didn't know anyone by that name, but it sounded pretty. "I don't know her."

"Yes, you do. Locasta turned Reva into her plaything to wreak havoc. She changed the way Reva looked, made her hideous so my last memory of her would be repulsive…" Crow closed his eyes, tears running down his cheeks. This was the first time she'd ever seen him cry, and her heart clamped up. "The

Wicked Witch of the West once had a name—Reva."

Dorothy inhaled a ragged breath, unable to release it. Her entire body couldn't move. The Wicked Witch. Reva was the Wicked Witch. Reva was dead. Because of Dorothy. Dorothy had killed her. She'd killed her own mother. And Reva had been the love of Crow's life. A wounded sob escaped her lips as both hands came to cover her face, to try and stop the ugly feelings from pouring out.

Crow folded his arm around her but she wiggled out of his grasp and stood. "I did this to you. I killed her when I could have come up with another way."

"It wasn't your fault, Dorothy. It was Locasta's."

Locasta had taken Dorothy and swapped her out with another baby, so she would have never known. Not when she'd met Crow and he talked in riddles and strange sentences most of the time. "What about the human I was swapped with? Where is the real Dorothy now?"

"I don't know." He placed a hand to his chin and shook his head.

"You don't know?" She raised her voice then, because the real Dorothy deserved to go home, back when Aunt Em and Uncle Henry were still alive. But the second part was impossible. "I've been gone for ten years! Haven't you looked? Didn't you *try*?"

"Of course I did!" Crow exclaimed. "Do you think I'm Lion? I'm not a coward. I went straight to Locasta after you left. She only laughed in my face, broke my wings, and told me she'd found the perfect place for the girl. All she wanted was for me to be her lover again. I left then and continued searching, but came up with nothing."

Dorothy would have to eventually go searching for her, after finding Langwidere.

"But…" Crow's brows lowered in confusion. "What I don't understand is how you managed to kill her with the water. It must've been the magic of the shoes combined with your power. You do have half of her, you know." He smiled, almost melancholic, as if he was recalling a memory. "Reva cared for the people of Oz. Before she was cursed, she wouldn't have done any of the terrible things she was forced to do. I know she didn't know what she was doing when she attacked you, attacked me—"

"I think I want to be alone for a little bit." Dorothy couldn't listen to any more of it. She'd killed her own mother who was actually *innocent*. Hot tears started to pour down her cheeks as she walked toward the front door.

"I understand," Crow said. "I'll give you some time to think over everything while I search for supplies to bring with us. I'll be back before the sun sets."

"All right," Dorothy whispered as they stepped outside.

"I love you. Deep down, even when my brain wasn't working properly, I knew you were my daughter." He wrapped his arms around her, but she couldn't bring herself to return the hug.

She watched as he walked away, slipping through the trees. As soon as she couldn't see the outline of Crow's—her father's—form, she released her tears fully.

After a while had passed, she gathered her courage and went back inside the house. The bedroom door was cracked, and the bathroom entrance stood wide open. She peered down at her filth and decided to get cleaned up, and possibly wash away how she felt.

As she stepped inside the mostly-clean bathroom, she took stock of the pale blue walls, the bright yellow floors, the tub already filled with fresh warm water. Tin. Tin had done that for her…

Dorothy couldn't think about him. She'd been trying not to all day. Even though she'd been avoiding him, she'd snuck glances his way earlier, too many to count. She couldn't help it.

Quietly, Dorothy stripped out of her clothes and stepped down into the water. Perhaps she could be all right about killing the Wicked Witch when she'd been wicked. *Reva.* The witch now had a name. But that wicked fae wasn't only her mother, she was Crow's true love, and she'd *murdered* her. Murdered the happiness that could have been. She sank her head into the depths of the water and cried once more. She watched as the bubbles floated to the surface, hoping Tin wouldn't be able to hear her. But she knew he had to have earlier.

When her tears were gone and she needed to breathe, she lifted upward and washed everything clean.

After she dried off and got dressed, Dorothy went out of the bathroom and stood in the middle of the house, unsure where to go. There was the living room and outside, but she didn't want to be alone again. Her gaze shifted to the cracked door leading to the bedroom. He'd left it open for her.

Dorothy chose to walk inside the bedroom. Mostly darkness spilled across the room because of the barricades. Tin lay on his side, bare-chested, facing the barriers of the window.

In case he was sleeping, she slowly got on the bed and curled her arms around his warm waist. "Thank you for the bath," she whispered.

He rolled over so he was facing her and draped his arm around her waist. "I'm the one who's supposed to be holding you."

"So you know…" She didn't meet his eyes. "You now know what happened to my mother and what a horrible person I am."

"Crow only told me your mother was Reva before he came to talk to you. Nothing else."

Dorothy needed it off her chest, out of her mouth, so she fed him the rest, the entirety of Crow's story. During it all, Tin's expression didn't change—he stayed watching her just the same.

"I'm horrible," she said when she finally finished.

"You're not horrible." Tin's arm tightened on her waist. "If anyone is, I am. Look at all I've done."

Dorothy moved her hand to his beating heart. The thump-thump sang against her palm. "But you didn't have this at the time."

"I didn't have a beating heart before the Wizard either. And back then, never once did I swing my axe to kill." There was something in his voice that sounded like anguish, and she knew he regretted everything.

"Losing a heart after you've had one would make murderers and monsters out of any of us." There were times when she was going to lose the farm that she'd wanted to go out and commit murder herself. If she'd had a heart of stone, perhaps she would have followed through with it.

"I told you your heart was kind," he said, kissing her forehead.

Dorothy shifted closer and he turned so she could rest her head against his chest. She tried shutting her eyes and sleeping, but that was when the memories decided to creep back in.

"Look at you, just a little girl." The Wicked Witch laughed, shrill and high-pitched. "One who no one would ever want. You'll give me those slippers or I'll find a way to pull all your bones through your flesh and let my winged minions lick them clean. Then I'll wear your skin as gloves while slipping on the shoes."

Dorothy trembled while studying the witch's emerald green eyes, the color matching her skin. The witch's nose came to a sharp curled point and her brown hair hung to her waist in matted waves. She didn't know what to do. Her friends were outside trying to get in, but they couldn't.

Her gaze fell to the bucket of water beside her. It was given to her to drink, the remainder of the room empty of anything. The water was the only weapon that Dorothy could use to distract the witch and give herself a chance to run.

Not taking her eyes from the witch, Dorothy picked the bucket up and jolted her arms forward. The liquid collided with the witch's face. And before Dorothy could sprint away, her slippers lit up a bright silver, growing brighter and brighter, until the room was nothing but the glowing color.

The witch screamed, a scream that Dorothy would never forget. The screams became howls until there was silence. When the silver went out, the room was clear again, and all that was left was the witch's black dress in a heap on the floor. Somehow, Dorothy, along with the magical silver slippers, had destroyed the enemy.

The door flew open and there stood Tin, Crow, and Lion, who'd come to rescue her, but she'd already won.

"She's dead," Dorothy said. "I melted the Wicked Witch."

Dorothy couldn't sleep then, not when her heart was beating too fast, not when her mind wouldn't let her rest. Her eyes remained open.

"Are you all right?" Tin asked.

"No," she mumbled into his chest.

"Me neither." Tin lifted Dorothy's chin so that her eyes met his silver irises. He had a lot going on in his head, too—she knew that.

And she would do something about it.

Her lips crashed to his in a desperate, aching, needy kiss. His eyes widened in surprise for a moment before he relaxed and kissed her back, his soft lips drinking hers in. Tin had been right—this would happen again.

The kiss deepened and Tin rolled to his back, taking her with him. She didn't pause as she straddled him in the familiar position that she had grown to love. Beneath her, she could already feel him hard and ready. She slowly moved against him while tasting the flavors of his tongue. He groaned inside her mouth. Dorothy could have sworn she tasted the flavor of that sound, too.

This, *this* was taking her away from everything that had happened—Crow's story, the memories. And *this* was something she could focus on and not have to feel sorry about.

Despite the kissing being heavenly, she needed more. Dorothy's hands went to her chest and she unbuckled her overalls with a soft click, then let the flaps drop to her waist. Tin studied her in wonder, staying ever so still, as she then unbuttoned the front of her shirt and peeled it off along with her bra, exposing her breasts.

Tin's expression grew hungry—he leaned forward and placed his hands at her waist as he pressed his mouth to her nipple, sucking and flicking it with his tongue, all while moving her body back and forth against his hardness.

Dorothy couldn't control herself—she ran her hands down his chiseled chest to the tie of his pants to unfasten it. With determined fingertips, she untied the strings while he shimmied them off, freeing himself.

He was well endowed, so much bigger than the one she'd seen before. She wanted to touch it, to taste it, to have it inside her. Her center throbbed at the thought of it all. Dorothy didn't care if she was a trollop—she'd done much, much worse than lay with a man.

His lips caught hers again, his tongue prying them open before it plunged in and out of her mouth. She angled closer and firmly gripped his cock, stroking it, the tip moistening her hand.

"Take my overalls off already," she begged.

And he did. He took everything off her until she was just as bare as he was.

Dorothy's arms wrapped around Tin's neck as he pressed his hand between her legs, rubbing the spot that needed it, rubbing it so perfectly. Then he pushed two fingers inside her. "You're so wet," he rasped against her lips.

Before she could respond, Tin rolled her over to her back, kissing his way down the side of her neck, in between her collarbone, the center of her chest, and down, down to the place calling for him. Dorothy's first instinct was to close her legs, because no one had ever been there like that, seen her like this. But her nerves disintegrated into a million pieces when his tongue stroked, licked, and prodded in between her folds. She interlaced her fingers into his soft hair, arched her back and moaned in pleasure when she swore she saw a constellation of stars.

With a low chuckle, Tin kissed his way back up her flesh to her lips once more, his hand cradling her breast.

Dorothy didn't want him to stop there, so she ran her fingertips against his iron scar, absorbing the warmth. "Just get inside me." She'd never talked like this to anyone in her life, but with him, she felt braver.

"Are you sure?" His silver eyes mirrored what she wanted. "I know—"

"This is what I need right now."

"Me too." He leaned forward, the tip of his nose skating up

the side of her neck as he murmured, "Have you ever been fucked?"

"Yes, I've been fucked," she whispered, running her nails down his spine. He shivered beneath her touch.

Tin lifted his head, his eyes locking with hers like before. "No, Dorothy, I don't think you have. Not in the way I'm thinking about."

The moment he spoke the words, she knew them to be true, especially after what he'd already done to her. "Then show me." The tip of his cock angled right near the place where it needed to be. "Please," she begged.

In answer, his hips rocked backward and he thrust forward, filling her the way she needed to be. She moaned as he continued to thrust, harder, faster. Her hands grabbed his buttocks, increasing the pace.

Neither one closed their eyes as they watched each other. He was fucking her and now she wanted to fuck him. Tightening her legs around his waist, she flipped him to his back and ground against him until the feeling started building and building. This time when the release took control of her body, creating planets and nebulas in the constellation, she shouted his name.

Tin grinned and returned her to her back. He deliciously plowed into her over and over until her name came out in a deep rumble from his lips. They were both a sweaty mess, and breathing the same heavy breaths, as he sank down on top of her. With a lazy smile, he held himself up by his elbows, looking at her. "Perhaps this is the first time *I've* actually been fucked."

Dorothy couldn't help but smile too as he adjusted himself beside her, both of them studying each other. Gently, he ran a hand down her cheek. "I told you to use me however you wished, and I meant that."

Did he… Oh God… Tin thought she had only done this to not have to think about things, as if she wouldn't have been with him otherwise. Hurriedly, she pressed her lips to his to show him that things between them had become more, even when she hadn't asked for it. She wrapped her arms around him because they both needed it. "Next time," she spoke softly into his hair, "it will be slow and beautiful, and I promise to make love to you like no one ever has. Because there will be a next time."

His arms folded around her, holding her tight. "There certainly will."

Dorothy could feel his length hard against her. "Already?" She giggled.

"For you, always." His lips went to the place right below her ear, kissing gently, making her body heat once more.

And for the rest of the night, neither's body would remain quiet.

CHAPTER NINETEEN

TIN

Tin woke just as the sun began its ascent. The warm light leaking into the room made Dorothy appear like a goddess as she laid naked beneath the blanket, her hair tangled from his hands. He wanted to weave his fingers into it again, tug her head back, and wake her with a deep kiss, but they both needed a break after spending hours devouring each other.

A break and food. With a smile that wouldn't leave his face, Tin slipped from the room to see what Crow had found for supplies. Had he ever felt like this? He'd never smiled like this, even when his heart woke for the first time. His stomach growled and his thoughts turned back to finding breakfast. There would be no rationing today. He and Dorothy both needed to regain their strength, and it would be easier to find food now that Dorothy was fae. His smile widened as he realized that meant she had a long future ahead since she wasn't mortal.

If things like this kept growing between them, and they became more, did that mean Crow would be his family one day? He inhaled sharply at the idea and his wayward thoughts, unsure how to feel, and cut a glance to the couch where Crow slept the night before last. It was empty, the blanket Crow used still folded neatly. *Strange*, thought Tin. But then he realized the likely reason—of course Crow wouldn't want to listen to Tin fuck his daughter. He and Dorothy hadn't held back their moans, and the slam of the headboard against the wall had nearly broken the old frame. Half the forest probably heard Dorothy cry out his name. Multiple times. He grinned, pleased with himself. Crow was most likely passed out in his hammock just out of earshot.

Tin crept through the small abandoned house, looking for the supplies. Surely Crow wouldn't risk taking them with him when they would be safe here from scavenging animals. He stepped outside and scanned the immediate area.

"Crow?" he called as loudly as he dared. He didn't want to attract Wheelers, but if any did creep out of the shadows, he'd chop their heads off to send to Langwidere. None had traveled past the house last night. If they had, they would've stopped to investigate all the noise he and Dorothy had made. "It's safe to come in now." Not even the wind dared rustle the leaves. "This isn't the time to be petty."

When silence was his only response, Tin eased back inside the house without turning his back to the woods. This wasn't good. Crow wouldn't go so far out that he couldn't keep an eye on the house. He slid the bolt, locking the door. It wouldn't do much to keep out any real danger, but it would slow an enemy down.

Tin returned to the bedroom and shook Dorothy's bare shoulders gently. "Dorothy, wake up."

She groaned with a sheepish smile. "As much fun as last night was, I need sleep."

"I would love to let you, but that's not why you have to get up." He left the bedside and began collecting her clothes as worry gnawed at him like a wild beast. "Crow hasn't come back."

She bolted off the bed. "What do you mean?"

"Exactly what I said." He handed her the clothes and she immediately slipped them on while he grabbed his axe from the floor.

"Maybe we scared him off?" She bit her lip, her face turning a deep shade of scarlet.

Tin shook his head. "I thought the same thing, but when I called for him outside, there was no reply. I have a bad feeling about this."

Dorothy met his gaze, her eyes wild. "Perhaps he didn't hear you. Perhaps he camped too far away. Or he could be sleeping very soundly like he did the other night. You two worked so hard burying the bodies and then he went for supplies… He had to be exhausted, so that's possible, right?"

Tin gently gripped her upper arms. "Breathe, Dearheart. We'll find him."

"But what if—"

Tin kissed her quickly, not out of passion but to silence her. "We will find your father, I promise. Stay calm and please, I'm begging you, listen to me. Can you do that?"

Dorothy, red-faced with worry, nodded.

He hoped she would this time—her track record with listening was abhorrent. "Good. Then take a deep breath."

Dorothy listened and Tin did the same. Once they had both exhaled, Tin collected one of her overall straps and buckled it over her shoulder. He made sure to use measured movements so as not to show how concerned he was. Having Dorothy panic would only make finding Crow harder and slow them down.

"There," he said when Dorothy was dressed and fitted with her machete. "Now we're going to search the woods for any sign of Crow or his belongings. Stay close to me and keep an eye out for his hammock."

Tin waited for Dorothy to nod before turning to lead the way. Her footsteps hurried behind him, barely noticeable over the echo of his pulse. If Crow was gone, the enemy knew where Dorothy was. Crow was the easier target between her protectors, especially if he had decided to camp outside. Now all Dorothy had was Tin, which would've normally been enough, but he was only one male. If an entire Wheeler clan came at them, if Lion had tagged along, or worse yet, Langwidere, there was no way he could win alone. Dorothy had a weapon now, but she wasn't trained in using it. Even her fae power was raw. She'd wielded it to escape Lion but that didn't mean she knew how to tap back into it.

Fuck.

As they walked, Tin shoved his iron-tipped gloves on and flexed his fingers. He was getting ahead of himself. Crow could've been eaten by a gremlin for all he knew which would've been a mercy compared to Langwidere. Just because something bad might have happened didn't mean Langwidere was behind it. But this was the South—a place that had become a land of blood and death because of her.

After ten minutes of searching with no luck, Dorothy grabbed Tin's arm. "I didn't say it back."

Tin paused. "I don't understand."

"To Crow," she clarified. "He told me he loved me before he left and I said nothing. I just let him walk away to gather supplies without telling him how I felt."

Tin's new organ cracked for her. "Dearheart," he whispered and used his knuckles to lift her chin. Her brown eyes glistened with unshed tears and her chin wobbled, but he refused to break their gaze. She had to know he meant what he was about to tell her. "Crow knows you love him. You didn't have to say a word. He understood that telling you about your mother would hurt and, I suspect, fully anticipated the reaction you gave him. Hell, he probably expected worse, but you're strong and brave and, most importantly, his daughter. Crow has known you loved him since you left for Kansas and he'll know you love him even if he goes another five hundred years without hearing the words from your lips."

Tears fell then, coating Dorothy's face. "I *have* to tell him."

"All right," Tin relented, drawing her in for a hug. "When we find him, you will, but for now, you have to continue to stay strong."

Dorothy sniffled against his chest before breaking away to wipe her face. "You're right. I'm sorry. We don't have time to waste on my crying when we could be finding clues."

Tin gave her a reassuring smile and turned his focus back to the search. It wasn't much longer before they ran across a fallen tree. Except, it hadn't *fallen* but had been cut down. Tin pushed Dorothy behind him and slowed his approach.

A piece of knotted rope was still tied near the top of the tree, just below the heaviest branches, with a small bit of ripped fabric clinging to the end. *Shit.* He already knew what he would find when he looked up, but he prayed Dorothy wouldn't follow his glance. There, dangling from a tree a few feet away, was the rest of Crow's hammock. On a lower branch, the overstuffed bag of supplies hung haphazardly, as if stuck there after falling. How Crow ever made it that high without being able to shift was a mystery.

"Tin…" Dorothy wheezed. "Look."

His eyes snapped to the ground where she pointed. Deep lines gouged the dirt. Dozens of them. And he knew, just as Dorothy seemed to know, that they came from the Wheelers. Tin studied the tree stump, taking in the sharp marks, and understood exactly what had happened. They had cut him down and took him. But where? Where were Lion and Langwidere?

"Damn it! Mother fucking Wheelers and their shit ass puppet master." Tin pressed the heels of his hands into his eyes. Their enemy was going to divide and conquer. Whatever it took to get Dorothy's head… Because, Tin realized with a start, *she* was the rightful heir to the West. He pinned her with a look. "*Fuck.*"

"The Wheelers have him," she said quietly. "Do you think he's still alive?"

"I don't know," Tin admitted. "But Dorothy, you're in more danger than I thought. If Langwidere knows who your mother is, she won't stop until she gets what she wants. Langwidere may not rule here yet, but she rules the West."

And what she wanted was Dorothy's head. A dead heir was no threat to her power grab, and why not add to her macabre collection while she was at it?

"What does my mother have to—oh…" Her eyes widened. "She controlled the West and, as her daughter, that makes me the next ruler, doesn't it?"

"Yes." Tin dug his gloved hands into his hair. *Fuck* didn't even begin to cover it. "We have to find Crow before it's too late. Glinda will have to wait a little longer so we can follow these tracks while they're still fresh."

"Of course." She jumped over the tree, following the map of lines. "Do you think they came this way, or went that way?"

There was really no telling based on the tracks alone. If they had followed Crow from the house, which Tin suspected they had, the tracks would lead away from it. "That way," he said, nodding in front of them. "Let's get our supplies first."

Tin would never be able to salvage the hammock, so he left it tied above them and grabbed Crow's bag from the branch. With a quick glance, he checked the contents. Fruit—now bruised—and a moldy heel of bread. He threw that over his shoulder. A rope, two canteens, a wrinkled map, and a small assortment of daggers. He handed one of the weapons to Dorothy just to be on the safe side and tucked another one into his boot.

He rose from his crouched position, swung the bag over his shoulder, and leaned in to kiss Dorothy's head. For a moment, he closed his eyes and breathed in her scent to calm himself. He wouldn't ask her to stay behind because he knew she wouldn't, but if anything happened to her… He swallowed a snarl and planted another kiss on top of her head. They had to go now if they had any hope of intercepting the Wheelers before they reached Langwidere.

Lion would likely be there too, that backstabbing coward of a fae. This time Tin did snarl. Dorothy had lost many things in her life, but he sure as shit wasn't going to let her lose her father.

Tin stepped away and gave Dorothy's hand a quick squeeze. "Let's go save Crow."

CHAPTER TWENTY

DOROTHY

Dorothy and Tin had been trekking through the lush foliage, following the maps of lines, heading deeper down into the South. But she didn't know if they were even going in the right direction. The Wheelers could have taken Crow anywhere, or he could be dead…

The current line they followed looped around and ended back at the yellow brick road with no other path to follow except the road itself. Dorothy gripped the handle of her machete and walked closely next to Tin alongside the road.

There was no other sound enveloping them besides the light buzz of bugs singing.

"I suppose we'll just go the way we were originally following," Dorothy said, gnawing on the inside of her cheek. It was the same direction Lion had run off in, but where was he now? It was obvious that Langwidere was just as cowardly as him if she had to send Wheelers to do her dirty work.

"We'll monitor the dirt in case we see Wheeler tracks veering off and giving any more clues." Tin raised his axe over his shoulder, and together they continued their journey to hopefully find Crow alive.

As they walked farther and farther beneath the powerful rays of the sun, Dorothy couldn't help but wonder what if Crow really was dead. And if so, it would have been exactly like her mother—Dorothy's fault. She may not have killed him, but she might as well have because he'd gone out searching for supplies to give her space. Then he'd chosen to stay away to give her even more space. She'd been selfish, wasting time skin-to-skin with Tin. One of the happiest nights of her life had led to one of the worst mornings. She didn't want to regret it.

The soft tap of a finger came at the side of her head. "Stop thinking like that."

"Like what?" she huffed, moving Tin's finger from her temple.

"Negatively." Tin grasped her upper arm, causing her to stop, his silver eyes flashing into hers. "What happened to the Dorothy who was going to conquer everything? What happened to the Dorothy who locked me in a room and snuck away to do what she believed was right? That confident Dorothy."

Her shoulders slumped. "She's hiding. That Dorothy didn't know she was fae, that Dorothy didn't know she killed her own mother, that Dorothy didn't know she could be the reason her father might be dead, and that Dorothy didn't know there was a lunatic fae female collecting heads and wearing them for pleasure!"

"Well"—Tin leaned forward until his nose was touching hers, his breath warm against her lips—"let *that* Dorothy know that if she doesn't get her ass out of hiding, she won't win." Lifting his head slowly away from hers, he pulled something from behind his back and pushed a round piece of pinkened faerie fruit in front of her face. "Here. Eat."

Eating was the last thing Dorothy wanted to do at that moment, but she took the fruit from his palm. "Fine," she grumbled. He smirked and she tried not to smile as she pressed the fruit in between her teeth and bit in. The sweet juice spilled into her mouth, tasting like honey, and it was the only heavenly thing that had happened to her that day. It was better than any fruit she'd had back at home.

As they continued on their path, they ate in comfortable

silence. She looked toward bright and colorful homes that appeared deserted. Like the other part of the South where Dorothy encountered the satyr, there were also grave markers, but too many for her to stick around and count.

The brick road curved down a sloping hill, then went up and dipped again, all while the sun beamed its burning rays against her skin. Up ahead, the trees seemed to grow closer, everything more wooded. A world of greens and browns and a dash of yellow. And still, no one in sight.

When they reached the top of the hill, Dorothy gasped. The yellow brick road was stained with splotches of dried blood. At least this didn't look fresh, but it couldn't have been that old, because the rain would have cleaned it away.

From the greenery to her left, a swish softly sounded. Dorothy paused, grabbing Tin's arms. His spine was already rigid, his axe raised. *Perhaps it was only the wind.*

With his axe, Tin crept forward and spread a red-berry bush apart. Dozens of flickering black and green bugs flew out.

Dorothy felt stupid, and she blew out a relieved breath.

"Come on," Tin said, returning his axe to its comfortable place over his shoulder.

She nodded, but her heart rate continued to spike as she scanned the area. Each step they took, the trees became even closer, until the sunlight could barely be seen through the overlapping limbs. Dorothy wished she had a lantern with her, but at least the sun wasn't eclipsed by the branches.

Dorothy stuck close to Tin—or perhaps he chose to be nearer to her. A rustle of branches came from above them, and she peered up, seeing nothing. With wheels for hands, she didn't think a Wheeler could climb up a trunk, but Lion or someone else could.

Directly behind her a squeak filled the air, and Dorothy's heart froze in her chest. Hurling herself forward, she whirled around to find a looming shadow sliding out from behind a tree. A pale-faced female with matted hair lunged at her. Dorothy darted out of the way while Tin lunged toward the Wheeler with his axe.

"Don't kill her," Dorothy shouted, her eyes wide. "We can question her!"

Right as the blade of Tin's axe was about to strike the killing blow, he swiftly angled his weapon to the side. In less than a second, he had the Wheeler down on the ground with the wooden part of his axe against her filthy throat.

The Wheeler bucked and jerked, her wheels spinning at a ferocious speed, but Tin had her pinned down, holding her steady. As Dorothy shifted closer, she brought up her machete and held it to the Wheeler's heart, not knowing if she even had one.

Dorothy studied the female with dark hair, shining pink irises, and crimson lips sewn with white ribbon covered in dried blood. More dried blood mixed with grime coated her skin, making her appear animalistic. The Wheeler's face looked like that of a human girl, but her body was disproportionate, with a beastly curving spine and too-long legs and arms. At the ends of her appendages were spiked wheels where her hands and feet should have been.

Dorothy leaned forward, pressing the tip of her blade harder against the Wheeler's chest. "I'm going to cut the ribbon from your lips so you can speak."

The female violently shook her head, her body convulsing in an irrational manner. Did she want to have her lips sewn shut? Did she actually *like* having it that way?

"I've got her." Tin held the female tighter while Dorothy lifted her blade and easily sliced through the ribbon. At the female's throat rested a white collar with something etched in the center. Dorothy squinted and read the word, *Zo*.

"Zo?" Dorothy's brows furrowed as she focused on the female's pink irises. "Is that your name?"

The Wheeler hissed savagely, baring blackened and broken teeth.

"I wouldn't do that," Tin's voice boomed at the Wheeler. "Where's Crow?"

The female's gaze slowly shifted to Tin, her lips gradually parting as though she was finally going to speak. Instead, a deep, raspy laugh escaped her lips followed by another hiss before a wild giggle found its way from her throat.

Dorothy shook her head, scanning the trees for anyone else. These Wheelers were truly mad if they were all like this one.

Zo's laughter came to an end and her head shook side to side, not focusing on Dorothy or Tin. "Never tell," she whispered in a growl. Her head going faster and faster. "Never tell. Never tell. Never tell. Never—"

Tin picked Zo up and slammed her body back to the ground. "Where's Langwidere?"

Another round of laughter came from Zo. "Waiting for you at her palace." She giggled and roared with more crazed laughter, the pitch growing higher and higher. "Your head will be hers."

Before Dorothy could ask her another question, Tin raised his axe and swung it down across the Wheeler's throat, decapitating her. Blood rained upward, splashing Dorothy and Tin.

"What did you do that for?" Dorothy asked, incredulous, jerking her head in Tin's direction. "She was *talking*." Zo got what she deserved, but Dorothy wasn't finished.

"We have our answer." Tin straightened, using the Wheeler's tunic to wipe the blood from the blade of his axe.

Dorothy held both her hands up. "We still don't know where Crow is!"

"She said Langwidere was at her palace." Tin shrugged. "Crow and I should've known after seeing her old place that that's where they would be headed."

"I still don't understand."

"They want Glinda's palace, her territory. That's why they're doing all this. And if so, Crow will be taken there."

Tin's words sank in. That made sense, and it was a better lead than anything they'd had thus far.

In the distance, the sound of squeaking filled the air. All the blood in Dorothy's veins stopped flowing as she looked further in the direction of the squeals. Tiny spots were heading their way.

"Oh no!" Dorothy whispered, praying and praying the Wheelers hadn't seen them.

"We have to hide," Tin said hurriedly, tugging her deeper into the woods. "Now!"

She grabbed hold of his hand and pulled him harder, her feet quickly moving over the dirt. While they dodged lifted tree roots, the squeaks grew nearer, more sinister. When the clanking of wheels and muffled howling reverberated across the foliage, Dorothy knew Zo's clan had discovered her body.

The Wheelers would never stop searching for them now.

CHAPTER TWENTY-ONE

TIN

There was nowhere to hide.

The trees in this part of the woods had no branches low enough to climb, but even if they did, the Wheelers had somehow managed to cut Crow down. There were no caves, no buildings. Tin stopped running and spun, frantically taking in their surroundings. A few Wheelers, like he'd faced at Langwidere's, wouldn't be a problem, but it sounded as if at least fifty tracked them deeper into the forest.

Shit!

The loud screech of their wheels and the maniacal, muffled laughter surrounded Tin and Dorothy. It pressed around Tin's body, squeezing every ounce of rational thought to its breaking point. Dorothy would die if he didn't get her out of there. Hell, they both would.

He spun and took Dorothy's face in his hands, looking into her deep brown eyes. They were just as wild as he felt. "Run. I'll distract them."

"What?" She gripped his wrists to hold his hands in place. "I'm not leaving you here to face those things alone."

"You will." He offered a weak smile—if this was the last time they saw each other, he didn't want her to see his fear. "Do it for me and for Crow."

"I can fight," she insisted, her grip on his wrists tightening.

Tin leaned in and kissed her. Her lips were warm and inviting, like what he thought home would feel like. Maybe that was what Dorothy could one day be. He put everything he had into it, willing his feelings into her for those few short moments, inhaling her very essence, then broke away. "If you run, there's still hope. Give me that. Give me a reason to keep fighting."

"I *won't* leave you," she said again.

The Wheelers were closing in. Flashes of movement in the distance caught his eye and he jerked his hands away from Dorothy's face. "Damn it, Dorothy!" He spun her around and shoved her in the direction of Glinda's palace. "*Run.* Go to Glinda and wait for me at her palace. If I don't come within a day, it will be up to you to save both me and Crow." *If Crow was still alive.*

That got her feet moving, but not nearly fast enough. She kept glancing back with uncertainty, pausing, and starting again. Tin growled and turned his back on her. If she wasn't far enough away from the Wheelers, he would be distracted. Distractions while fighting would only lead to his failure and none of them could afford that loss.

Tin took a deep breath, gripped his axe tightly, and ran toward danger. The screech of wheels became louder and louder until he couldn't hear his own thoughts. Individual shapes moved through the trees. Closer and closer. Tin inhaled and ran faster.

He trusted Dorothy to keep going, despite her track record of doing the opposite of what he said. She had promised to listen to find Crow, and this was part of that. Glinda would help her if Tin couldn't. As long as Dorothy was safe, he could do what had to be done.

Sooner than he'd expected, the enemy was upon him. But he was the Tin Man. This was what he was born to do: kill. Anything else he did was a conscious choice. His muscles coiled and his body slid flawlessly into a warrior's stance while his mind went completely silent. There was only an assassin and his prey. An axe and a target.

The first Wheeler fell with a single strike of Tin's axe through short, dark hair, and the second hit the ground without a head. Her pale face landed in a patch of mud with a squelch. He darted left, then right. Another Wheeler dead. The next dodged his killing blow and Tin's axe sliced through her arm instead. The dark-skinned female skidded across the forest floor, gushing blood.

That was the last easy swing Tin took. They were the leaders, faster than the rest of the pack, but the others were upon him then. Dozens descended at once. Their sharp wheels sliced his clothes. The kelpie scales held for a while, but even they weren't completely impenetrable.

While he swung his axe and dodged their attacks, a single well-placed blow tore into his calf. A pained roar ripped through the air and Tin attacked harder, dodged faster. He felt as if he were floating, his body moving while his mind watched. All of it instinct and years of honing his skill. But the Wheelers kept coming. More and more and *more...* Tin never suspected Langwidere had this many minions.

His breath became heavy, his movements sluggish. How long had he been under attack? At least thirty Wheelers had perished beneath his axe, but there were still twice that alive. Warm blood sprayed his face, blurring his vision, while more ran down the wooden handle of his weapon. Tin's grip slipped. His next swing came up short and landed in the back of a corpse as he stumbled to the ground.

Tin rolled to his back, bringing the weapon with him, in time to see a wheel slam down where his head had just been. He snarled at the female and lunged. The blade dug into her sternum. Before the life left her bloodshot eyes, she head-butted him. He hadn't expected that—hadn't expected the Wheeler to have that much strength—and the strike sent him flying back.

An instant later, a wheel pressed up against his throat. He froze, waiting. All it would take was slight pressure for the metal to rip open his throat. He hoped he'd given Dorothy enough time to escape, that she was far enough away to avoid his fate and would soon be safe within Glinda's walls. He had to save Crow and rid the South of Langwidere and Lion, if only he could make it there.

Mostly, Tin prayed Dorothy would remember him well, despite the life he'd led.

He stared up at the Wheeler, refusing to die a coward with his eyes closed, when something hard slammed into his temple. The world ceased to exist.

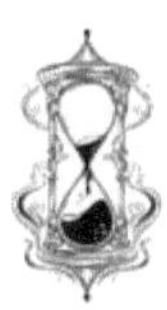

Throbbing pain tore through Tin's head. He winced, rolling from his side to his back with a groan, and cracked his eyes open. It was too dark to see anything, but the air smelled of damp earth and rot. He reached for his cloak, but it was gone—left back at the house. Luckily he carried a few emergency supplies in his shirt pocket, and getting stuck in caves, while hunting will-o-wisps, taught him to always carry a source of light. It was a small mercy he still had the flat, oval disk on him. Resting it in his palm, he blew a quick breath over its surface to activate the magic.

White light glowed around him. It smelled like damp earth because it *was*. A large round tunnel surrounded him. Two deep gouges ran down the center of the floor where wheels had passed countless times. Tree roots hung down like curtains, swooping sideways to cling to the dirt on either side of the passageway in a web-like network.

Tucked into the roots, like decorations, were heads in varying stages of decay. There were skulls picked clean, some that still had milky eyes and rotting flesh, and others with so many maggots beneath the still-intact flesh that the skin moved. Selkies, urisks, merfolk—all types of fae alongside the much smaller heads of rodents and other forest creatures. A fresh ballybog head stared out at him in slack jawed horror.

"Well, fuck," Tin croaked. There was loyalty to one's master and then there was… Whatever this was. Obsession seemed an understatement. It was a miracle they hadn't added him to their collection, though he wasn't going to question it at the moment.

He needed to escape and get to Glinda's before Dorothy did anything rash. But how? Tin climbed slowly to his feet but had to hunch over to avoid scraping the ceiling. His head throbbed again, sparking light behind his eyes.

"Damn Wheelers," he hissed. His hand fell to his hip where his axe should've been, only to find it empty. "They'll regret not fucking killing me."

A soft caw came from the dark tunnel behind him. Tin spun and pointed the disk outward. In the center of the tunnel, hopping pitifully on one leg, the other tucked against his body, and both wings dangling uselessly, was a black bird with flickering brown eyes. It cawed again, a pathetic cry.

Tin's eyes widened in shock and his heart thudded heavily. "Fucking hell, Crow!"

The bird—Crow—let himself slump to the dirt. His sides expanded rapidly with his breath. Tin hurried to his side and knelt.

"What happened to you?"

Crow blinked slowly. Shifting took a lot of energy, or so Tin had heard, and it didn't seem as if his old companion had enough to shift back. Crow's agitated reply about shifting while they'd searched for Dorothy made sense now. Apparently, these weren't fresh injuries. Tin found himself almost pitying him, but shut down the feeling as soon as it began. Why would Crow shift if it put him at such a disadvantage? *Fucking idiot.*

"We have to get out of here." Tin grimaced. There was only one option since he couldn't leave Crow behind. As gently as he could, Tin lifted Crow from the dirt. His bird form was nearly weightless. Brittle, thin bones poked against the skin beneath his smooth feathers, threatening to pop through, so Tin adjusted his fingers to press away from them. "Tell anyone about this, and I'll kill you."

A quiet caw came in reply.

Together, they navigated the tunnels slowly, pausing only when the distant squeak of wheels echoed. The tracks on the ground bent sharply at each turn, though some disappeared into soupy muck. Bones protruded from the dirt every so often. Tin recognized ribs and a partial spine, but he had no doubt there were more bodies stashed along the way—all the heads had to have come from somewhere. Where roots thinned, the Wheelers had carved out small den-like rooms with beds of sticks and hair matted to the ground. There was no way to tell how long they'd been down here or where *here* even was. The tunnels could span the entire south for all Tin knew. Maybe even farther.

Voices rose up somewhere close. A male spoke in low, hushed tones, piquing Tin's interest. The Wheelers couldn't speak with their lips tied, which meant they weren't the only ones to use these tunnels. If it wasn't the Wheelers, and it wasn't Langwidere, there was only one fae it could be.

"Lion," Tin rumbled. He set Crow down, tucking him carefully and safely into an empty nook within the tree roots, and stalked toward the voice.

Time to kill a coward.

CHAPTER TWENTY-TWO

DOROTHY

Dorothy hated herself, hated herself so much for leaving Tin. Why did she even listen to his self-sacrificing nonsense? She shouldn't have listened to him. It wasn't like she ever had before.

Tin was strong physically, and she knew that if anyone could take down all those Wheelers, he could. She'd tried to tap into the power that she supposedly had, but nothing came. Even now, as she ran across fallen leaves and patches of weeds, Dorothy couldn't call on anything. Perhaps she didn't truly have any magic. She didn't have power like her mother, nor could she shift like Crow.

Tears streamed down her face as she continued through the woods, only stopping for a few moments to drink water. As she came closer to the yellow brick road, all she could think about was how everything had gotten so much worse. Crow and Tin could both be dead, and now she was on her own again.

Dorothy stopped near a tree with several cobwebs hanging in its branches. Propping her back against the trunk, she caught her breath and tried to bring it back to a steady pace. The South needed to be saved more than anywhere else in Oz right now, and she desperately had to get to Glinda before Langwidere could invade her palace—if she hadn't already.

Gathering her strength for Tin and Crow, she pushed off the tree and continued. Even though she still didn't truly believe in herself, she needed to try, for her friends.

There wasn't time for her to stop, except to relieve herself, before night began to fall. She'd have to rest for the night, even though she didn't want to waste time.

Running alongside the yellow brick road was a town full of small homes shaped like mushrooms. Each one was a brilliant, neon color, some with polka dots, others with stripes. The town may have been beautifully decorated, but it looked just as deserted as everywhere else in the South. Yards were overtaken by weeds and dead flowers, and held clothing lines that appeared worn.

Dorothy stopped by a drinking well covered in gray stone along the bottom. She gulped down as much water as she could before striding up to one of the mushroom-shaped homes. This one was painted like a rainbow, and she wondered if there was a leprechaun inside based on its size. Gripping the handle, she twisted the knob—locked. She knocked a few times—no answer.

She was too tired to walk to any other homes so she shoved her machete through the glass beside the door, reached in, and unbolted it. The door slowly creaked open.

Quickly, Dorothy went inside, shut the door behind her, and locked it. A small sofa rested in a sitting room with an easel, canvas, and paint—some sort of art room. She collapsed on the couch, because her body was too heavy with exhaustion to do anything else.

As the silence enclosed over her, the tears decided to return, and she let them, because they were her only comfort as she fell asleep.

In the morning, Dorothy peeled her eyes open and focused on the dawn light spilling in through the window. Her gaze landed on a half-painted portrait of butterflies in a meadow. She hurried and sat up, remembering where she was, and that Tin and Crow were both gone.

Before she left, she decided to head into the kitchen to see if there was something worth salvaging to eat. Dorothy opened one of the doors and her body grew rigid. She shouldn't have been surprised.

In the center of the room, in the middle of the bed, lay two skeletons. A female in a violet dress, missing her head, and a male, completely whole, wearing a suit. Appetite gone, Dorothy quickly shut the door. One of Langwidere's minions must have taken the female's head and then by the look of things, the male possibly chose to end his life to stay with his lover in death.

She could barely breathe, and based on the couple's skeletons, even if there was food here, it wouldn't be good anymore.

Stumbling outside, Dorothy drank more water, then splashed her face with it to try and clear her head. She chose to pick a few pieces of fruit and nuts from the tree branches, and that would have to be good enough for now.

Carefully, she scanned the yellow brick road before crossing it. Once more, she stuck close to the trees.

The only sound in the woods was the soft humming of faerieflies. She didn't feel like getting stung today, so she stayed out of their swarming paths. During the night, she hadn't heard any Wheelers, but she wasn't sure if that was because there were none or if she'd slept through their squealing.

As she rounded a sharp curve, past white and lilac flowering trees, the palace came into view just ahead. Behind it, the looming ivory mountains rested. The building was larger than she could have ever imagined, with a steep sloping golden roof, and high magenta arches covered in bright yellow roses mounted along its trim. Dorothy couldn't help but smile as she crept closer and observed the pink glittering bricks—it was very like Glinda to have something so extravagant and colorful.

A pearlescent fence surrounded the entire palace, and the elaborately arched front gate was locked when she approached it. Where were the guards? *Shouldn't there be guards here?* She hoped she wasn't too late.

Dorothy gripped the bars and scaled her way up, gritting her teeth as she avoided the spikes at the top, before clambering down into the courtyard.

Brushing off her overalls, Dorothy surveyed the garden leading up to the entrance. Not a single space was without purple and blue pansies, except in the center. There, rising toward the skies, sat a shimmering light pink statue of Glinda, smiling.

Within the beauty, everything was quiet—most notably, no squeaks of any Wheelers. So perhaps Langwidere wasn't here yet—or maybe Glinda had already abandoned the territory like the other Southerners had.

The flowers brushed Dorothy's ankles as she trekked her way to the entrance. Large pillars connected to the front slope of the roof.

As she stepped to the porch, she expected to find the door locked, but it wasn't. She pulled it open, stepped inside the palace, and inhaled primrose. Dorothy would have expected it to smell of sugar, like Glinda herself.

The hallway was only a short length with more golden flowers in sconces hanging on a pale pink wall. As the foyer ended, Dorothy was met with a large open room, where a rectangular ornate golden carpet lay on the floor. Two chaises rested on one side of the room while four wooden chairs with white cushioning sat across from them. Along the back wall stood three sets of staircases, all leading upward to the next level.

Something wasn't right here, and Dorothy didn't hesitate as she brought her blade up. *Where is everyone?* In between the first two sets of stairs was another hall. As she approached it, a shadow peeked out from behind the staircase to her left.

A squeaking sound ripped across the floor as a Wheeler with dark raggedy hair charged forward. Dorothy didn't stop to think as she swung the machete—just as she would have if she'd been cleaving the corn stalks—and struck the Wheeler. He let out a muffled noise and toppled to the floor, blood spilling from his long arm. With swift precision, Dorothy brought the blade up and sliced through his neck with ease. She watched as the head plopped to the floor with a sickening thump. The body no longer jerked.

Dorothy gasped, and her eyes widened as she stared at the blood on her machete. She'd had it all this time but hadn't used it until right then. There wasn't an ounce of regret—none. And she would use it again if she needed to. She took one last look at the bloody ribbon stitched through the lips of the severed head as she passed it and continued down the hall.

Glancing side to side, she didn't see any sign of anyone else yet. What if Glinda hadn't left? What if she was still here—dead? Then what would Dorothy do? She couldn't think about that now.

Down the hall were open rooms, each unoccupied. At the very end of the corridor sat one closed door, and Dorothy's stomach sank with dread. Her heart thrummed in her chest and blood coursed through her veins as she followed the carpeted rug to the entrance.

Holding her breath and her weapon higher, Dorothy opened the door slowly with shaking hands. And she wished she hadn't. Inside were wooden cases, rows and rows of them. She covered her mouth to prevent herself from screaming, because they all contained heads. Blonde with milky skin, brunette with olive flesh, auburn with Grecian noses, pointed ears, some with curled horns—too many, all wide-eyed. Yet they were all perfect and beautiful—not an inch of rot to be seen. As her eyes continued to roam, they settled at the very end of the room, where a body wearing a pink glittery gown lay in a heap on the white marble floor.

Dorothy's hand clamped around her mouth as she hoped to God that Glinda's head was still attached. As she pressed closer, a relieved breath escaped her lips. Glinda was still whole, but she wasn't moving. Not a single twitch.

Jolting forward, Dorothy rushed to Glinda's side, feeling as though every eye in the room had followed her.

"Glinda!" Dorothy whisper-shouted as she picked up the good witch's limp wrist to check her pulse. "Glinda!"

Two emerald eyes slowly opened, focusing on Dorothy. "Who are you, young goose?" Glinda carefully sat up, her strawberry blonde curls bouncing beneath her flashy silver crown.

"It's me, Dorothy!" she exclaimed. "We need to get out of here."

"Ah, you've grown, haven't you?" Glinda lifted a hand and stroked Dorothy's pointed ears. "And become fae."

Dorothy didn't have time to answer those questions. "We'll talk about that later. What happened?" She clasped Glinda's hand and helped her to rise.

"It's Langwidere," Glinda said, stroking the high collar of her dress. It was the same gown she'd worn when Dorothy had met her. "I've been held prisoner in here for quite a while. She came in and took everything, leaving me without any power."

No power? This would make things even more difficult, but they could figure it out later. "I need your help. Crow and Tin have both most likely been taken by the Wheelers, Lion is a lying bastard who needs to be dead, and I'm fae as you've noticed. Everything is in shambles."

"There, there, my goose." Glinda folded her arms around Dorothy, holding her tight. A heavy scent of primrose invaded Dorothy's nose. Glinda had never smelled liked this—it was always sugar. Could someone's scent change? She supposed it could. Aunt Em's had over the years.

"Did you know you were a changeling this whole time?" Glinda whispered and pulled back with a giggle.

"No, I just found out." Dorothy noticed the expression on Glinda's face was no longer happy and giddy, but smug. She took a deep swallow and shifted backward.

"You're in luck because you can meet the human you were

swapped with. She's right behind me." Glinda smiled wickedly and stepped to the side. Before Dorothy, within the glass cabinet, rested a female's head. It was a human girl with brown hair the color of Dorothy's—she looked exactly like Dorothy had in her human form except for a slightly smaller nose and thinner lips. "You are much, much prettier as a fae and will be able to replace the real Dorothy perfectly."

Dorothy couldn't speak, couldn't breathe, couldn't do anything but stare in horror at this monster. "You're not Glinda," she whispered. Dorothy's pulse accelerated as the room seemed to spin.

"Why, young goose, I have her same dress"—she swished the material side to side—"her same words, and even her same head. I *am* very much Glinda."

"You killed her?" Dorothy raised the machete, her entire body trembling.

"But of course I did. Since I'm wearing her head, I hold all her magic." Langwidere primped her curls as though she was getting ready for a ball, not talking about *murdering* innocents. "Don't get all dramatic and weepy either, because Oz wanted Glinda dead as much as anyone. He was even the one who sent Lion to ask me to steal her head for him. But I chose to keep it for myself."

As Dorothy lunged forward, a sharp pain struck her chest, ran down her arms and to her fingertips, causing her to drop her weapon. Her knees buckled and she collapsed to the floor, feeling nothing but stabbing agony traveling throughout her body. A quivering cry that she hated slipped from her mouth.

Langwidere unzipped the back of her dress and pulled it down to reveal a white, silky skin-tight gown with a low v-neck, showing the curves of her breasts and a thin silver ring around her throat. *That must be where her head is attached.* She kicked Glinda's gown to the side. "That was a fun game to play with you. And for now, you will remain here until Lion arrives." Langwidere leaned forward and purred, "Then he will remove your head, and I'll wear it, along with your blood, as I fuck him for the rest of the night."

Dorothy was going to be sick. Even through the crushing pain, she tried to crawl forward to her blade, but Langwidere scooped it up. Then she stuck her hand into Dorothy's pocket and pulled out the small knife that Crow had collected and Tin had given her. Whatever magic the witch was using on Dorothy was too hard to fight.

"Thank you for bringing me these. Lion will enjoy using the machete when he arrives." Langwidere pivoted on her heels while Dorothy writhed in pain. The sound of a lock turning meant Dorothy was alone and trapped. But she realized with horror that she wasn't really by herself, because all the heads surrounding her seemed to be smiling.

CHAPTER TWENTY-THREE

TIN

Tin kept his steps light and soundless as he maneuvered through the tunnels toward Lion's voice. A dead Wheeler lay half-buried in mud and Tin stepped over its corpse. Farther down, a small furry animal bolted into a hiding place. His focus funneled, the heads lining the walls wholly ignored. It didn't matter that Tin's axe was gone—in fact, Tin preferred to take Lion out with his bare hands. His fingers flexed in anticipation. Strangulation was one of the most personal ways to kill, and this was nothing if not personal.

"My note was delivered?" Lion asked, his voice muffled. "Good. Langwidere will get to have a bit of fun with Dorothy before she collects her head. No one broke the order to leave her unbothered?" A short pause. "In that case, Dorothy should be arriving at Glinda's any time now." Another pause. "Stop fussing. I'll deal with our guests, but then I have to go remove Dorothy's head for Langwidere."

Tin fought to keep his breathing steady. They knew Dorothy was going to Glinda's and Lion seemed *pleased* by that. It was too late, then. Glinda must've fallen to Langwidere already, and Dorothy was walking straight to her doorstep.

Tin bolted forward in a blind panic. He made the next left toward Lion's voice in less than a second and found him alone with one Wheeler in a small circular room. Three other tunnels broke off behind the fae, but Tin barely noticed. He slammed into the male Wheeler, knocking him down, and broke his nose with the heel of his hand.

Lion jumped backward at the sudden commotion. His hair haloed his tan face with messy blonde waves, and his tail twitched nervously beside him. Faint light shining down from an opening hit Lion's bare chest. *An exit and Lion dead.* This kind of luck was uncommon. Tin grinned wickedly. The Wheeler struggled beneath him and Tin rammed his iron-tipped gloves into his throat without sparing him another look.

"Tin. You're awake." Lion spoke in a measured voice, but a slight waver gave him away. "I was on my way to see you."

"I'm sure you were," Tin said, standing. He took sideways steps to close the distance between them. "Crow as well. All your old friends defeated in a single day. How exciting that prospect must've been."

"We were never friends." Lion scowled. "Dorothy brought us together for a time, but we went our separate ways the moment we got what we wanted."

A flash of silver on Lion's hip caught Tin's eye. His axe. *That cowardly mother fucker.* He took a trophy before working up the courage to make the kill. "We all had our own lives to get back to."

"And look what you did with yours," Lion spat, now matching each of Tin's careful steps. "The fearsome Tin Man. The greatest assassin in all of Oz. Tell me, does the iron on your face still hurt as much as it did the day you received it? I watched the whole thing, you know. Your wretched screams were music to my ears."

Tin growled wordlessly. Much to his disdain, he had screamed while Oz's men dripped liquid iron onto his face, but it was the last time he'd let pain in. Now he embraced it like a brother. Too bad Lion hadn't learned to do the same. "I would expect nothing less from someone who warms the bed of a monster."

"Oh, yes," Lion said with a leer. "I've warmed it many times over the years, and one of my favorite faces to fuck is the real Dorothy Gale. The sight of her lips around my cock, the way her eyes flutter when I make her climax—"

Tin pounced. His gloved fingers drove into Lion's bare skin, missing his throat by inches. Damn Lion's quick reflexes. Tin slammed his forehead into Lion's with a resounding *crack*. Lion fell back into the tree roots. Skulls tumbled to the floor around them and Tin winced as one nearly smashed his nose.

Lion took that brief moment to snag a mandible, still stuck on a root, and slammed it into the side of Tin's face. The pointed teeth tore into Tin's flesh. He could taste the blood on his tongue, feel it racing to his chin where it dripped to the floor. But he didn't give an inch. Because he *was* the Tin Man and would remain an assassin for as long as it took to protect Dorothy.

"Is that all you've got?" Blood sprayed from his mouth as he spoke, speckling Lion's face. Lion pressed himself into the wall of rotting heads as Tin leaned closer. He knew he looked crazed—he *felt* crazed—as he ripped his axe from Lion's belt. "This is mine."

"Tin," Lion begged, the word a whimper. "You know better than anyone what it's been like. The gifts Oz gave us—"

"No," Tin said in an unrelenting voice. "You *never* stopped being a coward."

Lion's lips parted to deny it, or maybe to beg again, but time was running out for Dorothy. Tin pressed the head of his axe into Lion's throat, pushing it slowly with both hands, while Lion clawed at his wounded face. The fight was over before it really began.

Tin loosened a shuddering breath as Lion's head tumbled to the ground, joined shortly by his body. Part of him wanted to drag the head to Glinda's to throw at Langwidere's feet before he killed her too. But if Dorothy was still alive, he didn't want her to see this. She had loved Lion once.

Leaving the coward where he fell, Tin hurried back to Crow.

He'd managed to tangle himself in the root system in an attempt to get out of the nook that Tin had placed him in. "Where the hell were you going to go like this? Come on," he rasped, easing Crow carefully from the roots. "I sent Dorothy to Glinda's."

Crow cawed softly as if pleased Dorothy wasn't down there with them.

"Langwidere's already there," Tin added. "We have to hurry."

Crow struggled with his broken limbs, but Tin held him tightly against his side as he returned to the room with Lion's body.

"I won't apologize for killing him, but something tells me you don't want that."

Tin adjusted Crow slightly and, with his free hand, used the roots to pull them both from the tunnels. His muscles bulged as he supported his weight with one arm. The roots shifted beneath his boots as he tried to gather enough leverage to reach the exit. After a few tries, he found a solid foothold and shoved his upper body toward the sunlight.

Outside, the sun was high and warm. He'd parted with Dorothy in the late afternoon, which meant it had been nearly a full day he'd been underground, and it took less than that to reach Glinda's gates. Tin's heart rammed into his chest as he caught his bearings.

They weren't far from the yellow brick road—the entrance to the tunnels was at the base of a tree and resembled an animal den. He would never have noticed it, but they would need to keep an eye out now. If the Wheelers found Lion's body, they would report to Langwidere. Tin didn't have time to fight them off again, especially with Crow in bird form.

"Any chance you're going to shift back?" he asked. Crow struggled weakly until Tin set him down. Nothing happened for so long that Tin moved to pick him back up. "We're in a hurry, remember? If you can't shift back, I'll do this alone, but Dorothy would kill me if I left you behind, so just—"

A black cloud exploded with a *crack* and a few downy feathers floated through the air. When it dissipated, Crow was sprawled on his back, breathing heavily. "Go. Save. Dorothy." He was breathless and sweaty. "Now."

"Fuck you, Crow. It's not my fault you shifted when you shouldn't have. Get up and *help me* save her."

"I didn't mean to shift," he shouted. "But when you're suddenly free-falling from a tree, your body just reacts."

Not my body, he thought, because he knew how to control himself. The memory of how Dorothy drove him crazy all those nights hit him, unbidden. She hadn't even *done* anything to encourage his erections, but his body had rebelled. He bristled at the notion. "We don't have time for this."

"Have I mentioned how much I hate you?" Crow asked, dragging himself to his feet.

Tin rolled his eyes. "You and the rest of Oz."

"I don't approve of you and Dorothy." He narrowed his eyes. "She deserves—"

"Someone better? Kinder? More stable?" Tin laughed bitterly. He pressed a hand to his chest to feel the thump of his heartbeat, reassuring himself it was real. "Don't you think I know that? Dorothy deserves the world, but for whatever reason, right now, she wants me."

"Just because she brought your heart back to life doesn't mean she wants you."

The words hit Tin like a lightning rod. Crow was wrong; Dorothy wanted him just as much as he wanted her. "She's not going to be alive to want *anything* if you don't save the fatherly lecture for later."

"I can't believe you sent her to Glinda's on her own," Crow grumbled.

Tin strode down the yellow brick road before he could punch Crow. He was still too weak to withstand the blow Tin desperately wanted to give him. "Better than letting her end up in those tunnels with us, where she would've been hand-delivered to Langwidere," he shouted over his shoulder. "Now move your ass."

CHAPTER TWENTY-FOUR

DOROTHY

When the throbbing spasms shooting through Dorothy's body ceased, the first thing she tried to do was open the door. She kicked at the hard wood, then thrust her shoulder up against it. Nothing.

Her nerves were on fire and sweat coated her palms. The sick familiarity of this situation took her back to when she'd been all alone in that prison of a room. The one the Wicked Witch—her mother—had stashed her in. Only this time it was so much worse because she wasn't in an empty room, but surrounded by pristine, well-groomed heads with eyes that seemed to follow her wherever she stood. If she got out of this situation, she swore to herself she would light them all on fire.

In the middle of the floor, Dorothy sank down and cradled her legs against her chest, as though she was a child again. This time there wasn't even a bucket of water or magical silver slippers to aid her.

She kept her back to the head of the human she'd been a changeling for. Because if Dorothy hadn't been born, then the *real* Dorothy Gale would have still been alive and safe at home in Kansas. "It isn't my fault," she whispered. "That is all on Locasta and Langwidere."

The door clicked and Dorothy's head jerked up. She hurriedly got to the balls of her feet, prepared to barrel forward at whoever opened the door, when a wave of pain rushed through her veins. A choked cry escaped her throat as the door opened, revealing Langwidere in her silky ivory gown, the extravagant silver crown still resting neatly atop Glinda's golden curls.

"Don't try anything"—Langwidere smiled—"or I'll do that again."

Dorothy hated looking at that smile, those bright pearly teeth that had belonged to Glinda. "I thought Lion was coming to cut off my head," she spat.

"He's on his way." Langwidere yawned. "I grow impatient. Now, I want you to follow me into the sitting room. But if you try anything, you'll be down on the floor again, in worse pain than ever."

"All right." *For now.*

Grabbing the skirts of her dress, Langwidere sauntered her hips back and forth as the fabric dragged across the floor. Dorothy wanted to stomp on it and trip her.

Wondering if this was all a trick, Dorothy followed her down the corridor. All the doors that had been open were now shut. She would be obedient for the time, until she found the right opportunity where she could strike Langwidere without her throwing pricks of pain at her.

As Dorothy followed behind her, she asked, "Is your original head in one of those glass cases?"

"Only Lion knows how it was destroyed." Langwidere didn't even bother to turn around or glance at her.

Dorothy shouldn't have been surprised by this, but she still wondered how someone could easily toss aside a piece of themselves.

They entered the sitting room at the front of the palace. Langwidere arched her body seductively while stretching before she clapped her hands harshly. In answer, a loud squeaking of wheels came out from another hallway hidden behind the third set of stairs.

A female Wheeler, missing an eye and her hair shaved to the scalp, inched closer until she stopped at Langwidere's side.

"Where's Zo?" Langwidere asked, narrowing her eyes at the female.

The Wheeler shook her head and lifted a leg covered in sharp metal spikes.

Dorothy remembered Zo—she remembered Tin's axe coming down across the mad female's throat. "Who's Zo?"

Langwidere slowly sat down on the chaise, pushing her chest forward and crossing her legs leisurely. "My number one Wheeler."

Not number one anymore. But Dorothy kept her mouth shut, holding back a smile at her little secret.

"Sit," Langwidere demanded.

Dorothy sank down on the padded chair while Langwidere laid down like she didn't have a care in the world, as though she wasn't wearing someone else's head.

"Why all the heads?" Dorothy asked, glancing up at the vaulted ceiling and the glittery handrails along the staircases.

"You change clothes every day," Langwidere started, caressing the side of her face. "There's nothing different. It's all the same. I love my white dresses as much as I do my heads." She quickly sat up and leaned forward, studying Dorothy. "And I like your face, too. It's not quite as beautiful as your mother's, but close enough. If I could have had Reva's before she became monstrous, I would have taken it in an instant, but she was a tricky and powerful fae."

"You knew she was my mother?" Dorothy asked, trying to keep her talking.

"Of course I knew she was. Locasta and I have been working together for a long time, but our civility had to come to an end sometime. After I gain your head, the West can never be taken from me, and I'll have all I need to conquer her territories and the Emerald City."

After Lion's last words about Locasta before running away,

Dorothy should have realized that Langwidere had already known. She clasped her hands tightly together to keep her fingers from guarding her neck while desperately searching for a way to escape.

"Tora, bring me the blade!" Langwidere shouted and Dorothy stiffened.

The same Wheeler from earlier spun into the room with Dorothy's machete resting on her curving back. Langwidere's elegant hand curled around the handle of the blade. She rotated it in her palm, running her well-groomed fingers against the metal. Her demeanor appeared ravenous as she continued to silently rotate the blade while watching Dorothy.

There was nothing to attack Langwidere with. Her brain scrambled for a solution—*anything*. Dorothy's heart raced with too many emotions, her nerves flaring, her breath becoming uneven. Perhaps she could pick up the chair and throw it at her—no, too heavy.

"What are you thinking?" Langwidere asked slowly, toying with her lower lip.

"Nothing."

"When you lie, this happens."

A trickle of sharp aches, like spikes, struck at her flesh. Unable to hold back the cry, she screamed. It came again and again as Langwidere stood from the chaise with the blade, giving it a test swing. Tears pricked at Dorothy's eyes, and she couldn't even bring up her hands to swipe them away.

Langwidere inched closer—she was going to use the machete. Dorothy knew she was growing impatient waiting for Lion's return, and she wanted her head now.

Dorothy tightened her fists, her knuckles growing white. A familiar wave of silver flashed before her eyes and she almost gasped. The rush came to her like it had with Lion, with Reva— she needed to grab at that speck of light. But the silvery hands within her passed right through it. A memory slipped its way out from a hidden place within her. Dorothy was a baby and a female with her face hidden behind damp brown locks of hair held her for a moment, whispering something at her ear. *Thelia.* Then a door had burst open and another female, with hair the color of obsidian, entered the room.

Thelia. That was part of Dorothy's true name. And the female holding her had to have been Reva. The silver grew wider, wider and she grasped it, holding tight. Her true name came to her then. Thelia Tunok Turolla.

"Did you not hear me?" Langwidere seethed. "I said to follow me upstairs."

Dorothy's gaze locked on to Langwidere's and she shook her head, her expression firm. "No."

"No?" Langwidere cocked her head and arched a blonde brow. "Then I'll make you come."

Pain slammed into Dorothy and she fell forward from the chair, dropping to her knees against the hard marble. *Thelia Tunok Turolla.* She repeated the name over and over in her head, fishing it forward to control herself, to make herself do something to fight back against Langwidere's power.

A heavy fog of silver flowed out from her, and a loud boom reverberated off the walls, shaking the entire palace. Dorothy's body vibrated in sync with it.

Langwidere stilled, her mask of indifference slipping to where Dorothy could read the fright before she put it back up. "Your magic won't save you. You don't know how to wield it yet, but I'll know how. Once I have your head." Holding the machete out, she lunged for Dorothy.

Dorothy closed her eyes, waiting for the blade to strike, but she felt something burst out from her. She opened her lids, finding Langwidere on the floor, propping herself up with her elbows. Dorothy's magic must have thrown her back, like it had with Lion. Beneath Dorothy's feet, the ground rumbled, then the marble started to crack and split apart.

Small pricks floated across her skin—Langwidere was using her magic, but Dorothy could barely feel it. Dorothy thought about her name once more, and this time the silver fog filling the room turned into a heavy cloud of smoke. She couldn't see anything, but she heard Langwidere screaming and screaming.

Then silence, the cloudiness slowly fading.

As the smoke cleared, Dorothy spotted the machete on the floor and snapped it up. A few feet from her, Langwidere lay on the marble squirming, convulsing. Dark veins, almost black, pulsed against her too-pale skin. Dorothy rushed forward and slammed her fist into Langwidere's face—*Glinda's* face. Her head must have been loose from when she'd hit the floor because it popped off, revealing a metal disc. But the body was still *moving.* Drawing her arms up, Dorothy plunged the machete into Langwidere's chest, puncturing straight through the witch's evil heart. This time, nothing was left twitching as silver continued to pour around them.

Dorothy's magic wouldn't stop. The silver poured out of her more and more until she thought she was going to burst, and she didn't know how to shut it off. Was it possible to die from your own magic? Dorothy's knees buckled, and she sank to the floor, her body growing weaker and weaker.

After several long moments of lying there in nothingness, the room started to clear again. Two warm hands lifted Dorothy's head up slightly, and she didn't have the strength to stop it from being taken from her body to one of Langwidere's cabinets. Gently, fingers brushed the hair from Dorothy's forehead, like she was a child.

With all she had left, she tilted her head back to look into the two eyes that were going to murder her, where death awaited. Above her was an unfamiliar female fae's face. Pale skin, chestnut-colored hair, and emerald eyes that were mirrors of Glinda's.

"Thelia," the fae whispered, sadly smiling.

Another form crept forward with bright blue eyes and blonde hair cascading down to her waist. Dorothy jerked but stopped when she realized neither were Langwidere.

"It's okay," the emerald-eyed fae said. "This is Ozma. You saved us both from a lifetime of nightmares."

"What do you mean?" Dorothy's breath was coming back,

her body becoming less exhausted.

The fae sighed. "Ozma is the rightful ruler of Oz, but the Wizard hid her away before he stole her position by using the silver slippers. She needs to go home and reclaim it to correct all that has happened. I, on the other hand, have a journey of my own to make. To visit Locasta."

Oz again? The slippers were still intact after all? *He* had them? Langwidere had mentioned how he'd wanted Glinda's head. Another person Dorothy had once believed in, who needed to die. Then she focused on the fae's last word. Locasta. Was this fae going to go there to wreak havoc with her?

Dorothy narrowed her eyes. "Who are you?"

"I'm Reva." She smiled. "Your mother."

Inhaling sharply, Dorothy sat up and spun around. "No, I killed you. The water, the silver shoes, my-my magic—melted you. You looked nothing like this." She recalled the green skin, the long, pointed nose, the gangly arms, and curving spine.

"No, Thelia, you didn't kill me." She paused, her lower lip trembling as she clutched her thin black dress covered in holes. "You saved me from the curse but somehow banished me into darkness with your magic. And now, your power returned me here."

"So I had you trapped somewhere?" Dorothy asked, horrified.

Reva nodded. "Yes, but at least I met a friend there when Oz pushed her into darkness, too." She looked to Ozma. "We helped each other survive."

Ozma wore a sleeveless light blue dress with rips and holes. Her voice came out strong, regardless of what she'd gone through. "Oz wasn't the only one who did this to me. A witch named Mombi did a lot worse." She turned away from Dorothy, and at the center of her bare back was a hardened patch of skin. "Mombi cut off my wings and butchered them until they were shreds of nothing." Ozma looked as though she wanted to cry, but she didn't.

Reva peered down at Langwidere's dead body, her hand

covering her mouth.

"Langwidere killed Glinda and was wearing her head, and she planned on taking mine, too," Dorothy said.

The doors burst open and Dorothy and Reva hurried to their feet. Dorothy was ready for whatever was coming their way, but her arms fell back to her sides when she saw that it was Tin and Crow, both covered in grime and blood.

She didn't care how filthy he was—she ran toward Tin and threw her arms around him, inhaling his scent. "You two are late saving me again." Dorothy thought about the last time they'd come through the door right after she'd melted the Wicked Witch—Reva. *Reva.*

Dorothy released Tin and whirled around to find Crow staring at Reva, his lips parted.

Reva wore a neutral expression as her gaze held his. "I'm going to go to Glinda's room for the night and mourn my sister."

Her sister? "We need to see if there are Wheelers anywhere in here first," Dorothy said. Reva just came back, and Dorothy didn't want her mutilated by those monsters before she got to have a full conversation with her.

"I wouldn't worry about them. With their master dead, they'll be long gone soon enough."

Reva wrapped her arm around Dorothy's shoulders and kissed her forehead. "I'm sorry I didn't get to know you sooner." She turned around for the stairs.

"Reva!" Crow's voice sounded desperate, anxious, happy.

Reva's shoulders stiffened and she slowly turned around. The way she was observing Crow wasn't the sweet adoring way she'd looked at Dorothy—it was something furious and Dorothy wanted to shrink into herself, even though the anger wasn't focused at her.

"Don't you dare speak to me!" Reva seethed. "Don't you dare ever speak to me again. This, *this* is all your fault, and *you* are nothing to me." With those words, she spun around and hurried up the stairs.

Dorothy looked between Ozma, Tin, and Crow, the tension

in the room heavy.

"Let me go talk to her," Ozma said, studying Crow. "For what it's worth, I don't believe it was your fault." Then she turned and ran up the stairs barefoot after Reva.

"Who the fuck was that?" Tin asked, clearly confused.

"Her name's Ozma, and she was trapped with Reva. She's the true ruler of Oz."

Tin frowned. "I've never heard of her."

It seemed as if no one had.

"I'm glad you're safe"—Crow cleared his throat—"but I think I'll search the premises and make sure they're clear." He pulled Dorothy into a quick hug. His eyes were glassy when he released her, and she knew that it wasn't because of her.

CHAPTER TWENTY-FIVE

TIN

Glinda was dead, but her magic was still present in the palace. Flowers glimmered and, in the kitchen, food miraculously prepared itself. Candles flickered to life when the sun began to set. Tin wondered if there was anything in the palace Glinda *hadn't* enchanted, especially when he stood beside Dorothy in the bathroom.

Pearlescent bubbles floated through the air. They drifted off the top of a large in-ground tub, big enough for half a dozen people, and released different floral scents when they popped. One landed on his nose. He shook his head in surprise and swiped it off, leaving his face and hand smelling like daffodils. His lips curled in annoyance.

"You should get in," he said, wiping his palm on his pants.

Dorothy poked at the bubbles, mesmerized. "Why don't you go first?"

Tin placed his axe on the tiled floor and scooped Dorothy up over his shoulder. She gasped and grabbed at the back of his shirt as he stepped into the waist-deep water. Dorothy's laughter bounced through the room. Tin let out a low rumbling chuckle as he set her down before him, the front of her body sliding against his.

"You should take that off." Dorothy splashed at Tin's shirt.

Tin obeyed, pulling the wet material over his head, and advanced on her. "So should you," he growled playfully, and unbuttoned her overalls before she realized what he was doing.

Dorothy's deep brown eyes held his silver ones as she loosened the buttons of her shirt and tossed it aside. Tin stepped back to admire her body and worked the ties on his pants beneath the water. It wasn't easy peeling the soaking material off, but he had a slightly better time than Dorothy.

When she slipped backward during the struggle, she emerged a moment later with her hair full of bubbles. "Help?" she sputtered.

Tin laughed quietly and searched out her foot, prying the clingy pants of her overalls away. "There. Now we can bathe."

Dorothy reached over to where an assortment of soaps and oils were arranged and began smelling each one. Tin waited patiently while she chose, but once she had, he plucked it from her hands. "What are you doing?"

"Washing you," he said as if it were obvious. "Turn around."

She turned slowly, keeping an eye on him as he poured the purple liquid into his palms and rubbed it into a lather.

"Lift your hair."

She collected the wet locks. "You know, I can do this myself."

"What fun would that be, Dearheart?" Tin brushed a finger down the back of her neck and rubbed the soap over her skin. She sighed as his calloused hands caressed her back, her arms, across her stomach, and over her breasts. The sound lit a fire in Tin's stomach. He wanted her—he *always* wanted her—but first they needed to wash the horrors of the day off.

When he was finished, he quickly dunked his head underwater in an attempt to clear away all the dirty thoughts. There would be time for that later, he reminded himself again and again. He quickly scrubbed his body with the soapy water. Five minutes from now was *later*.

"Now you," Dorothy instructed the moment he resurfaced.

Later, later, later.

"Just the hair," he hedged. Dorothy opened her mouth but he silenced her with his thumb against her lips, tilting her chin up. He wanted her but he also wanted this tender moment. "Just the hair."

"Fine," she relented, rolling her eyes at him.

Tin sunk down so she could reach his head. His eyes drifted shut at the feel of Dorothy's fingers massaging the soap from his hair. She worked around the bits of blackened bone holding one side of his hair back and fanned the ends out to float on the bubbly surface.

All too soon, her warm breath tickled his ear. "I think I've gotten it all out."

"No." Tin reached up and gently held her hands to his head. "I think there's still a bit left. Keep going."

Dorothy laughed, the sound bringing a smile to Tin's face. "I'm going to rub you bald if I keep going." Her fingers resumed stroking his silver locks.

Tin closed his eyes again to revel in their peace a little longer. Soon, it would pop just like the bubbles. Langwidere was dead, Wheelers now ran loose through the South, and Reva was back with the true ruler of Oz. No one had talked about the emotional ramifications of what transpired or what would happen next. Because no one really knew, least of all Tin.

"Are you sure we shouldn't be helping Crow bury the heads right now?" Dorothy asked.

"He wants to be left alone," Tin assured her. Who could blame him? The love of his life had returned from the dead and seemed to loathe him with a passion. Reva and Ozma had barricaded themselves in a room and refused to see anyone—not that anyone but Crow had tried. "How do you feel about your mother?"

"I'm not sure yet," she admitted carefully. "I still don't understand what I did to bring her back. Langwidere was about to take my head and my power reacted to save me. I thought I was dreaming for a second when she told me who she was. I …

need to talk to her but I think tomorrow will be a better day to start."

Tin took one of Dorothy's hands and brought it to his mouth, kissing her palm. "That's probably for the best. It's been a hard day for all of us."

"It has," she admitted, her voice still downcast.

He hated to bring her mood down even more, but there was still something he hadn't told her. He'd already explained how the Wheelers took him into their tunnels and that's where he found Crow, but he'd left out details. The heads, Crow's broken body when he shifted … and Lion. He sighed. Better to get it over with.

"Dorothy." He sat up and turned around to face her. Water lapped against his abs with the sudden movement, and he forced himself not to stare at where her breasts disappeared beneath the layer of bubbles. "I need to tell you something."

All expression fell from her face, and she seemed to brace herself for more bad news. "What is it?"

Tin took a deep breath. "Lion was in the tunnels."

"Oh?" Something between fear and fury flashed through her eyes. "Where is he now?"

Shit. He almost didn't want to answer her. Yes, Lion was the enemy. He had planned to kill Dorothy and had hired Tin to deliver her so Langwidere could wear her head to conquer Oz. But once, long ago, she'd considered Lion a close friend. It was … complicated. *Everything* was complicated now that he had his beating heart back.

"Dead," he whispered without meeting her eyes. "I killed him."

For a few moments, the faint pop of bubbles was the only sound in the bathroom. Then Dorothy placed a hand on the unblemished side of Tin's face and ran her thumb along his cheekbone. "Good."

Tin looked at her to see if she really meant it and found steely resolve on her face. "Are you sure?"

"Of course I'm sure." She slid closer. "He wasn't the Lion I knew anymore. *That* lion has been dead for a long time."

Tin loosened a breath. He knew deep down that Lion's death pained her on some level, but what choice had he been given? If he had to choose between someone—*anyone*—and Dorothy, she would win every time. Besides, fuck that bastard. Lion deserved to die a worse death than Tin had given him.

"Let's get out of the water before I turn into a prune any more than I already have," Dorothy suggested.

Tin wasn't sure what a prune was, but he definitely didn't want Dorothy to turn into anything. He lifted himself from the tub and grabbed an oversized towel from the counter, holding it out for her to step into.

"Watch out, Tin. You'll turn into a real gentleman if you're not careful." Dorothy grinned and hurried into its warmth.

"Bite your tongue." He rubbed his hands over the towel, drying her body beneath it, and his cock twitched.

Dorothy stuck her tongue out at his teasing remark and he leaned forward, capturing it in his mouth. His tongue traced over hers in a dance and he tugged the corner of the towel so the front opened and she was naked against him. Her lips were warm and soft beneath his as he pulled her close, deepening the kiss. Dorothy leaned up on her toes to better meet him.

Tin pulled away and Dorothy whined. But then his lips kissed down her neck and across her collarbone. He flicked his tongue over the edge of her earlobe at the same time he released the towel so he could grab her ass. At her gasp, he moved back to kissing her throat.

Dorothy tilted into him, her pulse pounding beneath his lips. "Do you remember what I said before?"

"Can you be more specific?" he murmured.

A slight blush colored Dorothy's face. "I promised to make love to you like no one ever has, and I want to now."

Tin's breath caught. She had no idea how much he wanted that too. *Desperately.*

"Not here," she panted against him. "I want you in bed."

"Your wish is my command." He tightened his grip on her

ass and lifted her so her legs wrapped around his waist. "You're not cold, are you?"

Dorothy ran her mouth down the side of his neck. "I'm sure you'll keep me warm enough."

Oh, he would. Tin practically barged into the bedroom and set her in the center of the bed. Despite the throbbing of his cock, he leaned back on his knees to look at her splayed before him. Her nipples pebbled beneath his stare and the moisture coating her center had nothing to do with the bath. It was for him—because she wanted *him*.

"Hurry up," she urged.

Tin laughed. "You promised me *slow*."

"Not glacial," she replied with an amused huff.

He closed the distance between them and took her face in his hands. His lips molded against hers, lingering, exploring. Her tongue swept over his. *Slowly.* He smiled against her mouth and hovered over her naked form. Breaking their kiss, he brushed the hair from her forehead. His silver eyes swept over her features. "You're so beautiful."

One of Dorothy's legs wrapped around his thigh and urged him closer. "So are you."

"I've never done this before," he admitted, and Dorothy raised her brows at him. He chuckled. "Fucked, yes, but not … this."

"Neither have I. Not really." She leaned up on her elbows and set her forehead against his. "I think it's time for us to change that. Now."

"So impatient," Tin murmured. But so was he.

Their mouths met again, moving in perfect sync, and Tin pressed against her opening. His lips traveled over her jaw and down her neck, savoring the moment. When he ventured back to her lips again, he eased inside her.

Dorothy moaned and wrapped her arms around his neck, tangling her fingers in his hair. His movements were unhurried. Each tender thrust let him feel every inch of her as her hands slid over every inch of him. They learned each other's bodies for what felt like hours, switching positions and getting to know what the other liked. It was a long, exquisite torment as Tin held back, drawing out Dorothy's pleasure. When she cried his name, her body vibrating as she came around his cock, he spilled into her with a deep groan.

Tin rested his head on Dorothy's shoulder and fought to catch his breath. "I didn't know it could be like that."

Dorothy let out a satisfied *hmm*, apparently still unable to speak properly.

"I want to do it again," he said. Dorothy made a surprised sound beneath him and he quickly added, "later."

"Sleep first?" she breathed.

"Food first, then sleep." Tin kissed her damp skin. "*Then* again. In the tub next time."

She laughed and gave him a gentle shove off her. Tin rolled to his side. With a contented sigh, she snuggled into the crook of his arm. "Sleep first."

Tin pulled her closer and tugged the blanket over them both. If she wanted sleep, she would have it. He would give her the world if she asked it of him, though he knew she never would because Dorothy's heart was good. Much better than his. It was a miracle that she didn't care his was stained black around the edges—that it was beating again seemed enough.

He hugged Dorothy to him as his chest expanded. "I think I love you, Dorothy Gale." It may have been too soon to say it, but his heart felt it anyway.

She kissed his lips, then leaned her mouth closer to his ear. "I have a secret meant only for you. My name isn't Dorothy. That name never belonged to me. It's Thelia Tunok Turolla, and I'm giving that to you because I'm falling in love with you, too."

Tin froze. Her true name—she trusted him with her *true name*. And, just like that, his heart swelled until he thought it would burst from his chest. "My axe is yours, Thelia. My axe, my life, and my heart."

"I promise to take care of them," she replied with tears glistening in her eyes. "Always."

EPILOGUE

THELIA

"Thelia," she whispered. The name felt natural. As soon as she'd discovered her true name, it suited her more than Dorothy ever could. Then, when she'd heard it roll off Tin's tongue, she knew it was there to stay. The night before with Tin was different—it was the start of something more than she could have imagined. Even though the Land of Oz wasn't done being mended. The South and West may be free now, but Locasta still ruled the North and the East while Oz still reigned over all.

She studied each of the empty glass cases. No more heads.

Footsteps entered the room and she whirled around to find Crow carrying something in his hand. "You need to eat." He handed Thelia a pastry covered in heavy white icing and colorful sprinkles.

"Thank you for taking care of everything around here," she said, accepting the warm dessert from him. "I told you I would have helped." He'd spent the rest of the day digging up dirt, burying every single head, including Glinda's. No one knew what Langwidere or Lion had done with her body, but at least she could rest in peace now.

"I wanted to do it alone." He quickly changed the subject

before she could question him further. "Where's Tin?"

"Still sleeping." Tin had been resting on his stomach with her arm draped around him when she'd woken. She'd covered him with a blanket and let him rest because it was the first time she'd ever seen Tin appear so at peace.

"I still don't approve." Crow lowered his brows, sweeping his gaze across the empty cabinets.

"Why?" She tilted her head to one side. "Because he's murdered? We all have."

"No, I don't care about that." His lips tilted up. "It's because you're my daughter. But if someone has to be good enough, I suppose he'll do."

Thelia fought a grin. "You like him."

"Now, let's not be hasty here." He chuckled.

Bringing the pastry to her lips, she took a bite of the delicious sweetness. "So … have you talked to her yet?" She'd seen Reva's anger, but now that her mother had had time to sit and really think about things, perhaps she'd calmed down a bit.

"No…"

"Go knock on her door!" Thelia exclaimed. "What are you waiting for?"

"To be clear, I haven't talked to her. But I have knocked on her door. Three times."

Thelia folded her arms across her chest. "Tin would have broken down the door."

"Sorry, I don't carry around axes." He fought back a smile.

"Ah, but you do have metal claws that can extend. Perhaps try those next time." Thelia took another bite of the pastry. "I'm going to go talk to her."

Crow wrapped his arms around her. "Even if I don't have her, I have you, and that's enough for me." He was lying and she knew it.

"I really am glad you're my father, and I'm sorry I didn't tell you that before…"

"I know. We'll talk more later." He paused. "Now, go to Reva. I know she'd be happy to see you."

With a smile, she nodded before leaving the room to head to the stairs. After all these years, Crow was still in love with her mother. Her chest tightened thinking about the things that had been done to them.

As she grabbed the stair rail, she observed the sitting room. All the blood had been cleaned—Crow had done that too, and she knew it wasn't for his own benefit, but for her and Reva. The fracturing in the floor, and up the walls and ceiling, was barely visible. Only a hairline crack lingered. Somehow the magic inside the palace walls had mended itself.

Thelia climbed to the top floor and could tell right away which door had belonged to Glinda. Her door was the only one bright pink in color with silver flowers painted down its entire length.

Her heart beat quickly—she was going to see her mother again. Would it be strange? Would it be awkward? Raising her hand to the door, she softly knocked. "It's me, Thelia."

In a matter of seconds the door swung open, and Reva stood there with a smile. She was no longer dressed in a black cloth covered in holes. Instead, she wore a sparkling pink dress that was tight on top, accompanied with a poofy skirt, falling to her ankles. The sleeves were sheer with cloth cuffs at her wrists. Her hair, the color matching Thelia's own, was no longer a rat's nest but fell to her waist in a long, silky sheet.

"Come in." Reva waved her through the door, then looked down at herself. "This isn't something I'd ever wear. I prefer black. But my choices were limited—white or pink gowns."

Thelia thought about Glinda, and she tried not to let her eyes fill up with tears again. Glinda was not only Reva's sister, but had been Thelia's aunt. "I'm sorry about Glinda."

Reva sat on the bed and patted the spot next to her. Thelia studied the pink and silver room. More silver flowers covered pink walls. A cloth covered the top of the bed, forming a canopy. She walked toward Reva and sank down onto one of the softest beds she'd ever been in.

"Glinda and I got along well," Reva said. "Before the curse, it had been a while since we'd seen each other because we lived in different territories. But I should have taken the time. After the curse, I can see why she wanted me dead. I did a lot of terrible things."

When Thelia first came to Oz, Glinda had never mentioned that she was Reva's sister, only that the Wicked Witch needed to be ended.

"Was she your only sibling?" Thelia couldn't help but think about Locasta and the Wicked Witch of the East. When she'd first arrived by tornado, her house had killed the witch of the East.

"Yes, only Glinda. Our parents died when we were very young, so ruling the territories is all we ever knew."

Thelia had started work on a farm very young, but that wasn't anything compared to ruling territories. She glanced around the room. "Where's Ozma?"

"In the kitchen, baking," Reva said. "She was tired of being cooped up. For her entire life it's been like that, hidden as someone else or trapped in that dark place."

Poor Ozma. But then Thelia thought about Reva having to be in that dark place, too. "I'm sorry for what I did." The thought made Thelia want to fold in on herself.

Reva placed a warm hand against Thelia's cold one. "It's not your fault. I don't want you blaming yourself, especially when we have things we need to do."

Thelia met Reva's emerald gaze. "What do you mean?"

"I'm going to ask you for a favor." Reva blew out a breath. "I need you to hold down the forts of the South and the West. You rightfully won them from Langwidere, so they're yours."

Thelia shook her head. "You're back—that means they belong to you."

"No, Thelia, you are powerful, and I think you're the right fae to take charge here." She held up a finger before Thelia could protest. "I had a chat with Ozma and we have a plan. Once I defeat Locasta, because it will happen, I will take control of the North and East, then you and I will share the Emerald City. That only leaves Ozma to reclaim her throne from 'Oz the Bastard.' Then we can all work together to make the Land of Oz a better place again."

"You want me to take care of *this*?" Thelia's voice went up an octave as she pointed out the window. "A ghost town of headless bodies and loose Wheelers?"

"The Wheelers will return to the outskirts near the Deadly Desert. Then you can rebuild the South and West even better than it was before." The edges of Reva's lips lifted, her eyes shifting to the side. "And I think there might be a certain male who wouldn't mind helping you."

Thelia could feel her cheeks grow hot, and she didn't want to talk about Tin with her mother. "Ozma is going with you, then?"

"Only for a little while. She has a journey of her own to make before trying to retrieve the silver slippers from Oz. There's also a special someone waiting for her back home."

"*What?*" Thelia's eyes widened in disbelief. "You can't go alone!"

Reva wrapped her arm around Thelia's shoulders. "Who do you think you inherited your power from?"

That may be so, but Reva had also been overpowered before. "But Locasta…"

A trickle of green lightning pulsed in the center of Reva's palm and Thelia's lips parted at the beauty of it. "After having you, I was drained of magic, and Locasta caught me off guard." Reva's spine straightened and her jaw clenched. "It won't happen this time." The green faded from her hand as if it had never been there.

"Then take Crow with you. He's—"

"Crow can bury himself outside with the heads for all I care," Reva interrupted. "He will *not* be accompanying me."

How did she know Crow was burying heads if she'd been cooped up in the room? Had she been watching Crow from the window?

"Ozma and I will be leaving tomorrow morning," Reva continued.

"I just got you back, though." Thelia knew she could take care of the South and the West, but she couldn't help but fear what Locasta would do. "Let me go with you. I can help now that I have my magic, and you can help me learn how to use it."

"You can't." Reva pulled her close. "If something happened to both of us, then who would take care of this place? Besides, have faith, we will meet again, same as we did yesterday. While we have today, how about you tell me your story, and I'll tell you mine."

Thelia wanted to argue, but she could tell Reva wouldn't change her mind, just as Thelia wouldn't have. "That sounds wonderful," she finally said.

Kansas would always hold a place in Thelia's heart, but Oz was where she was always meant to be, needed to be, wanted to be. She had a lover, a mother, a father, and a home that she would choose to fight for eternally. Now that she was fae, forever was truly possible, and one day, all of Oz would be safe. And that was a promise.

CROW

BOOK 2

CHAPTER ONE

CROW

TWENTY-ONE YEARS AGO

Life was full of beautiful moments, though few as precious as the birth of a daughter.

Crow had known when Reva told him she was pregnant that his life would be permanently brighter. The small, wrinkled baby on Reva's chest had taken a single breath and, with it, his soul.

"What name do you think fits her?" Reva asked in a tired voice.

Crow shifted closer on the large, four-post bed and wrapped his arm around the love of his life. Sweat coated her face, her brown hair clinging to her forehead, but she had never looked more beautiful. His gaze drifted from the baby to Reva's emerald eyes and back again.

"We'll know it when it comes to us," Crow replied, placing a kiss on her temple. They hadn't spoken of names before—they couldn't without seeing the child. True names needed to fit the individual, and he was too overcome with the new, euphoric love to think clearly enough for such an important task.

The baby cooed and Reva lifted the child from her chest to

stare thoughtfully at her. Crow took in their daughter's gently pointed ears, identical to Reva's, and the chin that resembled his own. She also had his brown eyes, though her hair was too sparse to know if it was as dark as his or brown like Reva's. Their child seemed to have inherited the best of them both—not that Crow was biased.

"You have no suggestions?" Reva arched a brow and tilted her head.

When Crow took the baby's hand, her fingers wrapped tightly around his thumb. A name began to take shape in the back of his mind, still too vague to make out. When the time was right, they would *know*. All parents did. "I once knew a tree spirit named Gurbera," he offered playfully.

"Absolutely not!" Reva hugged the child to her chest and laughed. Then cringed. "Ow."

"Let me hold her," Crow said quickly. "You've labored for nearly a day. You should rest."

Reva sighed and snuggled closer into Crow's side. "I am rather tired."

"Sleep, my love. I'll have Whispa prepare something for you to eat when you wake."

"Let her rest too." Reva yawned. "She was up with me the entire time."

The pixie had been a lifesaver. Crow had no idea how to help with the delivery of a child. Fae children were so rare—he'd never even seen one so young before this day, let alone witnessed the miracle firsthand. But Whispa had seen Reva's family through multiple generations.

"Of course." Crow kissed Reva's lips quickly and slid from the bed while cradling their sleeping daughter. She was so small. So perfect. "Leave everything to me."

Reva offered a faint smile, her eyes already fluttering shut. His fierce, beautiful, powerful Reva. She appeared exhausted, but content. The labor hadn't been an easy one and it had taken almost every ounce of Reva's energy to see it through. When she woke, she would be ravenous. Making a warm meal was the absolute least he could do.

Crow laid his daughter down beside Reva instead of putting her into the bassinet. The smooth wooden basket hung from thick vines attached to the ceiling so it could gently rock, and the firm pillow inside was covered in the softest of furs. Reva and Whispa had spent a week weaving strands of delicate, enchanted wild flowers through the latticework. But Crow didn't want to leave such a tiny child so far across the room. Pausing in the doorway for a lingering look, Crow watched Reva pull their baby closer and shut her eyes. He left for the kitchen, feeling he might explode from joy.

"Oh!" Whispa gasped when they nearly collided on the staircase. Smoky gray hair skimmed her jawline and the first hint of fine lines showed near her honey-colored eyes. The red and blue patterned dress she wore was rumpled and stained after the delivery, and her thin, glimmering wings drooped with fatigue. "Is everything well with Lady Reva and the child?"

"Everything is wonderful." Crow lifted the four-foot pixie into a hug, and she squealed as he swung her in a circle. When he set her back down, she was blushing all the way to the tips of her ears. "They're both asleep. You should rest too."

She pursed her lips as if weighing the suggestion. "After I check on the lady, perhaps."

"You're too hard-working, Whispa." Crow smiled warmly and continued down the stone stairs. He glanced back before he lost sight of her and, in a serious voice, added, "You have to take care of yourself."

Whispa's good-natured *tsk* reached his ears as he continued his descent, followed immediately by the sound of glass exploding. Crow froze mid-step. "Whispa?" he called, hoping the pixie simply broke a vase.

But he knew she hadn't. The crash was far too loud for that. He bolted back to the second floor and skidded to a halt the moment he hit the landing. Whispa writhed on the floor among thousands of tiny glass shards, the large circular window at the end of the hall demolished. Her thin, crystalline wings were in tatters and blood spilled down her arms and legs from the cuts.

Crow's boots crunched on the glass, the sound echoing. "Whispa! What happened?" There were no trees near the house that could've caused this, and the weather was calm.

"Lady… Reva…" she croaked, curling into a fetal position.

Crow's world slowed as his gaze shifted from the pixie to the open bedroom door. *No, no, no, no, no!*

"Leave!" Reva roared from the bedroom.

A cold, feminine chuckle sounded in response, chilling the blood in his veins. Not *her.* Anyone but her… Stomach churning, Crow burst into the room he had vacated moments ago to find Reva shielding their child in her arms. The *Good* Witch of the North, Locasta, stood at the foot of the bed. Crow knew from experience that Locasta was as wicked as they came. He'd tried to leave her so many times after he'd realized *good* had nothing to do with the witch. She'd given out food to her people when they were hungry, but only enough to keep them from rioting. Offered cures that contained scant amounts of poison to fix the overpopulation. Fae that defied her were secreted away to be killed—some immediately, some after torture—but the Northern Witch assured the families that her guards were searching for their lost loved ones. She had frequently gone so far as to create *proof* of her efforts, or sentenced innocents to death for the crimes *she'd* committed.

Locasta had never accepted Crow leaving her though. The abuse had finally become so terrible that he'd fled to the West in search of help to stop Locasta. He'd found none before Reva. And now she stood in the home Crow shared with Reva on the night their child was born. That was too much of a coincidence to believe.

"Locasta," he barked, half in anger, half in fear. His daughter screeched in response. Hadn't they gone deep enough into hiding? How far did Crow need to take his family for them to be safe? "What are you doing here?"

"Ah, there you are, sweetheart." Locasta turned with a dramatic swoosh of her ruby dress. Obsidian hair shone all the way to her narrow waist and eyes, the lightest blue, pierced him. Her full lips quirked into an angry smile. "It's been too long."

Reva clutched the howling baby protectively to her chest with one hand and curled the other into a fist. Green sparks fizzled from between her clenched fingers, her energy too depleted from labor to conjure anything more. "Get her out of here, Crow. Now!"

If he had his choice, Locasta wouldn't only be out of their home, but banished from Oz completely. Unfortunately, she still had her claws in too many influential fae who believed her wicked lies. It would be nearly impossible to exile her through the proper channels. Forcing someone as deranged as Locasta to leave would only stoke the fire anyway, and his family was far too precious to risk her wrath. The situation was already dangerous enough.

"Locasta," Crow said gently, his hands outstretched. "Come with me."

His ex-lover laughed. "I've tried to get *you* to come with *me* for over a year now."

"I know." Crow swallowed hard and forced himself not to look away from her icy glare. She'd found him almost everywhere he and Reva went, sending him either letters proclaiming love, or threats accompanied by bloody appendages of random fae. "We can go downstairs and talk about—"

"The time for talking is over," Locasta seethed, her fists tightening. "You've offended me for the last time, hiding yourself away and breeding with this whore."

A wisp of green smoke streaked through the air toward Locasta, but she avoided it with a quick spin on her heels. It dissipated a moment later. Crow winced at his beloved's attempt to channel her power—that small, harmless bit had to cost her everything she had left.

"Reva, don't," he begged. She was too weak to battle Locasta right now, and his ability to transform into a crow wouldn't do much against the Northern Witch's magic. The best way out of this was to talk Locasta down. He would promise anything to get her to leave, even if it meant going with her. He'd escaped the North once and he could do it again if it meant protecting Reva and their baby.

Reva's eyes narrowed in his direction. She knew Locasta was unhinged—she knew *everything* Crow had suffered while he'd lived in her palace. He'd seen fae tortured on Locasta's orders, and endured the Northern Witch's rage multiple times. His feathers had been plucked, his blood drained until he was dizzy, and, whenever Locasta broke his skin, he'd been forced to take saltwater baths. Each punishment only ended when he was *sufficiently* injured. Sometimes not even then, because she would use her power to force him into his bird form and lock him in a cage. So why did it seem like Reva was angry at *him* for trying to protect her and their daughter? It wasn't possible that she thought he was standing up for his former lover, was it?

"This ends now," Locasta announced. Blue light filled the room and a shriek came from the hallway. *Whispa.*

"Stop." Crow tried to step toward Locasta, but his feet refused to move. The planked floor had transformed around them, shackling him in place. The wood slowly circled higher and higher, past his ankles and around his legs, digging into his flesh. He bent, trying to pry it away, but it was no use. "Locasta, *stop*! Release me."

"Crow!" Reva's desperate cry tore through his chest. When he saw the reason for her outburst, his heart nearly stopped. The bedsheets bound Reva's limbs, strapping her down, and the child… *Oh Gods…* Locasta held her with one arm, blue magic flowing endlessly from the witch's free hand.

"Pixie," Locasta called, chin held high, a victorious smirk on her lips.

Whispa lumbered into the bedroom then, only she wasn't a pixie any longer. Her willowy body seemed to have shrunk— now skeletal with thick, rubbery skin clinging to the bones. Jagged teeth protruded from tightly stretched lips, giving the illusion of a deranged smile, and her eyes had gone completely black. The worst part, however, was the change in her wings from beautiful, crystalline to black leather that hung in uneven pieces from a boney protrusion on her back.

Fear ripped through Crow—not for himself, but for the females around him. Locasta's power to transform anything had always unnerved him, but to see something so gruesome… She had never done anything so drastic before, and that terrified him most of all. The *Good* Witch seemed to have finally lost her senses completely.

"Locasta, please," Crow begged. "Stop this. Don't hurt them, and I'll go to the North with you, I swear. Just *please* don't hurt them." He would sacrifice himself for Reva and their child. Every. Single. Time.

"I begged you not to hurt *me* too," she said, spittle flying in his direction. "You"—she addressed the beast that was Whispa and held the baby out—"fly this *thing* North. Stop for nothing and no one. Wait for me in the highest tower and do not let it die."

"You stupid bitch!" Reva screamed. "If you dare take my daughter, I swear you will die a slow, painful death at my hands."

Crow struggled harder against the wood, now encasing his waist. Locasta couldn't take their baby. She *couldn't.* He had to stop this now before she handed her to the beastly pixie.

"Shut your filthy mouth," Locasta spat.

Whispa took the child, pulled her close, and darted out the broken window before Crow could even free a single splinter.

"No!" Crow and Reva cried in unison.

Crow fought against Locasta's magic with every ounce of strength he had. If he transformed into his bird form, Locasta's magic would snap him up and hold him tighter—he'd tried flying away from her temper before. But that was his daughter. *His daughter!* His heart shattered inside his chest.

"I will slaughter you for this," Reva spat, tears sliding down her cheeks.

"For your sake," Locasta said to Crow, "she'll become a changeling instead of a corpse."

"Give her back to me!" Reva's hands flexed and curled,

unable to create a single spark. "Give her *back!*"

The floor wove up to Crow's midsection, stopping just below his heart. "Take me, Locasta. Please."

"We aren't finished yet." With a swirl of her hands, Locasta sent her magic blasting into Reva's chest.

Reva screamed until her voice was raw, and Crow shouted along with her as Locasta's magic faded from the air. The sheets released their grip on Reva and she rolled, falling to the floor, unconscious—or nearly so. Her eyes rolled beneath their lids, and her neck muscles visibly tightened as she threw her head back at an unnatural angle.

"Reva," Crow whispered through tears.

"Look, sweetheart." Locasta walked behind Crow to whisper in his ear. "Watch as your beloved disappears."

Green pustules bubbled over Reva's face, popping, coloring her skin a greenish hue and leaving craters in their wake. Her nose elongated, twisted, making her look nothing like the female he knew, and the hands that had touched him with so much love extended into claws. A sickening snap filled the air as her spine arched, then curved in on itself. Finally, her body stilled as if she were sleeping. Every ounce of Reva's outer beauty had vanished beneath Locasta's curse, but Crow knew her heart. He knew that when she woke up again, she would still be his same fierce female, and he would love her regardless of what she'd become.

"Wait for it," Locasta squealed with excitement.

Reva's body flew upright with a gasp. Crow jerked toward her, but his restraints tightened. A weak, desperate sound escaped his throat. Reva patted her hands over her dark nightgown and looked up at Crow. Her emerald eyes, brighter than before, lifted slowly, landing on Crow with complete disinterest.

"Dance," Locasta ordered.

Reva immediately twirled through the room, hands stretched to the ceiling, her head reclined all the way back.

"Stop, Locasta. I'm begging you." Crow's voice cracked. Reva had just spent an entire day bringing their daughter into the world. She'd been exhausted and sore before the curse, but now… Crow felt a shadow of the pain Reva had to be experiencing deep in his bones. And she hated being told what to do. To be controlled like this, and by Locasta no less… "I'll do anything you want. Just… please…"

"All right," she cooed, then commanded Reva, "Come closer so he can have a good look at you."

Reva was instantly in front of them. Up close, it was worse than Crow could've imagined. The pustules left craters in her skin that oozed just enough to make them glisten. And they smelled—*Gods* how they smelled. Like death and decay. Her shoulders hunched, one higher than the other, and her hands—no, claws—were crooked and bent at every knuckle with black, pointed nails.

"Reva?" he breathed.

Her response was a cackling laugh that was *nothing* like the sweet rumbling sound Crow knew so well. His chest tightened, his heart crushed all over again. This was *his* fault. All of it. Damn his selfishness! He'd known Locasta would come for him eventually, yet he'd still brought Reva into hiding with him. Maybe if they had separated, none of this would've happened. Or, if he hadn't walked around his home unarmed, Locasta would be dead instead of Reva cursed and their daughter stolen.

"Don't worry." Locasta stepped between them and took Crow's face in her hands. The witch's eyes softened slightly, but the way her nails dug into his cheeks only reminded him that her anger would never be satiated. "I love you still, Crow, so I will grant you the mercy of Unknowing and curse you to the cornfield."

Crow's eyes widened and he gripped her wrists. The Curse of Unknowing didn't only make a fae forget something—it jumbled every tiny thought in their brain until they were little more than a slobbering creature. "Locasta, don't," he pleaded in a broken voice. He couldn't fix any of this if she took his mind.

Locasta simply smiled, her hands warm on his skin, blue light glowing in his peripheral vision. "One day you will be mine again."

The last clear thought in Crow's mind was how utterly sorry he was for everything.

CHAPTER TWO

REVA

This still didn't feel completely real. Reva was *out* of the dark place—because of her daughter's magic. Thelia had believed she was a human named Dorothy but, before killing Langwidere, discovered who she truly was: a fae.

Reva took off her late sister's frilly pink dress and slid on the only other clothing in Glinda's wardrobe that wasn't a garish gown. It was a one-piece: pale pink—still hideous—with poofy sleeves and loose pants that clutched at her ankles. Losing her sister to Langwidere's horrific obsession with heads had wounded Reva deep down, but she knew Glinda would want her to mend the Land of Oz, to end the wickedness. And that was exactly what she would do—keep her chin up like she always had before.

"Ozma, are you ready?" Reva turned and asked her friend, who had swapped her own tattered blue dress for one of Langwidere's white gowns. This dress wasn't as seductive as the other choices but still had a sheer diagonal v in the back that went from neck to waist, highlighting the raised scar where Ozma's wings had once been.

The one-piece itched at Reva's skin, but it was the only damn thing with pants that her sister seemed to own. Fortunately, it wouldn't be necessary for too long. She would swap it out for something else once they hit the brick road. Besides, she didn't want the distraction of Glinda to haunt her the whole journey. They may not have been thick as thieves, but they had loved and respected each other.

"Yes, I'm ready." Ozma ran a finger along her jawline, her bright blue eyes meeting Reva's emerald ones. "But I think you need to tell him you're leaving."

Reva clenched her jaw, trying not to bring herself to think about *him*. "No."

"No?"

"No." Reva peered down at Ozma's bare feet. "Still no shoes?"

Ozma wiggled all ten toes in the morning light spilling through the window. "Never." She handed Reva a leather satchel and placed another over her shoulder. Then she swiped her long blonde locks behind her back. "Plenty of goodies in there for the journey."

Reva pulled on her dark black boots—the one thing she still had left at Glinda's from the last time she'd stayed so long ago. She couldn't believe they were still here.

Reaching down by her waist, Ozma adjusted the dagger at her hip. Reva didn't need any weapon—she was her own weapon.

Reva walked to the door and quietly opened it, her eyes adjusting to the new lighting after being away from it so long. She halted as her gaze fell to a male body on the carpeted floor, curled on his side, asleep. Midnight locks, with dark feathers entwined, cascaded over his shoulders. Crow. He had always slept through anything.

Her heart didn't leap at the sight of him—she made sure of that. Reva narrowed her eyes, her magic beginning to crackle inside of her—a soft sound that only she could hear and feel. While down in the dark place, among trees that could move their limbs to rip one apart, and beasts that could do the same, she'd imagined hundreds of ways she would murder Crow when she saw him again. One of those ways was by her blasting lightning into his chest. Her magic had been gone then, but it wasn't any longer. Looking at him now, she thought of Thelia, and she could never follow through with it. Even though it was his fault Thelia had become Dorothy, his fault Reva herself had been turned into a cursed monster, his fault for not killing Locasta when he'd found out she was truly wicked.

Ozma pressed a hand to Reva's shoulder and cocked her head at Crow to wake him. With a quick motion, Reva placed a finger over her lips and waved her on. Ozma gave her a look that told Reva she disagreed with the choice she was making. She didn't give a fuck, not when the memory of Crow telling Reva not to use her powers against Locasta slipped into her mind.

Staying silent, they padded their way down the hall to the staircase and descended the wooden steps. At the bottom of the stairs, light shone down from the domed ceiling, casting its hue across a chaise and four chairs with white cushions. The room no longer contained Langwidere's dead body, Glinda's head, dead Wheelers, or the crack that had split the palace into two because of Thelia's magic. The palace's own magic, courtesy of Glinda, had mended the house, but Crow had done everything else. Cleaned the blood. Buried Reva's sister, Langwidere's heads, and the bitch's body.

A subtle movement caught Reva's attention. Waiting at the door with her arms crossed was Thelia. Her daughter. Her beautiful and caring daughter. Brown eyes—like Crow's. She was the spitting image of him, aside from Reva's ears and chestnut-colored hair. Even though Thelia's overalls were stained after a rinse, she was still wearing them. She had promised to go to one of the abandoned shops to find some new garments soon.

"So, you really are leaving without telling him?" Thelia whispered.

Reva had asked her to meet them here for a temporary farewell, but she should have known questions would ensue. If anyone could make her turn around right now, it was Thelia, but Reva *had* to do this. If she didn't, their fates—Thelia's fate—

could be destroyed by Locasta and Oz. The Wizard had the silver slippers and Ozma was going to make sure to get them back while Reva took care of Locasta.

"Yes," Reva finally said, "though I know you're going to tell him. At least give us a head start." That was all she needed, and she would make sure he couldn't catch up.

"I will stay silent until he asks." Thelia gnawed at her lower lip. "Which I can guarantee won't be long."

"I'll take it." He would sleep in if no one disturbed him.

Before Reva could say anything else, Thelia threw her arms around her, surprising Reva. She never would have expected for Thelia to embrace her so soon, but her daughter was different: more caring, more human. And she knew Thelia was this way, even from the little time they'd had with each other. Reva hugged her daughter in return, holding back the tears that were aching to come. But there would be no crying yet, not until they were tears of happiness after the Land of Oz was safe and free from the wicked. Then their world could prosper again.

"Take care of the South," Reva murmured in Thelia's ear.

"Tin and I will."

Tin… Reva didn't know him well. She only recalled him through her memories as the Wicked Witch of the West. The ones where she'd tried to murder him, murder them all.

A thrum to kill rocked through her, but not for the innocent—for another witch in the North, sitting daintily on her throne. Locasta would die for everything she'd done. Reva's lightning would burst the wicked one's heart to bloody pieces.

"I love you, Thelia," Reva whispered as she pulled back, calming herself with the knowledge that her daughter was safe, alive. For ten years within the dark place, she hadn't known. That uncertainty was part of what had made the hate for Crow fester. "When all of this is over, and Oz is safe, I look forward to getting to know you."

"I love you, too."

Ozma came closer and brought her arms around Thelia. "You will be a great ruler. I can feel the kindness of your heart."

Thelia wasn't the only caring fae—Ozma had a tender heart as well.

Releasing Thelia, Ozma stepped back and allowed Thelia to open the door to the morning sunlight. She winced at the brightness.

Reva expected Crow to rush down the stairs, sliding his palm across the ornate banister to stop them. He didn't. And she was relieved.

Outside, the sun bore down on them, its heated rays making Glinda's clothing itchier against her flesh. In the distance, past the ivory and lilac flowers, the freshly turned dirt, where the heads of Langwidere were buried, stood out from the rest of the ground. She remembered the bitch, remembered how she'd changed Oz from a selfish human Wizard into a greedy, deranged Wizard. Langwidere had deserved to die. Oz would eventually be dead too—by Ozma's hand. The silver slippers would then be returned to their rightful owner.

"Calm down, my good witch," Ozma soothed in a low whisper. "I can practically see the smoke rolling off you."

It wasn't a lie. Reva could see light gray steam rising from her skin. She managed to hold it in before the lightning and thunder followed.

As they walked out the gate, Reva tried not to look at the pale pink statue of her sister. She gave Glinda a silent, final goodbye.

Reva and Ozma started down the yellow brick road. They took sugary pastries from their satchels and ate and drank their canteens of water along the way, only stopping to find a new dress for Ozma: a pale blue one with a rope belt around the waist. There was nothing in the shop dark enough in color for Reva, and most appeared even more uncomfortable than what she was already wearing. She would deal with the pink and the itchiness a little longer.

While heading north along the yellow brick road, Ozma stared, mouth agape, at the world around them. The colorful trees, the cottages shaped like mushrooms, the winged bugs buzzing by.

Reva smiled to herself. She'd been trapped alone in that dark place for so long, for *years*, before a ray of light had fallen in—Ozma—illuminating the place with her words and her kindness. Seeing Ozma happy, *free*, after living in fear for so long, seeming like a completely different fae now that she was cleaned up, made her think back to how they'd met.

A loud crash sounded in the dark from not too far away. It was always dark here, but not to the point where Reva felt she were blind. It was in between the night and sunset. A rustle came from behind a blackened bush. Her magic still did not rise up to protect her, but she didn't care. She moved a branch to the side, spotting a blonde fae, her hair a tangled mess. The female's feet were bare, and a shredded tunic and pants covered the rest of her. Both garments appeared too small for her tall frame.

"Who the hell are you?" Reva snapped.

"I-I don't know," the fae stammered, sitting up and rubbing her eyes.

Perhaps this was an illusion, or a beast in disguise. But it couldn't be so, because a beast would have already tried to attack. They didn't trick here, and they didn't play nice or fair—they just wanted to tear one apart. No need for manipulation. "You don't know? Did you lose your memory or something?"

"No." The fae paused, staring down at her trembling hands. "I don't know. I was him and now I'm her. And I feel like her but I miss him."

Reva arched an eyebrow and took a step back. She had once been a fae who would've helped anyone in her territory of the West. But after the curse—the murders—she was hesitant to trust anyone in this nothingness of a place. She wouldn't have a problem killing this fae if she needed to. "What the fuck are you talking about?"

"I'm Tip." The female opened her eyes. "But I'm not Tip. I'm Ozma, the true ruler of Oz."

Reva scowled, studying the fae. "If what you say is true, you're not a ruler anymore. Not in this place."

"I didn't know. Not until Mombi. Not until Oz used the silver slippers..." Ozma turned away from Reva.

Reva didn't give a fuck about rulers, or Oz, or anything besides getting back to Thelia. She'd almost murdered her own daughter and Crow... Even if she hadn't killed them, she had slaughtered others. Lots and lots of fae.

She could remember her claws digging deep into the flesh of innocents, then feeding the bloody pieces to her flying minions. But that hadn't been the true her. The transgression she couldn't get over though, was how she'd almost murdered her daughter. It was her one haunting regret.

Her gaze fell to Ozma's back, where the dress was ripped, and even in the barely-there light, a raised patch of skin caught her attention. From the wound, bright blood oozed over her skin, as if whatever used to be there had been cut off. Wings. Reva knew right away, and perhaps she'd been too harsh.

In the distance, a low, fierce growl reverberated through the trees. "You're going to have to get ready to run," Reva said.

"Why?" Ozma stood on her tiptoes and peered around a large tree trunk.

"The beasts will be coming, and they'll smell your blood. Not only them. Beware the trees covered in thorns—their limbs can move and capture you."

Ozma stared again at her hands, furrowing her brow. "My magic is gone."

"So is mine." It had been gone for years now. Some days she was grateful, some days she was angry, and some days she just wanted the repetitive cycle to end.

"We'll protect each other then?" Ozma asked, stepping toward Reva.

"Perhaps. It could be our best chance to survive." Reva wasn't sure how long she'd been in this place, but she knew it had been years.

The sounds drew closer, trees groaning, everything around them ravenous with hunger. Reva yanked Ozma forward, and they both took off at a sprint.

Reva shrugged off the memory as a new sound stirred from all directions. *Squeak.* Unfamiliar. No. Not unfamiliar. She just hadn't heard it in years. They'd been followed.

"Seems like you'll see a living Wheeler for the first time." She should have known they would come, in need of a new master now that Langwidere was gone. The wheeled bastards should have returned to the edge of the Deadly Desert where they belonged, because she wasn't going to take care of them.

"Do you believe they're worth saving?" Ozma asked as the squeaking drew closer.

"No." She would have given them mercy if they'd chosen to

leave the South already, but they didn't deserve to live now.

The squeals echoed from the forest on the sides of the brick road. Wheeler after Wheeler rolled out from behind the trees, their arms and legs too long for their bodies. Most were covered in dried blood and dirt, leaves in their rumpled hair. White ribbon stained with crimson blood sewed their lips shut. They arched their curving spines in an animalistic manner as they edged closer.

A female Wheeler with matted auburn locks of hair shot toward Ozma. The minion lifted a spiked wheel, the speed increasing, turning and turning. Ozma leapt up and caught a branch, easily scaling the tree. In the dark place, they'd both grown used to climbing up boulders and trees that weren't murderous to make an escape. Ozma may not have her full magic back yet, but Reva did.

Reva smirked as she easily dodged a male Wheeler who charged at her. A raised scar ran from a missing eye to the side of his head where a mangled ear hung. "You should have gone straight to the Desert," she said, clapping her hands together, creating a thunderous boom that not only vibrated within her but shook the ground.

Not taking her eyes from the Wheelers—who no longer moved toward her, their expressions startled—she sparked a bit of green light in the center of her palm. It crackled, sang, and began to ignite. Some of the Wheelers started to turn, but it was too late for any of them. A blast of lightning shot forward, electrifying the world around her.

Everything was green, green, *green*—like her skin had once been—until the color dissipated and only a flicker of yellowish light remained. Then there was nothing but smoke surrounding her and the scent of charred bodies.

Reva's gaze flicked up to Ozma who sat safely in the tree, staring down at her with her head tilted to the side.

"What?" Reva chuckled.

A frown formed on Ozma's face as she jumped from the branch. She swiftly pulled out the dagger from her hip and jolted toward a tree. A twitching Wheeler was pushing herself up at its roots. Ozma lifted the dagger and plunged it through the Wheeler's chest, directly into her heart. The Wheeler collapsed to her side, unmoving, crimson pooling from the wound as she stared blankly toward the trees.

"Missed one," Ozma said, daintily cleaning the blood from the blade with another Wheeler's tunic.

"I suppose you were tired of hiding in the tree and had to steal my *thunder*," Reva teased, but she was also satisfied that Thelia and Tin would be safer with many of the Wheelers gone. Another male, with obsidian feathers laced in his hair, crept into her mind, but she pushed the bastard away.

"I'm going to miss your sarcasm when we have to go our separate ways."

"I'll miss you too." Reva didn't want to think about Ozma not being by her side just yet. "Let's continue before we lose light."

CHAPTER THREE

CROW

Crow stretched his stiff back, letting out a quiet groan. Sleeping on the floor wasn't what had left him feeling so sore—he'd done that hundreds of times when there weren't any trees available to hang his hammock from. It was from sleeping on the floor after being knocked out of a tree by Wheelers, transforming into a broken bird, shifting back, cleaning up after Langwidere's death, burying her and dozens of heads, then waiting anxiously for Reva to open the damn door. Which she still hadn't done yet.

A million questions swirled through his mind. The most pressing one was where Reva had been all this time. *Trapped in darkness* was so vague, but Dorothy hadn't been told more than that. Surely, with more information, he could figure out what had happened when Dorothy broke the curse. It had been an extra advantage to her killing Langwidere, but the sudden appearance of Reva and her friend, Ozma, threw him off his game.

Crow *would* stick to questions about what had happened when Reva finally came out of her sister's old bedroom—even if it killed him not to make more personal inquiries. He hoped Reva was comfortable surrounded by Glinda's things after learning about her death. Crow hadn't seen the Good Witch since before

Dorothy was born—she hadn't known Crow and Reva were together, and he'd had no other reason to visit—but time doesn't break familial bonds.

If Crow knew one thing about Reva's current feelings, it was that she seemed to loathe him with every fiber of her being. He couldn't blame her—and yet he *did* blame her. Crow settled his elbows on his knees and hung his head. Locasta had cursed her, taken away her daughter, but she had also cursed *him*. Taken *his* daughter. Reva had been completely aware of the risks when they'd gone into hiding together. Their entire relationship was spent with the threat of Locasta looming over them like a guillotine, its blade edging closer, but Reva had repeatedly assured him their love was worth the risk.

Crow ground his teeth together and shoved up from the floor. He would simply have to earn Reva back. Make up for everything that had happened. Somehow. Beginning with a nice, hot breakfast. It was a different meal than he'd meant to give Reva that fated night, but the thought was the same. Perhaps they could begin anew. Their daughter was back, their curses broken…

With fresh determination, Crow hurried down the stairs and through the foyer to the kitchen. Glinda's magic continued to keep the palace running even after Langwidere had killed her, and the room was full of baked goods. Stacks of buttery croissants, sticky buns, steaming muffins, and a variety of fruit-filled turnovers with syrupy filling covered the rose-gold marble countertops.

And, leaning over the various delicacies, loomed a shirtless Tin, his silver hair pulled back in a messy bun.

"Morning, *Father*," Tin said stoically without looking up from the turnovers.

Crow winced. Dorothy was far too good for someone like Tin—once a ruthless assassin with a stone heart. The Gnome King's curse was broken, but something told Crow that Tin was broken too. It was going to take a lot to get over the fact that Tin had brought Dorothy back specifically to hand her over to Lion and Langwidere. It would be a lie to say Lion's path hadn't come as a surprise, that he would willingly kill the female who'd once helped him—*saved* him.

Crow would try to forgive Tin for Dorothy's sake, but if the bastard ever hurt his daughter, Crow would kill him without an ounce of guilt.

"Don't be a jackass," Crow grumbled. "Also, put on a shirt."

Tin smirked, the iron scar on his cheek pulling his skin with the movement. "You look like hell. Did you get any sleep?"

"Did *you?*" Crow threw back at him, then paused at the thought of *why* he wouldn't have slept. "No. Don't answer that."

Tin snorted and lifted a full plate of pastries. "Thelia already ate, so the rest is all yours. I'd hurry before they disappear."

Crow's stomach growled at the reminder of last night's dinner. After he'd dragged himself inside from burying heads, he'd just sat down to a plate of gravy-smothered chops when every piece of food had vanished. Magic kitchens weren't all they were cracked up to be. "Who is Thelia?"

"Your daughter," Tin replied as if it were completely obvious. "You talked last night, didn't you? She remembered her true name."

They had talked, but it was mostly about the task Reva had given Dorothy—no. *Thelia.* The name fit her so well, so perfectly, that he should've known who Tin was talking about the moment he'd said it. *Thelia, Thelia, Thelia.* The name echoed through his mind, dragging a knowing feeling from the depths of his memory. He'd almost thought it on the night of her birth, but then Locasta… He had begun to think Dorothy's true name was lost forever due to his curse. *Thelia.* He smiled to himself.

"Guess she didn't tell you," Tin muttered at his silence. "It was a long night, with a lot of life-changing shit, so don't go getting angry with her."

"I'm not." Her name was incredibly important, but not as pressing as other things. He moved around the kitchen counter. "I'm going to cook up some eggs and sausages." Assuming there were any, but Lion had lived in the palace only days ago. Given his vulgar hobby of chopping off heads, he struck Crow as a meat eater. Reva certainly was. It was something they bickered about at least once a week when they were together. She always wanted hot, filling breakfasts while he wanted something light, like a bowl of fruit or oats, and she refused to allow Whispa to make more than one meal—even if it was simply tossing some fruit into a bowl. Unfortunately for him, Reva was an early riser so she nearly always won. Crow grinned, remembering her victorious, smug smile when he would finally stumble down from the bedroom. It was a smile that left him eating whatever Whispa made instead of preparing his own meal. "Reva prefers heartier breakfasts."

Tin tensed. "You're making Reva breakfast?"

"Of course." He picked a large skillet off a hook on the wall.

"Umm. Happy cooking." Tin eased away from the pastries with his lips pulled back in a grimace. Then he spun on his heels and bolted from the room.

"Tin!" Crow yelled, but the other male was gone. Something about it was suspicious, but Tin was nearly impossible to figure out, so he turned back to the task at hand. Pulling his hair away from his face, Crow studied the two dozen cupboards. "If I were a mixing bowl, where would I be?" he mumbled to himself.

"Crow?" Thelia asked from the kitchen doorway.

A smile instantly spread across his face. "Good morning."

"Morning." She hurried to him and placed a kiss on his cheek. "Tin passed me in the hall and said you were up."

Crow nodded and motioned around the kitchen. "I want to make Reva breakfast. She and I need to talk a few things out."

Thelia stood silently beside him, eyes fixed on the floor, wringing her hands.

"Don't worry," he assured her. "You're safe now."

"That's not it," she said with a halfhearted smile.

"Is it about us leaving then? You seemed upset when you explained your mother's plan to travel. As much as I would love to spend time with you—and I know Reva does too—we need to fix Oz."

"I know."

"Trust me, your mother is extremely powerful, and I'll protect her with my life." Like he hadn't last time.

"Crow, stop talking," Thelia snapped, then sucked in a breath. "I'm sorry, I didn't mean to be harsh. It's just…" She exhaled, her eyes blinking one too many times.

Crow patted her shoulder. His daughter's entire existence was new to her, and he didn't want her to worry about hurting his feelings. "We've all been through a lot."

"She's gone," Thelia whispered.

His hand fell from her shoulder. That couldn't be right, could it? His stomach sank. "What do you mean?"

Thelia rubbed a hand over her mouth as if she regretted opening it. "I promised not to tell you, but the thought of Reva out there alone, crossing through the Emerald City to reach Locasta in the North, terrifies me. She and Ozma left together, but will be separating to go fight their own battles while I stay here as she requested. I can't lose her before I've had a chance to get to know her, especially after I somehow banished her to darkness when she was the Wicked Witch."

Reva left? *How?* When? He'd slept outside her door all night, specifically so she couldn't leave without him. It didn't matter if she wanted him to travel with her and Ozma. There was no way he was going to let Reva go to the North alone to face Locasta, especially when everything that had gone wrong in the past was because of him. If he had simply escaped the Northern palace and gone into hiding on his own… If he hadn't gone to Reva for help in destroying Locasta. And what good had it done? They'd failed to stop Locasta from brutalizing her citizens in the end.

Crow might not have magic that could inflict the same sort of damage as Reva or Locasta, but he'd done more than train his brain over the last ten years. He'd learned how to fight, and fight well, so that one day he could take Locasta down himself. Reva coming back from the dead was never an option he'd thought possible, though he'd searched for answers about what exactly happened when Dorothy threw the water at the Wicked Witch.

There was no record of a simple pail of water melting a faerie—even with the silver slippers, it had seemed strange to him. If he knew Reva hadn't been dead at all, he would've found a way to bring her back so they could destroy the Northern Witch together. Hell, he should've killed Locasta years ago when he ventured back to her Northern palace. His desperation to find the real Dorothy Gale had driven him to visit his ex-lover, but he hadn't been strong enough to fight her then. Escaping was the best he could do, and that hadn't come without sacrifices. His only ally in the palace—a human changeling Locasta kept as a pet—had created the distraction he needed to cross the border into the West. The man's agonized wails fading to deathly silence still echoed through Crow's mind.

"How long ago did she and Ozma leave?" he asked. His throat bobbed, his palms sweating, but he made sure to keep his voice even for Thelia's sake.

Thelia took Crow's hand in both of her own. "I'm sorry I didn't tell you sooner."

"I'm not angry with you," he promised. With Reva, yes, but not Thelia. "How long ago?"

"A few hours. It was just past dawn."

Crow nodded once, placed a kiss on his daughter's warm forehead, and left the kitchen.

"Where are you going?" Thelia called after him.

"To find your mother," he called back, and hurried to gather his belongings.

He was going to find Reva and keep her safe. Something he couldn't do twenty-one years ago.

CHAPTER FOUR

REVA

After two days of traveling on the yellow brick road in the Southern territory, Reva's endurance remained high. She was used to constantly being on the move in the dark place, avoiding the trees that would attack and hiding from the creatures that wanted to rip them apart. Some days in the dark place they could rest for longer than others, and that was when hope had been the loudest.

Reva and Ozma ate, slept, and chatted on their journey. They walked around the areas of the yellow brick road where the Wheelers had left their bloody victims, torn apart and mangled. None of the bodies were new, though—perhaps a few days old. The deaths only made Reva more determined to heal the Land of Oz.

To Reva, the grave markers she'd passed of Langwidere's victims were a true punch to the gut. The South wasn't supposed to be this way. She and Glinda's parents had owned this territory, kept it flourishing—Glinda had continued the tradition. And now it had gone to shit. The colorful cottages were still intact, but that didn't mean anything because mostly everyone had left or was dead. *The South isn't dead, though,* she told herself. The Southerners could return to make it thrive once more. Thelia could do it. Reva and Ozma would help if she needed them. She would *always* help her daughter.

"What are you scowling about now?" Ozma asked, bringing a bright red faerie fruit between her lips. Crunch. Crunch. *Crunch.*

Reva needed an apple, but they didn't grow in the South. They were her comfort. She had a lot going on in her head, too much, and she was tired of thinking about the Land of Oz and how broken it had become. She hadn't seen what the other territories looked like yet, but from what Thelia had told her, the East was run down, and the Emerald City was full of dangerous, destructive fae.

"You chew too loud," Reva said, avoiding the question.

"You're going to make me dig for the answer, aren't you?" Ozma smiled and glanced up at the moving clouds.

Reva sighed. "I know the rest of Oz is going to be even worse than this."

"This isn't so bad." Ozma's gaze connected with Reva's. She was a dreamer and always one to see the positive in everything. Ozma would probably even find the good in the Wheeler she'd stabbed through the heart by saying the fae was better off dead— which was true.

"I think all the headless fae buried across this territory would have to disagree."

"What I mean is," Ozma said slowly, "it can always be worse. Those deaths will not be for nothing. They are the start of something, and that includes Glinda."

Reva's chest tightened at her sister's name. As young fae, Glinda would parade around in her frilly pink dresses and Reva would wear dark clothing. Glinda was the light and Reva was the dark but neither were wicked—only their personalities were different. Glinda was bouncier, Reva more demanding, but both made their territories a priority and took care of them.

The memory of Locasta barreling into her room after Thelia was born crept into her mind. Reva could once again feel the cracking, twisting, and manipulation of bones, muscle, and skin. Her nose stretching and curving, the pustules bursting over her flesh, causing the green color to spread.

Clenching her jaw, Reva tucked away that anger to use later when the opportunity came. "You're right, this is the start of something."

It had been Reva and Ozma together for so long. Now she was ready to see the fae from the West, or at least the ones who had survived her wrath as the Wicked Witch. But that would have to wait, too.

It didn't take long before they entered the Eastern territory. There wasn't much to see besides forestry and *no apples*. They trekked farther and farther, and Reva kept her guard up for creatures that might attack, but all remained silent.

Right as the sunlight was about to die for the day, Reva spotted a small village. Blue and black cottages, along with larger buildings, were tucked and covered by pine trees on either side of the yellow brick road.

Lit lanterns guided their way as she and Ozma passed the buildings. In the triangular windows, flames bobbed atop candlesticks. Outside an inn, two fae, with curled horns atop their heads, held each other close and walked inside. Next door, a nymph stood in front of the entrance to a brothel, drinking out of a silver goblet. She glanced at Reva and Ozma when they drew closer.

"I know you," the nymph said, ticking her finger back and forth as she stepped into their path. Dark hair, with ribbon laced throughout, framed her delicate features, and a yellow dress of spider silk hugged her lithe form.

Ozma's eyebrows lifted in surprise. "You do?"

"No, no. Not you." The nymph shooed Ozma away and inched closer to Reva, pointing at the Good Witch's chest. "You. I've seen *you* before."

Reva watched as an unreadable expression crossed Ozma's face. Possibly disappointment? Even if Reva had met this nymph before, nobody would have recognized her friend since no one knew she existed. All the years she'd spent in Oz, she'd been Tip, not Ozma. Enchanted to look like a male to hide her identity and keep the Wizard of Oz in power. Mombi had been the one to do the Wizard's dirty work—she'd stolen Ozma away as a baby and raised her to not know who she really was. If Reva could snap *that* witch's neck right then, she would. But it was best no one knew who Ozma was yet—she was without her power and throne.

Reva squinted her eyes, not recognizing the nymph in the slightest.

The fae leaned in closely, her breath reeking of ale. "You're Reva. How are you back? You're not monstrous anymore either."

The blood coursing through Reva's veins came to a halt. She couldn't breathe. With hurried motions, she grasped the nymph by her shoulders and shoved her against the outside wall of the brothel, knocking over a clay pail.

"Keep your mouth shut," Reva whispered, the lightning within her already crackling, creating waves of thunder in her ears. "It was a curse and the curse is gone."

"Reva," Ozma warned.

"Don't worry." The nymph smiled, not the least bit afraid. "No one will recognize you in these parts. Most who live here have never been to the West. But I was at Glinda's palace when *you* last visited, remember?"

Releasing the nymph's shoulders, Reva's brow furrowed. That would have been twenty-two years ago. The last time she'd gone to Glinda's palace, she'd only stayed the day and was supposed to return the next season, but had never gotten the chance. Things had heated around Oz because of the witch in the East, Inora. The Eastern Witch would slaughter anyone who came into her territory who wasn't from there, including families of Easterners who visited. But the last time Reva had walked into Glinda's room, she remembered her sister being pleasured by—

"Oh, you were the one in her bed!" The nymph's hair had been in a braid that day, and she'd been naked except for a pink glittering choker.

"How is Glinda by the way?"

"She's..." Reva shook her head.

The nymph seemed to understand as she nodded with melancholy sparkling in her eyes. "And Langwidere?"

"Dead."

"Good."

"We need a place to stay for the night," Ozma said, peeking through the window, lips parted in surprise.

The nymph stared at Ozma's odd motions and turned back to Reva. "I'm Falyn."

The name—she'd heard it recently. Reva lifted a dark brow. "You gifted Dorothy a machete. She saved the South."

Falyn gave a small smile. "I knew she would do something great again." She turned, opened the brothel door, and motioned them forward. "Well, come on. Enough chit-chat because I have money to be making."

They followed Falyn inside the brothel, where sex and incense filled Reva's nose. Her body normally would have tightened at the scent but she was too drained to feel aroused. She hadn't had a lover in years. Yet there had been the nights where she'd been asleep, high up in a tree in the dark place, and dreamt of Crow. His hands on her waist, sliding up to cup her breasts. Him so tender, her so wild. His mouth on hers, her fingers drifting down to—

Fuck Crow, she thought, shaking off the images stirring within her. She focused on several shot glasses on a counter filled with golden liquor. Grabbing one, she tossed the liquid into her mouth and relished the burn as it glided down her throat.

Reva glanced at Ozma, who stared with wide eyes at the fae around her. Some of them were naked, straddling males as they played games at the tables. Other males were mounting lovers against the walls. She smiled and nudged Ozma's arm. "Don't act like you're so innocent. I know you've seen a naked male before."

"Only myself when I was Tip. Then Jack..." Ozma drifted off, and Reva knew she was thinking about her true love.

"Now you've seen more." Reva's gaze carried throughout the

room as she followed the nymph toward a hallway. Paintings covered the wall of lovers fucking. Prostitutes and their clients appeared as if they were trying to mirror the positions depicted.

Ozma didn't look surprised anymore. She seemed inquisitive while watching the females and the males together, as if she were attempting to learn how it all worked.

"It will come naturally when you reunite," Reva whispered to Ozma as they turned down a hall filled with rooms and crimson curtains as doors.

"Would you like me to get either of you some company for the night?" Falyn asked while lifting one of the curtains leading into a room with a single bed and dresser.

"No, but would you have a change of clothing?" Reva pulled out a ring from her satchel. "Something black." She'd been ignoring the itching of the clothing but she couldn't handle it anymore.

Falyn waved the ring away. "Only if you replace it with what you're wearing. That clothing is far more valuable than anything I own.

"Are you sure?"

"Trade for anything in the closet you wish. I'm going to work for the remainder of the night, but you two can rest here." Falyn spun around to leave, but stopped to glance over her shoulder. "I'm glad you're back. Glinda mentioned what a wonderful leader and sister you were."

Reva didn't say anything—her fists tightened at what Langwidere, Locasta, and the Wizard had set into motion.

Chest heaving, Reva turned to find Ozma sitting on the bed, peering down at her hands. "What is it?"

"I just want to get back to him." Ozma sighed. "I've always wanted to get back to him."

Sometimes Reva wanted to roll her eyes because Ozma was more than who she used to be. She hadn't known she was the ruler of Oz—not until she'd broken free from Mombi's curse, then had been cast away to the dark place because of the Wizard. And now, there was so much more for Ozma than a single fae male. "You've known what"—Reva shrugged—"four fae your whole life before meeting Thelia and the others? Mombi, Oz, Jack, and me. I know Jack will be happy to see you from what I've heard of him, but you also have a whole new path now. It might not be a path that Jack would ever choose to walk."

"The Jack I know would. But I'm more concerned about my body." Ozma motioned at her breasts. "What if he doesn't like it? What if he doesn't like *me* anymore?"

"You did say he doesn't have a preference between males and females, so why wouldn't he? And if he doesn't, then fuck him. You're Ozma, Queen of Oz." Reva would strike Jack down with her magic if need be.

Ozma bit her lip.

Reva pressed her hands on Ozma's narrow shoulders. "When the sun rises, go to him and warn him about the Wizard. I'll be fine. After I deal with Locasta, I'll wait for you in the Emerald City and help you claim the palace. But if you arrive and there's still war over the territory, go back to Thelia in the South."

"I'll meet you there." Her blue eyes met Reva's, gleaming with determination. "Unless you need my help with Locasta first."

"No, you can't. Not with her ability to change you into something else. That's why I had Thelia stay at the Southern palace—we can't all be in the same place at the same time. If something happens to me, there will still be the two of you."

Ozma pressed her hand to her chest. "I only had my wings for moments, but I wish I had them now to help."

"You'll grow a new pair once you get the silver slippers. The shoes' magic will yield to you in whatever way you wish." The way Thelia had wanted Reva gone… Even though Thelia should have wanted her truly dead for everything Reva had done.

Ozma nodded and pulled back the red satin sheets. "Let's get some rest."

Reva removed her boots and slipped beneath the covers, but she couldn't shut her thoughts off. "Do you know what you're going to say to Jack when you see him?"

"I've gone over it a thousand times in my head, and I still don't have an answer. I still miss being Tip at times, but perhaps that's because I know Jack loved him. But I love myself now. I just hope Jack can too." Ozma stretched and closed her eyes, breathing slow and even.

Reva shouldn't have brought up the subject, because now she couldn't stop her thoughts from turning to her past lover and how they had first met.

Reva strolled down to the market because she preferred to pick her fruit herself. It had to be perfect. Not too soft, not too hard. She bid a passing hello to every fae she encountered on the way, only stopping to tickle a young brownie beneath her chin.

Merchants filled their stands with goods—dark clothing, obsidian jewelry, and fruit. Her favorite fruit stand caught her eye. Apples and oranges rested in baskets along the counter. Beneath the afternoon sun, a perfect green apple sparkled. That was the one. She reached for the luscious piece of fruit, but a male's hand grabbed it first.

Reva narrowed her eyes at him, first for stealing her apple, and second because he wore a mask shaped like a bird's head that covered half his face. Black hair with feathers entwined fell past his shoulders. "You're not from around here," she accused.

"How do you know?" he asked, cradling the apple closer to his chest, his brown eyes flashing impishly from beneath the mask.

"Because I know everyone in this territory." She looked at the stand's owner, Yovey, who was busy talking to another customer. His gold ring-covered fingers flashed as he gestured toward his fruit.

The stranger lifted his mask over his head, revealing a handsome face that made her catch her breath. He had a chiseled jaw, a light scar running across his nose, and high cheekbones. Reva came back to herself, not one to be swayed by a pretty face. She'd had plenty of those in her bed.

He arched a brow. "Every single one?"

"Every single one." Reva named each owner and customer at the stands circling the area, reciting the monikers like a shopping list. She held out her hand, palm up. "Now give me my apple."

He tossed the apple into the air and caught it again. "I was planning on bringing it to the Western Witch, Reva—I hear she favors pristine fruit."

Her eyes narrowed.

"And why's that?" She didn't do well with strangers entering her or her sister's territory—not with the Eastern Witch becoming more and more deceptive. Inora had already sent spies on multiple occasions, so the arrival of an outsider was never a good sign. If she had to kill him right then and there, so be it.

"Why does she like pristine fruit or why am I bringing her some?" he asked with a playful smile.

"The latter."

He shrugged. "I need to discuss a Northern problem with her, so I was hoping it would help put her in a helpful mood."

A Northern *problem? What was Locasta up to now? Everyone believed the bitch to be good, but Reva could see through her lies. She just couldn't prove anything—yet. Locasta wasn't like Inora, who didn't care about showing the Land of Oz who she truly was.*

"You want Reva?" She cocked her head. "Go to her palace, then."

He dropped the apple into her palm. "Do you really believe I wouldn't recognize you, Reva?"

Reva had never been caught off guard. Not until right then. "Who the fuck are you?"

"You can call me Crow."

"What do other people call you?" she asked.

"Crow. Though, I suppose it depends on who you ask," he said with a wink.

"I'm leaving," Ozma whispered, rousing Reva from sleep before kissing her on the cheek. "We will meet again soon."

"Stay safe, Ozma." Reva's heart beat faster, missing her friend already. "I know you can do this. You're strong and determined, and Jack will fall in love with you all over again when he sees you. It doesn't matter that your body is different. He will see *you.*"

"I hope so." Ozma bit her lip. "Now, try not to be too hard on Crow."

Crow…

Ozma smiled, pushed back the curtain, and left. Reva was alone again, as she had been in the dark place before Ozma had arrived. But this was for the better. Going after Locasta would be dangerous, and Reva didn't want anyone else to suffer from the witch's vicious curses.

She sat up and quickly removed Glinda's one-piece pink outfit to leave on the bed for Falyn, then walked to the wardrobe in the corner. Ropey vines were etched into the wood and heavy brass handles accentuated the doors. Reva pulled the doors open to sift through the nymph's clothing. She found black leather pants, a corset, and a tight tunic with lace around the collar and the ends of the sleeves. When she turned over the shirt, there were ribbons crisscrossed in the back. It was *perfect*.

Just as Reva finished sliding on the clothing and buttoning the front of the tunic, Falyn entered the room, wet-haired and more than a little rumpled.

"I would have returned sooner," Falyn said, "but my client paid me for the entire night and multiple rounds. I do hope he returns, because he was *exquisite*."

Reva ground her teeth as she thought about something distasteful. Crow's mind had been back for ten years—had anyone else found *him* exquisite?

"Something wrong?" asked Falyn.

"No, only thinking about the journey ahead," Reva replied, dropping her scowl and picking up her pack to head back out.

Falyn lifted Glinda's garment and hugged it to her chest. "I'm not sure I'll see you again, but stay safe. The Emerald City isn't as it once was."

Reva told Falyn goodbye, passing couples buried deep in each other as she left the brothel to venture north once again on the yellow brick road. The sunlight revealed that the road wasn't as pristine here as it was in the South, its color faded to a dull mustard.

The farther she traveled out, the worse the road became. Cracks in bricks, some missing, others uneven. She'd been traveling for too long when she stopped to eat berries and drink from a glistening stream. Brushing her hands clean against her pants and filling her canteen with more water, she spun around as a loud clicking noise reverberated off the trees. Whatever it was, it didn't sound small.

Reva's magic thundered, and she crept around a tree trunk. As she took a step forward on a bed of leaves, a crack echoed and she flew up off the ground, screaming. Iron-spun ropes with tiny holes surrounded her, the net swaying gently. It had been hidden by leaves—one that was used for hunting. The iron burned her hands and rendered her powerless.

"Fuck!" she shouted.

A rustle stirred the bushes, drawing her attention. Out came a harmless water fae with gills on the side of its neck, making the same clicking sound before darting on all fours into the river.

Trapped in iron with no one else around, Reva's only hope was for someone to pass by and help before she grew too weak and became something's prey.

CHAPTER FIVE

CROW

Crow trudged along the yellow brick road as dawn filtered through the trees. For fae who'd only gotten a few hours' head start, Reva and Ozma hadn't wasted a second. He'd pushed himself to walk faster, and sleep less, just to close the gap between them, but it had been three days. Given that Reva hadn't visited the Southern woods for decades, Crow figured she would keep mostly to the path. And that would lead to the same town where he'd finally found Thelia and Tin.

How ironic, he thought as he glimpsed a white-washed building. He would soon be asking around town for Reva instead of his daughter. It seemed Reva and Thelia had something in common—running, unknowingly, from him. Though Reva should've known better. There was no chance he would let her run off to fight Locasta alone.

He paused across the street from the brothel and set his pack on the ground to stretch. There were only a few places he could enter this early—eateries, galleries, and trade shops wouldn't open for another hour or so—which left the inn and the brothel.

"Hello," a nymph called brazenly from an upstairs window.

Ah, shit. With his luck, Reva had spent the night in town and would emerge just in time to see him chatting up a prostitute.

"I'm not looking for company, thank you," he called back.

"Are you sure I can't—"

The front door opened and a petite blond female emerged. She wore a simple blue dress, no longer one of Langwidere's. *Ozma.* "Fucking finally," he whispered to himself. But where was Reva?

The true ruler of Oz stared at him from across the road for a long moment before moving toward him. He felt frozen in place. If he moved, would she change her mind about approaching? Run and tell Reva they'd been found?

"Good morning," Ozma said cheerfully. She stopped in front of him and met his gaze. "It took you long enough."

He wasn't sure if that was an accusation or not. "I'm sorry?"

Ozma picked nervously at her skirts. "I… shouldn't be talking to you."

"Why's that?" he asked, as if he didn't know.

"Reva doesn't want you to go to the North with her." Her gaze fell to the ground. "I knew you were following us so I pretended to leave on my own mission first. I stayed behind to catch you even though…"

Crow waited for her to continue but only silence stretched between them. His heart went out to her—Reva was her friend. They'd survived some dark place together. And now, she was betraying that bond they'd built.

"I only want to protect her," he reassured Ozma. "Reva can't take on Locasta alone."

Ozma nodded. "That's why I stayed back. We survived too much for her to get herself killed so recklessly."

Crow swallowed a dozen questions about what exactly they'd survived. Where they had been. What was Reva like now? It had been *decades…*

"She went that way." Ozma pointed down the yellow brick road. "If you hurry, you'll catch up to her by midday."

Crow swept his pack off the ground and quickly flung it over his back. The movement sent his mask sliding down from the top of his head to cover his face. "Thank you," he said in a rush.

"Truly. Thank you."

"Don't thank me." Ozma sounded torn, but determined. "Just keep her safe."

"You have my word." He lifted her hand and planted a kiss on her knuckles. Then he took off after Reva with renewed energy.

Crow didn't slow his pace—not until he, finally, caught his first glimpse of Reva. The sight of her sent his pulse racing. She had ditched the pink one-piece outfit in favor of a black-lace tunic and leather pants. Seeing her in her favorite color again hit Crow with a wave of nostalgia. His body yearned to step out of the alley and go to her. He missed the days when they would walk side by side—arguing, touching, laughing, touching some more.

But it was nothing like old times. He would do whatever it took to make things return to how they'd been, to when she'd loved him, but first he had to find the courage to speak to her.

She was bent near the river, cupping water in her hands to drink. The sun beat down, caressing her long hair, and making the water behind her sparkle. She looked so magical. So lethal and beautiful. How had he ever gotten so lucky to win the heart of such a female?

Drawn forward by her presence, Crow stepped off the crumbling yellow brick road. A twig snapped underfoot, and he cringed. Reva would attack if she thought someone was sneaking up on her. He cleared his throat to call out to her, but stopped himself at the last moment. Announcing himself could send her running—being attacked would bring her right to him. And maybe help her work out some of the anger she clearly carried for him.

Before he could make a solid decision, another, louder snap echoed through the forest. At first, he thought he'd stepped on an entire pile of sticks. Then the sound was followed by Reva's scream. Crow's blades shot out from beneath his bracers, arching over his hands like claws, as he prepared to slay any dangerous fae that threatened her.

What Crow found instead stopped him in his tracks. Reva hung from a tree in a large iron net. His first instinct was to rush over and save her, as much as she would hate that, but he retracted his blades, chuckling silently. The indignity of it had to be killing her.

Crow's chuckle slowly gave way to a mischievous grin. Reva would *have* to speak with him if she wanted to get down. The question was, should he approach her now or wait until she was truly desperate to escape?

The answer was simple, though. She had suffered enough because of him and, while he needed her to hear him out, he wouldn't purposely terrify her. There was no telling what horrors she'd experienced over the last two decades, first as Locasta's monstrous puppet and then wherever she'd gone after the curse broke.

"Who the fuck is there?" Reva called as Crow strode toward her. Even trapped in a net, she didn't seem to be frightened of whatever predator prowled the forest.

"That depends." Crow paused beneath the net and waited for it to spin slowly around so she could see him. When she did, her face quickly morphed from shock to anger—likely because he had followed her, though perhaps also because she hadn't noticed that he was doing so. "Would you rather someone else save you?" he asked with a chuckle.

"Don't you dare leave me here," she seethed.

Crow made a show of releasing his blades and walking up to where the net met the tree trunk, then paused. "If I let you down, we'll talk?"

Reva mumbled something unintelligible, her eyes narrowing, and a harsh scowl formed on her face. "Why are you here?"

He wanted to admit that Ozma was worried about Reva but didn't want to cause a rift between them. Ozma had clearly felt disloyal when she'd found him. Instead, he pointed a finger playfully at Reva in the net. "You're as light on your feet as always, my love, and rather quick too. I didn't hear you leave your room at Glinda's which put me hours behind, yet it still took me days to catch up."

"I snuck out for a reason," she spat.

Crow shrugged as if it meant nothing, though he felt like a fire ignited in his chest. "I'm well aware that you wanted to avoid my 'tagging along.' I'm not stupid—my curse was broken too."

"Are you sure about that? It seems like you're having trouble taking a hint." The chains creaked and groaned as the net swayed.

Crow snorted. "That's nothing new, is it?"

"Far from it," Reva admitted. "Maybe if I'd been blunter before leaving Glinda's, none of this would've happened."

"It would've only endeared you to me more."

Her gaze shifted toward the sky and she let out a loud breath through her nose. "Get lost, Crow," she finally said.

He smiled and took a few steps away. Even now, she was as feisty as he remembered. "If you insist."

"I deserve to kill Locasta for what she did to me and to Thelia!" Reva shouted, her emerald eyes boring into him. "*I* deserve it! And *I* deserve to do it on my own terms."

He knew she was right. Locasta had been his burden to bear until he'd asked for Reva's help. Perhaps he should've stayed and taken Locasta's abuse so the females he loved would've never known so much pain. But then Thelia wouldn't have been born. Neither he nor Reva could've known the outcome of his trip to see the Good Witch of the West—the love that would blossom between them—but, regardless, he was the one who had brought Locasta's wrath down on Reva. Crow took a steadying breath and quickly sliced the rope surrounding the nearby tree branch. Spinning, he caught Reva in his arms, net and all. The iron burned his fingers but he found it hard to care as he clutched her tightly. It had been too long since he held her. "Reva," he breathed.

"Put me down," she growled, twisting in his arms and batting at the iron.

"Sorry." Crow set her on her backside and helped peel the net away. "Are you okay?"

"Just wonderful." She stood and blew a piece of ruffled hair from her face. "Now if you'll excuse me."

Crow swept an arm out to let her by, then promptly followed on her heels.

"That wasn't an invitation, Crow."

He laughed. "Since when have I ever needed one?"

"Crow—"

"Reva." He grabbed her hand and pulled her to a stop. She quickly yanked it out of his grip. "I understand why you're angry. I do. But Locasta came after our family because of *me*. If this is your fight, your … revenge, then it's mine too. You want to be the one to kill her? Fine. But I have my own vengeance to chase. It will benefit us both if we work together and, if I have the chance to make things right between us, all the better."

"There *is* no making things right," Reva gritted through a clenched jaw. Emotion flickered in her gaze for a brief second, then disappeared. She scanned him up and down. "You want to come? Then keep up. I won't wait. And I get to kill the bitch when we find her."

"Fair enough." They would be stronger together. Safer. He hurried after Reva as she started for the road again. "I can't fly anymore, but I'm more than capable of matching your pace."

"Can't fly?" She looked at him over her shoulder with narrowed eyes.

Crow shrugged. "I was looking for the human Dorothy and… Locasta didn't like that very much. My other form is completely useless now." Not that it had been any good the night Thelia was born.

Reva faltered. "Why didn't you get one of the Wizard's cures?"

"Oz destroyed them all before he disappeared."

"Like hell he did," Reva barked. "The only thing more important to him than his precious *medicines* is faerie fruit."

Could that be true? He'd gone to the Emerald City for a cure right after Locasta broke him, but the guards had turned him away to protect the Wizard's reputation. When he'd gone to the tavern to drown his many sorrows, the other patrons told him tales of Oz's outbursts—including one that destroyed all his potions. He'd been so disheartened at the time and the dryad had sounded so sure when she'd relayed the information. But if there was a chance the rumors were wrong—a chance they were really still in the palace....

"We have to go to the Emerald City," he said in a hoarse voice.

"Fuck no. I won't delay my vengeance."

"It will actually take us less time to cross through the Emerald City than it would to go around it," he reasoned.

Reva cast him a hard stare over her shoulder. "I may have only been back a few days, but I've heard what the capital is like now."

"If we can't survive the city unscathed, how will we hope to survive Locasta?" he asked. Then, without waiting for her to reply, added, "I need some of Oz's potions to heal my other form."

"You should have gotten them long ago."

"Reva." His voice cracked and he slammed his jaw shut. He wouldn't beg—if she insisted on heading straight to the North, he would go with her and get the cure after they killed Locasta.

She slowed her steps for a moment. "Fine. Since it's faster than going around."

A relieved breath fell from his lips. They had both already suffered so much over the years, and if there was a chance for his bird form to heal...

"Wait!" He quickly caught up to her, questions about the dark place burning inside him. "Thelia told me that her magic sent you somewhere else. What was it like?"

Reva pressed her lips into a tight line. "It doesn't matter. I'm here now."

But Crow knew that it *did* matter. It mattered very much.

CHAPTER SIX

REVA

Crow can't fly.

Reva told herself not to care about his strong, elegant bird wings being useless. Again, because of the Northern Witch… He'd asked about the dark place, and in that moment, she'd wanted to tell him, but she couldn't. She wasn't ready to speak of it to anyone, least of all him.

For now, they would need to cut through the Emerald City to gather potions to help Crow. To be honest, she didn't want to leave his bird form broken, but that didn't mean she wanted them to go together. Perhaps Glinda would have said Reva was being too harsh on him. Perhaps Thelia would have agreed. Perhaps Ozma would have said forgiveness was the answer. The old Reva would have fucked him right against the nearest tree trunk. But this wasn't then, this was now. She'd been a cursed, monstrous creature who slaughtered fae after fae, and she could forgive herself—and him—for that. But because of Crow, her daughter had been taken away from her.

Thelia could have died. There were so many times her life could have dissolved—a simple snap of the neck from Locasta was all it would have taken. In the human world, she could have met any number of unknown fates. Or worse, Langwidere could have been wearing Thelia's fucking head right now if Thelia hadn't drawn up her magic and defeated the bitch. All of this was because of Crow's scorned ex-lover—Locasta. The Northern Witch's vendetta against Crow. Reva wasn't an idiot—she knew it wasn't completely Crow's fault. But it didn't make things—or her—feel any better. Reva hadn't gotten to spend more than a few hours with her daughter.

Something green slid in front of Reva's face, interrupting her thoughts. It was round and bright. Her eyes shifted to the glistening apple. The perfect firmness. No bruises, no dents—the faerie fruit would taste divine.

Reva wanted to slap the apple out of Crow's hand and make him hurt again, make him feel the pain she'd felt while in that dark place before Ozma had come. But she was selfish in that moment, she was greedy, and she was *hungry*. So instead, she ripped the fruit from his grasp and pressed the apple in between her lips to bite into it. The sweet liquid drizzled out onto her tongue. Almost as good as sex.

"You're welcome," Crow said, fighting a smile while he watched her take another bite.

A cool breeze ruffled the ends of her hair as she side-eyed him with no reply and continued on. Reva wondered if he'd walked this same path with Thelia when her daughter had first come to Oz. She knew her silence couldn't last all of her immortal life, because she had questions.

Reva finished the apple and tossed the core along the edge of the yellow brick road. A swarm of tiny faeries flew from the foliage to finish off the core.

Taking a breath, Reva looked past the blooming trees at the clouds in the distance. "What was Thelia like?" She paused, her nails digging into her palms. "When you first met her?"

Crow didn't miss a beat, as if he'd been expecting the question. He had always known her better than anyone. "Even though the curse made it impossible to think clearly, I remember every moment I spent with her." He rubbed a hand against his jawline. "When I first met Thelia in the corn field, she wasn't frightened in the least. She was strong-willed and determined like you, a thinker like me. As a child, she already seemed fit to rule."

From the brief moments Reva had spent with Thelia, she felt he was right.

Another thing nagged at her, and she knew it would only bring about anger, but she chose to be a glutton for punishment anyway. "Why didn't you *tell* her who she was? After your curse was broken, you could have *told* her."

Crow inhaled deeply through his nostrils and shook his head. "Would it have made her life any better? Thelia was a child. Can you imagine telling a child that they killed their own mother? Young fae adjust differently, but she was raised as a human. It would have destroyed her at that age. As much as you hate it, Thelia had a home already, a life. People who loved her."

Reva curled her hands into fists, the lightning sparking off them as she slowly turned to face him. "Did you know when she went back to the human world, they thought she was mad? They poked and prodded her to try and make her better! When there was nothing wrong with her to begin with!"

Crow's eyes widened and his throat bobbed. "She—she didn't tell me about that."

"The people who raised her did it because they thought she was crazy and that it would help her." She held up a hand before he could interrupt. "And you know what Thelia told me: if she wasn't fae, the process could have either killed her or left her mind like yours was when you'd been cursed. Only, for Thelia, the damage would have been permanent."

"I only did what I thought was right for her." Crow's eyes glistened, his dark hair falling forward. "We all make mistakes."

"You more than anyone." Reva charged away from him before she spat out more than she wanted to—about wishing she hadn't met him. But that would be a lie… Thelia would never have been born. And she didn't let herself think about the good moments between them either.

He grabbed her by the elbow, turning her to face him.

"You've made mistakes too, Reva. It was *your* idea for us to hide in that house despite the number of fae living nearby who could see us. It was *your* idea not to have any guards with us for the birth. So you can't blame everything on me." He jabbed at his chest. "But you know what? I don't blame you. Because, like I said, we all make mistakes."

"Yet you brought it up." A part of her knew Crow was right, that it was her fault too. But that raging other part of her held on tighter. She'd been in that dark place for too long, and it still held onto a piece of her, more than the curse had.

"I—"

"Just stop talking," she said with a sigh, "and let's hurry so we can make it to the Emerald City sometime tomorrow."

Crow didn't say a word, only clenched his jaw and walked beside her.

Reva wondered how the Emerald City would look now. Thelia had told her what she'd seen from afar. It would be dangerous, especially if they went to the palace, but Reva was already used to that. She had her magic, and she could outrun almost anything.

They continued traveling for a long while, and she studied all the scenery they passed, trying to recall if it had changed since she'd been gone. It all seemed like a blur of greenery in her memories now.

As the light in the sky lessened, and the clouds turned gray from a storm brewing, Reva couldn't keep her mouth shut any longer. On the journey, they'd only stopped to eat and relieve themselves. Neither one had spoken another word to each other. She didn't know why it irritated her that he'd listened to her and stayed silent, but it did.

"So, how many people did you fuck while I was away?" she asked, her tone accusing.

Crow stilled, his gaze sliding to hers. "I'm not going to dignify that with a response."

She cocked her head as an influx of emotions rocketed through her. Hurt. Jealousy. Bitterness. "That many then."

Loud hooting blared in the distance, leaving Crow with his mouth hanging open, his words trapped inside. She knew that familiar sound, just as she knew the feel of her own heartbeat.

The storm clouds were blowing in faster than expected, quickly eclipsing the sky. A loud boom of thunder cracked and trembled above them.

The rumbling set the cursed pixies into a screeching frenzy. They had once belonged to her—another creation courtesy of Locasta—and helped the cursed Reva to do her merciless bidding. She remembered Whispa, her loyal friend, becoming the first of the night beasts. Her heart got stuck in her throat at remembering seeing what Whispa had become, flying Thelia away. Whispa had been with her family for years, and now Reva didn't know what had become of her.

The Emerald City was only a few hours away now, but she and Crow wouldn't make it before the darkness swallowed them whole—not even close.

One of the advantages the cursed pixies had was their keen hearing. And she knew they would recognize her scent, even if she wasn't the same wicked green creature anymore. Reva could control them back then, but she couldn't now.

She whirled to face Crow. "Shift!"

His gaze searched the tops of trees. "I can't fly. And even if I could, I wouldn't be able to carry you."

"You don't need to!" The cursed pixies were fast and they would arrive any moment. She knew just where to go and it would be much faster to carry him, while leaving the pixies with less opportunity to harm him. They were only small specks right now, but they were gaining speed. "Shift!"

In a flash of black smoke, as if his fae form had never been, Crow stood with one foot on the ground in his bird form. He ruffled his obsidian feathers, one wing hanging limply. Reva quickly scooped him up as the cursed pixies drew closer, their hoots echoing straight to her marrow.

Crow remained quiet, but his body fidgeted when she drew him to her chest. "This is as close to me as you're ever going to get again."

As the darkness set in and soft sprinkles hit her skin, Reva scurried from the yellow brick road and headed into the forest to where she'd last relieved herself. Deeper and deeper, pushing branch after branch out of the way, she searched for the shelter she'd seen earlier. Just up ahead rested a gray mound of rock with a wooden chimney and matching door. She didn't know if anyone was home—she didn't care either.

Around her and Crow, the hooting turned into vicious screeching. The cursed pixies, with their skeletal forms and elongated arms, surrounded her, swarming and swarming. Reva's thunderous magic roared through her veins, and the emerald lightning crackled onto her free palm. She flicked her left arm to the side, tossing a bolt of lightning at a beast baring its fangs, burning it to a crisp as it howled. Another pixie came, then another. But not as many as she'd thought would attack. Some appeared confused, their wings pumping in the air, their bodies unmoving, as though they didn't know if they wanted her to be their master once more or if they wanted to kill her for controlling them in the first place. Others didn't seem to care as one's claws struck the flesh of her neck and another sliced the top of her hand.

She spun the lightning so that it spread and spread, cocooning her and Crow within its depths. The cursed pixies jolted forward, bouncing off the current, too stupid to realize it would lead to their deaths. Sprinting forward, Reva dropped her magic when she reached the door to the rock mound. She turned the knob, finding it unlocked, and threw herself into the dark home before slamming the door shut with her boot. Chest heaving, she set Crow on the stone floor and a moldy scent hit her nose.

The cursed pixies screeched and raged on the opposite side of the door. Reva let a spark of lightning flicker in the center of her palm as she scanned the abandoned shelter. Whoever had once lived here must not have been around for years. Cobwebs and dust coated a wooden table without chairs. A feathered mattress with holes and a blanket was against a rocky wall. Broken cups were strewn across the dirt floor. Two logs rested in the fireplace in the back, and there seemed to be no other rooms.

Reva tossed a few sparks of her magic at the logs, flames instantly catching and rising.

The cursed pixies' cries still hadn't stopped. Rapid scratching came at the door, making her flinch. In the distance their wild howls continued, accompanied by pained screams—some of the cursed pixies must have found other victims to satisfy their hunger. A sense of guilt washed over her that this was happening to innocent fae because she'd led them here.

Crow still stood on the ground near the door, seeming to guard it. In that form, he wouldn't be able to fight off anything.

Reva pressed her hands on her hips. "You can shift back now."

In the glowing light of the fire, his brown eyes met hers, and he shook his small head. A low caw escaped his dark beak.

Her brow furrowed as she crept closer. "You never had a problem shifting back before."

With a tilt of his head, he used his beak to ruffle the feathers of his wing. She could see the misshapen areas of his fragile bones, and she almost gasped. Crow had told her that he couldn't fly, but he hadn't mentioned that it was this bad.

"The broken wings make it harder for you to change back?"

He nodded, his wing dragging on the floor.

"Come on then. Rest and shift in the morning." She sighed. No need to argue with him in this condition. "We're getting up early so we can make it to the capital tomorrow."

Reva carried him to the mattress and set him on top of it. She then threw one of the blankets on the floor, and made a nest out of the material before placing him there. He closed his eyes as she backed away.

Removing her boots, Reva lay back on the lumpy mattress. As the rain started to pour, the scratching faded. But the cursed pixies would be out there until dawn, prowling around for prey.

She knew this because she'd once been the worst of them—
a predator.

CHAPTER SEVEN

CROW

When the young Thelia left the Land of Oz, everyone had gone their separate ways. Lion holed himself up in the house the Wizard had gifted him, drinking himself into stupors and fighting whatever miscreant gave the slightest offense. Crow knew through observation that Lion was waiting for a worthy cause to swear his new-found courage to—if only Langwidere hadn't been the first one to make him an offer. Tin's decision to become one of Oz's personal guards had made less sense. The Tin Woodsman was skilled with an axe, but it hadn't been clear if he would be able to kill in defense of the Wizard, given he finally had a heart. Then his curse had returned. A terrifying thing, considering Crow's had been cured at the same time.

Crow, on the other hand, had only stayed in the Emerald City long enough to read every book there was on curses. Anything that could give him answers about Reva—his long-gone love. There was no bringing her back from the dead, but he'd wanted to know what happened for the sake of closure. The only useful bit of information he'd found was the existence of a red stone belonging to the Gnome King that could prevent a curse. A wonderful thing to know if he could get his hands on it for the future, but it hadn't answered his questions about Reva.

So, turning his attention away from the past, he'd traveled to the North and began his journey to find the human Dorothy Gale. It was a dreadful trip. Each step toward his former home felt heavier than the last, but it would be worth it if he found the girl his daughter had been swapped with.

In all the years between, he'd been to the capital only a handful of times. Each visit had been a little worse than the one before. Homes ransacked. Fae murdered. Cursed pixies haunting the night.

But now… Crow barely recognized the once-illustrious city.

More buildings were reduced to skeletons than were whole. Walls crumbling. Windows smashed. Roofs caving in. The yellow brick road gave way to emerald streets that had once glimmered in the sun. Now they were cracked, dented, and covered in so much filth that one would never know they were green. Death lingered in the air, decomposing fae with a hint of excrement. The buzz of danger rubbed against Crow's body.

"It's worse than I remember," he whispered to Reva.

She glared at him with wide, shocked eyes. "Worse than you remember?" she repeated in a strained voice. "The palace is little more than a pile of gemstone!"

Crow's gaze drifted to the iconic palace—missing peaks with holes in the walls large enough to see from this distance. The darkest black crept across the emerald stone like tainted veins. Whatever magic had once made it shine throughout the day and night had vanished, leaving it a dull, dingy green.

"Quit exaggerating. It's much bigger than a gemstone. However, it was whole the last time I was here—so, yes, worse." The palace had only been a little duller than before, thieves only struck at night, and the homes were in disrepair—not destroyed. But he hadn't been back in over two years.

Reva shook her head in disbelief. "I don't understand. I knew it would be bad here, but this? How did it happen?"

"As you know, Oz left—"

"Periodically, to make sure Ozma remained hidden in Loland, then he sent her to the dark place," Reva spat, eyes darkening. "And now he's abandoned the city all together."

"Apparently, yes." He cleared his throat as they navigated the muck-smeared streets. "The situation wasn't perfect before he left the city, however. The fae were growing tired of the Wizard ignoring them while he indulged his faerie fruit addiction. Work had been scarce and food low after a drought, so I believe a rebellion had been stirring. Which is likely why he'd suddenly thought to send Lion after Glinda. It would've left him virtually unopposed if he'd managed to take out all the territory leaders."

"It seems to have worked out quite well for him," Reva said in a low, sarcastic growl. "Ozma and I still don't know how he was able to get the silver slippers, though."

"A very good question," he agreed. "Maybe he's dead."

"He'd better not be dead—Ozma deserves the chance to show him *exactly* who he hid away all those years by ending his life with her own hands!" Reva scowled. "She never got to meet her father, Pastoria, and never will because of the Wizard."

Pastoria was the king before the Wizard murdered him and wasn't the brightest of fae. Crow wasn't sure if Ozma was capable of revenge. When she approached him outside the brothel, she'd seemed too sweet for such a bloody task, but then again, he didn't know her like Reva did.

After a few more streets, his stomach growled. He shielded his eyes and glared at the sky, trying to remember how long ago they'd eaten. The cursed pixies had chased them the night before, then he'd slept for hours in the nest Reva made until he woke to find her tossing and turning from a nightmare. And all through Reva's morning meal, he was still stuck in his bird form. She had offered to share the food, but his beak had healed from its break badly, just like the rest of him. While it looked fine, opening it wide enough to eat was too painful. They'd munched on fruit while they walked mid-morning, after he regained enough energy to transform back into a male, but he was more than ready for something more substantial.

"It's nearly midday," he said. "Would you like to find something to eat? I'm sure we could find a couple gremlins to skewer, or a redcap if you want something extra bloody."

"You're disgusting." Her nose wrinkled upward.

"This is the Emerald City. Fae eat fae because there's little else to go around."

"I'd rather starve."

Crow chuckled. "I was jesting." *Partially.* They did resort to eating each other on occasion, though he would also prefer starvation. "Are you absolutely sure there's a cure for my other form inside the palace?"

"When did I say I was sure? I said Oz would never destroy his potions." Her eyes slid over his body. "But if there's a way to fix your broken bird form, it will be somewhere in Oz's collection."

Crow swallowed hard. Reva appeared to hate him, but she'd still come with him for the *chance* of a cure. The question now was whether or not someone had ransacked the Wizard's private rooms. Odds might not be in their favor, but he didn't want to tell Reva that when she wasn't thrilled about coming into the Emerald City. Besides, she had to know that already.

"Forget about eating," Reva announced. "We're going straight for the potions and getting the fuck out of here."

A scream came from somewhere in the distance and Crow suppressed a shudder. He was in no mood for a fight, preferring this to be a stealth mission instead. Get in, get the cure, get out. Groups of fae lingered in the streets with swords and bows and spears. Their suspicious gazes followed Crow and Reva everywhere they went.

A feather-light touch brushed across Crow's side, and he leapt away from it, straight into Reva. A male sprite snickered, his spindly fingers wrapping around the ropes hanging from Crow's neck. "Spare some rope?" he asked, flashing pointed black teeth without a whiff of shame.

"The fuck?" Reva hissed.

"No, actually." Crow attempted to pry his clothing from the would-be thief's death grip.

"Just a little?" he whined. "It doesn't take much to hang a

nixie."

Crow let his blades drop. The sprite's eyes darted down to the gleaming metal and his smile froze. A nervous chuckle escaped his throat before he released the ropes and fled. "It could've been worse," Crow mused to Reva once the thief was out of sight.

"Let's not find out."

After that, they began walking a little faster and were soon at the perimeter of the palace. Groups of scarred, battle-ready fae gathered around small blazing fires, despite the sun shining brightly overhead. The kindling appeared to be broken planks from homes with odds and ends tossed in for good measure. A child's toy frog and a wooden portrait frame smoldered in a heap of embers, and flames still licked up the side of a broken mantel clock in another. There were mounds of dirty, blood-stained clothes, both adult and child, with an even larger pile of footwear nearby. Wooden crates formed a perimeter between them and the hardened fae and, past them, another row of crates ran in front of haggard-looking palace guards covered in grime.

"What's all this?" Reva whispered to Crow.

Crow nodded toward a painted sign that read *Onyx City*. It was appropriately named, visually and metaphorically. The heart of Oz was rotten—it was no wonder the rest of the territories followed. Crow's gaze traveled up the palace walls just a few yards away. The black lines seemed to pulse as if the building had a heartbeat. "They seem to have created their own headquarters," he said quietly.

"Not from around here, are you?" a male called from the nearest fire. The hobgoblin was larger than most at nearly five feet with black burn scars covering the left side of his face and neck. He wore layers and layers of clothing as if he were afraid someone would steal them otherwise. Given the piles of clothes, maybe that wasn't such a longshot. "There's no getting into the palace. Oz abandoned us, but Pastoria's magic is still strong as ever. Unless you can bribe a guard into letting you loot the place, no one goes in."

"And no one comes out," another fae, this one a leprechaun with wooden teeth, added dramatically. "We're the authority here now, if you want to petition us. 'Course you'll need vouchers for food and shoes and the like."

Crow and Reva meant no harm within the palace, but taking a potion could be considered thieving. The magic barrier could very well bar them entry unless there was a sanctioned escort. The guards looked utterly miserable at their posts, not that Crow could blame them. Who did they serve now that Oz was gone? Who paid their wages? Were taxes even making it to the palace? It was a miracle they hadn't abandoned their positions and let Pastoria's magic do their jobs for them.

"Not today," Reva told the leprechaun. Then she grabbed the ropes around Crow's neck and practically dragged him away from the surly fae.

"What's the matter?" Crow asked when they were out of earshot. Then, when his back hit the cool wall of a former eatery, the memory surfaced of her holding his bird form near her breast until they were safely inside the stone home. It wasn't like this the night before. Then it had been a matter of life and death, but now it felt more intimate. He lifted his brows suggestively. "Or could you not keep your hands off me another moment? Like last night."

"When I saved your life from the cursed pixies?" Reva *tsked* and quickly yanked her hand back from where it still gripped the rope near his neck. "You need to get us inside."

Crow chuckled without meaning to. "I'm open to ideas, my love."

"You're *Crow*. The fae who helped the savior of Oz kill … well, *me*. Are you going to pretend you don't have some level of notoriety? That there isn't a single guard who would escort us inside and take us exactly where we need to go?"

Crow opened and shut his mouth. She was right, of course, but he loathed using his status for favors. It always felt to him as if he hadn't done much of anything to help young Thelia. Sure, he'd protected her along the yellow brick road and rushed to save her from… He glanced at Reva and chewed his bottom lip. But that was something anyone would do, especially a father, even if he hadn't realized it until after the fact. There were exceptions to not asking for help, though, and he needed his bird form fixed.

"Won't you be jealous, seeing them fawn all over me?" he asked.

"I see you're starting to act like your old self again. Please don't." Reva rolled her eyes, groaning, and marched back to the palace.

He was feeling like his old self too. Reva brought that out in him, and he most certainly *would*. Too many days had been wasted focusing on earning Reva's forgiveness instead of saving Oz. Especially when one would lead to the other.

The fae of Onyx City all watched them return with wary expressions until Reva leapt effortlessly over a crate. The self-imposed rulers descended then—golems, bodachs, hags, and a dozen other species. Crow easily hopped over the barrier and released his blades.

"I don't need you to save me," Reva shouted over the sudden shriek of enemies.

Crow gave her a quick smirk before slicing out at a ghoul with his blades. Ruby blood sprayed from the wound on the fae's chest. A warm mist sprinkled Crow's face. "Maybe I want you to save me."

"You're assuming I'd bother," she yelled as lightning crackled along her fingertips.

A bright flash of green slammed into the hoard, knocking them backward. A slight prickle of Reva's energy struck him—a small jolt she must've given him on purpose. She had too much control for it to be an accident. Crow shot her a surprised look before throwing his head back with a laugh.

"Move before they get up," Reva demanded.

Crow followed her over the second barrier, where the elves on either side of the palace gates lowered into a fighting stance. "Good day," Crow called before they approached. "Lovely weather we're having."

They didn't react, their faces expressionless.

Crow sighed inwardly. This wouldn't work if they'd become someone's puppet—doubly so if there was someone within, ruling Oz quietly. "Any chance we could get inside? As a personal favor."

The two elves exchanged a quick glance and recognition lit their faces. "Crow?" the white-haired one asked. "You're … Crow, aren't you?"

"At your service," he answered with a flourishing bow.

The guards shifted nervously before the taller one spoke. "The Wizard isn't available for visitors."

"Oh, please. Who do you think you're kidding?" Reva growled. "I spent the last decade in another world and even *I* know he ran off."

At the mention of the dark place, Crow tilted his head to study her, to glean even the smallest hint of what it had been like there. But Reva gave no outward clue about what she'd lived through.

"Who are you?" the second guard asked.

"She's helping me," Crow answered before Reva could reveal her identity. Cursed or not, she had devastated countless families during her time as the Wicked Witch of the West. She needed to defeat Locasta before anyone discovered who she was. "We've just come from ending Langwidere's reign and are in need of a healing potion."

He felt Reva's angry stare on the back of his head, though he wasn't sure if it was because he hid her name from them or because he took credit for Thelia's kill. But the new victory might convince them that he was trying to help Oz yet again. They could clear up the misunderstanding later.

"Langwidere is dead?" the one with white hair asked, violet eyes bright with excitement. "The South is free?" When Crow nodded, the guard sheathed his sword. "I… I can send my family home," he whispered to his friend. "Our oaths prevent desertion, but our families can leave. It has to be safer for them in the South than it is here if Langwidere isn't there to steal their heads."

Then, to Crow, "What of Glinda? Have you seen her?"

Crow hesitated. The Southern fae adored Glinda and telling the guard that she was dead wouldn't earn them any favors. Yet, he couldn't lie. "Glinda fell to Langwidere," he whispered with sincere compassion.

Shocked silence followed before the taller male cleared his throat. "You just need a potion?"

"That's all," Crow assured him.

He nodded. "Take them to Oz's chambers. I'll keep watch here."

"This way," the white-haired fae beckoned eagerly. "I'm Avo, by the way."

"Nice to meet you, Avo," Crow said with a smile. Then he winked over his shoulder at Reva, receiving an eyeroll in return.

Inside, debris covered the once-illustrious courtyard. Large chunks of emerald were pushed along the palace walls in an attempt to keep the area clean, but small pebbles and powdered gemstone were ground into the bricks. The high arched windows were either smashed, revealing makeshift curtains hung inside, or webbed with cracks. Each stair leading up to the crooked main doors shifted beneath their feet, and the deep, earthy scent of the fires gave way to that of mold and decaying sea life.

Avo led the way through the deathly-quiet palace and began up a long, winding staircase. Patches of walls were ten shades darker where portraits had hung. The throw rugs, once vivid and plush, were halfway gone from what looked to be rabid wolves chewing on them. Vases appeared to have imploded where they sat, a shower of glass flowing out around their intact bases. Worn chairs were scattered in random places—in hallways and corners and stacked on top of each other. Overhead, broken chandeliers swayed on thinning ropes.

"There's a bit of a phouka infestation," Avo informed them as they climbed higher and higher. "But most of the guards broke their oaths and took off shortly after Oz left. We tried to open the palace to the citizens of the Emerald City at first, but none could make it through Pastoria's barrier."

"That says a lot," Crow mused.

"It does," Avo agreed, looking back at Crow and Reva every few steps. "The Oz you helped create was the true golden age for us. You aided Dorothy when she saved our world and rid us of the Wicked Witch."

Crow winced, but said nothing, though he desperately wanted to defend Reva. He knew she was most likely seething behind him.

"Everyone talks about how kind you are, both before the Wizard broke your curse and after. Always willing to help, they say. And you're the smartest fae they've met. I heard you studied every curse in detail."

"It's better to know how to break a curse before it's cast," he said casually. There was no need to explain that he was hoping to understand exactly what Thelia had done to defeat Reva. There was also his own curse—the Curse of Unknowing—that he wanted to avoid ever experiencing again. At least that particular research had ended with him learning about an object from the Gnome King that could potentially deflect it. He just didn't have it in his hand.

"And avoid getting cursed again, I'm sure," Avo continued. "You were the only fae of the Golden Four not to relapse or let it destroy you. If you ask me, you're the real hero, besides Dorothy. You have brains, heart, *and* courage."

"Brains, heart, and courage, my ass," Reva mumbled angrily under her breath.

Crow twisted around to smirk. "It was teamwork," he told Avo, but patted his chest over his heart and pointed at Reva. "Speaking of Lion, he's dead too. And Tin's broken his curse for good this time. He helped us defeat Langwidere and Lion."

He purposely didn't mention Thelia's return, though he knew the rumors were already circulating. That was how he'd learned she'd been with Tin.

"It's really true?" Avo asked desperately. "Langwidere and Lion are dead? And the assassin isn't heartless anymore?"

"It's true," Crow promised.

Tears glistened in Avo's eyes. "You're going to save us again."

It wasn't a question, which made Crow uncomfortable. That was too much pressure to work under when he simply wanted to focus on avenging his family for the moment.

"Here it is," Avo said, pointing at a bright green door with a darker emerald stripe down its center. Peeling gold filigree framed it from the top of the wall to the bottom. "Oz's private chambers."

"Thank you." Crow gently squeezed Avo's shoulder and strode into the room.

A large glass case of potions stood directly across from him, beckoning him closer. He hurried to it and scanned the fading labels with hope building in his chest. There was an assortment of differently-shaped vials in a variety of colors. Some had pointed tops, others completely round, and a few curved designs. There were cures that bubbled, potions that swirled as if being stirred, and liquid that glimmered in the faint light of the room. A row of tin boxes sat on the bottom shelf with glass tops, showing pellets and tablets to be ingested.

"Try that one," Reva said, stepping up beside him. "It says *mending*."

Crow plucked up the blue vial from Oz's personal collection. It could mean mending bones or mending literally anything else, especially with Oz being mortal. On occasion, he was known to call things by different names than the fae.

"Or this one." Reva lifted a brown vial reading *healing*.

"What do you think the difference is?" Crow asked, fingers nervously twitching. The realization that this could be dangerous slowly crept in. What if the potions crippled him further? Or, without knowing the proper dosage, killed him?

"This one says *bones*." Reva handed him a third bottle, this one clear with a tiny pebble resting at the bottom of the liquid.

Crow laughed without humor. "If you wanted to mutilate my body, there are easier ways to go about it."

"I'll keep that in mind if these don't do the trick."

Crow gently tucked the vials into his pack. "I'll have a healer look at them first."

"You say that like we have time," she said with an edge of annoyance.

"You say *that* like we have time to deal with my growing an extra limb."

"Your ability to shift isn't exactly useful," she snapped. "If it were, Locasta would've died the night she broke into our home."

Crow blanched. She wasn't wrong, but it stung more than her zap of lightning had. If he'd been stronger that night—had better magic—all their lives would've been different, so how could he be angry over the outburst? There wasn't a day that he didn't blame himself. "I'm sorry, Reva," he said quietly so Avo wouldn't hear her name. Most knew her as the Wicked Witch of the West, and even though no one had spoken her name after the curse, most still remembered it.

Some fleeting emotion appeared on her face. Regret? She opened her mouth to reply when a soft scratching sounded from inside the wardrobe beside the medicine cabinet.

"Shit," Avo called. "Hurry. That's the phouka!"

CHAPTER EIGHT

REVA

What the fuck were phouka doing inside the palace? There shouldn't be any of those blasted pests in the Emerald City—*Onyx City*—at all or anywhere near here. They belonged at the edge of the South near the Great Sandy Waste where they'd been banished.

Even though she missed Ozma's presence tremendously, Reva was relieved her friend wasn't here to try and combat these heinous beasts without her magic. Running or climbing away from them wouldn't be enough because they could fly. Nothing in the dark place had wings.

"Hurry!" Avo called as he whirled around and sprinted out of the Wizard's old room.

Reva clasped Crow by the elbow and tugged him out of the area.

Crow shot forward, and she followed him down the hallway, catching up with Avo.

"The phouka always rouse first before the night beasts come." Avo held his chest, breathing heavily. "We try to keep them out, but the sneaky bastards always find their way back in."

A buzzing picked up, joining the sound of clawing against the walls. Just as Reva turned, a swarm of ravenous creatures, with dark bloodred wings, blinding white eyes, large pointed ears, and brown fur covering their small bodies, barreled their way. Long tails curled behind them. Crow slammed the door, but she knew it wouldn't be enough to stop them.

Reva stood, prepared to destroy them with a single spark once they tore open the door, but her magic didn't ignite. She tried it again, waiting in vain for the thunder to rise. Lips parted, she stood stunned, unable to move, until she was lifted from the floor by Crow's strong arms.

"Why aren't you running?" Crow shouted as he set her on the floor. She didn't hesitate as she sprinted down the spiral staircase, its green gemstones flickering. The sound of the door being thrown against the wall echoed from above them.

As they reached the bottom, Avo swung open the front entrance and hurried behind the door. The swarm of phouka dodged down the staircase, screaming a high, distorted sound. Crow swiped at the air, blades extended. A creature with gnashing teeth came for him, and its blood sprayed as he ripped it to shreds with his blades. Reva rushed in his direction, knocking him to his back as the swarm flew over them at a quickening pace.

Reva waited to be torn to pieces. She continued to hover over Crow while trying to summon the lightning within her to life.

The sounds stopped. Everything stopped. The world around her had grown silent, just as her thoughts had. Magic surged within her before flickering out. The last ten years without magic had made her feel less than whole, and she didn't want to feel that again.

A loud bang came from behind her, and Reva turned her head over her shoulder to find Avo standing in front of the door that he'd slammed shut. Not a single phouka in sight.

"You saved my life," Crow said, and she knew he would have a smirk on his face.

She hurried to push her body away from his and stood, brushing off her jacket. "You saved mine first. The debt has been paid." If he hadn't picked her up, she would have still been standing at the door, frozen, attempting to use her magic.

Reva marched up to Avo. "Why is my magic not working? Where are the phouka headed?"

"They like to pick fights with the night beasts as soon as the sun sets. Langwidere unbanished them from the Great Sandy Waste to try and make this territory hers." His gaze flicked to her hands. "As for your magic, I can't say when it will come back. The Wizard's spells make it so that no one can do harm with their magic while inside the palace, but it's become unreliable lately with him gone. It will return at some point after you leave, but it won't be immediate."

Avo hadn't told them that earlier. She was about to use both her hands to do harm to his throat. Crow pulled her back before she could do it.

Unsheathing his sword, Avo put his opposite hand on the door handle. "I suggest going to Vronah's Tavern across the brick road, a few buildings down. You will still easily have access, Crow, but you will have to pull your companion through. The old magic there from Queen Lurline keeps it safe. She placed it there during the Wicked Witch's reign as a place to keep fae safe if needed, and it still holds to this day. If only all of the Emerald City could have had that magic… But as you see, the Land of Oz needs help. I would hurry before dark though."

Queen Lurline had become a victim to Langwidere sometime while Reva was the Wicked Witch. Reva was surprised Lurline's magic was still active, but at one point she had been a strong and powerful faerie. Lurline was Ozma's mother, but due to whatever spell Mombi or the Wizard cast, no one knew that particular truth.

The phouka belonged to Langwidere. That meant they were now Thelia's. Once Reva defeated Locasta. Together, she and Thelia could help the Emerald City. Reva could try and break the curse of the night beasts while Thelia could call the phouka back to the Great Sandy Waste. If they didn't, the destruction would only continue, and she wouldn't allow that.

Outside, Reva couldn't see or hear the phouka. After Avo left them at the gates to gather with the other guards, Reva and Crow crossed over the Onyx City barriers and stepped onto the path.

As they made their way through the city, they passed a tailor shop where she used to have her dark clothing made, but it sat empty. Then a pastry wagon where Crow had once taken her as a surprise, now rested abandoned, wheels missing, paint faded. Finally, they approached Vronah's Tavern. The walls of the magical barrier glistened bright white, like specks of glitter. She wondered if Queen Lurline's magic would truly allow them entrance, but Crow didn't seem to share her concern.

Crow easily passed through the barrier, as though it already knew him. He held out his hand, and Reva hesitated for a moment before pressing her palm against the warmth of his so she could go inside. The rules of this barrier were unfamiliar to her, but she still thought that her tainted past could have prevented her passage. However, it didn't.

Her gaze met his light brown eyes, and a familiarity washed over her. She hurried and dropped his hand, moving toward the tavern. It was a large turquoise building covered in diagonal yellow stripes. Its black roof flickered with tiny white specks across the top like a night sky. Thick vines, with dark purple flowers blooming, covered the bottom portion.

Crow slipped past her, not saying a word as he opened the darkened glass door. He continued to hold it for her until she walked inside. She didn't know what she'd expected the interior of the tavern to look like. Perhaps for the place to be deserted. But it wasn't. A few fae lingered at rectangular tables, peppermint and vanilla filling the air. The fae laughed, drank, and kissed while low music from stringed instruments played. She wondered if these fae ever left the building or if this was just their way of life—to remain hidden.

It seemed like madness that fae had chosen to linger in the capital, regardless of this sanctuary. But for them, she supposed, the Emerald City was their home—one that would become more dangerous as the night descended.

Reva stared at a long counter filled with pies, vegetable stew, and mugs brimming with ale. From the magic she felt swirling around her, she knew food could easily be prepared and beverages served in a never-ending supply. Behind the counter, two female dryads gossiped to each other, their shoulders and breasts covered in tree bark. Their hair flowed a grassy green with twigs and white flowers entwined.

One's flaming orange irises flicked to Crow and her whole face lit up. "You're here! We were beginning to wonder if we'd see you again."

The other dryad bit her lip and smiled. "You've returned to save us again?"

Something ugly pulsed through Reva's veins and none of it was her magic.

"Sauli! Milla! I've missed seeing your faces." Crow sauntered forward and winked at the dryads, scooping up a cup of ale. "The South and West have been reclaimed, and Langwidere and Lion are dead. My companion and I hope to liberate the rest of Oz next." He handed Reva the mug, shooting her a wink as well.

Reva rolled her gaze to the silver ceiling where yellow bubbles floated along the top. Taking a sip of the ale, then downing the rest, she walked away from the conversation and sat at a table in the corner with no other occupants nearby. Above her hung a portrait of a young Oz. His dark hair was swept behind his mortal ears and he wore a pathetic maroon suit from his world. A red, bloody mark had been drawn across his throat. She wanted to slash his real flesh herself.

"They gave us room 22 upstairs," Crow said, interrupting her thoughts. He placed a steaming bowl of stew in front of her along with the key.

Carrots and potatoes slowly spun within the liquid as she stared at it. "That's fine." She sighed, glancing over his shoulder at the dryads who were still batting their eyelashes at Crow's turned back. "Take the potions now."

Reva stuck the key into her pants pocket while Crow took out the three vials.

"Maybe I should drink them one at a time and give it a few

hours."

"Just take them, Crow." Her nails rapped impatiently on the table.

He chewed his bottom lip as he set the vials on the table between them. "I might have to be in my other form for them to work."

"Fucking drink them already." In all honesty, Reva didn't want to have to see his other broken form again. The thought made her stomach sink.

Crow grimaced but drank each one until they were empty.

"Do you feel any different?"

"Patience, my love." He flexed his hands as if testing them. "Do you know how many concoctions Oz made trying to become immortal? Who knows? Maybe he is now."

The possibility that Oz would never die unnerved her. "That wasn't my question."

"Nothing feels different yet."

Several worn books were stacked atop the table beside them. Crow reached across, plucked up the top tome, and cracked it open. She furrowed her brow as she watched his eyes shift back and forth across each line. Always reading. Even before his curse.

The night before, he hadn't known she'd woken in the morning before he had. He hadn't known that she'd had nightmares of the dark place, but not only that... She'd had a dream of him in his male form, touching her, tasting her. It had jolted her in a nostalgic way and caused her to have to face the other direction, sleepless. And he didn't need to know either.

Unable to study him anymore, she stood with her stew and walked to the opposite side of the room, past a table of raven-maids, their faces and arms decorated in feathers, their drunken singing followed by high-pitched laughter.

She continued to the back of the room where a bookshelf painted to look like tree bark took up the entire area. Reva started reading the titles as she ate her stew, the spices purely delectable—she didn't realize how much she'd missed their rich taste while trapped in the dark place. As for reading, it wasn't something she enjoyed. It had always been something she had to do. An endless chore. She could never enjoy stories, only ones that involved history.

"You look like you could use a bit of relief for the night," a deep male voice rasped.

She turned toward a tall fae male, not unattractive. But she preferred darker hair. His auburn locks were braided along the sides of his face and the rest flowed behind his back. Reva was about to turn around and walk away when she thought about the female dryads behind the counter. Crow had never answered her question from the day before. How many legs had he spread apart while she'd been away? Had he been inside one—or both—of the dryads?

Her fists tightened, her magic still gone. Reva wanted to forget, wanted to relieve herself. She set her bowl down on the shelf and fished out the key from her pocket. "My room?"

"She's mine," Crow rumbled beside her before the male could issue a response.

The auburn-haired male looked as though he was going to tell the new guest to fuck off, until his eyes widened in recognition. "Crow. You're back."

Crow rubbed his knuckles as though he wanted to extend those hidden blades of his. "For the night."

The male cast a glance between Crow and Reva, then cleared his throat. "Hope to see you soon." He turned and walked to the counter where the two dryads were now focused on the auburn-haired fae.

Reva clenched her jaw, chest heaving, and turned toward the sparkling emerald staircase in the corner. She left Crow standing there and marched up the steps. Only he didn't remain. His booted feet thumped against the planks, a minimal distance behind her.

At the top, the hall branched off in several directions. Lanterns lit up the walls with light pink flames. In between each lantern hung a letter—*N. E. S. W.*—representing the first letter of the different territories.

After she found door 22 in the Eastern wing, Reva pushed the key in and unlocked it with a soft click. She opened the entrance and stepped inside. Before she could shut the door, Crow's hand closed around the edge of the wood, preventing it from latching. She should have known he wouldn't simply sleep out in the hallway like he had at Glinda's. She could hear the frustration in his rasping breaths.

Reva stepped back, allowing him access into the room, then slammed the door and backed him up against a striped wall. "I can fuck whomever I choose."

Crow inhaled sharply and scowled. "You would've regretted it."

"And you don't think I'd regret fucking you?" she asked, incredulous.

"Not when I know what you don't like." He leaned forward and whispered near her ear, his warm breath caressing her neck. "What you *do* like."

Reva couldn't stop her traitorous body from heating at the words and reacting to his nearness. But then all she could see was Thelia being ripped away, the victims she'd killed in her monstrous form, and being alone in that dark place.

She leaned forward, close, closer, pressing her lips right beside his ear, stroking the curved point with her tongue. "And I know *exactly* what you like. My hand pressed in the folds of your ass, my tongue at the head of your cock. After that, you inside me, while I lick and nip at the spot right behind your ear." Gliding a finger gently down to the area, she pushed his dark hair out of the way. "Me on top of you, taking control, then you behind me to finish." As she drew even nearer, her body flushed with his, she could feel him hardening against her stomach. She smiled bitterly. "But alas, it's not happening."

Whirling around, she sauntered to the edge of the bed and sank down, realizing she'd not only done a disservice to him, but to herself as well. She refused to let it show.

Crow remained against the wall, chest heaving.

"We need to go to the Gnome King before we continue

north," Crow finally said.

"Why?" She didn't like how he so easily changed the topic when her body still felt on edge. "And now you want to suddenly take a second detour? You failed to mention this earlier. No."

"He has a red stone that can prevent Locasta from changing us into something else. I tried to find it several times before and couldn't. So, as of now, it's only hearsay but would be worth the risk. She'll be too dangerous for us without it."

Reva understood what he was saying but all she heard was Locasta, Locasta, Locasta. Even hearing the bitch's name from his lips angered her. "Why don't you just go back to being Locasta's whore?" And that was the first time she'd truly regretted something she'd said to him thus far. Because she remembered the stories he'd told her of how the Northern Witch had treated him.

Pushing off from the wall, he moved toward her, deadly silent. He pressed his fists on the mattress on either side of her legs, his nose almost touching hers. "You want to know who I've fucked for the last twenty-one years? No one. There's only ever been you—my *wife*—on my mind. So stop treating me unfairly. Even if we both think I deserve it." His eyes glistened with anger as they burned into hers.

Reva was at a complete loss for words. She'd assumed, with him thinking she was dead, that he would have moved on. Even after everything *she'd* done to him, to Thelia, to the Land of Oz, he still hadn't touched another. *Wife.* She'd married him. Loved him. But now she wanted to pretend it had never happened, not truly because of what he had done but what *she'd* done.

Her words were frozen in her throat as he backed away and turned for the door. He was going to leave her here. Alone. And it wasn't something she really wanted. Not again.

"Wait! Don't go!"

Clenching his teeth, Crow glanced over his shoulder. "I'm only going downstairs to get you an apple." He opened the door and softly shut it, despite the anger still rippling off him.

Outside her window, the sounds of the night beasts began to

rouse, growing louder and louder, but not any louder than her thoughts.

Reva had been awful to Crow and he was still going downstairs to get her a damn apple. Hot tears ran down her cheeks, and she remembered why she'd chosen to stay angry. Because this, this emotion, this *caring* hurt more than anything.

She leapt from the bed and threw the curtains closed, attempting to shut out the sounds from the night beasts as well as her thoughts.

CHAPTER NINE

CROW

The woven chair rocked unevenly when Crow plopped himself into it. His elbows went directly to the glossy wood bar top, and he hung his head in his hands. Reva's anger was understandable but to pretend they weren't married? It was a secret to everyone except them and Whispa, but that didn't mean it wasn't true.

"Rough journey?" Milla, one of the dryads, asked. Her deep brown skin was covered in pieces of mossy tree bark and green leaves were nestled in her carefully bound hair. Her friend, Sauli, from earlier was gone now, as were most of the other customers.

"You could say that."

Reva had taunted him so cruelly … then asked him not to go. Had she asked only because she'd been full of lust? The way he'd leaned in, close enough to kiss her, was so reminiscent of their first time sleeping together. She'd had a lash in her eye back then and he was trying to help get it out. Instead, the sexual tension snapped, and it had only taken seconds for their clothes to hit the floor. They'd fucked in front of the fireplace in her palace for hours. But tonight, Reva had tried to take a *different* male to their room. Crow loved her … he didn't want that to be how things were between them.

Crow lifted his head, ignoring the pain in his chest, and forced a smile so the dryad wouldn't pry into his current problems as any bar keep might. "It's good to see you again, Milla."

Milla's large eyes gleamed as she set a large, foaming mug down in front of him. "I wasn't sure you would remember me. It's been how long? Seven years? Eight?"

"Something like that," he agreed, regretting that he hadn't stopped in on his last visit to the city. The mead drew his attention with beads of condensation rolling down the glass. He shouldn't—clouding his mind was at the very bottom of his list—but his muscles were so tense. Perhaps just one drink to relax himself…

"It sounds like you've been busy, though. Ridding us of Langwidere and now you're heading north to face Locasta. The Land of Oz will never be able to repay you."

"The room and drink will suffice." Crow wiped the foam from his mouth and stared into his now-empty mug. Milla set another in front of him without missing a beat. "Besides, there are no guarantees that Locasta won't kill us instead."

Milla shook her head. "Don't underestimate yourself, Crow. You helped Dorothy all those years ago and now—"

"Now," Crow interrupted, "I have to find the Gnome King and convince him to give me something extremely precious and irreplaceable. What are the odds he'll be feeling generous?"

"Slim to none," Milla said stoically.

Another full mug found its way into Crow's hands. "I tried getting it from him a couple times. Without asking for it, obviously. Stealing it was much easier—or so I thought. It turns out that the Gnome King excels in setting traps."

The dryad winced. "I've lost a few friends to their nets. If the gnomes don't eat their catch, they use them to mine stone … then eat them later."

Crow finished his third mug of mead in a large gulp and sighed. His mind was a little fuzzy around the edges and he still had to figure out how to get out of the tavern without Reva following. There was no way he was taking her to the Gnome King's doorstep. He wasn't even sure why he'd mentioned it to her. "I need to go get some sleep," he mumbled. "Any chance you have an apple before I head back upstairs?"

"We do." Milla studied him for a moment. "You still look a bit wound up though. Would you like me to cut the apple up and sprinkle a sleep aid on it? It's completely harmless, but will give you a few hours rest, at least."

Crow opened his mouth to reject the offer, but then an idea struck. An awful, horrible idea that he knew he had no right entertaining. "That would actually be wonderful. Thank you, Milla."

By the time Crow returned to room 22, Reva was asleep on the far edge of the mattress. He set her sliced apple on the bedside table, the bruised pieces purposely missing. Not that he should care whether it was up to her standards, but that could've been due to the three large mugs of mead he'd downed as if they were nothing.

The drinks were, admittedly, a horrible decision. He felt no better about the fight with Reva, nor did it alleviate any of his guilt about the past. There was also the fact that he had to leave this sanctuary and find the Gnome King *without* Reva. The king had always been deviant—enslaving lesser fae in his mines, torturing his own subjects, raiding villages for gold, gems, and females—but ever since his queen was cut down by marauders, he'd killed any female who dared approach him. Locasta could simply curse them both again without the Gnome King's stone, though, so it was necessary for their victory. Crow worried about what he might need to trade the tyrant to get him to lend them the stone, but if it helped the Land of Oz and assured Reva her revenge, it was worth the price.

Crow eased himself onto the empty side of the bed, tucked an arm beneath his cheek, and watched Reva sleep. He wanted to reach out and stroke her cheek. Press his lips to hers. To *feel* her again. He wouldn't—not if she didn't invite him to—but that didn't keep his cock from stiffening.

Fucking mead. It had gone straight to his head. He knew he should still be frustrated with Reva.

"Did it work?" Reva mumbled without opening her eyes.

Crow jerked at the sound of her voice. Had she been awake the entire time? "Did what work?" he asked softly.

Her eyes cracked open, the slight glaze telling him she *had* been asleep. Or … Crow squinted. They were slightly puffy. Had she been crying?

"The potions," she clarified before he could question it further.

Crow rolled to his back to stare at the ceiling. "There's only one way to find out."

"Shift then," she said.

"Will you hold me close all night if I'm still broken? You know, to ease my disappointment." *Damn.* Definitely too much mead.

Reva groaned. "Perhaps I'll throw you out the window just to make sure you're not faking it." Something in her voice told him she wasn't serious.

Crow chuckled, but he wasn't about to call her bluff. He regretted downing all the potions at once slightly less than pounding drinks downstairs. If he needed to take them while in his bird form to work, their entire journey into the Emerald City was for nothing. He wasn't brave enough yet to find out the answer. Besides, if he shifted now—an extremely painful process given his shattered body—he wouldn't be able to shift back in time to leave Reva behind.

"Maybe tomorrow," he said to humor her. "Then you can carry me again while I get in a nap."

"You're insufferable."

"I do try my best." He rolled onto his side, suddenly

thoughtful. "If I asked you to stay here while I retrieved the Gnome King's stone, would you?"

Reva scowled, lifting one eyebrow as if to say *are you serious?*

He sighed. "I didn't think so. You are aware he kills every female he sees, yes?"

"And?"

"And, you're a female," Crow said, catching himself before adding *without power.* Her magic could return at any moment, but it didn't matter. Bringing her along wouldn't be wise.

Reva rolled her eyes. "We don't need his stone, Crow. Besides, you have no idea if it really exists, and even if it does, he won't just hand it to you. It would be more expedient to ambush Locasta without giving her the chance to curse us again."

Crow chewed his bottom lip. More expedient, yes, but he was less concerned with the speed of this mission and more so with their success. When he'd researched curses, a few books mentioned possible ways to avoid the Curse of Unknowing, but none were full-proof. The red stone belonging to the Gnome King was their best chance. All Crow knew was that he couldn't go through being cursed again. Not the forgetting and certainly not losing Reva. Thelia needed them, as well. They couldn't let their daughter suffer again.

"Reva?" he breathed. "Do you remember the last pub we spent the night in?"

"Not another word," she whispered without looking at him.

"Why not?" he asked. It was the same weekend Thelia had been conceived. "It happened, regardless of how you feel now."

Reva looked startled for a moment, and Crow couldn't understand why. But then her expression changed as she pushed up onto her elbows to peer down at him. "Whatever happened between us over twenty years ago happened to two different people. We are no longer them … nor do I wish to be."

Crow's lips lifted in a wistful smile. "Like it or not, my love, you're still my wife."

Reva pursed her lips, her cheeks and neck growing splotchy. Crow knew she didn't say anything because there was no arguing that he was right.

"I'm going back downstairs to read for a bit." He took the plate of apple slices from the small table and handed them to her. "You should eat this before it turns brown."

"The dark place I was sent to… I was alone. For years. Hunted incessantly. The constant running and hiding without magic was unbearable. I'd never felt so vulnerable. Not until Ozma arrived. You weren't there, Crow. You weren't there…" Her last word came out as a whisper.

Crow balled his hands into fists to keep from reaching out to her. Once again, Reva had been in danger and he hadn't been able to do a damn thing about it. "I'm sorry."

Reva turned away from him and bit into a slice of the apple. Swallowing hard, Crow slipped from the room. Instead of returning to the pub where a few fae still congregated, he slid down the wall beside the door, resting his elbows on his knees, and tipped his head back. "Until death," he whispered the final line of their vows to himself.

The full moon lit the clearing. Stones lined the circular area around Crow, Reva, and their friend, Whispa. The pixie smiled as she led the wedding ceremony, calling on the spirits of the forest to bless the union. Reva had never looked more beautiful. She wore a soft black dress with sheer sleeves and strips of leather crossing over her swollen belly while Crow had donned a simple black tunic. Whispa carefully tied Crow and Reva's forearms together with a green ribbon, signifying life. Once Whispa spoke, Crow's eyes locked with Reva's and they barely blinked as the pixie asked them to repeat her words.

They would seek to make each other happy.

They would be each other's confidant.

Honor. Respect. Love.

They would champion each other.

Until death.

Crow's heart exploded with joy when Whispa untied the ribbon from their arms, signaling their wedding was at an end. There were no witnesses, save the pixie—it was too dangerous with Locasta searching all of Oz for them—but one day, they hoped to repeat their vows in front of everyone they loved—including the child growing in Reva's womb. Until then, Crow would cherish his new bride in secret.

Crow shook himself back to the present. The phantom taste of Reva's lips remained, and he rubbed at the ache in his chest. Reliving those memories only tortured him, so why did he allow his mind to wander there?

Heavy footsteps started up the stairs and Crow stood. It should've been long enough for Reva to finish her apple slices—and the tasteless sleep crystals Milla had sprinkled over them—so he re-entered the room to avoid making small talk with whoever approached. The plate was indeed empty on the table and Reva was curled in a ball in the center of the bed, fast asleep.

"I'm sorry," Crow said as he approached. He bent to pull a thick rope from his pack. "I'd say you would hate me for this, but you already do." He tied one of the most complicated knots he knew around one bed post, then moved to the next. "What's one more strike against me? Especially when it's something as small as this?"

Crow frowned at his own words. In comparison to endangering her life, it was a minor offense to tie his wife to the bed and temporarily abandon her. It was still a completely underhanded move though.

"I'm doing this to save your life," he added as if that made everything all right. She was going to kill him for this, regardless of his motives, and he couldn't blame her.

Once each corner of the bed had a tight knot, he carefully stretched each of her limbs and tied the other end of the rope to her wrists and ankles. Reva had always found his knots hard to untie. She'd nearly chopped down her favorite tree because his hammock was blocking her garden's sunlight and the knots were impossible.

The fact that he was hiding her boots in the wardrobe behind the extra blankets only added insult to injury. Crow knew Reva would escape her bindings quickly—whether it was because her magic had finally returned or because she screamed for help, was yet to be seen. When she did, having her search for her footwear would buy him a little extra time to finish his business with the Gnome King before she caught up.

He shouldered his pack, but hesitated. There was a chance Reva would simply continue her plan to take on Locasta without him. She had never wanted to travel with him in the first place, and she'd been very clear about the Gnome King being a waste of time.

Fuck. This was a bad idea.

She would just have to get over it.

Or not.

But she would be alive and Locasta would be dead.

"Sleep well," Crow told Reva, and left her there, her face perfectly serene. He knew that the next time he saw her, the expression she wore would be far from peaceful.

CHAPTER TEN

REVA

The Western Witch moved lithely behind a tree as four sets of steps came closer. Three fae males and the pathetic human child. Even though the slippers weren't on the Wicked Witch's feet just yet, she could feel the thrum of the shoes' magic pulse inside her, as though they were calling to her. Once the slippers were on her feet, no one would ever be able to stop her. Not even the one controlling her—Locasta. She didn't want to be controlled anymore—she wanted to rage all on her own, then rule the entire world.

Closer and closer the interlopers inched. The girl wore her hair in braids, and the clothing draping her was disheveled and hideous. One male with silver hair held an axe and was still a youngling, not quite into adulthood yet. Another's golden hair shone beneath the sun, his tail twitching behind him, his gaze frantically shifting in all directions. He was even more pathetic than the other two. Out from behind the shadow of the girl came another, his black hair sprinkled with feathers, dirt covering his flesh. The Witch's gaze fell to his stomach, where a ropy torn tunic showed his glistening skin proudly. Something pulsed through her. A sense of wanting to lick that skin, touch him, taste him. Absorb his heat from the inside out. Unwind his intestines and discover their flavor. She'd never felt such an intense wanting of someone to die and become her meal.

"How far do you think we are from the Emerald City?" the girl asked.

"It could be this way," the feather-haired fae said. "Or this way, or this way, or this way, or this way—"

"It's this way," the one holding the axe replied, rolling his eyes.

The Witch smiled. They were now coming directly toward her, and her winged minions sat above her in the trees, waiting for her to give them the signal to attack.

Closing her eyes, the Witch let the magic stir within her. A thunderous boom from her lightning came, and a growing emerald fire lit in the center of her palm. She threw the flame at the golden fae. He screamed and dropped to the ground, cradling his legs to his chest. The other two protectively placed the girl behind them, all while a strange animal yapped and yapped.

But the fire spread and spread around the Witch and her prey as she stepped out from behind the tree, drifting closer. The flames looped around them in a wide circle. She was going to kill them all. Her life had been built on destruction and chaos and she wanted them dead. The small, furry creature continued its defensive sounds, grating on the Witch's ears. She was the Wicked Witch of the West and she wanted to destroy, destroy, destroy.

"You're her. The Wicked Witch of the West," the girl said, peeking her head around the silver-haired fae.

The Witch gave a shrill laugh, holding up her hand with another ball of flaming fire, calling to her minions. Out from the branches, the creatures rose, circling above them, screeching, howling, aching with hunger.

"You have nowhere to hide now," the Witch said, her eyes falling to the silver shoes. Their shine, their glisten, their sparkle. She needed them and couldn't take her eyes off the slippers as she lunged forward, ready to tear the girl apart and hand the bones to her beasts.

As she shot forward, the feather-haired male pushed the girl to the fae with the axe. He spun the girl around, protecting her. At any time, he could have come at the Witch with his axe, but he must have known that she could easily light them both on fire if she chose. She liked toying with her prey.

"I suppose she'll be last to be eaten instead of first."

The feather-haired male tilted his head, appearing to not truly see her, as if he were looking at nothing. Was he a halfwit? He continued to stare at her, stare and stare and stare and stare. Her anger rose. A sharp throb came at her ankle and she let out a yelp. The strange furry creature had bitten her! A hard shove came from the tailed fae, hitting her in the back.

Unable to hold her balance, the Witch fell to the dirt. Before the one with the axe could swing his weapon, her winged minions were upon them. But her prey was already running and running when she stood. Her circle of flames had burned out after she fell and lost hold on her magic. She threw a parting gift of flame that brushed the feather-haired fae's hand, but he didn't stop.

"You can't run forever! The shoes will be mine," the Witch screamed, lighting up again.

Reva jerked awake, her eyes wide, her voice coming out in a raspy shout. Something held her back from leaping out of the bed, the room, herself. Her wrists and ankles were bound with rope. She searched the room with desperation for Crow. He wasn't there. What if an enemy had taken him?

Reva's gaze drifted to her legs, then wrists, as she pulled, kicked, tugged, and ripped. None of the knots would loosen. She recognized those damn knots. *Crow.* She knew without a doubt that no enemy had done this to her—it had been *him*. Grogginess slowly started to seep its way into her as the high from her nightmare finally left. By the darkness through the slit of the curtains, and the night beasts' vicious noises, she could tell it wasn't yet close to dawn. Crow couldn't have gotten far yet.

All her guilt from the dream of him in her past vanished. And to think she'd felt *sorry* for how she'd treated him since her return—had told him about the dark place. She'd even been close to apologizing. Well, not anymore. The Gnome King may murder females, but that didn't mean he wouldn't torture the males until they prayed for death.

Reva's magic crackled inside her. Clenching her fists, chest heaving, she tried to release it, even a small spark to burn the bindings. She didn't have the fire like she'd had as the Wicked Witch, but lightning would have worked just as well. Relief washed over her as she felt her magic there, even though she couldn't tell when it would be at full strength.

With a hard thrust forward, Reva shook and rattled the entire head board, hoping to push the bed through the wall. "Open the door!" she screamed and raged as loud as she could. *Someone* would hear her.

After what felt like endless screaming, a rattle came as the door was unlocked and pushed open. It was one of the female dryads. Milla.

"Untie me," Reva demanded, still shaking the bed.

"I'm not supposed to," she said, her expression apologetic.

Reva narrowed her eyes. "What do you mean?"

"I gave Crow a sleeping aid, but I thought it was for him. Before he left, he said to make sure you stay here and remain safe."

The apple. The *apple*. The bastard had known there was something on her fruit to make her sleep. And he knew not to mess with her apples.

"Listen to me, and listen to me carefully," Reva said, low and dangerous. "You're going to untie these for me."

Milla shook her head.

"I can't tell you who I am, but just know I'm going to help Dorothy save the world." Reva hated using Thelia's name in that way, hated using her daughter to do this. Yet, Reva couldn't reveal that she'd been the Wicked Witch because the dryad would have not only left her there, but probably would have pushed a blade into her heart, too.

"I don't understand." The dryad took a step back, instead of closer, and crossed her arms. "That doesn't make me want to untie you. Dorothy can save the world with Crow like before."

Reva released a frustrated growl "Crow is Dorothy's father and I'm her mother. Dorothy isn't human—she's fae."

"Sure..." The dryad sighed, not believing her. Yet, she moved toward the rope. "But I think you should be able to choose for yourself what you want to do—not have someone choose for you, even if death is the result."

Reva was about to yell at the dryad to cut the ropes, but she was already using a jeweled blade from her hip to slash through the bindings.

Leaning forward, Reva rubbed at her wrists. "For that, when all this is over, I promise your position in the Emerald City will be great.”

“Wouldn’t that be wonderful?” The dryad watched her carefully as if Reva were drunk on wine or from the sleep aid, but no recognition set in.

Hopping from the bed, Reva reached for her boots. Her hand only grasped air. “Where *the fuck* are my boots?”

The dryad lowered herself to search under the bed. “Crow had no boots with him when he left, so they have to be in here somewhere.”

Blood coursing with rage through her veins, Reva opened the drawers of the dresser then threw open the closet door. In the back, behind extra blankets, peeked black laces. He was dead. So dead. But first she had to save his sorry ass before the Gnome King tortured him. Reva tugged on her boots and hurried out the door.

“He didn’t leave that long ago, so you should be able to catch up to him,” the dryad called.

When Reva rushed down the steps, into the dimly lit pub area, it was mostly empty, aside from a couple sipping on mugs while another fae male, with violet scales, sketched in a yellowing notepad.

The cursed pixies were still making their sounds outside, and she could hear the fighting escalating between them and the phouka. Perhaps they would be too distracted to notice her.

Another thought shot through her—Crow had really left during this? Her anger turned to fear. What if he hadn’t survived?

Reva took a deep breath and slowly opened the door, stepping into the cool darkness. The scent of fresh blood hit her, and she couldn’t help but think about how much crimson had truly been spilled here since she’d been gone. The entirety of Oz could have possibly been painted in it by now.

As she approached the protective barrier, she wondered again if Whispa was still alive in the swarm of cursed pixies. What about Ozma? Was she safe and whole on her own journey?

When a faint orange sun lit the horizon, the screeching from the creatures lessened. It wasn’t that the night beasts couldn’t survive during the day—they could—but their bodies would be in constant burning pain. When Reva was the Wicked Witch, she hadn't cared, hadn't worried about listening to their tortured cries. She'd made them carry out her duties, her searches, and her attacks without allowing them sleep, all while their bodies writhed from the sun's burn.

Reva shuddered at the memory of their screams. But then she remembered their elated cries as they lapped, bit, and tore into the fresh bodies she'd killed. Sometimes she hadn't killed them first—sometimes she would let the beasts fill their stomachs while her victims were still alive.

Reva hadn't realized she was still standing frozen at the magic barrier when a shrill shriek sounded not too far from her. Would the fae of Oz truly forgive her when they discovered who she was? Would they fear her? Or would they remember Reva, who'd fiercely protected the West. Either way, she would try to earn their forgiveness by ridding them of Locasta.

Taking a deep swallow and pushing her shoulders back, Reva silently crossed through the barrier. As the sun lifted higher and higher, the swirling yellows, oranges, and reds falling upon her, she didn't follow the green road leading back to the yellow. Instead, she ran to the back of the crumbled building, across from the tavern, and passed through the trees. The noises from the creatures of the night faded, but the Emerald City wasn't completely silent.

What Crow didn't know was that there was a shortcut to the Gnome King, so she was going to catch up to her *husband* much sooner than he ever could have thought.

CHAPTER ELEVEN

CROW

The skeletal pixies swarmed the trees outside of the Emerald City, their shrieks piercing his ears, but Crow had been expecting that. He wore his mask low, the beak covering his face, his head bent, as he slunk through the shadows. If he had more time, he would transform to see if his bones were healed so he could fly over the forest. It would take too long to regain the energy to transform back if the potions failed, though—and that was *if* the magic-depleting effects from the palace had worn off. When he'd left her, Reva's power had yet to return.

Crow plastered himself against a large tree covered in moss and held his breath. The beasts above him shifted on their perches, their heads cocking back and forth as they listened for the slightest sound. When a phouka crashed far away from him, the pixies took to the skies with an ear-piercing shriek. Crow used the noise and distraction to bolt.

On and on he went through the woods just outside of the Emerald City—running, waiting, throwing the occasional rock to send the cursed pixies investigating away from his hiding spot—until the sun broke the horizon. The mead was finally out of his system, but exhaustion replaced it. His mind was foggy, his limbs heavy. The little sleep he'd gotten since leaving Glinda's palace was broken and fitful, which made walking all night tip him toward the edge.

"Damn," he muttered as he stumbled over his own feet. *Just a few minutes…* A small rest, and then he had to keep moving. Crow pushed aside a sheet of vine-like branches to lean against the tree trunk. Hidden inside the natural tent, he tugged his mask down over his eyes and fell asleep.

Crow gasped, his eyes flying open. He looked frantically around for a threat but found none. Sun filtered through the trees and birds chirped overhead. All was serene. Except for Crow. Ever since the Wheelers had cut him out of his hammock when he'd been traveling with Thelia and Tin, sleeping outside had become nerve-racking. The few days that he'd spent tracking Reva were practically sleepless. Shaking his head, Crow eased himself to his feet. His pack was still fastened to his back, so after stretching quickly, he stepped outside of the tree's shelter.

His feet flew out from under him, his back smacking against the packed ground with a *thwack*.

He twisted his head as he was flung high into the air, trying to figure out what the hell had just happened, and found himself in an iron net. The net cocooned him as it swayed from one of the higher branches. On instinct, his blades shot out from his bracers, but they would do no good against an iron net. He rocked the net, shifting his weight around, forcing it to swing in an attempt to loosen the trap, but it held fast. After another moment of confused panic, he let out a long, shaky breath.

"Shit," he muttered. Why were so many hunters suddenly setting traps? He'd gone years without finding himself in one. Crow leaned on his pack to lessen the exposure of iron on his skin, but his arms still burned fiercely.

Just as he found a comfortable position and began looking for any weaknesses in the net, footsteps crunched on the forest floor. Crow's claws shot out again. His body tensed, ready to fight the owner of the trap.

"Well, well, well," a familiar voice purred from below. "Isn't this ironic?"

Reva.

Crow's heart slammed against his ribs. How had she caught up with him so quickly? "Hello, my love," he called as innocently as he could manage. "Fancy meeting you here."

"Yeah," she snapped. "Fancy fucking that. Since you allowed me to eat food with a sleeping aid and *tied me to the bed.*"

"If I remember correctly, there was a time you would've enjoyed being tied," he said with a sly smile. It had only happened once, but Reva hadn't complained. In fact, it was quite the opposite.

She rubbed at her temples and mumbled too quietly for Crow to make out her string of words. When her eyes flicked back up to him, she said, "I have half a mind to leave you up there while I go get the stone by myself."

"Only half? Besides, I thought you didn't want the stone?"

Reva's lips turned up in a wicked smile. "I'll come back for you once I have the stone."

Crow chuckled to himself, but then she walked off. The amusement faded the farther she got, followed by a sweeping sense of disbelief. She was *actually* going to leave him there? "Reva," he called. "This isn't funny!"

Her faint laugh reached him from a few trees away. She was serious? *She was serious.* Crow shook the net, the iron burning his fingers. But he didn't care. No way was he letting his wife seek out the Gnome King alone—not when it was an instant death sentence. And *especially* not if the rumors were true about him fucking beautiful women first.

"Reva Etain Westbloom!" Crow shouted, using her true name for the first time since he'd learned it. He'd wanted to use it so many times over the past few days to get her to listen to him but knew it was wrong. This was different.

Her footfalls immediately stopped.

"Get me out of this net right now!" he ordered.

Reva held a neutral expression as she crashed back through the forest to him and disappeared under the branches where Crow had just napped. A moment later, the net plummeted to the ground. Crow landed on his hip with a loud *thud*.

"As classy as ever," he said through the pain. "Reva Etain Westbloom, I release you from my control."

Reva flew out from between the hanging branches with fury swirling across her features. Her lips pulled back in a low growl as she ripped the net away from Crow. Her hands quickly curled into the strands of decorative ropes around his neck, and she twisted them until they nearly choked him. "You *dare* use my true name?"

"You left me little choice," he said earnestly. Though, he did regret calling it so loudly when there was no telling if other fae lingered nearby. "It's the *Gnome King*."

"Don't act like you're any safer going alone than I am. He would still torture you," she spat.

Crow pried Reva's hands from his ropes and stood, kicking away the net where it clung to his boots. "He would have to catch me first."

Reva looked pointedly at the net on the ground. "Clearly a manageable task."

"Untrue. I've snuck in a few times already without detection." Crow cocked an eyebrow. "Besides, you were in a net first, my love."

Reva *tsked*. "Consider us even. We're wasting daylight."

There was no arguing that point, and they resumed their travels in tense silence.

Creatures rustled in the brush, snorting, huffing, growling. It wasn't the ones that sounded disgruntled that they had to worry about, though. Between him and Reva, it would take a fae with critical thinking skills to pose a threat—unless they traveled in a large group or were massive in size, which they weren't.

The fresh, dewy scent of morning gave way when the sun reached high in the sky, and they decided to take a break at a riverbank. Reva snared a small boar and cooked it over a fire while Crow set his pack down at the edge of the water. He could see every pebble at the bottom of the river, and tiny blue fish swam leisurely with the current. The sun glinted off the surface and Crow's skin itched beneath the layers of sweat and dirt. He pulled his shirt over his head and glanced back at Reva to make sure she was still within sight. A small smile turned up his lips when he found her staring straight at him.

"Care to join me?" he asked, unbuckling his pants.

Reva rolled her eyes and turned back to the fire.

Crow took his time scrubbing himself in the crystal-clear river. The scent of roasting meat had him salivating as he drew himself out of the crisp water. He stepped onto the riverbank and slipped his pants back on.

"That looks good," Crow told her as he sat on a nearby log. His hair hung in wet locks around his bare shoulders and face, droplets of water clinging to the feathers.

"You're assuming I'll share."

She was obviously still angry that he'd tied her to the bed and used her true name, but he wouldn't lie and say he was sorry. Crow shrugged at her words and dug through his pack for the unblemished apple he'd snagged from the pub before he'd left. A preemptive apology snack.

Reva's eyes followed the fruit as he tossed it into the air and caught it. "Fine," she mumbled. "You can have some." He knew she wouldn't be able to deny the apple, just as he wouldn't have been able to deny her anything.

Crow gave her a knowing wink and handed her the fruit.

"It's not poisoned, is it?" She took the apple begrudgingly, giving it a whiff before setting it aside while she carved them each a piece of meat.

"Is your magic back?" he asked after swallowing his first bite.

Reva shook her head. "Can you shift yet?"

Crow chewed his meat instead of telling her he was too

scared to try. It was tender, but the flavor a little too grassy, yet fulfilling, nonetheless.

"Really?" she said, seeming to understand his silence. "After all we went through to get the potions? *Try it.*"

"There's no need to be hasty," he mumbled.

Reva sighed, some of her anger deflating. "I know you're fearful, but we need to know. The Gnome King is dangerous for us both, and I'm still powerless. If you can shift, it would at least give us *something* to work with."

Crow nodded. She was right—they needed to know. That didn't make it any easier, especially when he had a gut feeling that the answer would be unsatisfying. Setting his lunch aside, Crow closed his eyes and mentally prodded at his magic. When nothing happened, he poked at it a little harder. The part of him that contained his magic was brimming with it, but it simply rested there instead of responding.

"Are you going to shift or not?" Reva asked quietly.

Crow's eyes opened wide. "I… I can't."

"I should have guessed this." Worry lines formed on Reva's forehead. "But with the potions being for general healing, I thought perhaps you could. One of us should have waited outside the Emerald City Palace—"

"It's not that," Crow interrupted. "The magic is still there— I can feel it. It just seems to be paralyzed."

Reva stared down at the apple, turning it so the glossy skin caught the sunlight. "I think mine is getting better," she offered. "It's more awake than it was."

Crow blinked. Once. Twice. "What's more awake?"

"My power," Reva said as if it were obvious.

"Right, right," Crow said quickly to cover his building fear. Had they just been talking about her power? What was her power anyway? He could … turn into something. Maybe? Crow's lungs screamed for more air, but each of his breaths were hard won. His heart spasmed rapidly. "Reva," he breathed. He grabbed his head in his hands, desperate to hold onto her name before it vanished from his mind like it had when Locasta cursed him.

“Reva, Reva, Reva.”

CHAPTER TWELVE

REVA

"Reva," Crow murmured again and again, as though his immortal life depended on it. Reva studied him, her brow furrowing as he sat staring at the yellow flowering bushes along the riverbank.

Taking a hard swallow, Reva's chest tightened and her throat locked up. She'd never seen him this way, expressionless.

"Are you all right?" she asked, kneeling in front of him.

His head jerked up, his bright brown eyes meeting hers, wild. "I'm fine. I was just thinking about something. Go get cleaned up before we leave."

Perhaps his cursed past was haunting him the way hers had in dreams, in her thoughts. Something in her didn't want to leave him sitting there, but she nodded and stood.

As she stepped over small patches of faeriefly eggs in patches of flowers near the riverbank, she realized all her anger about Crow using her true name had vanished. And she knew why it had. Because she would have done the same damn thing. If he'd been in the room after tying her to the bed, she would have used his name to release her too. He could have left her behind when she'd been stuck in the net, and if he had tried, she would have used it then as well.

They were the same—both stubborn, both yearning for the other. Reva shook her thoughts away, feeling lightheaded. Why was she thinking about yearning? Her focus was on killing Locasta, and that was all.

Reva stared out at the glistening pale-blue river. Without another word, she slipped off her muddy boots and removed her clothing. She wondered if Crow was sneaking glances at her like she had with him when he was bathing. His naked chest, his toned arms, the smoothness of his backside. It was almost impossible for him to look better than she remembered, but he did.

"Stop," Reva whispered to herself. But her body was growing weightless, and she couldn't keep herself from looking back at him.

He wasn't peering at her, though. Instead, Crow sat in the same position, counting something over and over on each of his fingertips.

Those fingers she wanted in her hair, on her body, cradling her breasts, between her legs. Everywhere and anywhere.

Something wasn't right, but she pushed the feeling away as she stepped into the river. The cold water sent a chill up her spine, and gooseflesh sprinkled across her skin as she washed away filth from the journey.

She'd never felt like this before. Not with this *need*. She tried to wash her memories away again without peering at Crow, the way she had attempted back at Glinda's palace. But they always lingered, no matter how far she tucked them. They always would.

She needed to make herself think about something else.

It would take several days to get to the Gnome King. If he had still lived just past the Deadly Desert in his stone palace, it would have taken longer. The journey would've been a challenge to cross the desert, when touching it turned anyone's flesh to sand.

Once the Gnome Queen was brutally murdered, the king had never returned to his stone palace. Instead he'd stayed on land centered in the outskirts between the North and the West, luring fae females in, only to kill them in the end.

Because they weren't his queen. No one would ever be.

The females would go to him, believing they could change him, believing they could be his queen, that they could be the one to make him *feel*. But someone made purely of stone, with a hardened heart like Tin had once had, could never truly feel.

Thelia had told her Tin's story late into the night before she'd left. Oh, Thelia! Oh, how Reva wanted to spin in circles with Thelia and braid her hair and laugh together and eat baked delights.

Reva's excitement grew, her body becoming restless as she gazed at the sun, wondering how close she could get before combusting. She reached her hand up as if to touch it. Perhaps she could fly to the sun and find out. No, no, because that would mean she could die.

Her insides were alive, lit up with energy, wanting to burst free. The water was no longer cold, but hot, as if it would scald her skin. Her body felt off balance, like she'd drunk too much ale. She hadn't had any. Or had she?

Stroking and slicing her way across the lake to get back to Crow—*her Crow*—Reva could discuss all the games they could play with Thelia now that she was back. But they were supposed to go somewhere today. Oh, well, there were much more important things to do.

She sang to herself as she tugged on her clothes, not caring that they clung to her wet skin. As she tried to slip on a boot, she tripped over her own feet, dropping it. "Fuck those boots. I can be barefoot like Ozma." Ozma… Reva shrugged.

Smiling, she whirled around to find Crow in the same spot, but his eyes were focused on her now. For a moment, her stomach sunk, losing all its giddiness. The cornfield. That was where they would arrive next—the place where he'd spent ten years of his life.

Bah. She'd been selfish. For Crow, it would be similar to her revisiting the dark place. Oh, how she wished he'd been there with her in that lonely place. They could have played games there too. And possibly braided each other's hair. She laughed out loud, giddy, covering her mouth.

Crow moved toward Reva, on all fours like a baby dragon, his eyes never leaving hers. She laughed and laughed and laughed until it turned into a high-pitched shriek that reminded her of something.

Something bad.

Very, very, bad. "Naughty Reva, don't you worry, you aren't wicked anymore," she sang to herself.

As she spun and spun, she finally came to a stop, finding Crow on his knees in front of her. She gasped and released a giggle. He grabbed her hand and pulled her down to where he was.

"Something's wrong with me," he said, breathing hard. "I think—I think my curse is coming back."

Reva looked around, the world spinning and spinning, like she'd just done, except this time it was reversed. There was no game, there could be no games—she was becoming a wicked fae once more. She peered down at her skin. Was it just her, or did it glisten green beneath the sun? But even if she did turn wicked, she could have Crow be wicked with her this time. Be bad together. *No!*

This wasn't the curse—her body wasn't painfully shifting as if she'd just been torn apart. Reva was lighter and freer than ever before.

With wide eyes, she clasped Crow's warm and delicious hands. "I think we should dance. In the water. On top of the sun. Within the stars. And shine and shine and shine."

"Brighter," he said softly, stroking a thumb against her wrist, leaning closer. He chewed on his bottom lip.

Reva remembered the Gnome King again, but she didn't care about seeing him anymore. Or Locasta. She wanted to stay here beside the river with Crow, where they could run amuck, chase each other, and dance. Except they had too much clothing on. Why had she even gotten dressed?

Reva's gaze fell to the tan skin of Crow's throat. She leaned closer, until the tip of her nose pressed to the flesh of his warm neck, and inhaled his scent. From that single touch, she could feel his breaths. Him breathing into her, her breathing into him. He smelled so good, so fresh, like the forest.

"Reva," he rasped. "Please kiss me. Kiss me so I don't forget you."

Why would he forget her? "Stop being so silly," she said, rubbing her head along his bare shoulder. She could never forget him. But she had before… Green. Green. Green. Everything was green. Everything had hurt. Hurt. Hurt.

No more games.

Grabbing the sides of Crow's face, she straightened on her knees. "Don't let me forget you either."

His lips parted as her mouth crashed into his. And she pulled him toward her, one arm entwined and clutching his hair while the other gripped the bare skin of his back. Crow inhaled sharply before his lips finally moved against hers, like he was trying to remember how to do that too. Their mouths discovered each other as if it were new—she'd never felt so high before. Not even after their drunken night at the Summer Solstice.

Whatever was coursing through her body only heated it more and more. The world turned and turned as she kissed and kissed him, their tongues dancing, their upper bodies swaying. The only thing missing was music. But as Crow lifted her onto his lap and lowered them to the ground, fiddles played in her head.

Every hard inch of him was touching her, and her hand wanted to go straight to the part she hadn't seen, or felt, in so long. She continued to kiss him, allowing her fingers to venture between his legs, then stroking them against his perfect cock through his pants. Reva kissed her way down to the side of his neck, right behind his ear. She moved her hand up his naked chest, feeling each taut muscle connect with her fingertips, when she noticed his body was still, unmoving. Her head jerked up, making everything spin like before, and she found Crow's eyes shut.

"Crow?" she tried to yell, but it came out too tired to be more than a whisper. Her fingers reached under his nose, his warm breath hitting her fingers. He was *sleeping*.

A game of sleeping! She would love a sleeping game much more than the kissing and touching one, especially as her body grew heavier with each passing moment.

Reva pressed herself into Crow, slinging his arm over her so it draped around her waist, before resting her face in the crook of his neck.

They should be continuing somewhere over the rainbow, but she didn't care when she closed her eyes, because sleeping with Crow was her rainbow.

CHAPTER THIRTEEN

CROW

A heavy limb pressed down on Crow's abdomen and a rock jabbed at the center of his back. He yawned and opened his eyes, squinting. The sun was rising, chasing away the night. "Fuck," he shouted, sitting up too quickly. His head spun. "*Fuck.*"

A groan came from beside him. "What?"

Reva. Fuzzy memories flooded through Crow. His mind slipping away. Reva bathing. Him crawling like a fool. Reva *kissing* him. Sleep. Them waking to the sound of howling pixies and scrambling to find shelter in the woods like two drunkards. Sleeping again. Her arms around him. Her head on his chest.

"What happened?" Reva asked, groggy.

Crow rolled from beneath the shelter and stood. Sticks were woven together and fastened over four low posts to mimic the appearance of dirt from above. Or, close enough to dirt to fool the pixies. He searched the wooded area around them to avoid meeting Reva's heavy stare. She'd watched him break down, seen his fear. It felt shameful. He wanted Reva to see him as someone she could rely on, not a babbling idiot. It was bad enough the rest of Oz had seen him at his worst, but he wasn't cursed anymore. It was *him* this time. His cheeks burned.

"We left our supplies near the river." She stepped up to his side and ran a hand down her cheek. "Any chance you remember where that river is?"

Crow cringed. "I barely remember us waking up and finding this place." *And the softness of her lips against his.* But he didn't dare say that. Did she remember? Even if she did, she would surely prefer to forget it had happened.

Reva stretched her back and sighed heavily. "This way," she said, sounding mostly certain.

Crow studied the woods as he followed her, hoping to see something familiar. Purple flowers grew up from beneath a carpet of fallen leaves and nearly-invisible hanging vines captured the light, casting prisms over the dark tree bark. The body of a half-eaten fae lay partially under a large bush, too far decomposed to tell what it might have been. A tuft of light brown fur clung to a piece of the carcass, and the bones were scored with teeth marks. Bugs and beasts alike stirred for the day, chirps and snorts piercing through the forest around them, but Crow couldn't tell where they were or from which way they had come. What the hell had happened yesterday? One second, they were fine. The next…

"Here it is," Reva called. She had gotten slightly ahead of him and passed through the trees to the riverbank. Crow stepped over a fallen tree, then swerved to avoid stepping in a spot of stagnant mud. She spun to face him, righteous anger written all over her face. "Someone went through our bags."

Crow sprinted to close the distance between them. Their belongings were scattered over the clearing. Fruit—some nothing but a core, others untouched—and clothing were left in the dirt. But why go through their bags if the thief hadn't wanted to take anything important? Crow flicked his wrists to release his blades, in case the danger lingered, and realized his wrists were bare. He hadn't put his weapons back on after bathing in the river.

"Reva—"

She spun around, gripping a young faun by the scruff of his

neck. His hooved feet hung off the ground as he bent his arms and legs in a laughing fit. Small antlers barely poked out of his knotted, sandy blond hair and freckles dusted his high cheekbones.

"Explain yourself," Reva ordered the youth. When his wheezy laugh simply continued, she dropped him next to the pit where she'd cooked their meat. Turning to Crow, she motioned to the faun and asked, "Does this look familiar?"

Crow nodded. The fae looked as dazed as he'd felt the day before, but that only made it more worrisome that his weapons were missing. He stalked up to the child and crossed his arms. "Where are my bracers? My knives?"

The faun merely pointed to the log, still laughing, then rolled over onto his hands and knees. He clawed at the air with one of his hands, growling and hissing like a depraved beast, then fell to his side in a fit again.

Crow kept an eye on him while he crouched beside the log. All their weapons were stashed inside the hollowed end. He quickly pulled them out, fitting his bracers back on and returning his knife to his boot. After yanking his shirt over his head, he shoved everything else back into their bags. They'd already lost a day—there was no more time to waste.

"Nothing seems to be missing unless you count all the food he ate," Reva said as Crow stuffed the last piece of uneaten fruit back in his bag.

"No," Crow agreed, throwing his pack onto his back. He returned to the hysterical faun and crouched down to his level. "We aren't angry," he said calmly. At least, *he* wasn't. He'd committed innocent mischief in his youth too. The plates of pastries his neighbor had cooled on her windowsill were nearly always missing one or two desserts when she'd brought them back inside.

Besides, nothing was gone from their packs and they were the ones who had abandoned their belongings to begin with. There was no way the faun could've known they would return when it was possible the cursed pixies had found them. It made sense that he felt comfortable taking what he wanted. "Can you tell us what happened? Why you're acting like this?"

When the child threw his head back in a cackle, Crow noticed a piece of meat stuck between his front teeth. "Reva?" he asked carefully. "Where did you snare that boar yesterday?"

She made a low, thoughtful sound as if trying to remember. "A bit east of here, I think. Why?"

Crow hung his head. That made sense—the family of boars in that part of Oz fed on the poppies that had spread from the yellow brick road into the forest. The animals were well-known to those who traveled as often as Crow did. If they weren't passed out among the poppies, they were running wild while high, and there was no helping anyone caught picking their precious flowers. Why Reva hadn't hunted closer to the river where the boars ate mostly mushrooms was a moot point now— they'd eaten tainted meat without realizing it.

"Why?" Reva repeated when he didn't answer.

"The boars there eat poppies," he said in a low voice. There had been an unfortunate incident years ago where he'd tripped over one of the boars a few yards away from the poppies. The group had flown into hysterics, some so badly that they'd passed out, while several others must've had a bad reaction. Crow had to fly out of there before they'd trampled him.

Reva plopped onto the log, staring down at her hands. He thought she was going to burst into tears when a bark of laughter escaped her.

"Thank fucking goodness!" she said, jerking her head up to peer at the sky. "Being drunk over a few poppies is better than being cursed again. But I still don't have my magic back."

Crow eased out of his crouch and sank down beside her, watching the child giggle to himself. He had thought his curse was returning too. The poppies had fogged his mind. Everything that should've been important had flown straight out of his brain until all that was left were pure emotions. "I share that sentiment."

Reva shifted next to him and Crow knew she was about to

bring up their kiss. "We acted like that for a reason."

"We didn't lose our minds," Crow said in a flat voice. He didn't dare look at her, but he hoped she took the hint. Poppies or not, he didn't feel like celebrating. It *had* felt as if his mind was slipping away. He shook away the flicker of fear. "We should sit with the youngling until he's better."

"That could take all day," she argued. "We don't have that kind of time."

"If our daughter was in this situation, we would want someone to protect her." He turned to face Reva, but his eyes only reached her chin. He'd done what he could for Thelia after she arrived in Oz—guided her as best he could with his broken mind. All of the times he *wasn't* able to shield her still haunted him though. As did the moments he'd missed. "We're staying."

CHAPTER FOURTEEN

REVA

Reva stared at the sleeping faun in her lap. His clothing was full of tears and splattered with dried dirt. There were light scratches on his cheeks and he looked like he hadn't seen a home in weeks. She and Crow had been watching over him for what felt like seasons upon seasons, when in fact it had only been perhaps half a day.

The child had passed out from delirium. Crow had caught him after the faun had leapt from the forest floor and tried to scale a tree while laughing. His eyes had shut mid-climb and he'd fallen backward, right into Crow's waiting arms. But Reva didn't want the child to have to sleep on the hard earth, so she let his head rest in her lap while his knees hugged his chest. She wondered what it would have been like to hold Thelia when her daughter was this age. He appeared the same age that Thelia had been when she'd first come to Oz, so perhaps somewhere between eleven and twelve years old.

Reva hummed a song for him as she brushed her fingers through his tangled locks of blond hair. Poppies were dangerous, but especially for anyone who wasn't fully grown. She was surprised the poppies hadn't ended his life, but he must not have eaten much of the boar.

Smoke wafted around her, and the roasting scent of meat hit

her nose. Reva's stomach rumbled with hunger as she peered over her shoulder and watched Crow char an owl over a fire he'd built.

"Are you sure this one isn't filled with poppies too?" Reva asked, not really caring, because it smelled divine.

"I'm sure." Crow winked. "Birds are smart. They know not to eat poppies."

"Hmm. You're part bird and yet you still didn't detect it in the meat before." Her eyes darted to Crow's mouth, lingering before flicking away. She told herself they had just drifted there because she was thinking about him eating the meat. Not him kissing her. Or Gods, her kissing him first… Even though she'd been drunk out of her wits on poppies, she still remembered the softness of his mouth on hers. Her hands in his hair, his hands on her lower back. How hard he'd been.

Reva yearned for him the way she always had, and this was why she hadn't wanted him to come with her on this journey. Because he could indeed always win her over in the end. No matter how hard she tried not to be won.

A soft mewl came from the faun. Perhaps he would be stirring soon. She hoped.

"Here," Crow said, lifting a piece of blackened meat and lightly blowing on it. He started to give it to her and noticed her hands were still occupied with the child. "Part your lips."

She was too hungry to say no. As she opened her mouth, he placed the tender meat on her tongue, his fingers brushing her lips as he released it. There wasn't a grassy flavor like the day before, which she now chalked up to the poppies. It was savory and practically fell apart as she chewed.

"So," he said, taking a seat beside her and plopping a slice of meat into his mouth.

"So," she repeated, choosing to stare at the river instead of at Crow.

Before they could play their echo game anymore, another sound came from the child. His lids slowly opened to reveal orange irises and large pupils. When his gaze met theirs, his eyes widened. With a loud screech, he jerked up flailing, spitting, and flapping his arms to find balance. Was he still out of his mind? He pulled out a tiny blade from the back of his pants and held it up. Reva wanted to roll her eyes because she could easily kick it out of his hand before the youngling could even make another move. But she decided to let the faun have his moment, and Crow seemed to think the same, as he just crossed his arms and studied him.

A distressed expression crossed the child's face, his pale coloring becoming green. Dropping the knife, he turned around and expelled whatever had been in his stomach.

The faun stumbled backward and almost fell. Crow caught him like he had earlier that day. "We're not going to hurt you."

Reva scooped up the child's weapon, knelt in front of him, and held his blade up—with the handle toward him—to grab. "He's right. We're trying to help you. Now, where are your parents?"

The faun's bottom lip trembled as his hand shakily took the knife. "They're dead."

Reva slowly nodded in understanding. Since she'd been away, many children were without their parents or vice versa. Too many dead and too many separated. But when she was the Wicked Witch of the West, she'd separated families, too. She tried not to think of the blood she'd shed as she asked, "What's your name?"

His fingers gripped his blade, knuckles white. "Birch."

"I'm sorry, Birch." She knew she shouldn't say her name just yet, but she wanted to give him something. He was too young to remember her from before anyway. "I'm Reva and this is Crow."

Birch's gaze snapped to Crow's, recognizing his name, but hers must have indeed been forgotten with time, since no one had been allowed to use it in years. "Locasta killed my parents. She said she would protect us and she didn't. She's turning on anyone who speaks up. My parents wanted her to end the assault on the Emerald City, and she refused."

Reva pressed her lips together and shook her head. "She is

never to be trusted."

So the Northern bitch wasn't pretending to be good anymore. It seemed she thought her victory was near. If Reva's magic didn't return soon, Locasta may very well be victorious and rule over the Land of Oz. But no—Thelia was stronger than Locasta. Reva had felt Thelia's magic when it drew Reva and Ozma out from the dark place, had seen the strength in it. Yet it would take a while for Thelia to learn how to wield it at will.

The child was now studying Crow in awe, his hand no longer shaking. Perhaps she did need Crow after all. Everyone in Oz still looked up to him, to Thelia. Reva related most to the Tin WoodsMan in this quest, only her nature was even more questionable. Tin could be forgiven, but would the fae of Oz ever forgive her for what she'd done?

Birch needed to go somewhere safe, but there wasn't a trustworthy town nearby to take him to. The Emerald City had the tavern, but Birch actually making it there without someone killing him might be too tricky. Reva and Crow couldn't drag him through the cornfield on their way to the Gnome King either. He would be tortured.

An idea came to her then. One that would be perfect, and possibly selfish. But Birch was from the North and if he could learn to trust the other territories then maybe other Northerners would too… "How would you feel about going to the South?"

All the color drained from Birch's face. He rubbed the back of his neck and bit at his bottom lip. "Langwidere is there."

"She's dead," said Crow. "It's safe now."

"What if we told you it was now a haven?" Reva started. "That you could go to the palace and be safe. Crow and I will be helping to make the North safe as well."

"Glinda would never help the North."

"No. Not Glinda, but someone who loves all of Oz. She now rules the South and the West, and was a child like you when she saved us once before."

Birch lifted his chin, his blond brows all the way up his forehead. "Who is this you speak of?"

"Have you heard of a human girl named Dorothy?"

She'd expected him to look pleased, not narrow his eyes with distrust. "She's the cause of all this. The reason everyone's dead. That's what Locasta said."

And Locasta had murdered his parents, but she couldn't word it like that. "Do you believe everything Locasta says? Dorothy killed Langwidere and is now going to help rebuild the South. *We* trust her. Am I so bad? Is Crow so bad?"

Birch scanned her up and down. "I don't know." This was taking up too much time, and she needed him to head South already.

"Couldn't I have hurt you in your sleep if I truly wanted you dead?" she asked. "Couldn't I have left you here all alone and not given you this opportunity?"

"I suppose." Birch pursed his lips in a thin line. "Dorothy really is good, then?"

"The purest of hearts." A much better one than she, Reva, could ever have. "Are you brave enough to head to the South, her palace, alone?"

Straightening his shoulders, and lengthening his spine, he puffed up his chest. "I've been on my own for a while now and have been surviving just fine. Until I ate that meat..."

Gently, Reva placed a hand on his shoulder. "Avoid going through the Emerald City."

Crow pulled an apple from his bag and handed it to Birch. "For the road." Reva wanted to rip the fruit from his hand and give him a different one, but the child needed it more than her.

Reva removed her palm from his shoulder. "Dorothy will need a good guard, and I think you're just the fae to help her rebuild from the destruction Langwidere has caused."

"I'll do it."

She knew Dorothy would welcome him as soon as he showed up on her doorstep.

"And, Birch, if you help our daughter succeed, then we'll be most grateful," Reva added.

"Daughter?" His face was full of surprise. "Dorothy's your

daughter? But you're…" Birch looked at Crow. "He's… She's…"

"She's not human. Not really. She's fae, like us."

Birch studied his small hands, his brow furrowed as he peered back up at them. "I'll protect the daughter of Crow with my life. My parents told me to never make promises unless I mean them, and I mean it."

"You will be rewarded." She would make sure of it.

Crow pointed him in the direction of the yellow brick road and told him to remain on it as he headed south, except for the capital, which he needed to go around.

Birch turned away from them and took off in the southern direction without a glance back, not appearing the least bit afraid. Perhaps he'd already lost too much to be fearful.

"You didn't mention that Tin would be there," Crow said, stepping up beside Reva.

"I didn't want to frighten him. Thelia will help him understand. Besides, Tin wasn't as awful as me. He didn't kill for pure pleasure."

"It wasn't *you* doing it, though."

"I know," she whispered. "But it still hurts. It always will."

"Reva?"

She peered up at him. "Yes?"

"I promise not to leave you behind again. And if I could have come with you to the dark place, I would have. Even if it had to be for all eternity." Something nudged her fingertips. Crow had pushed an apple into her palm. "I didn't give Birch the last one."

Her heart thundered in her chest at his words. She lifted the fruit to her lips, and couldn't help but smile as she bit into the sweet juiciness.

Without another word, they adjusted their packs and drank from the river before continuing their journey. There wasn't much daylight left, but they could hopefully make it to the outskirts of the cornfield before dusk.

After pushing several branches aside, Reva and Crow entered an area with trees of white. But it wasn't the bark that made them that color—the entirety of the trunks and limbs were wrapped in ivory spider silk. A scream sounded above them, and REVA peered up to find a large spider with long, thin legs rolling a sprite into its web. *Good.* That species of sprite was a nuisance, using their fangs to suck blood from young fae and take bites from their flesh.

As more and more spiders poked out from places draped among the trees, Reva's instinct was to use her magic. But it still wouldn't spark to life. The spiders didn't venture any closer. Something told her that they recognized her as Reva, the ruler of the West, not as the Wicked Witch, and they knew better than to make a move.

Reva and Crow traveled in comfortable silence. She still couldn't help but think about yesterday, with the kiss—she needed to stop and not dwell on it. At least not until after what they needed to do was done.

She brushed away branches of tall leafy bushes, and up ahead, a silhouette spread like floating shadows swaying back and forth. The setting sun's rays shifted as they approached, revealing the cornfield. The field went on and on. It would take them forever to cross through it, so they would need to find somewhere within the field itself to stay the night the following evening. For now, they could find somewhere at its edge.

But as she shielded her eyes from the sun, she noticed something new. The once-yellow and green stalks, though still tall, had turned entirely black. The smell of rot permeated the air, making her almost lose her stomach's contents. As Reva and Crow stepped closer, she noticed yellowed skeletons, covered in dust, sprawled about the ground at strange angles.

"Was it like this when you were here?" Reva's voice came out angry, but not at Crow. At whoever had done this.

She whirled to face him when his answer remained tucked away. Something in his face appeared stricken, broken.

"Crow?"

He shook his head. "It was bad when I was here, but nothing like this."

CHAPTER FIFTEEN

CROW

Crow lay on his back, staring up at the cloudless sky. Millions of stars glimmered down upon the small camp he and Reva had set up. There was no fire for warmth, or to reduce the risk of night beasts finding them, but anxiety left him feeling uncomfortably warm, his muscles quivering at the nearness of the cornfield. It was right there—on the other side of the trees… He hadn't even been able to swallow the fruit Reva had sliced for him. She'd done it just the way he liked, too—thin but still thick enough to get a small crunch.

"You should sleep," Reva said softly.

His wife sat on a large boulder, facing out toward the cornfield, and cleaned her nails with the tip of Crow's knife. She looked so beautiful in the moonlight that it hurt, but his gaze kept trying to search for danger beyond her. In the field. In *his* field. A shudder ran through his body and he focused on his hands.

"I'll keep watch for enemies," she added.

He shook his head. "You should rest. I won't be able to sleep anyway."

"Try," she ordered.

Crow gave her the smallest of smiles. "I would usually make an inuendo here, but I'm afraid I'm all out of them at the moment."

Reva rolled her eyes and tucked his knife into her boot. "Why don't you tell me a story instead?"

"What kind of story?"

"About what happened to your wings," she said without looking at him.

Ah. That. He hesitated. She wouldn't like it—Locasta's name seemed enough to set off her anger—but if she wanted to know… "After exhausting every lead in an attempt to locate the human Dorothy, I went to see Locasta. She'd had Whispa exchange Thelia with the mortal baby, so I figured she would have some idea where to look—maybe the real Dorothy had been enchanted as a palace slave or given to another family. I don't know. It was foolish. When she finally realized I was only there for news of the girl and not to reconcile, she forced me to transform and snapped my wings. Then she tossed me down the stairs, where I barely managed to remain conscious long enough to shift back. Then one of her human changelings helped me escape, but he didn't make it…" He would spare Reva the little details, like the sound of his bird bones breaking, the intense pain that made white flash before his eyes, or the human's agonizing screams.

Reva sat thoughtfully for a moment before saying, "Sleep, Crow."

He shifted to his side to better see his wife. Just as he was about to insist that he take the first watch, she began to hum quietly so only he could hear. It was the slow melody of a Western song, full of drawn-out notes. Her voice was gentle and soft as it wove a wordless tale. Crow instantly relaxed as Reva's voice flowed over him. Closing his eyes, he let the music wrap around him like a blanket. He could have almost cried with relief in that split second before sleep took him. Because if he was sleeping, he wasn't thinking about the path through the corn that they had to take the next morning.

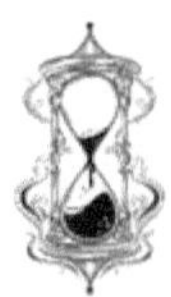

Crow stood at the edge of the cornfield, along with Reva, at the first light of dawn. He fought the urge to run from the place Locasta had trapped him all those years ago—to fly away from this horrible, cursed place. Spreading his broken wings and forcing them to carry him into the air would've been less painful than taking another step forward.

The stalks making up his former prison bars were no longer golden. They didn't sway in the breeze as they used to or carry the earthy scent which somehow still clung to him. The rustling of leaves that used to be his constant companion—a song seemingly sung just for him as he suffered through his days on the post—no longer filled the air.

Now, the field was as black as death and smelled of decomposing bodies. The ground, once rich, brown soil, had become dry and cracked. White worms crept over the fallen, rotting husks, and, beneath the outer layers, so many wriggled that it looked as if the corn were alive.

"You'll have to lead the way," Reva said, straightening her shoulders.

Crow jumped at the sound of her voice. "What?"

"You know the field, right? I don't want to get us lost and spend more time in there than we need to."

"Right." *Right.* It was a giant cornfield with no actual pathways. The trails that did exist were created by fae stomping through the field to find their way blindly to the other side, resulting in a maze of twists and turns. Going around it would take far too long. And yet… He spun to face Reva and reached out to her, freezing before he could grab her arms. "The thing is, when I was in there before, I wasn't in my right mind. And… And I wasn't, you know…" He'd spent eleven years tied to a wooden post until Thelia had happened upon him. She'd braved the field just to help him when she'd heard him crying in the distance. His legs trembled, remembering how weak they'd been when she'd cut him down as Toto barked at her side. "I wasn't mobile."

Reva studied his face. "We have to go through," she said, her expression soft.

"I know." Crow squeezed his eyes shut and steeled his nerves. He could do this. It would be fine. "Let's be quick about it then."

"As fast as our feet can carry us," she promised.

Crow adjusted his mask and extended his blades over his hands—it was better to be prepared for the worst. After bouncing on the balls of his feet for a handful of moments, he let out a harsh breath and barreled into the rotting cornfield. If he'd tried to walk at a leisurely pace, he never would've made it. Especially not when the stalks left a foul-smelling residue wherever they brushed against him. His stomach rolled when he noticed liquid oozing down each of the husks.

"Th-there's a shed at the center of the field," he said in a shaky voice. He'd told Reva as much the night before, but talking seemed to help his nerves. "If we can make it there today, that's halfway to the other side."

"We'll make it there before dark," Reva reassured him.

The patience in her voice continued to surprise him. He kept expecting her to snap at him to get over his fear or to stop talking, but this side of Reva was the one he knew best—the one she had only showed him behind closed doors. The fae of the West loved and respected her, but she'd still always felt the need to show them she was a strong leader. Strong leaders were kind without being soft, or so Reva had repeatedly claimed. He liked her softness though.

The sun beamed down on them as they walked farther and farther, seeming like they would never make it to the halfway point. They only stopped to relieve themselves. Crow's heart wouldn't stop racing, though it wasn't solely due to his past. Petrified corpses were entwined in the stalks. Elves and gnomes, goblins and kobolds, all with their mouths frozen open in horror.

Their skin had blackened and become leathery, their milky-white eyes wide. The only thing that gave Crow any hint about how long the dead had been there was the state of their clothing. While some hung in tatters, others were relatively clean and intact, which begged the question—how had they become mummified so quickly?

"I don't like this," Reva whispered at his side. "You said it wasn't like this before, right? Do you know what lives here now?"

Crow squinted as he tried to remember. After spending so long trying to forget, it wasn't easy to recall specifics of the days he'd been trapped here. But there was no imminent danger that came to him—at least none that frequented the field. He recalled seeing a giant and a redcap once or twice, though they'd barely spared him a glance despite his cries for help. Dorothy had been the exception.

"I've never seen it like this," Crow finally said. The corn had never withered, and no one had ever come to tend the crop. It was always simply there. A cursed place, always with a cursed soul to watch over it. Locasta had killed his predecessor, but there was no way of knowing the current resident. And he hadn't dared to look at the post rising from the field's center to see who kept the vigil now. "Something must've happened after I left."

Reva held her hands up, trying in vain to get them to spark. "I have a bad feeling about this."

She wasn't alone—Crow felt as if the corn itself were watching them. The sensation of eyes bored into his back, but it was nothing compared to the painful twisting of his stomach. Reva walked close enough to offer her support without making him feel like there wasn't room to defend himself if they were ambushed. To defend them both.

"The shed isn't far now," he said after what felt like a lifetime.

Crow swallowed hard. The shed was close, but his old post was even closer. He never wanted to lay eyes on it again. His heart battered the inside of his chest, harder and harder. He wasn't normally afraid of anything, but this ... this... *No, his* mind screamed. Their shelter was only a dozen or so rows away.

Beyond the…

The…

"Crow?" Reva put a hand on one of his bracers. The blades were extended, though he couldn't remember doing that. "Are you all right?"

Fuck. He was as far from all right as a fae could get. His throat was so tight that words refused to pass, and his mouth felt so dry he thought his tongue would crack. He stumbled away from Reva and through the final row between him and a twenty-foot post—a disturbingly *empty* post. Where was the scarecrow? There was *always* a scarecrow. How did his replacement escape his or her magic tethering? The post's wood was aged and full of tiny holes from insects. When it held him, the post had been pristine. At the top, a horizontal beam formed a T. Iron circles—now rusted—stuck from the posts where rope had once been attached, holding Crow in place for over a decade. His mind reeled and swirled until his thoughts became jumbled. If he wasn't careful, this *place* would ruin him in a way no curse ever could.

Reva stepped lightly up to his side. "Don't look at it…"

Crow felt the blood drain from his face. The post seemed to call to him like an old friend, but that was a lie. It was his enemy. A beast waiting to gobble him up. Still, his feet moved to its base. A shaky breath fell from between his lips as his hand rose to caress the wood.

The moment his fingertips made contact, his body went rigid. His mind was completely blank. A buzzing emptiness swept through him as the world spun. Or was he spinning? His back was suddenly on the ground. A dull ache throbbed in his head. Was it from the fall? Or the … the…

No words came to Crow then. Only pictures. Images of his past. A beautiful female. A baby. Another beautiful female with a cruel smile. Feathers. Feathers falling. Bones breaking. *He* was breaking.

"Crow!"

His eyes snapped open to find a female haloed by the setting sun. He blinked. Blinked again. Her face was white with worry, pupils blown wide, breath coming fast. Another blink. *Reva.* He recognized her. Loved her.

"Can you hear me?" She tugged him into a sitting position. "Are you all right? Say something."

"Reva," he breathed.

"Yes," she said with a weak smile. "That's right. I'm Reva. And you're Crow."

Crow. That was his name. She was right.

A black bird cawed overhead, and Crow followed its movement with a bitter feeling in his gut. *Fly.* He wanted to fly. The bird swooped down before them and exploded into a puff of black smoke. When it cleared, a gorgeous female in a green dress stood before them. Had he ever beheld such magnificence? She was flawless, with dark, shimmering hair, ruby red lips, and a smooth complexion. Crow's blood warmed as she took a few sultry steps forward, her cloven hooves leaving small grooves in the hard dirt.

"Crow?" she asked in the sweetest of voices. "I assume you to be *the* Crow who was trapped here?"

Trapped. Crow's lungs constricted as he tried to pull in another breath. His mind struggled against an invisible binding, locking his reasoning away.

"It seems this field traded one bird for another." The female's eyes flicked to Reva. "I'm the Baobhan sith. And you—"

"Fuck off," Reva clipped.

"Oh, dear." The Baobhan sith circled them predatorily. "You are both trespassing."

Crow shivered. His cock grew hard as the Baobhan sith ran a hand slowly down her body, caressing each curve. But wanting her was dangerous, wasn't it? This female meant them harm. So, why didn't he want to fight her? To protect Reva and himself? He only wanted himself inside the luscious female. Wanted her naked body straddling his, covered in sweat, stroking, touching, touching…

"As I'm sure you saw, I do not allow such offenses to go unpunished." The Baobhan sith smirked knowingly at Crow. Pointed canines poked over her bottom lip. "But I will deal with *you* later so we have time to enjoy ourselves first."

"Like hell you will!" Reva snarled.

The Baobhan sith lunged, her mouth open, fangs glinting. Crow looked down at his hands. Blades should've been there. A hiss filled his ears—the Baobhan sith, he guessed. Because Reva didn't *hiss*. He shook his hands, hoping the blades would appear. How did they work?

"Reva?" he called. "Do you know how to—"

The field exploded with green light. The magic tingled against Crow's skin and burned through a layer of the fog engulfing his brain. He gasped as information slipped through the cracks. He was Crow. She was Reva. Dorothy was Thelia. They were going to kill Locasta. Because they had a plan. Of some sort. Crow scrambled to his feet, desperately searching for a weak spot in the fog clouding his mind, where he could pull out something else. Anything else.

His gaze drifted up and caught on smoke curling toward the sky from the twitching body of the fanged female. Dead. *Maybe dead.* The limbs still moved. Dead meant still. He cocked his head thoughtfully. *Almost dead*, he decided after a moment. That seemed right. He puffed his chest, proud of himself for coming to a conclusion, and looked over the body to Reva. The sight of her made his cock throb. *That's right.* He didn't want to fuck the Baobhan sith at all—because he already loved *this* female.

"What's going on with you?" Reva asked, breathless from the brief battle.

"I…"

Reva studied him for a long moment. "We need to get to that shed."

"There." Crow pointed to the top of the roof, barely visible over the blackened stalks. He knew that answer—that was good. He knew things! But why did it feel so bad to be so pleased with himself? His head throbbed painfully, and another thought snuck through. *You're cursed.* His stomach twisted. *No.* This wasn't his curse. Because his curse wouldn't allow him to reason out problems. It wouldn't allow him to think at all. Or remember. And he remembered Reva. His wife. *My wife!* He was a lucky male. But he hadn't seen her in a long time. She didn't like him much anymore. He scowled at the vague memory of her walking away from him at Glinda's palace.

Reva stepped toward him as if she were going to comfort him, but he shuffled back before she could. He didn't want to be consoled when his mind was so scrambled, especially not by her. "Shed," he said, and marched toward it.

CHAPTER SIXTEEN

REVA

Reva watched as Crow awkwardly marched to the shed, his arms swaying differently than usual. Even his pace was off. If she didn't know better, she would have thought he was delirious from poppies again. But this was something else.

"Crow!" she shouted. "Stop!" His body came to an abrupt halt. He remained still, as though he were ready to obey her next command. Crow's head tilted toward the clouds in wonder, his jaw hanging open. Something in this field was causing him to not be himself. Locasta must not have only put a curse on him—but connected him to the field as well. Even though he'd been gone, replaced by a new guard, he still seemed to be linked to it somehow.

The trickle of thunder pulsed through Reva's veins, her magic stirring. It had come back, just in time to kill that bitch. She knew all about Baobhan siths. They would seduce a victim, making them feel good, aroused, loved, then rip their throat apart, draining all their blood. When she'd seen Crow's cock unwillingly harden in his pants because of the female, she'd known there was only one thing to do. Kill her. Even if she had to do it with her hands. Perhaps it was pure emotion that made her magic come forward—*finally*—when she'd needed it.

Crow was still staring up at the clouds. Had he done this most of the time when he was here, attached to that pole? She grabbed him by the elbow and tugged him toward the darkened shed straight ahead. "Try not to talk ... or get distracted by the clouds."

"Um." He released a chuckle but let her continue to lead him.

As she pushed a few blackened stalks out of the way, reeking of filth, the shed came into full view.

She sucked in a sharp breath and Crow covered his mouth. "It's dead. It's dead."

What he meant was that the entirety of the shed was covered in blackened skin and she could *smell* it. But it wasn't a whole sheet of skin wrapped around the building. Strips from what she assumed were numerous fae's flesh had been stitched together across the outside walls of the shed. Disgust filled her. Once Reva killed Locasta, the curse on the cornfield could possibly be lifted. What else had this bitch destroyed in Oz?

Around the field, birds cawed, their sounds echoing in all directions around them. She wondered if they were Locasta's minions or just kept to themselves. Either way, she and Crow would need to stay silent.

A strong breeze blew across the cornfield, shaking the stalks and rumpling her hair. The Baobhan sith was dead. Would another one be coming?

Straightening her shoulders, Reva grabbed the handle of the door. The texture beneath her fingertips squished when she turned the knob. The door creaked slightly as she pushed it open. She expected the inside to reek of dead flesh too, but it didn't. The scent of sweet pastries clouded the air and light shone through the two rectangular windows, cascading its glow over the area.

In the center of the room was a table and four chairs with a full meal spread across the top. She turned to Crow who was hungrily staring at the food.

"Is it edible?" she asked while sweeping her gaze over the area. A bed with a cream crocheted blanket was in the corner and not much else.

"Dorothy ate here," he finally said, and took a seat at the table in front of buttered rolls, juicy meats, jellied pastries, and glasses of wine.

He was back to calling their daughter *Dorothy*. Reva sighed as he started to stuff his mouth with pastries. Smacking and smacking, his sounds made her shake her head.

Ten years ago, when Crow had been with Thelia, he'd never once shifted, because his mind hadn't allowed him to remember. Not until the Wizard broke his curse. Thelia had told her that much. Perhaps if his magic was back the way hers was, he could shift and that could possibly snap him out of it.

Sinking down in the chair beside Crow, Reva leaned forward and pressed her hands against his warm cheeks, feeling the curves of his high cheekbones, then turned his head to face her. He stopped chewing as she studied the scar across his nose, his lips reddened from the jam, and the glaze in his stare that wasn't fully Crow.

"Can you try and shift now?" she asked slowly to make sure he could understand her. "My magic has returned and that has to mean yours has as well."

He tilted his head, eyes seeming to dance as he studied her.

The Wizard had fixed him the last time. What if Crow could never shift again? What if he was like this permanently? *No.* She reminded herself that this was linked to Locasta. He wouldn't always be this way. Perhaps she should have him remain in this shelter while she went to the Gnome King and Locasta. No to that too. She remembered how angry she'd been when Crow had left her at the tavern. Seeing him so unlike himself, defenseless, made her realize that she couldn't abandon him, especially not here.

"You're a bird. Think about your arms becoming wings, your body covered in feathers, having a beak, and being the color of the night sky. Imagine yourself whole, flying through the wind, above the clouds." Reva would lie in the field near her palace, watching him circle around her, bringing small gifts—

meaningless to others, but everything to her. Berries, twigs in the shape of rings, hair pieces created from leaves.

He pursed his lips. "A bird. Dorothy liked birds."

She had to do it, had to use his true name this one time. Besides, he'd used hers, so it was only fair. "Crowestyn Sennan Noloris, I command you to shift into your bird form."

His brown eyes shut as soon as she finished using his beautiful name. A flash of darkened smoke came, stronger than it ever had before. He was no longer directly in front of her, but below her. Dark and perfect, his feathered wings tucked against his fragile body, no longer dragging.

"Crowestyn Sennan Noloris, I release you." She prayed to the gods above that he would understand her. "Do you remember everything?" she asked hesitantly, kneeling to where there was barely any space between her face and his.

Crow looked up at her, his small, beady eyes meeting hers, then nodded.

Lifting one of his feathery wings, she stroked the softness, the wholeness. "You aren't broken anymore," she murmured. "The potions worked." Relief washed over her. This was one thing the Wizard had done right—abandoned his potions.

His gaze peered up at the half-eaten jelly pastry.

"Before you try shifting back, finish eating." Reva scooped him up from the floor and set him on the table. He'd had trouble eating in his bird form before, but he was healed now. "I don't want to see any more of your sloppy eating if you aren't yourself again."

Crow's tiny body vibrated, and a high-pitched sound escaped his beak, his way of chuckling. He gave her a wink before he started pecking at the buttery bread. She rolled her eyes and lifted a slice of meat to her mouth. The flavor was a tad bitter, and if she had to guess, she would bet that all the food here was glamoured. At that moment, she didn't care if she was eating leaves, or mud, because it was filling her stomach.

After Crow took a final peck at his meat, he flapped his wings and flew down to the floor.

"Now that your belly is full, try shifting," Reva said, standing and placing her hands on her hips. She hoped to the fae gods that his mind wouldn't revert to her having to watch over him like a child.

A darkened cloud came with a light swish, a few dark feathers falling to the floor. Crow was in front of her, closer than she'd expected. Possibly closer than he'd expected too, because he was silent, not blinking. Staring. Breathing. Saying nothing.

Damnit.

The curse Locasta put on the cornfield must be too strong, and now he was cursed once again. Her heart beat wildly, and she bit her lip so she wouldn't scream. Reva grabbed his cheeks between her palms and pressed her lips to his soft mouth. "Come back to me."

"I just needed to collect myself," Crow murmured against her lips. "That was all."

"You scared me!" Reva snapped, taking a step back. But more than anything, relief washed over her.

"I'd say the kiss was worth it." He smiled and winked.

She couldn't even be mad at him as she glanced out the window. "When we go back into the field, I'm going to have you shift so if anything happens again, at least I can easily carry you instead of dragging you through the corn."

A sizzling sound stirred from outside. She hurried to the window and froze. Dark gray smoke wafted from the ground, making it hard to see. But then something shifted, and she looked in horror as the darkened cornstalks started *moving*, as though they were hands reaching toward the shed to rip off the roof. "What the fuck is happening?" She turned with wide eyes to look back at Crow.

The cornstalks were bending, curving, and creating a barrier around them.

"The corn won't allow us to leave," Crow said, sidling up beside her. "Not until another fae is on the post. It won't take long. I came across that part of the curse while researching and, when one dies or leaves the field, another appears before the next sunrise."

"I'm getting tired of this shit!" Reva stomped toward the table and plopped down onto a chair. "Every second we're delayed is another second Locasta is breathing."

"No one said it would be easy." He rubbed his temple, headed toward the bed, and took a seat. "It's only until morning."

Morning her ass. With narrowed eyes, she watched as he tugged off his boots and fished out a book from his bag.

She took a knife from the table and went to the door, throwing it open. Before her was a barrier of corn—not even a hole she could peep through. The scent of decay struck her and she held her breath. Drawing up her magic, Reva sparked a jolt of lightning toward it. Nothing happened besides the bolt turning to smoke. With the sharp knife clenched in her hand, she tried to slice at the stalks. Nothing. Not even a dent. She released a frustrated noise.

"Are you done trying?" Crow called. "I lived here for eleven years, remember? Fae would pass through on occasion. It may be darker here now, but I still know how the corn works."

Reva crossed the shed and stopped directly in front of him, her shadow covering half his face and book. "How can you just sit here and read?"

He quirked a brow. "It's called a distraction."

She set down the knife on the floor, removed her boots, and took a seat beside him. "But your mind was just affected. Shouldn't you rest?"

"All the more reason to read."

He was worried. That was why he was reading. Perhaps he did need the distraction, but he truly didn't want to lose his mind again. She could relate. As the Wicked Witch, she could think clearly, but she had still, in a way, lost her mind, too.

Taking a deep swallow, she said softly, "Tell me what the story is about."

His eyes shifted to Reva's, and he batted his lashes at her. "A female is annoyed with a male but then she realizes she isn't and they…" Crow trailed off.

He knew she wouldn't leave it at that. "They what?"

"They make love. A lot."

"You're such a liar. Give me that." She yanked the book from his hand and fumbled to straighten it. She read the first page about a large cock and an innocent female orgasming, then tossed it back into his lap because it was indeed one of *those* stories. Reva hated them—she would rather feel the real thing than imagine it.

Crow let out a chuckle, almost musical, filling up the room. "Apologize for calling me a liar."

"I will not." Reva paused, turning serious as she remembered their night in the tavern. "You really didn't lay with another female while I was away?"

"Why would I? You were my wife before and you will always be, even in death." He lifted the book back up.

Reva could feel the heat rolling off her in waves. She took the book from his hand and tossed it to the floor with a heavy thump. "You can't say things like that and just go back to *reading.*"

He lifted a brow, waiting for her to continue.

She stared at the planes of his face, the angles, his full lips, his square jaw. Her body heated even more in that moment, a different kind of warmth, flames feeling as though they were licking at her insides. Aware, she was so very aware of every inch of him and his strong, muscular form. Leaning over him, she pressed a hand to his cheek. "Do you think we would still know what to do if we…"

"I would always know what to do with you." With quick reflexes, Crow rolled Reva to her back until he was on top of her, propping himself up on his elbows.

"Hmm, you may have to prove it." In open invitation, Reva spread her legs so that he could settle himself between them. He drew in a sharp breath and so did she when his cock hardened right against the spot that needed him the most. Yet the damn clothing was still in the way.

Reva knew she could hesitate, make him hurt in that moment,

say something awful. But she didn't want to. She wasn't angry anymore. Not to say that she wouldn't ever be angry with him again because that would indeed happen, but they'd always been meant for one another. He was the sun and she was the moon and his rays would light the darkness around her. Always. They had both endured enough. And maybe Crow had been through more than her because she'd known he had been alive, while he'd thought she was dead. He'd suffered in the light while she'd suffered in the dark. They were both changed now, but that didn't mean their hearts didn't still beat for one another.

"I love you," she whispered. "Even when I thought I hated you, I loved you. But you never deserved that. You never deserved any of this. And I'm sorry. I'm sorry for—"

His lips fiercely silenced her with a kiss. Her eyes widened in surprise while his shut. She closed hers then, and relaxed into him, his touch, his movements. She tasted him as he deepened the kiss, and she devoured it, his familiar flavor along with the jellied desserts. Crow's tongue entangled with hers and he nipped softly at her lower lip. She forgot how Crow's kisses felt—as good as if she'd just been fucked. She'd kissed him after the poppies, and the soft kiss when she thought he'd still been cursed, but this was different. This was a true kiss.

Reva drew him closer, her hands venturing up the smoothness of his back to the ripples across his chest. There were too many layers of clothing between them and she wanted them all off.

As she reached for his pants, he yanked at her shirt and corset. Their breaths came out heavy, desperate. Everything was shed, their lips never once leaving one another's, as if those body parts had known the painful abandonment of years separated from each other as keenly as their owners.

Their naked bodies pressed against one another and she couldn't control a shiver at how good it felt. As she kissed down his salty neck, Reva glided her fingertips to between his legs and gripped his hardened length. She stroked and she stroked. It was so familiar, like they'd never been apart.

Crow groaned and lifted his head, giving her more access to the place behind his ear where she licked and nipped.

His cock throbbed in her hand and she shifted him to his back so she was straddling him. He quickly sat up and adjusted her so she was flush against his chest, her nipples pebbling more than they already had.

"You're beautiful," she whispered as she trailed a finger down the light scar of his nose.

"That was supposed to be my line." He winked, placing his mouth around her nipple, licking, while he cradled the other.

The caresses, touches, and her hips rocking kept coming until she needed more, had to have *much* more.

Crow's hand drifted down between her legs, rubbing in blissful circles, her wetness pooling around his fingertips. "I'm going to please you more than I ever have," he rasped.

Reva arched her back and moaned as he pressed on her center. "Get inside me already," she said, unable to control the need in her voice. "We've waited long enough." Then she lowered herself to her back, taking him with her, his lips tasting hers once more.

"I love you," he murmured. With a single thrust, the way she liked, he pushed into her, filling her, making her gasp. As a lover, Crow always knew how to make her want more of him, even when she'd never planned to fall for him the way she had in their past.

He started pumping his hips, lighting up the nerve endings inside her entire body, creating a starry sky within her darkness. Reva grabbed his ass, driving him to move harder and harder, shaking the entire bed.

When that position fulfilled its duty, Crow lifted her with a firm swoop so that she was straddling him again. The friction increased and she kept her pace as they both sat up, his strong arms holding her tight, while he and his cock ravished her.

Reva's hands cupped his face. Their sweat-slick chests pressed together. The intense sensation was unfurling, like a flower opening and opening, until Reva gasped. The pleasure took over her entire body, vibrating it like thunder, more so than her own magic ever had.

Crow's hands tightened on her hips as she rode him even harder, knowing his satisfaction was nearing by the way he licked his lower lip. "Reva," he rasped when his orgasm followed suit.

Neither one moved from their position, their breaths coming out heavy. They stared at each other, and before tears could form, she put her lips to his, holding them there, thinking, for the first time, about not their past, but their future.

"We'll get back everything we had," Reva swore as her lips left Crow's. "And it will be better than before because we have Thelia with us again."

"We will." He lowered them to the mattress, and she placed her head on his chest, right on the spot where she could hear the musical sound of his heartbeat.

It was too early to sleep and she wanted more of him, not only the physical, but from his lovely mind, his voice. "Tell me about everything you did while I was away." She wanted to hear his entire story, the way she'd heard Thelia's. Not just the bits and pieces that she'd learned about. "Then, afterward, I'm going to make you forget you were ever cursed."

CHAPTER SEVENTEEN

CROW

A loud thud woke Crow with a start. He sat up to find Reva dressed from the waist down as she searched the shed. Crow leaned back on his elbows, completely unbothered by his own nudity, and watched as she kicked a chair aside, grumbling. She had been just as feisty the night before too, her lips around his cock while she gripped his ass. Crow grinned at the memory of having her again. She had tasted like he'd remembered—sweet, yet tart—and had felt even better.

As if Reva had sensed his stare, she whipped around to face him. "Finally. I thought you would sleep all day."

"Maybe if I'd gotten any sleep last night," he said with a sly grin. "Come here."

Reva inched toward him, too slowly for his liking, so he grabbed her arm and tugged her down. She landed on him with an *oof*, her breasts pressed against his chest. Crow's heart swelled at her nearness. He tugged a lock of her hair behind her ear and sighed silently. It had been so long since he'd held his wife, and for a little while, he had wondered if he ever would again. He swept forward and kissed her, his lips caressing hers.

Reva relaxed against him, returning the kiss, but only for a moment. "All right," she murmured, brushing his cheek before pushing herself up. "I need to find my corset and shirt, then we need to get out of here."

"I'm sure we have a *few* minutes," Crow complained at the loss of her warmth.

"When has anything only lasted a few minutes with you? A-ha!" She swiped her clothing off the floor near his head.

"Are you sure you need to put it back on? I wouldn't mind," he said with a wink.

"You're insufferable." She smirked and tugged the rest of her clothing on. "Get dressed. The stalks have moved, and we're losing daylight. I don't want to get stuck in the cornfield without shelter."

The thought of another night in his personal hell sent a shiver through him. He threw on his clothes quickly and shouldered his pack. Under other circumstances, he might've insisted they eat first, but he doubted he would be able to keep a single bite down.

"Ready?" Reva asked.

Crow paused and stared out the windows—clear of any stalks. Which meant only one thing… "A new scarecrow is waiting out there."

"Let's hope this one is planted to the post," Reva muttered.

She inhaled deeply and ripped the door inward. Crow followed her from the shed, trying desperately not to look at his old post. But he couldn't stop his eyes from straying.

A new scarecrow hung there without the slightest movement. The male had bright red hair, elven ears, and an expression of frozen horror. His ragged knit clothing drooped over his too-thin frame. It appeared to be mere fabric stuffed with straw at first glance, but the muffled sobs were undeniably real. It tore at Crow's already fragile state-of-mind. That had been him ten years ago. He hadn't been as lucky as the Baobhan sith who had somehow managed to break free of the post. Took *his* place. Every blazing hot ray of sunlight would land on him, every rain cloud or sheet of ice that fell from the sky. And he would *feel* it.

There was no way they could help the unfortunate fae, however. Not right then. It would take too long to discover how to break his personal curse. Even if they were able to, another soul would appear tomorrow if Locasta remained living.

"When we're finished with Locasta, we'll come back," Crow said as much to himself as to Reva. He would want to make sure killing her released the field.

Reva wove her fingers between his and squeezed. "Let's get you out of here."

Crow nodded and took off at a near run. He wanted *out* of there and every moment mattered. His mind buzzed. It was as if the field was trying to erase his thoughts again, but he kept hyper-focused on the feel of Reva's hand in his. She grounded him. Anchored him to reality. He could still taste her on his lips. Phantom touches lingered where she had caressed his skin the night before, leaving his entire body sensitive to the smallest breeze.

They plowed through the stalks all the morning and into the afternoon without a break. He tried to see nothing except the path directly before him, but glimpses of white bones caught his peripheral more than once. When they did finally stop, it was only to dig through their packs for food before continuing. The food taken from the shed was flavorless now that it was out of the building, but it still filled their stomachs.

Finally, as twilight touched the sky, turning it deep pink, they emerged from the cornfield. Crow sucked in a deep breath the moment his boots hit green grass. The stench of the field had nearly gagged him, but he didn't care. They were out. The field was behind them. On their journey back from the North, they would take an entirely different route.

After another few staggering steps, Crow fell to his knees and closed his eyes. His body quivered with exhaustion, his mind reveling at being free. He could still feel the maliciousness of the field's curse deep in his marrow. It wanted to reclaim him— wanted him to stay. Almost demanded it. But he would never willingly allow himself to be its prisoner again.

Reva's footsteps came to a halt in front of him and he reached out to her without opening his eyes. His arms wrapped around her waist and he buried his face in her abdomen.

Her fingers combed gently through his hair for a few minutes, comforting him, before she tipped his head back to look at her. "It's behind us," she said. "We keep going."

Keep going. She was right—the only thing they could do was move forward—and the farther they went, the better he was sure to feel. Crow nodded and climbed to his feet. Beyond them rose the Gnome King's mountain. A red haze hovered over the top of the rocky peak. Years of fae travel to and from the Gnome City had worn a path to the base. Tunnels ran through the interior of the rocky cliffs and eventually came out at a clearing surrounded by the mountain walls. That was where the gnomes had created their city, but the tunnels were where they kept their valuables. Crow knew because he'd searched them years ago, carefully mapping them out as he went, in an attempt to find the stone. This time, he planned to be less covert.

"Would you rather climb the cliff or go through the pass?" he asked.

Reva chewed her bottom lip as they walked. "I think that depends on how we want to approach the king."

"If we confront him in front of his subjects, he may kill us on the spot to maintain his image."

She tapped a finger on her chin as she seemed to mull it over. "So we sneak in and corner him when he's alone. I don't suppose you know where his private chambers are?"

"How would I know that?" Crow asked with a mischievous tone. When she shrugged, he slipped his pack to one shoulder and pulled out the folded paper, hidden in the seams of his pack. He held it out to her. "I do, actually."

Reva slowly unfolded the map and a smile crept over her face. "Well, aren't you full of surprises?"

"I told you that I've been inside a few times." He inched closer, so his shoulder rubbed against hers. The light scent of vanilla mixed with spices had his blood pumping faster. He pointed to an area at the top left of the map and forced himself to focus. "We scale the cliff and enter here. It's the closest entrance to his rooms."

"*I'll* scale the cliff." Reva handed him back the paper, and he tucked it into his pants pocket. "You should scout ahead."

Crow opened his mouth to say he wasn't any faster at climbing than she was when she smiled. *His wings.* They were healed. He could *fly* again. His bird form seemed to wrestle for control of his body, eager to take flight, but he couldn't leave her yet. There was still a half day's walk ahead of them. "Deal," he said, feeling lighter than he had in years.

Each minute of their walk was like ten. Crow knew he was going to fly when they reached their destination and it drove him mad to wait. But Reva did her best to distract him by chatting about Ozma. He tried very hard to stay engaged in the conversation, but it was difficult to care about Mombi and Oz being villainous in that moment when the sky was so bright. Mombi had always been rumored to be bizarre and Oz was a faerie fruit-addicted bastard. It wasn't all that surprising that they had joined forces to banish the true heir to the Land of Oz into the dark place. Once Locasta was dealt with, they would meet Ozma in the Emerald City. If Mombi and Oz were still alive then, they would decide how to change that.

When Crow and Reva reached the base of the mountain far from the tunnel entrance, he shifted anxiously from one foot to the other. The incline was steep but manageable. There were plenty of footholds along the gray stone. Smooth white rock peeked out from the dark gray limestone, offering Reva plenty of places to grab. Still, unease blossomed in his chest with her climbing on her own.

"Are you sure you're okay with this climb?"

Reva raised an eyebrow. "Is that a legitimate question?"

A vision of Reva scaling an even steeper mountainside surfaced in his mind. They'd been fleeing the West, seeking a haven from Locasta's wrath. The edge of the cliff had crumbled, and they'd fallen twenty feet to a wide ledge. It was either climb the cliff to safety, or edge along the ridge and hope it led somewhere worth going. Reva hadn't thought twice before launching herself up the stone wall.

"I'll be around if you get stuck," he said.

She scoffed. "I won't."

Unable to wait any longer, Crow willed his bird form forward. One moment, he stood beside Reva, the next he flexed his wings as wide as they could go. The muscles strained, shaky from lack of use, but he still felt powerful. He hopped once, twice, three times, testing out his now-mended body. He gave Reva a caw and launched into the air.

He gained height, then lost it. His body remembered how to fly, but it had been so long that it took a few extra moments for him to find the rhythm. Once he did, his heart soared higher than his wings could ever hope to carry him. The wind rushed over his feathers, welcoming him back.

Reva was only a few feet off the ground when he let himself drop. He swooped down just above her head and snapped his wings wide. They caught the air, carrying him upward again. "Behave," Reva shouted after him. His chuckle came out as a breathy *caw*.

But now that he'd given himself a moment of joy, there was a job to be done. He flew to the top of the cliff, a yard below the red mist. A bare, twisted tree offered the perfect perch. He landed on the sturdiest branch and squinted into the clearing below.

The stone buildings were so minuscule from this vantage point that they looked like children's playthings. Stone dots—the gnomes themselves—moved about like ants. There didn't seem to be any scouts where Crow perched, waiting, but he would stay put just to be sure they weren't making rounds.

Every few minutes, he sailed off the tree to check on Reva's whereabouts. She was making slow, but steady, progress and was nearly to an oval ledge large enough for her to take a break. He settled back on the branch and scoured the round entrances carved into the stone mountain, each leading to a portion of the tunnels. No guards. No civilians. It seemed as if all the gnomes were busy in the clearing or hidden inside, but that didn't seem right. There had always been at least a handful of guards when he'd snuck in. His talons clicked on the tree as he paced along the branch. Something was wrong. He needed to get to Reva.

Crow leapt into the air and plunged toward where she was. Where she *should've* been. But the cliffside was empty. He tucked his wings against his sides, and the wind whizzed over him. A panicked screech left his throat. Reva hadn't fallen—there wasn't a body on the ground below—but a spark of green leaked from inside a hidden tunnel entrance.

Shit.

Crow transformed into his fae form again before he hit the rocky ledge. He landed on his feet, dark hair falling in his face, and strode into the tunnel with blades at the ready. Another blast of green drew him farther into the tunnel entrance.

Crow found Reva around the first turn with two dozen gnomes surrounding her. They were varying shades and textures of stone—smooth obsidian, beige pockmarked felsite, tan dolomite covered in clear crystals, and striped sandstone—but all of them only came up to her shoulders. Their naked stone bodies had a vaguely elven shape, but their bulbous heads and severe underbites were uniquely *gnome*.

While the gnomes weren't what Crow would consider intimidating creatures, the iron spears they had pointed at Reva's chest were another story. Every blast of Reva's magic that slammed into their stone bodies only served to push them back. For each round gnome that retreated a step, another took its place.

Crow swept his blades across the nearest guard. White lines scarred the stone fae, who whirled on him. Sharp pain stabbed him between the shoulder blades at the same time the scarred gnome leveled his spear at Crow's chest.

"Stop," Reva shouted.

"Surrender your weapons," one of the guards said, his voice like gravel. "You," he said to another guard, "bind her hands behind her back."

Crow tensed, ready to leap to his wife's defense, but she

shook her head. She allowed one gnome to take her pack before her hands were tugged behind her, and she stayed utterly still as they shackled her with stone manacles. He sighed and retracted his blades. The gnomes quickly unbuckled his bracers, ripped away his pack, then ran their stone hands over his body in search of other weapons. Crow held Reva's gaze the entire time, hoping they would miss the knife in his boot.

They didn't.

But they didn't search Reva. He suppressed a grin, remembering how she'd used his other knife to clean her nails the night before they entered the cornfield and she'd never returned it.

"Move," a gnome ordered, shoving the tip of his spear into Crow's side.

Crow released a long breath and allowed himself to be led deeper into the tunnels. He memorized each turn they made to add it to his map later when they escaped. *With* the stone. There was no leaving without it. Not when facing Locasta empty-handed would undoubtedly end with both him and Reva cursed again. And Crow knew the Northern Witch well enough to understand there would be no breaking her curses a second time.

CHAPTER EIGHTEEN

REVA

"You mother-fuckers!" Reva seethed as the gnomes shoved her forward with the tips of their iron spears. The gnomes each had the same basic shape, their height reaching to her shoulders, their upper backs hunched, lower jaw set forward, and not a drop of cloth clung to their hardened bodies. Several of the gnomes' stony outer layers were full of large and small holes splattering their entire lengths, while others were as smooth as a newborn elf's skin. Each one varied in color. Some obsidian, others topaz, crystal, and so on. She'd never seen the Gnome King before, had only heard about him from other fae, but she wondered which of the gnomes he most resembled.

Crow's eyes locked on hers, and his expression told her to play along. They were outnumbered, her magic wasn't doing a drop of damage to them, and one gnome's spear was aimed right at Crow's heart. The gnomes didn't need to lock stone manacles on her wrists or try to attack her with their spears. They could have played nice themselves, but they hadn't. However, she needed to cooperate for the time being.

Another sharp jab came at Reva's back. She cursed under her breath but followed the gnomes as they led the way toward a narrow opening within the cave.

Inside, the tunnel opened into a wider space and a long strip of pale blue fire along the wall lit their way. Below the flames, trickles of water flowed down to the pebbled floor, creating puddles. An earthy smell surrounded her that wasn't at all unpleasant, almost intoxicating—the *only* thing that wasn't offensive here.

The tunnel led to a junction with three other oval openings. Gnomes seemed to appear out of nowhere as they pushed themselves out from the walls. These gnomes, made of limestone, took over for the others and shoved Reva and Crow down the tunnel.

"How much farther?" Crow asked.

"Remain silent or we eat your flesh," a gnome with half his face crumbled away bellowed.

Crow's jaw clenched, and Reva could tell he was trying desperately to hold his tongue.

The gnomes took them down two more flame-lit tunnels, the walls jagged and sharp, with protruding granite thorns. At the end of the tunnel was a whirling stone staircase leading down into the area below. Reva held her breath steady while taking the first step. She stared at the back of Crow's head, hoping nothing would come out of the shadows to cause him harm.

Once she descended the last step into a large room with sparkling quartz floors, she'd expected the Gnome King to be waiting on a stone throne, but he wasn't. There was no throne at all. In fact, the room was completely bare except for the twinkling gemstones that were worked into the stone walls. Sapphires, amethysts, diamonds, opals, and others she couldn't name.

On the other side of the room, a door creaked open, one that she wouldn't have noticed since it had blended in with the wall. Out stepped a looming figure, taller and more muscular than Crow. His hard, smooth outer layer was the color of ivory, and each muscle in his chest appeared chiseled to perfection. Midnight blue hair hung straight down to his waist in silken sheets and tucked behind his pointed ears. The male fae didn't much resemble the gnomes who still held her and Crow hostage, aside from being made of stone. Her gaze widened as it roamed to the area between his legs, which was on full display. Even his stone cock was practically a work of art.

The male bared his teeth into a smile, causing his high cheekbones to appear even higher. It was as if he'd been sculpted by beauty itself.

"Why are you here in my palace, maiden?" His voice came out stern.

So, this was the Gnome King. When maidens ventured here to try and make him fall in love, she wondered if any had thought about how it would feel to fuck a stone cock. It certainly didn't look like it would be comfortable, regardless of how good it might look.

The Gnome King's cobalt eyes drifted to Crow and hardened. "You dare to bring a male with you?"

You mean, I brought her, Crow mouthed to Reva.

Reva took a breath, trying to keep calm when all she wanted were the manacles to be removed from her wrists. "Gnome King—"

"You may call me Ceres," he interrupted.

"Ceres," Reva said slowly, "we need your help. Locasta is attempting to take over Oz, no matter who she ruins in the process."

"Why should I care who rules Oz?" Ceres shrugged and folded his arms over his muscular chest.

"Because you live here," Reva spat.

"No one can defeat me here." Ceres dropped his arms and moved to her in three quick strides. He lifted her chin between his cool fingertips. "Maiden, aren't you here because you think you can make me love again? That is why they all come."

Reva knew Crow was carefully watching, ready to intervene if he needed to.

"I'm not here for that. I couldn't give a fuck if you fall in love again or not." She paused, reeling her emotions back in. "I'm sorry. You've lost someone important to you. I understand. But that doesn't mean you should destroy every female who walks into your kingdom."

"Who do you think you are?" The Gnome King leaned his face closer to hers, his breath hitting her cheek. She held back a shiver from the coldness.

"We've never met before, but I know you've heard of me. I'm Reva."

Ceres's hand lowered from her chin as his eyes narrowed, recognition setting in. "Reva. The once-ruler of the West?"

Reva slowly nodded, keeping her eyes trained on his. She didn't look at her husband because she didn't want the Gnome King to see how much she cared for Crow. That could lead to torture, which was already highly likely.

"Locasta had placed a curse on me out of spite, then turned me into the monstrous Wicked Witch of the West." Even then she couldn't help but remember her taloned fingers, her green skin, the pustules, the need and desire to hunt, to kill, to torment.

Ceres's tongue scraped the inside of his cheek, the sound echoing. "I don't believe it. Dorothy killed the ruler of the West. She's dead."

There was only one way to show him, but with the iron poking at her flesh, she couldn't conjure the magic. "Remove my manacles and I'll demonstrate."

"She did have green powers outside," one of the gnomes hissed, his shoulders growing rigid.

Ceres tapped the side of his stone cheek. Reva guessed he was weighing his options—murder them there or let her prove herself. She wouldn't make it easy to kill them if that was what he chose.

"Free her," he finally said. His gaze shifted to Crow, his white eyelashes lowering. "But not him."

Reva held her breath. She had to remember if anyone tried to torture Crow down here, he could transform and save himself. But she knew he wouldn't leave her, no matter how much she would shout at him to do so.

A gnome shuffled behind her and unlocked her manacles. Reva rubbed at her wrists—they were sore and red from her yanking at them.

Stepping toward the Gnome King and taking a deep breath, she let the power crackle and churn inside her until the magic pulsed green on her palm, like emerald lightning flashing inside a darkened cloud. "If you want me to continue, I can strike the ground and make thunder rattle your walls."

"Stop," Ceres demanded, not removing his gaze from her hand.

Her magic ceased, the emerald color disappearing from sight. "Now"—Reva cocked her head and smiled—"I may not be able to end you or your gnomes' lives at the moment, but I can destroy your entire palace before you could ever end me."

Crow inhaled sharply in a way that told her to watch it. She ignored him.

"Will you help us defeat Locasta?" she asked, taking a backward step closer to Crow.

Ceres studied her, stretching the time out. "I need to think about it. First, I'll have to figure out what I want in return."

Reva held back a shake of the head. What all kings and queens seemed to want was more territory. "I can give you more land once I reclaim what's mine. All the land near the deserts."

He scanned her up and down, licking his lips. "I'm not sure more land is what I want, *Reva*. We'll discuss this more in the morning." His gaze shifted to one of the crystal gnomes. "Take them to a guest room for now."

The Gnome King turned away, but glanced one more time at her over his shoulder before sauntering through the same secret door that he'd used to enter. Reva turned to Crow, who was focused on her, the vein in his jaw ticking.

"Come on," a gnome grunted, removing Crow's manacles. He then waved at them to follow him back up the stairs. No iron spear this time.

"I don't like the way he's watching you," Crow whispered in her ear. He was jealous, but there was nothing to worry about.

She wasn't wooed by males who slit the throats of their females.

"It's nothing," she said quietly. "I'll bet Ceres looks at any maiden that way before he slaughters them."

"We're calling him Ceres now?"

Reva rolled her eyes. "Just remember what I told you yesterday. You know, in the shed?"

A side-smile formed on Crow's face and he pressed a hand to his chest, letting her know that he loved her too.

Neither one said anything else as they reached the top of the stairs and followed the crystal gnome. Once they reached the end of the tunnel, the other gnomes stayed at their posts while the crystal one continued to lead them down several tunnels. There was an elaborate crisscrossing arched design above them made from rose quartz, and protruding jagged stone poked out from the walls. An imaginary wind appeared to blow against the blue flames highlighting their way. The only sounds were the stomp of the gnome's feet and his heavy breathing.

The gnome turned the corner and stopped in front of what looked to be stone bars. He pulled open the door and ushered them in.

Reva and Crow stepped inside, and she wondered where their packs had been taken. He shut the caged door behind them, locking it. So much for *guest* room.

"If you're thirsty there's water over there." The gnome pointed in between the bars to the far corner, where water trickled into a large garnet bucket, before turning to walk away.

In the middle of the room was a rectangular stone that must have been the bed. Crow took a seat in the center of it. "We got farther than I expected. And you're still alive."

Reva sank down beside him. "And you weren't tortured."

"Not yet." He rubbed at a red spot on his arm where one of the gnomes had poked him too hard with the iron. "He's going to try something, Reva. I hated the way he looked at you."

"Let him look." She stared at the granite flooring. "The problem now is we're locked in a stone cage. I was expecting a room that we could sneak out of."

He winked at her, his smile lighting up his face. "You still underestimate me, my love."

It took her a moment to realize what he was implying. He could shift. "Oh, *oh*!" She smirked. "If we had time and we weren't here, I would kiss you all over."

"I'll take on the mouth for now." He leaned forward, stealing a quick kiss from her that tingled all the way down to her toes.

She then whispered in his ear, "I'll tell you when to go." Quietly, she slipped the knife from her boot and set it into his palm.

CHAPTER NINETEEN

CROW

Reva pressed Crow's knife into his hand. He winked at her as he tucked the blade into his boot, though he wasn't sure how much use it would be against stone. Still, it was better than nothing. "I'll be quick," he promised. Then he called forth his other form. One moment he stood six inches taller than his wife—the next, a black cloud exploded around him and he became a bird in the time it would take to snap his fingers.

Leaving Reva alone made Crow's insides squirm. The Gnome King could beat her to death, or drag her to a pit for a slow demise, or simply crush her with his bare hands. But they still needed to go through with their plan to get the red stone. Only, now they also needed a second plan to escape. Neither could be accomplished from inside a cell, so he gave her the softest of caws and, on her signal, slipped through the bars.

He hopped down the hallway, retracing their steps with the help of the enchanted blue flames that ran along the walls, until he found what looked to be an abandoned, dead-end tunnel. Cobwebs hung from the ceiling and a crack in the stone let in a trickle of water, leaving the floor slick with mildew. This was a safe enough place.

When Crow was broken, changing back and forth between

his forms had taken every ounce of energy he had. Bones either had to break or mend accordingly and it never failed to steal his breath away. But now, he shut his eyes and willed himself back into fae form as effortlessly as blinking. His clothes were just as he left them, his hair only slightly mussed.

Crow stayed hunched near the entrance and pulled the map from his pocket. He hadn't charted this part, but he was sure he wasn't far off from tunnels he *had* explored. Hopefully something would begin to look familiar on the map sooner rather than later. The dripping water was likely from the hot spring on the lower mountain ledge. There were a few areas with vegetation, but only one with a spring, which told him two things: they were being kept in the lower tunnels—perhaps even below ground—and they were on the east side of the city.

Crow studied the map, committing to memorize the most likely tunnels that this one connected to, before creeping out into the main halls. He was light on his feet as he explored, ducking in and out of small alcoves when the sound of stomping stone feet neared. A handful of gnomes passed, laughing and joking in Gnomish. Once the danger was gone, he continued on, all the while recording the turns in his mind. Left, right, right, left, right.

The tunnels seemed to stretch on forever before he caught his bearings. Each new passage looked just like the last, with blue flames and smoothly carved walls. The ceilings were left rough, as if to add character, and were the only thing that gave any hint of his location. A small x marked the top of a particular tunnel, so well-blended with the cracks that it was impossible to see if one wasn't looking for it. Crow, however, had been the one to score the stone when he'd explored last time. He quickly unfolded the yellow map, the creases wearing thin, and found the corresponding x marking which tunnel began there. Later, when he returned to Reva, he would draw the tunnels it had taken to reach that place and score another symbol on the ceiling in front of the cell.

"All right," he whispered to himself. "This way."

Based on his markings, behind him lay the cells, and before

him, nothing of value in regard to the stone. He was surprisingly close to the king's chambers. Only such an arrogant king would allow prisoners to be kept so near his own rooms. The tunnels were a maze to navigate, but Crow couldn't have been the only one to ever scout them.

With a quick glance at the map, Crow planned his route, but there was no telling how much time he had before the gnomes returned to the cell. He didn't want them to find Reva alone, so he would go back to her and then leave again after the guards checked on them.

"Did you send the message?" a familiar, deep, gravelly voice bellowed ahead of him—the Gnome King.

Crow bolted back to the last hiding place he'd seen, and without a moment to spare. Two sets of heavy footsteps trudged toward him.

"I did, Your Majesty.'"

"Wonderful. Locasta will surely reward us with more than a simple promise of land at some point in the future," the king huffed. "And land near the desert at that! As if we hadn't relocated for a reason."

"The Good Witch of the North will be generous, I'm sure," the other gnome agreed. "Especially given who the male is."

The king laughed heartily. "He probably thinks I didn't recognize him—the fool. What sort of help do you suspect they were going to ask from me?"

"We can only guess, sire."

"I think I'll do more than that," the king said. Their footsteps stopped just past Crow's hiding place, and his heart hammered in his chest. "Bring me the female tomorrow. We'll have lunch together in my chambers—alone. I'll get her to tell me everything."

"So you *don't* want us to prepare the blade or the hammer?" the gnome asked, confused.

"Not quite yet."

"Of course."

The footsteps sounded again, this time going in two different directions. Crow waited until he could no longer hear them and transformed into his bird form, flying back to Reva as fast as his wings could carry him. His small body slipped through the bars and he landed on Reva's shoulder with rumpled feathers.

"What's wrong?" she asked, seeming to sense all was not well.

Crow's beak opened as he tried to slow his rapid breathing. He was too wound up to shift—his body tense and his mind frantic, unlike the hyper-focused anger he'd felt entering the tunnels to save Reva. Still, he had to warn her that Locasta knew they were in Gnome City.

He hopped off Reva's shoulder and glided to the stone bed. There was nothing to write with inside the cell so he would have to do his best without language. He lifted a small piece of crumbled rock in his beak and puffed his chest.

Reva blinked at him in confusion. "A big rock?" she ventured.

In a way… Crow strutted around in a circle with his wings out.

"A gnome?"

Crow hopped in excitement, but he needed her to know it was the king. Flapping his wings, he landed on her head and set the piece of rock down, then hopped down again and cawed as if he were unequaled.

"Hat? No! Crown! The Gnome King!"

Crow flapped his wings and began delivering her small rocks from around the room.

"I have no idea," Reva said with a scowl. "Pile?"

Crow shook his head.

"The Gnome King smashed another gnome into pieces?"

Crow sighed. This was impossible. How else could he show *delivered*?

"Spell it out with these," Reva suggested, poking at the pile of pebbles.

Crow hadn't thought of that. He arranged the small stones into elvish letters. Finally, he'd spelled out *sent message to L.* He'd run out of stones to spell the rest, but Reva would know who he meant.

"The Gnome King sent Locasta a message?" Reva's eyes were wide and burning with unfiltered fury. "About us?"

Crow cawed.

"That son of a bitch! I'm going to turn him into rubble!"

Crow flicked at a rock with his beak. They still needed the stone.

"Yes, yes," she murmured. "The stone first, if we can find it."

Crow's body shuddered with exhaustion. He didn't have the energy to tell her his theory on the location of the stone, and there was the more pressing issue of the king wanting her to have lunch with him. He moved the pebbles to spell out *you lunch alone king*.

Reva's brows rose up her forehead. "The king wants me to have lunch with him alone? Why?" she mused, more to herself than him. She sat down beside him and lifted him into her lap. "Actually, this may work in our favor. I'll distract him while you keep looking for the stone. If he doesn't agree to give it to us, we'll steal it."

Crow wanted to tell her what a horrible idea that was. The Gnome King was far from stupid and, given that he killed every female who dared enter his city, also extremely dangerous. But Reva knew that and still wanted to go through with this, and Crow knew better than to tell her otherwise. So, he settled into her warm lap to relax enough to transform. It didn't help that he was no longer used to exerting so much energy to switch between forms. With an agitated huff, he ruffled his feathers and counted backward from a hundred to help calm his nerves.

CHAPTER TWENTY

REVA

It had taken a while for Crow to shift back to his male form the night before, but he'd finally transformed after multiple tries. As he straightened on the stone bed, Reva watched as beads of perspiration dripped down his forehead and neck. His skin even appeared paler. Neither one had gotten any sleep and they'd only had water, that had a strange taste, from the bucket.

"Will you be able to shift today?" Reva asked, her lips thinning as she continued to study him. "Perhaps you shouldn't try again. I'll just get the information from Ceres myself, then we can find the stone together."

He rubbed at his chin and arched a dark eyebrow. "There's nothing wrong with my shifting—I'm only wound up. I don't like this. Since Locasta knows we're here, who knows what will happen?"

Ceres just *had* to reveal to Reva's enemy that she was still alive. Now their plans would have to be altered.

"She won't come." Reva shook her head. "I know her well enough, and she hates to chance defeat, so she won't show herself—yet. Her minions will be the ones sent to do the dirty work." When Thelia was born it had been different because Locasta knew she could defeat Reva in an exhausted state. And once she'd been in the Northern Witch's control, Reva had been released into the wild, only secretly meeting when Locasta wanted to make her dance for her, or slap her across the face.

"And if she *does* decide to come?" Crow inched closer to Reva, brushing his fingers against hers. "Then what? I know her well too, and it won't be good."

"Then she comes." Reva grasped his hand and gave it a quick squeeze before letting go. "We fight."

"The gnomes are tricky to take down."

"That they are." She paused. "I didn't try for long, though. And I figured I should play nice, or *nicer*, so we could find the stone."

"There has to be a way to track it down." Crow chewed on his lip.

"If something was that important, most fae would keep it on themselves at all times." She would.

"He's naked, Reva." Crow cocked his head. "Unless you think he stuck it up his asshole."

"Now that, my dear Crow, could very well be the case." Reva laughed and covered her mouth. He was right. There wasn't a single stone or jewel clinging to Ceres's body. No rings, no necklaces, no bracelets. Nothing. Not even a crown.

He started to smile too, dipping his head toward hers. But then a clatter and heavy footsteps sounded from outside their cell and down the tunnel. Reva and Crow broke apart and watched as two gnomes stopped in front of their barred cell. Neither were the same gnomes from earlier. One was dark magenta with silver stripes across her belly and the other was entirely translucent with a hazy sheen.

"The Gnome King requests the female's company for lunch," the magenta one said, eyeing Reva and pointing a staff at her.

"A request can be denied," Reva answered, trying to make it seem as though she wasn't anxious to attend.

"Go or die." The clear gnome shrugged. "That's your choice."

"Well, then, with that sort of *hospitality*, I might as well attend." Reva stood from the bed and didn't look back at Crow as she stepped toward the door. It made a scratching noise as the magenta gnome pulled it open.

Crow had tried to return the knife to Reva, but she'd snuck it back on him, figuring he would need it more than her. It would be better than no weapon at all. At the very least, they could scrape it across the gnomes' eyes.

Reva exited the cell and followed the two gnomes down the jagged-stone tunnel. She knew as soon as the coast was clear that Crow would transform into his bird form—if he could muster up the strength.

The earthy scent of sandalwood from the stone itself enveloped her, stronger here than in the cell. Liquid dripped from the ceiling, a couple of droplets pelting her skin. The blue flames guided their way, the tunnels remaining silent as they walked down them and descended the stairs to the empty room where she'd first met Ceres. If this were meant to be where they were to eat, she wondered if they would be dining on the floor. As if answering her thoughts, the hidden door, from where the Gnome King had first appeared, opened in the wall with a soft groan.

The two guards waved their spears for her to follow them. Once she crossed into the new room, her gaze landed on the wall. It was covered in sparkling blue jewels, matching the color of Ceres's hair. Standing before them in a neat row were dozens of pale skeletons wearing blood-stained gowns. There was at least one dress of every color, all made of the finest materials, and ranging in size from pixie to troll.

Reva inhaled sharply, at a loss for words over the collection of the dead before her.

"These are the remains of the females who thought they could sway me," a deep voice rumbled.

Reva's gaze settled, unnerved, on the long rectangular table in the middle of the room, leading up to Ceres. He sat regally in his chair with one leg propped over the other. "I see," she said.

"I'm glad I didn't wear a gown then."

His cobalt eyes glittered with amusement as he watched every move she made on her way to the table. "You may sit across from me."

Strewn along the table were different rocks resting on stone plates, smooth in texture—gray, white, and brown in color. This must be their lunch… She believed him to be toying with her. Only a fool would believe she'd eat rocks.

"I have a better idea," Reva purred, sauntering toward him instead, and running her fingertips over the rocks.

He narrowed his eyes at her as she plopped down on the edge of the table in front of him.

"And what idea is that?" Ceres lifted his hand and drew a light line with his fingernail across her throat. "For me to bleed you out right here? It would add to the flavor of dinner."

Reva didn't let any fear show as she spread her legs apart. "We both know if you wanted me dead, I already would be." She unbuttoned the outer layer of her tunic, exposing the corset and curves of the tops of her breasts beneath. "How many of the maidens did you fuck before you killed them?"

With quick motions, he grabbed her from the table and set her on his lap, her legs open and cradling his. "How many do you think?"

"Too many." She could feel the hardness and twitch of his cock beneath her. She tried not to let the disgust show in her face as she leaned forward, pushing her breasts against his hard chest.

"The maidens—their *softness*—disgusts me. But I'll take the momentary pleasure anyway, then after I get my fuck, I remove their soft skin so only hard bone is left." He ran his hand up her face, through Reva's hair, and yanked her head back. "If my wife couldn't live, then why should any females be allowed to? Outside of my gnomes, of course."

Reva maintained a neutral expression, but she couldn't control the rapid beat of her heart. In that moment, she wanted to chip away at his hard skin, the way he'd done to those innocent females. Even though they'd known what he was capable of before trying to come and win his affection. "Do *I* disgust you?" she asked slowly.

Ceres released her hair, his gaze roaming over her as he ground his teeth together. "I'm intrigued by your power and more so by how much you've suffered. While your body is soft, your spirit is not. If you were to be my new queen, we would be unstoppable."

This mad king had just talked about slitting her throat and now he was talking about her becoming his queen? Reva thought about what he'd done to Tin's mother, how he had ruined an innocent child, even though he hadn't known she was pregnant. But, had he known the condition Tin's mother was in, Reva doubted it would have stopped him.

She pressed her forehead against his, pretending that it were Crow she was talking to, so she could sound sincere. "If I become your wife, will you give me the stone to defeat Locasta?"

"So, that's why you came here. For the stone." His vicious smile spread. "If you agree to be my wife, your body will become hard like mine, and only then might I relay the secret to you. Depending on how well you obey me first."

The door burst open, and Reva jumped at the loud bang. Ceres remained still as though he'd expected the gnome to enter all along. In walked the same crystal gnome who had originally taken them to their cell, but he wasn't alone—he held a stone bird cage.

Reva gasped at what—*who*—stirred inside, cawing in rage. Crow.

Gritting her teeth, Reva hopped from Ceres's lap. He stretched his hand forward and gripped her wrist before she could leave, squeezing tight.

"You think I didn't recognize him?" Ceres boomed. "Locasta had warned me that he may one day come, and described to me exactly what he looked like. She believed *you* were dead, however. But now she knows you're alive, and I know you love *him*. The only way you can be my queen is if he's dead. Locasta wants him for her own, but that would prevent me from getting what I want. You would never stop searching for him."

"No," Reva said with force.

"I think he will be a fantastic dessert. Don't you think? You aren't yet able to eat stone, so now I have something to force down your throat." The king threw his head back and laughed, the sound bouncing off the walls.

Reva couldn't help the horrified expression that she knew crossed her face, imagining him stuffing her throat with Crow's bloody meat. She spat at the Gnome King's feet. "Never."

"Guards!" Ceres growled. "Fire up the flames and cook the bird. Do it while he's alive."

"No!" Reva screamed, thrashing and trying to escape the grasp that Ceres had on her wrist. Nothing she did loosened his hand.

The gnome did as he was told, carrying the cage back toward the door.

Anger pulsed through Reva. Uncontrollable desperation and fury. "I said *no!*" The magic in her veins danced with furor, harder than ever, rattling the walls.

"You can shake the palace all you want," Ceres cooed, releasing her wrists. "I failed to mention before that whatever falls down here rebuilds itself."

Lightning rippled over Reva, not affecting the king in the slightest. She thought about Thelia and how her daughter's magic had split Glinda's palace in half. That was only a taste of what Thelia would be able to do one day. Reva knew—because her daughter had inherited that power from *her*. Rattling the mountain was just a hint of what Reva could do if she put her all into this moment.

Her magic shot toward the guard holding Crow's cage and knocked him on his ass. The guard's jaw opened, seeming stunned as he got back up, leaving the cage on the ground.

"You're just wasting time," Ceres said with a smirk.

"You forget what storms can bring." Reva whirled around to face Ceres. "There can be tornadoes, there can be hurricanes, there can be floods, there can be earthquakes." She'd never had to use this amount of power, didn't know if she truly could. The thunder roared around her, causing fragments of the ceiling to fall.

"I told you"—Ceres crossed his arms—"it will rebuild itself and I'll survive. But you'll kill yourself and your precious *Crow*. Your undying love for each other won't save you."

The gnome guard lunged at her and Reva roared, the quaking from her magic pushing into him, crumbling his body to pieces. Not giving Ceres time to make a move, Reva barreled forward, shoving her hands against the Gnome King's chest, and slamming him into the wall.

Reva felt him struggling to move, but the lightning held him in place. He stood frozen, like the statue he should have always been. Reva held her concentration, making his body shake from the inside out. A jagged line shot up his middle all the way to his scalp, splitting his face in half. He wasn't able to scream aloud but she knew he was screaming inside himself.

His entire body slowly separated, cracks covering every inch of him until he burst into hundreds of pieces, scattering to the floor. Dust filled the air.

"Rebuild *that*, asshole." Reva coughed, taking a step back. She reeled her magic in, her body still shaking. Red light reflected all over the walls of the room. Bright, so bright. Never before had she seen a red so vivid. Her gaze landed on the source—a heart-shaped stone laying in the rubble that was once the Gnome King. The stone they needed had been *inside* the Gnome King and now that she held it—his heart—he was no more. Was this what Tin's stone heart had looked like before Thelia had freed it?

Crow cawed from his cage behind her, and she quickly scooped up the red stone.

Reva cradled her prize and hurried toward Crow. She opened the cage, reached in with her free hand, and pulled him up toward her. "Are you all right?"

He nodded.

Her muscles relaxed and she placed him on her shoulder. "Don't shift. Not now. It will be harder for them to detect one fae.”

As she buttoned up her tunic, the door flew open again—gnome guard after gnome guard stood there, all holding their spears. None of them moved as they stared at the crumbled pieces of the king on the floor.

“Looks like I’m your queen now,” Reva said, holding up the stone heart. “If you want to remain whole, then I suggest you help me.”

“They’re almost here,” one of the gnomes covered with emeralds said as he broke from the group.

“Who?” Reva asked. “Locasta or her night beasts?”

“No,” another rasped, “she sent something worse.”

“Here’s the plan,” she said. “Assemble your archers, lock down the city, barricade any doors. After you’ve defeated this threat, march your forces to the Emerald City and help liberate it. Do what I’ve instructed, and you may come home and be free. I will leave you in peace as long as no other maidens are murdered, understand?” That seemed a fair bargain to her.

“Yes, my queen,” the gnomes answered in unison.

“Good. Now that that’s settled…” Deafening booms came from above and outside the stone palace. Reva sighed, staring up at the ceiling. “Fuck, can anything go right?”

CHAPTER TWENTY-ONE

CROW

orse. What could possibly be worse than Locasta and the cursed pixies?

Crow quickly transformed back into his fae form and watched as the gnomes followed the orders Reva had given. Spears in hand, the stone fae stormed into the tunnels, shouting directions at other gnomes to get to the top tunnels. He exchanged a worried glance with Reva. "Our packs?"

"You," Reva barked to the last gnome still inside the dead king's secret room. "Get our belongings."

The gray-stoned gnome backtracked through a second hidden door without a peep and returned, only moments later, with both Crow and Reva's bags. He held them up to Reva with his head bowed. She took them, tossed Crow his, then shouldered her own. "Well, don't just stand there. Go!"

Crow beamed at his wife. She was just as strong and decisive as he remembered. Anyone that dared confront her would learn their lesson the hard way—himself included.

When the gnome raced away, Crow slid closer to Reva. "What do you think is out there?"

"Fuck if I know," she grumbled. "It's just one thing after another, isn't it?"

Crow sighed. It really was. "Living as long as we do, life would get pretty boring if fate didn't keep us on our toes."

Reva leveled a hard stare at him. "We've both had enough shit thrown our way to last ten fae lifetimes. Now, let's get out of here while the gnomes distract whatever is making that ruckus."

Crow took the map from his pocket and unfolded it, his eyes following the multiple routes they could take. The closest to the bottom of the mountain—the easiest for Reva to make a quick escape—was one of the first Crow had explored. The twisting lines of black ink faded over the years, and he prayed the gnomes hadn't carved any new pathways between here and there.

"This way," he said, leading them through blue-lit tunnels.

None of the gnomes stopped them. They were too busy racing to their own destinations, shouting about closing off entrances and getting the females and children in Gnome City to safety. Crow's conscience nagged at him at the mention of younglings.

"Do you think we should—"

"No," Reva said in a hurried voice.

He snapped his jaw shut and followed her around a narrow bend. "You didn't let me finish."

"We are *not* helping them, Crow."

The corner of his lips twitched into a smirk at how well she knew him, but fell back into a frown at the loud screeches from outside. "You're their queen now," he said, hesitating. Kings and queens were meant to protect their territory. That was what they were fighting for—a better world with rulers who cared.

Well, that, and revenge.

"Oh, please." She snorted. "I officially abdicate."

Crow swung his pack off his back and dug inside for a better weapon than the knife in his boot. Thankfully, the gnomes had stuffed his bracers inside, so he quickly fastened them in place. "I'm fairly certain that isn't how it works. You need to name a successor and make the statement official before—"

"The only reason we're fighting anything is if we have no

other choice," she snapped.

Crow wrinkled his nose. It seemed to him there *was* no other choice unless they hid deep within the tunnels. And, in his opinion, being a coward was *never* an option. "Fine."

They came up to the exit, the light of the sun beckoning them forward. But the closer they got to escaping the tunnels, the clearer it became that the *worst* creatures had arrived in droves. Shadows flickered over the entrance in quick blips. One, then two, then a dozen. Then the sky blackened with their shadows.

"Do you want to wait for the gnomes to draw them away and make a break for it?" Crow asked. He hoped she said no—he didn't like leaving the gnomes on their own after Reva had just killed their ruler. They *had* been ready to serve him up to Reva like they'd undoubtedly done to hundreds of others, but it felt too much like genocide. Without their psychotic king and his orders, perhaps they would now change their ways.

Reva appeared to be seriously considering it for a moment before she gave a heavy sigh. "I can't fucking believe we're doing this," she hissed before charging forward with a faint crackle of green dancing along her fingers. Crow released the blades over his hands and followed.

They had only made it two steps outside when Reva stopped dead, her face paling. Crow pivoted, barely avoided slamming into her back, and followed her gaze. Thousands of large birds with brown and white speckled feathers soared overhead. Their massive talons were extended as if they had already selected their prey. Perhaps they had, as the mountainside was dotted with gnomes of every color. Arrows zipped toward them—the gnomes apparently trained in archery—but not many hit a target. The creatures were too fast, too agile.

Each of the agonized screeches shook Crow's bones and made his ears ring. The birds jerked from side to side, avoiding arrows as well as colliding with each other. Some of them dove closer to the mountain and landed. Gnomes screamed as the birds' heavy bodies slammed into the rock—and other gnomes—with enough force to shake the mountain. Pebbles scattered from beneath their massive feet.

"What are they?" Crow whispered, blades at the ready, and hoped they wouldn't draw attention to themselves.

Reva heaved a few deep breaths. "That goblin-fucking piece of shit!"

Crow's eyes widened. He tugged his wife back into the shadows. "What?"

"They're sluaghs from where the West borders the North," Reva said through a clenched jaw. "Locasta took control of them while I was wicked."

Sluaghs—fae left homeless in the afterlife that wanted to make the living feel their pain—were exclusive to the West. Reva had always kept them contained as much as possible, but leave it to Locasta to weaponize them. This wasn't simply a physical attack either. It was a power-play to tell Reva that Locasta owned the West—whether because she'd discovered Langwidere was dead or because she refused to accept Thelia's authority.

Crow licked his lips. As vicious as the sluaghs were, they were Reva's subjects. "What do you want to do?"

"I'm going to send them home." She shoved away from Crow and stepped out into the light. Green crackled down her arms, making her hair sway in sync with the electricity, and she shot her magic straight into the sky without hitting a single fae.

The sluaghs' wings continued to beat in a long, slow motion, but they hovered in place, seemingly searching. Another blast of green light drew the eye of every bird. Reva waltzed farther out of the shadows, crackling, glowing, like the ruler she was.

"Go back to the West." The sluaghs seemed to hear her despite the low tone of her voice. "Go back and wait for me, your true ruler. Locasta no longer controls you."

A handful of words was all it took—something Locasta should've anticipated unless she assumed the Gnome King killed her already. The sluaghs very slowly, almost uncertainly, turned back the way they'd come, and the gnomes ceased defending their city. When the sky was clear, Reva kicked a large boulder. Green light blasted around her like a bubble. The magic tingled over Crow when it caught him in its radius, but didn't sting.

"My love?" he whispered.

The glow shrunk from a single large dome into two circles as she sucked the magic back into her hands. "Come on," Reva said between labored breaths. "We have a bitch to kill."

CHAPTER TWENTY-TWO

REVA

Reva watched the sluaghs disappear into the distance, the beat of their wings fading. She patted the Gnome King's stone in her pocket.

"We need to leave," Crow said.

They had maybe a quarter of a day's light left. Neither Crow nor Reva had gotten any sleep or anything to eat while at the palace, but they would just have to suck it up and carry on.

If they needed to, she was certain the gnomes would leave them alone if they stayed one more evening. But that was what Locasta would expect them to do. Hole themselves away… Just like they'd hid from her before Thelia was born. Or tried to, anyway.

The last time they'd hidden, Thelia was taken from them, and both Reva and Crow had been cursed. Once the sluaghs didn't report back to Locasta, the witch would find something else to send after them.

An idea struck Reva then. One that could possibly help the gnomes as well as them. She grabbed a dark brown gnome by the arm and spun him around. He appeared surprised but said nothing.

"Will you do something for me?" Reva asked, hunching

down so they were of equal height.

He nodded. "Yes, my queen. Of course. What would you have me do?"

Reva placed her hands on both his shoulders, giving him her trust. "I told you if you followed my instructions, I would set you free. You won't be ruled by anyone anymore. Not a new Gnome King, me, or anyone else, understand? In order for Crow and I to save the Land of Oz, you can't mess this up."

"I will follow your orders." He clenched his staff. "To the ends of the world."

"You will not have to venture that far." Reva paused. "But your messenger will. I need a letter delivered to Locasta."

The gnome smiled. "You are a smart female. What would you like it to have?"

With a quick glance over her shoulder, she met Crow's eyes and could tell he already knew what she would say. She gripped the gnome's shoulders a bit firmer. "Don't tell Locasta that the Gnome King is dead. Send word that you killed me and in turn Crow escaped the palace. If you relay to her that Crow was murdered, she will retaliate against your kingdom. So make sure it's very clear he's still alive—just gone."

"I will do as you ask." He bowed his head. "Thank you, my queen, for your kindness. For allowing us to carry on."

Reva straightened, placing her arms back by her sides. "Good things will come your way—*if* you follow my instructions. Because I do believe in second chances. But only second chances, do you understand?"

"Yes, my queen. You're very generous." The gnome brushed past her and headed back inside the palace.

The sluaghs were now headed for their home at the Western border. Thelia would need Reva's training on how to handle them, but her daughter could do it. There was another reason that Reva had decided to give Thelia the West, rather than the East or the North, once she won them. The truth was she'd loved the West with every beat of her heart, but she'd destroyed it when she'd been cursed—hurt the fae she'd loved. So it had been for selfish reasons that she gave it to Thelia—because she was too frightened to return home, even though she wanted to see the faces of those she'd once known, who might still be alive. But she wanted a fresh start, and the West deserved someone in whom they could fully put their trust.

Crow brushed a hand through her hair, startling her out of her own thoughts.

"What's going on in there?" he asked, cradling the side of her head.

She grasped his hand and turned to face him, her gaze connecting with his. There was still so much unsaid between them and she wanted to give him this. "Thank you."

Crow arched a brow. "You know a fae is never supposed to say, 'thank you.'"

"Well, I just did." She shrugged. "Thank you. For always being the calm in my storm. Even after all this time."

He smiled, running his finger along her jaw. "Dearest Reva, did you actually give me a compliment?"

"Be quiet." She smirked. "Let's go before the sun sets. We should be able to get to Locasta's castle in less than two days. But we'll have to stop for the night, so I suggest we hurry."

"In that case, we run. We need to separate ourselves from the mountain as quickly as possible." Crow grabbed her hand then tugged her forward. She couldn't help but laugh as they sprinted out from the kingdom. It was no laughing matter, but this reminded her of old times, when she and Crow would chase each other and fall to the ground in a heap, then make love under the sun or the stars.

After running for a long while, they both came to a stop where bare trees were covered in light blue frost. Faeries in pale white gowns flew past her, creating snow flurries with their sheer wings. A cool breeze nipped at Reva's fingers, but her fae body was more resilient than a human's would be in this place.

They'd reached the North.

A crunching of twigs sounded close by and Crow yanked Reva from the path, behind a tree covered in ice. A few moments later a fae dressed in a Northern guard's uniform marched past them, sword swaying at his hip.

"I could have easily struck him down," Reva whispered.

"That would've only alerted Locasta when he didn't report back. And what if someone saw your magic?"

Crow was right. "Where should we stay the night?" she asked. "You know the North better than I do."

He smirked and tossed her his usual wink. "I know the perfect place, but you have to stay quiet until we get there. It won't be long."

Reva gave him a curious look. "Oh, so you have a secret place?"

"Mm-hmm." He held up a finger and smiled while waving her on. This had been his home, and while she'd heard most of his stories, uncovering new things about him was like meeting him for the first time.

With careful footsteps, she tried to avoid any sounds from the layer of frost, but that was impossible. Especially in a wooded area where wolves constantly darted by or ivory foxes would peek out from around trees and crawl up their trunks.

Eventually, as the sun lowered, a tiny village with a handful of cottages came into view. Each one was bright white like snow, with dark blue roofs twinkling with specks of silver. The wind picked up, and Reva shivered as she followed Crow to a home with a door that mirrored in color to its top. Icicles dangled from the arches, and Galanthus flowers were planted in a garden beside the porch, surrounded by patches of snow.

Smoke curled up from the chimney and lanterns shone through the lightly frosted window. Crow knocked softly on the painted wood. Almost immediately, footsteps sounded from inside. The door creaked open and a female poked her upper body out. Dark braids surrounded her head and brown eyes lit up when she gazed at Crow.

The female yanked open the door the remainder of the way and threw her arms around Crow, kissing his cheek. "You came home!"

"Home?" Reva asked, exchanging a look between the male and female. He'd told her he hadn't been with another female. Even before her, there had only ever been Locasta. "What *the fuck* is this?"

"Jealous already?" Crow inched back from the female and winked. "This is my sister, Calla."

"Sister? *Sister?*" Reva inhaled sharply. He'd never mentioned a sister, only that his parents had died from an avalanche when hiking in the mountains.

"Can we come inside, Calla?" Crow asked, already pulling Reva toward the door.

"Yes, yes." She let them both over the threshold and quickly closed the door behind them.

Crow chewed on his bottom lip. "I may have lied when I told you I had no family." He held up a finger. "But I told Calla never to tell anyone that she was related to me. If Locasta knew, she would use her against me."

Before Reva could say anything, two tiny fae children with curly black hair ran into the room grinning and chanting, "Crow. Crow." The two little females then stopped and ducked behind Calla's legs, peering around and looking at Reva. "Mama, who is that female?" one asked, the shape of her ears and cheekbones matching Calla's and Crow's.

Calla turned to her children, nudging them out from behind her. "Give him a hug and get back to bed."

With a quick swoop, Crow lifted them both, one in each arm. "Odette! Gemma! You've grown since I was here last. How old are you now? Fifteen? *Twenty?*" He gave each giggling child a kiss on the cheek before setting them down. They dashed back into their room with one last curious look at Reva.

Calla turned back around and placed her hands on her hips. "I'm curious who you are as well." Her smile was warm, one of the warmest Reva had ever seen. Reva tried to return the expression, but the grimace felt frozen on her face.

"This is my wife," Crow said softly so that only Calla and Reva could hear.

Calla's eyes widened and she covered her mouth. "Are you an idiot, Crow? When? The last time you came was a year ago and you mentioned no one."

"It's a long, long story, Calla."

"We have time. Sit." She pointed Crow and Reva to the settee as though they were children. Reva took a seat and fought back a smile at how Calla bossed her brother around. Along the floor in front of the fire was a rug made of wolf fur. Paintings of wintry trees and animals hung all over the room that she assumed were created by Odette and Gemma since they were each signed with an O or G.

Calla remained standing and continued, "You come back to the North, where you know *she* lives, and you bring a wife? Are you trying to bait Locasta into a fight?"

"Not just a wife," Crow said. "I never told you everything. This is *Reva*. I married Reva of the West over twenty years ago."

Calla's lips parted and her hand flew up to cover her mouth. "The Wicked Witch!" she exclaimed. "What did you do? She was dead!"

Crow stood and lightly grabbed his sister by the wrists. "Listen, she was cursed, like me. Only different. And she was never really dead."

"She nearly brought Oz to ruination!" Calla whisper-shouted.

In that moment, Reva lost all her confidence. This was the reaction she'd feared from anyone who'd heard about her return. She'd been lucky that Falyn had been sympathetic toward her when she'd met her at the brothel. But that was apparently the rare exception to the rule.

"Locasta found us the night Reva bore our daughter, Thelia. She hid our child away in the human world, and cursed us both."

"A child?" Calla nearly screeched. "Where is she now? You went for her after your curse was broken, I assume."

Crow smiled. "She's the one who broke it. Dorothy is Thelia."

"What in the ever-loving Oz…" Calla pressed her fingers to her temples. "I think I need to make us all a drink."

"Where's Jovie?" Crow asked.

"My husband's on guard duty for the next few weeks, patrolling the palace. Things are getting worse here. It had been the safest territory, but now it's becoming like everywhere else. Locasta is finally starting to show her true colors, the ones you've spoken of for all these years."

"So we've heard," Reva said, thinking about Birch and how his parents were dead because of Locasta. "I know this won't make you think differently of me, but we're going to try and make Oz better again. I vow it."

"If you were cursed like my brother was, it wasn't your fault." Calla turned around and headed into the kitchen.

"She hates me," Reva whispered.

"No." Crow chuckled. "She's making you a drink. That means she likes you."

Calla came back into the room with a bottle of rum and two glasses. For a moment, Reva wondered if Calla would attempt to poison her for all she'd done in her past, but she quickly brushed that off.

Crow's sister poured each of them a drink, then sipped from the bottle as she settled herself into one of the chairs.

"We're only staying for the night," Crow said after taking a swig from his glass. "But I promise, the next time we meet, I'll stay longer."

"You two can stay in my room and I'll sleep on the settee."

"No, no," Reva interrupted. "We'll sleep in here. And I won't hear another word of it." She was finally feeling a bit back to herself after downing her drink and letting it warm her a bit.

"If that's what you wish to do. I can't deny a ruler." Calla smiled.

For a while longer, they filled Calla in on their travels so far, while Crow's sister spoke of her husband and children. Then Calla left them alone in the sitting room while she turned in for the night. Reva hoped if everyone could see she'd been cursed by Locasta, they would accept her back. There was a nagging worry they wouldn't, but there was also the relief that Crow's sister had seemed to like her.

The evening was surprisingly quiet, but that must have been because the night beasts were busy terrorizing the Emerald City or other territories. Locasta had her guards to do that for her in the North.

Crow lowered himself on the rug in front of the crackling fire. He held an arm open and beckoned Reva next to him.

She got up and removed her boots before tucking herself beside him and placing her head on his chest. "Your sister's nice. I can see why you want to protect her, and I'm glad you allowed me to meet her." Reva's own sister was gone, Ozma was hopefully still all right, and Whispa either remained a night beast or dead. She couldn't allow herself to dwell on what she couldn't help, no matter how much it hurt.

"Of course, she's nice. She takes after me."

"You know how to ruin a moment," she teased, holding him tighter.

The Gnome King's stone felt heavy in her pocket and she drew it out. She held it up so the flames flickered against its red surface. "How do you think it came to be inside him?"

Crow exhaled. "I should have figured it out before. Ceres and his wife weren't always stone. They'd been flesh and bone once, though I could never find a reason for the change. It makes sense…"

"What does?" Reva fisted the stone protectively.

"When Ceres and his queen became stone, their hearts must've hardened too. Like Tin's, only more so."

"So if their hearts became such powerful stones—"

"That means someone has the former queen's heart," Crow finished. "And how the story must have been told. Although, a very vague story indeed since it failed to mention the stone was inside the asshole."

Reva released a low chuckle and held him tighter after tucking the stone away.

He drew light circles on her arm. "If we weren't at my sister's with little ones here, I would worship your body for the remainder of the night."

In a quick motion, Reva was on top of him, her nose brushing his. "There are different ways to worship a body."

Without further words, his mouth caught hers and he caressed her lips as if they'd just met, deepening and deepening the kiss. Despite the fact that they were married with a grown child together, this somehow felt like their first kiss all over again. She never wanted to forget this moment, or any with him, whether good or bad, and she couldn't help but remember their first kiss.

"You don't know what you're talking about," Reva spat. Trying to tell everyone that Locasta wasn't good would be harder than they'd thought.

"Oh, I don't?" Crow frowned.

Reva took the map of the North from Crow's hand. He stumbled back, taking her with him, and knocking them both to the floor.

"You're an idiot," she said, but couldn't control herself from laughing. She'd never laughed as much as she did around this male who had stumbled upon her weeks ago, requesting help from her.

"I rather enjoy your laugh." He laced his hands through her hair and neither moved. Not until he lifted his head and brought her face to his, then kissed her softly.

Reva pulled back, only a minimal distance. "I told you I wouldn't kiss you first." Then she pressed her mouth back to his.

There were kisses then and there were kisses now. Reva had told him that he was the calm to her storm. But right then, it felt like the calm before the storm that would end Locasta.

CHAPTER TWENTY-THREE

CROW

Bidding Calla goodbye was always difficult, but this time was worse. If Crow and Reva failed to defeat Locasta, this could be the final farewell he had always feared. Calla would be fine—he had to believe that. Their relationship was kept a secret for her sake, but Locasta's fury could affect the entire North. He'd finished the breakfast of warm oats his sister had made—repeating in his mind that her family would be safe—and now lounged on the floor with her daughters, playing a counting game with stones. The last time he'd visited, both Gemma and Odette had only wanted to build with their blocks. Hopefully they would play again one day.

"Are you sure this is wise?" Calla asked him quietly.

Crow darted a quick glance at Reva. She sat beside the fire, staring, unblinking, into the flames. "I'm rarely sure that anything I do is wise," he joked, winking at the children so they knew he wasn't serious.

Calla pursed her lips and tapped the younglings on their shoulders. "Go play outside for a minute, please." Their bottom lips stuck out in exaggerated pouts but they scurried off without voicing their annoyance, leaving their rocks behind. "You can't seriously think you should walk into the palace as if it were nothing."

Crow sighed. He and Reva had told his sister their plan before the children woke, and she was far from happy. But too many things in his life had been kept from Calla, Reva included. He had always wanted to speak with her about his beloved wife but worried about her reaction to *who* he'd promised his life to. Given all the horrible things Reva had done as the Wicked Witch, it was an honest concern. And if he had told Calla about Thelia, it would have raised the question of his child's mother. When Thelia was in the mortal world, there had been no chance of Calla meeting her, so he'd chosen not to burden his sister with the information. Now that he was marching to possible death, Crow wanted her to know what they were doing, and why, in case things went poorly.

"What would you suggest we do instead?" he asked.

"Not strut back through that bitch's front door as a distraction," she hissed. "There's bound to be another way for you and Reva to sneak inside."

Crow took her hand and squeezed reassuringly. "I'll come back, Calla. And when I do, the North will be free. *You*, my sister, will be free."

"Don't make promises you can't keep, Crow." She gave him a lingering look, her eyes glistening with unshed tears. "I hate that you keep putting yourself in this position. It isn't your job to save Oz."

He smiled a small, sad smile. She wasn't wrong—it wasn't his job—but someone had to step up. If not him, then who? "Oz is in this state because good fae did nothing."

Reva stood, the movement catching his eye. "We should leave before there are too many witnesses on the brick road to the palace."

Crow nodded, climbed to his feet, and embraced his sister. "Keep the rum out. We may need it on the way back through."

Calla sniffled into his shoulder. The last time she'd cried over his leaving was right after their parents died. It felt like ten lifetimes ago that he'd entered Locasta's palace to work as an official messenger—a task well-suited to his bird form. He'd had to support his sister back then, even if it meant living apart and sending coin home. If anyone discovered he had a family member solely dependent on him, he never would've gotten the job as a guard. For a moment, he held tighter. How different would things have turned out if he had gotten another job—*any* other job? Though, he couldn't wish away that part of his past. If not for Locasta, he never would've gone looking for Reva's help, and Thelia wouldn't exist.

"You be safe." Calla pulled away from Crow and turned to Reva, pulling her close. "And you too."

Although she appeared slightly uncomfortable with the hug, Reva wrapped her arms around his sister.

Crow and Reva stepped out into the crisp, cold winter air, sparing another moment for him to give Odette and Gemma a quick hug. They seemed to have warmed slightly to Reva's presence—though she received no embrace, they offered her smiles and waves. His heart grew heavier the more space he put between them and his sister's home. For all his brave words, Crow knew that Locasta wouldn't hesitate to reclaim him. But first there would be torture if Reva took too long with her part of the plan.

"You're clear on where to go?" he asked for what felt like the hundredth time. "Where to steal the servant uniform and how to get into the kitchens?"

"Yes," she said patiently. Then, as if understanding why he asked, she added, "It will all go according to plan."

It needed to. One slip up, one miscalculation, and, if the stone didn't work, they would both be cursed again. Or worse. It had all seemed like a much better idea when they'd discussed it the night before. What if Locasta only cursed him and killed Reva? He had already gone through that agony once. If it weren't for the other drastic changes last time, like his curse being broken and realizing who Thelia was, he surely would've followed Reva to the grave with a broken heart.

When the top of Locasta's palace came into view, Crow

tugged Reva off the yellow brick road. This was to be where they parted ways temporarily, but panic clawed at his insides. "Maybe we should find more help before we do this." His voice cracked slightly. "Tin would come."

"He needs to stay with Thelia," Reva reminded him. "And he's been through enough as it is. We all have."

Right. He knew that. It was more important that their daughter had Tin's protection since she couldn't control her magic at will yet. But the sight of his old home—his prison—left his mind spinning. For years he'd lived inside those pearly white walls, warmed himself by the fireplaces, nourished himself with fruit from the private orchards. But he'd also suffered. Locasta's temper was quick to rise and slow to fade. After years of trying to leave, he'd finally succeeded to break through her magic holding him there.

"I'll be right behind you." Reva cupped his cheeks with her palms. "Take the stone."

An image of her face covered with green pustules rose in his mind, and he shoved the memory away. "I told you this morning, no. And I meant it." Crow swallowed hard, then pressed a desperate, hard kiss to her lips. "Don't get caught."

"Who is underestimating who this time?" She gently pushed at his chest and lowered his mask from the top of his head to cover his face. "Let's get moving. The sooner we kill Locasta, the sooner we can truly start our lives together."

"I love you," he whispered, and forced himself to walk away.

Each step he took revealed another inch of the palace. The roof. Decorative, snow-capped trees. Curling parapets. Arched windows. Long balconies. Red winter-blooming flowers. Then, finally, the massive frost-covered doors. The guards weren't visible—Locasta wanted to appear confident in her safety—but they were there. Watching. Always watching. He felt the weight of their eyes on him as he neared a snowy drawbridge and paused. It was the last thing between him and Locasta's lair. Well, the bridge and, undoubtedly, dozens of guards.

It took everything in Crow not to extend his blades as he took that first step forward. He sensed the guards closing in on him when he reached the doors. Should he knock? It wasn't like they weren't expecting him at this point—they would have seen him walking brazenly up to the palace. He took a shuddering breath—possibly the last he would take as a free male—and shoved the doors inward. His stomach churned as he lifted his chin and waltzed into the palace.

The glittering entry was exactly how he'd remembered it. White marble floors so clean they looked like mirrors, columns of granite wrapped in sheer, flowing silver fabric, and a large table with an arrangement of winter flowers. A chandelier made of bone-white antlers hung from the high ceiling.

Guards were waiting, as he knew they would be, but only six. They were elves—Locasta's personal preference for those working within her palace—and wore pine-colored uniforms that hugged their lithe bodies. Rust-colored buttons ran down their chests in two rows and, inside, their jackets were lined with fur. The serrated swords they held were less worrisome to Crow than the palace itself.

"Good morning," Crow said as cheerfully as possible. If they could've heard his erratic pulse, they would've known how much of a lie his nonchalant tone was. "I believe Locasta has been looking for me."

The shortest guard eyed the feathers in Crow's hair and recognition slowly filtered in. He grunted in distaste. "She's waiting for you in the banquet hall."

Crow took a step forward and all six of the guards stiffened. "The hall is that way," he said with a casual wave of his hand. "I know the way, if you'll simply clear a path."

"You know we can't let you wander the palace alone," said a female.

Of course, they couldn't—he was a threat. But only warranted six armed escorts, apparently. That wasn't enough to clear the way for Reva. He needed every available guard looking at him so his wife could come in unnoticed. "Then, by all means…" Crow walked slowly toward them this time, hands raised to show he carried no weapon.

They stood rigidly at his approach but didn't move to stop him. Once he was in the middle of the guards—two in front, two behind, and one on each side—he let his hands fall to his sides. He held his breath for a moment before extending the blades from his bracers and spun with lightning speed, slicing four guards down where they stood. Blood sprayed against the pristine walls. The fifth, he pulled to his chest and placed the blades carefully against the artery in her neck. Warm liquid flowed over his fingers as he pressed the blades into her skin as a warning.

"Now, now," Crow told the last guard. The female froze mid-attack. "I mean you no harm."

He truly didn't, but some things were unavoidable. Four dead fae would undoubtedly bring the rest of the palace guards rushing to investigate, leaving Reva's path clear.

Boots slapped against the floors. Dozens upon dozens of guards. Crow smiled to himself. "It isn't polite to keep a lady waiting," he said, tossing the guard at her comrade, and raced down the glistening hall.

He ran past tapestries of gold and gilded mirrors. Deep blue curtains pleated around window frames. The rust-colored stains where Locasta had broken his bird form years ago still colored the tile at the bottom of a grand staircase. The guards closed in on him just as he caught a glimpse of a tarnished cage hanging in front of the highest window in the palace. One of *his* many cages. One of the many that Locasta had kept him in as a bird when he'd angered her. Another was bolted to the wall across the room.

"Stop," a male shouted.

Crow tore his eyes from the cage and then—finally—shouldered his way into the banquet hall. He slammed the doors shut behind him and flicked the lock. An enormous table stretched the length of the room with trays of food stacked high from one end to the other. Burgundy and bronze décor dripped down the walls and candles hung from the ceiling, their warm glow filling the room. The hardwood floors were stained ebony with a thick crème-colored rug covering the center.

But the splendor of the room failed to hold his attention when the female who had destroyed Crow's life stared at him from a high-backed chair.

Locasta's obsidian hair flowed over her shoulders and her fair skin practically glowed in the candlelight. She wore a dress of ice blue with silver gems sewn into the bodice. "Crow." Her light, airy voice made his skin crawl. It was an innocent voice, a deceptive one. She steepled her fingers, elbows on the lace tablecloth, and lifted her ruby lips into a savage smile. "I'd like to say this is unexpected, but, well…"

Guards slammed into the doors and the hinges rattled. Crow fought to keep his body from shaking. Locasta looked Crow up and down before standing and rounding the table. He wanted so badly to move away, but Reva would be there soon. He could endure long enough for her to avoid detection. "Is this my welcome party then?"

"Oh, my darling, if only it were. I've spent years thinking of new ways to break you after your last visit, but first…" Locasta knocked Crow's mask to the floor and slapped him across the cheek, the blood rushing to his face at the sting. She lifted a lock of his hair and ran it between her fingers. "I heard a rumor that a certain acquaintance of ours managed to resurrect herself, only to meet her end a second time."

Crow kept his breaths steady, hiding a smile. The gnomes had listened to Reva and passed on the news of her *death*. No one in the palace would be expecting her. "Don't speak to me about Reva."

"Is it revenge you really want? Because I don't think it is." She twisted the lock of his hair around her hand until his scalp throbbed. "I think you're secretly pleased. Now we can truly move on together. After your punishment, that is."

Locasta stepped closer. He felt her breath on his ear, then wet warmth as she licked the lobe. "Tell me, my lovely bird, do you want the chains or the ropes before we fuck?"

Crow leaned away from her, snapped his hand around her neck, and gave a firm squeeze in one fluid movement. "I could kill you now."

Locasta laughed, moving her hand from his hair to caress his red cheek. "How many nights did you lay awake, naked in my bed, and *wish* you could squeeze the air from my lungs? And how many times did you even try?"

Shame blazed through him. Countless times he had wanted to kill her, yet he had never tried. Not even once. But he would do it now. After everything Locasta had done to him, to Reva, and Thelia, he would kill her with a smile on his face.

But he kept his promises, especially those he made to Reva. His wife would be the one to deal the final blow to the Northern Witch.

"Precisely," Locasta cooed as if knowing he wasn't going to kill her. "Now is no different."

A shadow slipped along the wall behind Locasta. Crow released her throat, clutching her wrist instead. Squeezing and squeezing until he was sure the bones would snap.

"No," Crow started as a faint green light flickered to life. "Now *everything* is different."

CHAPTER TWENTY-FOUR

REVA

Another terrible experience to add to this journey—hiding in the shadows before knocking out a defenseless servant and stealing her uniform. It was too loose, the fabric itched her skin like Glinda's clothing had, and she already missed the black. The white hue reminded her of Langwidere's obsession with that color, only this was nowhere near seductive.

As she slipped through the back entrance of the palace, into the kitchens to which Crow had given her directions, she spotted a single female with her hair in two braided buns. She kneaded dough along a silver counter in front of a blue and white striped wall. "Laundry's over there," the female said as she shaped the bread, then glanced up. "Another new face—I'm not surprised. Hopefully you last longer than the others."

Reva spotted a bowl full of fruit on the edge of a table and pressed an apple into the pocket of her apron. She would need something sweet to bite into when this was all over. *If* it ended well.

"I'm sure I will." Reva picked up the large wicker basket filled with soiled clothing and towels. The smell of peppermint permeated the air as she walked through the kitchen and entered a pale blue hallway covered in black feathers. The feathers were attached to the walls in artful, swirled patterns. Her stomach sank at the sight of them. These weren't just any bird's feathers—she recognized them right away. *Crow's.*

Reva had heard the stories from her husband. Locasta wouldn't only use the feathers for her *art* that he'd shed—she would pluck them from Crow's bird form when she was livid with him. But Reva hadn't known that Locasta was obsessed enough to hang them as decorations in her hallways. This would not go on any longer—no matter if she had to rip the Northern Witch to shreds with her own teeth and hands.

The stone rested in her apron pocket beside the apple, and she stroked her fingers against its cool surface to reassure herself that it was indeed still there. Crow had refused to take it, even when she'd tried to sneak it into his pocket.

After leaving the basket of laundry behind, she turned down another long hallway with a neat line of paintings on each side of the walls—all of Locasta in seductive poses—naked. Before Reva lost her stomach, two familiar voices echoed from behind the servants' entrance to the banquet room. Crow and *the bitch.*

Tiptoeing as quietly as she could, she pushed open the door and peered in, her gaze landing on the duo. Crow's hand was latched around Locasta's throat and all the bitch did was smile at him, seeming to not believe he would end her life. Reva focused on Locasta's hand. The witch's fingers twitched, and Reva knew she was about to do something tricky.

The magic thrummed through Reva, lightning crackling as she slipped through the door and stepped into the room.

Crow said something to Locasta as he released her throat and grabbed her wrist.

The Northern Witch looked up at Reva, her lips parting and brows lifting in surprise. "You're supposed to be dead." Locasta's fingers twitched again and worry spread across Crow's face.

Reva shook her head. "I wouldn't try that, Locasta."

"I should have known those gnome bastards were traitors." She elbowed Crow in the ribs, causing him to gasp and free her.

"You're going to the bird cage now. Then perhaps to the cornfield until you crawl back to me with broken bones."

"Stab her!" Reva shrieked.

Crow didn't hesitate to release his blades and thrust them into Locasta's stomach with a squelch, spilling crimson down her blue gown.

Shimmering, pale-blue light flickered around Locasta as she thrust a hand out. Crow's skin changed to the same color as Locasta's magic, and he transformed into his bird form before vanishing.

Reva started to cry out when a *caw* came from a cage bolted to the far side of the room. Reva flung a burst of magic at the Northern Witch. Despite gripping her wounded stomach, Locasta still managed to turn the green lightning into bright white snowflakes.

"Ah, this brings back such wonderful memories," Locasta rasped, a thin line of blood trickling from the edge of her mouth. "Are you so desperate to become my plaything again?"

A flash of blue magic barreled toward Reva. She dodged to the left, but a hard hit struck her arm, turning into a sharp ache. It spread and spread, growing hotter until she couldn't bear it. A scream broke free from Reva, and she glanced down at her skin as Locasta laughed again. Green rippled up Reva's flesh and pustules bubbled.

Why isn't the stone working? It was supposed to prevent Locasta's shifting magic. In that moment Reva couldn't help but worry for Thelia. What would Locasta do to her daughter this time?

With a shaking hand, Reva reached into the front pocket of her apron. As soon as her fingers brushed the stone, a warm energy spread through her, taking away the scalding sensation. Her skin was no longer green and bubbling, but smooth and pale.

"What have you got there?" Locasta asked after Reva tugged out the Gnome King's glimmering heart.

Reva focused on Locasta, who was growing paler with each passing moment. She wasn't willing to let the witch lose consciousness and die in peace. Not after everything she'd done.

"It's a gift from the Gnome King." Reva smiled, baring her teeth. "After I reduced him to rubble."

Locasta hurled another ball of magic at Reva. It hit her in the chest, but this time she didn't even feel it.

"You'll never take him from me again!" Locasta shouted, blowing the doors wide open with her magic. "Guards!"

As the guards burst into the room, Reva let her energy spill out, lightning crackling all around her. "Do you really want to mess with me? I am Reva and was once the Wicked Witch of the West because of your ruler. Everything that has happened is because of her."

The guards didn't move—only stared in horror at Reva, likely knowing they would be helpless against her magic.

"Seems like they will easily choose my side over yours, bitch," Reva spat at Locasta. She launched another bolt of lightning at Locasta, which again turned into bright white flurries, falling to the floor.

She clenched the stone tighter, and a heavy quake erupted beneath their feet. The rumbling sounds reverberated within the room, rattling the frames hanging on the pearly white walls. Green lightning wove around Reva, like snakes crossing over one another. She smiled with menace and walked toward Crow's cage to open it. Locasta hadn't moved a muscle toward them, yet she watched with fury blazing in her eyes. Crow flew out, flapping his wings fiercely. She opened a small space in her magic, allowing Crow to pass through and perch himself on her shoulder.

"You're right." Reva grinned wider. "Crow will watch. But it will be as I repay you for all you've done to him, my daughter, and *me.*"

"Ah, yes." Locasta coughed, specks of blood spotting her chin, her eyes filled with rage. "Your *daughter.* However, I did raise the true Dorothy Gale for a long time, toyed with her until she wasn't worth my time anymore, then handed her off to Langwidere. The game isn't over yet." She glanced toward the top of the stairs and screamed, "Kill her!"

Reva glanced upward as a storm of wings rose and drew closer. The night beasts.

Howls carried through the room as cursed pixies shot out, one after another, and Reva thought it would never end.

Above her and Crow, the cursed pixies' skeletal forms swirled in a circle, waiting for the right opportunity to attack. One with a twisted spine and a row full of sharp teeth took the chance, and struck Reva's magic, which sliced the pixie in half. Another flew in at the same time, scratching Reva across the cheek with its deadly claws, just before her magic darkened it to ash.

The night beasts continued to hover—but something was awry. Same as in the forest when she'd run from them with Crow, more of the pixies appeared hesitant to attack than not. And she didn't think it was because of her magic.

"Kill her now!" Locasta seethed, falling to her knees. "Or tonight, I shall rip your wings from your bodies and feed them to Crow."

"Without your power to use against me, you are *nothing*," Reva said in a low, but deadly, voice. "Even after your curse when I was without my magic, I was something. I've been through worse things than you, and you've mistreated our land long enough."

"What a sad, sad speech that was." Locasta cocked her head, chest heaving. "But just remember, I fucked Crow first."

Crow's talons dug into Reva's shoulder and her blood boiled at the taunt, more so for her husband than herself. He'd been through enough of this shit already. She flicked her gaze at the cursed pixies once more and shouted, "If you want this to be over, then end her."

Locasta cackled. "You're a fool! They won't listen to you."

A few moments passed, and Reva started to believe Locasta was right. But then one pixie, with uneven leathery wings, finally parted from the pack and barreled toward the Northern Witch. Another broke from the group, then another. More continued to follow. Reva reeled her magic in enough to give the cursed pixies room as they shrieked and tore through Locasta. But not all. A few tried to get to Reva and Crow, failing as their bodies flopped to the floor with a sickening plop.

Howls of agony escaped Locasta's lips as the pixies ripped into her flesh. Blood speckled the walls, and pooled along the marble floor as skin, muscle, and organs were torn away from her bones. Reva had wanted to kill Locasta herself, but having Crow stab her and the pixies finish her off was the right choice. The cursed pixies had been slaves to Locasta even longer than she'd been.

As the cursed pixies broke away from the body and roared with glee, there was nothing but Locasta's skeleton left behind, her jaw open as though still screaming, even in death. *Good.*

Low wails came from the cursed pixies as they dropped to the floor with thump after thump, trembling until their bodies stilled. Were they dead? Reva reeled her power back in, lightning no longer crackling. Crow flew from her shoulder and transformed in a cloud of smoke, a few black feathers cascading downward.

Reva tucked the stone into her apron and hurried to a small skeletal pixie. Its eyes were still open, its chest moving. The dark color of its body slowly started to fade to a light brown. Its spine straightened, teeth no longer fangs, wings thinning, skin thickening. The curse was broken, and the beast returned to his pixie form—with pointy ears, light hair, and a handsome face.

"Reva? Crow?" a female pixie whispered from behind her. Reva's eyes widened and she whipped her head around. This one wore a tattered red and blue dress that fell to her ankles. Her gray hair was mussed and her honey-colored eyes exhausted, but there was a smile on her face.

"Whispa!" Reva shouted, her heart racing with excitement. "You're alive."

"I don't think I want to do that again." Whispa pushed herself to her feet and brushed her matted hair out of her eyes. "And I don't think you do either."

Tears streaked Reva's cheeks and she swiped them away as

she stood. She rushed toward her old friend and folded her arms around the pixie, squeezing her tight.

Circling her, all the pixies—now uncursed—were silent, watching them. And so was Crow. Whispa removed herself from Reva and gave Crow a similar hug. "I'm sorry I couldn't have prevented this, but I was the first to go after her this time."

"That was you who broke from the pack first?" Reva asked. "You did good, Whispa. As for the last time, no one could have stopped Locasta that fateful night." They'd tried to hide and had done the best they could at the time. She turned toward the others, who seemed to be waiting for her command. "You're free. Go home."

Some nodded and left the room, but most didn't. They stayed, surprising her. A female with bright red curls and a heart-shaped face shifted forward. "What do you want us to do next?"

Reva smiled at the determination in the way they stood with their spines straightened and chins lifted. "How about we start by cleaning up the North, then working on the East?" She looked back at Whispa. "Can you send word to our new leader—Thelia—of the South and the West to meet us at the protected tavern in the Emerald City in two weeks' time? I have a good feeling the capital will be safe by then. Thelia is located in Glinda's palace."

"Of course." Whispa bowed. "For you, my friend, I will always help."

Taking a step back, Reva turned around to find Crow looking at the walls, the marble floor, and his *cage*. Reva wondered for a moment if she'd been selfish. She'd told herself she would take Locasta's palace and make it her own, but did Crow even want it to be his? After all he'd gone through here?

She would choose to go wherever he wished. "We can leave if you want, Crow. We can build our own palace somewhere else in the North or stay in the East."

"No," Crow said firmly. "The palace never made me feel unsafe. It was *her*. Always her. The North was home to me, but so was the West. I say we make this ours, not hide from her shadow. We can easily paint everything black." He winked at her. And with that wink, she knew he would eventually be all right.

"You know me so well." Reva bit her lip and pushed her hand into her apron pocket, fishing out the apple. "My gift to you." She handed him the fruit.

"Oh, you must really love me." He grinned, taking the apple and biting into it.

"Once you finish that, we need to get this bitch out of here." She pointed at Locasta's remains, believing the witch still merited worse, but this would have to do.

"First, take a bite. You deserve it."

Reva opened her mouth and Crow pressed the apple between her teeth. It tasted like victory.

CHAPTER TWENTY-FIVE

CROW

The room slowly cleared of pixies. Reva had appeared much more collected than he'd felt in those first few minutes after Locasta's death—giving jobs to those who remained—while his mind was a whirlwind of thoughts.

They'd won.

Whispa was back.

The North and East were free.

His sister's family was safe.

And yet, there was still so much more work to do to return Oz to its former glory. That was for another day, though. It was all he could do not to collapse with relief. Locasta was *dead*. She'd gotten exactly what she deserved when Reva sent the pixies after her. He hoped that they felt half as good about ripping into Locasta as he had felt stabbing her. The blades hadn't inflicted nearly enough pain to make up for everything she'd done to him over the years, but it was better than nothing. Vengeance had needed to be shared among those she'd wronged, and that was a long list. Thelia deserved to share in it too, but she was doing far greater things than seeking revenge against a female she'd never known.

"Are you all right?" Reva asked again when the door clanged

shut behind the final pixie.

A red stain was all that remained of Locasta now—her bones carried away by grateful palace guards. Crow wondered briefly what they would do with them, but couldn't find it in himself to care. "Yes. I'm fine," he assured her, tossing his apple core onto the table. He was more than all right—just shocked. "Though, I almost think I'm dreaming."

Reva leaned up and kissed him on the cheek. "You're wide awake."

Crow's lips quirked into a smile. "If we're staying here for the night, I want to show you something."

Reva's brows rose. "Now?"

"You can order the guards around some more on the way," he joked.

She took his hand with a huff. "I think I've given them enough tasks for the moment."

"The next moment?" Crow laughed as he led her from the banquet hall. "They'll be busy for days, and I *know* you're not done yet."

"You know me too well."

Crow kept his eyes on the marble floor, not wanting to see the familiar décor again. Once Reva changed things, he would feel comfortable in the halls, but not truly until then. Especially not when his feathers hung like tapestries, and cages loomed in almost every room. The guards seemed hard at work on removing them, as per Reva's first order as Witch of the North, which was a relief.

"Not even Locasta knew about this place," Crow whispered when they turned the final corner toward their destination. "I found it completely by accident."

Reva's eyes gleamed with interest. "Oh? What kind of accident?"

Over the years, before their curses, Crow had shared many stories of his time with Locasta, but he wasn't sure he wanted to tell Reva this particular one. He'd been in his cage for days when Locasta finally decided to free him, and she only did that because she was leaving the palace and didn't want him to starve. Anger drove him to destroy multiple paintings in the hallways while she was away, tearing them from their frames and lighting them on fire. When he'd come upon a hideous, dust-covered statue, he'd intended to push it over. Break it apart. Destroy it completely. But it hadn't budged, which had only angered him more. He'd found the switch because his next attempt was to pry it apart piece by piece. The tale didn't paint him in the best light, but it ended well.

"A happy one." Crow winked and stopped in front of the statue. Pieces of smooth driftwood were held together with copper spikes forming a five-foot egg shape. He'd always hated the statue, up until he'd found the secret it contained.

"Prepare to be amazed," he told Reva, and released her hand so he could kneel to reach the hidden lever.

A moment later, a panel of the wall lifted smoothly into the ceiling, revealing a rather large room. Floating yellow lights flickered to life as they stepped inside. The walls were unpolished dark stone and the floor was covered in a plush brown throw rug. Stacks of dust-covered books lined the walls. In the very center of the room sat a round bed covered in gold silk. How many hours had he spent curled up there? Countless. Whenever Locasta was away or when she was preoccupied, he would slip inside and read until his eyes grew heavy. If it was the latter, it was too dangerous to fall asleep there and risk Locasta noticing his absence, but the precious moments of freedom spent within these secret walls had kept Crow going.

"It feels like you in here," Reva said.

He knocked a cobweb down from the ceiling and grinned. "Old and dirty?" Reva's eyes widened as he slid an arm around her waist. "Shall we see which is dirtier?"

"Crow." She batted playfully at him. "There's so much to do before we—"

He swooped in and kissed her fiercely. There would be plenty of time to set things in motion, but standing there, in his space, knowing they were done for a moment... He *needed* her now. He deepened the kiss, his fingers tangling in her hair.

Reva melted into him. Her lips were hot on his, moving as urgently as his own, and he knew she needed this too. When his tongue skated along her bottom lip, she moaned into him before greeting it with her own, causing Crow's hard cock to press painfully against his pants.

His breath hitched when she slipped her hands beneath his shirt, searing his skin. And that was it. He couldn't stand waiting any longer. One moment they stood in the entrance of his sanctuary, the next Reva was pressed against the wall.

"Clothes," he growled against her mouth. He needed her *now.* "Off."

Reva shoved him back a step and their heavy breaths filled the room. Fabric tore loudly. Crow couldn't tell which article of clothing had ripped or who it belonged to because they were both moving as frantically as the other to rid themselves of the unwanted barriers. Neither of them bothered with their shirts.

The second Reva stood after pulling her pants from her feet, Crow lifted her. Her legs automatically wrapped around his waist, holding him tightly. The tip of his cock rubbed against her wetness, teasing him. Her tongue then ran up the side of his neck and he nearly lost control.

Using the wall to brace them both, Crow slipped inside her. His moan echoed through the dusty room. Reva threw her head back, her nails digging into his shoulders. A string of mumbled words fell from her mouth.

Crow pulled back until he was nearly out of her, then slid slowly inside again. He ground his teeth, forcing himself not to lose control. At least, not until Reva was satisfied.

"Crow," Reva whispered in his ear. One hand left his shoulders to scrape down his back. "Stop playing around and fuck me!"

A small grin found its way to his lips. "If you insist."

Crow moved faster. Slammed harder. The floating lights seemed to shimmer brighter with each thrust, until he buried his face in Reva's neck, and pressed his eyes shut. Just a little longer before he could let go… He wasn't sure he could make it…

Reva cried out in pleasure and he released the harsh breath he was holding. Then he released something else, a stream of vibrations soaring through him as he shouted her name. They both froze, panting. His heart felt as if it would break through his chest. It had been a long time since he'd experienced such a desperate need—or the pure exhaustion that followed. His legs quaked beneath him and, if it weren't for the wall behind Reva, he might've dropped them both to the floor.

"I love you," he breathed. The scent of Reva mixed with sweat and dust and pleasure. "So much."

"I love you too," she said, wrapping her arms around his neck to help support her weight. "Can you put me down now?"

"Do I have to?" he teased as he set Reva back on her feet. He brushed the hair out of her face. There were no words that could express how he felt about his wife, and the gravity of their love slammed into him like a bolt of lightning. If he had things his way, he would never let Reva out of his sight again, but that wasn't realistic. Nor would she allow it, which was another reason he loved her. His strong, independent, beautiful, powerful—

"What's that look for?" she asked. "It looks like you're plotting something that will get us both in trouble."

Crow shook himself back to reality. "What look?"

"Never mind," Reva said with a roll of her eyes.

"So…?" he asked with a crooked grin.

Reva wobbled slightly before stepping into her pants and shot him a quizzical look. "What?"

"Which is dirtier? Me, or the room?"

She rolled her eyes. "I know which one is *older.*"

He leaned in and kissed her cheek. "You're older than I am."

"Crow!" Reva swatted at him. "Get dressed. We have plans to make."

Chuckling, he did as she asked. They did have plans to make—plans for a peaceful life together. But before that could happen, there was one more fight to win. In two weeks, they would meet Thelia in the Emerald City, so there was no more time to waste. He took Reva's hand in his and smiled.

"Lead the way, my love."

EPILOGUE

REVA

Little had changed visibly in the Emerald City. The tavern stood before Reva and Crow, the magical barrier still flickering a glittery white. All the surrounding shops needed rebuilding. The palace still held King Pastoria's barrier. Yet this time, everything was quiet after the gnomes had taken control of the capital. No fights in the streets. No battling in the air. The fae outdoors had faces filled with hope instead of despair once Crow told them Locasta and Langwidere were both dead. Soon, the Wizard would be dead too and then the palace would be Ozma's.

Reva didn't know what had happened to Ozma or when she would show up here to claim her palace. A small hint of doubt nagged inside her head—what if she didn't? But Ozma had survived so much—she would have to survive this too. Reva would give her more time, and if Ozma didn't show up, then she would have to cross the desert to find her friend.

"Are you ready?" Crow asked, interrupting her thoughts.

Reva nodded. "Yes. I'm just overthinking things."

He intertwined his fingers with hers and kissed her knuckles. It calmed her for the moment. Giving her hand a squeeze, he pulled her through Queen Lurline's magic barrier and toward the establishment.

Two male centaurs stood outside, chatting and sipping from mugs, both fae giving them a smile as they passed. Crow opened the door, allowing Reva to enter first.

Once she stepped inside, a tangy scent hit her. Reva spotted one of the familiar dryads—Milla—talking to a young male faun with blond hair who was eating pie over a plate. She recognized the child right away.

"Birch!" Reva called, striding up to the counter. Had he gone to the South like she'd asked?

Spinning around, his gaze met hers. A grin spread across Birch's face before his lips pulled down into a frown. He poked his fork at the air. "You didn't tell me the Tin Woodsman was in the South."

Reva exchanged a glance with Crow as he came up beside her. "Would you have gone if I'd told you?"

Birch appeared deep in thought when his eyes ticked side to side. "No."

"Well, then there's your answer," she said. "How was he?"

"Eh." Birch shrugged. "He's not as bad as everyone says."

"Are you sure about that?" Crow mumbled.

"What are you saying about me?" a deep voice boomed from behind them.

Crow glanced around with a sigh. "Do you always have to lurk?"

"Only because it bothers you so much." Tin ran his gloved fingers against the iron scar on his cheek. He was dressed the same as when she'd seen him last, with kelpie scales artfully sewn into his black tunic and pants, only less bloody. An axe rested at his hip. His silver hair was pulled back in a low knot and his hungry gaze was focused on the pie in Birch's hand.

Reva's heart practically stopped when her eyes drifted from Tin to the smaller female coming up beside him. She wore a lavender dress, simple, but with stitched floral designs down the sides, and her hair in a single braid. *Thelia.* She was more beautiful than Reva remembered, and she looked more like Crow than ever.

Before Reva could move forward, Thelia threw her arms around her. "You're late meeting us here. I was worried sick."

"It took longer to set things up in the North than we'd expected." Reva smiled, letting go of her and stepping back. Not to mention that they'd had to visit Calla on the way. "With or without us, you would have been fine. You're a stronger daughter than I ever could have asked for."

"The same goes for my mother." Thelia turned to Crow next and gave him a hug before they started chatting about her meeting Whispa.

After Whispa had given Thelia instructions to meet them in the Emerald City, the pixie had returned to the Northern palace, where she was now watching over it with the other guards until Reva and Crow could return.

Since Locasta no longer reigned, the Northerners had accepted Reva despite the menacing things she'd done while cursed. It didn't hurt that she had Crow by her side, who they loved.

She'd have to work on relations in the East soon, and she hoped they would grow accustomed to her too. Apparently, Locasta had started attacking fae there with the night beasts, even though it had been her own territory. Over the years, while Reva was in the dark place, it seemed the dead witch's desire to torture had grown.

"May I talk to Thelia alone for a moment?" Reva asked.

"Of course," Crow said.

Tin didn't move.

"That means you too, dumbass." Crow shoved Tin forward. Thelia chuckled as Tin cursed under his breath. Reva watched as they went with Birch back to the counter and asked for drinks.

Reva and Thelia walked over to a table in the far corner, near the one where she'd sat the last time she was here with Crow. She pulled out a chair and took a seat across from her daughter. "How's the South been?"

"It's taking a little adjusting, but some of the fae have returned and there hasn't been any new sign of Wheelers."

"*Good.*" They were either all dead by Reva's hand when she'd killed the large group of them, or they had fled back to the outskirts of the Deadly Desert. "If Ozma doesn't meet us here in a few weeks, I may have to go searching for her." Or the Wizard.

Thelia leaned back in her seat, folding her arms. "I'm not staying back this time if you do."

"I wouldn't dare ask that of you again." Locasta would have been too dangerous and tricky for Thelia. Oz was manipulative too, but he was still mortal—silver slippers or not. "But let's hope she comes soon." Reva's gaze traveled to the counter and settled on the smaller fae. "So really, how was Birch when he first came to the palace?"

Dorothy grinned. "Tin greeted him at the door by asking who the hell he was. It took him a moment to recognize Tin before he tried to run. I had to catch Birch and persuade him to stay by giving him desserts while Tin thought I should have just let him run off."

Reva chuckled.

"I suppose we should do another story-time. How about you go first?"

"I don't think so." Thelia paused, still grinning, and shook her head. "You and Crow seem to be getting along better. I need to know more about *that.*"

Reva couldn't help focusing her attention on Crow. "Of course. I'll tell you half while my husband tells the other. We'll do it together."

"*Husband?*" Thelia's brows rose all the way up her forehead, her eyes bulging. "I knew you two would find a way back to each other, but you got *married?*"

"It happened a long time ago, actually—before we had you. Sometimes you just have to let the storm pass before the calm takes over." Reva smiled as Crow noticed her watching him from across the room. He gave her a quick wink as he took a sip from his glass and held up an apple in his other hand. "The day I met your father started with my favorite piece of fruit."

OZMA

BOOK 3

CHAPTER ONE

OZMA

TWO YEARS AGO

Pumpkin innards slid through Tip's fingers as he swirled his palm around the carcass. He ripped the guts out, threw them in the grass at his feet, and pressed his digits back inside. The pungent odor wafted into his nostrils.

"I can think of a better use for your hands than that," a deep voice said from behind him.

Tip rolled his eyes and turned to face Jack with a grin. "The pumpkins are keeping them a bit pre-occupied at the moment." But they were itching to be somewhere else, *on* someone else.

Jack walked around Tip until he stood in front of him, his orange hair damp from his bath in the lake, his hazel irises greener than ever. Any lingering scent of Tip after they'd made love in Jack's hut had been washed away. Tip still needed to bathe himself, but why bother when he was required to gut pumpkins? Mombi had to make her pies for the market so there wasn't much time left.

They were well hidden on the side of Jack's hut, diagonally across the field from the one Tip shared with Mombi. Both were the only homes within the witch's magic barrier, and Mombi's spells kept Tip and Jack from escaping. Tip had tried running away before, on numerous counts, and it was impossible.

Not taking his gaze from Jack's, Tip slowly pressed his hand inside the pumpkin. Jack swiped his tongue against his lower lip, took the fruit from Tip's hands, and set it to the side. Then Jack caged Tip against the hut and nudged Jack's nose gently with his own. Blood rushed straight to Tip's cock.

"Again?" Tip asked, inching closer to his lover.

"Again," Jack whispered, softly licking Tip's lips before pressing his mouth against his lover's in a starved kiss.

Greedily, Tip kissed Jack back and pulled him down to the ground. Bits of pumpkin smeared Jack's wet hair as he gripped it, making him dirty all over again.

Their mouths glided over one another, and Tip felt the firmness of Jack's back as he slid his hand up his tunic. A groan escaped Tip as Jack reached between his legs and stroked him over his pants. The rush, the feeling, he needed him.

"Turn over," Tip rasped, bringing them both forward.

"I like it when you're demanding." Jack grinned, kissing Tip right below the jaw.

Tip preferred when Jack mounted him, but there were moments, like these, where he *needed* to be inside Jack, desperately.

As Jack got onto his knees, he reached to unbuckle his pants and stilled, a glazed look appearing in his hazel eyes.

No. Not again. Tip sighed. He already knew there was nothing he could do to prevent Jack from leaving. Mombi enslaved his mind whenever she needed Jack to cross the barrier, and it terrified him and Tip.

"Jack, just be careful," Tip urged.

"I always am." Jack smiled, but it wasn't his real smile.

"I love you."

Jack didn't return the sentiment as he scowled at the patch, hurrying to gather some of the pumpkins they'd collected that morning. He then placed them into a crate, his body twitching with the need to perform Mombi's tasks.

"We'll get the fuck out of here one day," Jack finally said, peering over his shoulder. He released a heavy breath and headed off in the direction of the red-flowered trees, toward the barrier, to freedom for a little while. But Jack wasn't free, just as Tip wasn't. Jack had told him that he may be able to get out to run errands, but it didn't mean anything, because he was still a slave while doing it. As soon as he crossed the barrier, he was compelled to finish Mombi's tasks. He couldn't remember things clearly—it was as if his mind was in a fog.

Tip groaned as he sat up—his length had softened, but he still missed the feel of Jack's touch. He shoved his hand back into the pumpkin and finished cleaning it for Mombi. But his worry for Jack wouldn't relent, so he focused on the one memory, years ago, that had changed everything between them.

Tip picked a few small pumpkins from the patch and set them aside. A thrashing of footsteps caused him to glance up and catch a head full of bright orange hair. He stilled and watched as Jack entered the pumpkin patch, his lips red and swollen after running errands in town. Again. Tip wasn't as confident as Jack, always feeling like he didn't fit in his body, so how could he expect Jack to find him attractive when he didn't feel it himself? Blood coursed through Tip, and he felt it pumping at the vein on the side of his neck. He was angry. Hardly anything could make him truly angry. Not even Mombi. Not when she slapped him across his face, or when her nails bit into his flesh until he bled. Yet Jack's swollen lips once more had Tip's fists tightened and his jaw clenched.

Well, Tip was going to find a way out of his entrapment. And, when he did, Tip would be the only one making Jack's lips red.

"Here," Tip spat, picking up the shovel and throwing it into Jack's hands.

Jack didn't say anything, only narrowed his eyes at him. Tip had never let his emotions get to him this way, never been this harsh with Jack. But he didn't care.

Tip could feel Jack's eyes burning into his back as he headed out of the pumpkin patch and away from Mombi's hut. After a day of work, Tip always walked back to Mombi's. For sixteen years, he always had—he wasn't one to disobey. But now he would. He would break through her magic barrier somehow. That was a promise.

After he stepped over the last row of newly bloomed pumpkins—still not yet orange—Jack's hand clasped Tip's wrist and tugged him back to his chest. "Where are you going?"

"Out of this cage," Tip said sharply.

"Mombi's barrier won't allow it." The tone in Jack's voice was melancholic. Tip knew his entrapment bothered Jack because he had repeatedly said that Tip should be free to roam wherever he wished. Jack wasn't truly free either, though. Yet Tip was still envious that Jack could leave. Get touched, caressed.

Tip whirled around and pulled his arm out of Jack's grasp. "I'm going to go and get kissed."

Jack lifted a brow, a smirk slowly spreading into a smile. "I don't think so."

"And why not? You get kissed all the time when you run Mombi's errands." And who knows what else. He'd probably tumbled all of Loland judging by his rumpled state.

"Even if you could leave, you're too ... innocent." Jack's smile still remained.

Tip narrowed his eyes, his fists shaking. "Not for much longer." He spun around and trudged toward the forest. "We can't all get pleasured on our way home."

A low growl came from behind him. Then Jack appeared in front of Tip, placing a hand at his chest to prevent him from walking away. "When I leave the barrier, Mombi's magic makes me forget—you know that. She can't have me telling anyone about you. All I know when I'm out there is that I need to deliver pumpkins or get her supplies and come back. I never choose to go."

"And yet you can stop to fondle someone?" Tip's voice came out high-pitched. "Every time?"

Jack smirked again, his freckles glinting under the afternoon light as he took a step back. "Oh, I see now."

"What do you see?"

"You're jealous."

"No, I'm not." Tip's cheeks heated. He'd overreacted and had given

himself away. With each passing day, it had grown harder and harder to keep his feelings for Jack hidden.

Jack sighed and shifted closer, angling his face near Tip's. "When I'm out there, and my mind isn't clear, I search for dark hair and eyes as blue as the sky. No one's eyes are as bright as yours, Tip. No one's. I don't know why I'm looking for this fae, when I should only be running Mombi's errands." He paused, his hazel gaze latching on to Tip's. "All right, the first part was a lie, I know why. It's not them I kiss. It's you. It's always you. But I'm not good enough for you."

Jack turned away and started walking back toward his hut, leaving Tip with more questions than answers.

"You can't do that." He jogged up to Jack, grabbed his upper arm, and spun him around. Jack was at least a head taller than him as he peered up. Tip's chest heaved and his hands shakily clasped both Jack's cheeks, bringing him closer, their lips merely a hairsbreadth from touching one another's. It wasn't outspoken Jack who made the move first. It was Tip, innocent *and* shy *Tip.*

He pressed his lips to Jack's, more hard than gentle. Desperate. Hungry. Ravenous as his mouth moved over Jack's. Tip had known he loved Jack as soon as Mombi had first brought the orange-haired fae home when he and Jack were both younglings. There had never been anything brotherly in their relationship. Only a strong friendship, a bond, and whatever this was.

Together their lips caressed, together their tongues danced. When Tip pulled back, Jack's eyes were glazed and looked to be full of stars, just as his own had to be.

"All the times I've dreamt of that kiss, it was nothing like this," Jack rasped.

"Me either. This was much better."

Tip smiled at the memory and finished the second pumpkin. He took the fruit into his arms and walked them across the field to Mombi's hut.

As he entered her home, the scent of spices hit his nostrils, along with several rotten things. Possibly a dead faerie she'd let decay for days. Who knew what else she kept behind the protected barrier of her bedroom—no one could get through the door but her.

The strong smells signaled that it was another potion for the Wizard to pass off as his own creation. Mombi came scowling out of her room after Tip closed the door. Her gray hair was pulled into a bun, and deep lines were etched in her face, more so around her lips and eyes. The sort of magic she continued to use was draining her of life, arching her spine, hunching her shoulders. One day, Tip knew the dark magic would kill her. And he and Jack both eagerly awaited that day.

"It took you this long to clean two pumpkins?" Mombi ripped the fruit from his hands and smacked him hard across the cheek. His head swung to the side. The slap burned, but he was used to it.

The best thing to do was stay silent. He started to turn but Mombi grabbed his shoulder to halt him. "You didn't answer my question." Her dim blue eyes bored into him as she leaned closer and inhaled.

Tip held his breath, his heart beating wildly in his chest. His bath. He hadn't bathed before coming here. *Damn it.*

Mombi took a step back and slammed her hand against his cheek, harder than before, the sound reverberating through the entire hut. "You've been fucking the slave!" she shouted and moved back, swiping a clay jar off the table. It crashed to the floor and shattered.

Tip took a deep swallow and shook his head. "No, I haven't."

"You're lying. I *smell* him all over you."

"No." She would be able to hear his lie again, but he tried to keep his voice even. "I'm not lying."

Mombi stepped over the broken pieces of the jar and held her arm out toward him. She tightened an invisible hand around his throat, her magic biting in, cutting off his air supply.

The magic continued to squeeze, and he clawed at the air, trying to get out of its wicked grasp. *Air.* He couldn't get any in, and he could feel his face turning red, his lips blue.

Tip was going to die. Mombi was going to kill him. He wouldn't be able to tell Jack goodbye. The last thing he'd told Jack was that he loved him. At least Jack knew Tip's feelings.

Something pulsed through Tip then. Love. More than love. A thrum of power he'd never felt. Tip's body shook, his skin glowing. *Glowing?* It was glittering with blue flecks, like stardust.

Mombi's eyes widened, her lips parting, and her grip on his throat dropped. She twirled her hand in the air, drawing up her magic, and shooting sparks of various colors at him. But none of it connected with his body.

An itch tore at his back, then built into something else, as though his skin were painlessly spreading. They broke from his flesh, ripping his tunic, freeing themselves. *Wings.* Bright blue, feathery wings. It didn't stop there. His body started *changing*. His black locks of hair grew long, to his waist, lightening to bright golden hues. Tip's body seemed to stretch, as if he were growing taller, the sleeves of his tunic and ends of his pants becoming shorter. At his chest, breasts formed beneath his shirt, and he gasped. His body shook and his eyes widened with fear, not understanding what in all of Oz was happening.

Mombi covered her mouth and hissed as she stared at him in horror. "Ozma," she growled. The horrified look on her face turned to rage and she jolted forward, knocking Tip to the floor.

Tip wrestled out from under her and stood back up. He'd lost hold of whatever power was there, his body weakening. A rush of magic came from Mombi as she rose, barreling straight for Tip's back, severing his wings. Pain rocketed through him and he let out a high-pitched cry.

That wasn't his voice at all, but a female's. Behind him hung a large oval mirror, and he took a glance at himself, while straining to breathe. Higher cheekbones, plumper lips. Nothing about himself looked like Tip at all, except the color of his irises. He was truly female.

Mombi hurled a ball of orange magic at the severed wings, burning them to ash. Tip didn't have time to mourn what had just happened, when the front door burst open. *Jack.* He was back. And he'd come to save him. But it wasn't his beloved. It was Oz. The only other individual who could cross Mombi's barrier.

"What have you done?" The Wizard seethed.

"What are you doing here?" Mombi snapped back.

"The slippers felt her curse break and whirled me here with their magic." He jabbed a finger in Tip's direction. "Now, explain!"

"You knew she couldn't be hidden forever," Mombi screeched. "With both Pastoria and Lurline dead, you should have killed her."

"You know I can't do that. Has her magic returned yet?" Oz moved toward them, his lips curled to show blackened teeth.

"Not all of it."

"Good." Oz shifted his cape to the side, revealing the silver slippers—flat and glistening—on his feet. "I suppose I should tell you that you're Ozma, born of Pastoria and Lurline. You're the true queen of Oz, but it will remain our little secret."

"Wh—what?" Tip croaked. Shock left him rooted in place. "I'm who?"

"No one … anymore," the Wizard answered.

With those words, Tip—Ozma—froze as a blast of coldness exploded around her. It was as if ice were slowly encasing her body. But it wasn't. Instead, she was falling through the floor of the hut. Falling and falling through wintry coldness, until she collapsed onto a hard surface. She was not in pain. The only thing that ached was her back, where her wings had lived for a few brief moments.

But that wasn't completely true. Because so did her heart. That ached even worse.

CHAPTER TWO

JACK

TWO YEARS LATER

The sun beat on Jack's bare back, sending rivulets of sweat down his spine. He did his best to ignore the heat as he cleared weeds from between pumpkins. His bucket was nearly full with invasive sprouts and he still had half a field to clear.

Jack leaned back on his heels, his knees digging into the soft dirt, and wiped his forehead with the back of his hand. This had been much faster when Tip was there to help. Or maybe it only seemed to be faster because of the company. The conversation. The stolen heated looks when Mombi was certain not to see. A promise of more when they were finished with their chores. His gaze traveled across the field to where a crystal-clear pond was hidden among the trees. Mombi had refused to let Tip into her hut until he washed the dirt off, which had given them both the perfect excuse for privacy every night.

Running a hand down his face, smearing dirt over his freckles, he choked back a wave of tears. It had been two years since Tip had died. No amount of crying would bring him back, but they *would* bring Mombi's wrath down on him. She could smell the grief on him, smell the salt of his sorrow, and he was supposed to have gotten over Tip. *Shit*—he was never supposed to have mourned in the first place.

If only it were that easy. If only he hadn't been about to ask Tip to marry him. If only he hadn't planned his entire future around the male he'd loved so much. Tip had been his first lover—the only true one of his life. But, when given the choice to leave, he'd run so recklessly that he was torn apart and eaten in the Shifting Sands. Jack rubbed at the ache in his chest. Why hadn't Tip said goodbye? *Why?* Tip could've at least given him *that...* He would've fought for him to stay, would've done anything. Or maybe he would've helped him figure out a way to get around the Sands because Tip deserved his freedom—even if it was without Jack. His goodbye wouldn't have made a difference in the long run either way, but at least he could've asked Tip why he didn't love him anymore.

Jack stood slowly and carried the bucket toward the magical barrier. When he was close enough, he chucked the contents to the other side and swiveled toward his small hut instead of going straight back to work. He couldn't drown his heartache with tears, so he would drown it with something else.

Jars of pumpkin ale lined more shelves in his pitifully small pantry than food did. There was a wedge of cheese from his last trip to the market and half a loaf of bread, along with a couple glass jars filled with vegetables. Meat was a rare pleasure and he'd eaten so much pumpkin that the thought of eating more made him want to vomit—though he had to force it down to survive. *Tip would want me to live*, he thought. Even if he chose not to live alongside him. Besides, the ale distracted him from his hunger most of the time.

The lump in his throat worked furiously as he gulped down an entire jar. Jack's blood instantly warmed. The ale tasted like shit as it slid over his tongue, but it was oh-so wonderful. It made him forget there was a Tip-sized hole in his heart.

Almost.

With a low, pained scream, he hurled the clay jar across the hut. It hit the wall over his bed, *cracked*, and shattered. Shards scattered over the thin woven blanket on his bed. The bed he and Tip would fuck in when Mombi went to town alone, or when she was holed up in her hut working on potions.

"Why?" he mumbled to himself as he slid down the wall. "Why did you have to die? Why did you leave me here all alone?"

Why did you make me love you?

Jack didn't voice the last question because it was unfair. Tip hadn't *made* him fall in love—he'd simply been himself. Kind and funny and generous. If Tip lived in town, everyone would've loved him. Jack felt beyond lucky to have had Tip love him back, even if it was only for a little while. But *damn*. It hurt. It hurt so much he thought he would die too. Day after day after fucking day. For two years. He thought the pain would lessen over time, but it hadn't.

So why did you leave *me?*

Maybe Jack was the problem. His parents had left him too, after all. They'd placed him beneath a tree on the side of the road and told him to wait there. Three days later, Mombi had found him. Stolen him away to be her *thing*. The only affection he'd ever received was from Tip, but they were the same in that way. Mombi loathed them both. If he and Jack hadn't loved each other, no one would have. Perhaps that was why Tip left. To find someone to love for more than convenience. Could Jack blame him for that?

No.

Yes.

It was easier to drown out the question with his ale than decide which answer was true. Ale and fae. Whores, mostly. Whoever he could find with dark hair and blue eyes when he finished with Mombi's errands. Males or females, tall or short, horned or covered in scales. It didn't matter. None of it mattered as long as they resembled Tip. But none of them were *him*. They were each simply a way to forget for a moment—now that Mombi no longer made Jack forget his life on the farm when he left, compelled. There was no reason to keep Tip a secret now that he was dead—not that he understood the reasoning when his lover was alive.

Fucking heartless bitch.

"Jack!" Mombi screeched outside, pulling him from his thoughts. "I see your bucket—I know you're in there."

He sighed and rested his head against the wall behind him. There was no point hiding from the witch. The barrier trapped him on the farm unless Mombi sent him out to do her bidding— selling pumpkin pies and cakes and soups. Buying bread and seeds and eggs. Acquiring herbs for potions and bottles to put them in. But without her intentionally letting Jack out, there was nowhere for him to go.

"Get out here!"

I'll come out there and bash you over the head with a pumpkin, you evil bitch.

Jack shoved himself off the ground and stumbled. Perhaps drinking the entire jar in one go was a bad idea … but today was a bad day. Not that any of them were *good* anymore. Sometimes he just woke up feeling worse than others. Perhaps it had something to do with the dreams he had—if they included Tip or not.

"What?" he snapped, pushing through his door.

Mombi leaned on her cane at the edge of the pumpkin patch. Her hair had turned from gray to white over the last two years and thinned considerably. The wrinkles deepened around her mouth, and her back had become so hunched that she appeared nearly bent in half. If only her magic had withered as much as her body had, then maybe Jack could've escaped her barrier. There was no reason to stay—nothing keeping him there except for Mombi's barrier. By the looks of her, she wouldn't live much longer if she continued dabbling in dark spells.

Old hag.

Sharp pain lanced across Jack's chest and he yelped. A red welt swelled from his right shoulder down to his left hip where her magic struck.

"Watch your tone," Mombi warned. "Go finish those weeds,

slave, or I'll slice off a patch of skin."

Ooh, more threats. What the hell else is new?

But even the alcohol couldn't bring Jack to say that aloud. The punishment would be far too severe. So, he bit his tongue and stumbled over to pick up his bucket.

"You're good for nothing," she mumbled. "Tip never gave me these problems."

Jack blanched at the mention of Tip's name. Mombi brought it up just to be a bitch and it never failed to give her the reaction she wanted. Tip had always been one to follow the rules… To keep him in line. It felt nearly impossible to do on his own. Everything did. He sighed silently and turned away from her.

"When you're finished, come to my hut," Mombi said to his back.

Jack's shoulders stiffened. That was never good. "Why?"

The wooden cane cracked against his lower leg and he winced at the pain.

"Don't question me."

If Mombi didn't want to tell him her reasoning, he wasn't going to change her mind. "All right," he said and returned to the same chores he'd done a million times. Over and over. Day after day.

Hours later, with the field clear of any unwanted growth, Jack tossed the empty bucket in the work shed. It landed with a loud clatter and knocked over a rake, which sent pouches of pumpkin seeds tumbling from a shelf. He dug his fists into his aching lower back and the thought of leaning over to collect them filled him with dread. It would be a miracle if he was able to stand again after an entire day on his knees. Besides, he was expected at Mombi's hut. *Damn witch.*

"Tomorrow," he said to no one. The seeds were sealed and

it wasn't like they would go anywhere.

He shut and locked the shed, pocketing the keys. Mombi would demand that he give them back now that his work was done. Likely so Jack wouldn't get any ideas about murdering her with a trowel in the middle of the night. Not that he hadn't imagined it before. A trowel, a spade, a cultivator… If they had it, he'd dreamt of killing the witch with it. The only thing holding him back was the barrier and what would happen to it—to him and, once, Tip—if she died. Would they be trapped inside forever? Her spells weren't made using normal fae magic.

Jack sighed again and turned toward the hut on the other side of the field. *Might as well get it over with.*

Trudging toward Mombi's, he kicked at the pumpkin leaves that crept over onto the grass. Maybe he should've stopped for another jar of alcohol first. His mind was too clear now, his tongue feeling too sharp. Deep down, he knew he was about to get himself in trouble. Trouble that Tip would've been able to talk him out of creating. But Tip was dead. Jack knocked loudly on Mombi's door and it instantly swung open. The witch poked him hard in the chest with the end of her cane.

Poke me again and you'll find that cane shoved so far up your—

"Get the wagon," she snapped.

Jack ground his teeth together. He'd *just* been at the shed beside the maroon and blue wagon, the bed of it covered in curving wood, forming an arc, but he returned for it without a word. Mombi usually moved it with her magic until she located the stag she'd enchanted. How the hell was he supposed to push it on his own? Even if she'd had the damn thing when Tip was alive, the two of them wouldn't have been able to move it together.

Jack went behind the wagon and pushed with his shoulder. *Yeah-fucking-right.* Then he tried pulling from the front, digging his heels into the dirt, but it didn't budge. Finally, heaving from exertion, he stomped back to Mombi. "Look," he said more harshly than was smart. "That's not moving unless I get some help."

"You're pathetic. Always have been." Mombi tossed a fabric bag at his face.

He caught it with an *oomph*. "Pathetic or not, your wagon's not going anywhere unless you do it yourself."

The witch grumbled under her breath and shot a streak of yellow magic across the field. It hit the wagon with a small *crack*. Mombi circled her hand in the air, reeling the wagon up to the hut in less time than it had taken Jack to attempt the same thing.

"Load my belongings," she barked when it creaked to a stop in front of the hut. "Quickly now."

Jack opened the back of the wagon and set the bag inside. "Are we going somewhere?" he asked, his brow furrowing.

"I'm leaving." She disappeared into the hut and glass clinked together. "Dorothy has returned to Oz and I have to help the Wizard prepare."

Dorothy? Who the fuck was that and what did she have to do with Oz?

"What are you waiting for?" she snapped.

Jack hurried to grab a large trunk and heaved it out to the wagon. Mombi was leaving? For how long? Did that mean he was free? His mind spun and spun with possibilities. Even if she was only leaving for a short time, he would be alone. He would be *free of her*. For more than a handful of hours.

"When will you be back?" Jack asked hesitantly. His palms sweated with anticipation—if she was gone long enough, he could *really* examine the barrier for a weakness. Maybe he could escape too.

"When that little bitch is dead."

That didn't explain a damn thing about how long it would take. "What should I do?"

"What you always do!" she cried so loudly that her voice cracked. "Do I have to tell you how to breathe? How to shit? Oz have mercy, you're not a youngling anymore. Even then, you were always *pitiful*." Mombi hobbled out of the hut and slammed the door behind her. She set a crate full of jingling glass containers on top of her trunk and used her magic to push the wagon toward the barrier. "Where is that damn stag? I'm not pulling this wagon the whole journey myself!"

Probably looking for a hunter's trap so it doesn't have to drag your ass across Loland.

"I haven't seen him," Jack said. He'd only seen the stag a handful of times, and never on the farm. Mombi always released him outside the barrier, enchanted him to return when she needed him, then hauled the wagon home with her magic.

Mombi grumbled to herself and sent out a small burst of power. To call the stag, Jack assumed, but he didn't question it. His mind was too busy racing over the possibilities before him. Of what it could mean. Unless she never returned and he couldn't find a way to escape… He swallowed nervously.

Pulse racing, Jack watched her walk through the barrier. As much as he hated her, he didn't want to die on this farm. Alone. Trapped. The further Mombi got, the faster his heart thumped. *Fuck! I do* not *want to become pumpkin fertilizer.* Perhaps it wasn't too late to call out and offer his services. She could enchant him to help with this Dorothy and then he would be outside the barrier. The chances for escape would be greater… But then he would be stuck at Mombi's side for who knows how long.

Before he could make a decision, a shimmer of magic rippled over the pumpkin patch, disintegrating the spell that held him captive. The invisible cage was gone. His jaw dropped in disbelief. "What the fuck just happened?"

CHAPTER THREE

OZMA

PRESENT DAY

ree. Ozma was free. She'd never known what that meant. All her life she'd belonged to Mombi, or had been a prisoner in the dark place with Reva—the Good Witch of the West who had been forced into becoming the Wicked Witch for a time. Trapped within Mombi's magical barrier around a small pumpkin farm in Loland, Ozma had never been able to venture out into the rest of Oz. There was a possibility that she could get stuck inside the barrier of the patch again, but she would try to get Jack's attention from outside it.

Loland was on the outskirts of the Shifting Sands, across from the Eastern Land of Oz. The Wizard had used the silver slippers to send her to the dark place, but Ozma was unsure how and when she'd been changed into Tip. But it had to have been sometime as a baby, because Reva had never known King Pastoria and Queen Lurline to have had a child. Her guess was that Mombi or Oz had stolen her, but then what? Why hadn't her parents gone searching for her or spread word that she'd gone missing before they'd died? She'd learned from Reva that Langwidere had taken Lurline's head and Oz had murdered

Pastoria. That made Ozma the rightful ruler of Oz, and she had never known, not until she'd been angry enough to somehow break the curse that Mombi placed on her.

Ozma was going to kill them both, retrieve her slippers, and then her kingdom.

Seeing the world as it truly was, not from Jack's maps or Reva's stories, was no comparison. And it was nothing like the dark place—that nightmare world where only a mad dash and a climb to the tops of the tallest trees brought a moment's relief from the threatening creatures. The South had been deserted but it was still beautiful, and she'd come across live Wheelers! Killed one. Felt that rush of doing something good. She'd been inside a brothel with Reva, seen fae pleasuring one another out in the open. It had given her a shock, but also made her want to know more, understand how she might bring pleasure to Jack in this female body. She'd never even explored it much herself because of the constant danger in the dark place, and the endless running. Jack had always been attracted to males and females, while she had only ever been attracted to Jack. Though, she supposed, he was the only fae she had ever been around.

Since parting ways with Reva at the brothel, and waiting around to make sure Crow—Reva's husband—could catch up with her friend, Ozma had only stopped to rest in the branches of trees for the night. But she hadn't slept much. She wanted to stay awake not only to be prepared to run if need be, but to see the Land of Oz in the moonlight.

Ozma adjusted the blue dress she'd gotten from an abandoned shop with Reva before they'd left the South. She hopped over a rotting log, then another, the map of the vast land pulsing through her veins. Though Ozma didn't have her magic, something was there, guiding her in the right direction. The moment when Thelia's power had brought Ozma and Reva back from the dark place, she'd felt every inch of Oz within her. Perhaps this was a bit of magic. She wanted to explore everything, but not yet. Not when she had to prove herself worthy to the fae that depended on her success.

Even though Thelia had already defeated Langwidere and Reva was on her way to vanquish Locasta, the biggest threat still remained. If Oz wasn't stopped, none of the other good things mattered. And worse, he would find a way to get rid of Thelia and Reva to keep his throne.

Ozma couldn't let that happen. She needed to cross the desert to see if Mombi was still in her hut. Her heart thump-thumped with the name Jack over and over. What had Mombi told him? That she gave her away? That Tip broke through the magical barrier and made a run for it? Did he think she was dead? But he would never trust whatever lies Mombi had told him. She believed that down to her bones.

Every night in the dark place, for the past two years, she'd thought about him, wanted to see his lovely face, feel his calloused hands against her naked body, his strong hugs that could always calm her fears.

While Reva would try endlessly to forget Crow, Ozma had never once wanted to forget her Jack. Not the orange of his hair under the morning sun, the light sprinkle of freckles on his nose—like flickering stars in a night sky—his high cheekbones, the plumpness of his lips. His *kisses*.

She. Loved. Him. And he loved her. Only, she hadn't been Ozma then when he'd spoken those words to her in his bed, in the lake, beneath the night sky, as the sun rose. She'd been Tippertarius and had been unknowingly forced to live in a male's body. At times, she still yearned to be Tip, but only because he was who Jack had wanted. Not who she wanted to be. If she had a chance to be a male again, it wouldn't feel right.

When she found out she was Ozma, after falling into the dark place, it took some time to get used to, but also felt like she was always meant to be this fae. She was a female, one destined to rule the entirety of Oz. On the day Ozma had broken her unknown curse, she finally felt true to herself. Being a queen was another matter—she didn't truly know if she could succeed at it.

Ozma tried to shove away her too-many thoughts as she squeezed through branches covered in thick moss and stepped over patches of polka-dotted mushrooms and flowered shrubbery. A few birds flew from the trees, pumping their… *Wings*. She'd only had strong, feathery wings for moments, but she knew with her whole heart that she needed them back. They were a part of her, and Mombi had burned them to ash. But once the silver slippers were on her feet, it was possible they would grow once more.

A sparkling river came into view and Ozma stopped at the water and gathered the cool liquid in her canteen. The internal map told her she'd be at the Shifting Sands soon. Even though Mombi's pumpkin patch hadn't been far from it, the Sands had never been possible for Ozma to see because of the barrier, but Jack had told her about its bright multi-colored grains. Still, she had never wanted to cross its sandy peaks. Not after the stories Mombi had told her about creatures emerging from its depths, biting the heads off fae and eating them from the inside out.

As Ozma brought one last handful of water to her lips, the raised scar on her back throbbed. The phantom pain of her wings was always a reminder of Mombi. After stewing so long in the dark place, Ozma was sure she would have the strength to outwit the witch who'd ruined her life. Only one good thing had come from Mombi keeping Ozma from her destiny, and that was Jack. But he'd been stolen away from his family, just as she had.

Determined, she placed her satchel's strap over her head and thought of him as she wandered through the forest toward the desert.

Ozma pressed her fingers to her lips as she stared out at the Shifting Sands. The color was so intense, it made it hard to keep her eyes open. There were so many hues, from dark blues to light purples and bright pinks. It seemed to sway, rhythmically, creating a dance of colors. The light breeze floating across the mounds seemed to sing as if luring its prey.

She shivered at the sight, even though she didn't want to be afraid. All she had to do was get to the other side. The distance across wasn't far, but width wise, it stretched on and on.

She wiggled her toes in the grass, the blades tickling her skin. The Sands could make her see things if it wished, make her *feel* them. Ozma always thought Mombi had lied, but once she'd fallen into the dark place, after swapping her shredded clothing for a blue dress off the skeleton of a dead fae, Reva had told her that the story was true. Each Sand territory had its own hidden dangers. Thankfully, she wouldn't have to cross the Deadly Desert, because she didn't know if being the true queen of Oz would keep her from turning to sand.

"Let's do this, Ozma. Let's go to Jack. He's your home." Blowing out a breath and squaring her shoulders, Ozma pressed one bare foot onto the warm sand. She expected the touch to burn her heel, but instead, it was a light caress. She knew not to trust it. Whichever way the Wizard had crossed, whether the Shifting Sands, the Impassible Desert, the Great Sandy Waste, or even the Deadly Desert, he had to have used the silver slippers or Mombi's help to do it. Otherwise, his mortality would have prevented him from surviving the trip.

Ozma would get the slippers from him, and she would only ever use them for good—if she decided to use them at all after her world was safe.

The winds kicked up, swirling around her, faster and faster. She kept focused, trudging ahead, the grains stinging her eyes and scratching her skin. Beneath her feet, the sand shifted, making it seem like she was walking on water. Ozma knew it wasn't the sand moving on its own, but what lay hidden beneath. *Please stay below until I finish crossing.*

A roaring sounded in the distance, muffled by the sand. If she sprinted, the creatures below might notice her sooner and chew her to pieces. The sand quaked. The world rumbled. In front of her, a head shot up from the grains. Large black wings flapped. Thick yellow saliva dripped from sharp teeth set in a wide mouth, and thorn-like spikes ran from the top of its head down its massive, blue-scaled body. It wouldn't be the short, clawed arms that grabbed her, but the mouth. And she bet it would be quick.

Ozma's heart seemed to skip a few beats as her body trembled. If only she had her wings, then she could have easily avoided this situation. She genuinely wanted to keep her head attached to her body. All she had was a dagger at her waist that wouldn't do much damage if she used it.

She caught the look in the beast's eyes and jolted out of the way just as the creature's teeth tore into the sand with an ear-piercing shriek. There was no hesitation from her—she sprinted. Pumping her legs as fast as she could, Ozma thought of Jack's face, his eyes, his lips, him pulling her across the sand, though it was really only her who was doing this. On her own.

With a quick glance over her shoulder, she watched as the spiked tail of the beast swished in the air while the rest of the body vanished into the sand.

The edge of the desert wasn't far now. A few moments and she would be safe, but the beast shot up again. Followed by a second. Both studied her with predatory skill, then scrutinized each other, as if neither wanted to share. One dove, mouth wide open, sharp teeth glistening, aiming for the other's throat with a loud growl. A wailing screech echoed.

Ozma suppressed a shudder at the thought of them deciding to divide her and ripping her in half. She took the chance to run again while they were distracted. The heat of the sun beat at her skin as she held her breath, and she didn't breathe again until her feet met grass.

Dropping to her knees, chest heaving, she hurried to turn around. In the small stretch of sand, the two beasts were still fighting, bright red blood pouring from deep wounds on both their bodies. One of the blue creatures buried its fangs into the other, spraying more crimson. The beast unlatched its mouth and let the second creature collapse to the sand, unmoving.

There was victory in the beast's flaming-orange eyes until it spotted Ozma across the barrier of the Sands, safe. A heavy roar escaped the creature's mouth as it dove back into the sand, taking the dead beast with it.

She was so close to where she needed to be, so close to Jack.

Ozma rose from the ground. The tall trees surrounding her were drawn so tightly together that she couldn't glimpse anything through the red flowers growing along the branches.

She pushed a limb out of the way, then another and another until she came across her first sign of life in Loland. Faeries with clear glittery wings sang and danced in the leaves above. Ozma smiled as she watched. The joy that radiated from them would soon spread through Oz. It would take time, and fae would need to rebuild, but the happiness would come. Ozma had experienced her share of darkness—as had Reva, Crow, Tin, and Thelia. But each of them still held hope, and she prayed others would too.

The farther she got through the trees, her heart raced more. Decaying logs full of holes were sprawled across the ground and she hopped over each one, pep blooming with each step. Her smile didn't drop, not once.

A sprinkle of orange peeked through the trees and her smile grew wider. Hot tears streamed down her cheeks and she let out a giggle.

But then her laughter caught in her throat, the smile dropping from her face when there was no flicker of blue where the barrier should have been—it was *gone*. Mombi had never once let the barrier drop. Even the pumpkins seemed to be sparser than they had in the past.

Focus, Ozma.

Something was wrong, and she needed to not worry about getting to Jack first—she had to see if Mombi was still in her hut. Revenge on the witch would have to take priority, unless she wasn't at the patch.

Her gaze settled on Mombi's light brown home resting in the distance. Mombi's and Jack's huts both appeared the same, as though they remained occupied. The clay pots were still on Jack's porch, the plants in full bloom with blue and purple hyacinths, like always. And Mombi's rocker continued to rest beside her door with her favorite blanket thrown over its back. She hesitated for a moment to go farther, then shoved the nervousness away.

From her waist, Ozma drew out her dagger. Part one of her plan would be to kill Mombi. Part two would be to find Jack. And part three would be to kill the Wizard.

Ozma hovered along the edge of the forest, behind the row of trunks, even though she wanted to run through the field. She doubted Mombi was looking out a window, waiting for Ozma to approach, but she needed to sneak up on her for this to go smoothly.

When she reached the hut, Ozma slipped out from the trees. Mombi didn't keep a single flower around her home. The beds in front of the hut were nothing but dirt gardens with weeds as they had been before. It fit Mombi's personality quite well.

The porch was bare except for the single wooden rocker where Mombi used to sit and watch them work the fields. In that moment, Ozma could hear Mombi screeching at them to work faster and she shoved that aggravating voice away.

Ozma crept in front of the grime-streaked door and pushed open the entrance as quietly as possible, but a teeny squeak sounded and she froze. Gripping the dagger, Ozma stepped inside—the house still smelled of Mombi: nutmeg, ginger, and rotten eggs. The sitting room appeared unchanged, with a canary-yellow settee and a table covered in empty glass bottles and vials that Mombi would use to store antidotes for the Wizard.

Ozma's door was open and she could see that nothing of hers remained. Her wool jacket no longer hung on the wall, her wardrobe of clothing was gone, and the blanket from her bed was now used as a curtain over the far window. It was as if she'd never lived there. But that didn't surprise her.

Slowly, she went toward Mombi's room, her door shut, always protected from anyone going inside. Only, like the barrier around the patch, there was no flicker of blue around it. The barrier had vanished here too. Her lungs stilled as her eyes widened. Something was wrong—Mombi would never leave her room unprotected.

Ozma took a deep swallow, turned the knob, and cracked the door open, a light creak sounding. Her eyes remained widened as she inhaled a mixture of the witch's scent, faerie fruit innards, and lavender. She'd never seen Mombi's room before because of the spells that had been placed around it.

The space was filled with stack after stack of books, several with loose sheaves of paper sticking out. Spellbooks. Besides those, there was only Mombi's bed with rumpled sheets, a wardrobe, and several silver pails for her mixtures.

Jack. What if he wasn't at the patch either? What if he'd gone somewhere else? What if she could never find him again?

The map in her veins could lead her to places, but that was all—she'd tried to feel him before and she couldn't, just as she wouldn't be able to locate Reva. A wounded sound escaped her as she closed the door and rushed from the room, tearing her way out of the hut, back into the heat of the day.

Leaping off the porch, she rushed toward the gray hut on the other side of the patch. Thick, curled vines from the pumpkins struck her legs as she hurried, and she ignored the slight stings at her ankles.

Ozma came to a stop at the edge of the patch, her face hot, catching her breath before she took a step onto the uneven porch. The hyacinths caught her attention again—he had to still be there.

Hand shaking, she gently opened the door in case Mombi was here. The witch had never set foot in Jack's hut, but things seemed to have changed over the last two years and she needed to remain cautious. She gripped the dagger in her hand as she entered the tiny sitting room. The settee and small kitchen table were still in the space, but it sat empty. Paintings hung on the walls that were hers and Jack's, of places they'd wanted to go and visit one day. They weren't very good, but they were theirs. She couldn't help but smile because he'd kept them.

A stirring came from the only other room in the hut, followed by muffled noises. Clenching her blade tighter, Ozma tiptoed down the tiny hallway to the open door.

She furrowed her brow and stopped in the doorway, peering inside. Orange hair, brighter than the pumpkins outside, stood out like a beacon in the room. Her heart rose with elation just as fast as it dropped to ruination the moment that she stepped inside. She couldn't comprehend what she was seeing. Jack's naked body was atop another male with dark hair. And he was thrusting inside him.

With a sharp inhale, Ozma covered her mouth, the dagger dropping from her hand with a loud clang. She backed into the door frame instead of out of the room, making more sound than she'd wanted to. Deep down, Ozma should have known that Jack wouldn't wait for her. She didn't know what Mombi had told him, but she should have known either way.

Jack's head angled over his shoulder from the commotion, his body stilling as his hazel eyes met hers. "Who the fuck are you?"

Tip. Tip. Tip. Ozma just stood there, body trembling. She couldn't look at the male beneath him, only Jack, but anything she wanted to say was lodged in her throat. *Just say who you are.* "Tip's sister," she finally stuttered. And with those words, not waiting for him to respond, she whirled around and took off for the front door.

Her heart pounded with too many emotions as she fled out of the house and over the pumpkins. A large vine snagged her by the leg, tripping her, and ensnaring her there. Tears rushed down her cheeks while she tugged at the vine.

This was not home. Jack wasn't her home any longer.

CHAPTER FOUR

JACK

Market day had been a success. All of the ripest pumpkins sold—for far less than Mombi would've accepted but fuck her—and Jack had traded forgotten potions from Mombi's hut for a new handcart. Once the rest of the crop matured and Jack sold everything on the farm, he would leave. Find his own place in the world and start anew. The Enchanted Isle of Yew, perhaps, or the Isle of Mifkets. He and Tip had dreamed of traveling to both, and he would love to live by the sea.

But those plans had to wait another week, until he had enough coin.

It was an amazing feeling that the coins in his pocket were all his. He didn't have to sneak a few out to pay for a tumble because the scraggly old hag had been gone for a fortnight now. *Bless whatever happened to bring the barrier down.* It had to be related to how weak Mombi had become lately, but he didn't give a damn. This little taste of freedom was only a drop in the bucket. After buying a celebratory *real* bottle of ale—none of that homemade pumpkin shit—there was only one thing missing before he left town.

A body to warm his bed. And he knew just the one.

"Elidyr," he greeted as he approached the male leaning against the corner of a pub. A hanging lamp swung lightly over his head with the gentle night breeze. The elf was shorter than him and taller than Tip, but height didn't matter when he was pressed into a bed. The dark hair and blue eyes were what made this particular prostitute a favorite.

Elidyr smiled coyly and played with the ties holding Jack's shirt closed. "Hello, Jack. It's been a while."

Jack shrugged. "You've been busy."

"Aye." Elidyr's smile widened. "I have. Some trooping faeries passed through and decided to continue their revelry here for a few days."

"Who could blame them?" Jack closed the distance between them and lifted Elidyr's chin. "With a face like this."

Elidyr lightly ran his fingertips up Jack's torso and slid inside the loose ties crossing over his chest. The skin-to-skin contact made him shiver. He wanted more. Needed it. He leaned in and flicked his tongue over Elidyr's bottom lip. The male's fingers curled into his shirt in response.

"I want you for the entire night," Jack breathed. What did he care if it cost more than he could truly afford? He meant to save as much as he could, but desperation clawed at his chest, erasing all reason. A quick fuck in the back alley wouldn't cut it this time. He wanted someone to sleep beside him all night, and be there when he woke in the morning, just so he could pretend he wasn't completely unloved. "I can pay."

"A whole night is expensive," Elidyr said.

"I can pay," Jack repeated and held the bottle of ale up between them. "Help me celebrate."

Elidyr's brow lifted. "Celebrate what?"

"Freedom." Jack tugged at Elidyr's waistband. "Come home with me and I'll pay extra if you wake me up with your mouth."

Elidyr reached up and rapped on the window behind him. "I've got a client for the night."

A portly redcap flung open the window and stuck her head out. "Ah, Jack!" The madam's pleasant expression turned to a scowl. "You can afford an entire night? What will Mombi say? Elidyr is one of my best males and I can't have him injured."

"Mombi's gone." He dug into his pocket and tossed her a silver coin. "Half now. Half when he leaves in the morning."

The redcap caught it midair, bit the coin, and nodded. "Where is Mombi then?"

"Damned if I know," he said with a shrug. After fourteen days, he hoped she was dead.

The redcap licked her lips and stared at him as if trying to detect a lie. Finally, she waved them off with a quick, "have fun."

Oh, we'll have fun. Jack's cock stiffened slightly at the thought of Elidyr's lips wrapped around his length. *All night.*

"Lead the way," Elidyr said with a playful grin.

Jack turned on his heel and started out of town with Elidyr trailing behind him. His heart thumped wildly at the promise of pleasure, but it was tainted by something darker—longing. For Elidyr to be Tip. For someone to tell Jack it was all a lie. That Tip had never left him and was alive somewhere. Waiting for him. Wanting him as badly as Elidyr wanted his money. That Tip needed him with every bone in his body.

But no one could tell Jack those things.

Because Tip didn't choose him. Tip chose to abandon him to a life enslaved to Mombi, so fucking someone who closely resembled his ex-lover would *not* make him feel like he was betraying their relationship. He would *not* feel guilty.

Not even a little.

Jack woke the next afternoon to Elidyr's wet tongue gliding up his swollen cock. His lips twitched and a moan slipped from his throat. Opening his eyes was out of the question, at least for the moment. He could pretend better if he didn't see. Pretend that the breath skating over his glistening head came from a different male. Pretend that, if he *did* open his eyes, he would see the brightest blue ones looking up at him.

"Morning," Elidyr said with a sleep-filled voice far too deep to belong to Tip. "Or perhaps more like afternoon."

The image of his ex-lover vanished from behind Jack's eyelids. It wasn't Tip—it was a fae he *paid* to show him attention. The realization of what he'd done, how low he'd fallen, always struck the hardest when he first woke. Before the ale could drown out the humiliation. *No.* He would. Not. Feel. Guilty. If Tip loved him, he wouldn't have left. There was no reason Jack shouldn't enjoy himself. No reason not to seek momentary pleasure.

He sprung from the bed with a frustrated growl and jerked his chin to the headboard. "Hold onto that."

Elidyr inched up the bed, his dark hair rumpled, and bent over to hold onto the wooden frame. Jack took in Elidyr's lean form and pale skin. He hadn't noticed just how pale he was in the shadowy alleys where they fucked, but the sunlight made it painfully obvious. Tip's skin was darker from working in the field all day. Golden and beautiful.

Just close your eyes, he told himself as he knelt behind the fae and gripped his ass. Elidyr pressed back into his touch. Jack fisted his own cock, pumping until it was completely hard, and grabbed the oil from the bedside table.

Elidyr moaned the moment Jack slid inside him. The sound rang false to his ears, but he would ignore that too. Ignore, ignore, ignore. And simply *feel.* Feel each thrust. Thrust after thrust after—

A loud clang sounded behind him, followed by the shuffle of feet and a softer thud. Jack froze and his eyes flew open. Over his shoulder stood a young female in a blue dress. Blonde hair, blue eyes. *Gorgeous.* But no one came here. Ever. Unless she was new to the brothel and came to collect Elidyr on behalf of the redcap.

"Who the fuck are you?" he demanded.

She stared at him with a pained expression before blurting,

"Tip's sister." Then she whirled around and fled the hut.

Tip's sister? Tip's *sister*? Her words immediately made him go limp. He pulled out of Elidyr and scoured the floor for his pants. There was never any mention of a sister or any other family for that matter. Not from Tip. Not from Mombi. "Shit," he muttered.

"Here." Elidyr lifted his eyebrows and threw Jack's pants across the room. "Your lover?"

"Not even close," he said, panting, as he tried desperately to get his legs in his pants. Why was one leg inside out? "Damn it!" His hands shook as he fixed the fabric, his pulse echoing in his ears. "You should leave."

Elidyr began collecting his own clothes. "The other half of my money?"

He shoved a hand in his pocket and tossed him a coin. Without bothering to buckle his pants, Jack raced out the open door. The female was halfway across the pumpkin patch, sprawled in the dirt with her foot caught in the vines.

Jack sprinted after her, leaping over rows of pumpkins, while holding his waistband in place. The female saw him coming and scrambled to her feet.

"Wait!" he called. But she was already bolting straight for Mombi's hut. Jack pushed himself faster until he was close enough to grab her wrist. "Please wait."

"Let go of me," she cried.

"Okay," Jack agreed slowly. She couldn't simply show up, claim to be Tip's sister, and disappear. He needed answers first. "But … wait. Okay?"

"Fine," she grumbled and Jack released her.

For a moment, they faced each other, steadying their rapid breaths, before Jack asked, "You're Tip's sister?"

"I…" She swallowed hard. "I'm Ozma."

"Ozma." Jack looked her up and down. She looked nothing like Tip. They had the same vivid blue eyes but that was where the resemblance ended. Where his hair was nearly black, hers was so blonde that it could've been spun from sunlight. She was taller than Tip, too. Her features were delicate, her lips full, where Tip's cheekbones and jaw had been sharp-edged, his lips wide. "I'm Jack."

"I know," she whispered.

Jack cocked his head and ran his free hand through his hair. "Sorry about back at the hut. I wasn't expecting company."

"Of course not," she said in a harsh voice.

At a loss for words, Jack simply stared at Ozma. A sister… Tip had a sister. But how did she find this place? And why did she come now? Was it Mombi's doing? Had she sent this female to taunt him? Or check on him, perhaps? What kind of game was this?

He was torn between being patient and shaking the answers from Ozma. But mostly, he wanted to hide in his hut so she wouldn't see his shame. The first time he'd brought someone back home, fucked someone other than Tip in his bed, and Ozma caught him. Of all the fae… He quickly buckled his pants.

"You should get back to your lover," she snapped.

"He's not my lover." When Ozma glared at him, he added, "Not in the way you're thinking."

"Sure," Ozma mumbled, barely loud enough for him to hear.

His breath caught. "What's that supposed to mean?"

"Nothing." Ozma's voice crackled with emotion. "I'm just here for Tip's things."

"Tip didn't *have* things," Jack growled. A few changes of clothes and essential items, but nothing more. Especially not two years later. *Patience.* Scaring her away wouldn't get him the answers he needed. "Did Mombi send you? Are you going to report back to her? Tell her that I brought someone here?"

Ozma's eyes widened. "Why would I need to report to Mombi when she can see you for herself?"

Did she really not know Mombi had left? Could she be who she said she was? His gaze fell to the ground as he ran different explanations through his mind, and Ozma's bare feet caught his attention. "Tip never wore shoes either," he blurted before he could stop himself.

Ozma huffed and turned toward Mombi's hut again, then ran.

Jack stayed where he was and watched her go. There was a familiarity about Ozma. Not her blossom aroma, but beneath that lingered sugar and crisp autumn leaves, just as it had with Tip. And there'd been something in her eyes... It was like she *knew* him. Like she was personally offended by what she had walked in on.

Had Tip survived the Shifting Sands? Had he found his sister and told her about their relationship? Had they laughed at the idea of him alone with Mombi? No... Even if Tip didn't love him, he wasn't *that* cruel. Perhaps Tip sent Ozma here so he wouldn't have to see Mombi again? Or so he wouldn't have to face Jack? Jack looked up just as Ozma disappeared into Mombi's hut and felt the cracks in his heart breaking open again.

CHAPTER FIVE

OZMA

Jack had run after Ozma. But of course he did—a strange female barged straight into his hut while he was... She shook her head, trying to escape the vision of Jack with the other male. *What was I thinking, telling Jack I was Tip's sister?*

She wanted to leave, should leave, but she couldn't. Instead, she ran toward Mombi's because that was the only place where she could lock herself in for the moment. Ozma was the true queen of Oz and she shouldn't be wasting time hiding in another dark place to cry. However, she needed to regain focus. This was all Mombi's and the Wizard's fault and, more than ever, she needed to run a blade across their throats. For making her feel this way, for making Jack so easily turn to a new lover. Perhaps Jack didn't love her as much as he'd claimed.

A small voice rang in Ozma's head, whispering to her that Jack likely believed Tip was dead. She batted at her ear—the voice of reason—as she sprinted, leaping over pumpkins. It didn't matter because she'd *seen him* mounting another and she couldn't unsee that.

Ozma knew she was being deceitful, but if she did tell him the truth, it would always be Tip, Tip, Tip. Jack might not say the words aloud but he would compare her to Tip, to who she used to be. But she wasn't that fae anymore, in body or mind. From being in that dark place with Reva, learning things, discovering the world—even though she'd yet to see it in its entirety. Stars above, she couldn't stop seeing Jack *thrusting* inside that other male.

With shaking hands, Ozma threw open the entrance to Mombi's and rushed inside. The door slammed, echoing within the hut, rattling the walls as she bolted the lock. She didn't want to be back in this place. This hut. This *patch*. Earlier, she'd been so focused on having her blissful reunion with Jack after murdering Mombi, to be overly bothered by being here, but neither had happened. Too much time had passed for Jack.

Standing alone, in the middle of this familiar room, seeing the glass vials, the switches in the corner that Mombi would use to slap Ozma's knuckles, she shivered. Ozma could feel the stings now, along with the painfully vicious strikes against her cheek. No, *Tip's* knuckles, his cheek. Her body trembled—it was too much. She didn't miss being in male form, especially now with the memories resurfacing.

Ozma cupped her nose and mouth, to stifle any more crying. As her chest heaved, she dreamed of shattering Mombi's glass vials to pieces, setting fire to the hut. Not now, though. She only had the strength to release an ear-shattering scream. What could Mombi do if Ozma did destroy her things? What could be worse than what she'd already done? Put Ozma back in the dark place? Kill her? Make her forget? Perhaps that would be better than the betrayal and hurt consuming her at that moment.

A tapping came at the door and Ozma froze, knowing it wouldn't be Mombi because she wouldn't knock at her own hut. Why couldn't he just leave her alone? But she knew why… Ozma should have just told him she was someone else. *Anyone* else.

She didn't want to see him. She did want to see him. No. She *did not* want to see him.

The knob turned and the door rattled as Jack tried to open it, insistent, urgent, like the frantic beat of her heart.

Taking a deep breath, she went to the door and unbolted it

before yanking it open. "Yes?" she asked, voice soft, too soft. Ozma should have snapped, asked him why he'd been tumbling another. It had been two years, but Jack *knew* Mombi, and he shouldn't have believed anything she'd said.

Jack ran a hand through his hair, grabbing at the short curls before a lock fell right at his brow. He stared at her, throat bobbing, his eyes dancing with an uncertain emotion. "I wanted to give you a moment to yourself, but you can't stay at Mombi's."

Ozma opened her mouth to say she needed more than a moment when he pressed a finger against her lips. To shush her. She narrowed her eyes, clenching her teeth, but her heart kicked up at his touch anyway. Until a familiar scent of oil hit her nose and she took a step back, away from him. That single digit that had touched her body everywhere … but not *this* body. He'd been with another male only minutes ago.

"Now," Jack continued, dropping his hand and licking his lower lip, "we're going to have a little chat. You're going to tell me why you're here, *how* you're here, and if Mombi truly didn't send you. I want the truth."

The truth… He wanted the *truth*. Before, she would have told him, she would have confided everything to him, but after seeing what she had, she just couldn't find the words.

"I'm not working for Mombi," Ozma whispered. She straightened so she was closer to his height and lifted her chin. It was strange to now see him almost eye to eye instead of having to look farther up at him. "I came here to kill her, not to collect Tip's things. And yes, I'm Tip's sister. Whether you want to believe it or not is up to you, but I am." And in a way, she believed her words. She'd been Tip in the past, but it felt like another fae now, one she didn't want to go back to. Perhaps Jack was just part of that old world, that broken place. Perhaps Jack was her lover then, but not meant to be hers now.

Jack cocked his head and crossed his arms as he leaned against the doorframe. "You being his sister doesn't make a damn bit of sense. Tip died while crossing the Shifting Sands so there's no way you could've known Mombi held him captive once." He paused, a glimmer of hope crossing his face. "Or are you telling me he's still alive? Is that how you knew to come here?"

That was what Jack was hoping for. To have Tip back. Because he believed that, maybe, Mombi had lied to him, that Tip was still out there alive somewhere. Tip was Ozma so it was true... She almost told him in that moment. Almost. *But* if he'd believed there was a chance Tip could be alive, then why was he taking a lover to his bed—the bed where Tip and Jack had been together, time after time—instead of searching for him. The barrier was gone so there was no excuse.

"Mombi didn't lie to you about that," Ozma finally said. "Tip is dead, but it was she who killed him."

Jack pushed off the doorframe, his shoulders dropping as he inched close, closer. She couldn't tell if he believed her. "Then tell me, pretty blossom, how do you know all this?"

She could give him a partial truth. "Because … because Mombi stole me too." Her eyes focused on the spot where she'd become Ozma: across from the decaying wooden chair, where a large oval mirror hung on the wall. She locked her gaze on her own image. "Only, I was held in the mirror here all this time." She pointed to the glass. "Tip had an argument with Mombi and his magic somehow came to life, but before he could use it, she turned him into ash. So, Tip may not have known about me, but I knew everything. After Tip died, Mombi sent me somewhere else, a dark place, and before you ask how I got out, it was because Dorothy returned." She paused, tears pricking at her eyes. "So that's why I'm here, to murder Mombi for what she's done, to Tip, and to me."

Jack took a step back, rubbing a hand over his mouth and jaw. "I don't know what to say. Mombi isn't here—she left when she heard Dorothy had returned."

Ozma's eyes widened. "She knows?" Of course she would. Word must have spread like wildfire when Thelia came back to Oz. This wasn't good. Ozma hadn't known who Dorothy was when she'd lived in Loland, but she'd learned all about her in the dark place from Reva. "What happened to the barrier?"

"I don't know. It vanished a few minutes after the bitch left to go to the Wizard."

Perhaps the witch was growing weaker. Why would Jack stay if he wasn't trapped inside? But she didn't ask him. "Has the Wizard been here recently?"

He shook his head. "I haven't seen him in years and don't know where he is."

"I'll have to find Mombi then."

Jack arched a brow, scanning her up and down. "Show me your magic."

"What?" She wrinkled her nose, confused by his sudden change of mood and question.

"Show me"—he stepped forward, lifted a lock of her hair, twirling it around his finger—"how you're going to defeat Mombi. Because if you've watched her from that mirror most of your life, then you'll know you need to have a pretty damn good amount of magic."

She closed one eye, squinted the other, and cringed. "Um, I don't have any at the moment."

"Let me understand this." Jack dropped his hand from her hair and shook his head. "You have zero magic and think you can defeat one of the most powerful witches in Oz?"

"Listen," Ozma said, determined. "I have a blade and I've learned how to be sneaky, how to kill someone." She thought about the Wheeler she'd stabbed through the heart after Reva had struck the rest of the clan dead with her magic. "It wouldn't be that difficult if I were fast, if Mombi was unaware."

Jack stared at her for a long moment, studying her face. "I see that hate burning in your eyes, the way it did in Tip's, the way it does in mine. And I believe you really are Tip's sister, only because you have the same eyes as him. I would recognize that bright blue anywhere. But, if he were still here, and he knew about you, he wouldn't want you to do this."

Before she could reply, Jack scooped her off the floor, making her gasp. He cradled her in his arms as he strode out of the hut, closing the door with his boot.

"What are you doing?" she screeched when she finally found words.

"You're coming to my place for the night," he replied with an easy shrug.

"I will not!" She tried to wriggle from his hold. "Not with a … lover there."

"He left, so it's just you and me." Jack stepped over several pumpkins as he walked in the direction of his hut. "If you promise not to run again, I'll set you down, though."

"Fine." She honestly just needed to go somewhere and rest. The day was catching up to her. Not only the day, but the past two years of constantly being on the move and trying not to be killed. Now that she was at the patch, she could relax for a moment, even if nothing was ending up as she'd planned.

Jack lowered her to the ground and she walked beside him, leaving a two-person gap between them until they reached his hut.

Her lids fluttered, the exhaustion washing over her, as she peered at him in front of the door.

He stared at her, a line settling between his brows like he wanted to ask more questions, but he didn't. "Go inside and get some rest. I have a few things to take care of before heading to the market tomorrow. By the looks of things, you'll get to join me."

Ozma didn't have the energy to argue as she nodded and stepped into Jack's hut. She didn't focus on anything around her, just went to his room and scooped up the dagger she'd dropped earlier. She set it on top of his dresser beside an unlit lantern. Even though she wanted to collapse on the bed, she just couldn't. Not after Jack… She sank to the hard floor, curled her knees to her chest, and imagined she was in the same place, but back in time with Jack.

Ozma opened her eyes, surrounded by darkness and shadows swaying across from her. She jolted up with a gasp, her gaze settling on a flickering lantern. For a moment, she thought she was back in the dark place with Reva. But then she recognized the rafters of the ceiling and ugly frayed curtains. She was in Jack's hut.

How long had she slept?

She stood from the floor and stretched her spine. In front of the lantern, beside her dagger, was a bowl full of fruit. Jack had left this? Turning, she searched the bedroom for him, but he wasn't there.

Tiptoeing to the door, she peered out through the narrow crack. Light snoring came from the sitting room, signaling Jack was there and asleep.

Now that Ozma was rested, her head clear, she remembered Mombi's room, the stacks of books. There had to be something inside them—a location spell, one she could use to track down the witch.

Ozma tucked her dagger at her hip, then collected a piece of fruit and the lantern before going to the window. Little by little, she lifted the glass, each push releasing a soft creak. As Tip, she'd snuck out of this window too many times to count, so Mombi wouldn't catch her leaving out the front door.

Outside, all was quiet, except for the flutter of faerie wings somewhere in the forest. The barrier had been out past the trees and around the lake, but not even the small faeries could slip past Mombi's magic. She wondered if they tried to now or if they assumed the barrier was still in place.

Trudging quietly across the patch, she bit into the sweet fruit and attempted not to let herself think of Jack. Only focus on the next step, which was finding Mombi.

The hut stood quiet and dark as she opened the door. An

eerie feeling poured over her as she stepped inside. Darkness always made things worse. Ozma's hands trembled as she thought about trees from the dark place reaching out with thorned limbs.

The sweet, rotten scent assaulted her as she entered Mombi's room. Holding the lantern higher, she surveyed the space and the messy stacks of books.

There had to be something here she could use. Ozma lit the candles along the wall with the flame of her lantern, giving herself more light. She picked a book up and thumbed through its yellowed pages, the drawings of mutilated bodies, blood spilling from fae babies' mouths. The things Mombi had done in the past with these spells churned her stomach.

After finding nothing useful, she searched another and another. Most were spells that involved conjuring up the dead or opening doors to dark worlds.

There had to be a location spell somewhere. Mombi always had an alternate plan and letting Jack go to town—even compelled—was a risk. The witch would want to track him down if he never came back. She closed her eyes, the map of Oz lighting up within her, hoping that she could possibly find Mombi this time. But she couldn't, nothing had changed.

Her hand halted when she discovered, not what she was looking for, but something else, circled in what appeared to be faded blood. A curse to take away a fae's true identity, which would allow them to have their magic hidden too. As she turned the page, a withering folded note, tucked inside, caught her attention. She opened it and read:

Steal the child growing in Lurline's belly.
Use magic to alter the child's identity.
Find silver slippers to draw magic from the child.
Create immortality.

Ozma placed the note in the book and slammed it shut. That must be why Mombi had changed her instead of killing her. The

Wizard… The shoes had brought him to Mombi's the last time because of the burst of Ozma's magic. She didn't have any now, though… And according to the note, it had to be because the slippers were drawing the magic from her right now, the way they must have been while she was locked away in the dark place.

Chest heaving, she put aside what she'd uncovered about herself for now. Because it didn't matter in that moment. Finding Mombi did. After going through several more books involving hearts of sprites, heads of gnomes, fingers and eyes of fauns, she came across something that could potentially work. All she would need to do was create a concoction with a piece of skin from herself and something personal from the other fae, along with a few other things that Mombi would already have there. Then chant the spell words and she would be able to follow a magic trail to her target that only she could see.

This is it. She grinned as she tore the pages from the book and placed them in her satchel for safekeeping. Tomorrow she would come back and create the mixture.

Ozma left the house and glanced at Jack's. Her chest tightened, and she realized she didn't want to go back there for the remainder of the night. She wanted to bathe from her long journey, then she would sleep beside the lake until morning.

While staring up at the night sky, Ozma studied the full moon, and made a wish for Reva and Crow, then Tin and Thelia. For their safety.

Pushing past several trees, she slipped into the forest. The crooked limbs seemed to stretch up to the stars as she walked around the group of small boulders and stopped in front of the lake. The moon reflected off the glassy surface while the liquid rippled. Setting down the lantern in a patch of grass beside the log that was hers and Jack's, Ozma removed her satchel, the rope across her waist, and dress. She caught a whiff of herself and she nearly choked—bathing was the perfect choice.

As she stepped into the cool water, the liquid swaying against her, Ozma ignored the shiver that rolled through her body. She swam out to the center, practically feeling the grains from the desert wash away. Once she found Mombi, Ozma wondered how exactly she should kill her. The dagger through her heart? Across her throat? Through her eye? Her first kill had been the Wheeler with Reva. Before she'd changed into Ozma, the thought of murder would have terrified her. But Reva had taught her that sometimes it was necessary. To make things better, it was sometimes crucial.

Once she cleaned off well enough, Ozma started to swim back to the edge of the lake when a *click, click* sound erupted from behind one of the trees. She stilled mid-swim, breaths halting, and whirled around in the water. It came again, louder than before. She'd never heard anything like it. The moon gave off light but not enough to illuminate the entire forest. Shadows enfolded around her as the wind blew.

A splash into the water made her suck in a sharp breath. She didn't linger—she swam, faster than she ever had. Behind her, the thing thrashing through the lake drew closer. Two hands grabbed her by the waist, claws digging in, drawing blood. Ozma released a terrified scream as she was yanked beneath the water, her attacker pulling her down, deeper and deeper.

She shoved her elbow back and struck the soft flesh of whatever it was. The claws loosened and Ozma swam rapidly to the surface. Just when she caught a gulp of air, the creature snatched her ankle and hauled her down again. A hand clamped around her mouth, and she bit it, but the creature didn't relent.

Her heart pounded harder, her lungs growing thirstier and thirstier for air. Ozma fought to hold her eyes open, but she couldn't. This wasn't the way she'd ever expected to die, not in this lake that had always been safe. The last thought that came to her was if she could so easily be killed, then perhaps she wasn't a true queen after all.

CHAPTER SIX

JACK

The slide of wood-on-wood woke Jack. He knew exactly what that sound was—*the bedroom window*. He stayed where he was on the worn, tattered rug, feigning sleep. Ozma was sneaking out and he wanted to know why. If Tip's sister was running off to report to Mombi, he needed to know. The floor creaked and the rustle of her skirts filled the air as Ozma slipped through the window.

Jack's pulse raced as he forced himself to continue lying there. *One. Two. Three.* He cracked his eyes open. The moth-eaten curtains were closed so she wouldn't be able to see him moving about. Slowly, he got to his feet and crept into the bedroom. The spot on the floor was vacant where Ozma had been sleeping and the window was, indeed, open. Peeking out into the night, he caught a glimpse of Ozma's golden hair weaving through the pumpkin field toward Mombi's hut.

"What are you doing, Blossom?" he whispered to himself.

He waited until she was halfway to the hut before darting out the window after her—the door would make too much noise. His bare feet landed quietly in the dirt and he slipped through the shadows, watching her sprint. If Ozma wasn't working with Mombi, what did she want so badly inside the hut? And why would she need to sneak away to find it? Sure, there were a lot of things of the witch's that many fae would desire, but some fae were more nefarious than others. He'd been impulsive when he'd scooped her up and brought her home with him, but she'd looked ready to collapse. And perhaps he'd been hoping a good rest would make her more eager to speak to him. He had so many questions—the mirror she lived in, the dark place, who her and Tip's parents were…

Ozma disappeared into Mombi's hut and shut the door behind her. Jack ran as silently as he could, until he reached the witch's hut. He pressed his back to the rotting wood walls and slid closer to the window where a crack marred the glass. Inch by inch he moved, afraid she would spot his bright orange hair. He vaguely regretted not grabbing a shirt to shield against the chilly night.

Too late now.

Jack poked his head up and squinted into the dark hut. A lantern—*his* lantern—illuminated the corner bedroom, followed by the sudden flicker of more candlelight. *Mombi's room, eh?* Suspicious. He hadn't tried to go in there himself after the barrier dropped—hadn't cared to—but he regretted that now. Did Mombi have some sort of communication apparatus in there? Or was Ozma tasked with bringing her forgotten items? He *wanted* to believe she'd been trapped in a mirror but… He let out a quick huff. *But nothing.* Perhaps he only believed Ozma because that meant Tip hadn't left him at all—though it did mean there was no room left to doubt his death. Mombi's tale had always left the smallest crack of hope that it was a lie, that Tip hadn't died, but Ozma's…

Shaking his head, he returned his focus to the flickering light with a growing sense of anxiety. He wished Mombi had a window in her bedroom so he could sneak around back to see what Ozma was doing in there. A shadow moved now and again, and items sailed across the room as she threw them, but Ozma didn't reappear in the main room of the hut for ages. When she did, the candle flames danced across her face. She looked …

unnerved. Her features pinched, her bottom lip pressed between her teeth, she studied the hut as if she'd never seen it before. Jack narrowed his eyes. Surely there were some strange things inside Mombi's room, but if Ozma truly had been trapped in the mirror, a witness to everything the witch had done, he doubted a few pickled body parts would upset her.

Shit.

Ozma was heading straight for the door. Jack sprinted around the side of the hut and waited. The door opened and shut. Light fell over the ground, swaying with her steps. *The woods?* Why the fuck would this female go into the woods in the middle of the night? And to be moving so confidently, as if she knew exactly where she was going… How, if she'd been trapped in a mirror, would she know the layout of Mombi's property so well?

Even more suspicious…

A kernel of contempt grew within Jack. Ozma had shown up here … and lied to him. But why? To what end? Her eyes truly were the same unique hue as Tip's, so he believed they were related, but that didn't mean Mombi wasn't controlling her. If that were the case, it wouldn't be as if Ozma wanted to lie to him, only that she had to. Still, it cast the shadow of doubt over everything she'd said. She wanted to kill Mombi, did she? He had always wanted the same thing, yet Mombi was still alive. And not because there hadn't been a single opportunity. Dooming himself to a potential life stuck inside the barrier wasn't on his list of goals. He fisted his hands at his sides.

What the fuck do I do? Who am I supposed to believe?

He'd only ever trusted one fae—Tip. And then he'd either left or been killed. Whatever his fate, it had destroyed a part of Jack. The very small, almost non-existent side of him that had wanted to have faith in others, had been smashed beneath the boot of sorrow.

So he followed Ozma, a shadow among the trees, until she came upon the lake. The moon lit the clearing around the shore where the softest grass grew. A fallen log had been rolled up to the water's edge by Tip long ago and remained there as a bench. They'd spent many hours there, baring their souls, and eventually, their bodies.

And now Ozma was setting her lantern down beside it as if it were the most natural thing in the world. *How did you know the way to this place if you were trapped somewhere else?* Jack took a step forward to demand the answer when her dress fell from her shoulders to pool at her feet. His breath hitched at the sight of her bare ass, the exposed curves, and … was that a scar? A jagged oval marred the center of her back, the healed patch of skin appearing thick and almost glossy. His heart softened slightly at the agony that wound must've caused her.

Ozma flipped her long hair over her shoulders and stepped toward the lake. Jack retreated into the woods far enough so she wouldn't notice him, and so he couldn't be accused of spying on her if he was caught. Not that he wanted to see her naked body— though his cock definitely wanted another peek—but he couldn't let her vanish. Not without figuring out everything she was hiding.

Though clearly a fuckable backside is on that list.

No.

He could *not* lust after Tip's sister. Even a whore like himself needed to have some restraint.

A loud splash sounded from the lake, and Jack leaned against a tree to wait for her to finish bathing. He yanked a red leaf from a low hanging branch and ripped it into tiny little pieces. How should he go about demanding answers? Ozma didn't seem overly excited to share what she already had and would likely give him issues when he tried to fill in the holes.

Fuck this shit.

He would just voice his doubts and wait for the pretty blossom to reveal the truth. He'd kiss it from her if he had to. Dip his tongue between her lips and taste the flower's nectar. Gently spread apart the petals to see what lay within. His cock stiffened again.

Whoa. Stop it, he chastised himself. *She's Tip's sister and a liar.*

A damned beautiful liar, though.

A scream broke the night air. The hair on Jack's arms stood on end as he bolted toward the lake. There had never been anything nasty living in the water, but Mombi's barrier was down now. Not only could Jack get out, but other creatures could get in.

Jack skidded to a halt in the clearing just in time to see Ozma get completely dragged beneath the dark water. "Oye!" he screamed at … whatever it was. "Don't even fucking think about it!" Before the words finished leaving his mouth, he was knee deep in the lake without realizing he'd moved. "Ozma!"

Shit. Shit shit shit shit shit.

Where was she?

He dove, searching. And searching and searching. All he saw was endless dark water and swaying plant life.

His heartbeat echoed in his ears and his frantic movements kicked up the muck. A scream built in his chest. *Fuck no, you don't!* he thought at whatever had Tip's sister. He needed to save her for Tip's sake. For himself.

He surfaced for a gulp of air and dove again. This time his hand brushed something soft and string-like, and he gripped it. A hard tug came from the other end. *Gotcha.* He used his other hand to grip what had to be Ozma's hair, then worked his way down until he found her head. The fact that she wasn't grabbing for him set his blood pumping faster and faster, but if he could get her to shore, it would be fine.

It had to be fine.

For Tip.

There was no other choice but for her to be okay.

Jack found Ozma's hands, moved his grip up, and hooked her under her arms. Then he kicked hard for the surface of the lake. A high-pitched screech flowed through the water, echoing down to Jack's bones. He almost released Ozma as his body tried to curl in on itself.

His gaze met a pair of white eyes, within a strangely human face, glowing through the dirt, illuminating the area. *Undine.* A particularly nasty water faerie that could also roam the land in search of a new home. He bared his teeth at the fae and aimed his next kick at her face. The heel of his foot connected with her nose. He felt a satisfying *crunch* and blood further clouded the water around her head.

Jack used the undine's moment of surprise to yank Ozma up, up, up, not stopping until they were both completely on land where the undine wouldn't hunt. He flipped Ozma to her back and started pressing on her bare chest in even compressions.

"Come on, come on," he urged. "Don't die."

As if hearing his desperate words, Ozma coughed. Water spewed from her mouth and she rolled to her side, sputtering. Jack leaned back on his heels, gasping for air along with her, and ran both hands through his wet hair.

"Shit, Blossom," he wheezed. "What were you thinking coming here alone? Anything could be living in there now that the barrier's down." Even though he wouldn't have expected an undine to move in. But this was *his* lake. His and Tip's. He would have to come back later and kill the undine because there was no way he was giving this place up.

She shot him an angry, sideways glance.

"So you *weren't* thinking," he spat.

"Stop. Talking," she said in a hoarse voice and sat up.

Jack unconsciously flicked a glance at her chest and the peaked nipples that greeted him. He hadn't meant to look. It was absolutely inappropriate given the circumstances, but he couldn't stop his eyes from sliding downward.

"Look somewhere else." Ozma quickly crossed her arms over her chest as though she were ashamed of something.

"Sorry! I didn't mean to." He squeezed his eyes shut and willed away the image of her breasts, nipples hard from the cold, before opening them again. "Are you … okay?"

She seemed to think for a moment, a line creasing her brows. "Something grabbed me."

"An undine," Jack supplied. "She must've been searching for a new home and found the lake uninhabited."

Ozma slowly nodded, her teeth chattering.

Jack stood to gather her satchel, dress, and the lantern. "Come on. Let's get you inside so you can warm up."

Ozma eased back to her feet and took the dress from him, pulling it over her sopping wet body. When they returned to his hut, Jack would give her one of his shirts to sleep in so her dress could dry in front of the fireplace.

"You didn't answer my question," he said when they started walking back toward the field. "Are you okay?"

"I think so." She licked her lips. "Thanks for … saving me. How did you know I was there?"

"Of course," he mumbled. "I heard your scream and came." He wouldn't tell her that he'd only been able to do so because he'd followed her. Or that he was more concerned with getting answers about Tip than he was with her personally. Because, though he was a selfish asshole, he couldn't let her know that.

Yet.

CHAPTER SEVEN

OZMA

Sunlight spilled through the window, shining in Ozma's left eye, causing her to squint. She'd been staring at the ceiling of Jack's hut for most of the night after he'd patched her up. Then, without her asking, Jack had changed the tumbled sheets of the bed. Ozma still couldn't bring herself to sleep on it, though.

A dull throb pulsed at her waist from where the undine's claws had dug into her flesh, but Jack's healing ointment had done its job.

During the night, she couldn't stop thinking about what would have happened if Jack hadn't come to the lake. Too much of Oz would've been let down because she'd failed before she even started. Each passing day, the weight on her shoulders was growing heavier with the Wizard and Mombi out there, still alive.

Magic would have helped her, but she had to settle for her own smarts, her dagger, and Mombi's spell books.

The door swung open, and she lurched forward to find Jack, head cocked and mouth turned up into a smirk.

"Rise and shine, Blossom," he purred, motioning her forward with a finger. "Come on."

Ozma's heart pounded harder at that voice, his gesture, that new pet name he called her yet again. Then there was him without his shirt on the night before. Each muscle was taut and firm, and she knew it was from the work he did on the farm. She shook the image away and refocused on how he was acting.

"Why?" Ozma asked hesitantly.

"Did you forget we're going to the market today? You get to help me with the pumpkins, and in return, you'll get another meal." Jack tossed her a deep blue fruit and she easily caught it. "Chop, chop! I want to make at least two trips today."

The market. Of course. But part of her interest was extremely piqued by this wild concept. Now she would get to see if it was truly how she'd imagined it. "Let me get dressed first."

His eyes seemed to linger on her, expression unreadable, before shutting the door. The previous night hung between them—him *seeing* her naked body, his gaze resting on her then too. But she hadn't wanted him to see her body for the first time like that, all at once. She glanced down, noticing Jack's tunic. *Is he annoyed that I'm still wearing his shirt?* He'd given it to her when they'd returned to his hut since her dress had been too damp to sleep in.

Making a low groan of frustration, she tugged off his tunic and shimmied back into her dress. She bit into the piece of fruit as she left the hut and walked outside into the patch. The sun lay hidden behind the clouds and the sky was turning a light shade of gray. A gust of wind swished past her, blowing the vines of the pumpkins, near where Jack stood.

Beside him were mostly empty crates and one filled with small pumpkins. On his other side rested a cart on wheels loaded with larger ones. She hadn't missed having to gut the fruit day after day for Mombi's spells and pies.

"I think it might rain," Ozma said, padding up beside him.

"A little water never killed anyone." Jack peered over his shoulder, lifting the crate of fruit. "Can you take that one?" He pointed at the cart, then paused and reached for it. "Never mind. I don't want you pulling at your wounds."

"I'm fine." She arched a brow and grabbed the wooden

handle, tugging the pumpkins forward. They jostled side to side. Her wounds stung for a moment, but she didn't let it show.

Jack wiped the sweat from his brow with the back of his hand and they started walking toward the forest.

Ozma practically held her breath as they skirted around narrow tree trunks where the barrier should've been. And, even though it wasn't there, she still couldn't believe that she was able to go into uncharted territory of Loland.

Once outside the former boundary line, heart still pounding, she took a deep inhale, the woodsy and sweet scent enveloping her. She wondered what the buildings would look like, and what the world outside her entrapment held. And now she would finally know—get to see the places Jack went when he'd been commanded to leave the patch.

Past rocks and boulders, a creek trickled with water. Bushes full of pink and purple berries surrounded the edge of it. The trees seemed to grow wider the farther they got. A tiny brown and green rose goblin covered in thorns leapt out from a crooked hole in a tree, baring its teeth.

Jack hissed back. The rose goblin yelped and tucked its head back inside. Ozma couldn't control her chuckle.

"So," Jack drawled. "Tell me about this dark place you were at…"

He was digging for information from her because he still didn't trust her. Nobody else would be able to tell, but she could. Ozma needed to avoid his suspicion until she could make the potion at Mombi's.

"After Mombi removed me from the mirror and banished me from Oz, I fell into a place with darkness all around. There were things down there that made it so you wouldn't want to sleep. I was constantly on the move, fleeing from beasts that could rip you apart in one bite, and trees that could tear you in half. But I wasn't alone—that's where I met Dorothy's mother, Reva." They'd never seen another living soul there other than the beasts—only skeletons of dead fae, like the one she'd taken her clothing from.

His lips parted and this time she placed a finger on Jack's mouth. To shush *him*. Even though she hadn't meant to do it, the movement was a habit. Jack's warm breath struck her digit and her nerves lit up everywhere, so she hurried and dropped her hand.

Ozma then explained Dorothy's story—how she was really a fae named Thelia, and how she'd defeated Langwidere. She continued to explain how Reva had been cursed as the Wicked Witch of the West and was traveling with Crow to defeat Locasta. Or at least she hoped Crow had caught up to her.

Jack's brow furrowed, confused. "News reached here from across the Sands, but I never really listened."

"Why not?" Ozma ducked under a branch and stopped when her foot pressed onto a blue bricked road, similar to the yellow one. A layer of dust coated the faded bricks, but not a single crack or fracture marred them.

"Because I never plan to go there anyway." Jack helped her lift the cart over the edge of the bricks and changed the subject. "What about your parents? Tip always wondered about them."

He was right. As Tip, she always had, but as Ozma she knew what had happened to them from Reva. King Pastoria and Queen Lurline. While thinking about them—regal images without faces—she didn't feel the way she thought she should, as a daughter, as a queen. If Ozma had known them, she would have loved them, but there was only the want to be sad, not the true, fragile emotion. "They're dead." She sighed. "The Wizard killed my father and Langwidere took the head of my mother to wear as her own."

Jack made a coughing sound. "I'm sorry, *what?*"

"I'll tell you all about Langwidere and her collection of heads later." Ozma had seen Crow burying them outside Glinda's castle. She'd wondered if her mother's had been in the collection or if Langwidere had already destroyed it.

His face turned serious. "I'm sorry you and Tip didn't get to know them."

She nodded, wishing she had.

As they rounded a curve up ahead, past fruit trees, light gray smoke curled upward. There were huts spread all across the land. Not in a single neat row, but anywhere and everywhere. The blue bricks led them closer and closer, and she found the huts to be neat and tidy. Emerald green leaves and dark purple branches made up the roofs, and each home was painted shades of yellow and red.

Her eyes widened at everything around her: the elves in front of their homes washing clothing in large silver buckets, the tiny fauns chasing each other in some sort of game, and another fae who looked to be preparing to go to the market with a cart full of flowered headdresses.

This part of Loland was much different than the stories she'd heard from Jack. He'd thought it drab, but perhaps that was because he'd seen it so many times and she hadn't. Even though he'd been compelled, he had still seen some of the world.

"You really were telling the truth about being hidden away," Jack said, his voice soft.

Had he truly not believed the story she'd just told him? She peered at him, his hazel irises shining, a glimpse of a smile forming on his lips, the first she'd seen from him since she'd been back.

Her annoyance vanished and she mirrored his smile. "I told you I was."

"Yes, you *told* me." Jack adjusted the crate as they passed a group of laughing fae. "But now I see it, Blossom. The way the world is dancing in your eyes."

She shrugged, not sure of what else to say.

A sweet scent hit her nose, and a large grassy area covered in wagons and carts caught her attention. Merchants chatting, customers purchasing what they needed.

As she passed the sellers, she observed each item they had. One fae stitched a cotton dress while another rolled a spool of spider silk. Sugary pastries, buttery rolls, meats, fruits, glass figurines, sapphire rings, ruby necklaces, tools, jeweled swords. So much, and too much—she wanted to run her fingertips across *everything.*

Jack grasped her by the shoulders and turned her in a different direction. "This way, Blossom. We want to make coin sometime today. Not tomorrow."

Ozma rolled her eyes and followed him down a lopsided path. "Why haven't you left the patch for good since the barrier is gone?"

"I'm saving up." He bit his lip. "Actually, it's not just that. I've practically been there my whole life. Tip and I always wanted to leave but now that I can… It sounds strange but I don't know, maybe it's the nostalgia. The pumpkins are all I know."

The past conversations between Tip and Jack came to her mind—the wishes, the dreams, and the death of those things. But she could relate to Jack on that level. It was all Jack had ever known, but he couldn't stay there forever. "Seeds, Jack. *Seeds.* Take them and run before Mombi returns and the barrier goes back up."

Before he could answer, a merchant called his name. "Jack! Hurry. I just sold the last pumpkin and had to send two customers away. My other items don't sell as fast." The centaur's arms were covered in beaded bracelets and golden loops decorated his ears. Dark green hair was braided down his back and his yellow gaze focused on Ozma, scanning her up and down. "Who's this?"

"His lover," Ozma rushed out. He wouldn't recognize her name, but that didn't mean it couldn't somehow get to the Wizard or Mombi before she had a chance to end them. She needed the element of surprise if she had any hope of succeeding.

Jack wrinkled his nose, looking at her strangely and then must have decided to take pity on her because he answered nonchalantly, "This is Blossom. And no, you can't have her. I don't share." One of his long fingers trailed down her arm and she suppressed a shiver.

"A beautiful blossom indeed." The centaur grinned, then motioned to the baskets of oranges behind him, propped on a small table. "You want to buy any? Half price today."

"You mean every day. But no." Jack set his crate on the ground beside the centaur and unloaded the pumpkins into empty buckets in front of the wagon.

Ozma did the same with her cart as the centaur fished out a handful of coins and handed them to Jack.

He told the centaur he'd see him later, then pocketed the coins and placed the crate in the basket before pulling it along.

Ozma rushed up to him. "You didn't let me look around."

"That's because the bastard tries to get you to buy goods so he doesn't have to pay for the pumpkins. But we can look around if you want."

"No, perhaps another time." She needed to focus on getting back and doing the location spell anyway.

As they rounded a wagon with a brownie inside playing a flute and selling glass chimes, thunder boomed from the sky. Within moments, the rain started to pour, soaking them from head to toe.

"Told you it would rain," Ozma said, liking the feel of the light pellets against her skin. Even in the patch, she and Jack would work during storms. Mombi had made them, but Ozma never minded.

"Have you not seen that either?" He side-eyed her, running a finger across his well-formed lips.

"Of course I have!" The last time had been them naked together in the rain. And that had happened time and time again.

They stayed in comfortable silence, the only sound coming from the rain and tiny creatures scurrying for shelter, until they reached Jack's hut. The sky cleared as soon as they got to the entrance, as if by magic. He left the cart outside and pulled open the door for Ozma.

Beads of water slid down Jack's face and neck as he grabbed a bottle of homemade pumpkin ale from the table. He took a deep swig, not looking at Ozma. "Want some?" he asked.

She'd never drank alcohol before. Only pumpkin cider or water, but it was time for her to try new things. With a nod, she grabbed the bottle and took a long drink. A burning heat lit up her tongue and throat, causing her to cough. "Maybe not," she rasped, shoving the bottle back to him.

"Ah, not a fan, huh?" Jack smiled, and it dropped almost as quickly as it appeared. Clearing his throat, he stepped toward the door. "I'm going to gather more pumpkins to bring to the market later. You can come if you want."

This was the perfect opportunity she needed. "I think I'm going to lie down for a while. My wounds are aching a bit."

"Do you need me to change the bandages?" He reached out as if he meant to check for himself.

"No!" she practically shouted, then softer, "No."

"All right," he said with an amused smile. Then his lips slowly turned downward. "You're going to rest, right? If I leave you alone? You won't go back to the lake or do anything else to cause trouble? I won't be here to save you …"

"I'll rest," she lied.

With a nod, Jack went out the front door, and Ozma waited several moments before heading to the back of the room. After packing up her satchel with fruit, she slowly drew up the bedroom window and hurried to slip outside. Checking each direction, she darted into the forest behind the hut so she would be hidden by trees. She took out her dagger as she rushed to Mombi's, remaining vigilant in case a dangerous creature appeared like the night before.

Ozma avoided any crackling leaves until she'd made it safely to the area behind Mombi's hut. She peered around a tilted tree with decaying limbs, and spotted Jack, his back turned, seeming to be gutting a pumpkin.

Before Jack had time to turn around, she lunged out of the trees toward the front of the hut and pulled open the door, not making a single sound as she pressed inside.

The scent of Mombi's past concoctions hit her nose again as she entered the witch's bedroom. She took the pages she'd torn out of the book from her satchel. First, Ozma gathered a bucket and filled it with pumpkin water. Mombi kept at least ten jugs of the stuff in the sitting room at a time. The cabinet was only half full of the jars it usually held, most likely due to Mombi taking some with her on the journey. She then gathered a few strands of Mombi's hair—the something personal—still stuck to her pillow, followed by gremlin blood and salamander feet.

Finally, she lifted her dagger and pressed it to the flesh of her ankle. She bit the inside of her cheek when she pushed in and sliced off a sliver of flesh. A low squeal escaped her lips as she tossed the skin into the bucket. The last things she needed were her saliva and blood, so she spat into the pail and used a few drops of scarlet from her throbbing ankle before bandaging it with cloth from a pile of clothing.

As she stirred the liquid with a wooden spoon, she chanted the words from the spell book page. A blue light flickered, and she chewed her lip as she poured a small amount of the mixture into a vial. Gripping the glass, she chanted the words again.

The blue light became a thin line, like yarn unraveling, before shooting out of the area, and through the sitting room to outside, connecting her to Mombi. Ozma opened the front door and peeked out, finding the light stretching right past Jack as he loaded pumpkins into the cart. He wouldn't be able to see it— only she could.

Ozma couldn't wait until nightfall to go hunt down Mombi— she was going now. She hoped Jack wouldn't notice her as she dashed back into the forest and out of his view. Quickening her pace, she retraced her steps into the forest and flew through the trees, wondering how long it would take for her to get to Mombi.

Ozma said a goodbye to Jack inside her head, but it wasn't forever. She would see him again, at least to let him know she'd killed Mombi so he would be completely free. But her heart still felt heavy.

The light guided her past faeries circling overhead and other tree fae watching her from branches or inside trunks. Ozma didn't stop once, not until she reached the market. Fae kept asking her to purchase their goods, but she ignored them, until a female troll with deep wrinkles, and one eye lower than the other, grabbed her shoulders.

"Sit," she demanded and shoved Ozma down onto a velvet-padded chair.

"I don't have coin," Ozma said, trying to escape the hands clamping her into place. "I'm—I'm in a hurry."

"On me. Your hair is in much need of attention. It can easily be grabbed or unwillingly chopped off and sold."

Before Ozma could utter a word, the troll quickly braided her hair. She relaxed under the female's practiced movements as she effortlessly pressed braids into a crown around her head. The troll then plucked flowers from a painted vase and entwined them in sections of Ozma's hair.

"There." The troll clucked her tongue. "Much better."

Sliding her fingers into her satchel, Ozma drew out a fruit and handed it to the troll as payment anyway—the female had been right. Mombi didn't need any more advantages than she already had.

Ozma brushed a velvety petal in her hair and resumed following the light out of the market, down a long sloping hill. In the distance, more forestry and huts took up the area, but the light wasn't taking her there, it was leading her to the right, toward an unlit tunnel, reminding her of the dark place. Her heart hammered in her chest as she studied it for longer than she should have.

As she took a step forward, a strong hand hauled her back against a solid chest. "I've let this charade go on long enough. What are you up to, Blossom?"

CHAPTER EIGHT

JACK

Jack dropped the handles of the cart in front of Antair's stall and stretched, his back popping three times. "That's it for the day," he told the centaur. And probably forever. There were smaller pumpkins left and, though he would've liked more coin first, Ozma was right. It was risky to stay too long and have Mombi return. Waiting another week was asking for trouble. He should run with as many seeds as he could. If he allowed himself to become her slave again—

No. He would never. There were other ways to fill his pockets, even if he had to whore professionally. He did enjoy a good fuck anyway, especially when it took his mind off things. It would still be better than being trapped in that damn field.

"I wish Mombi had left you some pies to bring before heading off," Antair lamented.

Jack shrugged. He wouldn't wish those pies on anyone. There was no telling what that fucking masochistic witch put in them. There were probably crystallized bat wings or petrified gnome shit mixed into the batter. He ate Mombi's cooking only when he *had* to, but here these fae were *missing her pies*. Probably due to some sort of addictive powder, as her skills over a fire were mediocre at best.

"Your friend from earlier isn't helping you this time?"

Jack shook his head. "She's at the farm." Sleeping, like he wished he was, though he regretted not checking on her before he left. Her wounds from the night before were deep and, though he'd put ointment on them for her, they still had to bother her a bit. He hadn't wanted to wake her by stepping on a creaking floorboard. Before going back, he should find a stall selling a potion to prevent infection and maybe some herbs for pain.

"Is she now?" the centaur asked with a mischievous grin.

"Yes." Jack narrowed his eyes. Why did it feel like Antair was implying something else? Ozma had lied and said they were lovers, so it couldn't be Antair hinting that there was *more* between them. When Antair only continued to smirk, Jack's patience snapped. "What aren't you telling me?"

"Oh nothing." His beaded bracelets clicked together as he lifted a pumpkin from the cart. "Only that she's sitting at Asie's right now, getting her hair braided."

Jack's heart nearly stopped. "She's ... *what?*" he nearly shouted. But that might alert Ozma to his presence and he wanted to see what she was up to. How did she get past him? *When?* Why? If she wanted to get her hair done, there was no reason she couldn't simply *tell* him that she was going for a bit of pampering. After years of being trapped, he couldn't blame her, but why wouldn't she *tell him?*

Wait.

How was she paying for this? Jack patted his pockets and the heavy clink of coin from earlier sounded. He sighed, relieved, though it was stupid of him to work in the field with a pocket full of money, but the thought of leaving it unattended somewhere made him uneasy.

Antair chuckled and waved him off. "I'll watch your cart if you want to catch up with her."

Jack hesitated. He wanted to confront Ozma, but what right did he have? If she went to the market to have her hair braided, who was he to complain? She wasn't his prisoner. *She is a liar though.* And he'd just begun to believe her.

That's what you get, Jack.

Believe someone and they use it to ruin you.

"Thanks," Jack told Antair through a grimace. "I'll take you up on that, actually."

He wandered as casually as he could toward another part of the market. Food shops gave way to tables covered in rouge made from berries, then gems fashioned into jewelry. Clothing took up nearly half of the street: woven skirts, hooded jackets, hats, and boots. Then came artists inking skin, either permanently or with a paste that faded over a few weeks. Ozma sat at a booth nestled between a table covered in hat pins and a pixie who would pierce any part of a fae's body. Her back was to Jack as an elderly troll carefully arranged her golden locks. Tiny blue flowers that matched Ozma's dress were woven into the intricate braids.

Sneaky, Blossom.

She hadn't been joking when she'd said she had learned how to get around unnoticed.

Ozma stood, the troll having finished her work, and hefted a satchel from the ground. She quickly handed a piece of fruit to the troll before continuing down the bricked path. There looked to be a fresh pep in her step as she walked. Jack trailed her at a distance, his cart safe with Antair, to see what she was up to, but a troubled feeling came over him the farther they got from town. When Ozma paused to stare at a daunting black tunnel, the feeling only intensified.

Don't you dare, Blossom. I'm not ready to die yet.

And die they both would—probably. Jack would give them a five percent chance of survival if they went into that tunnel. Places like that were where fae went to conduct nefarious business such as trading younglings for coin or hiring an assassin.

Or to eat other fae who were conducting nefarious business.

They would be an easy snack for any number of bloodthirsty creatures. So what the hell was she doing? What reason could she possibly have to visit a place like this?

Ozma seemed to steel herself and took a step toward the

tunnel.

Oh, fuck no!

Jack lunged forward and grabbed her wrist, hauling her back into his chest. "I've let this charade go on long enough. What are you up to, Blossom?"

She struggled against his hold, but Jack didn't give an inch, so she finally stilled. "What are you doing here, Jack?"

"Well, I *was* dropping more pumpkins off at the market, when what did I see?" He paused, though he didn't expect an answer. "You. Getting your hair braided when you claimed that your wounds were aching too much to help me."

"The rain ruined my hair," she said with forced casualness.

Jack spun her to face him, keeping a grip on her upper arms. "So, you walked all the way to town to get it fixed without a coin to your name? Don't fuck with me. What's going on?"

She studied his face, her blue eyes roaming over his features. He hoped she could tell how angry he was, hoped that his face showed the depth of the rage. She lied again and again. Put herself in danger. But mostly, he was upset that he wanted so badly to trust her. That she got under his skin so much. And Tip… Jack would never forgive himself if anything happened to his sister.

When her gaze met his again, she appeared completely emotionless.

What am I doing? Why do I care?

Why is she doing this to me? Stirring up old feelings. Playing games with him. It wasn't fair, nor was it in the least bit kind. He'd had enough cruelty in his life to allow for any more.

Jack growled. "Speak."

"I don't know what you want to hear," she said quietly.

"The truth!" he demanded. "You storm onto the farm, lie to my face, then get it in your head to run off—through *that* tunnel, no less—and you think I don't deserve to know what you're doing here? What if I hadn't found you and you'd died? What then? I would be forced to wonder what happened to Tip's sister for the rest of my life. Forced to worry if you were still out there, in pain, and if there was something I could do to stop it."

"Okay, okay," Ozma said quickly. "I'm going to kill Mombi. Happy now?"

Happy? Was he fucking *happy* that she was embarking on a journey to get herself killed? "You are nothing like your brother," he seethed.

Ozma's jaw dropped. "Wh... What's that supposed to mean?"

"He was never this insufferable," Jack snapped, letting go of her arms. "Or this stupid."

"Perhaps because he was *trapped* in that patch. Perhaps you didn't truly know him," she retorted.

How dare she... Clenching his jaw, he stormed around her toward the tunnel and kept going without looking back. He was nearly halfway to the entrance when Ozma caught up.

"What are you doing?" she asked.

"Going with you. Obviously."

"You can't—"

"I can do whatever the fuck I want, Blossom. No one has a claim over me anymore." Not since Mombi's barrier dropped and Tip died. Jack was a completely free fae—his body *and* his heart.

He picked up the pace, making it to the foreboding tunnel much faster than he expected. It was eerily silent there. Long, sweeping vines swooped down over the oblong entrance and moss clung to the large rocks peeking out from the packed dirt. A musty, metallic scent wafted from inside.

"You don't have to come," Ozma whispered.

Jack ground his teeth together and reached down to grab a thick branch from the dirt. It was better than going in there with only a small carving knife, dull from use on so many pumpkins. At least the branch gave him range. "I wish that were true, but Tip would never forgive me. And that I *do know* about him."

Ozma looked up at him, blinking, unspoken words filling the space between them. Jack cleared his throat to distract himself from studying the shape of her lips. He was having *none* of that bullshit. Did he want answers? Yes. Did he have an unexplainable urge to kiss some sense into her? Also, yes. But, that was a hard no. If only she were anyone besides Tip's sister…

"Damn," he muttered and headed inside the tunnel. He had to calm himself before he did or said something completely moronic.

Before the light faded behind them, he took note of the thick wooden beams running across the ceiling and down both sides of the tunnel, holding everything up safely. *The only safe thing in here,* he thought. Scratching sounds filled the darkness. Dubious laughter bubbled. A muffled scream.

There was no telling if the creatures lurking around them could see in the dark or not. But on the off chance the predators were equally blind as them, there was no sense giving away their position with a light.

"This way," Ozma whispered, tugging him along, when they'd been walking for what felt like hours.

Jack stumbled over something on the ground—a root perhaps, or a severed body part. He winced at the thought. "How do you know? I can't see shit."

"I used a spell before I left the patch," she admitted.

Jack stumbled to a halt. "A spell? One of *Mombi's* spells? Is *that* what you were looking for in her room the other night?"

There was a long pause before Ozma asked, "You followed me? That's how you saved me at the lake."

"Of course, I followed you. Not only do I not trust you, but you went out the window. There's no reason to sneak about unless you're up to no good." He huffed out a breath. "But to use one of Mombi's spells? She uses dark magic—tinkers with forces that should never be messed with."

"It's just a tracking spell," she scoffed. "It's leading me to Mombi with a trail of light."

A tracking spell using *dark magic.* That was probably why nothing dared attack them—the beasts could sense whatever evil was at work. But it was too late to talk Ozma out of it, so he kept his thoughts to himself. "This isn't some wild guess, then?"

Ozma snorted softly. "Not so stupid after all, am I?"

"Don't go getting ahead of yourself, Blossom. This is still foolish."

"Say that again when she's dead." Ozma gripped Jack's hand and steered him in the right direction as the tunnel curved.

"Let's make a deal." Jack squeezed her hand, feeling a little more comfortable touching her when he couldn't see a fucking thing. Her skin was smooth, though callouses dotted the pads of her palm. They were smaller than his but no less prevalent. "If she dies and we don't, I'll take back what I said."

"Which part?"

Was … that hurt in her voice? He had been angry with her and lashed out, but he hadn't meant what he said. Not really. His mind was being pulled in a million directions. Believe her, or don't? Trust her, or don't? Help her or… *No.* That one he was certain of. He was helping her whether she wanted him to or not. But he wished that it didn't feel as if she were keeping something important from him. Wished she would lay everything out—her motive, how she knew her way around the farm so well…

"All of it, Blossom," he answered.

"Good. Because she's there."

Jack jerked, expecting the witch to be standing directly in front of them, but instead noticed a faint trickle of sunlight. They were almost at the other end of the tunnel now—completely unscathed, physically. Having unseen fae hissing and growling at him from the darkness had his hand shaking around the branch. The knife in his boot would only be helpful if something was close enough for him to use it, though he didn't want to wield either weapon if he could help it.

Nothing attacked. Just threatened to. It felt impossible. There were creatures in there and the two of them were practically defenseless. Something didn't feel right, but nothing involving dark magic ever did.

Still, he followed Ozma through the last bit of tunnel and out into the light once more. Though, *light* was a stretch. The sun was half obscured by land with night hot on its heels, and the realization that they would be stuck out there hit Jack for the first time. He'd never spent an entire evening away from the farm before.

Ozma gave a hard yank on Jack's hand and they tumbled into the prickly brush.

"Shit," he mumbled as a particularly pointy thorn scratched his arm. Blood welled on his skin. "Why did you do that?"

"There," Ozma whispered, pointing overhead at a large overhang made from rock. "We have to climb."

As if going through the tunnel wasn't bad enough, now they had to climb over it? *Fuck…* He held back a groan as he stood, hands on his hips, watching Ozma hike effortlessly up the steep hillside. It was only when she disappeared onto the overhang that he scrambled up after her, dropping his branch. When he reached her side, hunched behind a fallen log, they both peered wordlessly over the bark as the soft padding of hooves struck the ground.

A familiar blue and maroon wagon, the wood curved in an arc over the bed of it, came around a bend with a gray stag pulling it. And, holding onto the reins, was Mombi, wearing the same clothes she'd left in. Jack swallowed hard at the sight of her. What were they thinking, confronting her? Both he and Ozma ducked down when the wagon neared. As it passed their hiding place, Jack caught a whiff of the smokey scent of burning wood mixed with the acrid odor of burning hair.

Up to your dark magic, as always, you horrid bitch.

The wagon creaked to a stop and Jack held his breath, peeking out again, sure she'd seen them. But Mombi didn't seem at all fazed. She hummed off-tune as she leapt down from the seat with all the grace of a newborn foal, nearly falling. The witch caught herself on the spokes of the mud-slicked wheel and shifted a small woven basket over her arm. With her other hand, she removed her cloak and placed it on the bench where she had been sitting.

Each of her steps came with a grunt as if it pained her to move. It probably did. She'd left the farm to help the Wizard, which meant she was using her magic more often. Probably daily. By seeing her again, it hit Jack just how much of a fool he'd been to stay at the farm. Money could be made anywhere—not just from pumpkins.

Setting her basket down on the steps leading into the rear of the wagon, she pulled a large cleaver from her skirts. "Yes, yes," she mumbled to herself, trailing her thumb over the blade. "Sharp enough. Now…"

The witch turned her gaze to the top of the wagon. Jack's eyes traveled upward to see what was so interesting and froze. Sprites in cages. Dozens of them hung along the sides of the wagon like decorations. As if sensing Jack's stare, the sprites started screaming, their weak voices somehow still sounding like a crack of thunder across the small clearing.

"Help! Please, sir, help us!"

A chorus of cries, all directed at him.

"Fuck," he breathed.

Mombi looked over her shoulder and her beady stare landed directly on him where he still watched over the fallen tree. "Jack!" she screeched so loud it hurt his ears. "How did you get off the farm?"

She hadn't realized the barrier fell?

Fuck, fuck, fuck, fuck, fu—

"Get over here, you disobedient little bastard!"

As Jack stood, resigned to the witch's wrath, a rock flew through the air and pelted Mombi right in the temple. She flailed about for a moment before using her powers to balance herself. Regaining her composure, she blasted her magic in the direction the rock had come from.

And hit the empty ground.

"Time to go," he said quickly while Mombi was distracted by some miracle attack. He glanced down to hurry Ozma back the way they'd come … only to find himself alone.

"No." His eyes shot up, scouring the area. Mombi appeared to be the only fae there. *Where are you, Blossom?*

Another rock.

Another answering blast of power.

He caught a flash of blue fabric dart behind a wide tree.

Stupid female—I'm never taking back what I said! Never! Foolish, impulsive—

Mombi's power wrapped around Jack's throat and dragged him forward. He clawed at the invisible hand, choking, his heart thumping wildly. "Jack, Jack, Jack," she scolded. "You should've run when you had the chance."

He should have. Should have run and never looked back.

And now he was as good as dead.

"Come out here or I'll kill him!" Mombi screamed.

There was a long moment where nothing happened. Nothing but the fading of color. From the sunset? *If only.* Stars sparked in his vision. Air. He needed air. But he hoped Ozma wouldn't rise to the bait. If she ran, saved herself, then he would gladly die. He had nothing to live for anyway, so if he could save Tip's sister on the way out…

"I'm here," Ozma called. When she stepped out from her hiding place, appearing as a blue blur with golden hair, Jack's heart dropped.

"Ozma?" Mombi hissed in surprise, her eyes impossibly wide. "You're not supposed to be here…"

"Let him go," she commanded.

"I think I'll kill him instead." Mombi's grip tightened. "Then I'll shrink you to the size of a doll and keep you locked in a box."

Jack's hands went numb, his arms too heavy to keep clawing pointlessly at his neck. The world was fading. Fading, fading…

Mombi let out a loud squeal at the same time a deafening *boom* sounded. Her magic released him and he fell to the grass, gasping desperately for air. With a quick glance, he saw the wide tree tilt. It fell in slow motion, one branch tumbling, dragging down another and another.

"Got you," Mombi crowed.

Jack's gaze instantly cleared at the words as the adrenaline kicked in. Mombi had Ozma by the throat, holding her three feet off the ground, while her other hand moved in a swirling motion.

A spell.

Jack watched the air darken around Mombi's fingers. His chest became so tight he was sure it would crack open against the roaring beat of his heart. Knees shaking, he climbed to his feet and threw a hand out. "Stop!"

A swirl of green, blue, and yellow burst from his palm. *What the fuck is this?* But there was really only one logical answer: *magic.* The pressure of it nearly snapped the bones in his hand, but he was too shocked to do anything other than stare.

He watched as vines curled forward from the trees and snapped around Mombi's limbs. As grass grew higher and higher around her body. The witch screamed as a tree branch extended downward, piercing her through the shoulder. Blood immediately seeped into the fabric around the wound.

Ozma dropped to the ground in his peripheral, but he couldn't drag his attention away from the scene before him. The witch shrieked again as the grass cocooned her. The vines went taut, pulling her arms and legs. Her cries became muffled as the grass tightened.

Jack's breaths came in heavy pants and his weak legs buckled. He tried to pull his hand back, close it into a fist before whatever was happening killed him too. But it revolted. Forced more, more, *more*, from him.

Until the vines ripped each of Mombi's limbs from her body. Blood shot out like geysers, coating the grass around her. Jack's mind went blank at the sight. Crimson dotted the area. Pooled around the body. The grass-wrapped witch tumbled back in slow motion, rolling slightly when she finally hit the ground, and the magic retreated into his palm.

Dead. Mombi was dead.

Jack shouted in triumph. He'd killed her! *Fucking yes, I did!* But the excitement was short lived as his body quivered with exhaustion. A hollowness spread through him. Used up.

"Jack!" Ozma shouted.

At least, he thought she did. His hearing had followed his vision—fading and fading and fading…

CHAPTER NINE

OZMA

Mombi was dead. But so was Jack. Ozma let out a choked sob and rushed to Jack's side. Beads of perspiration lined his brows, his hair damp and skin pale. Even his freckles seemed faded.

All around her, plants had sprung up, grown in size, like nothing she'd ever seen before, not even at the pumpkin patch where only the crop grew unnaturally fast. Whatever it was had come from Jack, his outstretched hand. *Magic.* But how?

Ozma couldn't think straight as she shook his shoulders. "Damn it, Jack, come on! Wake up, so you can say you don't trust me again. Wake up, so I can tell you how much I love you!"

Jack's eyes remained closed as she pressed her palm to his chest. *Thump thump. Thump thump.* His heart beat rhythmically against her hand, his chest gently rising. A soft groan escaped his lips, but his lids stayed shut. Had he broken out of a curse, the way she had? She'd always assumed Jack didn't have magic, but in the dark place she'd wondered if Mombi had done something nefarious to him too. And she'd been right.

Screams exploded from the wagon behind her. She whirled

around to the dozens and dozens of sprites locked in iron cages. Their bright wings were unable to flap with the tight fit of how many Mombi had shoved inside together.

The enclosed wagon was light blue, and a curving arch accentuated it, while the front was painted maroon, with gold flowers and emerald vines crawling up its length. A gray stag stood harnessed to the wagon, appearing ready to lead it if commanded.

"Mombi carries the key on her," a female sprite, with light pink hair, chirped, pointing in the direction of the witch. "In her left pocket."

Ozma peered up at the darkening sky—night would be falling soon. Too soon. The blue light tracking Mombi had vanished once Jack ended the witch's life. She'd secretly hoped that the Wizard would've been there too. It would be impossible to perform another location spell because she had nothing of his. But one dead was better than none.

Pulling the dagger from her waist, Ozma held it up as she padded toward Mombi. She would free the trapped sprites, then get Jack loaded in the wagon so she could bring him home before figuring out a plan to find the Wizard. It was lucky that Mombi had been so close, but they couldn't risk staying on the farm for much longer. Not when the Wizard could come looking for the dead witch.

The grass still cocooned Mombi's body—or what was left of it. All her limbs had been ripped away, the ground soaked in scarlet. Ozma lifted her blade and swiped a clean line down from the top of the witch's head to her navel. Mombi's bloodshot eyes stared blankly up at the sky. She hadn't gotten to kill her, but she pierced her weapon through Mombi's heart anyway and released a scream of her own. "You *bitch*!" One melancholic cry that spoke of despair over missed opportunities, a life that could have been more for her, for Jack. Then she slammed her hand across the dead witch's cheek like Mombi had done to her so many times.

Tears slid down Ozma's cheeks and she brushed them away.

She wiped the blood from her dagger on Mombi's tattered dress, then placed it back at her waist. A raised outline of an object in the left pocket, over Mombi's breast, caught her eye. Ozma fished out the silver key.

She walked back to the wagon, stopping at the first iron cage. "Tell me," Ozma asked the pink-haired sprite, "do you know which direction Mombi came from, and where the Wizard is staying?"

"She journeyed from the seaport after going to Orkland. That's where he is." The sprite paused and shook her head. "But you don't want to go to Orkland. Everyone there is under an enchantment, doing what the Wizard orders."

Ozma remembered the maps Jack drew of the places outside Loland. Orkland was an island, not too far from here. Just go through Hiland and sail across. She could feel the correct path in her veins but not where the port was along the sea.

"I have to go." Ozma shrugged. Of course Oz wouldn't be in Loland anymore. "Which way leads to the seaport?" With a sigh, careful to avoid touching the iron, she unlocked each cage, one by one.

The sprite hesitated but rattled off the directions.

Loosening her shoulders, Ozma peered at Jack and hoped she could lift him into the wagon. Once they arrived back at the farm, she would have to gather more supplies and spells before heading to Orkland. She didn't know if she would leave him there or if he would decide to come with her once he was awake. He had come with her to stop Mombi… She wasn't going to sneak off again, and he'd earned the right to choose whether he wanted to accompany her or not. The truth was, she wouldn't mind spending more time with him.

Ozma went to the wagon door and opened it. Something burst out, shoving her aside, and she let out a scream. A hobgoblin flopped to the ground as she caught herself. He rolled with a growl, dried blood caked around a half-missing ear. He got up to run, and tripped, his hands bound behind his back.

"Wait," Ozma said. "I'll untie you."

The hobgoblin stopped and slowly turned around, eyeing her with suspicion. "She took my ear. Wanted my arms next."

Ozma calmly nodded. "Not anymore. She's dead." Taking out her dagger, she walked toward him and cut the rope. "There, you're free."

"What do I owe you? Though I suppose, now that I'm unbound, it's enough that I don't eat you." He cocked his head, staring at her like he wanted to rip out her heart and feast on it.

A shiver ran down her spine at the thought of his filthy hand thrusting inside her chest. She shook off the image, pulled back her shoulders, and motioned at Jack. "Help me put him in the wagon and I'll consider it a fair trade."

With a low grunt, the hobgoblin stumbled toward Jack and lifted his legs while Ozma hauled him under his arms. She was close to Jack's height, but he still wasn't light enough for her to carry.

Inside the wagon, mold permeated the air. Amidst dried herbs, was mostly empty space, aside from a stack of books in the corner and two baskets full of fruit, some rotten.

After they placed Jack on the floor, Ozma shut the door and the hobgoblin grunted again as he scurried off into the woods— most likely to find something to shred apart.

At the front of the wagon was a teal wooden plank to sit on with Mombi's cloak sprawled out along the edge. Something hard poked at Ozma when she sank onto the cloak. Crinkling her nose, she tugged out a shiny red stone in the shape of a heart. "Strange." If Mombi'd had it in her cloak, perhaps it could be useful. She shoved the stone into her satchel and tossed the cloak on the ground.

Grabbing the reins to the stag, she snapped them for the beast to go. The stag didn't move.

"Oh, come on!" she screamed, the crescent moon already pushing up into the night sky. Nothing. The stubborn beast just sat there with its chin lifted.

From her satchel, Ozma took out a purple fruit, then hopped down to go to the stag. He leaned forward, his antlers almost brushing her face as he sniffed at the fruit, finally biting into it. Ozma quickly pulled her hand back, not allowing him another taste. "I'll give you the rest once we get home." A huff of air escaped his nostrils as she hopped back onto the plank, bringing down the reins once more.

This time the stag stomped his feet and dragged the wagon forward with a jolt. Ozma's back struck the wagon, and she straightened in her seat. As they moved through the dark, the wagon bobbed side to side, and she hoped Jack would be all right in there until they got home.

Ozma wished the vial's light still worked, the way it had when they went through the tunnel earlier. What Jack hadn't known was that the blue light from the magical line had lit up the area for her. She'd seen what was in there. The beasts clinging to the walls, blood staining their mouths and sharp teeth, hissing, prepared to strike. But they hadn't. She thought it had something to do with the light from the vial, like they were afraid of it, even though she wasn't sure if they could see it.

The stag pulled the wagon into the tunnel and Ozma shivered, the inky black sweeping closed like a curtain around her. It wouldn't take too dreadfully long for them to get out, but what if one of the creatures decided to attack? As if in answer to her thoughts, hissing reverberated off the walls. A hard thump dropped down on top of the wagon, rattling it, and Ozma yanked out her dagger. But she couldn't see a damn thing.

A small body landed beside her, the plank she sat on shaking as sharp talons clawed her arm. She thrust her blade into whatever part of the creature it was, and the beast released an agonized howl. Another crashed behind her onto the wagon. As she prepared her dagger again, a bright light swirled around her, and for a moment, she thought it was from her, that her magic had returned.

But it hadn't.

Before her, the gray stag glowed a bright yellow, body and antlers, lighting up the tunnel like rays of sunshine. The creatures hissed, baring their fangs, rumpling their wings as they scurried up the walls. Their spines protruded through their thin skin, and she wasn't sure if they even had any eyes. The light yellow of the stag turned to a pale blue, shining, and he continued straight down the path, unbothered. All the while, the creatures growled, driving their talons at the walls in rage.

"You saved us," Ozma said in awe as she watched the colors of the stag change from one shade to another. His brightness remained until they exited the tunnel, then the hue dimmed to his usual light gray.

As they traveled toward the market, it was mostly quiet. A couple of fae with curling horns outside a wagon were groping each other while kissing. Shops stood dark and empty. Lit lanterns hung on several of the wagons where the owners were probably sleeping inside, waiting to begin again the following day.

The sliver of moon shone brighter than before, the sky full of twinkling stars as they rode off the bricked road and entered the forest toward the patch. Ozma thought again about Jack. It had to be the same thing that had happened to her. Perhaps he'd been angry enough to break free from whatever curse Mombi had placed upon him.

She wondered, if Jack hadn't been there, would she have been able to kill Mombi on her own? That was the second time he'd saved her since she'd been back in Oz. It seemed she was always being rescued. Even Reva had defeated all the Wheelers, aside from the one that was an easy kill for Ozma. She'd escaped the dark place because of Thelia. With the beasts in the Sands, she'd only gotten away because one had attacked the other. A tinge of doubt spread through her that maybe she couldn't defeat the Wizard. Not without Jack or Reva or Thelia. Or a color-changing stag, apparently…

Blowing out an exaggerated breath, Ozma pulled on the reins as they neared Jack's hut. When the wagon came to a stop, she leapt to the grass and released the stag from his binds.

"Go wherever you wish." Ozma took out the fruit from earlier and gave it to him, then moved toward the wagon door.

A nudge came at her arm, the stag following her. "Are you still hungry? I'll give you more fruit if you help us on one more journey."

The stag stomped its feet against the ground and threw back its head as if in agreement.

"There's a creek we passed, if you want to get something to drink. We'll leave in the morning, but only if Jack is all right." The stag seemed to understand, but studied her for a long moment before venturing toward the forest.

Ozma clasped the handle to the wagon door and drew it open, finding Jack still asleep on his back. What if it wasn't fatigue from using his magic that made him sleep? What if Mombi had cast a dark spell with her last breath and he never woke up?

Stepping inside the wagon, she knelt next to him. Jack groaned, his shoulders moving, like he was trying to stir himself from a nightmare. Out the door, a sizzling sounded, growing louder and closer by the second. She surveyed the patch, and her eyes widened. Around the wagon, the vegetation started to grow, spread. Shadows shifted as pumpkins bloomed to full-size, some getting bigger and bigger, larger than she'd ever seen.

She shook Jack wildly, attempting to wake him before things got completely out of hand. "Jack!" she shouted.

He jerked forward, his eyes bursting open, settling on her. Clasping her wrist, his voice came out raspy. "It was a dream..."

Ozma glanced out the door, at the hovering silhouettes from the giant pumpkins. "No, Jack. It wasn't."

CHAPTER TEN

JACK

The night passed in a haze of fever sweats and vivid dreams. In one, Jack had a pumpkin for a head and a chicken for a friend. Another forced him to watch Tip explode into dust over and over again. All were fucking terrible, but Ozma never left his side. She was there with a cool cloth for his forehead or to run her fingers through his damp hair to calm him.

Jack watched her now. She had pulled one of his rickety dining chairs to his bedside and rested her head on the mattress beside his thighs. There was a vague memory of waking inside a wagon and her insisting the events that had played out weren't a dream. Then he'd stumbled inside with her help and collapsed again on the bed.

It was a shock to find out that Mombi had suppressed his powers. That he *had* powers. That was the only reason he could think of for what had happened—fae didn't often gain abilities after maturity. He had always thought he was born without magic, but to have it blast out of him like that… And for that magic to deliver such a bloody death. Even now his muscles ached. His head was clear though. Clear enough to know that Mombi was finally fucking dead.

Breaking out of a curse is a bitch, though.

Jack had left his cart at the market, but he didn't give a shit about that now. He eased himself up with a soft grunt, and flicked the tip of Ozma's pointed ear. She leapt up with a squeak. *Cute.* Jack grinned and his chapped lips cracked slightly.

"Jack?" She rubbed the sleep from her eyes. "How are you feeling?"

"Better," he said. He felt less heavy and his breaths didn't hurt like they had the night before.

She let out a relieved sigh. "You had me worried."

"Sorry, Blossom. You won't be rid of me that easily."

Ozma rolled her eyes and stood, stretching her back. Jack didn't bother to hide that his gaze was drawn to her chest with the movement. What could he say? He was a horny bastard. No matter how many fae he was with, no one truly satisfied his hunger since Tip. She crossed her arms and glared down at him, spearing him with a trace amount of guilt. *Tip's sister*, he reminded himself again.

"I'd apologize but…" He shrugged.

"I'd smack you if you hadn't just been at death's door."

"Don't exaggerate," he said.

Ozma swatted lightly at him. "Are you hungry?"

"Famished, but I need a bath more than food." He could smell himself—old sweat and dirt—so he knew it was bad, and he hated feeling sticky. "Pack a lunch and meet me at the lake. We'll have ourselves a celebratory picnic."

Ozma lifted the chair, assumedly to return it to the table, and shot him a glare. "The lake with the undine?"

Jack lifted his lips in a knowing smirk. "Exactly."

"Ah, okay. I see. You have a death wish." She set the chair back down.

"Don't worry, Blossom." Jack flung the thin blanket off and stood slowly, testing his strength. *Back to normal.* "I won't get in the water until she's dead."

"And I suppose you're up to fishing her out of there?"

"I've never been good at catching fish." He was going to test his magic. It flowed through him now like a second set of veins, and he was curious to see what he could do with it. Make sure he was able to summon and control it. If there were ever a time when he needed to use it, like with Mombi, he wanted to be sure he could. "Go on. The fare is up to you."

"Are you sure this is a good idea?"

Jack bopped her on the nose as he passed wordlessly out of the bedroom. Was he sure? Hell no. But he was going to have fun testing his limits.

Outside, over-sized pumpkins dotted the field as a testament to his strength. Physical proof that everything had actually happened the night before. Excitement fluttered through his stomach.

The path to the lake felt extra long with the sun high, air crisp, and leaves just beginning to change color. Not because of his slight aches and pains, but because he wanted to unleash himself. His fingers flexed at his sides as he tried to conjure up a spark of magic on the way. The power beneath his skin stirred, but it seemed trapped.

When Jack reached the lake, he stopped a few feet from the still water. "Okay," he told himself. Maybe he simply had to hold out his hand again. He scanned the grass until he found a small yellow flower with liquid droplets resting on its petals. Pointing his palm at the flower, he pushed at the magic. Nothing happened.

Seemed too easy anyway.

Grow, he thought at the flower, trying to be more specific. Still nothing.

Again and again he *tried.*

Again and again he *failed.* It had come so naturally before...

Releasing a sigh, Jack plopped to the ground. "Please grow," he whispered, coaxing the little bud to bloom bigger. A tiny bit of the pressure left his palm, easing the tension that built there, and the flower shot up an inch.

"A-ha!" he cried and jumped to his feet. "That's more like it!"

"Amazing," Ozma said in awe from behind him, and he whirled around. When had she shown up? "Do it again."

Jack took a deep breath and, using his magic, coaxed the flower to rise even higher. Again it worked. Biting his lip, he closed his eyes and spread his magic wider. He held up his hands, the magic begging the grass to grow, and every blade woke as his power touched them. It was like a thousand butterfly wings brushing through him. Fluttering faster and faster until he felt numb to all other sensations.

Ozma inhaled, an impressed sound, and grabbed his elbow.

Jack snapped his eyes open to find the grass along the lake was nearly as tall as they were. *Oh shit.* "I guess I got a little carried away," he said. But that was fine. It would take practice to perfect.

"Maybe a little," Ozma drawled with a light laugh.

"There's one more thing I want to try," he told her in a serious voice.

"What?"

"Killing the undine." Because it was *his* lake, so where better to try?

Ozma said nothing as he turned toward the water and focused his power on the plant life swaying at the bottom of the lake. He didn't ask any of it to grow—not until he found a patch of grass near the center that felt trampled upon. *The undine's nest.* While he couldn't see it, he knew the undine was lying there. Sleeping or, perhaps, just waiting patiently for prey to enter the water, but the weight of her body was suffocating the plant life.

Now, he would turn the tables.

Grow, he thought at the swaying grass along the edge of the nest. *Grow and hold her.*

The grass lengthened, knitting together into a net around the undine. He felt the creature as if the grass was his own skin.

Tighten. As tight as you can. Cover her gills. Immobilize her hands.

And the grass did. Phantom movements echoed against his palm. Air bubbles rose to the surface in what Jack imagined were the undine's dying screams. The last bits of air squeezed from her lungs, her gills unable to bring in any more. He held the power in place until the strain of the undine's struggles ceased. Then he held it some more just to be safe.

"There," he said after a handful of moments, and released the magic. "She's dead."

His body shook slightly, the aches worse than before, but he hadn't blacked out. *A damn improvement.* He knew that so much more would be possible once he learned to better hone the power. Mombi, he assumed, used the siphoned magic for the pumpkins, but he would put it to much better use.

Probably to grow some shitty pumpkins too, though.

Whatever.

"I'm going to take a bath," he told Ozma.

She flicked a look at him before eying the water as if she expected something terrible to surface. "Okay…"

He quickly shed his clothes and stepped into the water, completely unfazed by his nudity. The thought of Ozma seeing him bare didn't cross his mind until after the cool water lapped over his skin. It sent a shiver up his spine, goosebumps rising, and he dipped beneath the surface, eyes closed. *My lake.* He scrubbed himself, removing the layers of sweat and dirt, while his body got used to the temperature.

A pair of hands grabbed his arm and for a brief moment, horror filled Jack. Had he not really killed the undine? But then wisps of blonde hair caught his attention, floating around Ozma like a halo. Jack let out a relieved breath and followed the bubbles to the surface.

"What?" he gasped, wiping the water from his eyes.

"You were down there for a long time," Ozma said. "I thought maybe you were in trouble."

Jack's eyes caught on her bare arms skimming the water's surface and he smirked. "So concerned that you took off your dress first?"

She scowled. "I got in to bathe since I was interrupted last time, *then* thought you needed help."

"Right."

Ozma splashed at him. "You're welcome."

Jack laughed—a real laugh. His first in two years. He flicked water back at her. She gasped and flung an even bigger splash at him. Again and again, until the entire surface of the lake rippled around them and they were both winded, their chests heaving. The swells at the tops of her breasts drew his attention. Ozma stopped first, ducking beneath the water—*cheater!*—and waited for Jack to cease before reemerging. Grateful for her quiet surrender, he took only seconds to stop.

"You know," Jack started once the lake had calmed again, "I used to come here with Tip frequently." He cast an unsure glance at Ozma, worried she wouldn't want to hear about his relationship with her brother.

Ozma's eyes flashed with interest, but she quickly lowered her gaze. The hair that had come loose from her braids clung to the sides of her face, making her appear younger. "Since you both needed to bathe, I'm not surprised."

"We didn't just come here for that."

Ozma blushed. It was a good color on her—he wanted to see more of it.

"We also came," Jack continued, "to give ourselves a moment to breathe." She stared at him wordlessly as a crease formed between her brows. "It was too far for Mombi to walk, so we had to fill a tub for her instead. Which was fucking backbreaking work, but it was worth it because we could really be ourselves here. Talk about anything, dream about escaping, kiss…" *Fuck each other senseless.* He paused to see if the information made her uncomfortable, but she simply watched him as if waiting for him to continue.

"Tell me about him," Ozma said when he remained silent, lowering herself so the water skimmed her bottom lip.

Jack ran a hand through his hair. It twisted his insides to think of Tip in detail, but it also hurt not to. "As I'm sure you know from your time in the mirror, we grew up here together. He was all I had, and I was all he had, too. Except, I could sometimes leave under Mombi's control, so I suppose he had it worse than me.

"Still, he didn't let it bring him down much. Tip always had a smile for me, always told me not to worry. His laugh was like the sun and his eyes were even brighter. Tip was the purest soul I've ever met—not that I've met many—and I didn't deserve him."

Could I sound more like a sap? But, damn me, it's fucking true.

Jack's gaze locked on the ripples widening along the surface of the water as he willed away his pain. He missed everything about Tip. The way he hummed while they worked the field and how he tugged on his ear when he was nervous. When his jealousy tinged his cheeks pink. The softness of his hair, the tingling sensation Tip's touch put in Jack's chest, and the silly faces he would carve into pumpkins.

"It must've taken you a long time to get over him," Ozma said with a question in her tone.

Jack huffed. "I've never gotten over him. Believe me, it would be better if I could."

She watched him carefully. "But the other day—"

"A prostitute from town," Jack said quickly, and winced. *Great thinking, asshole. Dig yourself a deeper hole, why don't you?* Not that Ozma should care. "That doesn't sound good, I know, and the next part is even worse. But I… Well, I fuck whores that look like Tip to bury my pain. And, before you ask, no, it doesn't make me feel better. It makes me feel worse, in fact."

"Then why keep doing it?" she asked, her eyes like saucers.

"Why?" He took a deep breath and searched his mind for the answer. "I don't know. Maybe I hope that, if I keep trying, one day it *will* work. That some of my pain will lessen for longer than it takes for pleasure to come and go."

Ozma swam forward slowly, as if she were afraid he would flee, and smoothed a lock of wet hair from his face. "You're wrong."

Fucking hell—her eyes were just *like Tip's.* He wanted to lose himself in her gaze. Lose himself in other parts of her too. It had been ages since he'd felt the warmth of a female, and he couldn't help feeling drawn to her. But she was Tip's sister. If he were going to screw his way through Loland to forget Tip, he certainly couldn't entertain the idea of adding Tip's sister to the mix. And yet…

"Wrong about what?" he croaked.

"I can tell how much you still love Tip after all this time. If that doesn't prove your devotion, nothing would."

"I never claimed otherwise, so what am I wrong about?"

Ozma swam backward toward the shore. "You deserved him."

Jack felt frozen in the water as she reached the edge of the lake and walked, naked, into the tall grass. The twitch in his cock told him *she* was wrong. Lusting after Tip's sister made him extremely unworthy, but the pang in his chest was harder. A crack formed and tears stung Jack's eyes. He quickly ducked beneath the surface again to wash them away.

CHAPTER ELEVEN

OZMA

Ozma squeezed the water from her hair as she walked back toward the farm with a happy—albeit confused—heart. Jack still loved her... Or no, it was *Tip* that he still loved. It didn't matter, because it was her either way. And there had been a reason he'd had the male in his hut—a prostitute—who had looked like Tip. Ozma hadn't taken the time to study the male's face, or similarities, since she'd been too focused on Jack, sweat-slicked and thrusting inside another. Perhaps that was why there'd been so many clients at the brothel where she'd stopped with Reva when they journeyed. *Loneliness*. She could understand Jack feeling that way, even if she hated what he was doing to fill a void.

It didn't mean anything that Ozma was Tip because she'd changed so much over the last two years that she was hardly the same fae inside. She hadn't even confessed to Jack who her parents really were, who *she* was. Not *only* Ozma. Not *only* a female who had responsibilities. All she'd been focused on before was her love for Jack, not the pressure that her royal status would put on him.

Fisting her hands, Ozma walked inside Mombi's hut. Jack's magic was beautiful, the way he could get things to grow, make the grass appear like it was dancing, even when going in for a kill. How could Mombi have done this to him? To her? She wanted to stab the witch in the heart over and over again.

Now that Jack was no longer in and out of sleep, Ozma needed to formulate a plan and gather any spells she could from Mombi's so she could head to Orkland for the Wizard. Blowing out a breath, she went into Mombi's room and started collecting the spell books. Piling as many tomes as she could in her arms, Ozma took them across the patch and loaded the books into the wagon. After all the books were out of the hut, Ozma grabbed the jars of ingredients, until she was certain she'd plucked away everything she could possibly use.

Once she returned to the sitting room, she gathered candles, created from goblin skin, and lit one, then another and another. She put a flame to the remaining candles in Mombi's room before knocking them, one by one, to the bed, then to the floor with a thump. Black and orange fire spread its way across the blankets, the filthy walls. As it engulfed the room, Ozma set flames to the curtains in the sitting room, watching as they crawled throughout, going past the spot where she'd discovered her true self.

Ozma remained in the middle of the sitting room, studying herself in the mirror, the bright orange, black, and gray around her, until the heat became too much against her skin, the smoke too heavy for her lungs. As she turned to leave, the door swung open with a *crack*.

"What in the ever-loving fuck are you doing?" Jack shouted. He motioned his hand back and forth through the smoke as he hurried toward her. Before she could say anything, he lifted her from the floor and cradled her against his chest, then rushed outside.

Ozma couldn't contain her emotions anymore. The tears came, her sobs echoed throughout the patch. "Put me down! Stop trying to save me when I can save my own damn self! For once."

"Okay," he breathed, setting Ozma down and cradling her

face, his gaze latching onto hers. "Okay. But what am I supposed to think when you're standing in the middle of the hut, watching it burn around you?"

"Ask me if I need help before swooping in," she whispered, not being able to shift her eyes from his hazel irises.

"*Do* you need help?" he asked, lifting a brow.

She did. Jack had magic, and she didn't. Even if he hadn't had any magic at all, she still needed him on this journey.

"Will you come with me to kill the Wizard in Orkland?" she asked softly, as his hands released her face. "It wasn't only Mombi who sent me away to the dark place. It was him, and if he doesn't die, then Reva and everyone else will be in danger." Ozma paused, taking in a deep breath. "I do have magic, but I learned from Mombi's spell books that the Wizard's been absorbing it with the silver slippers. He must have somehow gotten them from Thelia when she left Oz."

Jack stared at her, cocking his head like he didn't fully understand. Behind them, the crackles of Mombi's burning home sounded, the smoke curling into the air, the flames ripping through the hut to the outer layers.

"Thelia is Dorothy, remember?" she pointed out. "Anyway, I promised Reva that once I defeated the Wizard I would meet her back in the Emerald City. You don't know Reva—if I don't go there, she'll come looking for me. But I understand if you choose not to go." She would just have to hope that the spells from Mombi's books would be enough.

"If you had magic, I'm assuming Tip did too, and Mombi did the same thing to all of us."

Ozma slowly nodded. *Truth.*

"You're not telling me something." Jack took a step closer. "I still feel like you're leaving out information."

"Do you want to come or not?" There were some things that Jack still didn't know the truth about, but she wasn't going to tell him. One day he would learn she was a queen, but she was too far into the lie to tell him that she was Tip.

"Yes," he finally said. "I'll come with you."

"You do know you're free now, though," she whispered. "Free, Jack. Just because I'm asking you to come doesn't mean you have to. Mombi's dead—you aren't bound to do anything you don't want to."

"I was never very good at taking orders." He smirked. "From the bitch, anyway."

Ozma turned from that face she yearned to touch and walked away from him, toward the wagon.

"When did Mombi get a wagon?" As she tugged open the door and lifted one of the spell books, Jack stopped at the opening with his arms crossed.

"After Tip died, she sent me out of the barrier to collect one. She used it for the last couple of years when she journeyed out more by herself." He watched her flip through two of the tomes before asking, "Are you going to pass one over or hoard them all?"

She picked up a tattered sickly-green one and tossed it at Jack. He stepped out of the way and the book landed on the ground with a plop.

"You were supposed to catch it." She rolled her eyes and threw him another.

He easily caught it then picked up the one from the ground. Licking a finger, he turned a few pages before meeting her gaze. "What am I looking for here, Blossom?"

"Just anything that might help us." Ozma bit the inside of her cheek—nothing so far appeared useful.

"I'm pretty sure making fae lust after pumpkin pie isn't going to save anyone." He crawled into the wagon and sat across from her.

Ozma let out a huff and sifted through more pages. Raising the dead, putting someone under the spellcaster's command, shifting someone into an animal. She tore out those pages and set them aside to stick in her satchel. The rest of the books didn't seem like they would be worth anything, unless she wanted to rot herself from the inside out while using dark magic or cheat fae at the market.

The note from before, about Lurline's baby being stolen, caught her attention again when she thumbed through its book one more time. Something in her didn't want to put it back in between the pages, so she stuffed the note inside her bag too.

The night started to darken and Ozma hadn't realized so much time had passed. She peeked out at the twinkling sky, at Mombi's smoldering, collapsed hut across the field, and stretched her arms. When a book hit the wagon floor with a *thump*, her gaze darted to Jack.

"How about we get some rest and head out in the morning?" he asked.

Even though she'd been up for most of the night, watching over Jack, she wasn't tired enough to sleep. "Go ahead. I'm going to stay out here a little longer."

"All right." Jack hopped out of the wagon and walked off toward his hut, leaving Ozma to wonder if she'd said something wrong.

Shrugging off the odd feeling, she slipped out of the wagon, trekking over vines and around the large pumpkins Jack had created with his magic the night before. In the middle of the pumpkin patch, she lay down on the grass, letting the fruit surround her, and the stars hover above. This was something she'd always liked to do—count the stars, connect them with an imaginary line to make shapes, while hoping to one day escape the patch.

Footsteps sounded and she sat up, spotting Jack with a lantern and a bowl of something in his hand.

"Here," he said, giving her the bowl filled with pumpkin-seed brittle and two plums. "You know, Tip used to like lounging in the middle of the field at night too."

I know. "Really?"

"Yeah," he said quietly.

"Hmm." She took a piece of brittle and bit into it, surveying the shifting silhouettes of trees in the dark. Jack sank down beside Ozma, the pumpkins practically cocooning them closer together so that his thigh brushed hers and his pinky finger grazed her wrist. Neither spoke as they both gazed up at the sky.

Her heart thumped, harder, *harder*, her chest tightening at his nearness, his scent. She couldn't breathe, her body aching as a warmth spread through her. There were times she couldn't control herself as Tip, just as she couldn't now. Seized by her old reckless habit of needing to kiss him, she grabbed his face and pressed her lips to his. Soft. His mouth was always soft, perfect.

There wasn't any hesitation as Jack kissed her back, urgent, spreading her lips with his tongue. He gripped her by the waist and lifted her with one easy swoop into his lap, her legs cradling his hips. Her center was right against his hard length, and a moan escaped her mouth as emotions rushed through her body, like a magical tornado taking down the entire world. It had never felt like this—this sensitive, this *good*, as he moved her hips forward, again and again. And his cock wasn't even in her yet. Her tongue licked and danced with his as she ran her hands in his hair, grasping, tugging it. He released a low groan, and she responded by drawing him even closer. She couldn't stop kissing him, that familiar taste, those movements, that body she needed to see bare again like earlier at the lake, that—

"Tip," Jack murmured, sucking and nipping at her bottom lip.

Ozma froze, then leapt from his lap. What was she doing? She'd said she would let him be free and then she'd done this. And he'd called her Tip… Who she *was*, but he didn't know that.

Jack blinked, his mouth parting, seeming to be at a loss for words as he stared at her. "Ozma," he finally said, as if that would make everything better.

"It's fine." Ozma took a swallow, tugging at her ear. "I've gotta go to sleep. See you in the morning, Jack."

She didn't want to hear his apologies as she whirled around and hurried across the patch to his hut. Jack didn't chase after her—she was sure he was hating himself for calling her the wrong name and thinking he'd kissed Tip's sister.

Why had she made up this ridiculous lie?

CHAPTER TWELVE

JACK

Jack sat among the pumpkins, watching Ozma hurry away from him, with the taste of her still on his lips, the roof of his mouth, his tongue. *What the hell just happened?*

She'd kissed him.

She kissed me.

He hadn't initiated anything, though he'd wanted to. He knew damn well his cock had wanted to. But he'd tried to behave. Then her lips touched his and that was it—he didn't give a flying fuck anymore. He wanted to take and take and take until Ozma had nothing left to give.

And then she ran. Because he'd, stupidly, called her Tip. *Fuck me.* She tasted just like him though. Savory and just a little bit sweet. Her tongue stroked his, her hands waking every inch of skin she touched. For the briefest moment, it had made him forget that it was Tip's sister he was kissing.

Jack lay back and dragged a hand over his face. Maybe it was for the best. Nothing could truly happen between them while he was still so in love with Tip, and yet... He closed his eyes and unapologetically replayed the kiss anyway. The first press of her warm lips, the way her tongue danced with his, how they seemed to melt together. It felt like they'd kissed a thousand times before.

Jack's eyes flew open at the unbidden thought. Ozma … tugged her ear. His pulse raced. Tip did that—exactly like that. Two quick pulls followed by a longer one. And she knew the way to the lake without hesitation. That was impossible if she'd spent her life inside a mirror, and then the dark place. The look of betrayal on her face when she'd seen him with the prostitute…

Mombi's dark magic could do just about anything.

No… It wasn't possible, was it? Could Ozma be Tip? Would she admit it if he confronted her? If it were true and she wanted him to know, she would've told him. Right? He ran his thumb over his bottom lip. *No.* Ozma was a liar. Which meant Tip was a liar. But Tip *never* lied, at least not to him. The thought of Tip hiding a truth so large left him feeling cold inside. There was only one way forward—get Ozma to admit the truth. And, to do that, he would need to arm himself with proof.

Jack leapt up from the ground and sprinted to the wagon. With a quick glance toward his hut to make sure Ozma wouldn't see him, he slipped inside, leaving the painted door open a crack to use the moonlight. The scent of dried herbs with a hint of sweat assaulted his senses.

"What did you take from Mombi's hut, Blossom?" he asked aloud.

Flipping through each book, he found nothing surprising. Dark magic spells for this, dark magic potions for that. But then he glanced at Ozma's satchel, still resting inside the wagon, practically calling to him. He shouldn't. *He should.* With hurried motions, he unlatched the flap and collected a few of the notes resting inside. Spells… Then a handwritten note.

Steal the child growing in Lurline's belly.
Use magic to alter the child's identity.
Find silver slippers to draw magic from the child.
Create immortality

"What the fuck?" he whispered. Was this talking about Tip—

Ozma… Which identity was true? And who was Lurline? The slippers and the immortality had to be regarding the Wizard, just as Ozma explained before. Altering the child's identity would explain Ozma being Tip too.

"What are you doing?" Ozma asked. She stood in the open door with a bundle of blankets, staring with wide eyes at the note in Jack's hand.

Jack turned the paper so she could see it. "Why do you have this?"

"In… In case it helps destroy the Wizard."

Liar. Or, if not a lie, then she was holding something back. "Who is the baby?"

Ozma hopped into the wagon, dropped the bundle, and quickly took the note and the other spell pages from Jack's hands. "How should I know? It also isn't polite to go through someone's things." Jack watched in silence as she tucked the page away inside her satchel. "We should get some sleep."

"Right," he said carefully. "Sleep."

There was no way he would be able to shut his mind off tonight, but his body begged him to try. So he followed Ozma back to his hut and nestled down in front of the fireplace so she could take his room again.

Tip.

Ozma.

Mombi and the Wizard…

He mentally tried to piece everything together as his eyelids grew impossibly heavy. None of the pieces fit—not yet. But he wouldn't stop trying until they did.

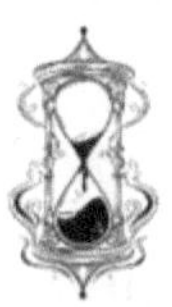

Sleep did nothing to erase the insane thoughts running through Jack's mind. He hoped it would bring him to his senses. Hoped that it was simply residual exhaustion from what had happened with Mombi that put strange ideas in his head. Ozma was Tip. She couldn't be … but she was. He was almost certain of it. If he could just make her admit it…

Jack sat in a wobbly chair and watched Ozma pick through his paltry shelves for something other than his home-brewed ale, stuffing anything edible into a sack for their journey to Orkland. She moved differently than Tip had. Smoother and less awkward. And she didn't need to stand on her toes to reach the higher shelves. Could Mombi adjust a fae's height? He scowled. If she could change everything else about someone, was that even really a question?

"If I didn't know any better, I'd say you were a drunkard." Ozma turned toward him and froze. "What's with that look?"

Jack rapped his fingers on the tabletop. "If you didn't know any better?" She *would* know. Better than anyone else.

"I'm not judging you. Living with Mombi almost required a muddled head," she said with a shrug.

"But why *would* you know any better? Why wouldn't you assume I *am* a drunkard?" Ozma wouldn't know if he drank once a year or every night if she'd been in Mombi's mirror. *Tip* would've known that Jack only drank on the really hard days, but that wasn't exactly true anymore. Every day was a hard day since Tip had died.

Or didn't *die.*

Was Tip stuck as Ozma, or was this her true form? Any curse Mombi placed on her should've broken when she died. Unless dark magic was used… So had Tip always been Ozma? The note mentioned altering a child's identity, so the infant would have had to be born as Ozma. He chewed his bottom lip.

What a mind fuck.

"I don't understand." Ozma's brows knitted together. "Are you trying to tell me that you *are* a drunkard? Sorry, but you need a clear head on this journey. All the jars stay."

Jack swallowed a frustrated scream. Was she really this good at acting? He already knew she was a liar, but this was extreme. Why wouldn't she tell him if she'd been Tip?

Because she caught you with your dick in someone else.
Shit.

Orkland was a two-day journey—one by land, another by boat—so Jack would have to pay close attention to gather proof. Ozma would slip up again like she had when she'd tugged her ear. "I don't need to bring any," he said as casually as possible.

Maybe one or two…
No.

He would sober his sorry ass up on this trip if it was the last thing he did. Ozma was a sly one—getting the truth would require him to have all his wits about him.

"Then I'm ready if you are," Ozma said, hefting the sack of food over her shoulder.

Jack reached out, took the heavy bag from her, and swept an arm toward the door. "After you."

He followed her from his hut, then took one final look around the small, worn shelter. Would he ever be back? It was the only home he'd known, so even though he'd been forced to live there, leaving felt bittersweet. Every moment he'd had with Tip had been on this farm. His eyes narrowed. But, apparently, they could keep making memories together—as Jack and Ozma. The idea of having more time together sent prickles of warmth through him, but he shut it down quickly.

He had to be *right* before he allowed hope to settle in.

After depositing the sack of food in the back of the wagon, Ozma whistled. The stag trotted from the woods and stood calmly as she hitched him up. Jack took note of her sureness as she connected the straps properly—something else she wouldn't have learned inside the mirror. But Tip would've known. As very small younglings, they'd had a wretched, swayback mare to help turn the soil for a few years before it dropped dead.

Jack climbed up beside Ozma to begin their journey, gnawing his bottom lip. He let her navigate the way to the sea. The forest he knew so well gave way to sparser trees with tall, umbrella-like leaves, and the dirt road lightened to white clay. Homes were made from brick with thatched roofs. Instead of lush grass, it grew tall and wispy with tiny tufts at the top of each blade.

Every turn Ozma made was done with a sureness he couldn't begin to grasp. If she was in the mirror, and then some dark place, she would have no idea where to go. He already knew the mirror was a lie because she walked around like she owned every inch of the farm, but what about the dark place?

Pain shot through his chest. If there was no dark place, where had Ozma been the last two years? Because Tip wouldn't know his way around Loland either. Not when he'd been stuck on the farm. So, if the dark place was a lie, why had she waited to come back? Was it because of Mombi? Or was it because she hadn't wanted to see Jack? Warmth flooded over him, a mixture of fear and embarrassment. He'd longed for Tip for two years … but when he'd returned as Ozma, there were only lies. Lies about who she really was. Lies about where she'd been. His mind twisted and twisted around itself, tying complicated knots of nerves.

"Do you want to stop and stretch your legs?" Ozma asked quietly as the sun sank below the tree line, breaking the silence between them.

Jack shook his head.

"And to eat?" Her voice became even more uncertain.

"I'm not hungry," Jack told her coolly.

She swallowed audibly. "We should give the stag a rest, at least. There are a few more hours before we reach the sea."

And how would you know? Jack crossed his arms over his chest. "Maybe we should camp here for the night."

"Here?" Ozma scoured the area. There were plenty of places to steer the wagon off the road. Though the trees wouldn't offer any coverage, they hadn't seen another traveler all day. It seemed safe enough.

"Why not?" he asked. "You can sleep in the back of the wagon." *Not we.*

"Me?" Both her brows lifted. "Where will you sleep?"

"Out here." He motioned to thin woodland. The ground was flat, the dirt dry and packed, with leaves scattered about. It would've been preferrable to sleep inside the wagon, but there was no way he could rest being so close to Ozma.

She hesitated. "We should keep going. There will probably be somewhere nearer to the port so we can catch the first ship to Orkland."

"Why does it have to be the first ship?" he asked in a flat voice. They had no solid plan of attack to defeat the Wizard, which sat uneasy with Jack. Neither of them had fighting skills—at least, that he knew of—and Ozma had no magic. Unless that was a lie too. His magic could grow things, but it was still highly untested. Killing one undine didn't make him battle-ready. It felt more like they'd gotten lucky with Mombi than anything, and the Wizard wasn't one to be messed with. Jack hadn't seen him in two years, but before that the mortal had aged over the time he visited the farm, grown frail and crazed from his fruit addiction. Yet still, he exuded power. The hair on Jack's arms always stood on end when he visited and the sense of unease lingered long after he left.

"I suppose it doesn't," Ozma conceded. "But you want to visit the sea."

Jack quirked a brow. "Do I?" *Keep calm.* The only one who knew about his desire to set eyes on the sea was Tip. "Maybe I hate water."

Ozma blushed and gave him a shy smile as she steered their wagon onto a flat, grassy area beside the road. "I just assumed… Since you've been on the farm your entire life."

Jack studied her carefully, desperate to see some physical sign that Ozma and Tip were the same fae. Nothing. Only those fucking blue eyes he loved so much. "I gave up wanting anything a long time ago."

Ozma's smile fell. "Don't say that."

"Tell me"—he leaned closer and closer, then lifted her chin—"what do you think is left for me, then?"

Her eyes dropped to his mouth as she spoke. "You have your whole life ahead of—"

Jack snorted, releasing her face. "Don't bother, Blossom.

Unless you can tell me Tip is still alive…"

Take the bait.

Take. It.

Ozma opened and shut her mouth. "I'll get us something to eat from the back," she said, sounding defeated.

Jack hung his head as she climbed down from the seat beside him. Was he wrong? Was it wishful thinking? He squeezed his eyes shut before they could threaten him with tears. There was no explanation other than Ozma being Tip.

I'm not wrong.

But why was she still lying to him?

CHAPTER THIRTEEN

OZMA

Jack had been acting differently toward Ozma the entire day… And it had to be because of the night before, in the patch, beneath the stars. That damn kiss. That beautiful kiss. The kiss she couldn't stop thinking about, even when she'd disappeared into Jack's hut to try and get some sleep. Instead, she'd explored her body—her breasts, the slick folds between her legs, feeling things that were good—but could be even better, when done by another's hands. Then she'd gone outside to check on him and had found him in the wagon, holding that note of Mombi's that she should have burned instead of kept. Luckily, she'd been quick to have an answer about it.

Ozma straightened in the seat of the wagon, shaking off the night before, and focusing on the trees blooming with bright fruits and nuts. The map in her veins lit up, and she knew if they took the shortcut through the forest, they could make it to the sea sooner. Pulling the reins, she steered the stag off the sandy road.

"Where are you going?" Jack asked, grabbing onto her wrist.

"It's faster this way. Trust me." She smiled as he gave her an unsure look. Then Ozma cursed herself because that was the reason Jack was acting funny, not because she'd kissed him. But because he still didn't fully trust her, and he probably thought she'd been trying to seduce him for some nefarious reason. No, that wouldn't be right, because she hadn't asked a thing while she'd been planted against him, feeling every inch and curve of his delicious mouth. Hurriedly, Ozma tucked that down and focused on the clear sky.

As she glanced at him, she inwardly sighed, knowing she should just give him something else. "I know where to go, Jack, because, while I don't have magic, there is something within me that knows where lands and seas are. Like an internal map. Perhaps that is magic, or perhaps it's just a part of me. So that's how I know."

"Oh. We shouldn't get lost then." Jack bit his lip, appearing conflicted, as though he wanted to say something different but held back.

Ozma arched an eyebrow at him. "We certainly won't."

They traveled deeper and deeper into the forest until trees with their tops in the shape of mushrooms covered its entirety. Branches intertwined and curved like snakes, the sun's light dimming and squeezing through the narrow slits from above.

"Listen … Ozma," Jack said, placing his hands behind his neck.

"No more *Blossom*?" she asked, trying to make things light as she tightened her grip on the reins. But something about his tone made her nervous.

He chuckled and snagged a few leaves from a branch, tearing them to small pieces as he spoke, "Oh, you're most definitely sweeter than any flower." Then his expression grew serious, his lips forming a thin line. "I want to apologize for last night. I didn't mean to call you Tip."

So he wanted to discuss that… "It was all my fault anyway." She winced. "I shouldn't have … done that."

"I don't know." Jack smirked.

Ozma furrowed her brow at his response. He didn't know what? Did he want her to do it again? He was tumbling prostitutes and guzzling pumpkin ale as a means to get over Tip.

But even if he did see something to desire in her, she needed to keep to her decision and not shackle him with a crown. Still, those lush lips and those long fingers kept drawing her gaze.

The wagon bounced up and jolted to the side as a loud snap echoed. Ozma and Jack lurched forward, the stag grunting while trying to turn before coming to a halt. A sudden shift to the right caused Ozma to slide off the seat, releasing the reins, and clawing at air as her backside hit the ground. She groaned as a sharp ache ran up her spine. Jack almost landed on top of her, but grabbed her and rolled her with him to his back, until she was above him.

"Are you all right?" Jack rasped, lifting her chin. "Did it worsen your wounds from the undine?"

"I'm fine," Ozma lied. Her back still throbbed, but it was slowly dissipating. She searched around to see if anyone had attacked the wagon, but only the stag stood there. "And you?"

"I've been through worse." Jack's smirk returned as he sat them both up with her in his lap. "This reminds me of last night. Your body against mine, your legs cradling my hips." He tugged on a lock of her hair, twirling it around his finger. "Have I told you how much I like the gold?"

Something felt off here. The way he was looking at her, as though he wanted to kiss her right then. "Did you sneak pumpkin ale on the ride, or did you hit your head?" Ozma quickly stood, leaving his heat, and brushed the dirt from her dress. She glanced at the front of their ride, where one of the wheels had fallen off, making the wagon tilt to the right.

"Just lightening the mood." He scanned their means of transportation and walked to a nearby tree where part of the wheel lay broken. "At least we weren't being attacked."

"This is only going to slow us down. Couldn't the wagon have at least made it to the port first?" Perhaps she should have just taken the longer route and stayed on the sandy road. But it would take them longer to turn back now.

"Apparently, the wagon wasn't made for softer terrain." He tapped the closest tree with his knuckles.

Ozma shot Jack a dirty look as she strode toward the stag.

He bucked his head and stomped in place. Hot air hit her face from each of his heavy snorts.

"Quit being antsy," Ozma said, reaching out a hand to calm the stag, stroking his soft fur. She looked from the broken wheel to Jack. "You don't have anything to fix it, do you?"

"Yes, I carry huge pristine wheels in my pocket." He patted his pants and shook his head. "Of course not. I wouldn't know how to replace a wagon wheel if I tried. Mombi always used magic to do things like that. She assumed I would have left it loose." A wicked grin spread across his face, stretching his freckles. "Not that I wouldn't have."

Ozma gave him a small smile. She was good at repairing things back then and now, but even if she could change out a wheel, there wasn't one for her to use.

The stag released another annoyed huff.

"All right. All right." She reached for the reins and started to unbuckle the straps from his body. "Now you can be free." There was no reason for the stag to stick around longer than he had to.

"Hold on now." Jack lifted a hand toward the stag. "We can still ride him to the port and not lose any time."

Ozma peered up at the stag, unsure if he would let them ride him, but they could try.

A loud shriek sounded in the distance as she took a step forward. Something like branches cracking reverberated and the stag jerked, barreling off in the direction of the road. Ozma stood frozen beside Jack before yanking out her dagger. He held out his hand, as if prepared to release his magic.

When nothing else came, Jack rolled his eyes. "Or not. Could have at least given us a goodbye first, stag."

She was just glad he'd taken them this far. Blowing out a breath, Ozma opened the door to the wagon, collected her satchel, and handed Jack his pack. Inside, the wagon was mostly empty, except for the extra fruit they'd brought. Before she and Jack had left that morning, she'd cleared out Mombi's spell books and burned them. No one needed to find those tomes and use that sort of darkness on other fae. No one deserved to go through what she and Jack had.

"Ready?" Ozma asked.

Jack opened his pack and fished out a plum. "Now I am." He bit into the thin skin as they walked deeper into the forest. The mushroom-shaped trees seemed to get shorter, and the trunks wider, the farther they trekked. Dryads—with leaves for ears and bodies covered in thorns and twigs—would poke their heads out, large eyes blinking, then scurry back inside the trees.

"So," Jack finally said when a lavender-winged sprite flew past them. "Is Ozma part of your true name or was it one Mombi gave you? Tip could never feel his true name."

Ozma closed her eyes briefly, recalling how she would say Jack's true name—Jackseith Arel Diosyll—to try and force him to escape Mombi. But Mombi's magic was always too strong for it to work. She thought about her own true name and tapped into it. The one she hadn't known until after she'd met Reva, but it hadn't mattered then, and it didn't now, because she still couldn't draw up magic. *Ozma Emeraldis Dynasia.* Her heart sped up as she silently repeated it over and over. Nothing.

"Yes, it's part of my true name." She shrugged. "I didn't know all of it before, not until the dark place."

"I think I like Blossom better." He pressed a red flower into her hair that he'd taken from a small patch on the forest floor.

She left it there, her heart speeding up from how gentle his movement had been.

Neither spoke for a long while as they skirted around trunks and dodged vines lined with sharp spikes.

In the distance, there were several huge trees, forming a half-circle, stretching into the sky, taller and wider than she'd ever seen. Gnarled branches bloomed from the tops and sides of the charcoal-colored trunks. Dark blue leaves grew across the limbs while others decorated the ground where they'd fallen. Long brown vines with scarlet leaves dangled over the large openings—similar to a cave entrance—at the front of each trunk.

Ozma glanced up at the sky, noticing it would be dark soon.

She didn't know how safe it would be staying the night here, but they would have to make do. Besides, she didn't think Jack would be able to handle sleeping at the top of a tree like she could. The wagon would have been ideal, but that was far behind them now.

"You want to stop there for the night?" Ozma pointed to the tree in the middle. "Or go farther and hope we find something better."

Jack squinted as he lifted his chin, seeming to search around the trunks.

Ozma smiled, latched onto a shorter tree beside her, and quickly scaled her way up until she was near the branches at the top.

"You're quite fast at that," Jack called up to her. "Even in a dress."

In the dark place, a dress was all she'd had to wear after she'd abandoned her old clothing, so she'd grown used to it, rather liking the loose fit more than trousers.

"Two years with Reva," she shouted down, then studied the surrounding trees and past them into the distance. "I can't really see anything. Only foliage and more foliage."

After Ozma touched ground again, she and Jack gathered twigs and dried leaves to start a fire outside, near where they were staying, to give them light without burning the whole tree down. They set the things on the ground to start the fire later, then headed inside the large trunk in the middle. Ozma pushed aside the vines at the entrance, allowing Jack to enter the dark space first. A smoky smell struck her nose as she stepped next to Jack.

From the outside, a small bit of light entered, making shadows dance along the wall. Jack moved forward, examining the trunk's walls. Ozma glanced down just as his foot was about to step into nothingness.

"Jack!" She rushed to grab his arm and yank him back. But it was too late—his body fell forward, taking her with him.

A squeak escaped her mouth at the same time he shouted, "Fuck!" Her stomach was somewhere down in her knees and she couldn't get a scream out.

Above them, the opening fell farther and farther away. Small bugs with glowing blue bodies scurried along the dark walls, the only light guiding their way as they continued their descent.

Into the darkness below.

CHAPTER FOURTEEN

JACK

Down, down, down, they fell.

Jack couldn't pull in air. Couldn't cry out another curse. *Fuck!* Twisting, he managed to hug Ozma to his chest, his back to whatever fate lay beneath them as the blue glow of bugs blurred around them. His stomach rose, the plum he ate earlier threatening to make a reappearance. All he could do was hold onto Ozma. Hold on and hope there was a soft landing.

Because if there wasn't, they were dead.

Pain seared across Jack's back. A breath was torn from him, only to be met with a mouthful of freezing cold water. Too stunned by the razor-sharp sting and frigid temperature, he didn't immediately try to surface as the pool of water swallowed him.

Them.

His grip on Ozma had become steel—a reflex against the shock. It was her struggling against him in an attempt to swim that finally snapped him out of it. With a powerful kick, Jack catapulted them upward until they found the surface. They both gasped, the sound echoing off the cavernous stone walls. Specks of blue light reflected off the water's rippling surface and the sound of sloshing water filled his ears.

"Are you okay?" Jack choked out.

Ozma nodded, teeth chattering. The blue light dancing on her face gave her an ethereal appearance. "You?"

"I'll live." Assuming there was somewhere to exit the water. If not, they would quickly exhaust themselves swimming and drown. His back hurt so tremendously from slapping the surface of the pool that he couldn't inhale deeply. He needed a place to lie down for a moment and collect himself.

Jack scanned the area, more than grateful for the glow of the bugs. They cast everything in breathtaking wonder. If it weren't for their situation, Jack would've loved to gaze up at them in awe all night long. But they *were* in a situation. A fucking bad one.

Smooth rock curved up to the hole they'd fallen from. It was impossible to tell how far they'd tumbled, but far enough that the opening seemed no larger than an average pumpkin. Vines hung around the edges like fringe. There was no climbing back up, even if the walls offered footholds.

"Fuck," he mumbled. "Fuck. *Fuck.*"

"There," Ozma rasped, pointing. "Shore."

Jack's eyes found what she meant, but he hardly considered it a *shore*. A slab of stone stuck out from the wall, large enough for perhaps a dozen fae to sit comfortably, but there was no obvious exit. "There's—" His words caught when he found the spot beside him empty. Heart stumbling over itself, his eyes quickly landed on a blonde head already gliding toward it.

A relieved sigh fell from his chest as he started after her. He swam as fast as he could with the ache radiating through him. It took more out of him than he would admit aloud as he caught up to Ozma at the rock. Jack heaved himself over the ledge first. The stone was warm—too warm considering the cold water and lack of sunlight—but he wasn't about to complain. Taking Ozma's hand, he hauled her up beside him and collapsed on his stomach.

"Jack?" Ozma touched his back and a hiss escaped from between his teeth. "You said you were okay…"

He grunted. "I said I'd live."

"Let me see." Ozma began sliding his shirt up his back.

"Blossom," he said, rolling slightly away, "relax. Let me catch my breath, then we'll look for a way out of here."

She sat back, releasing his shirt, and exhaled loudly. "You catch your breath while *I* find a way out."

"Sure," he said, too tired to argue, and closed his eyes.

A few minutes of careful breathing and Jack felt slightly less winded. He lifted his head, rested his chin on his folded hands, and watched Ozma flip through her satchel then scour the cave for an exit. The fabric of her dress clung to her curves in a way that made him want to touch her—if only moving didn't hurt as much as it did. The kiss, the feel of her body last night, only made the desire worse.

"We're trapped," Ozma finally declared. She spun on her heel and looked at him with fear in her eyes. "There's no way out of here."

"There's always a way," Jack told her. He wouldn't let them die in this place. Too many unseen things were left on his and Tip's list to perish now.

She chewed on her bottom lip and peered up at the opening. "If I had my wings…"

"Wait—what?" He winced as pain prickled worse with his stunned shout. "Wings?"

Ozma pursed her lips, not meeting his gaze. "Mombi cut them off with her magic. The scar on my back…"

Jack remembered the scar. It was large enough for him to see from a distance that night he'd followed her to the lake. "I'm sorry," he whispered. The words seemed louder with the way they echoed through the cavern—or perhaps it was only because his mind was reeling. First, she had a map inside her, and now she had severed wings.

"Don't be." Ozma returned to kneel at Jack's side. "I'll get them back once we find the silver slippers."

If they got them, though Jack admired her tenacity.

"Jack?"

At her nervous tone, he turned his head so he could study her better. "What?"

"We should get out of these wet clothes so they can dry. Don't—" She said when he grinned. "Don't make comments and *don't* peek."

"Fine." He sighed and pushed himself up. The rock would dry their clothes quickly, and they would warm faster if they shared body heat—skin-to-skin, preferably. There was a blanket in his pack they could spread out and— "Shit!"

Ozma jumped at his sudden shout. "What?"

"My pack! It's gone!" He was on his feet in less than a second, looking all over for it but finding only Ozma's satchel. His gaze traveled across the water's surface. "I must've dropped it when we fell."

"Did you have anything important in it?"

Jack raked his hands through his hair. "Food, a blanket, and a…" Grief burned through his chest. "Yes. There was something important in there." He could remember the day he'd gotten Tip's final gift like it was yesterday.

Tip snuck across Jack's hut in an untucked white shirt and pants two sizes too big without a belt. He'd been pressed up against Jack's side only moments ago, stealing a little extra time together before they had to part ways. Tip must've thought Jack was asleep because he'd slipped so carefully from his embrace, but if the creak in the bed hadn't given Tip away, the door would've.

Jack watched him through the open bedroom, his curiosity growing as he forced his expression to remain blank. Why are you sneaking about? Tip didn't have a devious bone in his body and Jack had no secrets, so it didn't set off any alarms when he heard Tip lift a loose floorboard near the fireplace. Jack kept all his important things there—not that he had many. A few stolen coins and a book of short stories he'd found discarded in the woods.

Tip was welcome to any of it. They'd read the book together too many times to count, traveling across Oz through the eyes of a fictional hero, and Tip had no use for coins. Not when he was never allowed to leave the farm. Regardless, Jack knew Tip wouldn't take anything without asking.

Tip shuffled about with something and settled the wood back in place with a soft thunk. *Jack closed his eyes and pretended to be asleep as Tip made his way back to the bedroom. The mattress dipped when he climbed onto the edge of it.*

"Jack," Tip whispered. "Wake up."

Jack cracked his eyes and pretended to yawn. "What time is it?"

"Mombi's not looking for us yet," Tip said in a rush. Pink tinged his cheeks and he tugged nervously on his ear. "I... I made you something."

Jack shifted up onto his elbows. Tip was always bringing him little presents that he thought Jack would like to see. An extra-large pine nut or an especially colorful leaf—things no one outside of Mombi's barrier would think twice about. But Tip had never made him something. "Oh?"

"It's not very good," Tip continued. "I've been working on it at night after Mombi falls asleep, but—"

"Give it to me," Jack interrupted. Whatever it was, however poorly crafted, he already loved it. Because he loved Tip.

Tip set a rectangular, cloth-covered present into his hand and fidgeted nervously.

Jack smiled at him and moved the fabric away to reveal a small house made of sticks, tied together with twine. Each stick had been snapped off at almost the same length and a pitched roof hung low over the sides. The front door swung in and out with the pull of a pebble. Perfectly imperfect, like most pumpkins in the patch. But better. Because Tip had made it. For him.

"It's ... our house," Tip mumbled nervously. "Or what our house would be if we weren't trapped here. Something like that, anyway."

"It's wonderful." Jack beamed at Tip. "I love it."

His blush deepened. "You don't have to say that just because I made it."

Jack clutched the house in one hand and wrapped the other around the back of Tip's neck. "I'm not." He pulled Tip in for a gentle kiss.

Tip smiled against Jack's mouth. Bliss filled Jack's heart at the sensation. In the whole, wide, cruel world, his only shining light was that they'd found each other. That they could make each other so happy without trying. Jack knew he could search a thousand years for another soul like Tip's and never find it.

"Thank you," Jack whispered.

Tip slid a finger along Jack's jaw. "Anything for you."

"I'm sorry, Jack," Ozma said with a hand on his arm, pulling him out of his memory. "We can see if it's at the bottom of the water, if you want."

"No." He swallowed the lump in his throat. Judging by the distance they'd fallen, and the fact that they hadn't hit the bottom of the water, it was too deep and too dark to dive all the way down. And besides, it likely would've broken in his bag. Even broken, he would've treasured it. "We'll never find it."

Ozma hesitated. "What was it? The important thing."

"My seeds," he lied. There *were* pumpkin seeds in his bag so he could potentially begin a new life, but he didn't care about those. He wanted his house. The one he and Tip—*Ozma*—would share a lifetime in once they had the chance. But with her lies, that house felt just as lost as the one in his bag. He forced a small smile and a shrug. "It doesn't matter. I'll find something else to grow."

Ozma nodded and tugged up the skirt of her dress, exposing her legs, when she caught him staring. "Do you mind?"

Jack's gaze traveled over Ozma, which earned him a scowl. He chuckled, keenly aware of the fact that he'd seen her naked already, and faced the opposite direction to undress himself. "Feel free to peek at me all you want," he said with a laugh. When Ozma didn't scold him like he expected, he started to glance back then stopped.

"Jack..." Her voice came out annoyed but he could hear something else there too. Desire?

She was able to see him in all his glory. Jack felt her eyes roaming his strong back, his firm ass, and his broad shoulders. Unashamed as he was, he wanted her to look. Wanted her to see more.

She's lying to you, he reminded himself. *She's Tip and she's lying.*

But it didn't stop his body from reveling in the fact that she was clearly still attracted to him.

When a freezing hand landed on his upper back, he yelped both from the temperature and the pressure against his raw skin. "Have mercy, Blossom. You're cold as ice."

"So are you." Her breath was warm on his neck, sending

shivers down his spine. "Turn around but keep your eyes on my face. We'll warm each other up—*not like that*," she added before he could make an innuendo. "Just … snuggling."

"I can do that," he said in a raspy voice. Though another part of his body was much less certain.

CHAPTER FIFTEEN

OZMA

Snuggling? *Snuggling?* Why had Ozma said that word? Gooseflesh covered her from head to toe, and her teeth chattered with a rhythmic pattern of their own. Jack's were doing the same, his hazel eyes glowing beneath the bugs' blue illumination.

Ozma had never been this cold in her life. Not in the dark place during the freezing nights, not when winter winds blew across the pumpkin patch while she'd worked alongside Jack.

She studied Jack for a moment and peered down at his chest, his stomach, his length, even though she'd told him not to look at her. Jerking her head up, she met Jack's gaze again.

With a smile, he held his arms open as he settled on the ground. "You coming or not, Blossom? I'd suggest hurrying up unless you want us to die down here."

Ozma wondered if anyone else had fallen in this hidden pit of a place. There weren't any skeletons in sight, but that didn't mean there weren't any dead below the surface of the water. A shiver rolled through her, not from the thought, but the coldness.

Taking a deep swallow, Ozma lay down and shifted closer to Jack. Closer. Closer. She didn't even know why she'd overreacted with him about her body—he'd seen her bare at the lake. Anyone else who saw her naked, she wouldn't have cared about, yet this was Jack. Reva had seen her in a state of undress all the time when they'd bathed in murky lakes. But Reva hadn't known Ozma before, hadn't laid her eyes on every inch of her old body, to which she could compare things.

"You're taking too long." Jack wrapped his arm around Ozma and drew her the rest of the way to him. "I'm practically dead already."

Neither said a word as he held her close, his chest to her breasts, his calloused hands pressing into her back, his forehead touching hers. Heat spread through her entire body as he rubbed soothing circles up the length of her spine. Her teeth slowly stopped chattering.

The bugs' light seemed to have grown brighter, their steady soft glow shining across the walls. It was like starlight. If only there were a shooting star that she could wish upon to get them out of here. But in that moment, she didn't want to be anywhere else, only in Jack's comforting arms.

"How's your back?" Ozma asked, not wanting to put too much pressure on it as she moved her hands to his neck.

"Perfectly fine," Jack said. The hit to the water had rattled her entire body, stealing her breath for moments.

"If it changes, let me know."

"Careful. I might think you truly care about me."

Ozma felt her face grow hot. "You wish."

He chuckled then, and it was the same musical sound that he only shared when they'd been alone in the past. She couldn't help but smile in return because she loved that laugh.

They both stayed quiet, their breaths increasing. The expression on his face was much better than the somber one he'd held when he'd discovered his pack was long gone. She could dive into the water to search for it, but Jack had been right. There was no way they would be able to locate it, not with how dark the lake was or however deep it went. Her satchel was wet, but everything in there was still intact when she'd checked, including the ink on Mombi's spells.

Their fruit wouldn't last forever though. With no apparent way out, except for the hole practically a sky's distance away, she didn't know what they could try in the morning to escape.

All around her, the bugs' light seemed to lessen, making the area dim, slowly descending into what she feared would be darkness. Every time the world eclipsed of color, she thought about the dark place. She wondered if she died, would she somehow be sent back there again. Her heart beat harder against her ribcage, slamming into Jack's chest.

"Hey"—Jack shook her shoulders—"are you all right?"

"I don't know. It's hard being in the dark sometimes." Ozma's chest heaved as she stared at the fading blue color. She sighed in relief because it hadn't eclipsed completely, but it still unnerved her that it could.

He ran a hand over her damp hair. "Do you want to talk about it?"

"You already know Reva and I constantly ran from things." She bit the inside of her cheek and listened to the slight movement of the water beside them.

"But you never mentioned if you'd been hurt while there," Jack said softly.

Perhaps it would help for her to talk about her experience more instead of keeping such a tight hold on it. After Thelia had pulled them out of the darkness with her magic, Ozma hadn't been able to think about how she truly felt. There had been too many important tasks that needed to get done, beginning with her short journey with Reva before parting ways.

"At first, yes. Mostly scratches and cuts, but I was also bitten a few times. That's when Reva taught me how to climb trees quickly. Up in the branches, I could steer creatures away from Reva. Other times, she would do the same for me."

"I'm glad you had someone there with you." His gaze connected with hers, as they lay on the ground on their sides, and the edges of his lips tilted upward. "Your eyes are even brighter under this light. I like them."

Ozma frowned. "Because they remind you of Tip?"

"No," he drawled. "because they're *yours*."

Before she could speak, he placed that finger over her lips and continued, "It's not just your eyes I like." His hand drifted into her hair. "The color of your hair I *like*, your blossom scent I *like*, your height I *like*, the way your body arches into mine I *like*. Do you want me to go on?"

Her heart pounded faster than it had this whole time, even more so than when she'd been falling down the hole.

"Have you … *tumbled* anyone before?" Jack cleared his throat as if he were hesitant to ask. He'd never used that term when talking about sex—only she had.

"No, I've never *fucked* anyone." *Not in this body anyway.*

"Ah, a beautiful word from a beautiful mouth." Jack's hand slid down her side until it rested at her waist. His nose brushed softly over her lips, his mouth came next, his lips grazing over hers so gently that she wasn't sure if she'd felt them at all.

With a light touch, Jack's other hand moved up to her neck before skimming the curve of her ear. Her body arched into his. For now, there was no way out of this hole, and there was a possibility that they would die down here. If so, then Jack would never get to be free. And neither would she. But perhaps for a while, they could be. She could pretend they weren't trapped, just as she had in the pumpkin patch when Mombi's barrier had kept her hidden.

Jack's mouth hovered over hers, and he lightly licked her bottom lip with the tip of his tongue. "I forgot to mention that I *like* the way you taste."

Done with words, she gripped his hair and kissed him. Slow, too slow, agonizingly slow, but she wanted to taste as much of him as she could before devouring him. A low groan escaped his throat when her tongue entered his mouth, caressing his.

As Jack's lips and tongue lit her body aflame, his cock swelled against her stomach. She wanted to know what it would be like to have his length inside her, how it would feel when she stretched for the first time. Reva had explained to her how tumbling worked as a female, but listening was different than experiencing.

"You're not close enough, Blossom," he rasped, placing her leg around his waist.

"More," she whispered as her center rubbed against his cock.

In a quick swoop, Jack lifted her into his lap and pressed his back against the cave wall. Ozma moaned when his hardness settled perfectly against her core.

As she rolled her hips forward, they both released moans that reverberated around them. Jack's finger glided down the valley between her breasts to slightly above the aching spot between her legs.

"Can I touch you?" he asked, kissing her until both their lips were swollen.

"Please," she murmured, unable to deny whatever he asked right then. "It's been far too long."

Jack froze, halting her from shifting her hips forward again. "What did you say?"

Ozma took a deep swallow, playing back what she'd said, realizing what she'd done wrong.

"You're a liar," Jack said in a low voice. He licked his lower lip and studied her with an intensity that she couldn't begin to describe. "A pretty liar. Lie to me again. Lie to me for all eternity as long as you're here with me. *Alive*."

That finger went up again over her lips, trapping her words in. But she didn't have any to say as they were lodged in her throat, her head, her heart.

"Tell me the truth so I can fuck you however you want. I can't go along with this charade anymore, and before I worship all of you, you need to know that I already knew. Until the day I die, I will never stop fucking loving *you*." Tears welled in his eyes after he said the last word, his voice a whisper.

Her hands shook, the sentence finally forming as she moved to get off of him and stood. She could tell he wanted to hold her down, but instead, he got up directly across from her.

"You know I'm Tip." Her voice came out shaky.

He nodded. "It was the letter in your satchel that made me certain, but there were other things. It was the way you tugged your ear, knowing where things were, the look on your face when you found me with the prostitute. Did you really think I wouldn't put it together? You could be in dragon form, unable to speak, and I would still recognize you soon enough. I know you better than anyone."

"I know," she said softly. And if Jack had been in her position, she would have detected who he really was, too.

"Then why didn't you tell me? Why make up such an elaborate story?" His voice grew louder, angrier. "We never lied to each other!"

"Because you were fucking someone who wasn't me!" She rushed forward and cupped a hand over his mouth. "And I'm glad you did because I realized how selfish it would be if you knew the whole truth anyway. You deserve to be free, Jack. *Free.* So I'm going to give that to you now. Jackseith Arel Diosyll, forget that I'm Tip. I release you, Jackseith Arel Diosyll."

Ozma slowly dropped her hand, watching Jack's gaze focus on her. Tears of her own pricked at her eyes at what she'd done.

A cold smirk crossed Jack's face. "Sorry, Blossom. True names don't work like that."

CHAPTER SIXTEEN

JACK

Jack's anger exploded through his chest. Ozma tried to use his *true name* to make him forget! As if he wouldn't realize the truth all over again. As if he didn't have a right to know. If she wanted him to be free, she never should've come back to the farm. She should've continued to let Jack think the Tip he knew was dead.

"Please forget it," she practically begged.

"How dare you?" he seethed. "How dare you do this to me? Did you think you could just sweep back into my life, lie through your teeth, and leave? No harm done?"

"I had to come back to kill Mombi and the Wizard."

Jack winced. She came back from the dark place and, instead of seeking him out, returned only for revenge. "You never loved me at all, did you?"

"Of course, I did," she said with tears in her eyes. "I *do*. But you deserve to be free."

A growl slipped through Jack's teeth and he stepped closer, grasping Ozma's shoulder. "Don't tell me what I deserve. My choices have *never* been my own—none except to love you. And now you want to take that decision from me too?"

Ozma's hands closed around his forearm, tugging until his

grip loosened. "That's not what I'm doing."

"It's exactly what you're doing." His heart thumped painfully and he stumbled back a step. "But I can never be free of you, Blossom. No matter how much you push me away or lie, my heart is yours."

When he thought Tip was dead, he'd wanted to live to honor him. Not with his actions, because sleeping his way through Loland was a desperate attempt to numb his own pain, but to *remember*. Everyone died twice—once when they passed away and again when no one remembered they'd ever existed. Jack had wanted to keep Tip alive in that way… But if there was no *first* death, then there was no reason to worry about the second.

Jack looked urgently into Ozma's eyes, imploring her to see how much he loved her. It didn't matter what she looked like—Tip was her and she was Tip. But she said nothing as she held his gaze.

"You're killing me," Jack whispered.

"I'm sorry," Ozma said, her chin quivering. "I *never* meant to hurt you."

Jack laughed humorlessly. "You're doing a hell of a job of it anyway."

If they weren't trapped in an underground cave, he would've left then. Hid himself away somewhere and allowed himself to have a good cry before he decided what to do. Though, if he were being honest with himself, he already knew that he would forgive Ozma. After his anger ebbed, he would forgive her lies if she only loved him. *Really* loved him. None of the self-sacrificing bullshit.

But there was nowhere to go to nurse his wounds, so instead, he swept up his wet clothes and pulled them back on—freezing be damned. His churning emotions would keep him warm until he could figure out how to save them both.

Jack paced, his gaze sweeping from one side of the cave to the other in search of a way out. Smooth walls. Sky-high ceiling. *Think, Jack, think.* His thoughts refused to drift away from Ozma though. He tried not to notice her near the wall where she had lay down and curled in a ball, shivering, with her dress pulled tight around her shoulders like a blanket. Goosebumps covered his own body and his toes were numb. *Find a way out.*

If he froze to death, an escape route wouldn't matter.

"Shit," he mumbled to himself and stalked back to Ozma. She peeked up at him and his heart thudded heavily. *Those damn eyes.* How many times had he begged the universe to bring his lover back? How many times had he promised to do *anything* for just one more day? Too many times to count. And what was he doing now that his prayers had been answered? His chest caved, taking all his walls with it.

"I'm sorry," he blurted.

A crease formed between Ozma's brows. "For what?"

"Losing my temper."

"It's not like I didn't deserve it," she said between chattering teeth.

Jack removed his clothes once again and knelt beside her so they could warm each other. "Let's not talk about it anymore, okay?" He laid down and inched closer.

"Fine." Ozma immediately wound her arms around his waist and snuggled into his chest. "I have to confess one more thing to you," she mumbled, "and then you'll understand. But I never stopped loving you, Jack. Not once."

One more thing? What else could there be?

"Tell me tomorrow," he said.

Tomorrow he would ask. Now he would allow himself a few hours of happiness. *She still loves me.* He sighed into Ozma's hair and pulled her flush against him. This time, he would make sure nothing happened to her.

The lack of light in the cave made it difficult to tell how long they had been asleep. Jack pried himself away from Ozma's body, his back still cold from the lack of skin-to-skin contact, and stretched. He'd slept on worse, but it didn't make the stone any more comfortable. It was pure luck that his arm hadn't lost circulation.

Ozma curled in on herself at the loss of his shared warmth, covering her breasts in the process. Jack wished he could've seen them again, but hopefully there would be another chance soon. Ozma *loved him* and had seemed willing to show him that. Maybe she would again.

Thoughts of them fucking in the past flashed through Jack's mind. Tip bent over. His smooth back. His soft moans. The taste of him on Jack's tongue and the feel of Tip's lips all over his body, his cock. They had always worked well together. He very much wanted to see her beautiful face flush as he pleasured her and tangled his fingers in her silky golden hair.

Shit.

Now was not the time to get himself overly excited.

Once his back cracked twice, he glared up at the opening they'd fallen through again. They were well and truly fucked. If only the walls weren't so smooth, there would be a chance they could climb out. But the vines were too high up for—

"Ozma!" he shouted despite her nearness.

A small shriek echoed through the cave and a few of the blue bugs went dark. "What happened? Are you okay?"

"Sorry, I didn't mean to frighten you." He scooped up his now-dry clothing and began tugging it on. "Get dressed. We're leaving."

"What?" Ozma patted around for her dress. "How?"

Jack yanked his shirt over his head and grinned, then wiggled his fingers. "Magic."

He couldn't believe he hadn't thought of it the night before. Maybe it was the pain of smacking into the water, or the shock of the cold, or the revelation of Ozma's truth that had kept the magical option from his thoughts.

Jack quickly spun on his heels and held his palms up toward the opening. *Grow,* he urged the vines. They crept down, down,

down like snakes, groaning from the quick growth. Twisting and curling, they slowly descended from the top of the cave. When the ends were nearly at the water, Jack stopped them.

Form a net. It would be quicker and safer than climbing.

The vines slid over each other, up and down, making neat rows as if it were a basket they wove. They kept going until the edge of the vines reached their rocky platform.

With a cocky smirk, Jack turned to Ozma and held out his hand. Ozma's mouth dropped open in awe.

"After you, Blossom," he said with a chuckle.

Ozma brushed her fingers against the net and gave the vines a tug. "I've scaled worse. It seems sturdy enough." She shrugged, stepping out onto the vines.

Let's hope so. There was no reason it shouldn't be though, so he simply followed her carefully onto the net. "Going up," he said once they were both steady.

Lift us, he thought at the vines. Their energy pulsed through him like a second heartbeat. The vines creaked under their weight as the net rose, inching closer and closer to the surface. When they were near enough to pull themselves up, Jack reached out mentally to tell them to stop their ascent. The magic tingled through him and the vines eased to a jerky halt.

Ozma went first, climbing free of the cave as if it were nothing more than hopping over a fallen log. She seemed more agile than she'd been as Tip. More free and sure of herself. It was a wonderful change to witness after all he'd seen her go through in the past. He wanted to know more, see what was different about her, learn how she'd grown into the fae she was now.

"Onward," he said with a flourish once they both stood outside the tree. It had looked so inviting the night before, but now he would steer clear of trees with caves.

The farther they walked, the more the sun thawed the last bits of him. Jack's joints no longer felt stiff and his shoulders relaxed as he finally stopped hugging himself. There was only one uncomfortable thing left to deal with.

"So…" Jack hesitated, unsure whether he wanted the answer

yet or not. *Better to get it out of the way.* "What's the last thing you have to tell me?"

Ozma twisted her hands together. "Wait until we get on the boat, and I'll explain everything."

Jack clenched his jaw and nodded. What were a few more hours when he probably didn't want to know anyway?

CHAPTER SEVENTEEN

OZMA

Ozma and Jack trekked through the forest until midday. With each step, the map in her veins pulsed, pointing her toward the sea, her destination. Hours ago, they'd crossed into Hiland, but it seemed no different than Loland, only more dips and even taller trees covered in leaves the size of Ozma's head.

She hadn't spoken to Jack, and he hadn't spoken to her. The silence between them was tangible, and she knew he had questions. But he wasn't the only one—she did too. The night before flashed in her head—his mouth on hers, her body pressed to his, her attempting to use his true name to forget.

How could she have done that? But it would have been for him. Perhaps it was unfair for her to have even tried that, but she loved him enough to let him go.

Now he knew who she was, though. She should have known it couldn't be kept a secret forever. And he'd been right about one thing. If she'd truly wanted him to be free, then why had she come back for him? Why hadn't she realized it would've been better to let him be? Either way, she'd always known she had to free him from Mombi. She'd spent the last two years thinking about her reunion with Jack. A childish dream.

The quiet—his quiet, her quiet—spread and spread around her until it became too much. She opened her mouth to finally speak when he grasped her arm, pulling her to a stop.

"I hear it," Jack said, biting his lip as he stared ahead.

"Hear what?" She drew out her dagger from her hip and lifted it. They were so close to the shore and she didn't want to be slowed down again.

"The ocean." Jack released her arm and took a step forward. "Do you hear it too?"

She tilted her head and perked her ears. When an almost magical sound floated around her, she lowered her dagger. The lapping of water against shore, sea birds cawing, the wind singing. "It's beautiful."

A smile spread across Jack's cheeks, reminding her of how he'd been before she'd gone to the dark place. "Remember when we talked about seeing the sea one day?" he asked.

"One day we'll visit the sea, and I'll worship your body in it until you've come as many times as you wish, not caring who sees us fuck."

Tip felt his cheeks heat. "I hope that's a promise."

"Oh, it's more than that," Jack said, swiping his tongue against the glistening pearl at the head of Tip's cock, then placing his lips around the length.

Ozma swallowed hard, the memory drawing a warmth in her like it did back then. "Did you still plan on coming here?"

"No…" The smile fell from his face. And she knew it was because he hadn't wanted to go alone, without her.

Something about seeing that broken expression made her heart hurt. She was here now, and they would look upon the sea together. Perhaps not worship each other's bodies there, at least not this time.

"Well"—Ozma shoved him playfully—"looks like I'll be seeing it first."

His lips parted and his eyes widened. With a laugh, she took off at a heavy sprint, just as she used to do when they would race to the lake.

"You're such a cheat!" Jack yelled.

She threw her head back and laughed again when a few curses flew from his lips. Clumped branches decorating the ground slowed her pace. As she was about to regain her lead, Jack's strong arms gripped her waist, lifting and whirling her around. After setting her down, he took off, chuckling.

"You!" she screamed, skirting around trees and ducking under branches, until she finally caught up with him.

Ozma yanked him to her by the back of his tunic, and they both stopped when voices echoed ahead.

"The port," she said, heading in the direction of the sounds, shoving aside shrubbery blooming with fragrant red and black berries.

The world before her opened to a silver sea, reflecting the sun's rays, and a gasp escaped her mouth. It was nothing like she'd imagined and more amazing than she could have believed. Ships and rafts of all colors lined the sparkling water, the soft swells bobbing them in a rhythmic motion. Glittery golds, sparkling blues, shimmery pinks. All with bright white sails flapping in the wind. Numerous fae carrying crates or barrels loaded up their ships for travel. Other fae delivered their supplies by foot, stag, or wagon.

"We have to find out which ship is heading for Orkland and sneak on board." She surveyed the area, reading the names on the sides of several green ships flecked with yellow.

"Not a raft." Jack squinted and pointed straight ahead. "I think that's our prize."

Ozma focused on a dark charcoal ship and studied the side where letters were painted in a deep red, forming the words, *The Wizard.*

She rolled her eyes at the name, but she was almost sure it would be destined for Orkland.

"Let's blend in, shall we?" she said, straightening.

He nodded and motioned her forward. "Follow me. I have an idea."

As she remained alongside Jack, crossing the soft lavender-colored sand, several fae with horns sprouting from their heads carried baskets of jewels past them.

"Excuse me," Jack called to a female draped in pink silk, her horns wrapped in matching ribbon. "Which ship is headed for Orkland?"

"Right there." She pointed at the charcoal ship. "Perhaps you would care to join us on our boat instead? For a cost, I can take you to the Isle of Phreex where there will be endless pleasure." Her tone came out silky as her gaze roamed over Jack in a flirtatious manner. Jealousy stormed through Ozma's veins, and she drew her hands into tight fists.

Jack made a tsking sound. "Not today."

"Your loss." The female shrugged and sauntered, her hips swaying seductively, toward a golden boat.

"You weren't tempted?" Ozma asked, turning to face Jack, fighting the clench of her teeth.

"Mmm. Having my spine ripped through my throat sounds really pleasurable to me." He grinned. "How about you?"

Ozma's eyes widened when she recalled the tale so long ago about the Isle of Phreex. The female fae who lived there would bring males back to tumble, which hypnotized their prey, causing the males to crave more and more pleasure, until they slowly went mad, chopping off pieces of their own selves to feed to the females.

"Let's go," she said and barely missed stumbling into a group of brownies headed toward *The Wizard*.

Jack and Ozma stood at the pier and watched as fae carried empty glass vials in buckets onto the ship. Ozma followed them onto the deck, and Jack yanked her down behind a stack of wooden boxes, just as a tall male elf with red eyes, a shirt to match, and golden studs along his pointed ears, rounded a corner. The fae was tall and broad with golden skin and hair the darkest of blacks.

"This was all we could bring, Tik-Tok," a brownie missing two fingers said.

He ripped the vials from the brownies' hands before shooing them off the ship and slipping somewhere out of view.

"Now what?" Ozma asked.

"Below deck?" His answer sounded more like a question.

She cocked a brow, eyeing the obsidian door and its sapphire handle. "And what if someone's there? Or what if it's locked?"

"We'll figure it out soon enough, won't we, Blossom?"

Ozma puckered her lips, wondering if it would be better to just remain right where they were.

"Ah, I missed that look too," he purred, tugging her toward the door.

She kept her feet feather-light beside him. Holding her breath, she drew open the door. A set of wooden stairs lay before her and a flowery scent hit her nose. No shuffling sounds came from below, so she quietly walked down the steps. Jack trailed closely at her heels after he closed the door behind them.

At the last step, Ozma breathed again while Jack searched the large space. The walls were lined with wooden barrels and crates of wine bottles cluttered the area. There were several open rooms without doors that held more crates, stacked high—these filled with faerie fruit and vials containing different colored liquids. Some sort of potions?

A scuffing of footsteps sounded from the other side of the door at the top of the stairs.

"Fuck," Jack whispered, pointing her to one of the rooms as the door creaked open.

Ozma slipped inside and darted beside Jack into a corner behind the crates. She peered out a narrow crack between the crates as two fae entered the room. The male from before—Tik-Tok—and another female with short red hair. They each set down sacks of something.

"The Wizard keeps demanding more fruit, but don't they have enough over there?" the female asked. Silver hoops pierced the entire edges of both her pointed ears.

"You would think. But the fiends' cravings keep getting stronger." Tik-Tok raked a gloved hand through his sleek black hair.

"I don't see how fruit does anything to the fae," the female said. "It should only affect the humans."

"It just does. Quit asking questions unless you want to end up like them when Mombi returns for our next shipment." He shrugged. "And don't forget to lock the door this time. We don't need the fucking wine disappearing again."

Their feet pounded up the steps as they exited, followed by the echo of the lock turning.

Ozma relaxed against the wall of the ship. They would be trapped down here for a while, but they'd made it.

"Cozy place we have here for the night, isn't it?" Jack leaned back beside her, stretching out his legs as much as he could.

"Is that sarcasm?"

"No." His warm breath brushed her ear, and she held back a shiver at his nearness. "Now that we're here … what did you plan on telling me? There's nothing you could say that would make me leave your side. I'm the freest when I'm with you."

The boat eased forward, the hull rocking side to side. Ozma's nerves were on edge, but not because this was her first time on a ship. She had no idea how Jack would react to what she was about to say. She bit the inside of her cheek as she spoke, "I'm the queen."

"That you are." He tapped the end of her nose. "We can play all the games you want later, Blossom. But for now, tell me."

She needed to be straightforward and tell him the entire truth—he deserved to know. Should have known earlier, but she couldn't change the past several days. "Lurline, my mother, was a faerie, which is why I had wings before Mombi burned them. My father was King Pastoria, and because they're both dead, that makes me queen."

Jack's brow furrowed. "Queen of *what?*"

"Oz…"

He blinked several times, his mouth parting. "Oz," he finally repeated.

"Yes. All of Oz."

When he didn't say anything else and remained still as a statue, she continued, "You've always wanted to be free, Jack.

And I came to the conclusion recently that this would only be trapping you again. I wouldn't be able to travel the world anytime I wanted. Like we'd talked about…"

"Is being queen something you want, though?"

Ozma had thought about it over and over, and had even contemplated giving the throne to Reva. But something in her couldn't, as though she were created for this purpose—to make Oz good again and keep it that way. "Yes, it's something I want."

"I'm not worthy of you, Blossom. It took me forever to believe I was before, but now you're a queen. *The queen.*" His shoulders remained tight, his throat bobbing.

"Jack, you're not Mombi's slave anymore. She made you feel this way—she made you believe you were nothing." *Made me believe I was nothing too.*

"I've already proved what a bastard I am." Jack's head drooped. "While you were banished by Mombi, what was I doing? I fucked and I fucked and I *fucked*. I'm such a piece of shit. But you, you can do anything you want. I always knew that."

Her chest sank at his words because he truly believed this of himself. "You're not nothing—you're everything, and a king to me. You always have been. Even that damn pumpkin patch felt like a kingdom at times because you were by my side. But now we have choices. You can get to know the world … other fae." As much as it ached to say it, he deserved to make his own decisions.

"That's the thing." He held her gaze. "I've been around other fae and know that there's no one I'd rather have than you. Yet you haven't—you've only known me. Perhaps it's me who should free you to discover if there's someone better suited." He clenched his jaw, as though those last words had to be forced from his perfect lips.

"Damn it, Jack," she whisper-shouted. "You know I choose you. Every time." She threw her arms around him, holding him tight.

He lifted her into his lap and rested his chin on her head, his fingers interlacing with her hair. "Then we have that matter solved.”

For a long while, they stayed in that position, and even though the room remained silent, it was as if their bodies were speaking to each other, comforting, apologizing.

Finally, Ozma peered up at him, the angles of his face, his hazel irises. Those eyes that could sweep her anywhere.

Jack’s gaze fell to her and he smiled. “So, since you’re my queen, what are you going to order me to do first?”

Ozma shook her head, about to give him a sarcastic reply, when his lips crashed to hers, taking her by surprise. She inhaled, savoring the flavor of his lips as she kissed him back with equal hunger, her tongue tasting every inch of his mouth.

“I don’t think there will be much time for kissing once we get to Orkland,” he rasped.

“Keep kissing me then.” *And don’t ever stop.*

Jack’s strong body shifted as he lay her on the floor, hovering above her. A naughty grin formed on his face as he leaned forward and whispered in her ear, “I don’t want to kiss *only* your lips. I want to kiss here.” His tongue flicked the side of her neck. “Here.” He moved down her body, kissing her through her clothing, above her breast. “Certainly here.” Then he traveled to her navel, pressing his lips gently there. “And, finally, here.” His fingers skimmed up her dress, against her uncovered thigh, so very close to the place that desperately wanted to feel his caress.

“Remove my dress then.” She didn’t care how he got it off as long as it was gone—now.

In answer, he drew up her dress, agonizingly slow. She pulled it from her body and lay completely bare before him. He’d seen her several times like this, but somehow it felt different.

Ozma placed her hand against his heart, feeling the thudding pulse against her palm. “Do you really like me in my true form?”

Jack tugged his tunic up and over his head, then rested his chest against hers, their hearts beating in sync. His warm skin ignited hers like a flame held to a candle. “How could I not?” His hands shook as he held her. Jack had never been nervous about anything.

"Why are you trembling?" she asked, wondering if she'd done something wrong.

"I lost the house you built for me," he whispered, his voice cracking. "That was the important thing in my satchel."

Ozma's hands trembled then too, because he had always loved her as much as she loved him. "It doesn't matter. A house is what you make of it." No longer was she worried about what he would think about her body, or if he would compare it to her old one. She knew he would love it regardless.

She reached between them, unlaced the tie of his pants, and shoved them down. Jack kicked them off the remainder of the way until there were only their bodies sinking into one another.

Jack slowly kissed the place at her neck, grazing it with his teeth, and sending a shiver through her from head to toe. He again drifted to her breast, her navel, until his lips connected with the tender spot on her inner thigh. Her hands entwined with his soft hair, wanting him to come closer, to taste her.

As his hot tongue stroked her center, an intense feeling swarmed through her that she hadn't expected. It was much different than having a cock—more intimate, as his tongue pressed inside her, swirling, licking. Her nerves lit up, creating their own blue starlight. She tried not to moan too loud as his lips moved between her folds. Ozma's hands tightened in his hair as his rhythm picked up—she didn't want him to stop. Not now. Not ever. But she wanted something else—*harder*—to fill her.

"Jack." She lifted his head from between her thighs, his lips shiny from devouring her. "Give me everything."

His gaze dilated with understanding. "Are you sure? We don't have to yet."

That was true. They were on a ship, behind stacks of crates, with guards above them. But she was used to sneaking around with Jack and them pleasuring each other in secret places, hoping not to be discovered. "It's been two years. I'm plenty ready."

"As you wish." Jack grinned mischievously, his wicked tongue traveling up her stomach as he planted kisses. His lips closed around her nipple, sucking and licking. Her body tightened with need as he moved to the other one, repeating the motions before coming to her mouth.

She gently bit his bottom lip, making him groan as his lower body drew closer. The tip of his cock skimmed her entrance, and her center throbbed at the caress. A nervousness poured over her as it had when she'd done this the first time with him as a male. But yearning overpowered that. His hardened length pushed into her, the pressure causing her to gasp, her back arching.

"Are you all right?" he asked, his thumb brushing her cheek.

Ozma nodded and Jack pressed farther in, little by little, stretching her until the pain relinquished. Her gaze held his as he slowly moved. Then, when she needed more, she gripped his ass, urging him on.

Jack smirked. "I knew you would get tired of this pace." He rolled his hips forward, shaking them both, filling her with pleasure. He thrust again and again, her legs wrapping around his waist as he drummed into her, until she needed even more.

She rolled them over to his back, her legs now cradling his hips. They stared at each other, his hand cupping her breast, his thumb drawing subtle lines over her nipple.

Holding back the desire to grind her hips forward, she leaned closer, kissing him ever so gently on the lips. "I love you," Ozma murmured, her breath striking his mouth.

Before he had time to return the sentiment, Ozma rolled against him, his cock rubbing her center in a delicious manner. This position was new for her, and she wasn't sure if she was doing it right. As if knowing what she needed, Jack gripped her waist, helping her ride him with steady back and forth motions. When she became more attuned to it, confident, she arched her back, rolling her hips in slow circles, over and over.

Their pace kicked up, faster and faster until a strong heightening sensation, enveloped her, consumed her. She had to control herself from screaming Jack's name as a blissful wave of pleasure stormed over her. Ozma's body shook as miniature earthquakes rocketed from her center to her toes, her fingertips, *everywhere*. But she didn't stop, not until Jack also felt the beautiful euphoria.

A moment later, Jack groaned, seeming to hold back his shout too as his cock jerked inside her. Before pulling out of her, he sat up, holding her against his chest, both breathing hard.

"I love you too." He pressed his lips to hers in a delicate kiss and smirked. "My queen."

Rolling her eyes, she rested her forehead on his. "My king."

CHAPTER EIGHTEEN

JACK

The ship gently rocked beneath Jack and Ozma. They'd both dressed quickly after they'd finished fucking in case anyone came back downstairs, but Jack wished circumstances were different. He wanted to learn every curve of her body with delicate touches. To brush his fingertips over her bare back, her shoulders, her arms, her breasts. To skim his lips and tongue over her collarbones and up the side of her neck. He wanted to feel her heartbeat beneath his hand as she calmed after they fucked.

A queen.

He winced. Was he really up to the task of ruling the land of Oz at her side? On one hand, it felt almost like protection. A shield for the future if they were lucky enough to win. After everything Mombi had put them through, he desperately wanted that. But… Ozma was a queen. A literal queen. With subjects to rule and laws to make and everything else that came with that.

Fuck.

There would probably be assassins lining up to kill her. And him too if she truly made him her king. *Oh shit.* He was *not* ready for that kind of responsibility. What did he know about the world? He'd been confined to the farm and the market. At least

Ozma had learned how to survive in the dark place and about the world from Reva. A king had to manage foreign affairs and … and … other things Jack had no idea about. Because they hadn't been in their hidden adventure book and he was a fucking clueless farmhand. A *slave*.

Jack's stomach heaved. They could be caught at any moment and, though he hadn't noticed until minutes after dressing, the ship's movements weren't settling well with him. The musty scent of the ship and the salty tang of the ocean swirled through him like poison. He could *not* be ill here. The loud retching would undoubtedly bring attention below deck, as there were fae directly above them. A light shower of dust rained down with every metallic *thunk* of someone's footsteps.

"Are you well?" Ozma asked, brushing the hair from Jack's eyes.

He licked his lips. "Nauseous."

"You're sick?" Her palm pressed against his forehead. "Did you eat something strange before we left? Or did you use too much magic getting us out of the cave?"

"I don't—" He paused to swallow the excess saliva flooding his mouth. *Fucking hell.* Jack shook his head, which only made everything worse. He lay back and closed his eyes. "How much longer?" he asked, fully aware there were hours ahead.

"It feels like less than a day by boat," she said. "Do you need anything? Some fruit?"

"Shh," he managed, but that was all he could force himself to say. If anything else left his mouth, it wouldn't be words.

Ozma settled beside him and ran her fingers through his hair. "Perhaps it's just the motion of the ship. Once, in the dark place, Reva and I thought to cross a lake using a giant lily pad. Turned out that they were attached to creatures beneath the murky surface. I think it felt us climb aboard because it started swimming in circles so fast that all we could do was hold on. We didn't stop for nearly two days. I was sure we were done for."

"What was it?" he whispered. Being trapped in this ship with danger above them was bad enough—he couldn't imagine what she'd felt then.

"What was what?"

Jack cracked his eyes to look at Ozma. "The fae beneath the water. What was it?"

"I'm not sure the beings there were fae, but we never saw what it was. As soon as we passed close enough to shore, we jumped off and ran in case it was able to follow." She smiled gently down at him. "Now, let me distract you with details of what our home will look like once the Wizard is dead."

"Like a palace," he said with a smirk.

"Hush," Ozma said, playfully smacking his shoulder. "We might have to live there sometimes, but it won't be our home. We'll have a secret place away from the city with a short stone fence around the yard. There won't be a gate, though—nothing to close us in. I'm going to fill it with flowers of every color and, outside the fence, we'll plant vegetables and fruit orchards, but *not* pumpkins. Any fae will be allowed to take what they need. We'll plant everything far enough away so we have privacy. Inside, we'll have a large bedroom and a library full of adventure books."

Jack's smile widened. *A life.* As they'd planned—only now, it was truly possible. "Just like the book we had before?"

"Like that," she agreed. "But different ones too. All kinds of adventures."

Jack closed his eyes and focused on Ozma's gentle voice as she described in precise detail what else they would have. All of it sounded perfect … assuming they survived long enough for it to become a reality.

"Jack," Ozma whispered. "Jack, wake up."

He cracked his eyes open—when had he fallen asleep? "Hmm?"

"I think we're here." She stood and tilted her head to the ceiling. "They're shouting."

Jack forced himself to get up, his stomach a bit calmer than before, and listened. A deep voice called out to drop anchor and tie down the sails. Then a loud *splash* hit the water on the other side of the hull. Feet pounded back and forth and wood scraped against wood. More shouts rang up, a mixture of voices, giving directions he couldn't quite make out.

"How do you want to get out of here?" Ozma asked. "Once they unlock the door, they'll probably start unloading all of this."

And catch us. "Guess we'll have to play it by ear." There was little else they could do besides hide and try to get out of there unseen. If they had anything of value, perhaps they could've bribed a brownie or two to look the other way. Sadly, all they had was Ozma's title and that meant nothing until she retook the Land of Oz.

Ozma yanked on his arm, pulling him behind a barrel with her. She quickly put a finger to his lips to stop his protest. "Shh. Someone's coming."

Jack's heart thumped wildly in his chest as he crouched behind the fruit. Two sets of footsteps hit the stairs in tandem, one heavier than the other. "Grab the food first," Tik-Tok ordered. "Make sure the fiends are fed so we can make it to the shelter without killing any of them."

"Yes, sir," a squeaky brownie replied.

"Get started and I'll send the others down."

Tik-Tok's heavier feet thumped upstairs again and Jack peeked around the barrel. The brownie shifted one of the crates from the top of a pile. It tilted precariously and her small, withered hands struggled to balance it again.

An idea sparked in Jack's mind as the first apple tumbled down on the brownie's head. She let out a small yelp of fear and Jack gave Ozma's hand a squeeze. "She's going to drop that," he whispered, "and we're going to use it as a distraction to get out of here."

"What? No!" Ozma replied. "The commotion will only bring

more of them down here."

And the more fae that came, the better their movements would blend in with theirs. Jack nodded once. "Exactly."

The crate finally toppled on the brownie, apples rolling everywhere, and Jack prepared to run. "Stay with me," he said and crept toward the stairs.

"What was that?" someone called from above. "Everything all right down there?"

Jack tucked Ozma beneath the stairs and squeezed in beside her, just as a handful of brownies and elves hurried into the storage rooms.

"Shit," Tik-Tok shouted. "What *the fuck* did you do now?"

The crushed brownie stumbled over her words as the others quickly gathered the apples.

Now, Jack mouthed. His hands shook slightly with nerves, but this was their chance. He sprang out from behind their hiding spot with Ozma right behind him. Keeping one eye on the brownies, Jack took the stairs two at a time. The distraction worked as well as he'd hoped—the crew's attention was focused wholly on the mess, and his and Ozma's movements were lost in the frenzy to pick up the fruit.

But that was where the success of Jack's plan ended.

More pirates worked the rigging, lugged ropes, and lowered small row boats from the side of *The Wizard*. And every eye swiveled to Jack and Ozma—the pair of fae bolting from the bowels of the ship as if their lives depended on it.

Because they did.

"Jump," Jack yelled as he reached the side of the deck. And he leapt, trusting Ozma would follow. The waves sucked him under just as another body sank down beside him. The warm, salty water stung his eyes, but he kept them open, waiting to see if it was Ozma or someone else. Once the bubbles cleared, he found his beloved reaching out for him.

Jack grabbed Ozma's hand, his lungs begging for air as they surfaced. He glanced at the shore—the distance seemed manageable, but he didn't want to be wrong. "Wait," he rasped.

Turning back toward the ship, he fixed his gaze on one of the lowered row boats that was within reach. Jack tilted the side of the boat toward them. "Get in, *quick*."

Ozma heaved herself up over the side and helped Jack in beside her as dozens of fae looked down at them, shouting. Tik-Tok loomed above the rest with an expression of pure fury.

"Leave them," he yelled. His lips curled into a cruel smirk, his red irises blazing. "They have nowhere to go."

Nowhere to go? *The Wizard* was anchored farther out since there wasn't a pier, hence the row boats, but there was most definitely a landmass.

"That's not good," Ozma breathed as Jack was about to row.

"What's—" Jack's gaze landed on the shore. Aquamarine sand sparkled in the fading sunlight and, beyond that, black skeletal trees loomed like shadows. But that wasn't what Ozma was talking about.

On the sand walked dozens of fae. Fae and—Jack squinted—humans. They wore dirty, torn clothing, their hair unkempt. It was the blank expressions paired with ravenous eyes that set Jack's pulse racing though.

"Shit."

"What are they?" Ozma asked.

Damned if I know. Jack swallowed hard. "A huge fucking problem, that's what."

CHAPTER NINETEEN

OZMA

Hisses and growls drifted over the silver sea. Ozma couldn't take her gaze away from the fae and humans hovering at the edge of the forest and on the shore. She hadn't been around many others until recently, but she knew they were not supposed to look like this. The faes' skin had a purplish hue, their pointed ears drooped over, their cheeks sunken. Everything about them appeared hollow, a shadow of what they once were.

As for the humans, their gazes seemed unfocused, their bodies leaning to one side, as though they might topple over at any moment. From what Tik-Tok had said aboard the ship, they were all addicted to faerie fruit on the island. The sprite had told her that there was an enchantment over everyone here, and this wasn't what Ozma had been expecting at all. Perhaps she'd imagined them with pupils dilated a little more, like how Mombi's would get when she ate certain mushrooms. This was so much worse.

Ozma swallowed, her eyes roaming from the fae and humans, to the skeletal black trees with their glistening white leaves and long ivory vines, and back to the crazed faces of the victims, their lingering movements. She chanced a glance over her shoulder toward the ship, its sails down, unmoving.

Tik-Tok still stood there, his arms draped off the side of the ship, his red eyes lazily watching them. A wicked grin spread across his face, replacing his earlier anger.

"Go on. I won't stop you," he called, daring her, then swiping a lock of obsidian hair behind his gold-studded ear. His face was beautiful in a vicious way, and she wondered about his part in all this.

"Ignore him," Jack said.

She focused back on Jack, his hands on the oars, the boat bobbing against the silver water.

Closing her eyes for a moment, she thought of the dark place, the beasts she and Reva had escaped from. Although there had never been as many creatures as this, the beasts there were much faster, their movements unpredictable.

A splash came from near the shore, drawing her gaze straight ahead to two female humans with matted hair hobbling into the water. Ozma placed her hand on the dagger at her hip, but the humans didn't swim. They continued to walk forward, hissing, until their bodies, inch by inch, were taken by the water.

She waited for them to rise to the surface. But they didn't. Not until moments later when their unmoving bodies floated to the top of the swells.

"I wasn't expecting that," Jack said, one orange brow lifted.

Ozma's heart thudded rapidly. They couldn't continue sitting in this boat with Tik-Tok gloating down at them. And if they lingered near the ship too long, would he hunt them down himself?

The vines on the island gave her an idea. She clasped her hand around Jack's arm. "Can you use your magic from here?" He'd been able to do it in the cave, but the vines there had been much closer than these.

Jack thrust a hand forward and twisted it to the side, his teeth clenching. His fingers tightened and loosened, then he shook his head. "No. We're not close enough for me to feel the life in them."

The swarm of corrupted humans and fae opened their mouths wide, hissing, baring their teeth. Their skin was peeling away in areas, revealing inky black muscles. *Rotting.* They were alive but decaying. Another idea came to Ozma, one that would hopefully work. Besides, it was her turn to save Jack.

Standing from the wooden seat, she faced Jack. "I want you to row to shore. Let me distract them."

"Oh no, you don't." Jack reached for her, but it was too late.

She jumped into the warm water, then kicked her legs and pumped her arms, swimming beneath the waves. The sea seemed to caress her flesh, as though it were trying to lure her into staying below the surface.

Silently, she said Jack's name over and over inside her head to not give in to the temptation to turn back. Cutting through the liquid with long motions, Ozma stayed underwater. She would do it for as long as she could before needing air. This was as familiar to her as walking or sleeping. She'd done it at the lake by the pumpkin patch and beneath the eerie waters of the dark place.

Below her, purple and blue striped eels laced through one another. But she couldn't see anything much farther than that— the water wasn't clear enough because of the silver tint and the glittery sheen.

A slow burn started to develop in her lungs. She would need air soon, but she held on a little longer, stroking harder, faster, before finally rising to the surface. As her head broke through the swells, she gulped in as much air as she could. Her gaze darted to the shore, so very near.

The fae hadn't seen her—all their focus was on Jack, who was rowing and glaring at her at the same time. She smiled and shrugged, because he would see her purpose soon enough.

Ozma cut across the water, until she could touch the ground, then ran the rest of the way, her bare feet finally striking dry sand. Her body was soaking wet, her dress heavy, as she drew the blade from her hip. "Over here!" she shouted.

All eyes turned to her in sync. Ozma bounced on the sand,

waving her hands in the air. "That's right! Come on!" As soon as the swarm started toward her, she jolted for the trees. Two fae, with black gore dripping from their lips, pushed out from the forest before she could get to her destination. As they growled, their bodies swaying, Ozma lifted her dagger and drove it through the male's chest, then the female's heart. Dark red blood oozed from the wounds as the two fae slumped to the ground with a thump.

A human crawling near Ozma's leg snapped her blackened teeth, and she drew a blade across the female's throat. There'd be no saving any of these humans. Whatever Mombi did to them was too dark to bring them back. Unintelligible noises escaped the human's lips as Ozma lunged for a tree, striking it with her foot to give her leverage. Her arms easily caught the branch above, just as another fae swiped at her legs and missed.

Swinging herself up, Ozma folded her legs around the branch and quickly scanned the area for Jack. The boat stood empty at the edge of the water, but then she spotted him farther away, moving toward her with both his hands raised, shaking, like using his magic was too much.

The swarm must have heard his footsteps because they stopped batting their hands at the air below her branch. Slowly, they turned to face him, hissing, their jaws unclamping.

Ozma was about to leap from the tree, when a white thorn-covered vine shot forward, piercing a fae through the eye, spraying blood. It drove out the back of his head and struck two more behind him. Then two more behind them. More vines came, snaking and curving around the remaining fae and humans. The vines snapped and cracked, and with one fluid motion, they pulled tight, cutting all the bodies in two through their middles.

Jack continued to slash his shaking hands in the air, making the vines whip, then slicing the heads clean off another group. Blood splashed across the sand until all that was left were torn bodies.

In the distance, growling reverberated within the trees.

More… And they would be heading this way. This time it sounded like too many.

"I think we need to go." Jack ran toward her, his curls damp with sweat. "My magic is still too new, and I don't know how much longer it will last."

"Let's hurry." Grabbing a twisted branch above her, she swung across it to another and another, then let her feet hit the ground a bit farther into the forest. She wiped the blood on her arm, from her kills, against her dress.

Jack was already beside her, brow arched. "I like how you move."

She grasped him by the tunic and yanked him forward.

As they hurried past trees, stepping over fields of black mushrooms with lavender spots, she still wondered if Tik-Tok and the others from the ship would come after them.

"I hope we find the Wizard soon, so we can get off this fucking island," Jack said, hopping over a log.

"Shouldn't be too long." But she wasn't sure. By the map in her veins, she could tell the island wasn't large, yet she didn't know if Oz would be close by or at the opposite end somewhere.

Above them, shriveled, blackened fruit dangled. Mombi's doing. They all oozed dark liquid that matched what coated the swarm's mouths.

Jack wrinkled his nose. "Whatever you do, eat nothing here."

Ozma rolled her eyes when a crunching sound came from ahead, along with something like gurgling and a horrid odor.

"Jack, stop!" she whisper-shouted, latching on to his sleeve. "And don't use your magic." It would be too easy for them to be detected if the Wizard was staying somewhere close by. Hopefully, their incident at the front of the island wouldn't get back to Oz too soon.

They both stopped, listened, then slowly walked the mushroom path. Keeping her feet light, Ozma took a few more steps toward an opening in the trees. Her eyes widened at what she saw through the slits in the leaves.

Dead bodies of fae, rotting and festering, were sprawled

across the forest. Their stench permeated the air, and Ozma covered her mouth so she wouldn't lose her stomach. However, there weren't only dead fae, but live ones too, feasting and sucking on the blackened bodies.

CHAPTER TWENTY

JACK

*W*hat. The. Actual. Fuck.

Fae and human addicts attacking them was one thing—Jack and Ozma were live prey—but *this?* Jack's gaze latched onto a particularly ghastly human with more exposed muscle than skin, and a black hole where his nose should've been. The human snapped a dead fae's finger off, tendons stretching as the digit was pulled free, and stuck the rough end into his mouth.

And sucked.

Bile burned its way up Jack's throat. This was too much. Far, far too much. The gods-forsaken pumpkin farm seemed like fucking paradise to him now. Even being enslaved to Mombi was better than any of this, though he knew the witch was responsible for these creatures. She must've used her black magic on the fruit which created monsters, likely to quash any threats to the Wizard that reached the island. But, on the farm, there were no monsters—only a nasty old crone who was too fond of swinging her cane. Usually at him. Not to mention, the farm didn't smell like the inside of a dead swine's asshole.

"We should go before they notice us," Ozma whispered in Jack's ear.

"Right." Jack forced back a cough and nodded to his left. It was the direction they had been heading when they'd paused. Going toward the monsters was clearly out of the question, as was going back toward the beach. They could only hope the only way left was the *right* way.

Ozma followed him as they crept around the field. He kept his eyes and ears trained on the rotting horde, expecting them to attack at any moment. So, when Ozma lunged and knocked him to the ground, he was completely caught off guard.

A growl vibrated above him, sending fear straight down to his marrow. Ozma let out a strangled scream. Her legs thrashed where she lay across Jack's back. He tried to shove himself free, but the weight of her and the addict was too much. He was pinned. Suddenly, he felt Ozma rip her dagger from her waist.

Jack clawed at the ground and managed to drag himself a few inches out from beneath the fight. Then everything was silent. The weight baring down on him doubled. Jack struggled to pull the rancid air into his lungs. *What the fuck is going on?*

"Get"—Ozma growled and shifted her weight—"off."

A body rolled down beside Jack's head. One Ozma had clearly just slaughtered, and the sight left him light-headed. He could've lived the rest of his life without seeing a toothless kobold, blue eyes milky and skin molting, with a dagger jutting from his forehead.

"Fuck," Jack spat, rolling to face Ozma. "Are you all right?"

Ozma stood over the dead kobold with blood sprayed over her face and neck. Her breaths came in great heaves as she nodded and retrieved her dagger. In the distance, predatory snarls carried through the air. "Are you?"

"Yes." He rose from the ground and wiped the blood from her cheeks. She'd saved his life. Drove a blade straight through the fae's skull. If it didn't appear to be half decomposed, he would've said it were impossible, but the bone seemed to crumble around the weapon. "I need to keep what's left of my magic for Oz or I'd cage the field off."

"Yes," she agreed as the growls deepened into something

more feral. "But we can't stay here."

They needed to move, and fast. Jack and Ozma sprinted away as quietly as possible. Every so often, one of them would step on a stick that had fallen from a skeletal tree and the crack rumbled like thunder in his ears. There were a few leaves on the ground that crunched below their feet, sounding as if someone was ringing a dinner bell. *Here we are. Come and get us.* A shudder ran through Jack's body.

After what felt like ages, they stopped near a shallow stream and guzzled the cool water. Black fruit hung within an arm's length of the bank but none of what dripped from the rotten skin reached the clear water. Oz would need to keep the fresh water supply disinfected for his own purposes. The fading sunlight shone off the surface, showcasing the smooth pebbles at the bottom and the tiny red and yellow turtles that hurried far from Jack and Ozma's cupped hands. *Cute little buggers,* Jack thought. Probably the only cute fucking things here.

"Look," Ozma called. "There."

Jack followed her gaze and caught a glimpse of green light glowing through the trees on the other side of the stream. *The Wizard of Oz.* Jack had only spoken to Oz briefly the times he'd come to the farm, but leave it to that smug son of a bitch to hide on an island while using obvious magic to give away his location. Ozma led the way closer and paused at the edge of the clearing.

A green, domed barrier glimmered faintly over a small stone house, smoke billowing from the chimney, with six smaller sheds spaced out along the outer edges. Each smaller building was painted black with different symbols carved into the walls. The grass was worn away where someone had walked back and forth between them and the house, while the rest of the lawn grew too tall. Flowers poured down the sides of boxes beneath the windows, rose bushes needed pruning, and weeds covered a small vegetable garden. Two chickens pecked aimlessly at the ground near the other side of the barrier. Jack wondered if they were there for the eggs or to sacrifice to whatever strange gods the Wizard worshipped.

"Don't touch the barrier," Ozma warned him. "It might alert him to our presence."

"Hadn't planned on it, Blossom." With his luck, it would melt his hand off or send his entire body into shock. That would've created quite the scene but done little else. They needed to get inside somehow—break the barrier or figure out how to get through it unnoticed. Or perhaps it would be easiest to lure the Wizard out… But this was Ozma's plot, so he would let her decide. "What now?"

Ozma chewed on her bottom lip. "It's getting late. Let's make camp and try to think of something helpful."

Jack felt a pang of regret at burning all of the witch's books, despite how dark their magic was. He knew they couldn't cart them all across the Land of Oz, but he just *knew* the answer to this problem would've been in one. There wasn't enough luck in the world for the barrier spell to be on one of the few papers Ozma had saved.

Resigned, Jack nodded. They hadn't heard any feral addicts in a while now, and maybe a bit of sleep would restore some of his power. The magic in his veins still felt weak and what was left ached in the same way his back hurt after a day of pulling weeds. "Let's just be sure to keep an eye out for—"

Cold iron pressed against Jack's neck. It bit into his skin and a line of warm blood trailed down toward his collarbone. Ozma froze where she stood a few steps ahead of him. Her eyes were wide and wild, her jaw hanging open with a mixture of shock and fear that echoed Jack's feelings.

"Hello, little stowaways," a deep voice purred in Jack's ear. The same voice from the ship. The elf with red eyes, jet black hair, and a cruel smirk—Tik-Tok. "I must say, I'm impressed."

CHAPTER TWENTY-ONE

OZMA

Ozma's heart was stuck in her throat as Tik-Tok held his blade to Jack's neck. She'd seen Jack in predicaments with Mombi, but never as bad as this. But he had magic now. And she desperately wished she did too. She pleaded with wide eyes for Jack to use it, to take a vine and rip Tik-Tok's head clean off. But then she focused on the blade cutting into Jack's flesh, drawing a thin line of crimson. *Iron.*

Jack's hands flexed at his sides, seeming to try and draw magic, but failing.

"So, your magic is with nature? You reek of it." Tik-Tok only smirked. "Useful. But not right now."

While on the ship, Ozma had gone over the spells in her head, memorizing the words. There was one she could possibly use here, but only if his eyes focused on hers. It would be like holding his true name, ready for her to command him. Mombi had used it on her before but it only lasted moments, so the witch had found it worthless. It could buy them time here, though. Tik-Tok's burning red irises finally met hers, and she whispered the spell, urging him to obey her.

"Look at you." Tik-Tok smiled vengefully, exposing his back teeth. "Your pathetic spells aren't going to work on me. I'm protected. *So,* what are you going to do, darling?"

"He's not going to do it," Jack ground out. "If he were going to slit my throat, he would've done it already."

Ozma's eyes bulged, silently telling Jack to shut up. Even with Mombi, he'd never held his tongue, and that only made things worse.

"He's right, but my patience has its limits." Tik-Tok's red gaze bored into Ozma and he licked his lower lip. "I want to know why you're here first. Then, if I like what I hear, I may offer you a trade."

Tik-Tok didn't seem like one to be trusted, but with a blade at Jack's throat and a protection spell, what choice did she have? "Aren't you on the Wizard's side?"

"I'm on my own side. And, right now, it doesn't appear advantageous to help you." He cocked his head, his dark, sleek hair shifting forward. "Here's your chance to change my mind."

Ozma tilted her head right back at him, even though fear still pulsed through her veins for Jack. "One of my friends has taken back the South and the West in the Land of Oz, while another is in the process of redeeming the North and the East."

"How sweet," Tik-Tok purred. "But why would I give a fuck when I spend a majority of my time on the water, owned by no one." His blade dug into Jack harder, making her lover wince.

"Even if you kill us, our friends will come to end the Wizard, and I don't think you'll want to be on their bad side—which is exactly what will happen if you harm me." Ozma caught a glint of something gold at his wrist, where his gloved hand gripped the knife, beneath the fading sun. "We're here to reclaim Oz and stop the Wizard's darkness from spreading."

"I'm not sure his darkness *can* be stopped. Why fight a battle you can't win? It's much easier to join the winning side."

Ozma wondered what had made him decide to be a part of this. The money? Was he more than a pirate? A mercenary?

"She's the rightful queen of all of Oz," Jack interrupted, and Ozma glared at him. "You should be bowing down to her."

"Is she now?" Tik-Tok's gaze flicked up and down her body,

as though starved for something—power.

"I am." Ozma lifted her chin, though she was frustrated with Jack for revealing her true identity to an enemy. But perhaps it was better this way, possibly an advantage. "The Wizard is only human, so even if we weren't to kill him, he'd eventually die of old age anyway."

"Is that what you think, darling?" Tik-Tok chuckled deeply, beautifully, viciously. "Not with the slippers. He's immortal now."

Ozma took a deep swallow, because she'd known he wanted to live forever. She'd known Mombi had been making him darker spells. That day he'd shown up at the witch's hut, he'd been wearing the slippers, but she hadn't known they'd been a part of the spell to make him immortal. "Mombi's dead. We killed her, and we'll do the same to him."

"Good. I never liked the bitch." He shrugged. "It's not as though the Wizard needs her now anyway."

Before Ozma could respond, Tik-Tok shoved Jack to the side. Instead of moving toward her, Jack stood frozen. An oddly dull texture—the color of slate gray—seeped up his skin, hardening him to stone. A statue.

"What did you do to him?" Ozma spat, keeping her voice low as not to alert anyone or any*thing*. She ran up to Jack and placed her hands against his rough cheeks, begging his worried expression to move. "Come on, Jack!"

"He's a distraction." Tik-Tok was suddenly behind her, his breath at her ear. "But don't worry, he can hear everything we say, see everything we do. And if you try to harm me, I won't change him back."

Ozma pushed the pirate away, her gaze catching on the gold of his wrist again—his skin was *metal*. "What happened to your arm?"

"It was a gift." He clenched his jaw and tugged his sleeve down. "Now, hand me your satchel."

She slowly removed the strap over her head and tossed the bag at his face.

He caught her satchel before it struck his nose. With a smile, he leaned his back against Jack's statue and motioned a finger at her to come closer. "Join me."

"No." She watched as he undid the clasp to her bag. "So that's your magic? Turning things to stone?" It seemed like a useful power—one she wished she had.

"I can do a lot of things."

"Then why didn't you stop us before?"

"I prefer to watch. But then I was impressed, and it wasn't hard to sniff you two out. I have a wicked sense of smell that's very useful in finding whomever I want." His nostrils flared when he inhaled. "You smell as though you have *no* magic."

Damn it. She couldn't even pretend to have power if she wanted to. "The Wizard is absorbing my magic. For the time being."

As if he wasn't listening, Tik-Tok slipped his hand into her satchel and started flipping through it. He tossed things to the ground, piece-by-piece, like they held no value. Loose papers flew through the air, fruit rolled across the grass. He lifted something up, glinting red, and stared at the heart-shaped stone that Ozma had taken from Mombi's cloak after Jack had killed her.

Tik-Tok arched a dark brow. "This can be part of the trade."

"Why ask? Couldn't you just take it?"

"I could."

"Fine." What did it matter? She didn't know what it was used for anyway. Linked to Mombi for protection? A magical amplifier?

"The Wizard refuses to return an object that belongs to me, hence why I'm open to other deals. I will help *Jack* get what is needed to break into the Wizard's house, then give you something that will allow you to share your lover's magic, but that's all. If the Wizard kills you both, I'll do nothing to save you."

"Why haven't you turned the Wizard to stone?" Perhaps she could find a way to persuade him to do just that.

Tik-Tok tossed the stone up, caught it, and tucked it into his pocket. "Oh, darling, my magic won't work against him. It was part of my trade with Mombi."

"And what was it you traded?"

He rested the back of his head against the stone of Jack and peered up at the sky. "That's rather irrelevant now that she's dead, don't you think?"

Ozma wasn't going to press further—he wasn't going to answer anyway. "What is it you want from me, then? A palace? Money?"

"I didn't know you had either of those things before I approached you, did I?" He pushed off Jack and took a step toward her, arms crossed. "There's a prophecy about a female with silver hair and dark eyes who hasn't been born yet. She'll be able to open portals through the sea. I will take her when I say it's time, and you will allow it. The female wouldn't be of your blood."

"Why would I let you kidnap some poor female?" she scoffed, knowing what it was like to be trapped herself.

"Yes? No? Or we're done here." There was a finality in his tone, and she knew she wouldn't be able to question anything else.

This was tricky. Too tricky. On one hand, Ozma would be sacrificing an innocent's life. On the other, she could potentially save the entirety of Oz by agreeing to this bargain. Images of Reva and Thelia slid into her mind, as did the few other good fae she'd met along the way. To save them all, she would have to agree to the deal. Even though she didn't know what he would do with the female, or with access to the portals.

"I agree." She pursed her lips, not knowing if she truly did the right thing. But it was the right thing to do in that moment. As a queen, she would have to make many more difficult decisions.

Tik-Tok waved his hand in the air, and a scratching sound came from Jack, like rocks rubbing together. The gray stone across his skin faded lighter and lighter until his flesh was pale and soft once more.

Jack stirred, and a choking noise came from his throat. Ozma started for him when Tik-Tok grabbed her by the arm, turning her to face him.

"Now"—he grinned—"it's your turn to rest while I chat with Jack."

Ozma's heart raced as his meaning sunk in. She opened her mouth to protest, finding her body unable to move, and seeing a gray hue spreading across her skin in the periphery of her vision. Everything around her grew heavier and heavier until she was completely still.

CHAPTER TWENTY-TWO

JACK

Jack's body slowly loosened from being a statue, but his mind raced. His heart was beating hard enough to bruise his ribs as his lungs strained to pull in enough oxygen. He'd seen and heard everything, but watching Ozma darken into stone was the worst part. It felt like his future was fading along with her body. He wanted to scream, to cry, to lash out and save her. But there was nothing he could do. His joints were still stuck, his voice still trapped.

Tik-Tok turned toward him and smirked. "Almost there, sunshine."

I'll destroy you, you cocky piece of shit!

Jack's fingers twitched. Then feeling flooded up his arms. The second his shoulders tensed, proving he had full range of motion, he swung a fist. It connected with Tik-Tok's jaw with a *thud*. His head snapped to the side from the impact and Jack rubbed his aching knuckles. "Bring her back." Jack commanded the vines to hold Tik-Tok captive, but they only swirled and moved around close by, none touching him.

Tik-Tok chuckled as he rubbed his face. When he looked back at Jack, he licked a drop of blood from the corner of his lips and smiled. "So much fire in you. I *like* it. Now, put the vines down. I'm protected from that too."

Jack dropped his magic, lunged forward, and fisted Tik-Tok's shirt in his hands. "Son of a bitch! Bring Ozma back!"

"Now, now," he said calmly. "First, my mother *was* in fact a bitch so that isn't exactly an insult. And second, the same rule applies to you as it did to Ozma. Try to hurt me again and she remains an ornament."

Jack instantly released him and stepped back. As much as he wanted to beat the hell out of Tik-Tok, he couldn't do that to Ozma. *And I'm also a lousy fighter.* Another perk of being stuck on a farm his entire life. What had he punched? Pumpkins? They never swung back, and this foe looked like he fought everything that moved.

"Pity." Tik-Tok smoothed his shirt out. "She's quite lovely to look at. I could've tucked her in the corner of the captain's quarters to liven the place up a bit."

Jack bared his teeth.

"Calm your bits. No harm will come to your queen if you behave." His red eyes flashed with humor. "I'm one male and the two of you aren't trustworthy. This is easier. There will be no colluding behind my back or having to choose who to chase down if you run in different directions."

"Easier for you," Jack snarled. As far as he knew, Tik-Tok didn't realize how terrifying it was to become stone. It was as if his whole body had seized up, the air slowly squeezed from his lungs.

He shrugged. "*Meh.* It doesn't matter. Let's get moving."

Jack turned, following the pirate's nonchalant movements. "We can't just *leave* her here like this."

"Why not? It's not as if the fiends can eat her like that." He didn't even bother glancing over his shoulder as he spoke. "Don't fall behind."

Jack stared helplessly at Ozma, her face frozen in shock. He wanted to wipe the fear away with a kiss as he always did, but there would be no changing her expression until she was no longer stone.

"Chop, chop!" came Tik-Tok's voice from farther away.

"I love you," he told the statue, cupping her cool stone cheeks. "I'll be back as soon as I can. I swear." Then he raced after the bastard.

Jack felt the distance between himself and Ozma grow as he caught up to the other male. It was a tangible weight, pulling him back. Leaving her out in the open with so many monsters prowling felt wrong. Just because they hadn't followed them all the way to the Wizard, that didn't mean they wouldn't eventually wander that way.

She's stone, he reminded himself. The asshole was right—they wouldn't want to eat her. *Couldn't.* But what if something else happened? An animal or one of those addicts could accidentally knock her over. What if she broke? *Would* she break? He'd felt pretty solid when he was frozen…

It was getting darker by the minute. For all he knew, there were other dangerous fae lurking about. If he and Tik-Tok were attacked and something happened to either of them, what would become of Ozma?

"I give you my word that no harm will come to Ozma," Tik-Tok said in a sincere tone. Jack hadn't known he was capable of speaking that way. Then the fae clapped his hands together and smirked. "Now. Focus."

Focus. I'll focus … on how to kill you the second Ozma is back.

"You said the Wizard has something of yours," Jack said, recalling Tik-Tok's conversation with Ozma.

"Not for much longer. That's what you're for."

"What is it?" Jack asked with a scowl.

"An enchanted object."

He leveled a stare at the back of Tik-Tok's head. "You don't say."

"I'd prefer to say *nothing* until we get there," he replied casually, but the implication was clear. *Shut the fuck up.*

Jack balled his hands into fists. He would listen, not because he was afraid of the fae, but because Ozma's life depended on it. If he were being honest, Tik-Tok's plan was smart. Put one of them in danger to guarantee the other behaves. *Fucking asshole.* He bit his tongue and trudged farther into the woods.

Orkland wasn't a huge island judging by the maps he'd seen, but that was in comparison to all of Oz. It could take days to cross it for all Jack knew. It had taken one just to find the Wizard, but there was no telling how far from the other coasts they were.

The longer they walked, the worse the forest became. The skeletal trees with dripping fruit slowly lessened. In their place stood rotting stumps covered in black sludge. Each stump was hollow except for more stagnant goop, and the bark that was left clinging to the outside protruded in jagged strips. Tiny flies floated, dead, on the surface.

The ground was soggy beneath Jack's boots, and he'd never been so glad of his worn footwear. With the sun nearly gone, Tik-Tok hurried his pace, causing the thick liquid to splash up onto their pant legs.

In front of him, Tik-Tok kicked something from his path. A skull skidded across the ground in front of Jack, cracked and covered in muck, with pointed teeth.

Fucking hell.

There would be no getting this stench out—especially if it was partially made of dead bodies. He would have to burn his clothes after this. Perhaps it was better that he wouldn't be able to see much going forward. He could pretend the ground was made of fertilizer after a heavy rain and the smell was simply rotting pumpkins. Nothing new there.

"Your power is rather handy," Tik-Tok said conversationally, breaking the silence that had lasted uncomfortably long. He slowed to walk beside Jack instead of in front of him. "Can you do anything else?"

Jack shrugged. He wasn't aware fae regularly had multiple abilities, but if they did, he wanted to find out what else he was capable of. *Later.*

"Hmm." Tik-Tok's eyes practically glowed with the last rays of sunlight. "It's a new power for you—that's why you exhausted it so quickly—so maybe you'll come into more later. You're young yet."

"Not that young," Jack grumbled.

"No? A decade past maturity, I'd guess."

Accurate, you kelpie scum. "It's really none of your business."

"I'm approaching my first century now. By the time I was your age, I had at least three abilities. My first was feeling weather before it happened—quite useful on the sea. Then I—"

"What happened to not talking?" Jack snapped. He *was* curious about what else this asshole fae could do, but he was more concerned with finishing their quest without attracting any of the rotting creatures.

"You piqued my curiosity, but fine. That's our destination." He pointed to the lone silhouette of a tree.

It was free of both fruit and leaves, its branches reaching skyward in perfectly straight angles. As they approached, Tik-Tok took an orb from the pouch at his waist. It lit up in his palm, casting them and the immediate area in a soft white glow. The orb highlighted the razor-sharp edges of the branches and the rough, gritty texture of the bark. The tree was variegated brown and white instead of solid black like the ones on the rest of the island.

"Okay," Jack said slowly.

Tik-Tok motioned to a round knot jutting from the middle of the trunk. "Use your magic to open this and take the object inside."

Jack crossed his arms. Telling him how low his powers were seemed like a fucking horrible idea. The pirate had implied that he knew Jack was running low, but not *this* low. He wouldn't be able to defend himself for long if anything went wrong, but why give him the advantage of *knowing* that? "Why can't you do it? Hack at it with an axe or something."

"Hack at it with an axe," he repeated mockingly. "As if I haven't spent years trying to crack it open? Oz spelled it against me and my crew specifically to ensure my loyalty."

"Why does it feel like it's better to leave this thing where it is?" *Because it probably is.*

"It's mine," Tik-Tok said through a false smile. "And I want it back."

Jack hesitated. The enemy of his enemy wasn't his friend … but they could be temporary allies. Whether he was lying about the object or not wasn't important. They needed to kill Oz, then get the hell off this island. Not that he had much choice in helping if he wanted Ozma safe.

"And the thing inside will get us into Oz's house?" Jack asked.

"It will," he replied with a stiff nod.

Jack licked his lips. There should be enough magic for the task, but he wasn't sure how much would be left to fight the Wizard afterward. Especially if he had to share it with Ozma—however that worked. But no one would be fighting Oz if they couldn't *get* to him. Jack sighed and lifted his arm.

Open.

The knot struggled to obey. Maybe he needed to be more specific. Instead of using words, he imagined the knot peeling back. The edges unfurling. The center flaking away. And, this time, the tree listened. Inside, a glint of gold sparkled with the light Tik-Tok held.

"Take it," he urged.

Jack stepped closer and carefully plucked the octagonal piece from its hiding place. It was large enough to fill his palm, no thicker than the shell of a regular-sized pumpkin, and surprisingly light.

Tik-Tok held out his free hand. "Give it to me."

Jack turned it over to the other male and watched him carefully for a reaction. The pirate clutched the object tightly with his gloved hands, held it to his lips, and whispered inaudibly. Jack only knew he spoke because his lips moved. And then the object popped open.

Tik-Tok grinned wildly. "It still works."

Jack leaned forward and caught a glimpse of the needle spinning around inside. The face was marked with North, South, East, and West, with tiny scores around the outer edge. "A compass? How will that get us into Oz's house?"

"This isn't just any compass," he said in awe. "It's *my* compass."

Jack lifted a brow. "And that means…?"

Tik-Tok shot him an irritated look. "Never mind. Let's get back to your precious Ozma and I'll keep my word to get you in to see the Wizard."

"Wonderful," Jack said flatly. His muscles ached and his body felt void of any magic. Completely tapped of energy in general. When had they last gotten a decent night's rest? When had they eaten? It felt like a lifetime ago. But there was no way he was going to delay the return trip.

Not when Ozma was in torment inside her stone body.

CHAPTER TWENTY-THREE

OZMA

The dark night wrapped around Ozma's stone flesh, and the stars shone through slits in the trees, allowing her to see straight ahead. It was strange, not being able to move, yet somehow still feeling the wind blowing against her. In the dark place, Reva had spoken of gnomes made entirely out of rock—was this what they felt? Their nerves still coming alive beneath hardened flesh?

Time passed and passed as she worried about Jack, wondering if Tik-Tok would betray him. Even though the pirate seemed like a selfish prick, she prayed he wouldn't harm Jack.

Finally, as night bugs swarmed past her, the sound of footsteps and leaves crunching echoed, interrupting her thoughts as they drew closer. If she could hold her breath any more than her stone lungs were already doing, Ozma would have done so. She hoped it wasn't fae or humans from the swarm. She relaxed when a flash of orange hair appeared in the silver of the moonlight, followed by Tik-Tok's dark mane.

The pirate stroked the sword at his hip and sauntered toward Ozma. "Wake up, darling." He flicked his hand in the air, and a sizzling noise sounded in her head as her skin became lighter, freer. Her body jerked forward, feet stumbling, until Jack's hands wrapped around her waist, catching her.

"Are you all right?" he whispered, his hazel gaze holding hers.

"I'm fine," she choked out, her voice raspy. Ozma's throat felt scratchy as she took a deep swallow, then another.

A twig snapped behind her. Ozma withdrew her dagger and whirled around.

Tik-Tok lifted a brow and bit into one of the fruits he'd tossed from her satchel earlier. "Sorry, did you want this back?" he asked, slowly chewing with a smirk.

Ozma released a frustrated sigh and focused on Jack. "Did he retrieve what we needed to get inside?" She didn't know what exactly it was the pirate had gone to find. He could have been lying when he'd said that the object would allow them access to see the Wizard.

Jack ran a hand through his hair, his eyes sliding to Tik-Tok. "So he says."

"I'm wounded you still don't trust me." Tik-Tok took another bite of the fruit, then fished out something golden from his pocket. "It will work." She only caught a glimpse of its octagonal shape before he pressed it back into his pants.

Jack ignored Tik-Tok and knelt on the ground. He plucked up the last couple pieces of their fruit, then tossed her a plum. "We'll need some strength before we try to go in."

Ozma sank her teeth into the sweet fruit and peered up at the full moon mounted in the sky, the constellations of stars clustered together, and the small wings of night creatures pumping across the treetops. "Should we wait until morning?" she asked, not knowing if the time of day would really make a difference.

"The fiends can find you more easily at night," Tik-Tok started. "Their sight works better in the dark, so I say move now. Kill Oz when he's least expecting it."

The Wizard would most likely be asleep, and perhaps there were a way she could catch him easily, then cut his throat. But if he wasn't asleep… "What about sharing magic with Jack? How are you going to make that happen?" Ozma needed something more than a dagger and a few spells that wouldn't even work against the Wizard.

Tik-Tok grinned secretively, and tugged off his glove, revealing a hand made entirely of gold. The color was an exact match to the object he'd flashed her a moment ago. His hand appeared to be a real appendage, and as he flexed his fingers, she noticed it even moved like one. The only differences aside from the coloring were the tiny screws in areas where the joints bent, and the overlapping folds that could be seen when he shifted his digits and wrist. She couldn't see how far the metal stretched up, and if it was his entire arm—or only to the elbow.

Thin silver rings with jewels of different hues decorated all of his fingers, except for one in the middle that was entirely of silver. "I don't give anything away lightly. Or at all." He removed the silver ring from his middle finger and held it up in front of her face. It shone brightly as if flecked with glitter. "I'll want it back when I collect the female."

Ozma reached to grab it, but he delicately moved her hand away. "No." He bit his lower lip. "Give me your hand. It has to be transferred with freewill."

"Hold on—" Jack interrupted, anger lacing his words as he stepped in front of Ozma. "What kind of sick game are you playing? You aren't going to place that damn thing on her finger, then say she's your wife."

"If I didn't already have plans for another, she would do well," Tik-Tok purred. "But your queen is safe from such things."

Jack's hands clenched at his sides and Ozma pulled him back beside her. As she took a deep swallow, her stomach sank at the thought of the unknown fae belonging to this male in the future. Straightening her spine and lifting her chin, she placed her hand into his anyway. His cool metal fingertips gently held her as he slid the silver circle onto her middle digit. The ring was loose at first, but it tightened around her finger, the color changing from silver to gold, by some sort of magic.

She went to twist it to the side, to examine, but the ring

wouldn't budge. Ozma's eyes widened, her heart accelerating as her gaze darted from Jack to Tik-Tok. "What did you do?" Her voice shot up an octave.

"It will stay on. Even years from now, the ring will remain there, until our agreement is complete. But it will also allow you to share another's magic as long as they are without a protection spell. Just study whom you want to borrow from while whispering, 'divide one's magic and make it as though mine,' to ignite it."

Ozma whispered the words, while staring at Jack, and something stirred within her. *Magic.* It didn't feel attached to her, though. The power seemed to be floating, and perhaps this would make it so the Wizard couldn't absorb that from her too. Lifting her arm, she studied a vine above and twisted her hand. She squinted and focused on it to move until the vine slowly slithered forward, its pointed end curling.

"Where did you get this from?" Ozma asked, releasing the vine, pushing it back into its original place. She wanted to use more of the power, test it, but would hold off until inside Oz's home.

"One of the sea witches gave me the ring as a gift to assist with the prophecy. I did have to fuck her to keep it, but she's a good female. Like you." Tik-Tok reached for a lock of her hair and Jack slapped his hand away.

"Stop trying to touch her," Jack seethed, narrowing his eyes.

"Perhaps"—Tik-Tok's smirk grew wicked with delight—"two females in the future might suit me better than one. What do you think, darling?" His fiery, red gaze lit with playfulness. He didn't even glance at Jack.

"Quit toying with Jack when we've already made a deal," Ozma said.

"That wasn't necessarily a *never.* But don't worry, Jack. You did a good deed for me, so I'll leave you your queen." Tik-Tok chuckled and motioned them forward. "Come on then. I'll help you get past the Wizard's barrier."

"Why don't you just give us the compass," Jack grunted as he walked beside Ozma through the forest.

"How about … I give you nothing?" Tik-Tok peered over his shoulder with a smirk, sliding his glove back on and flexing his fingers. Ozma wondered what it would be like to have a metal arm, one that still moved just the same. Could he feel with it?

Loud chirping noises echoed as the trio traveled further, the moonlight guiding their way down twisting paths. The area was bright enough to see their shadows reflecting across the moistened dirt and grass, along with the outlines of trees and shriveled branches. As they drew closer, she could see a flickering of green flashing into the sky, emanating from the Wizard's home.

In the distance, growls and rustling stirred, but they weren't near enough for Ozma to be worried, although her heart still pounded ferociously. She also knew Jack was running low on magic, so she hoped whatever creatures were out there stayed where they were.

As they approached the Wizard's house, the emerald light glistened even more in the darkness, like a beacon. The swarm didn't sound any nearer, their noises remaining in the distance.

As they came to the edge of the barrier, Ozma halted, but Tik-Tok pressed his metal arm forward, and the barrier didn't stop him. His fingers brushed a wooden pole and pushed something. A hidden button? Around the Wizard's sanctuary, the barrier flickered once, twice, then vanished, as if it had never been there at all.

"It helps to have a metal arm," he cooed.

"So I suppose you didn't really need the compass to get us in here," Jack grunted.

A shuffling came from the back of the house, then a figure rounded it, slipping into view. Before Ozma could draw magic from Jack, a dagger sailed past her from behind and planted itself into the guard's head. His knees buckled, and his body folded to the ground with a thud.

"Looky there, you don't have to worry about the guard now," Tik-Tok said.

Ozma frowned but took a step forward at the same time Jack did. She'd thought that maybe an invisible barrier would still be there, yet they passed through unharmed. With a glance over her shoulder, she noticed Tik-Tok hadn't moved.

Tik-Tok reached into his pocket and tugged out his object. While cradling it, he brought it to his mouth and whispered something in another language. The object shifted, as though alive, unfolding until she recognized it as a compass. The dial in the center glowed a pale gold as it started spinning around and around.

"Are you coming?" she whispered.

"No." He shook his head. "I'm headed for my ship. My crew will leave a rowboat on shore for you. If you're still alive, use it by dawn to get back on board. Otherwise, we'll retrieve the boat and you'll be trapped, as I won't be coming back." With those words, he turned around, striding straight toward the sounds of the horde in the distance, leaving Ozma and Jack alone once more.

This time, to face the Wizard.

CHAPTER TWENTY-FOUR

JACK

Before Jack knew it, Tik-Tok had strutted out of sight. A portion of Jack's power had transferred to Ozma, leaving him feeling slightly weakened, and they were alone inside the barrier with a dead guard. Unless Oz counted—in which case, it was hopefully only him, Ozma, and a soon-to-be-dead immortal. *Fucking insanity.* Were they really doing this? The most dangerous thing he'd fought before Ozma returned from the dark place were stubborn weeds. Now they were about to face *the most dangerous being in Oz.* Stealing Ozma's power had made the Wizard that way, but unless they could revert the magic to her, there was little hope of winning.

"Ozma," he said, his voice shaking slightly.

She looked up at him with her large blue eyes, and he saw his own fear reflected there. "We'll be all right. We just have to get the slippers and everything else will work out."

That seemed overly simplistic, but there was no turning back now. "I suppose, we're off to kill the Wizard, then," he said with forced lightness.

Ozma nodded and, together, they crept closer to the house. The outer walls were made of black wood, assumably from the surrounding trees, but the rounded door and shutters were painted emerald green. Only faint candlelight burned through the windows and no smoke billowed from the chimney, despite the growing chill in the air.

Every step Jack took beside Ozma felt like it would be his last. A trap would spring, or an alarm would go off, and then it would all be over. So, when they made it up to the house without incident, it was almost too good to be true.

Ozma stretched up onto her toes and peered into the window. Jack's scant meal from earlier threatened to reappear. *Don't see us,* he prayed as he joined her at the glass. *Please don't fucking see us.*

Inside, light filtered into a living room from the hallway. A rug was rolled up beside an unlit fireplace and most of the furniture was covered with white sheets. An overstuffed brown couch and a dark, low table were the only things exposed. Papers were scattered across the table beside a glass half-full of amber liquid.

A small vine had managed to flatten completely and work its way into a narrow crack under the windowsill, with the help of Jack's power via Ozma. He'd barely felt the small trickle of magic pass to her. The vine unwrapped itself from the latch now that it was open, and slithered back to the flowerbox.

"It's unlocked now," Ozma said with a proud smirk. She placed her palms on the window and slid it upward. To Jack's surprise, it didn't stick or creak.

"We can't just crawl in through the window," he hissed.

Ozma shot him a perplexed look. "Why not? It's not like we haven't done it a thousand times before."

A smile tugged at Jack's lips but didn't fully form. It was true—they'd both snuck out of the window in Jack's cabin more times than he could remember—but the consequences were very different. Mombi would beat them for disobedience or possibly make them go hungry for a day or two, but the Wizard would kill them. At least, he would kill Jack.

Jack took Ozma's face in his hands and pressed a desperate, wild kiss to her lips. He drank her in as if she were the last breath of a dying male, which was possibly true. She returned the kiss with equal vigor, but broke away too soon, panting.

"We'll finish *that* later," she promised. Then, without waiting for him to agree to her plan, she slipped easily through the open window. Jack scrambled in behind her less gracefully but just as silent.

Over the pounding of his own heart, a cheerful hum carried through the room. It was slightly muffled by the walls but became clearer the closer it came. He quickly darted behind a covered settee with Ozma right beside him. They hid not a moment too soon as the chandelier flashed magically above the center of the room. Two flashes later and the candles remained lit, casting the room in ghostly white light.

Now what? he mouthed.

Ozma held a finger to her lips and peered between a gap in the furniture as someone walked into the room. A gasp left her lips a moment later and she slapped a hand over her mouth at the tiny sound. *That's a fucking great sign.* What had she seen, *exactly*? He wasn't in a position to look without being caught and he couldn't very well ask her.

The humming hit a crescendo before ending abruptly in favor of a soft *thump* followed by a loud yawn. "Right, right, right," the Wizard mumbled to himself. His voice sounded different than Jack remembered. Less raspy. *Was* it the Wizard? Or perhaps another guard?

"Where was I?" he continued with a shuffle of papers.

Ozma tapped Jack's knee and, when he looked at her, she motioned beneath the settee. There was a decent sized gap between the cloth and the floorboards. Jack eased himself down to his hands and knees and peered beneath.

In front of the brown couch were two feet.

And on those feet, the silver slippers.

The material sparkled with every small movement the Wizard made. They hugged his feet tightly, showcasing large bunions that stretched the sides outward, and the flat soles tapped on the bare floor with a soft *tick, tick, tick*. It *had* to be him if he wore the slippers—there was no chance he would allow anyone else to put them on. Ozma nudged Jack's knee again and made a cutting motion with two fingers.

She … wanted to cut the slippers from the Wizard? Even if it were possible to cut the shoes, it would ruin them. She needed their magic to get her power back—and her wings.

Seeming to sense his confusion, Ozma made the cutting motion again, this time against his ankle. Was she serious? Cut his *feet* off? Why not simply kill him and take the shoes from his corpse? It seemed safer. Though, he supposed, in order to kill Oz, they needed to strip him of his power first. Which meant slippers first, death second.

Just fucking great.

Ozma nudged him gently with her elbow.

Jack pointed to his chest, silently asking *me?*

Magic, she mouthed.

His mind raced over what he could possibly do with his magic to *cut someone's feet off.* Even if any plants were inside, it would take far too long to squeeze through flesh and bone with a vine. Surely someone as powerful as Oz would have a way to stop them if given even a moment's chance. Killing him first was really the better option.

Jack held Ozma's stare and slid a finger across his throat. Not that he cared if they slit his throat, set him on fire, or poured poison down his throat. The bastard just needed to die.

Ozma bit her lip and nodded. After a moment's hesitation, his magic tugged in his veins as she drew out part of his power. Her eyes narrowed in concentration and a drop of sweat rolled down her temple. Whatever she was doing, it was big. Jack could feel the life of the plants outside swell within him.

"I know you're there," the Wizard said suddenly.

Ozma's concentration faltered and Jack's heart tripped over itself.

"If you're going to sneak in, you might want to close the window next time."

Fuck. Fuck fuck fuck fuck fuck.

Oz heaved an agitated sigh. "Your foolishness is growing old, Tik-Tok. The compass is yours once the Land of Oz is secured as mine."

He thinks we're Tik-Tok. Relief flooded over Jack in waves, but, as each wave receded, terror screamed through him again. They weren't Tik-Tok, but they were still caught. If they didn't make their move *now*, it would be too late.

Jack squeezed Ozma's hand, her palm slick against his. She returned the motion, then slipped free of his grasp.

And stood.

"Sorry to disappoint you," she said in a level voice. If Jack didn't know her so well, he wouldn't have noticed the small tremor. "The pirate ran back to his ship."

"Ozma," the Wizard growled. "How the hell did you get here?"

She flicked her hand at Jack behind the settee as if telling him to hurry, then she stepped away. Closer to Oz. "It's a long story, though you may find it interesting."

Jack crawled to where Ozma had previously sat and looked through the same crack she had. It was indeed the Wizard of Oz. Only, it wasn't.

The man Jack had seen picking up Mombi's spells at the farm had white hair, age spots, and rotting teeth. Plus, the gleam in his eyes had looked absolutely insane. But this … this human was in his early twenties at most. Carefully coiffed dark hair set off his pale, porcelain skin and perfect white teeth. His full lips had dropped in shock—and maybe a little in awe of Ozma's return—though his blazing green eyes showed only fury.

"In the dark place"—Ozma began—"I met Reva. The Wicked Witch of the West, as you likely remember her, though she wasn't wicked at all. Or maybe she was. She *did* teach me all sorts of ways to kill."

She's distracting him. Jack swallowed hard at the realization and scrambled to come up with a plan. Slippers… He needed the slippers. *Think, Jack!*

"That bitch survived eight years on her own?" Oz said with

a surprised laugh.

"And two with me."

The Wizard leaned into the settee, resting his arms on the back as if Ozma's presence wasn't a threat. "What a triumphant return you've made," he said in a flat voice.

"Our return is credited to Dorothy Gale—or Thelia, as her parents named her."

The Wizard's face drained of what little color it had.

"But, regardless of the method, I wouldn't exactly call our return triumphant." Ozma licked her lips and stalked a bit closer. "Not yet, anyway."

Jack wanted to leap out and pull Ozma away from him. She was too close. The Wizard could lunge at her, throw a potion … anything, really. His magic throbbed as Ozma tapped into it again. A message to hurry. He wished there were more of his magic to spare…

Fuck it.

Immobilize the ass, then worry about the slippers.

With a single blast of power, Jack plucked the thorn off every un-pruned rosebush outside and sent them sailing through the window. Once in the room, he forced more magic at them, doubling each thorn's size. Tripling them. They instinctively flew around Ozma, aiming straight for the Wizard's chest.

"What the fuck is this?" the Wizard shouted.

Oz was on his feet, his hands thrown outward toward the incoming thorns. Ozma ripped into Jack's magic supply, painfully gouging out almost every ounce he had left, and the floor buckled beneath them.

A black, jagged tree burst upward and didn't stop until it broke through the ceiling. Branches speared outward at nearly every angle. One sliced through Jack's thigh and he let out a strangled cry. If it weren't for the Wizard's own scream, it would've given him away. He grimaced through the pain and looked up to find a large branch had struck through Oz's left shoulder. It pinned him to the far wall like an insect.

"This isn't your magic," Oz shouted between painful gasps.

"Where's the slave hiding?"

Ah. So he was exposed either way.

Jack struggled to his feet, blood flowing freely from the wide gash in his leg. "I'm no slave, *mortal.*"

"Young love." Oz smiled a wicked smile. A smile that promised something. "Once a slave, always a slave, eh? Though your master is admittedly better looking this time."

Ozma quickly drew the dagger from her belt and gripped the handle so hard her knuckles turned white. Who was Jack to stop her if she wanted to hack away at the Wizard's feet before Oz was dead? It wasn't like Oz didn't deserve it. In the scheme of things, he was getting off easy. Still, his gut churned. This was *too* easy…

Oz slapped his open palm to the wall behind him and green light exploded through the room.

CHAPTER TWENTY-FIVE

OZMA

Ozma screamed and dropped to her knees as the green illumination around her grew brighter and brighter. Sharp pain lanced her right eye, and her vision went black on that side. Her wailing ended as she lifted her hand and felt warm blood leaking down her cheek. Fingers shaking, she brushed against a hard object planted in her eye. With quick motions, Ozma ripped it out and released a cry. The room spun, her head dizzy, and she heaved.

Her gaze settled on one of the thorns that Jack had sent riveting into the Wizard's home. Somehow, when the Wizard threw his green light back, it must have sent some of the thorns soaring again, piercing her eye.

The emerald light remained bright, flickering across the room, against the large tree that had exploded in the room with Jack's power. Her uninjured eye could only squint in the intense brightness.

Ozma dropped the thorn and felt around the hard flooring to get to Jack. She crawled forward, widening her good eye as the light around her dimmed a fraction. Two hands wrapped around Ozma's neck, lifting her by the throat, then shoved her against a wall. The room cleared of green and the stark white light returned. She met the cold emerald eyes of the Wizard. There wasn't a single wrinkle or blackened tooth on him. The shock of discovering him this way—so different—still hadn't worn off. No longer withering, but young and full of life. Like he must have been when he'd first come to the Land of Oz. This had to be the reason Mombi had appeared frailer than ever—she was using more and more dark magic to restore his youth, while the shoes and Ozma's power had been making him immortal. Even the wound where Jack had struck him with the tree appeared to be healing.

"Ozma, you beautiful thing," Oz said pleasantly, his body firmly against hers. "Aren't you wondering why I haven't sent you back to the black pit yet? Did you really think I didn't know you were attempting to distract me earlier? I knew exactly what you were doing."

She had wondered it, but she wasn't going to start asking. Instead, she whispered a spell that would make Oz obey her, but all he did was cluck his tongue at her. Tik-Tok hadn't been lying about that—the Wizard *was* protected from spells. She moved to shove her dagger forward and he easily confiscated it, sliding it into the belt at his waist.

Oz tsked. "That wasn't very nice."

She would have to wait for the right time to get it back. "Where's Jack?" Ozma searched past Oz, around the room and the tree, the couch, the window, but she couldn't spot him anywhere. Why wasn't Jack taking the opportunity to attack the Wizard? Unless the thorns had done something worse to him, taken more than his eye. Her heart struck her rib cage and her stomach dropped at the thought.

"Your precious slave will make the perfect guest at our wedding." Oz's smile grew wide, his white teeth glistening from the chandelier's candlelight. "I just need to wait for Mombi to return so we can cast the spell to give her your body. The slippers' magic wouldn't have let you die from the dangers in that darkness."

Ozma's eyes widened in horror. "*What?*" Gritting her teeth, she tried to dip into Jack's magic, needing to find the power to draw forth a tree branch or vine, *anything*. But nothing stirred within her.

"You arrived sooner than expected." He pressed his nose to her hair and inhaled. "Mombi was supposed to get the remainder of her potions, summon you back to Oz herself, and bring you here."

"Mombi's dead." Ozma tried to wiggle out from his grasp, but he was pressed too tightly against her.

Oz's brows lifted, and his lips formed an O of surprise. "A pity we can't use your body for her now." He shrugged, staring hard at her. "But there's always another option, isn't there? You're still here." With motions too quick for a mortal, Oz spun her the other direction and squeezed his hands around her wrists behind her back, then walked her forward. "Let's get you dressed now."

"No," she shouted, kicking back at him.

Oz's other hand came to her throat, his fingers digging in at the sensitive area right under her jaw. He twisted her head to the side so her stare fell to a lump on the floor. A body of gnarled twigs with thin fingers and toes, and a pumpkin for a head. An emerald green leaf rested near the stem at the top of the pumpkin. As Ozma recognized the clothes the horrible creation wore, tears of anger burned down her cheeks. *Jack.*

"Fix him!" she screamed, wanting to claw at the Wizard, but his hold was too solid.

"I don't think so," he spat, tightening his grip even more as he pushed her forward into an open bedroom.

Spell books and jars filled with body parts were neatly placed on wooden shelves against the walls. It smelled of Mombi—her room. Two wooden wardrobes stood beside a bed on the opposite side of the room. A white gown lay sprawled over the mattress with hideous yellow jewels stitched into the bodice. Beside it rested a crown, sapphire and emerald jewels embedded in the gold.

An awful thought slammed into her. Mombi had been

planning to use Ozma's body to reclaim the throne and ensure no one could take it from Oz in the future. Ozma knew Mombi hadn't been in love with Oz—she'd wanted power, most likely believed it was owed to her for all the help she'd given.

The Wizard thrust Ozma onto the mattress, taking her by surprise, and she flipped over to face him.

"Unless you want me to set fire to the slave, get dressed," Oz snapped, inching closer, the silver slippers alight with magic.

Ozma's heart thrummed frantically in her chest as she thought about the closeness of the Wizard, and about what had happened to Jack. "Why have me marry you? I won't obey you or help you rule Oz."

"Dear girl, is that what you think I'm still doing?" The Wizard released a loud chuckle, echoing maddeningly off the walls around her, his handsome face training on her with an ugly expression. "You're going to fuck me willingly so I can absorb your magic permanently. Then I'll free your slave."

Oz leaned forward and swiped a long finger slowly down her cheek, making her shudder. His digit came away coated with crimson from her wound, then he tenderly licked the blood clean from his fingertip. "Even with one eye, you'll make a pretty fuck, and I'm sure you'll taste as good as your magic."

Ozma held back another shiver. She wasn't going to put on that dress and let him press his cock inside her. Even if she did as he asked, Ozma knew he would never change Jack back. No matter how much she loved Jack, she couldn't do as Oz wanted. If the Wizard took whatever power she still had, he would use it to destroy everyone, including her and Jack.

Oz was protected from spells, but it was obvious by his shoulder wound that he could still be harmed.

"You promise to return Jack to his fae form?" Ozma whispered.

"I will." He grinned savagely. "The last time I had a good fuck was Langwidere, and you'll need to make it better than that."

Closing her eyes, Ozma took a deep swallow. "Fine." She

grabbed him by his collar and drew him close.

The Wizard was immortal now, appeared youthful, but no spell would take away the lingering scent of decay. Holding her breath, she pressed her lips to his and pulled him down on top of her. A low growl escaped his throat as he kissed her back, his lips devouring her. His lower body rocked into hers, and she could feel the swell of his length. With each movement of his mouth and each rolling of his hips, she yearned to murder him more, tear his body into pieces.

"Your sole purpose in this world was to belong to me. Your power was always meant to be mine," he cooed in her ear, then crashed his lips onto hers again, tasting, licking, probing. Repulsion washed over her as he lowered his hands between them to unbuckle his belt, and she fought the desire to rip off his cock.

This was the moment. She reached for the dagger at his hip and quickly drew it out. His eyes bulged, but he wasn't fast enough as she slashed a smile, reflecting her own, across his throat. A burst of magic knocked her back, holding her to the bed, as Oz choked on his own blood. She pushed through the power as Oz's magic seemed to weaken.

Ozma sat up, grabbed her dagger again, and lunged for the Wizard, knocking him to the floor. Bringing the weapon up, she plunged it into his throat.

He struggled for a few more moments, then his movements stopped, his breathing ceased, and any life that was in his eyes was now gone.

The Wizard might have been one of the most powerful individuals in Oz but that was only because of others. And behind all that glamour, he was still just a human male, thinking with his cock first.

Ozma's gaze settled at the slippers on his feet and she hurried to tear them away, but they wouldn't budge. She peered around Mombi's room for something she could use, but the witch had never kept weapons before. She didn't appear to now, either. If Ozma could only use the dagger to saw through Oz's bones, she would have, but the blade wasn't large or sharp enough.

Not wanting to take her eyes off the Wizard's body longer than she had to, she barreled out of the room and into the one beside it.

This room was messy, with notebooks and maps thrown everywhere. Rumpled blankets were clumped on a bed against the wall. Beside it was a nightstand with two emerald-jeweled swords resting against it. Buckets and buckets of faerie fruit, unlike the shriveled ones of Orkland's trees, were stored in a corner. Ozma ignored the sharper smell of decay, in what must have been the Wizard's room, as she snatched one of the weapons and darted back to where his body lay.

Oz was just the same—he hadn't roused back to life. Rapid healing wouldn't have helped with a fatal blow, but with Mombi's dark spells, she hadn't been sure.

Lifting the blade high, she swung it down across both ankles, severing them from the bastard.

A blast of something rocketed through Ozma, and she inhaled sharply. It was what rightfully belonged to her, what she'd only truly felt once. *Her* magic.

It spun and it spun within her, connecting to each nerve in her body, attaching to every inch of her. But, unlike before, feathery wings didn't emerge from her back.

Ozma dropped to her knees and picked up one of the Wizard's feet, removing the first blood-speckled slipper, and rushing to place it on her bare foot. It tightened around her flesh, then the dull silver lit up, like it had on Oz, and a pulse of magic stormed through her. Releasing the bloody foot, she grabbed the other one and ripped off the second slipper. She didn't care about cleaning the crimson right now—she slipped the shoe on, and it illuminated with bright flecks of silver.

Brushing off her dress, Ozma stood and turned to go to Jack but stopped when another blast of power ignited within her. A hard jab came at her back, then another, and another, as though something were pounding at a door behind her skin. As she reached to touch the throbbing scar, two pale blue wings shot through her flesh, ripping the back of her dress. The feathered wings folded around her as though hugging her.

Tears sprung from her eyes, because this was the part of herself she'd mourned the most. With a sigh, she smiled and drew them back into her body before sprinting out of the room toward Jack.

Nothing had changed with him since the Wizard's death. His head was still a pumpkin, his appendages thin sticks that could easily be snapped and broken for good. It had been Oz's power that had made him this way. But that wasn't right—it was *her* magic the Wizard had used. She should be able to change him back with that same power. *Please.* Cradling the outer shell of his head, Ozma murmured to him, "Jackseith Arel Diosyll, return to me."

Glittering blue smoke swarmed around her, spinning in a circle. Jack's body fidgeted, his stick hand squeezing hers. A muffled cry came from somewhere within the faceless pumpkin—Jack struggling to somehow speak.

Ozma's hands shook with fear, but then she realized what she'd done wrong. "Return to your fae form." Magic spilled out of her, wrapping around Jack like a blanket. The bluish color became a cloud of orange smoke.

The smoke vanished as though it had never been there at all, revealing hair the color of a morning sunrise, freckles across tan cheeks, pointed ears—*Jack.* Sweat glistened on his forehead as his lids snapped open.

"You're okay," she whispered, pressing a hand to his cheek. "Jackseith Arel Diosyll, I release you."

"I rather preferred being a stone statue," he rasped, slowly sitting up. Then his eyes widened as he focused on her. "Your eye!"

"It is what it is." Ozma softly kissed his lips, then pressed her forehead to his. "The Wizard's dead, and my magic and wings are back."

He wrapped his hands around her and hauled her into his lap. "I'm taking the bastard's head and feeding it to the wild fae in the forest. There's no way he'll ever come back from that."

CHAPTER TWENTY-SIX

JACK

Outside the Wizard's house, Jack took a moment to pat his hip to be sure his knife was still there. To return to the ship and get the hell out of Orkland, they would have to venture back through the swarm of rotting fae and humans. It wouldn't be possible to outrun them this time. Not when his leg was sliced open and they would be heading straight into the horde, which was why he clutched the Wizard's severed head in one hand. A distraction. A … snack. Still, they should've loaded themselves up with weapons inside. Magic was all well and good, but so was a blade.

Jack turned to tell Ozma as much and froze. She stood calmly in front of the open door with blue sparks flying from her hand. Large rips ran down the back of her dress, the frayed edges moving with a force that seemed to be coming from her body. Locks of her hair lifted and fell gently as the sparks became light that swept over her. A true *queen*.

"Ozma?" he asked in a dazed whisper. Was this supposed to be happening? She had the slippers so she would have her magic, but was this right? It looked … ethereal.

Then, her light exploded outward. Jack flung his arm up against the brightness of it, squinting. A loud crack vibrated the ground as white-blue flames engulfed the Wizard's house.

I guess we're not getting a shit ton of weapons then…

Ozma turned toward him with a satisfied glint in her eye. The other was hidden behind a strip of fabric they had ripped from the furniture coverings. Blood was already seeping through, the sight of it tearing at his heart. She hadn't complained, but it had to hurt like a bitch. And, more than that, Jack hated that Ozma seemed to lose something every time she regained what was rightfully hers. To regain her true body, she'd lost two years of her life to darkness. To regain her magic and her realm, an eye.

"Just in case," she said, peering at Oz's burning home.

Jack simply stared at her. The beauty of Ozma stole his ability to think. To speak. She was extraordinary… And too good for him. She had chosen him, though, and he wasn't stupid enough to let his lack of self-worth ruin that.

"One more thing before we go." Ozma stepped closer and two shadows emerged behind her. "I want you to see them."

Jack's jaw dropped at the sight of her elegant, feathered wings. The iridescent sheen glistened in the fading firelight as she flexed them wide. "Shit," he breathed. Something inside of the house exploded, interrupting his fascination, and they both ducked, his ears ringing. "*Shit!* We need to get to the ship. Can you fly?"

"I don't know, but it doesn't matter. We're sticking together."

Ozma reached out for his hand with her own and he clasped it. Together they bolted back into the forest. His leg throbbed with each loping step. The wound on his thigh burned and stretched, but they had to get to Tik-Tok's ship before they were trapped.

Jack took comfort in knowing that Ozma could *feel* her way back to the shore, because he still felt slightly disoriented. The spell the Wizard had cast on him was broken but the effects seemed slow to fade. With the buzz in his head and the revelation of Ozma's power—her *wings*—Jack needed a minute to collect himself before putting his brain to work.

Growls reached their ears every so often—a grave reminder

of the danger they were still in. After running for what felt like hours, the pain in Jack's leg forced them to stop and he lay down in the dirt, breathing heavily. "Sorry," he muttered to Ozma. She had to be in worse pain than he was after what she'd suffered with her eye.

"Don't be." She sat beside him and adjusted the stained cloth. He had stuffed extra strips in his pocket for when it needed refreshing.

I should've grabbed some for myself, he thought as he pushed aside the rip in his pants to see the wound. It was red and angry and far too deep. One of the brownies on board the ship would hopefully know how to stitch him up.

The snap of a twig sent both Jack and Ozma to their feet. *Oh, come on! Can't I get a moment?* A nude, rotting human female stumbled toward them through the trees. Her left arm hung by a few tendons, intestines bulging from a hole in her stomach. Two more silhouettes moved behind her.

Ozma lunged forward, kicking Oz's head where it lay on the ground. It sailed through the air, spinning as it went, and whizzed past the woman's ear. The female whirled around and chased after it.

"Hurry," Ozma said, and Jack obeyed.

When they finally reached the sandy shore again, Jack expected to be surrounded by enemies. He would've questioned the lack of monsters earlier if he realized how close they'd gotten to the water. But, instead of finding a hungry horde ready to tear them apart, dozens of bodies greeted them. They were spread across the beach, limbs twisted, with black liquid oozing from their orifices.

"What the hell?" he asked.

Ozma tugged him across the sand. "Don't question it. Let's just go."

She was right—it didn't matter, as long as they got out of there in one piece. Jack ushered Ozma into the row boat that was left for them and shoved it into the glistening silver water. Once it was far enough out to float, he jumped in beside her. Gentle waves bobbed them up and down while Jack gathered the oars, reminding him how ill he'd felt the last time they were on Tik-Tok's ship. He squinted through the bright moonlight at the hulking shadow of a ship. *Fuck.* It was better than being stuck in Orkland though, so, resigned, he rowed toward the pirates.

"How's your leg?" Ozma asked as he pulled the oars. "I can row if—"

"I'm fine," he assured her. *Or I will be.* As soon as someone took a needle and thread to him. And gave him the largest bottle of ale available—mostly to drink, but also to disinfect the cut.

Ozma pursed her lips. "You're a horrible liar."

He smirked. "I'm an astounding liar, Blossom. You just know me too well."

"I do," she agreed and glanced over her shoulder at the ship. "Why does it still feel so far away?"

Because we're both fucking exhausted.

But he kept rowing. If he stopped, even for a moment, he wasn't sure that he would find the strength to start again.

"You're alive." Tik-Tok popped his head over the side deck when they reached *The Wizard.* "And they say there's no such thing as a miracle."

Fucking asshat. "Just throw us a rope or something."

A rope ladder almost immediately fell and slapped against the side of the ship. Jack grabbed the ladder and held it steady for Ozma. She climbed ahead of him, her wings spread wide as if helping her balance, and he scrambled up behind her.

Once on the deck, Jack collapsed to his knees and sucked in the salty air. *Safe.* Or, relatively. Tik-Tok was still suspicious as fuck and he knew from books that the sea was fickle. No one greeted them with weapons though, so it was a good start.

"Wings, eh?" Tik-Tok leaned nonchalantly against the side of the ship, staring at Ozma. His gaze landed on the bloody cloth covering her eye for a moment before returning to the feathered wings behind her. "Interesting."

"We'll be taking your quarters." Ozma's tone brokered no room for argument.

Tik-Tok lifted one brow. "You know, the last fae to have wings like *that* was a royal."

"Don't act like we didn't tell you who she was," Jack snapped.

"Oh, please." Tik-Tok rolled his eyes. "If I had a coin for every fae claiming to be a true heir, I could dock my ship for life. But if you were going to kill the Wizard, I didn't give two shits who you were. Whatever allowed me to start calling my ship by her rightful name again and get the fuck away from Orkland. *The Temptress* sounds more pleasant to the ears than *The Wizard*, doesn't it?"

Ozma ignored his comment about his ship's name. "Why make that deal with me, then? For the unborn child?"

"Bad odds are still odds, Your Highness." He tossed a key at her and gave a flourishing bow. "My rooms are yours until we reach the mainland."

"A healer." Jack got to his feet and stumbled slightly. "And food."

"Is that a request?" Tik-Tok asked. He caught a brownie by the back of her shift. "Hoist the anchor."

"A demand," Jack clarified. "Something substantial."

He laughed. "You're on a pirate ship, my grungy little carrot." Then he strode across the deck, stopping crewmembers every so often to bark out an order. "Kaliko! See to their wounds."

An older brownie with crooked fingers hobbled over, gave them each a once over, and made a soft *hmm* sound. "Don't move."

As if he had anywhere to go besides Tik-Tok's quarters. Still, he plunked down on a large wooden barrel and waited. Ozma did the same, tucking her wings into her back. The brownie returned with a leather sack a few minutes later.

"I can't say this won't hurt," he said, plunging his hand inside the sack.

"Wonderful," Jack mumbled. Then a splash of liquid hit his wound and he clenched his jaw tight to keep himself from screaming.

Ozma wrapped her hand around his and gave a reassuring

squeeze. He forced a smile for her benefit and swallowed a groan as the brownie began poking at the skin around the gash. However painful it was for him, her eye would be worse.

"You should drink this now so it starts working while I stitch this one up," the brownie said to Ozma. He tossed a bottle at her. "It'll numb you up."

"I don't get any?" Jack asked.

The brownie scowled as he resumed his painful examination. "It's a flesh wound."

I'll show you a flesh wound.

The first prick of the stitching needle stopped him from saying so. It was best not to anger the fae already stabbing him with a pointy object.

After the brownie had attended both their wounds, stitching his leg and redressing Ozma's eye, he gave them both vials of medication to take. The pain lessened shortly after and they were shown to Tik-Tok's private bathing chamber. It was small and held only the essentials, but they were clean. And *starving*.

"Come on, Jack," Ozma said gently.

He followed her to the captain's quarters and, when she locked the door behind them, lights flickered to life as if sensing their presence. The warm cinnamon scent reminded Jack of the farm—of pumpkin pies and cakes and cookies. A large desk took up the center of the room with two chairs in front and one behind. The dark wooden seats were partially covered in red velvet with gold studs. Trapped beneath a piece of glass on the desk was a map, and more hung on the walls. A white, half-dead flower sat in a vase on the windowsill, and the other side of the room was made of cupboards that stretched into the back of the space. There, white gauze curtains swept over a large corner bed.

Jack went to the cupboards first and opened them until he

found what he wanted—a glass decanter and two glasses. He poured them each a decent amount. "A celebratory drink," he told Ozma when she joined him. He really just wanted to slow his racing thoughts enough to dull the adrenaline rush.

Ozma opened a few cupboards until she found a wedge of cheese and bread. "This is probably the best meal we'll find for now."

Jack's stomach growled loudly and he chuckled. "It seems you brought me back with a real appetite."

She stepped closer, holding the food in her hands, and stretched up to kiss him. Jack kissed her back, set the glasses down, and pulled her to his chest in one fluid movement. Their lips came frantically together, gliding, their tongues colliding. It almost felt like another battle—though this one promised a pleasurable ending. Jack groaned into Ozma's mouth, hunger forgotten, or rather, a new one taking shape.

The bread and cheese thumped to the ground as Ozma tugged at his clothes. "I need you inside me. And I know the position I want. Don't be sweet about it." She released him and slid her dress over her head, exposing her perfect breasts and every other inch of her.

"You don't have to tell me twice, Blossom." He didn't think he had it in him to be *sweet* at the moment anyway. Hell, he didn't even have the patience to remove his own damn clothing.

Jack spun her around and bent her over the desk. The twitch of his cock reminded him how desperately he needed the release. He gripped her naked hips, his fingertips digging into her soft flesh.

"I love you," he rasped.

"Show me how much." She panted, looking at him over her shoulder with a lust-filled eye.

Jack grinned and quickly released his cock. In one motion, he slid inside her, and could have come right then. But he held back and began thrusting at a fervent pace. She pushed against him, matching his rhythm, her tight ass slapping him, her firm breasts bouncing. The desk scraped back and forth across the floor with each push.

"You feel so good." Jack leaned down so his chest was against her warm back, and he nipped at her ear. A moan escaped her as he let go of one hip to circle her clit with his fingers. Again and again, he stroked. "Fuck."

Without warning, her core contracted around him and she gasped his name, still moving rhythmically along with him. The sensation built and built until it pulled him completely over the edge and he groaned, "Demand this any time you want, Blossom. Any time." Jack collapsed over her and kissed her neck.

"Do you think they heard us?" Ozma asked.

Jack chuckled into her hair. "They definitely did."

Ozma arched back as if she wanted to stand, so Jack slid away. She threw her head back and laughed.

"Care to share the joke?" Jack asked, already smiling over the infectious sound.

Ozma pressed a soft kiss to his lips. "We're alive."

"Indeed."

Ozma reached around him and grabbed the drinks. "To the Land of Oz."

"To *us*," Jack corrected, clinking his glass against hers.

"To us." She grinned and yanked at his shirt with her free hand. "Now let's get out of these clothes."

When Jack stirred awake a few hours later, his stomach queasy but full of bread and cheese, he focused on the female in his arms. Ozma's long lashes swept across her cheekbones as she slept, and her lips parted ever-so-slightly. He brushed a stray piece of hair from her forehead and replaced it with a kiss. *I love you.* He didn't speak the words, not wanting to wake her just yet, but his heart swelled at the mere sight of her. There wasn't a day over the last two years that he hadn't wished to have his beloved back. Now that she'd returned to him, he would make up for each moment they'd spent apart.

With a quick flick of his magic, Jack called the dry, vine-like leaves of the dead flower toward him. They moved slowly, almost painfully, and Jack felt what very little life was left in them. He sent a silent apology through the bond and coaxed them into a twisted, three-ring circle.

Ozma stirred. "What's going on?"

Jack snatched the ring from the air and hid it in his palm. "Nothing. Why?"

"I can feel you using your magic," she mumbled against his bare chest.

"We're giving that ring back to Tik-Tok," he grumbled.

She laughed. "You don't want to share with me? I'm sure it works both ways."

"We're giving it back," he insisted jokingly. "How am I to surprise you with anything if you can tell every time I grow a flower?"

Her blue eye slid up to meet his hazel ones. "Surprise?"

Jack licked his lips. "A question, really…"

Oh gods. His hands shook. *What if she says no?*

"A question?" She pushed up onto one elbow, her hair gliding over her bare breasts.

"You know I love you." He cleared his throat. "I'd do anything for you."

"And I you," she said, brows lowered in confusion.

"So, I was wondering… Or… Hoping, really…" *Spit it out, idiot.* He held his hand up between them and uncurled his fingers to reveal the ring. "Will you marry me?"

Ozma blinked down at his offering.

Seconds ticked by without an answer and Jack nearly jumped out of his skin. "I'll get you a better ring."

"No!" She snatched the twisted vines from his palm. "I want this one."

Jack's heart hammered in his chest. "Is … that a yes?"

"Yes." Ozma pushed the ring onto her finger and gripped his

face. "Yes." She pressed her lips to his. "Yes." Climbing onto his lap, she showered him with kisses. "Yes, yes, yes!"

Jack let out a relieved breath and placed his head to her chest, listening to her heart beat. "Thank fuck."

They shifted together beneath the covers, pressing closer. Ozma avoided touching his injured leg and he gently shifted so her eye wasn't pressed into his arm. His cock stiffened again, but he shoved down the desire. For now, they needed rest. Forever lay ahead of them. A life together. Happiness. Everything they had always wanted and didn't know was possible. Until now.

EPILOGUE

OZMA

As Ozma and Jack drew closer to the Emerald City, she peered down at the ring on her finger that he'd crafted. It was perfect, and it would remain on that digit for as long as they lived. Beside it rested the gold token from Tik-Tok, a reminder of a debt that still needed to be paid. But for now, she would have to push that thought aside.

On their journey, Ozma had purchased a new dress from the market in Loland and a shimmery blue eye patch, along with some ointment for Jack's leg. She wasn't used to having one eye yet, but she would adjust. Jack had returned to their farm and gathered a few of his books and clothing before they'd departed again on foot. They didn't take any of the pumpkin seeds—they would rather plant new things at their secret house once they settled in at the palace.

Crossing the Shifting Sands had been much simpler with magic. The beasts had remained hidden when Ozma sparked her blue power to life, willing it to create a barrier of protection.

Jack wrapped one arm around her waist as they walked the yellow brick road and brushed her hair aside with the other. He gently kissed his way up her neck, and she could feel every inch of his strong body behind her. His warm breath caressed her ear as he spoke, "Are you going to try and fly yet?"

She had told Jack she would attempt it once they reached the outskirts of the Emerald City. Her wings were still too new, and she didn't know if they were strong enough to lift her yet.

"Fine." Whirling around, she circled her arms around his neck. "But catch me if I fall."

"The branches will be ready." He flicked his tongue over her lips. "However, you won't need them."

Closing her eye for a brief moment, she let the magic stir, the blue energy raging inside her. Her wings released from her back, the wind from the movement rumpling Jack's hair. This time she was able to use her magic so her clothing wouldn't shred.

Ozma took a step back from him, pumping her wings, once, twice, until her feet lifted from the ground into a wide-open space.

As though she'd always had them, Ozma flapped her new appendages, going up and up until she was near the tops of the trees.

Jack's hand hovered at his forehead, blocking the sun, as he watched her in the air. "See! You don't need my help, Blossom."

Slowly, she retreated back to the ground, her silver slippers crunching the leaves. She stumbled forward and Jack caught her around the waist.

"Or maybe you do, just a bit." He smiled the brightest of smiles. "Ever since I've known you, you've been beautiful, but you've never been more radiant than you are now."

She pressed her lips to his, tasting the fruit he'd eaten earlier. "Tonight, pick your pleasure, and I'll do what you ask."

His pupils dilated. "Yes, my queen."

Ozma chuckled and tugged him forward so they could head into the Emerald City. The journey through the East had been quiet during the nights, not a single sound from the cursed pixies. Reva must have defeated Locasta—she could feel it all the way down to her bones.

Beneath their feet, the yellowed bricks became a sparkly shade of green as they entered the Emerald City. She watched

Jack peer around at the crumbled buildings with wide eyes. Her heart accelerated, not at the destruction, but because there were fae outside repairing the broken architecture. Hammering, sawing, painting. The Emerald City beat like a heart inside her veins with each step, drawing her closer and closer to its center.

Ozma looked at the different shops—broken windows being replaced at a bakery, a new door being put in at a flower shop, and fabrics being carried from wagons into a building. Each street they walked was bustling with renewed life.

Eventually, they rounded a corner and Ozma held back a gasp. There it stood—the palace. Even from a distance, she knew it wasn't in perfect condition. There were holes in the green walls and blackened areas that would need to be mended. Even though it was in need of repair, it had the potential to be glorious.

"Sure you don't want to turn around?" Jack teased.

"We're used to a little hard work." Ozma rolled her eyes.

The palace door swung open and two guards walked out from the building: one male fae with long silver locks cascading down his back and the other with feathers intertwined in his obsidian hair. No, not guards—she *recognized* them.

Tin and Crow.

The silver-haired fae focused first on Jack and lifted his axe, his face like stone. Jack was already raising his hand in defense, then Tin's gaze shifted to Ozma. His expression didn't soften, but he gave a brief nod as he lowered his axe a fraction.

"Quit being an ass," Crow grunted to Tin. He sauntered toward Ozma. "You made it just in time. We were going to leave in a couple days to search for you. There were guards under oath to the Wizard, stuck here by that bond, but then a few days ago they were able to go home."

"Where's Reva?" Ozma rushed out the words, moving toward the palace.

"She's not in there." Crow tilted his head in the direction behind her. "But she's coming this way."

Ozma whirled around, spotting three fae in the distance. Thelia, who wore a lavender dress and her brown hair pulled into a single braid, with a young faun beside her. On her other side was Reva, dressed in her usual black, her long sleek hair falling to her waist.

"Did it work out for you two?" Ozma whispered to Crow.

"The entire palace can hear them fucking almost every night, so I'd say so," Tin grunted.

"Fuck off." Crow fought a smile.

"Ozma?" Reva shouted. Her friend took off at a sprint, leaving Thelia and the faun behind. Once she was close enough, Reva threw her arms around Ozma, squeezing her so hard she could barely breathe.

With a smile, Ozma returned the hug.

Reva froze when she pulled back, a horrified expression crossing her face. "Why are you wearing an eye patch?"

"One of us was bound to lose an eye." Ozma tried to make her voice sound light, but rushed to change the subject. "I heard the good news about you and Crow, and I suppose you have me to thank for him catching up to you."

"I should have known he had some help." Reva's gaze slid to Crow, a smirk forming on her lips.

"It isn't as though I wouldn't have found you anyway," Crow said with a wink.

"We had a little help from the Gnome King." Reva fished something out of her pocket and tossed it in the air. "We killed that bastard, too."

Ozma could only focus on the shiny red stone shaped like a heart. Her lips parted, and she snatched the stone before Reva could catch it.

"Where did you get this?" she asked, her voice shaky. The last time she'd seen it was when she'd given it to Tik-Tok.

"From the Gnome King's chest." Reva shrugged. "Whatever spell turned the Gnome King to stone apparently also gave him a heart that prevents curses."

Ozma clenched her teeth. Tik-Tok had known the entire time what she'd held, and he hadn't said anything. But why would he? "Mombi had one and I traded it." She handed the stone back to

Reva.

"The Gnome Queen's heart," Crow said softly. "That's where it was."

"Now it's with a pirate named Tik-Tok." Ozma sighed. A rush of anger fired up in her. She could have used that stone against the Wizard if she'd known sooner. Though she'd defeated him anyway, she still couldn't help feeling a little bitter about it.

Reva narrowed her eyes. "I know Tik-Tok. He's a sneaky, cocky bastard, but he shouldn't be a threat."

Yet he would be a threat for someone… One day.

"Glad you made it," Thelia said, strolling up with the faun. "This is Birch. Part of my new guard." The youngling straightened his spine and lifted his chin, his small antlers peeping out from his hair.

Ozma could feel Tin rolling his eyes behind her.

"You will do well in keeping Thelia safe." Ozma smiled and locked her gaze onto Thelia's brown irises. Taking a deep swallow, she glanced over her shoulder at Tin, at his silver hair. A nagging feeling washed over her—she quickly shook away the thought. It was just a coincidence. Lots of fae had silver hair and brown eyes.

"Please tell us the Wizard is just as dead as Locasta," Reva said.

A weight lifted off Ozma. The wicked had been defeated. All of them were now gone. That didn't mean that there weren't others out there who would attempt to rise, but the ones who had driven Oz into despair were gone. "The Wizard and Mombi are both slain."

"Fuck yes." Reva grasped Ozma by the shoulders and smiled. "We did this." She spun and looked at everyone standing there. "We all did."

They all smiled back, except for Tin, who appeared as though he were done with this conversation.

"It was a bitch removing the spell from the palace that was suppressing our magic," Reva continued, "but Thelia helped me wipe it out. A protective barrier from King Pastoria remains, though. Has your magic returned?"

Pastoria—her father whom she would never know. At least part of him was still here. Ozma lifted her hands and called on her power. The blue glittery fire rocketed through her until two orbs of flame rested on her hands. She quickly flexed her spine, the wings shooting out from her back.

"I have to say I'm envious." Reva chuckled. "It's beautiful."

"She is," Jack finally spoke. And all eyes turned to him.

"This is my Jack." Ozma grabbed his tunic sleeve and tugged him closer. "He's going to be my husband."

"A wedding!" Thelia clapped her hands together.

"Before we start discussing wedding plans," Ozma started, "I think we'd better talk about our next steps in rebuilding Oz."

"The three of us together, ruling, will become enough," Reva said.

"It will remain enough," Thelia added.

"It will forever be enough." Ozma sucked in a breath of true victory. They'd all been a part of liberating their world. Now, she and Jack were both free, and, with their freedom, they had still chosen each other. Soon, the rest of Oz would know what it meant to be truly free too.

Ozma turned to her beloved, his smile mirroring hers when she said, "Welcome home, Jack."

TIK-TOK

BOOK 4

CHAPTER ONE

TIK-TOK

TWENTY-THREE YEARS AGO

Sand was a pain in the ass.

Literally.

That was what Tik-Tok got for letting the sea witch, Celyna, ride him, buck-naked, on the beach all afternoon. Decades upon decades of yearly trysts and still, he hadn't learned his lesson. Against a tree or in her glass house were the only reasonable options on the island of Isa Poso. There wasn't anything *but* sand here—save for trees, sea life, and an occasional patch of salt grass. It didn't matter if they kept their clothes mostly on because the gritty particles snuck into every crevice.

Celyna was worth the irritating chafe between his ass cheeks though. Her light blue skin, the iridescent scales scattered up and down her arms, how her dark green hair floated around her head as if she were underwater, the fluid way her body shifted over his. His cock twitched despite the fact that he had just come inside her minutes ago. She fucked gracefully, each movement as smooth as if she were swimming. Honestly, he'd be willing to make the trip to Isa Poso twice a year instead of once if she were willing to use her second-sight that often.

The silver waves of the Nonestic Ocean gently rocked the sea witch where she floated, sprawled on its surface. As Tik-Tok treaded water beside her, the middle finger of his left hand grazed over her abdomen. Up and down, leaving goosebumps in its wake, teasing. Tracing her hips, gliding along the curve of her breast, circling her hard nipples. If he were the sort of male to settle for one female, he might be tempted to ask for more, but he wasn't. And neither was she.

Thank the sea gods. There was nothing worse than a clingy female.

Celyna's dark, orb-like eyes turned languidly to his red ones, just as his fingertips met the curls between her legs. "You should head back to your ship before it gets dark."

Tik-Tok took in the setting sun and let his hand drift lower. "Aren't you forgetting something?"

"Am I?" She ground against his palm. "Perhaps I need another reminder."

Tik-Tok growled playfully as he grabbed her hips and pulled her toward him. Her second-sight worked only during an orgasm and he'd given her multiple. "I would love nothing more than to bury myself in you a third time today, but"—he paused to stroke his tongue up the length of her sex, tasting her sweet flavor—"as you pointed out, it will be dark soon."

With a dissatisfied grunt, Celyna lowered her legs into the sea. "You must bargain with an unknown queen for two things," the witch said as if she were suddenly bored with his presence. "First, the ring I gave you."

"My ring?" He held his right arm up—the low rays of sunlight gleamed on the golden surface, the joints clearly mechanical—and stared at the silver band. The ring was always cold where it circled his digit, his metal hand having no body heat to transfer, but he'd grown accustomed to the sensation. Celyna had given him the trinket the year before with the instruction to keep it close—a useless task that left him restless all year. At first, he'd assumed the reason would make itself known as the months stretched on, but it had only served to calm the clash of different powers inside himself. It also had the power to transfer magic between fae, but there was no way in hell he was doing that. Tik-Tok's gaze darted to the other rings he wore, all gold, some with gems and some plain. "Which?"

Celyna rolled her eyes. "You know which, pirate."

He grunted. There was a bigger picture to keep in mind—a portal to find. To open. To explore. Among ... other, more important things. "And the second thing?"

"When you retrieve the ring from the unknown queen, you must exchange it for possession of a female who has yet to be born."

"Come again," he blurted, jerking back. There were a lot of calculating things Tik-Tok didn't mind doing, but *possessing* a female? No. He didn't want a slave, nor did he want anyone on board his ship who wasn't part of the crew.

"Do you want your portal or not?" she asked, impatient.

Of course he wanted his portal. He'd spent far too long and sacrificed too much to let the quest fail.

When Tik-Tok said nothing, she continued, "You will collect your ring from the queen at the same time you collect a female with silver hair and brown eyes. She will be well-known to the queen. Bargain for both things at once or the queen will not let the female go."

His nostrils flared. "And what am I supposed to do with her?"

The witch smirked. "She's the only one who can open the portal—but not until she's ready."

She can open the portal? His pulse raced. *Finally*. Everything was about to pay off. All he had to do was find an unknown queen. How hard could that be? While he was stuck doing the deranged Wizard's bidding—another one of Celyna's tasks—he'd sailed the entire world. The fae he must bargain with was bound to show up eventually—they always did if Celyna saw them in her visions.

Celyna slid forward and pressed her lips to his. His fingers tangled in her hair, holding her close, extending the kiss a few moments longer. As they broke apart, he nipped playfully at her bottom lip.

She nipped back and used one finger to push his body away from hers. "I'll see you next year." Then she sank beneath the silvery waves, her form disappearing from view.

Tik-Tok let out a warm, victorious laugh as he swam back to shore for his clothes. The portal was within reach.

Find the queen.

Acquire the female.

Fulfill his life's work.

A devious grin spread across his face.

CHAPTER TWO

NORTH

Tonight was the night. North was going to confess her love to Birch. Then kiss him anywhere and everywhere. Be it her room, his room, the grass, the water, wherever he wanted.

Birch.

She'd been in love with him for as long as she could remember. His short blond curls, his dark orange eyes, his muscular body, his skills with a bow… But it wasn't just how he looked. He was gentle, kind, strong, and valiant. He was *everything*.

Birch was there when her father—Tin—was too strict, when her mother—Thelia—was too demanding. He'd brought her wildflowers when she'd felt lonely, sad, or just because. There were nights when Father and Mother were sleeping so deeply that she would sneak out of her room to watch him get in extra practice with his bow. Then, after, her body was always so wound up with wanting his kisses, his hands stroking her bare flesh, him inside her, that she would seek release from her own fingers. For years, she'd known he would only see her as a youngling, but she wasn't anymore. North was twenty now. She wasn't as shapely and alluring as her mother or grandmother, but she hoped he was able to see *her*.

In personality, North wanted to be more like her grandmother—Reva. Bold. Daring. But she wasn't as powerful as Reva or Thelia. She was without magic, while everyone else in her family could bring the Land of Oz to its knees if they chose.

Thelia could tear the world apart, Tin was able to open portals and wield an axe better than anyone, Reva created storms, and Crow—her grandfather—had magic that allowed him to shift into a bird. While she had nothing…

Outside her window, the night had already swallowed the world—it was time. Birch would be where he always was when they visited her grandparents in the North: behind the palace, practicing his archery near the stables. North had already told her family she was tired and would retire for the night, while Thelia and Reva played a game of cards, with Crow occasionally joining in, as her father watched. Tin and Crow rarely spoke to each other unless they had to, but they tolerated one another in the same room. An improvement from her youth when they'd constantly instigated arguments.

North wiggled into a simple yellow dress with pearl buttons lining the front. She ran her hands through her silver wavy hair.

Quietly, she tied the corner of her sheet to the bed post, then knotted a few more together before carrying them to the window. She pushed up the glass and let the sheets spill over the side. Giving it a sharp tug to make sure the fabric was sturdy enough, North grabbed onto the cloth and shimmied down the side of the palace. Green vines speckled with blue and white flowers covered the Northern palace walls. A cold wind blew fiercely, disheveling her hair as tiny snowflakes swirled around her. The cold didn't affect her though, not as it would a human's sensitive flesh.

Once her feet hit the ground, North craned her neck to search the garden. Trees with ivory blossoms and pale azure leaves enveloped the area—icicles caught the moonlight where they hung across the curved branches. Snowdrop flowers cloaked almost every inch of the landscape at the palace, aside from the winding paths leading to the entrances. Stars painted the sky around a sliver of moon, giving off a bright yellowish radiance.

In the distance, faeries sang a slow, melodic song. A blue glow flickered from small snow bugs as they danced above the faeries. North inched to the side of the palace and peered around to the back where two guards chatted with one another.

"Gods," she muttered under her breath, knowing if the guards found her, they would report her to her grandparents right away.

North hesitated, deciding to go the longer route, but then a faerie with iridescent wings hovered above her, seeming to notice her predicament. Holding her breath, North motioned her head at the guards. The faerie gave her a beaming smile and darted forward, spewing an elaborate question. As soon as the guards' attention fell on the faerie and her inquiry, North hurried past them on light feet to a cluster of trees, then straight for her grandmother's stables.

She trekked across the hard ground, wearing her warmest boots, and skirted around the icy trunks. In the distance, she caught a glimpse of soft light spilling over the field.

North sidled up to the dark building, its obsidian bricks glistening from the glow. The light coming from the field turned out to be dozens of lit candles, forming a circle, with two lanterns in its center. The flames highlighted Birch's golden hair, the deer-like antlers at his forehead, his tight tunic and pants. Was this for her? Did he somehow know she was coming to confess to him how she felt?

"Birch?" North called, taking a few steps forward.

He whirled around, his eyes wide. "North?" he said. "You shouldn't be out here."

Shouldn't be out here? Her stomach sank as realization struck her. "This isn't for me…" She should have known—he'd never treated her as more than a sister.

"For you? It's for Gemma." He paused, moving toward her. "I'm planning to ask her to marry me tonight."

Her cousin. Not North. Her *cousin*.

She hadn't even known that he and Gemma were more than friends. Hurt bubbled inside North, laced with anger. She turned, sprinting back toward the palace. But she wasn't fast enough. Birch gripped her elbow, halting her. Her back struck his chest, and she couldn't stop the butterflies from storming through her, even though he was going to propose to her cousin. North had always looked up to Gemma, and she could see why he would want to marry her, but that didn't make it any better.

"What are you doing?" Birch asked, the first to pull away. Otherwise, she would have stayed pressed up against him for all eternity.

North looked around for her cousin, but she wasn't there yet. Gemma probably knew about her infatuation. Both Reva and Thelia could tell, but North had always denied it.

"You're asking her to marry you?" North whispered.

Birch bit his lip. "Yes."

"Why?" She could have said anything else, but apparently, she was one to relish in humiliation.

"Why does anyone marry?" His tone came out low, steady. "Because they love one another."

"You can't." Why couldn't she just stop talking? Why did she have to appear more like the child he saw in her, instead of the grown female she was?

His face softened as he studied her. "North…"

"I love you," she rushed the words out. "I always have." Her heart couldn't hold it in any longer, and if it did, it would break. More than it already was.

Birch placed his hands on her shoulders, and she hoped this was the moment. The one where he realized they were meant to be. His throat bobbed as he watched her, not seeming at all surprised at what she'd just confessed. "You don't," he finally said, his voice gentle.

"I do." She felt the tears pricking at her eyes, wishing he could slip directly into her heart, her mind, and see how much she did, because maybe then, he would love her too.

"North, I can't."

She winced. "You're only saying that because of my father."

Birch released a sigh, not taking his hands from her shoulders. "I would sacrifice my life for you, you know that. You're like a sister to me, and I love you, but I don't feel the way you want me to." He paused and gnawed on his lip. "Please go home before Tin finds you out here."

North inhaled sharply, her gaze darting everywhere but Birch's face. Something in her broke … shattered. "I understand," she forced out the words, even though she didn't mean them. "I'll go."

Turning out of his grasp, she started for the palace. North ducked behind a tree and glanced back as Birch slowly spun to go, as if he'd been debating whether to escort her home himself. She continued to watch while he walked back to his candles. And she knew that he would worship Gemma's body right in the circle of flames after he proposed to her and she said yes. Taking a deep swallow, she wiped the hot tears from her cheeks.

North peered at the castle, her chest as hollow as the collection of her grandmother's vases inside. She couldn't go back right now, simply to sit in her room alone, crying herself to sleep.

Instead, she would do something *daring*. She'd been saving herself for Birch, for when the time was right. But it would never happen now.

Blowing out a breath, she hurried to the front of the castle, across the bridge, to the part of the woods where fae went every night to have a good time, to not have to think, or worry.

Faeries filled the air with laughter while dust from circling sprites lit up the night. The wind continued to bite her skin, but she barely felt it as she slipped past icy trees and snow-covered bushes to join the revelry.

Fae skidded across the frozen lake, some half-dressed despite the cold evening. Along the bank, couples chatted, drank, and danced. Others were naked, mounted atop one another, their hips rolling. She lifted her chin, trying not to seem inexperienced, as she crept closer.

A fae with bark covering most of his body glanced up as she passed and held out a vial full of emerald dust. North nodded—her usual set of rules didn't apply tonight. He sprinkled some glittering flecks onto her wrist and she licked it clean, letting the high wash over her. Grabbing the full mug of mead at his side, North drank half of it before strolling off. The world seemed to brighten.

She needed to find someone, *anyone*, who would serve her purpose. A fae stepping off of the ice caught her attention. He was already shirtless, his red hair spilling down over his shoulders. Beautiful was the only way to describe him. He wouldn't be forever hers, and she didn't need him to be. Whatever happened next would only be to keep the ache from her heart for tonight. Before anyone else could claim him, North sauntered to the male and grabbed him by the wrist.

"Come on," North said, not meeting his eyes. She would be brave while the dark of the night helped to conceal her nervousness.

The male arched an eyebrow as he studied her. "Which tree?"

With a false grin, she brought him to the nearest trunk. The drug pulsing through her made her too high to care if anyone watched—she only wanted to feel better.

"Open your mouth," he said, pressing a finger to her lower lip.

North listened as he pulled out his own vial of emerald dust from his pants, sprinkling some on her tongue before coating his own with gold from a different pouch. He licked his tongue against hers, mingling the dust, and warmth spread through her, so much so that she forgot everything. It didn't take much time to learn how to match the movements of his lips. Then, as she discovered what to do, their kisses became frantic, desperate, as the dust soared within her. She loosened the tie at his pants, pushing her hand inside and squeezing his length. It felt different than she'd imagined—smooth and soft, yet hard.

And even though she didn't want to think about Birch, his face still haunted her as the male hiked up her dress, then lifted her so her legs wrapped around his narrow waist. North wanted to pretend Birch loved her, that she had her own magic, that she was good enough—even compared to her family. But she couldn't. Shame spread through her.

"Stop!" she shouted, desperate.

The male froze, releasing her as though she'd burned him.

"I can't." Avoiding looking at him, she adjusted her dress.

"I thought… North…" His voice came out gentle.

Of course he knew who she was. Everyone here did. How could they not? She was the granddaughter and daughter of the Land of Oz's leaders. Not only that, but she was like a daughter to the Queen of Oz. Three powerful females. And she was nothing.

"It's fine. It's not your fault. It's mine." North turned to leave and swayed unsteadily as the woods spun around her.

The dizziness remained until she reached the castle walls, thankfully avoiding any guards, and approached her window. Only when she looked up to climb the tied sheets back to her room, did she realize they were gone.

Gods.

"You snuck out," a voice growled behind her.

Closing her eyes, she sighed and turned around, trying not to wince. "Father, I—"

"You said you were *tired*." Tin's silver irises burned brighter than the stars as he glared at her. "You lied."

"Father…"

"You really thought Birch wouldn't tell me what happened?" Her father's gaze remained hard.

"He had no right," North murmured. She supposed Birch didn't stay to propose if he'd already tattled to her father. A desperate part of her liked that he had.

"He cares about you."

"Like a sister, I know." North didn't want to think about it anymore.

Tin's shoulders relaxed. But then they tightened again as she stumbled, no longer able to maintain the charade of sobriety. He caught her by the arms and took a whiff—his entire face became stony.

Her tongue felt heavy. "Father...."

"You're never leaving my sight again."

CHAPTER THREE

TIK-TOK

There were times when Tik-Tok thought the sea witch was fucking with him. Mostly in the last few years. *It isn't time,* Celyna had told him last year. And the year before that. And the one before that. Every single one of his yearly trips to the seer had met with the same three words for over two decades now.

It isn't time.

Like hell it wasn't.

Tik-Tok had done everything Celyna had told him to do for *decades*. Every year, she'd given him a new task that was meant to bring him closer to his dream. He'd tracked down a magical compass, held a mutiny against his old captain, severed his own arm, and helped that cunt of a mortal wizard—*who had held his compass hostage.*

Running the Wizard's errands was easily one of the darkest parts of his history. Willingly helping keep the Land of Oz under the mortal's oppressive rule, giving up even a sliver of control over his choices, made him want to murder someone. And those monstrous addicts guarding Oz in Orkland. *Damn.* It was enough to make even the most hardened of fae squirm.

But then, as Celyna had promised, he'd reacquired his

compass. Followed immediately by making the fated deal with an unknown queen—for a female with silver hair and brown eyes. Ozma and Jack had been unexpected but a relief. Not only had they wanted the Wizard dead—something Celyna hadn't mentioned—but they'd been desperate enough to take his ring and promise him a female with little convincing.

All of that just to hear the sea witch tell him *it wasn't time?*

No. To hell with that. He wanted to open the damn portal to another world just like the witch had promised. Celyna didn't personally care about the portal—as long as she got a good fuck in—so the lack of forward motion didn't bother her. Tik-Tok could wait another fifty years for all she cared. That fact had somewhat soured their yearly tryst.

Palming his magic compass, Tik-Tok flicked the golden top open. "Starboard, ten clicks."

"Aye, Captain," Rizmaela, his first mate, said from where she stood behind the ship's wheel.

He'd picked up the cynical female dwarf a few years back after watching her take out three males singlehandedly when they wouldn't leave her alone at a tavern. The three dwarfs started by asking to buy her a mead which she refused, so naturally they thought she would agree to join them for a foursome instead. *Idiots.* He'd never seen a dwarf pull a dagger from their boot faster than Rizmaela had.

When she merely removed an ear from each instead of killing them, Tik-Tok knew he needed her on his crew. He'd lost numerous males and females to their egos already, so he valued someone who knew the meaning of restraint. Rizmaela rose through the ranks faster than anyone else on board. Most of the crew were brownies—not cutthroats—but he'd also recruited others. Two elves, Respen and Dax, who were both irreplaceable to his sanity out at sea. Cyrx, a goblin he'd met playing cards, and, perhaps most surprisingly, a siren named Echo.

Now all he needed was the sea witch's next set of instructions. A bone-deep tingle told him he would get his wish this time. It was as if fate were reassuring him. Coaxing him to hope. He wasn't sure if the sensation was trustworthy, but he wanted it to be.

Tik-Tok propped the elbow of his gold, mechanical arm on a rain barrel, letting the sea breeze whip his black hair around his face. "I have a good feeling about today," he said more to himself than to Rizmaela.

"I hope you're right," she said in her usual gravelly voice.

He grinned at her. "Am I ever wrong?"

"Is any male?" she joked.

Tik-Tok barked a laugh and checked his compass again. Right or wrong, he did what he wanted, when he wanted, and his crew knew it. If they didn't like it, they were free to leave whenever they docked. Or, if they were particularly defiant, *before* they docked.

"Port, two clicks."

"Aye, Captain."

The final leg of the journey took half a day, and the closer *The Temptress* sailed to Isa Poso, the more restless Tik-Tok became. His fingers rapped against the rain barrel, and he felt the prick of what would've been a splinter poke at one of his gold fingertips.

"Land!" a brownie, Kaliko, shouted from the crow's nest.

Tik-Tok's heart slammed into his ribs. The tingling sensation that gave him hope now bubbled and foamed inside him. Slipping the compass into the pocket of his dark pants, he strode toward his quarters.

"Prepare to drop anchor," he commanded Rizmaela over his shoulder.

The dwarf was already shouting orders to the crew when he kicked shut the door to his room. He shrugged a deep blue jacket with gold buttons on over his loose white tunic, changed out his good boots for his old, and tugged on a pair of gloves. Finally, strapping one of his swords to his hip, he returned to find the crew tying down the black sails of *The Temptress*.

"Will you be long?" his first mate asked, rubbing her gnarled hands down her leather pants.

He shrugged, watching the brownies prepare the smaller boat he would use to row to the island's shore. "As long as it takes."

Sometimes Celyna made him wait, sometimes she met him on the beach and quickly ushered him away. Either way, they always ended up fucking—even if it was a quick tumble on the sand—so she would have the vision he needed.

"Let the crew relax while I'm gone, but stay aware. No ale for anyone," he said in a stern voice. The last thing he needed was to return with a clear purpose only to have a ship full of useless drunkards. "We'll be departing as soon as I return."

Rizmaela jerked her chin in understanding and he strode toward the rowboat. "Ready?" he asked, climbing in. With a final tug on a knot, the brownies nodded. "Lower away."

As they slowly eased the boat down onto the shimmering silver water below, Tik-Tok took in the island. The aquamarine sand reflected the sun like a mirror. From far away, the island looked like a floating blast of light, but close up, the sand shimmered beautifully. Tall trees with smooth, white trunks grew a variety of exotic fruit while, farther on the island, the trees barely stood taller than Tik-Tok. Their leaves were crystalline blues and greens, in contrast to the pink salt grass that sprouted in patches all over the sandy beach.

Once the boat landed safely, the pirate untied the ropes holding it to *The Temptress* and gathered the oars. He eagerly sped through the quiet waves. Celyna would have a task for him today—she had to. Enough had been sacrificed for his goal— friendships, limbs, sanity—that waiting any longer would send him over the edge. And that wasn't taking his crew into consideration. He'd promised them a portal and their patience would only last so long. Unfortunately, he couldn't man a pirate ship on his own.

The boat scuffed against sand a few yards from shore. Tik-Tok hopped out, water splashing up his legs and seeping into his old boots. Dragging the boat the rest of the way, he toed a few bright red crustaceans from his path and followed the familiar stone walkway to the sea witch's home. The island was small, the witch the only permanent resident, and even she spent most of her time in the water. He skipped over the stepping stones while ignoring the cries of sea birds circling above. His gaze was fully focused on the glass building ahead.

Nestled into a thick patch of the smaller trees, Celyna had built her home in the only somewhat livable place on the island. Purple flowers flowed down the roof and hung from the eaves like curtains. Coral grew in a small pond nearby, surrounded by a collection of sea glass in all shapes and sizes.

"My favorite pirate has returned," a female said from the side of the home. "I expected you yesterday."

Tik-Tok stalked forward, rounding the corner of the glass house, to find the sea witch using her magic to carefully weave water into a basket. Her familiar dark green hair drifted around her head and her two fin-like ears peeked out on both sides. As she worked, her scales sparkled over her blue skin and, finally, she raised her black, orb-like eyes to meet his.

He cleared his throat, struck by her beauty as he was every time he visited. Their meetings were a simple transaction. He thoroughly enjoyed fucking her until she forgot her own name— the other fae he had made scream with pleasure throughout the years were nothing in comparison. But that was all he and Celyna were to each other. *A great fuck.* "The sea is unpredictable."

The witch smiled, revealing each slightly pointed tooth.

"You seem talkative today," Tik-Tok mused. Sometimes she greeted him with endless tales, other times, no more than *it isn't time.* "Do you have my next task?"

The witch watched him thoughtfully. "Will you not seduce me first?"

Tik-Tok crossed his arms. Would he give her an orgasm so she would have a vision of his mystery female? Yes. Many. Was he feeling particularly *giving* at the moment? Not at all. "I've fucked you for the last twenty-two years without reward."

"It isn't *payment* for what I see," she growled.

Tik-Tok shrugged. *No.* It wasn't payment—they both genuinely enjoyed the pleasure, no strings attached, but the weariness of waiting had put his libido on ice. "Is it time yet?"

The sea witch stood, her seaweed skirt bouncing with the sudden movement. She sauntered forward, took Tik-Tok's chin in one hand, and kissed him harshly on the lips.

Surrendering to the taste of her—both salty and sweet—Tik-Tok nearly forgot his question. It wasn't until she nipped his bottom lip, drawing a drop of blood, that he pulled away. "Feisty witch," he growled.

Lifting Celyna, he pressed her up against the glass of her home and slid her upward until her legs rested over his shoulders. She was bare beneath her skirt, giving him unimpaired access to her slit. He shot her a knowing smirk at how wet she was. "Seems like you missed me."

"I missed your body," she crooned, grabbing his hair and bringing his face to her sex.

His tongue flicked her bundle of nerves and he grinned at her gasp. But, as much fun as Celyna was, he was too impatient today. His tongue ran down her opening, plunging inside, swirling as she ground against him. A groan slipped from his throat at the taste of her and his cock begged for attention, but his mind refused to release him to the pleasure.

Portal, portal, portal.

Increasing his pace just like Celyna liked it, he tore an orgasm from her in no time. Her legs spasmed on the sides of his head, her back arched. It felt as if she would pull every hair from his head as he licked her clean, but he didn't mind. He knew, as the fluttering continued, she was seeing exactly what he needed her to. Finally, her grip on him loosened and he carefully set her on her feet. She reached for his pants with a dazed expression.

Tik-Tok brushed her hands away and stepped back from her. "What did you see?"

With a sigh, the witch bent and lifted her new basket. "Visit the queen and force her to make good on your agreement."

"Queen Ozma?" His pulse hammered in his ears. "The female is finally mine?"

"That *was* the deal you struck, wasn't it?" She cast a look to his gloved hand. "Don't forget your ring was part of the bargain."

Tik-Tok rubbed his chest, his heartbeat painfully fast. *It's time. She's mine. The* portal *is mine.* "Yes, that was the deal."

"Then go to the Emerald City and claim your prize."

It was hard to catch his breath, his focus zeroing in on the end goal. How many more tasks would come after this one? How many more *years?* He shook his head. *It doesn't matter.* His next task was ready.

And, just as he'd sensed the witch would have good news, he felt a tether to the unknown female. A link tying their destinies together. Gentle vibrations of an undeniable bond locked into place, warming his chest, beckoning him nearer.

"I'm expected by the merfolk," the witch said, interrupting his thoughts. "Next time, come earlier and we can finish what we started."

He grinned, his libido suddenly in overdrive. If he wasn't in such a hurry to get to the Emerald City, she would completely miss her meeting with the merfolk. "Promises, promises," he told her, winking.

But, before the year was up, he hoped there would be no need to visit again. Because he would sail the Nonestic Ocean and find his portal long before that.

CHAPTER FOUR

NORTH

“If I could, I would tie you to the chair and make sure you stayed here where it's safe, but your mother wouldn't allow it,” Tin said, his silver eyes boring into North as he leaned his head against the door of her room. “You're lucky I'm not going to tell her that you snuck out of your grandmother's palace. Tomorrow we leave to celebrate Brielle, so please try to behave.” This would be her first time meeting Ozma and Jack's daughter since she'd been born a month ago.

North hated disappointing her father, but she wasn't a child anymore. She wasn't the youngling who constantly followed him around and hefted his axe as if it were her own. While she still wanted to make him proud, she was also finding herself, becoming an individual.

“I'm sorry, Father. But you don't understand what it's like to not be enough or to make mistakes.” Her head drooped as she clasped her hands together in her lap.

Tin took heavy-footed steps to her bed and knelt in front of her. Under the orange orbs' illumination from the ceiling, his iron scar seemed to glow. As usual, his hair was pulled back in a knot.

“You think I haven't made mistakes? I've told you the stories. You know I've felt the same.” His voice came out gruff, yet soft, as he lifted her chin. "North, magic doesn't always come right away, and if it never happens, then it doesn't. There's more to life than power."

By her age, if she was going to have it, she should have already.

"Are you still angry?" she asked.

Tin rolled his gaze to the ceiling and let out a long sigh. "Fuck yes, I'm angry, but I love you. Even when you act without thinking. Oz isn't perfect, and there are dangerous fae out there." He pressed a light kiss to her forehead and stood. Adjusting his axe on his hip, he turned to leave, then peered over his shoulder. "There are guards below your window now too. I know you're not a youngling anymore, but it's for your safety. Strangers are traveling through the area to reach the capital, and you know I trust no one."

North smiled. "No one but Mother."

"And you." He shot her a hard stare like she should have known better. "Goodnight."

"Goodnight."

North fell back onto the mattress, letting her body bounce as she stared up at the ceiling, watching the light orbs gently sway. Tugging back her hands, she pretended to throw axes over and over at the center of each invisible target, hitting its mark. This, every night, was the only way she could get herself to fall asleep. She was decent enough with an axe, but that was only because she'd wanted so much to be like her father. Even so, she missed the marks when she hurled one. However, she could twirl an axe and slice someone down if they were close enough.

Shutting her eyes, still throwing pretend axes, North tried to stop feeling sorry for herself. To pretend as though she'd never gone to see Birch or had her first kiss, and more, with a male she didn't love. At least she would get to see Ozma, Jack, and Brielle soon.

North pulled dress after dress after dress from her traveling trunk. Each one ended up on the floor of her bedroom in the Emerald City Palace. Loose, poofy, tight, awful, awful, awful—nothing ever fit right. A knock came at her door, making her drop the fabric.

"Come in," she called, not bothering to look up when the door creaked open.

"You're not dressed?" Thelia gasped.

North whirled around to find her mother, perfect as ever. Thelia's chestnut hair fell to her shoulders and a silver dress covered in sparkling jewels concealed her body, the cloth of the arms flaring out at the ends. She bet her mother had been dressed for hours, tapping her fingers together while waiting for the event to start. Her gaze dropped to Thelia's swollen belly. North would have a sibling soon, and this child might possibly have magic. She hoped her sibling would, so he or she wouldn't have to feel the way North did. North already had a softness for the child—she'd always wanted a sibling. But it had taken her parents a long while to conceive again, and they'd thought it would never happen. Then twenty years later it had.

"I don't have anything good enough to wear." North blew out a hard breath, pushing the silver locks away from her face. Even after everything that had happened with Birch, she wanted to appear beautiful for him. Not like a child.

"Let me help you then," Thelia said, pity forming in her brown eyes. In that expression, North knew something was wrong.

"What is it?" North asked, picking up the dresses from the floor.

"Birch is engaged to Gemma."

"I heard he was going to propose." And she supposed he had.

"Are you all right?" Her mother pressed her lips together, and North could tell she was worried about her.

North took a deep swallow, tears brimming at her eyes, and she shook her head. She hated that she needed someone, but right then, she really needed her mother. North dropped the dresses and threw her arms around Thelia, holding her tight. "I thought… I thought…"

"I know. I've always known," Thelia said softly, stroking North's hair. "And if I'd known Birch had fallen in love, I would have warned you."

Love… North's heart felt as if it had just spilled out of her chest and dropped to the floor with a sickening plop. She lifted her head and peered up at her mother, determined. "Can you at least help me look as though I'm worthy?"

"You're the worthiest female in all of Oz." Thelia smiled and turned North around. "Let me start with your hair." With practiced motions, she began to braid her daughter's hair.

North kept quiet as Thelia styled the top half of her hair into a full crown, pressing flowers into sections from the vases on her nightstand. The rest of her locks hung just past her shoulders. Thelia took a silk dress of deep purple, handed it to North to put on, then said she would be right back.

After North finished slipping on the purple silk, Thelia returned with a few things to accentuate it. A sheer copper skirt to layer the bottom half of the dress, then a soft chestnut leather piece that covered her shoulders and arms, leaving a gap of bare skin above the tight bodice of her gown.

"There." Thelia grinned, taking a step back. "Beautiful as always."

North turned to peer at herself in the oval mirror hanging on the emerald wall. Within the glass, she still appeared childlike, due to her height, heart-shaped face, and doe eyes. All she could focus on were her flaws and how, if anything, she was possibly cute. But beautiful…? "It's perfect," she lied to her mother.

Thelia clapped her hands and drew North into a hug. "I love you."

"I love you, too, Mother." North wished she could be like Thelia, but she knew she would never live up to it. And her mother's heart was so brilliant that she would love North with all her flaws and misgivings anyway.

"We have a celebration to attend." Thelia waved North to follow her out of the room, then walked beside her down the emerald hall. North's heart pumped with elation at finally getting to see Brielle for the first time. Ozma and Jack hadn't arrived at the palace yet—they'd been at their secret cottage for the last month.

As she descended the steps, her hand touching the cool glistening marble of the banister—she wished that she were still high from the emerald powder. She didn't think she could handle seeing Birch with his betrothed this evening.

Music floated through the air, fiddles and flutes, swift and gorgeous. Laughter accompanied the welcoming sounds. With each step, the noise grew until she reached the bottom of the stairs, her gaze falling on a crowd of various fae filling the ballroom. Even in a space cluttered with bodies, she spotted Birch's tall frame and blond hair across the room right away.

North stood on her tiptoes to see if anyone was beside him— her cousin—but she couldn't tell.

"Get closure," Thelia whispered, knowing, and patted her shoulder. "I'll see you in a while."

Closure. Perhaps that was what she needed. He was still her friend, even though she would war with herself about wanting more.

North nodded and skirted around bodies dressed in fine spider silk gowns, decorative head coverings, shoes of the finest leather. Chandeliers of silver and green hung from the ceilings, and along the walls were paintings of the various territories of Oz. She followed the high archway of the ceiling until she came upon Birch. Thankfully, he was alone, guarding the area, a sword at his hip and his bow across his chest. His hooves were bare, and he wore a light gray tunic and tan pants.

He met North's stare, cocked his head at her and smiled, his eyes dancing playfully—even though he knew what she'd confessed to him. How she'd looked a fool.

"Does this mean you're not ignoring me for all eternity?" he asked, holding out his hand to her.

"Perhaps." North placed her palm against his and he pulled her beside him. The fact that he didn't act different toward her made her heart sing.

"If this is ignoring, then I'll take it."

She smiled, wishing she could stay touching him for the entire night, but he was in love with someone else. *Bah.*

"So you'll still be my guard, right?" she asked as she watched fae placing honied desserts into one another's mouths, gulping down wine, kissing.

"To serve you is my first duty." He bent his knees so she and he were eye to eye. "Always."

And that would have to be good enough.

"May I borrow her for a bit?" a voice called behind her, drawing her attention away from Birch.

Reva.

Her grandmother was dressed in the darkest of blacks, a tight gown with a train trailing along the floor, heeled boots, and the swells of the tops of her breasts for all to see. She looked wickedly perfect, like a dark enchantress. If North had worn that, her father would have chopped off the head of anyone who so much as looked in her direction.

"Love doesn't always happen the way we want it to, does it?" Reva murmured, draping an arm around North's shoulders. Of course someone had told her grandmother, and she was sure it had been Thelia.

"It did for you," North mumbled. Shame washed over her for saying that because she knew the story of how long Reva and Crow had been separated from one another before reuniting. Twenty-one years, and both Reva and Crow had not been themselves for eleven of them. They hadn't reunited with Thelia until that time either, when North's mother had discovered who she truly was and had conjured Reva and Ozma from a dark place with her magic.

"You don't even want to know how many males I went through to find Crow." Reva laughed. "You're young, and there will be more. Enjoy the pleasure. Have fun. Live."

"Easy to say when Tin's not your father." She had a feeling that Tin would have had a hard time accepting Birch, and he'd known him for years.

"Tin is just protective, that's all."

Something landed on North's shoulder and talons scratched lightly through the fabric of her dress, causing her to jump. Her eyes fell to black feathers and a sharp beak. "Grandfather." North grinned.

Crow let out a low caw before leaping from her and transforming in front of them in a cloud of smoke. A few obsidian feathers trailed to the stone floor.

"Haven't started trouble yet, have you?" He chuckled, lifting a beaked mask and pushing it to the top of his head, revealing the light scar over the bridge of his nose. His hair was entwined with feathers, and he wore a deep blue tunic paired with dark pants.

Before she could give a snarky response, a horn blew, its sound long and loud right outside the closed entrance. The entirety of the room silenced, everyone spinning to face the opening doors. North stood on her tiptoes again, so she could catch a glimpse of Ozma, Jack, and the baby when they entered. But someone's melon of a head blocked her view.

"Need me to lift you on my shoulders like I used to?" Crow chuckled.

North rolled her eyes but almost took the offer.

Still chuckling, Crow grabbed her by the elbow and tugged her to the side for a better view. "Look here."

She peered through a space between a gray-haired pixie— Whispa—and a dryad, to see two fae guards enter the room in uniforms of blue and emerald. Behind them followed a female with long blonde waves cascading to her waist and an orange-haired male with freckles. Ozma and Jack. In Jack's arms was a child swaddled in a light blue blanket. Gold crowns with blue and green jewels sat atop their heads. Ozma was draped in an emerald silk gown with a sapphire cloak, the silver slippers shining on her feet, and her wings hidden for now. Over her eye rested a patch that matched her cloak. Jack smiled brightly in his knee-high boots, leather pants, and silken tunic while Ozma greeted each fae as they passed. They walked down the ornate velvety carpet to their glistening gold thrones awaiting them at the far wall.

The fae of Oz hadn't known who Ozma was until she defeated the Wizard and regained the slippers. Then the world discovered that Queen Lurline and King Pastoria had been cursed to forget they'd conceived a child.

Beside the thrones, the guards stood tall as Ozma and Jack took their seats, beaming as they peered down at their child.

Reva nudged North forward, knowing she wanted to see the baby as much as anyone, even though Reva, because of her close friendship with Ozma, had the right to greet the child first. North knew she couldn't argue, so she made her way forward until she stopped in front of Ozma.

The Queen of Oz's dazzling blue eye scanned her over, and something like pride shone brightly on her face. "You look just like your mother and father," Ozma chirped, motioning her forward. The queen rested her gaze on her child in Jack's arms. "Brielle has been waiting to meet you."

"Hello, Jack," North said, wanting to hug him, but his hands were too full. "Hello, Brielle."

"We have a few gifts for you." Jack grinned. "I'll grab them from our room after the celebration."

Jack always had the best gifts. Beautiful writing quills, adventure books, seeds for unique flowers.

"May I?" North asked, reaching a hand forward, antsy to hold the baby.

Jack nodded, holding Brielle forward. North pressed a hand to the child's soft cheek, hoping she would have as much strength, magic, and gentleness as Ozma. That she would be just as giving and caring as Jack.

As she was about to pick up Brielle, the doors burst open with a bang. North straightened, leaving Brielle with Jack, and whirled around, focusing on a male entering the hall. His hair was obsidian and sleek, his red irises blazing. Gold studs lined his pointed ears. He sauntered toward them as if this were his palace and he was a king. Thick-soled boots clunked against the floor, and the jingle of the metal adorning both his cobalt coat and the ruby sash around his waist echoed through the now-silent room. His hand hung too close to the golden sword dangling at his hip.

Two of Ozma's guards rushed forward. The male twirled his hand in the air, and a gray hue flooded across their bodies, casting them into stone. "Anyone else care to become a permanent fixture?"

"Everyone stop!" Ozma shouted.

No one else rushed forward, but the other guards, including Birch, were poised for Ozma's next command.

"Tik-Tok," Ozma said, her voice hesitant when he came to a stop before them. "Change them back."

Tik-Tok. North recognized the name immediately—he was the pirate from Ozma and Jack's past who had helped them break through the barrier around the Wizards home.

"All in due time. You know how it goes." He winked at Jack where he sat, frozen with fear, on his throne. "I've come to collect the female"—he held out his hand—"and my ring. A bargain is a bargain."

What bargain?

"You're not taking the child," North gritted out, narrowing her eyes. She lunged forward and shoved the male's firm chest. She may not have magic, but she would create the best barrier she could between him and the infant. With his next breath, he would probably turn her to stone too.

But Ozma wasn't even looking at the baby. She was looking at North.

"My apologies," Tik-Tok cooed, studying North up and down with a smirk. "It seems I've come to collect *you*, darling."

CHAPTER FIVE

TIK-TOK

Chaos erupted in the ballroom. It all seemed to happen in a single heartbeat—one teeny promise to take the female that he was owed from Ozma, and everyone lost their shit. The rest of the guards surged forward, nobles fled, and a loud *caw* echoed off the walls. Tik-Tok narrowly avoided a bolt of green lightning followed by a blast of gray magic. His enchanted arm protected him against magic which was helpful in a room of so many powerful fae, but that didn't make getting blasted by it fun.

Not that he was worried—his enchanted arm wasn't all he had at his disposal. His own magic was just as strong as theirs.

Silver flashed in his peripheral and he pivoted. It was too late to completely avoid the silver-haired male from cracking him with an axe so, instead, Tik-Tok flung out his power with a flick of the wrist, turning every remaining fae to stone.

Everyone except for Ozma, Jack, their child, and *her.*

Though, judging by the murderous look on the young female's face, he wondered if that wasn't a mistake. *No.* It was more fun this way. He would get to see how she reacted under duress before dragging her in front of the entire crew. She was a captive, after all.

Tik-Tok slowly swept his displaced black hair behind his shoulders and stood straight again. He looked over the axe with an appreciative nod as he edged around the now-stone male. *That was close.* The fae would be worth fighting if Tik-Tok wasn't in the middle of something much more important.

"A friend of yours?" he purred to the wide-eyed female. A gentle tug came at his center as he met her stare.

"Her father," Jack replied through gritted teeth. "Tin."

His brows rose. Tin was infamous—an assassin like no other—until his curse was broken by Thelia. And he was about to kidnap their daughter. Smart? Probably not. But Tik-Tok never claimed to be the wisest of fae. He needed the female. End of story.

"He'll kill you for this," Ozma warned. "And I won't stop him either."

"*Mmm.*" Tik-Tok stepped closer to the thrones. "He will definitely *want* to, but we had a deal. So, if he comes after me for taking her, he'll need to come after you for giving her away. I highly recommend spinning whatever tale necessary to keep him … subdued until I've finished with her. *If* I finish with her."

"No," Ozma and Jack said in unison.

"Suit yourselves." His red eyes slid back to the silver-haired female. "What's your name, darling?"

"None of your business," she spat.

Despite her bravery, it was impossible not to notice how violently her hands shook. Yet she didn't move to attack him or to defend herself. He couldn't decide if that was disappointing. "*None* for short, then? It's rather a mouthful otherwise."

She opened her mouth to reply, but Ozma reached back to grab her hand. "North," the queen said quickly. "Her name is North, but she's not the fae we bargained for."

"Isn't she?" He scanned North up and down, feeling the tug again. Silver hair that looked softer than a cloud, deep brown eyes, and known to the queen—exactly what the sea witch had told him. It wasn't her rosy lips, curvy waist, or creamy skin that made his cock twitch. It had been the way she'd risked being turned to stone to shove at his chest. She was a dainty thing, but his attraction to her wouldn't tempt him to change his plan. He would take her and she would open the portal. Nothing more.

Well, maybe… He couldn't deny a good seduction. If she found him half as attractive as he found her, having her naked flesh against his could become inevitable.

"Please," Ozma said with an edge of desperation. "She's the daughter of Tin and Thelia, the granddaughter of Crow and Reva. They have the allegiance of all four territories so, if I let you take her, they'll use all of Oz to take her back. Our deal was before she was born, and if I would have known—"

Tik-Tok snorted. If they wanted to chase him down with their armies, let them try. They would need to pass through at least one other country on their way out of Oz, which wouldn't sit well with the rulers there, then find an entire fleet of ships to reach him. *Good fucking luck.*

"North has no power," Ozma continued. "There are other females who meet your requirements."

"She meets my requirements well enough," he said with false nonchalance. North was the one—he could smell the magic in her, even if they believed she was without it. The pull he felt toward her was undeniable. Fate had linked them, he was sure of it. "I won't harm her, if that's your concern. I may be a pirate, but I'm an honorable male."

"Honorable, my ass." Jack stood, clutching their baby to his chest. "Ozma, we can't…"

"You don't have a choice." Tik-Tok was suddenly in front of Ozma, seething. "We made a binding deal for the unborn female in order for you to defeat the Wizard. If you break it, who knows what will happen." His eyes slid toward Jack and their child in a silent threat. The consequences of breaking a vow were unknown until it was too late, but it was nearly always worse than keeping one's word. Body parts could fall off, loved ones often met an untimely end, or, of course, your own death. Afflictions were common consequences and the sort that made one *wish* for death. "You have an infant to think about now. Denying me isn't worth the risk."

Ozma gasped, her gaze darting to Jack and the baby. Tik-Tok could practically see her thinking as she drew her bottom lip between her teeth. The indecision and guilt. Her inability to say the word *yes* even though it was the only real option.

"I'll go," North said, her voice wavering.

Tik-Tok's breath caught. He hadn't misheard, had he? She was willing? Then why the fuck was he still standing there, arguing?

"North, no." The Queen's voice was hard and unyielding. "You're not going anywhere."

She forced a small smile and squeezed Ozma's hand. "If anything happens to you, Jack, or Brielle, I would never forgive myself."

"If anything happens to *you*, I would never forgive myself either."

North eyed Tik-Tok so hard that he felt it in his core. *What a bold little North Star.* He liked her already.

"He said I'll be safe," she reasoned and scanned the room of stone fae with uncertainty. "His word will have to do."

"I said *I* wouldn't harm you. Same goes for the crew, but no promises on being safe." He was riling the female, but he couldn't help himself. With a smirk, he added, "It *is* a pirate ship, after all."

"Do you want me to come with you or not?" she hissed, then looked back to the queen, her gaze softening. "Let me do this for you, Ozma. I'm not angry with you—you've been like a second mother to me. The deal you made was to save all of Oz from the Wizard so this isn't such a steep price. Besides, you couldn't have known the bargain was about me. And I'll find a way back home."

Ozma nodded once.

His smirk grew. *She was his. The portal was* mine. "That's all settled then."

"We haven't settled anything," Ozma growled.

"Blossom," Jack whispered. "As much as I hate this, there's

nothing we can do right now. You agreed to the bargain."

"I don't know how long we'll be gone," Tik-Tok said, meeting North's gaze. There wasn't a single tear in her eyes as she straightened, and that … intrigued him. The sea witch had told him he needed the female, and now he had her. Besides, she would get used to life on *The Temptress*, and nothing she did would thwart his life's work. "If you want to gather any of your belongings, do it now. Be quick."

"Don't hurt them," North pleaded.

Tik-Tok glanced between North and the rulers of Oz. "Why would I hurt them?" When her eyes flicked to the sword at his hip, he had to bite back a laugh. If he wanted the queen and king dead, he wouldn't achieve it with a blade—not when they'd both grown so well into their powers. "I wouldn't waste time arguing about you if I had plans to murder them."

North hesitated before bolting around Jack's throne, putting as much space between them as possible, and fled the room. He wasn't concerned about her fleeing—not when she had already agreed to join him. Had argued in favor of it.

"Now"—Tik-Tok held his palm out toward Ozma—"my ring, please."

She clenched her jaw, leveling a steely glare at him, and reluctantly held her hand out, fingers shaking with rage. The gold ring he'd placed on her finger was untarnished with time. It had allowed her to share Jack's power when she'd had none of her own and was the only reason she'd been able to kill the Wizard. Without Tik-Tok, she and Jack would've been eaten by those vile fruit-addicted creatures, or met their doom at Oz's hand. He'd practically given Ozma her crown—temporarily borrowing one of her subjects wasn't much to ask in return.

Tik-Tok gripped the ring and pulled, but it didn't budge. "You have to willingly surrender it, Your Royal-ness."

Ozma closed her eyes and took a few deep breaths, seeming to calm herself, then nodded.

Tik-Tok pulled again, and the ring slid from her finger. Having it in his possession after all these years was more relieving than he expected. It kept his different powers from getting too jumbled inside him, making them easier to wield separately.

He took three steps back and removed the glove covering his gold hand. When the ring was seated on his digit, the color shifted back to the original silver metal. He flexed his fingers, admiring its return, before replacing his glove.

Behind him, the doors banged open and a huffing, puffing North stumbled back into the ballroom with a small, handheld luggage case. "I'm back," she said as if they hadn't noticed. "Can I … say goodbye?"

Tik-Tok looked over to where Tin was frozen, axe in the air, snarl on his face. Behind him was Reva with her hands outstretched, lightning balled against her palms, a crow frozen midair, and a female, hands twisted as if calling upon a large storm of magic.

No way in hell was he releasing them from their stone prisons. Once he was far enough away from the palace, this particular magic would fade on its own and then they would be Ozma's problem.

"Sorry, my star, but I'm not interested in fighting my way out of here. You can have five minutes with the queen and king to pass along any messages." He nodded to Ozma and Jack. "I'll release a handful of guards now to help you move the others. When we're far enough away, the spell will break, and you won't want their magic hitting the wrong target when it does."

Ozma ignored him, pouncing on North with the tightest hug.

Jack nodded. His face was grim as he took in the room of statues. "Release Whispa now as well," he ordered, pointing to an elderly pixie. "She's harmless and can take our child to safety while we deal with…" He glanced around the room.

Tik-Tok waved a hand at the pixie without a word, releasing her. A shriek fell from her lips, but he was already weaving his way around the others to carefully select which guards seemed the least skilled.

Better to play it safe.

The royals spoke in hushed whispers, the pixie replying

through crackling sobs, as he made his selections. He worked slower than he would've liked, to give North a few moments longer. Not that he cared, really, but if she was willing to cooperate, it could make opening the portal easier. So he would play nice until she gave him a reason not to.

"Time to go," he called from the ballroom doors when he'd finished his assessment.

Ozma clung tighter to North as she started to step back. Whispa stood behind them, crying silently while gently rocking the baby. North finally moved away from the queen and buried her face in Jack's chest before stumbling her way over to Tik-Tok.

He held a hand out to North, but she brushed past him without taking it. *Insolent!* He pressed his lips together to hide a smile. As long as she didn't take her attitude too far, he was *really* going to enjoy this.

Slowly, Tik-Tok backed out of the room, taking the knobs of both double doors in his hands. He half expected one of the royals to lash out at the last minute, to demand North stay.

Instead, feathery wings burst violently from Ozma's back, blue light, otherworldly, and shimmering. She whirled on him, her voice coming out low and deadly, the first time he'd seen her truly angry. "Don't think this ends here."

Tik-Tok would've been disappointed if there were no repercussions. As long as he got his portal opened first, he welcomed Ozma's revenge attempt.

With a flourishing bow, he took the final step from the room and closed the ballroom doors. A small, effortless burst of magic tingled from his fingertips as he released the chosen guards from his spell. Almost instantly, Jack's order to stand down came. North clung to her luggage with her lips pursed, a deep line between her brows. But even while scowling, he saw her eyes growing glassy.

"Shall we?" he asked.

Her only answer was to pierce him with a stare.

He chuckled. *Oh, this* will *be fun.* "After you, then."

CHAPTER SIX

NORTH

Everyone North loved had been turned to stone. The only goodbye to her family would be through Ozma and Jack. Her father, mother, grandfather, grandmother, Birch…

North hadn't known Ozma had struck a deal with the pirate. Ozma had bartered a female from the future in order for Tik-Tok to help her save Oz, but hadn't known who it would be. Hadn't known because North hadn't been born yet. North didn't know how to feel—her life had been given away before it even started. But it was what it was.

Before she'd left, Ozma had told her that Tik-Tok's magic would wear off when they got far enough away, but she wouldn't know for certain.

North walked out of the palace and through its protective barrier. A lot of good the magic did to keep nefarious fae out since Tik-Tok had found a way to slip past it. How *had* he done it?

Her steps came to a halt and her eyes widened as she noticed guard after guard had been turned to statues. That was how…

She took a deep swallow and picked up her pace again. It was already darkening, and the streets stood empty. All fae living in the Emerald City seemed to be within the palace walls or celebrating Queen Ozma and King Jack's child inside their own homes.

The sound of booted feet echoed beside her, but she avoided looking at the male. Wouldn't let him see her tears. She'd tried to hold onto the anger she felt earlier in the palace, tried to be strong like her family would have been, but as soon as she'd left the ballroom, realization that she was alone struck, and hot tears slid down her cheeks.

A red cloth slipped in front of her face, as crimson as Tïk-Tok's irises. She ripped the fabric out of his hands, threw it on the ground, then stomped on it for good measure. Taking her sleeve to her cheeks, she wiped away the wetness instead.

"Was that really necessary, my star?" Tïk-Tok asked as if she had offended him by throwing his gods-forsaken cloth on the ground. *Good.*

"Leave me alone." North kept staring ahead, avoiding his face as she tightened her grip on her luggage. She wondered how Ozma and Jack had been able to tolerate him when they were trying to save Oz.

"You can have some time alone once we're on my ship, but not until then."

They were still in the Emerald City, only a short distance past the palace walls. Traveling to the sea was no easy feat. How would they even cross the sand barriers surrounding the Land of Oz? But if Tïk-Tok could turn whomever he wished to stone inside the palace, then she supposed the rogue could get them across. However, it would still take days to reach the sea. Days and *days*...

Hope filled her chest.

Days.

It would take days.

Her father would come for her regardless of who told him not to, who told him to wait. Then there was her grandfather—Crow could easily fly and spot them from above, then send word to the others. Someone would reach them before they got to the sea.

"Come out," Tik-Tok cooed.

Who was he talking to? Or *what?* North inhaled slowly, peering around as the sunlight dimmed.

Above them, an elf wearing a deep green tunic hovered in a large tree. He leapt from the branch, landing directly in front of them. Light brown eyes met hers and blue hair brushed his shoulders.

North took a deep swallow, glancing back in the direction leading to the palace.

"Ah"—Tik-Tok tilted his head—"you thought your loved ones would catch up and rescue you, didn't you? They won't today."

North clenched her jaw. "I hate you."

He grinned, baring all his teeth, appearing like a wild fae beast. "Hmm. I don't hate you, though." He snapped his gloved fingers at the elf, and the other male pressed a hand to each of their shoulders, digging his fingers in.

"I'm Respen," the elf said. "Just remain relaxed."

Before North could wiggle from the elf's grasp, her head spun, her feet touching nothing. A strong gust of wind smacked her face and the whole world was a blur. Her scream stayed silent, way down in the pit of her stomach, trying to claw its way out. She closed her eyes until the spinning stopped and her body no longer felt like it was swaying.

North gasped, her heart pounding wildly. They were no longer in the Emerald City, but on a hard surface, slightly rocking. A ship. Below her boots was a long and wide deck, and curving pristine rails lined the edge of the ship. Tall poles that met at a sharp point held triangular sails and netted ropes—all a dark charcoal shade.

"I'm going to join Dax and Cyrx." Respen said, releasing their shoulders. She watched as he walked to the opposite side of the ship, his blue hair swaying, where he joined another elf and goblin. The elf was tall and slender with dark brown skin, long blond hair, and blue eyes. Deep scars ran across the goblin's orange flesh, his muscles bulging against his tunic, and large teeth poked out of his mouth.

North frowned as she met Tik-Tok's smirk. "You could have at least given me a heads up."

"And risk you trying to run?" He shrugged. "I don't think so."

"I agreed to come, didn't I?" she bit back, her silver tendrils blowing around her face.

"You did, but that doesn't mean you won't try to flee. Or murder me. I wouldn't try either of those things, for the record, because I have an alternate plan if it happens."

North stumbled a few steps to the rail as the ship rocked, and glanced at the last light of day catching the silver swells of the sea, just before night touched down on the water. Except for a few orb-lit areas of the ship, the stars, and the moon, they were surrounded by darkness. She felt Tik-Tok sidle up beside her, closer than she would have liked.

"We're here," she finally said when he remained silent, "so what is it you want me to do? Because I don't have any magic."

He turned to face her, studying her, his eyes roaming her features, his nostrils slightly flared. She stared at him, growing annoyed at whatever it was he was doing. But for the first time, she took in his face. She knew his hair color, his eye color. But this close, those red eyes were like blood, his long, flowing hair the darkest of blacks. Gold studs lined his pointed ears. There wasn't a single blemish or scar she could see. His face was wickedly beautiful. And she hated that too.

"I smell it. The magic deep, deep down inside you. It's there, waiting to burst free. It will come soon, and I'll be waiting." His gaze shifted away from her. "Rizmaela, show our guest to her quarters downstairs." He focused back on North. "I'll meet you there shortly." With that, he shoved from the rail and sauntered to the front of the ship where Respen stood with the two other crew members.

Tik-Tok smelled *her* magic? He was mistaken.

A dwarf with matted copper hair, murky brown eyes, and a bulbous nose hobbled to her. She wore a worn tunic, loose trousers, and scuffed boots, her stocky height coming to about North's shoulder. *This must be Rizmaela.*

"Come on, then," Rizmaela grumbled, taking North's luggage. "The captain didn't tell me he'd be returning with a prostitute today."

North's eyes widened, and she drew in a sharp breath. "I'm not here for that!"

Rizmaela grunted. "Any other female would appreciate being taken by the captain."

What other female? A hobgoblin? "And I suppose that's how you got here?" North fired back.

"I'm here because I earned my place." Rizmaela struck her chest. "After my husband was murdered, I left my home. Chose this."

North didn't say anything else, wouldn't have known what to say to that anyway. She wondered how the dwarf's husband had been murdered. Even if North had wanted to plan an escape, the ship was somewhere in the middle of the sea, land nowhere in sight.

A pole hung across the deck and North ducked under it, then stepped around a few barrels as she followed the dwarf to one of the doors. Rizmaela pulled it open and motioned North down a ladder that appeared sturdy enough.

Gripping the rails, North headed to the bottom and waited. Rizmaela tossed down her luggage, narrowly missing North's head, and it landed with a *thunk*. The dwarf slammed the door shut again.

North rolled her eyes and picked up her case. She took in the small room with a single bed covered in satin sheets and fur blankets. Orbs from the ceiling gave off pale-yellow light. But there was nothing else.

It was a prison.

North let out a sigh but didn't shed any more tears as she rested her luggage beside the bed and sank onto the mattress. At least Ozma, Jack, and Brielle were safe. She truly hoped everyone would be freed from the spell that had made them stone. Tik-

Tok had said as much. But could she trust Tik-Tok's word? Ozma seemed to trust him on that matter, so North had to believe her family would be released from his magic.

This wasn't Ozma's fault, even though North knew she would blame herself. North thought back to the story she'd heard as a child about how Ozma and Jack helped save the Land of Oz and Tik-Tok's part in it. Ozma hadn't completely trusted Tik-Tok back then, but he'd done his part in assisting her. Even as a child, North had wished for the multiple abilities he held. Had wanted to go on a ship and sail the sea. Well, here she was…

Her family wouldn't be the only ones looking for her. Birch would be too. She still wished things were different between them. But, as her friend and her guard, he would risk his own happiness, his life, to bring her home. North knew she couldn't get out of this situation on her own, but she couldn't have anyone get hurt because of it.

Since she couldn't flee and wouldn't possibly be rescued for some time, perhaps there was another way… What would her grandmother do if she was North? She would seduce, then kill the pirate. Tik-Tok hadn't hurt her, and North had agreed to come, so killing him felt wrong. Besides, she'd never murdered anyone. But maybe North could try to tempt him, the way Reva would have. And once he felt something for her, when she wasn't a stranger, then there was a higher possibility she would get home this century.

North may not have much experience with physical touch, but she'd imagined every way that she had wanted Birch against her. Then there had been the other night by the tree… She could at least kiss … and grasp a male's length… North sighed at the last part because she wouldn't know what to do after that, but she could try. Tik-Tok was hard to read, yet perhaps she stood a chance. At least he hadn't looked at her like a sister, the way Birch did.

The door flung open without a knock, and North jerked her chin up to watch as Tik-Tok slid gracefully down the ladder. He grinned as he turned to face her.

"How about you knock next time? I could have been naked," North said, annoyed by the way he came in like he owned the place. Even though she supposed he did.

"I would have closed my eyes." His grin grew wider. "Maybe."

She narrowed her gaze.

"Relax, I knew you wouldn't be changing." He ran the tip of his gloved finger along the empty wall as he inched closer to her.

"What power do you think I have?" North asked, trying to figure out the right opportunity to put her plan in motion.

"Portal magic."

North had already tried to open portals while accompanying her father in the South. She could never do it. "I don't have that."

"Not portals on land, but the sea."

"No one can open portals here," North said.

Tik-Tok looked her over thoughtfully. "No one in Oz, perhaps, except you. Hence, why I've waited so long."

Why was he so worried about opening portals in the sea anyway? She lowered her brows, trying to focus, to see if she could feel any movement of magic within the water. If she did, then maybe she could open a portal, be finished, and then he would send her home. But there wasn't a single stirring of power. Nothing. "I *don't* have magic."

"Rest tonight and I'll help you try another time." He shrugged and turned on the heels of his boots to leave.

"Wait!" she shouted, desperate. "Come sit."

Tik-Tok slowly spun to face her, his brow arched. He didn't leave, though—he took a step forward and sat beside her. Too close. Each time she'd been near him, he'd been too close. Like he didn't understand proximity.

This was perfect though, because if she'd tried to kiss him standing, it would have been awkward with him being over a head taller than her.

With lazy motions, Tik-Tok leaned back, his elbows pressing into the fur blankets. A sandalwood scent enveloped her. "What is it you want?" His words rolled off his tongue like knives wrapped in silk.

She remembered the motions of the drunken kiss the other night, the way she'd instinctually moved her lips, her tongue. North's gaze drifted from his scarlet eyes to his lips, and it wouldn't be the worst mouth she could have kissed. Plump and shapely. A pretty mouth on a dangerously pretty face.

"This," she finally said, placing a hand to his warm cheek before pressing her mouth to his. There wasn't any hesitation or startle from him as his lips moved against hers. He parted her lips with his tongue, then swiped it along her teeth, the roof of her mouth, softly flicking it against her own tongue like he had done this a million times. He probably had. His lips caressed and took and gave. This was nothing like the kiss the other night, not a drunken dance but something she couldn't describe. And his hands weren't even touching her...

Tik-Tok drew his lips from hers and pressed them to her throat, then inhaled. "You most certainly do have magic in there."

Then he stood, peering down at her with a smirk. "I seduce, my star—I am not *seduced*. But, this once, I'm willing to make an exception. Shall we continue? I can keep you up all night, writhing in pleasure, or you can stop playing games that you know nothing about."

Bastard... Her fists tightened as she tried to wipe the kiss from her lips. "I hate you."

"I seem to have that effect on fae. But North, it doesn't stop me from getting what I want. Try making progress with your magic." And with that, he headed up the ladder.

The door gently shut, not like when Rizmaela had slammed it. Even though the click of a lock never came, she was still a prisoner.

North would find another opportunity to make this work.

CHAPTER SEVEN

TIK-TOK

Days of sailing without a destination had Tik-Tok pacing his quarters. The crew didn't mind—it was par for the course. Unless there was a particularly wealthy ship setting sail that they could plunder, they mostly meandered the sea, stopping at nearby ports as they came about.

But now he had North.

North who was going to open the portal for him. North who had tried to seduce him. Her kiss had caught him by surprise, but not more so than the fact that he had *liked* it. Soft lips that tasted like berries drew him in and, despite how innocent she seemed, made him want more. He still wanted another taste—to slip his tongue between her lips and devour her flavor.

But the little star hadn't once left her room since she'd boarded *The Temptress* nearly a week ago, and she'd barely eaten the meals Kaliko had brought down to her. Tik-Tok had left the door unlocked for her because, although she was a captive, there was nowhere to run. But he was growing tired of waiting. She had a job to do, and it was necessary for her to find her magic.

Of course, it didn't matter how willing she was to open the portal if Tik-Tok couldn't *find* it. He knew it needed to be opened in the northeastern part of the Nonestic Ocean thanks to his compass, but that was still a massive area to work with. They had already sailed across it countless times in an attempt to see or feel *something* that would give him the exact location, but to no avail.

"You're going to wear a hole in that rug," Respen said as he magically appeared in the cabin with a tray of salted meat and ale. The elf's blue hair slipped over his shoulder when he bent to set the meal down on the desk.

"Thanks for knocking," Tik-Tok grumbled. *I let my frustration show for one minute, and someone just* had *to walk in.*

Respen glanced over his shoulder at the door leading to the deck. "Sorry, Captain. The door wasn't open and I didn't want to spill anything with the sea as rough as it is today."

He grunted and continued to pace. Would sailing the entire northeastern sea again, this time with North present, change anything? Perhaps being in proximity to the portal's location could rouse her magic. Because it *was* there. The scent of it lingered in his mind, calling to something inside him. It was almost like she wasn't even *trying* to awaken it, holed up in her room as she was.

Respen hesitated at his desk. "Something bothering you, Captain?"

"No," he snapped, continuing to pace. How could he admit that he had no idea what to do with North now that he had her? Not when she willfully refused to acknowledge she had magic. They'd been waiting for her for more than twenty years. "Why are you bringing me food? Where's Kaliko?"

"He's preparing tea for your female and then had some inventory to check so I offered to help."

Tik-Tok spun on his heel, eyes narrowed. "*Tea?* This isn't a damn teahouse, Respen. Why is Cook lighting the fire when the sea is rough?" All it would take was a single ember to fall and the whole ship would go up in flames.

Respen blinked. "I … don't know, Captain. Kaliko told Cook to make sure North was comfortable. Since it's extra chilly today, I suppose he wanted—"

"We have a closet full of fucking blankets below deck." He pinched the bridge of his nose. "And I have a fool on board who would rather burn down my ship!"

Tik-Tok stormed past Respen and thundered down into the bowels of the ship where Cook was bustling about. The brownie was young—but old enough to know better—with a jagged scar running across her neck after a failed murder attempt before she'd joined him.

"Are you trying to kill us?" He slammed his palms down on the heavy table, the legs nailed down.

She whirled around with a yelp. "Captain! I don't understand?"

He scanned the kitchen, lips pursed at the lack of a fire. There wasn't even the hint of smoke in the air—just a warm herbal scent. "How did you heat the water?"

"I asked Dax," she replied with wide, horror-filled eyes.

Tik-Tok felt the anger rush out of him, then roar back to life. Only, now he was angry with himself. He didn't want to take his frustrations out on his crew—they didn't deserve it. If it were anyone else but the found-family on board this ship, he wouldn't have given two shits about who deserved what.

"Right." Tik-Tok smoothed his hair back. The elemental elf, Dax, couldn't create a spark, as his skill lay more solidly with air, but he had enough talent to heat water without fire. He slid the steaming teacup across the table. "Is this ready?"

The brownie nodded.

"I'll take it to her," he said in a gruff voice.

And she better have made some fucking progress with her magic.

By the time Tik-Tok reached North's room, half of the warm tea had sloshed out of the cup. It was still more than he ever would've given her, when water was better for hydration. Maybe Celyna truly *was* fucking with him—sending him after a female without the ability to access her power. He gave two quick raps on the door to announce himself to North before pushing it open and climbing down the ladder.

"What's that?" North asked, scowling up at him from the center of her bed. "Come to poison me now that you've realized I'm telling the truth about my lack of magic?"

Tik-Tok gave her a strained grin. *Get yourself together.* It wasn't like him to lash out like this, but he was *so* frustratingly close. His heart kicked as a memory threatened to surface, but it was quickly locked away again. He had everything he needed—so what was the problem? The sea witch might be seeing him sooner than expected.

"Oh, my star. If I wanted to poison you, I would simply pour it down your throat. Not hide it in tea." He set the cup down on the bottom rung of the ladder and flopped down beside her on the bed. "See, this"—he motioned between them—"only works if we're honest with each other."

North inched closer to the end of the bed, putting space between them. "I will *honestly* kill you one day."

He licked his lips and smirked. "I look forward to the attempt. What shall you do? Kiss me again, then bring a blade to my throat?"

Her nostrils flared as she studied him.

"Well?" He turned to his side, propping his head up on one hand. "Or … will you use magic to kill me?"

"I told you—" she said slowly.

Tik-Tok lifted a piece of her soft silver hair and let it slip slowly through his fingers, meeting her brown eyes. The eyes he'd dreamed about for years. Eyes that belonged to the female who would open the portal so he could get what he desired most. He leaned in, his nose almost brushing hers as he took her chin between his fingers, and inhaled that magical scent. "Your magic carries hints of the sea and sweet, tangy fruit." He released her. "With subtle notes of mint. Unlike your body, which smells of vanilla."

Deny it again, he silently dared her as he inched back to give her space. *Tell me you have no magic.*

"How can you smell it?" she asked in a careful voice. "And if it's true, then why can't I use it?"

Damned if he wouldn't find out. There was something in her tone that sounded as if she *wanted* the magic, that she really thought she didn't have it, and judging by her desperate expression, he believed her. Perhaps she needed a trigger to tap into the power. Something to break the locks off whatever held it back. He stared at her, taking in her perfect features, her alluring scent. *Yes,* he decided. She simply needed help. And that was what he would do to occupy his time until they found the portal. All his frustration could be funneled into something useful.

"I want you to try something." He pulled the golden compass from his pocket. Oz had held it hostage to ensure his allegiance, but it had been unnecessary. Celyna had told him to help the Wizard, and Tik-Tok wouldn't have walked away until it served his purpose. Which was what had brought him to Ozma, and Jack, who had retrieved the compass for him. Then North. "Take this."

"What is it?" she asked, lifting it by the edges with two fingers.

"A compass." He reached out when she settled it in her palm and flicked the top open. Curling black letters—N, S, E, W— marked the face with a spinning gold needle pinned to the center. It was spelled to show him which direction he needed to travel to find what he wanted most, but no matter how often he'd looked at it since North's arrival, the needle never settled. Something about her portal magic must've been messing with it. "It's supposed to point to what I desire most."

She stared at the open compass. "What is it you want?"

"All in good time." There was no point scaring her with the truth of his desire just yet. He peeled the glove from his gold hand and heard her sharp intake of breath. Flexing his fingers, he held it higher for her to better see it. He had a love-hate relationship with the appendage—getting it had required him to cut off his own arm, but it constantly protected him from the magic of others. "Like it?"

She scanned the arm, lingering on the pinned joints. If it weren't for the small pins and the fact that it was gold, it would've looked like a regular arm. Interest sparked in her eyes but she said nothing.

Tik-Tok slowly drew the ring, that he'd only just retrieved

from Ozma, off his finger. The instant jumble of power inside him pulled a small grunt from his throat, but it was just for a little while. Minutes, at most, though he should've been used to it after the last twenty-two years.

"Give me your hand," he instructed. North slowly held out the one not holding the compass and he slipped the silver band onto her finger. Unlike Ozma, he didn't need to whisper to distribute his magic. He simply pushed a little of his power toward the ring to allow her to share it. Not enough to do any harm should she want to, but enough to get a sense of what magic felt like.

"What's the point of this?" North asked, taking her hand away. "I'm not sure—"

The needle of the compass whirled faster before coming to a sudden stop in North's direction. Tik-Tok's heart hammered in his chest. The compass knew she was the key. *It knew.*

"Do you feel anything?" he asked breathlessly.

North dropped the compass to the bed and tugged the ring off, handing it back to him. "No. Should I?"

Tik-Tok never removed his eyes from the compass as he slid the ring back onto his finger. "I don't know," he admitted. Whether she felt it or not, the compass had responded to her when they shared his magic. "We'll begin training soon."

"Training?"

He made a low *mmm* sound. "How are you with a sword?"

"I trained with an axe."

"We don't have those here. You'll need to learn how to use a sword, or a dagger at the very least." He nodded to himself. In case there was ever a time someone attacked her and he wasn't immediately there to help, she should know how to stab someone. Perhaps it would boost her confidence too— sometimes it was as simple as the lack of self-assurance that kept a fae's power dormant. There were a lot of things they could try. "And we'll continue to practice with … this…"

"What is *this?*" she asked, sounding a little more nervous.

"Magic." He swept the compass up, the needle spinning once

more. "Drink your tea. I'll be back later."

He didn't wait for her to refuse the drink or for her to tell him to stay the hell away from her. Honestly, he couldn't give two shits about the tea that Kaliko prepared. And it was *his* ship. He would go where he wanted, when he wanted, and no spirited—albeit extremely attractive—female would tell him otherwise.

The door to North's room had barely shut behind him before he shouted for Rizmaela. A moment later the dwarf appeared at the top of the stairs leading to the storage rooms. "Man the helm," he ordered.

"Aye, Captain," she said. "Where to?"

"Northeast."

"You sound certain. Did the female have a breakthrough?" she asked, walking beside him to the helm.

"Something like that. For a descendant of Thelia and Reva, her lack of power is surprising," he admitted, spinning the ring around his finger. "Tin has portal magic, so it makes sense that his daughter would too, but speaking truthfully, I'd expected someone with a bit more flare, given her mother's lineage."

"Her father is the assassin?" Rizmaela rasped.

"Former assassin." Tik-Tok shrugged. There was something to be said about a male who could completely turn his life around. The memory of Tin's attack back in the Emerald City made him smirk. "His axe seemed well-kept as he swung it at my head though."

"I see." She placed her hands on the helm, eyes unfocused, and cleared her throat. "Captain?"

"What is it?" He couldn't stop the smile from spreading across his face. This was good. Very good. If he had to pry the lock off North's magic, he would do it.

"Should we go around The Palace of Romance?"

"The Palace of Romance? Why?"

"It's … just that if we head in that direction, from where we are now, it will send us straight through Captain Salt's territory."

Fuck. His old captain—the one he'd stolen *The Temptress*

from, along with his entire crew. The fae who went along with the mutiny were long gone, not that it mattered. Not to him and certainly not to Captain Salt. The old bastard was a cutthroat with absolutely no morals, so when Celyna told him to take the ship and leave the overbearing fae behind, it had been no hardship. Disloyalty sat uncomfortably with him for a few years, but once it faded, he had vowed loyalty to himself alone.

But, despite the rumor that Captain Salt had reformed himself, Tik-Tok knew that sailing through his territory wouldn't go unpunished. He already had a metal arm—he wasn't keen on having a matching set, if he even lived through the experience. But going around Salt's territory would take an extra three weeks. *No.* Twenty-two years was long enough.

"It's only a problem if he catches us," Tik-Tok mumbled, more to himself than his first mate. "No detours."

CHAPTER EIGHT

NORTH

North lay in bed, throwing her imaginary axes at the ceiling, only this time it didn't help her fall asleep. She'd been down in this room for a week now, pretending it was her sanctuary instead of her prison.

Only a brownie named Kaliko and Rizmaela had made appearances. Kaliko had dropped off her food then left, while Rizmaela would open and slam the door throughout the day—North assumed to make sure she was still there. But where else would she go? Dive over the ship and swim until she either made it to land or drowned? Whichever came first. North, of course, had thought about it.

Until a few hours ago, she still hadn't seen Tik-Tok since the day she'd arrived. The prick had been as cocky as ever. Still, he stirred something in her that no one else had—not even Birch. She felt *important* around the pirate. There'd been a moment where she believed him, that there could be a touch of magic within herself, that perhaps he wasn't mistaken in taking her aboard his ship.

Then she'd second-guessed everything again after he'd left. Her mother's magic had been hidden behind a glamour when she was cursed to be a changeling. So it made sense that Thelia hadn't felt her magic until she'd broken the curse.

Maybe North did have something buried, deep, deep down. But then why couldn't she sense it if she wasn't cursed or glamoured?

Focusing on the floating yellow orb above her, she threw a pretend axe at her mark. *Strike.*

With a sigh, she peered up at the door, wanting to clear her head somewhere else. Perhaps she would finally explore the deck, go out into the night to look at the sea and the sky. Breathe the freshness of the outdoors.

Peeling herself from the bed, North slipped on her boots and headed up the ladder. The crisp air rumpled her hair, and the waves beat against the ship's hull, singing a ravenous song. As she passed under the sails, she glanced up to see Kaliko hovering at his post in a circular space with open slits, the top wider than the bottom. He gave her a nod, his dark eyes shining, as she walked beneath him to the railing.

Not another soul was in sight—most must have retired for the evening to prepare for their shifts the next day. She rested her arms over the rail and stared up at the sky, sprinkled with hundreds of stars and a plump silvery moon. One star stood out, shining brighter than the rest.

North felt a body come up beside her, and she rolled her eyes without turning to face Tik-Tok. She wondered how he moved so quietly. "I'm not jumping off the boat tonight."

"I should hope not, North. The hippocampus and other sea beasts will rip you to shreds," a female sang, her voice silky, her body lightly humming.

North squeaked and whirled to the side to find a female, lithe and shapely, matching Tik-Tok in height, standing before her. Her hair was short and almost as red as Tik-Tok's eyes. Silver hoops lined her ears. The lit orbs of the ship made her green irises appear to glow. North found herself mesmerized, focusing on each angle and curve of the female's delicate face. She couldn't look anywhere else, didn't want to look at anything besides this perfect creature forever.

A veil seemed to lift and North's mind cleared. She quickly

shook her head and took a step back, her eyes drifting down to an unclothed body. The female was *naked*. Large, perfect breasts, a narrow waist and hips, the longest legs she'd ever seen.

Siren.

North reached up to cover her ears, rip them off if she must, because she knew what sirens would do when they hypnotized someone. She could ask North to slice off her own flesh and North would gladly do it if under her spell.

The siren grinned and yanked North back just as she was about to run.

"That won't be necessary," the siren said, not singing this time. "It was only a test to make sure I could protect myself if need be. I'm Echo, by the way, and I'm with the captain."

North scowled, unable to stop her thoughts from turning to Tik-Tok slowly peeling off his gloves and clothing to tumble this female. She had probably just come from his bed and knew North had tried to entice him the other day.

"Not like that. I'm part of his crew." Her grin grew wider.

North tried to keep her gaze on Echo's face as the siren leaned on the handrail, arching her back against it, making her appear even more alluring. "Why are you out here so late?" she stammered, struggling to collect herself.

"Each night, I take in the sea when the ship is quiet before going back to sleep beside Respen."

"Oh." She and Respen… How did that happen? How had he learned to have faith in a siren? How had Tik-Tok?

"Tik-Tok is a cocky son of a bitch, but you can still rely on him."

"He took me from my home," North bit out. She remembered the horror of seeing her family and all the guests in the ballroom turned to stone. How could she rely on someone who would do that?

"He saved me from mine." Echo shrugged. "There was an invading force in my underwater village. When he found me, I tried to sing him into doing my bidding, thinking he was like the others who'd murdered my clan. It hadn't worked, and he asked me to be part of his crew. That was before I knew he was protected from magic, of course. Try to trust him."

He hadn't given her a reason to. "I'll trust you before I ever do him."

"I'm surprised. I'm usually the last one anyone wants to." Echo pushed off the handrail and stepped past North. "I hope to see you on deck in the morning instead of hiding in your room."

North watched the siren's naked form saunter toward the back of the ship to a door leading below deck, where she supposed the female would curl up beside Respen.

North turned to the water again, shut her eyes, feeling for a possible portal, but there wasn't a single stirring of magic. A splash sounded below and her lids flew open as she shoved her head over the side, thinking she had performed some sort of miracle. But she only caught the scaly skin of a creature's back, jagged spikes lining its spine, and a broad tail as it sank below the swells.

Hippocampus. *Great. Just great.*

Lowering herself to the floor, she propped her back against the railing and let the waves sing their melody while she tried to tap into any spark of magic. Until she was too spent to even head back to her room and drifted to sleep on the deck.

Something nudged North's arm.

She cracked her eyes open to bright light and the tip of a boot beside her cheek.

"Rise and shine, my star," Tik-Tok purred. "Time to train."

She let out a yawn and pulled herself up to a sitting position, the salty air filling her nose.

As her gaze scanned up Tik-Tok's form, she took him in from boot to firm body to wickedly beautiful face. He looked pristine, and she wondered how long he'd been waiting for her to rouse. She hoped a while.

North stared down at herself, appearing as if she just rolled out of a bird's nest. She ran her fingers through her hair to comb out the tangles instead of going downstairs to get her brush.

"Do you want to put on a different dress yet? I can help if you want. I'm quick with my fingers when it comes to unfastening buttons." Tik-Tok grinned, his eyes dancing.

She shot him a glare, and her stomach decided to do the speaking when it let out a loud growl.

"Eat." He tossed her something red from his hand. She tried to catch it, but, of course, she dropped it onto the deck. Arching a brow, he watched as she scrambled to pick up the apple and bite into its juiciness.

She thought of her grandmother while taking another bite—they were her favorite fruit and she always had bowls of them at her palace.

"Here." He fished out a silver flask from his pocket and held it toward her.

She eyed the flask with suspicion but took it from him anyway. She brought it to her face, inhaled the strong scent, and wrinkled her nose. "What is it?"

"Do you not drink alcohol?" He reached to take it back.

She pulled it away before he could think her too innocent, like everyone else did. "I do." *The one time.*

If it were possible, his dark brow arched even higher.

North threw her head back and took a swig of the liquid. And holy gods did it burn as it slid down her throat. It was like fire, lava, and beasts' claws. How did he drink this? She managed to hold back her cough, but she could feel red staining her face.

"That color suits you," Tik-Tok commented with a wink. "I'll have to share my ale more often." Before she could tell him what a bastard he was, Tik-Tok unsheathed an extra sword attached to his waist, then threw it down in front of her feet. "Ready?"

North puckered her lips and stared down at the sharp blade, the golden handle, the sparkling encrusted ruby jewels. "I already know how to defend myself."

"With *all* weapons?"

"Just the axe." And her gods-awful aiming with a dagger and a bow.

"That isn't good enough. Lift it," he instructed.

With or without magic, most of the guards at her palace carried swords. Others, like Birch, used a bow. She thought of him now, already missing his face, his kind words. Even though he was worlds away, she imagined he was speaking to her. *You can excel at anything you want to. You just have to try. Want it bad enough.*

She picked up the sword, its weight heavy in her hands as she held it up, and prepared herself.

"Why are you standing like a hunched hobgoblin?" Tik-Tok motioned to her body with the tip of his sword. "Straighten your shoulders, adjust your feet, bend your knees slightly."

Hobgoblin, indeed… But she nodded, figuring she would learn what she could, take in the necessary skills she was lacking so she could defend herself better. No one had been able to teach her thus far, but she would try again anyway.

North held up the sword, the blade shining beneath the sun's rays. Tik-Tok swung his weapon, striking hers, metal against metal echoing. Her body lurched forward and the sword shot out of her hands, flying to the floor of the deck.

"Pitiful." A grunt came from Rizmaela as she passed them, carrying a large barrel almost the size of her body. "She would be better suited as a prostitute."

North wanted to knock the barrel from her hands and punch the dwarf in her face. Tik-Tok's gaze traveled up North's form, making her feel that he believed Rizmaela might not be wrong.

"I hate you," she said to him as she scooped up the fallen sword.

"Were you planning to tell me that the other night as I made you quake with pleasure?" He chuckled, his shoulders shaking.

She could feel her face heating again, but then she focused on his laughter. It was different than she would have expected— musical, beautiful. Not vicious or cocky, but pleasant. North attempted to block out the sound. "It wouldn't have gotten that far."

"Oh really?" He sauntered forward, backing her up until she was caged in by his arms at the rail. "Tell me, my star, how far would you have allowed your seduction to go?"

Gods. That was a very good question. Would she have spread her legs for him and allowed him entrance? Or would she have wrapped her hands around his length like she had the male in the woods, then realized she couldn't go through with it? She hated that she wondered what Tik-Tok's hardness would look like compared to the one she'd seen, felt.

She shook the image away. Birch. Birch. *Focus on him, even though he doesn't love you the same.*

Tik-Tok was studying her, and she realized that she'd inched closer to him in the cage his arms created around her, her chest brushing his. *She'd* done it. Not him. Realizing their positioning, she shoved him away. "Let's train."

Tik-Tok raised his weapon. She lifted the sword and he swung, and like before, her blade was knocked out of her hands, clanging as it struck the deck.

"Your turn." Not a single bead of sweat dotted Tik-Tok's face or neck, while perspiration was already sliding down her back and forehead. If an axe was in her hands instead, she wouldn't have dropped it, grown tired so easily.

Gritting her teeth, determined, North plucked the sword from the floor. She didn't even step into her stance, and with everything in her, she swung at the blade to take him by surprise. Tik-Tok didn't even blink as her blade gave his a fierce kiss—his hand didn't move an inch. He cocked his head at her, willing her to try again.

Gods, she hated him.

She eyed the gloved hand holding the sword, remembering how the gold had gleamed the night before. It was shaped like a real hand, moved like one, but it had been metal with small bolts attached to the joints.

"How did it happen?" she asked, unable to hide her curiosity about it any longer.

Tik-Tok hesitated, his lips curling into a half-smirk, half-sneer. "I cut it off."

"Why?" She couldn't hide her horrified expression, her gasp. "Was it too far gone from infection to be healed?"

"It was by choice. Because of it, I'm immune to magic and cannot be controlled." He was no longer smirking and had slipped into a neutral expression that she wished she could replicate. "Enough talking. Again." His gaze dropped to her sword.

So again and again she swung. Again and again he blocked. His sword didn't budge. Her sword fell to the floor. Every. Single. Time.

They practiced for the entire day, only stopping to eat or relieve themselves. Though she'd desperately wanted a break, she hadn't asked for one because she'd been so determined to beat him. Knock his sword from his hands just once. Then she could die happy. But she hadn't, so there she was, practically dead, her legs aching, her arms throbbing, and her entire dress drenched.

"One more time," she demanded as Tik-Tok sheathed his sword.

"Go rest," Tik-Tok said while she swayed, her hands shaking and gripping the hilt. "Echo will show you where to get cleaned up. Then we'll try again tomorrow."

North wanted to argue, but her tongue felt thick, and she was too tired to even talk. Echo strolled toward her, dressed in tight leather pants, a shelled top—lined with shimmery pearls, covering her breasts—and knee-high boots.

"You did well," Echo said, leading her to the back of the ship.

What was the siren talking about? North had been awful. It had taken her years to become decent with the axe, but she would never be good with *all* weapons. Especially if it had to do with aiming.

"I'm serious." Echo laughed when she hadn't said anything. "Most would have given up already."

That didn't mean much, because if an enemy came at her with

a sword, even if *she didn't give up*, she'd be dead. "I'll be practicing again tomorrow."

Echo lifted the hatch in the floor, then showed her down the stairs to the bathing chambers. Smooth wooden walls surrounded her, and high-back chairs with towels folded in their seats rested at the opposite end. Two large rectangular tubs stood side by side in the middle of the space, while a vanity with an oval mirror and wardrobe took up the wall across from them. Pale yellow orbs swayed along the ceiling, giving off a calming light.

"Some advice?" Echo started as North turned to face her. "I watched you up there this afternoon, and you were driving with emotion. You can't do that. You're small, right?"

North had heard it her entire life. "Yes?"

"Use it to your advantage. With practice, you can be nimble, light on your feet, duck and roll more easily than the captain." She pressed a finger to her lips and smiled. "But don't tell him I told you."

"I won't." North smiled in return.

"Dax already warmed the water in the bath, and there's soap for you to use. I also left you a sack filled with clothing from an old crew member if you need them. They're all about your size."

North had only packed a nightgown and the filthy dress she was already wearing. She normally wanted to look nice, usually for Birch. This time, it would be for herself.

"Thanks, Echo," North said as the siren headed back up the stairs.

The siren glanced over her shoulder before shutting the door, her grin widening as she stared past North toward the sack on the floor. "Don't thank me yet."

North's gaze lingered on the rough material of the sack, her interest piquing at what was inside. She knelt to untie the string, then drew the sack open. She dumped the contents on the floor and gasped at each piece of fabric.

She would never normally wear any of these revealing garments. But they were clean, so she would put something from

the pile on. And perhaps, with these, she could revisit her plan
to tempt Tik-Tok.

CHAPTER NINE

TIK-TOK

Tik-Tok tensed at the sight of North walking toward him with a new swing in her hips. Or, perhaps it was the same swing, just no longer hidden beneath flowing skirts. Now, she wore a deep red dress that clung to her curves. The material twisted and pleated in all the right places, accentuating her small waist. Thin gold-braided rope swirled beneath her breasts, looping upward over her shoulders in an intricate design. The sides were cut out, displaying skin down to her hips and the edges of her stomach. Two high slits in the skirt showed nearly her entire leg with each step.

"Why are you staring at me?" she asked with false innocence.

"What are you wearing?" he blurted.

North spun slowly. "Do you like it?"

Like it? He fucking loved it. That was the problem. Everyone on board would be gawking at her previously hidden attributes and thinking exactly what he was: *I want to fuck her.* But that wasn't why she was on *The Temptress*. Besides, if anyone was going to mix business with pleasure, it would be him and him alone.

"No," he growled. "Go change."

North grinned. "Sorry, I rather like this."

"I let you pack a case." He was overcome with a sudden urge to stand between her and his crew so they wouldn't see her looking so delicious. Stepping closer, he widened his stance. "What did you bring?"

"I brought a nightgown. Would you rather I wear that? The material is thin, practically sheer." Her soft lips tilted up. "Or should we end this discussion and begin our training for today?"

Practically sheer. A sudden desire to see the outline of her chest, her rosy nipples hard with the cool sea air, slammed into him. *Shit. Focus.* Tik-Tok swallowed hard and tossed a sword at her feet. "You'd better hope it doesn't limit your movements. I won't go easy on you."

North bent slowly to retrieve the sword, her cleavage begging to be set free as she glanced at him from beneath her lashes. "I'd never expect you to."

His mind filled with the image of her holding onto his headboard as he filled her—as he *didn't* go easy on her. *Damn.* In a desperate bid to rid himself of his mounting thoughts, he lunged into the first attack.

Day after day, Tik-Tok continued to work with North on her swordsmanship. And, day after day, she continued to flail around like a baby bird pushed from the nest too early. His patience was wearing thin. Sure, he had decades of practice, but how hard was it to *block*? To *duck* when a blade came flying toward your head?

Extremely fucking difficult, apparently.

But he had a potential solution. Respen had whirled himself to the market in Merryland an hour ago. The daughter of Tin had practiced with an axe—so an axe she would have. If there wasn't some form of improvement, he would simply chain her to his side for protection and focus on training her magic instead. That was more important, anyway.

"Captain," Respen said from behind him. "I'm back."

"Did you get it?" he asked, spinning to face him. North could only focus on mental exercises to find her magic for so long every day, and he needed to know she could wield a weapon. *Any* weapon. If there was ever a time he couldn't defend her, he needed to know she could defend herself. She couldn't open his portal if someone killed her first.

Respen nodded and held out the handle of an axe. "Merryland is busy today. Should we wait to dock?"

They needed an enchantment to conceal their presence from Captain Salt, and Merryland was the best place to get it. Tik-Tok loathed the crowds with their hustle and bustle, the pickpockets, the loud-ass hawkers, but he would make an exception this time if it meant getting his portal even one day earlier.

"No." Tik-Tok spun the smooth axe handle in his gold hand, his gloves forgotten in his room, testing its weight. It would be another forty minutes or so before they reached land. Maybe the crowd would thin by then. He turned toward the helm where Rizmaela stood, checking her own compass. "We'll go as planned. Who knows how long it will be before we dock again? Let the crew have some fun while I take care of business."

Rizmaela grunted and eyed the axe. "Is that for *her?*"

"Watch your tone, Riz," Tik-Tok replied. "Without her, there's no portal. Naturally, I'm going to take extra steps to make sure she's safe."

His first mate's top lip curled into a sneer, but she said nothing else. Tik-Tok watched her for a moment, swinging the axe gently at his side. *Not jealous,* he decided. There was no reason for her to be, of course, since there had never been anything remotely sexual between Rizmaela and himself. But this reaction was unexpected.

"Straight to Merryland," he said deliberately. "Call Dax if you need him to create enough wind."

"Aye, Captain," Rizmaela grumbled.

Respen caught Tik-Tok's eye, and the elf lifted a brow, sharing a knowing look. Apparently, they had both noticed the dwarf's unexpected dissatisfaction. "Want me to get North for you?"

"If you don't mind," Tik-Tok answered, returning his glare to Rizmaela until Respen disappeared. "Something you'd like to say now that we're alone?"

"No," she snarled.

But, clearly, there was. He scowled at the dwarf, rubbing his jawline. If she didn't want to tell him, it was likely something he didn't want to hear. Still, he was curious, but not curious enough to push the issue, so he checked his compass instead. *Still spinning.*

"You summoned me?" North said from across the deck.

Tik-Tok ground his teeth at the sight of her in yet another new outfit. Each one showed more skin than the last. If she kept it up, he wouldn't be surprised if she walked across the ship stark naked by the end of the week. Today's outfit was dark green and left a large strip of bare skin across her midriff. A wide golden ribbon circled the top of the skirt and beneath her breasts, bringing his attention straight to her stomach. He wanted nothing more than to lick the expanse of it. To nip and tease. *Damn.*

"It's time to train," he grunted.

North's gaze fell to the weapon in his hand, and her eyes brightened. "Is that for me?" she asked, a hint of excitement entering her voice.

Tik-Tok's chest swelled a little at seeing her happy, the more lecherous thoughts fading. She'd never smiled like that before. "You're shit with a sword so I sent Respen after an axe."

"I thought I needed to learn *all* weapons." Her grin widened, reaching for it.

"Using my words against me, are you?" He released the weapon to her and turned to point at the mast. Shutting his eyes for a moment, he willed away the image of that dress on his floor. Of what she would feel like beneath both his calloused hand and his gold one as he slid the top of her dress off to palm her breasts. "Throw it there," he instructed, his voice rougher than he would've liked.

When the axe didn't automatically soar past him, he crossed

his arms and looked over his shoulder. North stood, pretending to toss it, but not releasing when her arm came down.

He waved at the target again in a silent order to let go. "We have other things to do today, my star."

She sighed and, after pretending twice more, let the axe fly. It flipped repeatedly in an expertly thrown arc … then landed ten feet from the intended target, right between Dax's feet.

"The fuck?" the elemental elf called, his hands frozen mid-air where he was creating wind. The strong breeze he'd already built blew his light blond hair around his face, his vivid blue eyes wild with surprise.

Tik-Tok blinked. Then blinked again. She … missed. By *a lot*. Whirling, one brow hiked up his forehead, he studied North as if he'd never seen her before. "You…" He rubbed a hand over his mouth, unsure of what to say. Had she missed on purpose? *No.* Judging by her flaming red cheeks, she had actually tried to hit the mast. "Your father is *Tin.*"

"I am aware," she said through gritted teeth.

"But…" He watched Dax pry the axe from the deck. "You said you could handle an axe. So I got you an axe…"

She took a deep breath and tilted her head in an attempt at being coy. "I never said I was *good* at it. I said I *trained* with one."

"No shit. What the fuck was that?"

"You told me to throw it," she said with a shrug.

A surprised snort escaped Tik-Tok. "If you were honest with me, you wouldn't have almost killed one of my crew."

"I *was* honest. I simply left out the details." North shrugged. "And I may not be able to throw one, but I can swing them well."

More than anything, he wanted to see her fight well. Not so he knew that she could defend herself, but because it would undoubtedly send blood rushing to his cock. He licked his bottom lip.

"Here, Captain." Dax passed the axe back to him with a withering expression. "Maybe it's a good thing she can't access her power. She'd probably blast us out of the water."

Tik-Tok suppressed a laugh, knowing it wouldn't gain him

North's favor. While he enjoyed a good, old-fashioned hate fuck, he couldn't risk her agreeing simply because she had concocted some insane plan to seduce him. It was obvious she'd never sought male attention in this way, but had she fucked many others? Not that it mattered. He wanted her no matter the answer, but he wouldn't take her until she desperately *wanted* him to—until she begged him for release.

"Show me," he dared North, handing her back the axe.

A twinkle lit North's eyes as she found her grip on the wooden handle. Tik-Tok barely had time to draw his sword before she lunged forward. He brought his blade up to block and, an instant later, the hook of the axe twisted it from his hands. The sword clattered to the deck, leaving him wide-eyed, mouth parted.

"Have I shown you enough?" she asked with a smirk. "Or shall we go again?"

Tik-Tok stepped over his sword, into her space, and took in the sight of her. It had been so quick, so skillful, and made him fucking hard. It was all he could do to not steal a kiss right there on deck in front of the whole crew. "Oh, my star, I haven't seen *nearly* enough." When she blushed, he stepped back and reclaimed his sword. "But it will have to wait. We'll be arriving in Merryland's capital shortly."

North scanned the horizon. "I've heard stories of that city. Isn't that where pirates go to sell their stolen goods?"

Mostly. He shrugged. "Until you open the portal, you're my first priority. No one will harm you."

North leaned slightly to the side to see around him. "Are you sure about that?"

Tik-Tok followed her gaze to Rizmaela, who was studying North with fire in her eyes. "Don't worry about her."

She mumbled something he couldn't quite hear before turning on her heel.

"Where are you going?" he called after her.

"You said training was finished."

Tik-Tok hurried to her side, his gaze stuck on her ass the

entire time. "That doesn't mean I'm finished with you for the day. Wouldn't you like to get off this ship for a while?"

North stopped walking and turned to face him, eyes narrowed. "Why?"

"So suspicious." He tapped her nose with the tip of his golden finger. "We're docking soon for food and supplies." *Very specific supplies so Captain Salt doesn't locate us.* "Most of the crew are going into town, and I can't very well leave you here with a couple of brownies."

She folded her arms, inadvertently drawing his attention to the swells of her breasts. They had been concealed before, but this dress clung to them, lifting them, drawing the eye. They were the perfect size to fit in his hands.

"Why not?" she asked. "I've proven I'm capable with an axe."

Because she was too important to risk, even if that risk was infinitesimal. The best way to protect her was to have her beside him. "What if the ship is boarded by thieves while we're gone?" he asked, cocking his head. "How many can you fight at once? The brownies are hard workers, but hardly warriors."

"*Will* it be boarded?"

He laughed at the concern in her words. No, his ship wouldn't be ransacked. Ozma likely had the entire continent looking for them too, but he *dared* someone to try taking North. Besides, his reputation was too great to attract thieves and his stolen treasures well-hidden elsewhere. "Let's use this opportunity to get to know each other," he offered, "since we'll be spending a long time together, it seems."

"We'll see about that." Her gaze locked onto his, seeming to dare him to press the issue.

Tik-Tok grinned and gently pushed her hair behind her shoulders. "This dress suits you," he said in a quieter voice.

And makes me want to rip it off.

His cock jerked at the thought. Of seeing her flesh. Touching it. Listening to the little sounds that he would draw from her. He bit his lip to keep from groaning in anticipation. They were indeed going to be together a long time… It wasn't irrational to think she would end up in his bed. Enough females from the ports had sucked and fucked him on his sheets over the years, but none had made him anticipate the act as much as she did.

"You wouldn't prefer the nightgown?" North asked, matching his tone.

He laughed brightly, genuinely. "You may succeed in seducing me, after all."

"I—"

"Don't worry." Tik-Tok winked. "As I told Ozma, I'm the most gentlemanly of pirates."

"Land!" Kaliko called from above in the crow's nest.

"Land," Tik-Tok repeated with a grin. "Are you coming with me, then?"

"Do I have a choice?" She arched a silver brow.

He held out his gold hand for her to take. "Not really, no."

She placed her hand in his and shivered slightly when her palm touched the cold metal. "Fine, but you're buying me a better axe."

"I'll buy you anything." He leaned closer. "All you have to do is ask."

CHAPTER TEN

NORTH

North adjusted the axe at her back—it was a little heavier and bulkier than she would have liked, yet the weapon had worked well enough for training. She smiled to herself, remembering the look on Tik-Tok's face when she'd knocked the sword from his hand, then winced when she thought about how she'd hurled the axe and almost sliced off Dax's malehood.

The sun shone bright in the sky, not a cloud in sight, as she walked down to the dock behind Tik-Tok. He was discussing something with Dax when someone slid up beside her, and she recognized the hum Echo's body emitted.

The siren ran a hand through her short red hair and grinned widely. "Who knew you'd be so good with an axe? When I saw you knock the sword from the captain's hand, I almost shit myself." She laughed, draping an arm around North's shoulders. "No one has ever done that to him."

"My father trained me." North thought about him and how, when she was younger, she'd wanted his axe for her own, even though it had been too heavy. Her father had surprised her one day by having an axe like his made, except in her size. After placing it in her tiny hands, he'd wrapped her fingers around the weapon and shown her how to swing. It hadn't come easy, but she'd practiced every morning with him. Not because he'd told her to, but because she'd wanted to. Tears pricked at her eyes, thinking about him. Stone. Her family as stone. They wouldn't be that way any longer, but the image of her father frozen, holding his axe in mid-air to save her lingered in her mind.

"You won't be with us forever, North. The captain needs you to open the portal and then you can go wherever you want," Echo said softly. Her tone lightened again. "I'm glad you decided to wear my gifts."

"I should have known she got them from you," Respen piped in, wrapping his arm around Echo's waist and tugging her to his side.

"Joria's old clothing was still below deck in her sack, practically screaming to be worn by her." The siren's grin grew wider.

North smiled, finding that she liked Echo more and more with each conversation. When it came to clothing, North had never worn anything close to revealing until Echo had given her these. Growing up, she'd always chosen loose, pretty gowns, usually adorned with pearl buttons. The night of Brielle's celebration, when her mother had accessorized North's gown, had been the only time she'd ever dressed differently.

Perhaps North had worn the dresses that she thought would please everyone else, instead of choosing for herself. The tighter fabric felt more like *her*.

As she'd moved with the axe, the slits in the skirt made it easier for her to shift and lunge. When practicing with the sword, she had still perspired, but there'd been better airflow and the material hadn't clung to her flesh like a wet starfish—much.

"Do you want to come with us? We're going to pick up some goods at the market. I'm famished." Echo stepped from the long pier onto a grassy trail leading in two different directions.

"She's coming with me," Tik-Tok answered, as if he'd been listening the whole time, which he probably had been.

Dax rolled his eyes and sauntered up beside Echo and Respen. "She'll be fine with us. I'll keep her safe."

Tik-Tok glared at him. "You'll keep her safe as you fuck a

female in the middle of the market? She doesn't need to witness that horror."

North *did not* want to watch Dax take a female while she stood by, whistling to herself, waiting for him to orgasm. And judging by the direction Respen's hand was venturing on Echo, they would be doing the same thing.

"I'll go with you," North said to Tik-Tok, surprising herself. She'd already spent days training with him alone on the ship, and even though he aggravated her at times—or all the time—it wasn't uncomfortable being around him.

Echo gave her a wave and tugged Respen with her while Dax walked beside them.

"Ah, you can't deny my company, can you, my star?" Tik-Tok grinned. The smile said she would be in for trouble, but good trouble. Did she *want* trouble?

North flicked her gaze from his to the trees surrounding them. *This is the perfect moment to be a little more charming.*

"So," North purred, toeing at the grass. "Where are we going?"

Tik-Tok furrowed his brow. "Something wrong with your throat? We can find a healer."

North sighed at another failed attempt and shifted closer to him, purposely brushing her arm against his. She palmed her forehead when he didn't seem to notice, or did he not feel it in his gold arm?

He lifted his hand and waved her to follow him. "We can't waste time. I'm meeting a friend and getting a real meal while we're at it."

"What friend?"

"Aren't you the inquisitive one?" He fished out a gold pocket watch from his pants, then looked ahead. "The less you know, the less you'll worry."

Of course... But that only made her worry more.

They walked side-by-side down the narrow, grassy trail, and North studied the trees. The foliage there wasn't as lush as the flora across the Land of Oz—it was duller and more muted in coloring. She passed bushes covered with shriveled yellow berries that didn't appear appetizing. Even the small bugs seemed to avoid them, which probably meant their juice was poisonous.

A rustling stirred, shaking the leaves behind her. She turned around, thinking Echo or one of the others had come back. But as she scanned the trail, the trees, no one was there.

"What is it?" Tik-Tok asked. "You stopped walking."

Taking a deep swallow, she squinted. "I heard something."

Narrowing his eyes, he took a step past her, tilted his head, and inhaled. "I don't smell anything unusual. They have all sorts of birds and tree spirits in these parts—could have been one of them."

North shrugged, knowing she was being foolish. She'd heard plenty of rustling sounds in her life. But she wasn't at home. This was an unfamiliar place with more new creatures and fae than she could imagine.

"So," Tik-Tok drawled once they started walking again. "How is it being born of the greats?"

The question always reminded her that she didn't have any magic, but it made her think of all the good things too. "I have everything I could want in a family. They care fiercely about me, as I do them, even though at times we don't always see eye to eye. But in those instances, I've always had Birch."

"Birch?" Tik-Tok lifted a brow. "A lover?"

"No…" She could feel her cheeks heat, and she wished they would stop doing that around him. "He's one of the guards, mostly mine. A friend."

"Yet you blushed when you said his name." Tik-Tok smirked, not one to pretend he hadn't noticed how red she probably was. "Tell me. Who is this Birch, really?"

"Someone who has always seen me as a sister. My grandparents found him when he was a youngling, then sent him to my parents, who turned him into a guard. I recently made the mistake of confessing how I felt to him, but he was about to propose to someone else, so I—"

"Went and found someone else to fuck," Tik-Tok finished for her, giving an all-too-knowing nod.

North's entire body grew hot. She didn't want to reveal all that had happened in the woods after leaving Birch—how she'd acted like a fool when she should have gone home. And she certainly didn't want him to learn how inexperienced she truly was.

In the distance, a light sound drifted closer to her, tickling her ears. Laughter, music, talking. The pleasant aroma of fresh baked bread hit her nose, and she wanted to tear into the food like an animal. All she'd had before meeting Tik-Tok this morning was a piece of dried fruit.

As they curved around the trail, her stomach softly rumbled at the scent of roasted meat. The town was bustling with fae. A group of centaurs trotted beside blue and yellow buildings, carrying baskets of fruit. Tall faeries laughed and danced in the center, their wings not feathered like Ozma's, but smooth and iridescent. Sheer fabric dangled from their wrists.

Shops of different sizes lined a stone path—tall, curved lanterns stood in front of each building, unlit. Everyone seemed to be going about their daily tasks, shopping, eating, or... Her eyes widened at the side of a building where one female was being ravished by three different males, her head tilted back in pleasure.

"A lot of females travel here specifically for the brothels. The male prostitutes are willing to do anything their patrons wish. *Anything.* For a price of course." Tik-Tok's voice came out silky, then he chuckled and motioned her in the opposite direction. "Come on. We're going somewhere quieter."

He led her behind a yellow and blue striped building with a balcony on its second floor. As they rounded the shop to the back, North's gaze fell on an area with four rectangular tables and benches pushed beneath them. A pale pink awning provided the perfect amount of shade.

She could still hear the sounds coming from the other street, but it was less noisy than she would have expected.

"I always reserve this side when I visit." He pulled out the bench for her with his boot.

North took a seat as the back door cracked open. A voluptuous elf wearing a strapless dress of deep blue feathers stepped out. The front of her hair was pulled up into several buns atop her head, forming a neat row, while the rest hung loosely to her waist.

She cast a bright smile to Tik-Tok. "I saw you through the window." She leaned in to whisper something in his ear and he smirked.

Her eyes turned to North. "You have a new guest? I haven't seen this one with you before."

"She's temporary, Drusile."

North frowned. *Temporary?*

"Do you want your usual? Glazed boar and roasted potatoes?" Drusile asked.

"We'll both have a plate and also two bowls of the vegetable soup."

"Maybe I'll bring dessert to your ship later?" She winked and swayed her hips as she walked back into the building.

North knew exactly what kind of dessert she was talking about, and she didn't want to be around for any of that. She avoided looking at Tik-Tok, not wanting to see what expression he'd given to the elf.

"I'm going to step away for a bit," Tik-Tok finally said.

North jerked her head up. He must have not been able to wait for *dessert*. "You're leaving me here alone?"

"I'll be close." He pointed to a garden surrounded by decorative trees, near enough so he could see her but still far enough away where he wouldn't be able to catch her if she wanted to run. "Will you be all right?"

"I'll be fine." She pointed to the weapon at her back. "I have my axe, remember?"

He leaned forward, his face close to hers, never understanding personal space, but her heart thumped at his words. "Don't worry. I won't have dessert with Drusile, but my door will be open if you feel like something sweet later tonight."

North blinked, and he chuckled.

"I hate you."

"I love hearing those words from you." His face grew serious. "Order anything else you'd like while I take care of this."

As Tik-Tok sauntered toward the garden, Drusile brought out two bowls of soup and set them down on the table. "I always welcome new guests to join for dessert as well." She winked at her, and North choked on her own spit as the elf grinned before heading back inside.

North smacked her chest to clear her throat, and her coughing ceased. She focused on her steaming soup, not wanting to hear any more about dessert, and brought a spoonful to her lips.

"Hot!" North whisper-shouted and dropped her spoon. "Gods!" She should have blown on the liquid or tested it out first. Fanning her mouth, she looked around the table for water, *anything* to cool her mouth. Nothing.

Tik-Tok was already talking to a male with curving dark horns protruding from the sides of his head. He was too far away for her to see his other features.

Just as she was about to push up from the table and go inside to get something cool to drink, footsteps crunched from behind her. North whirled around and reached for her axe, when her gaze landed on matted copper hair. "Oh, it's you, Rizmaela."

The dwarf plopped down beside her on the bench, her expression moody as always.

"I owe your father something," Rizmaela grunted.

"My father?" North's brows drew together.

"I owe him this." The dwarf's hand moved so fast that North didn't have time to blink. Sharp pain sliced at her chest. "For murdering my husband and exchanging his head for payment."

The words sounded far away as blood bubbled up her throat, suffocating her. North peered down at the crimson blooming from her chest where a dagger jutted out. The voice inside her head screamed to grab her axe, defend herself, but everything was growing fuzzy.

Then Rizmaela ripped the blade out. An agonized gurgle escaped North's mouth, and her gaze met Tik-Tok's as he rushed toward her.

The world spun.

And she found herself falling, falling, falling.

CHAPTER ELEVEN

TIK-TOK

Tik-Tok's body moved without thought. His steps were so hard and so fast that he felt the impact of each footfall vibrate through his legs. But his mind—that was suspended. Floating. Frozen.

Before he even finished properly greeting his contact, Rizmaela brandished a dagger. Shoved it into North's chest. Despite the distance between them, North's muted gasp echoed through his head. A low, gurgling sound. Tik-Tok's answering roar ripped from his center and burned up his throat, sending his contact fleeing into a dark alley with the spelled object they needed to avoid Salt.

No, no, no.

Not North. He *needed* her. She didn't deserve such a violent death. And by his first mate? He had vowed she would come to no harm. *Vowed it.* And now that oath was broken.

His hands slammed down on either side of the dwarf's head. One twist, one resounding *crack*, and Rizmaela's dead body slammed to the pebbled ground before she could utter a single word in her defense.

There were no excuses for this.

One of North's hands gripped the table's edge, the other

pressed to the gushing wound in her chest. Her eyes fluttered shut and her body swayed. Tik-Tok caught her as she slumped backward, nearly falling from the bench.

"North," he bellowed into her pale face. "You do not get to die. Wake up."

Blood bubbled in the corner of her mouth as her chest heaved. Each inhale was a rasp. Every following exhale, a snap.

"Fuck!" He stood, hoisting her up and cradling her small frame to his chest. *Respen.* They needed Respen—but the elf was on the other side of the market. He could take her to a healer faster than anyone else. Tik-Tok didn't even know where to fucking find one. "I need a healer!" he yelled in desperation.

Drusile burst out the door and gasped, her eyes widening. "What happened?"

"She needs a healer," he barked. His insides twisted and tightened. Panic clawed at his chest in a frantic bid to escape. "*Now!*"

Drusile darted back inside and her shouts seemed far away. He didn't know what the hell to do. Should he wait for a healer? Should he race through the streets until he found one? There wasn't time.

No time!

With each passing second, North grew paler and paler. He refused to look at her chest. Couldn't bear to see it. To watch the life seep out of her, knowing there was nothing he could do to stop it. If he turned her to stone to stop the bleeding, it could make the wound worse. Perhaps he should risk it…

"North," he demanded. "North, please."

"Out here," Drusile called, racing toward him with Respen beside her. He didn't know how she'd found him so quickly— didn't care.

"Move!" An elderly woodland fae shoved between them with a large black, leather bag. Long pale scars and deep pockmarks marred his brown flesh, shimmering green wings hung limp on his back, and there was a large depression on the side of his bald head. "Lay her on the table."

Respen knocked the bowls of soup out of the way for him, but Tik-Tok simply held North closer. "Captain," his crewmate urged.

"I want another healer," he growled. If the woodland fae hadn't been able to heal himself, how could the male hope to heal North? No. He needed someone better. *The best.*

"There's no time for this," the fae snapped. "Put her down and step away, or let her die."

The next moment felt like ten as he ran through his options. But there were none. North was dying, her breaths slowing, so he set her on the table. He brushed her silver hair away from her face and didn't budge from his spot. His knees hit the cobblestone beside the table so he was at her level.

"Don't you dare die," he whispered. "I don't give you permission to leave."

The woodland fae ripped the fabric of North's dress to expose the wound and chanted words in another language. His eyes were pressed shut, thin lips barely moving, veins protruding on his forehead. A strong odor—one of death and decay—filled the air, followed by the intense tang of herbs.

But Tik-Tok still didn't look. He didn't listen to Respen begging him to move away so the healer could work. Didn't pay any heed to Drusile's shocked sobs. Instead, he gripped North's freezing hand and continued to whisper that she wasn't allowed to die. Not after he'd waited so many years to find her.

By the time the healer was finished, the moon was rising and a crowd had gathered. The old fae stumbled away from North, wiping the sweat from the back of his neck. "I'm unsure if it will be enough," he wheezed.

"It had better be," Tik-Tok growled.

Respen leaned into the healer's side, pressing a few gold coins into his palm. "Thank you."

"She will need to stay hydrated," he said while Tik-Tok remained kneeling at North's side. He dug through his bag and handed Respen a vial of brown liquid. "If she develops a fever, give her this. The magic I used was strong, but it will still be another day before she's safe from death's clutches. Take her somewhere warm and dry. No traveling via magic."

"Respen," Tik-Tok said in a hoarse voice. "Secure us a room at the Willow Inn."

"Aye, Captain." He hesitated a moment before stepping closer. "What shall I tell the crew?"

Tik-Tok stood, his knees aching from the hard cobblestones. "The truth. Rizmaela betrayed me, paid with her life, and I will return to the ship once North has healed. You're my new first mate." He lifted a tired gaze to Respen. The elf should've been his first mate from the start, especially since he knew the reason Tik-Tok wanted the portal open so badly. But he'd insisted he wasn't ready before. They both knew he was now. "Keep them calm and don't let any of them run off. While I stay with North, you need to find out if Rizmaela was working alone or if there are more traitors on board."

Respen took a deep breath and nodded. "Leave everything to me." Then he was gone.

Tik-Tok carefully eased an arm beneath North's knees and shoulders. She moaned at being jostled as he lifted her, and he offered a gentle *shh*. Finally, with North tucked securely against him, he made his way toward the only decent inn in town.

Respen secured the largest room at the Willow Inn before returning to the ship. Tik-Tok knew Respen could handle the crew. Otherwise, he wouldn't have promoted him. If anyone from his ship started a fight in a tavern or fell overboard after overindulging, that was on them.

North, on the other hand, hadn't done anything to Rizmaela. So why? What caused his first mate to shove a dagger in her chest? And would someone else on the ship try to finish the job? Tik-Tok's mind kept circling back to that thought. Respen would find out—but what if…? Tik-Tok had led a mutiny against Captain Salt. Was this a cruel twist of fate? To have his crew turn on him? But why *now* when he was so close to opening the portal?

Tik-Tok tucked the wool blanket around North again despite the fact she hadn't moved since he'd put her down. She would need a clean dress before they left—one that hadn't been torn open, nearly exposing her breasts. A square, white bandage dipped in healing herbs covered the wound, but once it was removed, her chest would be fully on display.

One day.

The healer said the danger would pass by then. For such a wound, it sounded too good to be true. But North's breathing was now steady and she no longer bled. He'd been too hasty judging the healer by his appearance.

Setting the vial on the small table beside the bed, Tik-Tok eased down to the floor with a grunt. He rested against the bedframe, his head leaning back on the edge of the mattress. The ache in his knees had spread through his body, throbbing most painfully where his golden arm met his shoulder.

He plucked off his blood-stained gloves and tossed them into a corner. His metal fingers clicked against his palm as he made a fist. The pain of losing his arm had left him incapacitated for weeks. In fact, he'd almost died of infection—something the sea witch never bothered to mention being a concern. Only after a skilled healer removed the remaining few inches of his arm, taking it right up to the shoulder, had he healed enough to commission the enchanted arm.

"You can't die," he murmured to himself.

He'd done too much for this portal to fail now. But … not only that. He genuinely wanted North to be well. To live and sass him another day. Maybe he would even cut her some slack. *Or not.* It was amusing getting a rise out of her. More amusing than usual.

With a sigh, he shifted to touch her forehead, ensuring the fever was still at bay, and settled back to stare at the ceiling. His thoughts continued to bounce frantically between North's health, Rizmaela's betrayal, and what was happening on *The Temptress*. Rizmaela's actions were bound to affect morale, if nothing else. It should be the least of his worries. It *was*. But his crew was his family…

His eyes slid shut and he forced them open. Again and again. Until the worries had drained him too much to fight the pull of sleep.

It wasn't clear how long he'd slept before jerking awake. He spun and reached out for North, only to find her staring at him. His hand froze before making contact with her forehead. "North?"

She shifted in an attempt to push up on her elbows, but Tik-Tok placed his palm on her forehead, holding her down. A small huff left her mouth, followed quickly by a groan. "What happened?"

Tik-Tok removed his hand, satisfied that her skin didn't feel overheated, and sat back on his haunches. "You don't remember?"

"I…" North scowled and gingerly poked at the bandage on her chest. "Rizmaela stabbed me."

Tik-Tok nodded. "How do you feel now? Should I call the healer?"

"I feel stiff," she said, moving slightly as if testing herself. "My chest aches like I was punched. Hard."

"Punched is better than stabbed," he said with a smirk.

She glared at him. "Did you know?"

"Know what?"

"That my father killed her husband." Her hands gripped the wool blanket. "That's why she wanted me dead."

Tik-Tok's eye twitched but fought to keep the surprise from his face. Rizmaela only knew that North was Tin's daughter because he'd mentioned it—but the dwarf had known that they needed her. Rizmaela had set her selfish revenge ahead of the portal—a portal that would earn everyone on his crew a hefty payday. Rage filled him, churning and thickening in his veins. He wished he hadn't killed Rizmaela already so he could take his time. Make it hurt. Tin murdered her husband—so fucking what? That wasn't North's fault.

"I didn't know," he said, meeting her eyes. "Even if I had, your father's deeds aren't yours. You're innocent and her vendetta was with him—not you."

North studied him for a moment before nodding. "Where is she now?"

"Dead." His lips curled into a snarl, before he forced himself to calm down. There was no changing what had happened. He didn't want to frighten North with his anger. He peered down at his hands and sighed. "I owe you an apology. You nearly died when I promised you would be safe with me and my crew."

"You also said there was no telling what could happen because you're a good-for-nothing pirate," she grumbled.

A short laugh escaped him. "I'm fairly certain you're twisting my words."

"I'm fairly certain my words are *true*." She looked around the room, licking her cracked lips. "Is there any water?"

Tik-Tok was on his feet in an instant, pouring water from a ceramic pitcher into a glass. Wordlessly, he lowered himself on the edge of the bed and helped her sit up, letting her lean on him for support as she drank. When she finished, he refilled her glass and she drank again.

"Do you need anything else?" He settled her back onto the pillow and tugged the blanket into place, both to hide her mostly-bare chest and keep her warm. "Are you hungry? I'll find whatever you'd like."

"I'm tired," she whispered. "Have you been here with me this whole time?"

He shrugged. "It hasn't been *that* long. Less than a day."

"You must really want me to open that portal," she said with a roll of her eyes. "Where does it lead anyway?"

"I don't know exactly, but I know I need to go. It's the only thing I want." Tik-Tok sat on the floor again, resting his elbows on his knees. Everything he'd done was for the portal. His entire life. He *needed* it open so he could claim his revenge. "But, if you think that's the only reason that I've taken care of you, then you're wrong."

"Then why?" North turned her head, meeting his red eyes with her brown ones. He'd imagined that gaze in a thousand different faces. Obsessed over what silver-haired female would possess them, but somehow, he'd never imagined North.

Tik-Tok ground his teeth. Did he want to tell her? To open up about his own pain? It was dangerous to let this female in when she so clearly wanted to escape him, but he couldn't stop the words from leaving his mouth.

"I told you I cut it off myself," he said in a deeper-than-normal voice as he held up his gold arm. "But what I didn't tell you was I tied a thin iron wire around my upper arm and tightened it with a block of wood. It took hours, and I lost consciousness twice."

North gasped, her hand cupping her mouth. "Why would you do that?"

He gave her a wolfish grin. "I'm a masochist. Couldn't you tell?"

"Tik-Tok," she said, exasperated.

"Celyna—the sea witch—told me I needed to do it if I wanted the portal. Every year she has a vision of what will bring me closer to opening it, and a few decades ago, it was to remove my arm."

Her scowl deepened. "And this year it was to steal me away?"

"A task I gladly accepted—I'd rather keep the rest of my limbs." He continued opening and closing his fist. *Click click click.* "We're getting off track, my star. You wanted to know why I looked after you?" He paused, meeting her gaze. "When I was bleeding profusely, when my arm was infected, when the wound was finally healing but not yet well enough to replace, no one helped. A healer, yes, but only enough to keep me alive. My crew was new at the time and things were ... uncertain."

"You—"

"Shh," he admonished lightly. "I don't want whatever pity you're about to give. I'm only telling you this so you know that I understand. I know what it's like to suffer when you have no one you love to comfort or care for you. Besides, there's powerful magic built into the arm, so it worked out rather well in the end despite the fortune I had to give the Tinker Witch who made it."

"Well, then." North's eyes took on a slightly softer edge. "Thank you. For saving my life."

"You're welcome," he said with a shrug.

"Even though I wouldn't have been stabbed at all if it weren't for you." She cleared her throat, taking on a forced arrogance.

"Cheeky," he huffed.

North shifted slightly and he could feel her eyes on his arm. "Can you feel with it?"

"Of course." He ran his fingertips over the woolen blanket, feeling the roughness of the thick fabric. "It's the same as a real arm, only flashier."

"And magical," North added and her stomach growled. "I think I'll take you up on the food now. Something hot. And it had better not taste like what you've been giving me on your ship."

Tik-Tok chuckled softly and rose to his feet. "Anything else, my lady?"

"Clothes." She tugged the blanket higher. "Nice ones. And if you don't get me the axe you promised, I refuse to step foot back on that awful ship."

"Now, now." He took her chin gently and turned her to look at him. "Say what you want about me, but leave my ship out of it."

"Food," she demanded, shoving his hand away with what might have been a smile.

Tik-Tok bit his lip to keep himself from laughing and left the room to find the innkeeper. Such spunk, even now. Idly, he wondered how far she would push her demands—how far he would let her—and it spurred something in his chest. Such a difficult little star.

His difficult, challenging, spirited little star.

CHAPTER TWELVE

NORTH

A *sharp axe sliced clean through his neck—blood sprayed into the air. North couldn't see the victim's face, but by his short, stocky build, he was a dwarf.*

An ear-shattering scream screeched from behind her, and North whirled around, finding Rizmaela watching in anguish, tears flooding her eyes.

North peered down at her hands, where her fingers tightly gripped the axe, her skin coated in bright crimson.

North's eyes flew open and she jerked forward.

"Are you trying to reinjure yourself?" a deep voice rumbled from beside the bed, his hands holding her by the shoulders.

Tik-Tok.

Taking a deep swallow, she slowly leaned against the headboard as he took his palms from her skin.

Rizmaela was dead. The dwarf shouldn't have tried to murder her for something she hadn't done. But North's father had taken someone important from her in the past...

Tin had never hidden his past from North, not once. She knew what he'd done when he was cursed, when his heart was stone. About kills he'd done for money, and how he'd brought her mother to Oz and had planned to take her to Langwidere so the obsessive female could wear her head. North had been horrified for days, but it hadn't made her love him any less. It only proved how far he'd come since then.

But even though she understood his past, it didn't mean the families he'd destroyed could forgive him.

"What are you thinking about?" Tik-Tok knelt so he was eye-to-eye with her, his scarlet irises shining brightly, reflecting the sun's rays that spilled in through the window.

North should have been fearful of that bloody shade, but she only wanted to inch closer, and see the flecks of silver in them.

Shaking off the thought, she flicked her gaze away and lied. "Birch."

"Ah"—Tik-Tok stood and folded his arms—"you still love him."

North would rather talk about that than other things, like Tik-Tok's eyes or the nightmare she'd had about Rizmaela. As for Birch, she'd been in love with him for years, but perhaps that love was meant to fade more easily because it was unrequited, while their friendship was like iron. Over the past few days, she hadn't thought of him or her family much, not while training with Tik-Tok before collapsing into her bed from exhaustion after the long sessions.

"As family." She sighed, pressing a hand to her chest where it still ached from the wound. Her fingers traced the raised scar, finding it smoother than she would have expected.

Tik-Tok nodded, his expression unreadable. "We should get back to the ship. Either I can carry you, or I can retrieve Respen from the shop across the street. He's picking up a few extra things before we leave."

"I can walk."

"You're not walking." Tik-Tok plucked up a long piece of fabric from the back of a wooden chair. He held it up with a smirk, letting the fabric unravel—a dress—hideous. "Respen got this for you. An improvement from your latest choices, don't you think?"

North scanned the bright orange clothing, the different sized beads and jewels covering its entirety, the high-collared neckline. "It's, um…" She chuckled, and the movement made her scar throb.

"I can help you change into it if you want," he said in a low, teasing voice.

"I'll be fine."

"No clever comeback?" Tik-Tok grinned as he handed her the dress. "Where's my star hiding?"

"Go get Respen. I'm not going to let you carry me." She rolled her eyes.

He nodded, leaving the room and shutting the door behind him. As she stood from the bed, her body felt like it hadn't been used in months. She twisted to the side, then stretched and shook out her arms and legs. An unpleasant smell wafted from her body—blood, sweat, and grime.

The dress skimmed the floor after she threw it on, and the material seemed to scratch away a layer of her skin, but it would do for the time being. The door squeaked open, drawing her gaze to Tik-Tok. She hadn't noticed before, but, for the first time, his hair didn't appear as silky as usual and purple circles underlined his eyes.

"Can't you knock?" North cocked her head.

"I *can*, actually."

"That's unproven." Respen pushed past Tik-Tok and entered the room.

"How are the others?" North asked, wishing she could see Echo's face.

"They've been watching the ship." Tik-Tok stepped beside her while Respen stood in front of them.

Respen scanned her over. "Are you going to be all right if I use my magic now?"

She remembered the last time Respen had used his power on her, and how she'd felt as if she'd been riding backward on a stag, consumed with nausea. How there had been nothing beneath her feet, her body filled with the rush of falling. North grasped Tik-Tok's hand without thinking, perhaps because she wanted something to ground her for the short journey.

Tik-Tok peered down at their joined hands and arched a brow. She started to pull her hand away, but he gripped it firmly. Her body relaxed into his touch.

"Close your eyes," Respen said. "It will be easier that way."

As soon as she closed her lids, Respen's hand curled around her shoulder. Not a second passed before the spinning started, and she felt like she was plunging into the darkest pits of Oz. She clenched Tik-Tok's hand so tightly that she feared she would break every single bone in it. And then the world stilled, but her body continued to sway like a flower in the wind.

"You can open your eyes now," Tik-Tok whispered.

"I know. Give me a moment so I don't hurl on your pristine boots." Then she peeled one lid open, followed by the second, after Respen's hand left her shoulder. Her chest heaved as she focused on the deck of the ship. "I want a bath."

"Dax, heat the water!" Tik-Tok shouted toward the elf who was cutting rope across the deck. He turned back to North. "But you're not going down there alone."

North furrowed her brow. "I was alone before."

"You weren't recovering from a stab wound last time."

"I'll go with her," Echo said, sliding up beside her. "And I'll also get her out of this hideous dress. Who the fuck picked this out?"

"I did." Respen tilted his head. "There's nothing wrong with it."

"You have no taste."

"My tongue would say differently."

"No one wants to hear about your tongue," Tik-Tok spat, his hand jerking in hers.

North realized she was still holding onto him and dropped his hand as though she'd been scalded.

Echo didn't miss the movement, and she blinked several times before motioning North to follow her. "Let's go."

North didn't so much as glance at Tik-Tok, her cheeks still hot, as she caught up with the siren.

"How are you feeling?" Echo asked. "I was going to come and visit you, but I needed to help Respen and Dax question the crew about Riz. If I had known that dwarf bitch was planning to kill you, I would have sung her a song to rip out her organs."

North's eyes widened, both terrified and impressed at the things Echo could do if she willed it.

The hatch leading into the bowels of the ship was already open and Echo led her down the steps. Dax hovered over the water, his fingers swirling within it. Steam wafted from both metal tubs and he pulled his hand out.

"Water was already in each, so I heated them both. Take your pick." Dax peered up at North, his brow furrowed. "I wish I had taken you to the market, damn it."

"One good thing came out of this," Echo said. "We found out Riz was a traitor sooner rather than later."

Rizmaela could have tried to kill North in her own room, where she wouldn't have had a weapon, where no one would have found her in time. North shook away the image of her lying in bed, drenched in blood with a blade sticking out of her chest.

"Tell me if it's not hot enough." Dax headed up the steps then shut the hatch.

"Let's not waste the heat since he warmed them both." Echo peeled off her clothing and stepped into a tub. "I already brought a dress down here for you. Figured you would want a bath when you returned."

North glanced at the maroon and deep purple fabric folded on the counter beside a stack of towels. Shimmying out of the orange monstrosity, trying not to feel shy about her smaller breasts and narrower hips, she hurried into the warm water. North settled into the tub with a sigh, the liquid relaxing her flesh and aching muscles.

"I've never seen the captain so rattled." Echo tapped the side of the tub with her fingers.

"The portal's important to him." North thought about how Tik-Tok had cut off his own arm for it. She hadn't asked why he wanted the portal open so desperately, but there had to be a good reason if he'd done something so drastic.

"It is to all of us," Echo said as if reading North's thoughts.

"Why?"

"I can't speak on the captain's motive, as it's personal—but for the crew, it's the fortune he promised. It will set all of us up for ten lifetimes."

North nodded, sinking down into the water. She wondered where the portal would lead and what would be on the other side of it. Would the world be like theirs? Would the inhabitants be welcoming, or would it be like the human world that thought no others existed?

She reached for a bar of soap and scrubbed away the dried blood, the sweat, the healing herbs, the day, the feeling of Tik-Tok's hand in hers, Rizmaela's expression when she'd pierced North's chest. She traced the pink scar between her breasts, and relief at being alive washed over her.

Once the water cooled, North got dressed and left Echo resting in the tub. The siren's serene expression made it seem as if she were absorbing energy from the liquid while her hands hovered over her stomach. North shut the door to the bathing chamber softly so she wouldn't disturb her and searched the deck for Tik-Tok. He was nowhere in sight. Two of the brownies were separating buckets of dried fruit and placing them in crates. She gave them a small wave as she passed and climbed down the ladder to her room.

Her body sank onto the mattress and sudden tears surprised her when they rained down her cheeks. So much had happened in such a short amount of time.

North stayed in her room for the rest of the day. She'd been too exhausted, both physically and emotionally, to join the others. Respen had come down to bring her food, then Echo had dropped off a bottle of spirits.

"I brought you a gift to help you unwind." Echo smiled. *"Don't drink too much, though. A little goes a long way."*

She hadn't seen Tik-Tok since the morning, and something bothered her about that. But why should she care? If he hadn't taken her from Brielle's celebration, then she would've been home now, and … feeling lost. She would have been in the same place, struggling with having no magic. North still didn't have any now, but there was a speck of hope that *maybe* she could.

Another light ache throbbed from her chest. North took a deep swallow as Rizmaela's angry face flashed before her.

What would Tin have done if the roles were reversed? He would have decapitated the fae who dared hurt her mother, not taken an innocent life. If Rizmaela had come after Tin instead, North would have defended him with her axe. She would always protect her family.

Yet, still… The images, the thoughts, swarmed through her, and she needed to clear her head. Get out of this room. Do something… Throwing pretend axes wouldn't help her fall asleep tonight.

North straightened her dress, grabbed the bottle of spirits, and headed up the ladder to the deck. Outdoors, it was only North, the sea, and Kaliko keeping watch up in his spot behind a sail. The salty air calmed her, but it didn't take away everything she felt.

North lifted the spirits to her mouth and took a long swig, allowing the liquid to glide down her throat. She walked to the rail and leaned over, staring down at the sea, the waves. The night sky reflected off the water, making the liquid glisten. She fisted her free hand and concentrated, tapping into her true name. *North Talina Selain.* Quiet lingered. Silence stayed. Not a stir from any hidden magic inside her. Again, North lifted the bottle to her lips, drinking the sweet liquid. More and more. She drank until she felt as if she were floating, as if her mind thrashed like a wave.

North wasn't all right. The alcohol intensified her turbulent thoughts instead of numbing them. Where was Tik-Tok? Why hadn't he thrown open her door without knocking at least once?

She stumbled her way to the back of the ship, curious to see what his room looked like. Grasping the curved handle leading to the captain's quarters, she jiggled it and found it locked.

The door jerked open to a scowling Tik-Tok. "What do you want?" His gaze settled on her and his lips parted in surprise. "North? What are you doing here?"

Her gaze traveled from his face to his bare chest. His skin was golden, his shoulders broad, his abs ripped, and she couldn't stop staring. The only clothing he wore were his pants—even his feet were bootless.

"I want to see your room," she slurred.

Tik-Tok smirked as he sniffed the air. "Who gave you spirits?"

"It was only a single bottle."

"You drank the whole fucking thing?" He drew her inside and shut the door. "I can't have you walking around the ship drunk."

She peered around the room, taking in the cabinets, the desk cluttered with maps, and a large brass bathing tub. And, of course, his bed. White gauzy curtains hung from the four large posts. Silken black and red sheets covered the mattress, which led to a headboard etched with swirled designs. Setting the empty bottle on his desk, she walked to the back corner of the room. North crawled onto the bed before sinking into the mattress, finding it softer than anything she'd ever felt.

Tik-Tok studied her as she patted the spot beside her, remembering what it had felt like when she'd kissed him.

He gave her a sly grin and sat down on the mattress next to her. The room was growing blurry, but he was clear as day. His lips were the perfect shape, and she recalled how nice they'd felt against her own.

"Why didn't you come see me earlier?" She adjusted a pillow behind her back.

"You needed rest and I needed to think."

"I wanted you to come see me."

"Mm. And why is that?" The edges of his lips tilted up.

"I don't know." She lifted her hand and swept a lock of his silky black hair behind his ear. Then she inched closer, her mouth so very near to his.

"I'm not going to kiss you, North."

"Why not?" She jerked back. It was like Birch all over again, the rejection. It made her want to sink farther into the bed, completely disappear.

"You drank a whole bottle of spirits, for one thing." He leaned in, his hand resting on her shoulder. "For another, you were just stabbed."

She couldn't stop the tears from flowing again as she folded herself around his warm body, wrapping an arm around his waist. "What if I could have talked to her? Made her understand that my father was cursed, that he's different now, that so many others had been damaged back then too."

"It wouldn't have mattered," Tik-Tok murmured, tugging her closer. He trailed a finger lightly down her cheek. "Rizmaela made her way to the top by being spiteful. I never cared about other's pasts as long as they shared my goal and were loyal to me. Anyone who's disloyal will die by my hand, and she knew as much. She should've ignored the fact that you are Tin's daughter."

"I want to see him." North cried into his chest, and he held her even tighter. "And my mother."

"I'm sorry." He sighed. "I promise I'll bring you home as soon as possible after the portal is open."

"Why do you want it open so badly?"

Tik-Tok hesitated. "Once it's open, you may understand."

A low growl escaped her throat but she was too exhausted to fight back. She settled on his chest and closed her eyes.

Tik-Tok ran his hand through her hair, tenderly. "After this is over, you won't have to see me again, if that's what you wish."

But a part of her didn't wish that at all.

CHAPTER THIRTEEN

TIK-TOK

Tik-Tok slid himself out from beneath North's sleeping form in the middle of the night. The warmth from her head on his shoulder remained, and the feel of her silky hair made him wish that he could twine her locks through his fingers forever. He gazed down at her, rubbing at the strange new ache in his chest. What was happening? North was his key to the portal—*maybe* a decent fuck if things went that way—but she wasn't someone to get emotionally attached to. She was there for a purpose—a captive who was trying to seduce her way into escaping. If she hadn't been so completely drunk when she'd shown up at his door, Tik-Tok would've assumed it was all part of her grand plan.

Quietly, he lifted a white tunic from where it draped over a chair, and snuck from the room. The salty, cool air bit against his skin as he padded over to the helm. The goblin, Cyrx, stood at the wheel, keeping them on track. Large bottom teeth protruded from his mouth, pressing over his top lip. His deep scars seemed to stand out more prominently against his orange-tinged skin, and his bulging muscles pressed against the tight sleeves of his black shirt.

"Evenin', Captain," Cyrx said in a guttural voice.

Tik-Tok nodded a greeting while tapping his middle finger against his golden palm. *Click, click, click.* "We need to detour to Isa Poso."

Cyrx's eyes widened. "Celyna? Already? Did something happen?"

"No." Just a certain female wedging herself between him and his plan. He didn't hate it as much as he should. Hopefully after fucking Celyna in exchange for a vision, he would be able to think a little more clearly about North. "I couldn't get the shield to keep Salt from detecting us when we docked, so wandering aimlessly through his territory is too much of a risk."

"In that case…" Cyrx turned the wheel, steering them west toward the sea witch.

The crew didn't want or need to be in the middle of Tik-Tok's feud with the fae who had saved him from a life of pain—the fae he'd betrayed. Salt was seeking revenge against his former-first-mate-turned-traitor, just as Tik-Tok was seeking revenge for his past. He understood it, but if Salt caught up with *The Temptress*, there was no telling what would happen. Only that it wouldn't be pleasant.

The silver-capped waves slapped against the hull and a spray of water rained down across the deck. Cyrx wiped the droplets from his face. "You think the witch will give you answers?"

The last time he'd tried to visit Celyna before their yearly appointment, she'd hissed in his face before disappearing into the sea. Tik-Tok scowled at the memory. This time, he wouldn't give her the chance to run off. If she could give him even the smallest of clues, this could all be over soon. All he needed was a clue—something to help him unlock North's power or tell him where, exactly, the portal was. The portal would open, revenge would be had, and North could return home. Then, he could finally rest.

"I have to try," Tik-Tok said, shrugging.

He didn't wait for the goblin to give his opinion on the matter before striding back to his quarters and shutting the door with a soft thud. North was exactly as he'd left her—mouth open, small snores escaping, her hair spread over his pillow. Her sweet vanilla scent would linger once she left his bed. His heart sped at the thought. *Damn.* What was wrong with him?

Rubbing a hand over his face, he eased onto the mattress and turned on his side to face her. His gold fingers traced the air over the planes of North's face as she slept, never touching, only *almost.* When his middle finger grazed the sweep of her lower lip, she snapped her mouth shut. He whipped his hand back as her eyes fluttered open.

"Tik-Tok?" she mumbled.

One side of his mouth lifted in a grin. "Were you expecting someone else?"

"What are you doing here?" She rubbed a fist against her lids.

"In my own bed?" He lifted a brow. "I *was* sleeping until you decided to join me."

North sat up quickly, eyes darting around the room. "I'm in *your* room?" she asked, despite the obvious answer. She shifted to her knees and peered down at herself. "Why did you bring me in here?"

Tik-Tok's answering laugh was both warm and mocking. "That's rather presumptuous. You came here, *drunk,* because you wanted to know what my quarters looked like. So—" He rolled to his back and motioned to the room behind him. "Are you satisfied? Does it look as you thought it would?"

"Oh." She paused, squinting as if in deep thought. "*Oh.* Echo gave me a bottle of spirits."

Tik-Tok smirked. "And you'll soon regret drinking the entire thing."

"Fairly certain I already do." She rubbed at her temples. "I should probably get back to my room."

"Stay," Tik-Tok said, surprising himself. "You're already here and, besides, I have a gift."

"A gift?" Her brows lifted as she studied him.

He rose and crossed to one of the cabinets lining the wall of his quarters. The axe he'd acquired while she was bathing, before they'd departed Merryland, was from the finest bladesmith he knew. It would be easier for her to grip the slim handle, and the metal was nearly weightless. Carrying it back to the bed, he wondered if he should've skipped having the butt of the axe engraved with a star.

"Here." He tossed it onto the bed where he'd lain moments ago. It landed, sinking slightly into the thick blanket. "You can't say I don't keep my word."

She lifted the axe without looking at him, turning the weapon over, examining every inch, her delicate fingers slowly running up its length. Tik-Tok felt her careful scrutiny all the way down to his groin. Felt the imaginary touch of her doing the same thing to him—caressing, admiring. *Fuck.* If she showed his throbbing cock even a fraction of the attention she showed the new weapon, he would burst all over her pretty face.

"It's perfect," she whispered after what felt like an entire voyage across the sea.

Tik-Tok released a small, relieved breath, and joined her on the bed. He sprawled across his half of the mattress and tucked his hands behind his head. "I know."

"It has a star…"

"I know," he said again, closing his eyes. "Now, go back to sleep."

He kept his breathing shallow as he waited for her to decide whether or not to listen. She could return to her room and he wouldn't stop her, but he hoped she didn't. He wanted her to stay. Even after the portal was open, she could choose to remain beside him. The irrational thought pierced him. *No.* She was going home. She missed her family—his enemies. She'd said as much.

Finally, North shifted, leaning sideways over his abdomen. *And she would leave now too.* Of course, she would. Why wouldn't she? But a soft thunk hit the floor instead. Tik-Tok's eyes cracked to find her face hovering over his chest. "What are you doing?" he asked.

"Putting the axe on the floor so we don't injure ourselves." She struggled to balance over him without touching—there was

only an inch of space between his hip and the edge of the bed
for her to hold herself up. After a moment of trying to shove
herself back to her side of the mattress, she gave up and placed
a hand on his lower stomach, below his navel. He wished he'd
left his shirt off.

Tik-Tok's gold hand immediately landed on top of hers,
holding it there. "Careful, my star."

She rolled her eyes and scrambled gracelessly away. When her
head hit the pillow, Tik-Tok glared sideways at her, taking in the
sight of her in his bed and enjoying how perfect it looked. He
would have her there every night if he could.

North yanked at the covers, pulling the material from under
his weight, and shimmied beneath them. "Don't get any ideas."

Tik-Tok chuckled. "I should be the one saying that, don't you
think?"

"Go to sleep," she said with a tired groan.

"Land!"

Kaliko's call radiated through the walls inside Tik-Tok's
quarters—which did, indeed, still smell like North despite her
having left hours ago. She had tried to sneak away, but it was
impossible not to feel her climb over him. He had kept his eyes
closed, however, letting her believe it was all done in stealth.

Grabbing his jacket, he stalked onto the deck. Respen and
Dax stood near the helm, working in tandem to bring *The
Temptress* as close to Isa Poso as possible, while North used her
new axe to spar against Echo and the siren's narrow blade. He
paused only for a moment to watch her move effortlessly in a
light pink skirt and a brown button-up bodice that showed her
stomach. The scar on her chest was hidden beneath the bodice,
and the silky skirt was knotted, bringing the fabric up above her
knees. Her braided hair whipped over her shoulder as she spun

to block one of Echo's attacks.

"The boat's ready for you," Cyrx informed him. When had the goblin come up beside him?

Tik-Tok turned his back on North to find the brownies tying down the black sails. He'd been watching the sparring match longer than he realized. "I won't be long," he said loud enough for Respen to hear, and went straight for the rowboat.

"Wait!" North called. She ran up to him as he stepped into the boat, chest heaving, beads of perspiration clinging to her smooth skin. "Where are you going?"

His red eyes rose to meet her gaze. The look of longing on her face cut straight through him, but he brushed away the spark of pain. Who was she to question him and his methods? She was only there because he'd *forced* her to be. What did it matter if he pleasured Celyna?

It didn't. And North wasn't accusing him of wrongdoing. That was him—putting words in her mouth. Why? Did he feel guilty about what he was going to do?

Absolutely not.

"To fuck the sea witch," he said in a low voice.

The curious spark drained from North's eyes, her cheeks burning bright red.

"Stay put and listen to Respen," he added, then nodded at the brownies waiting to lower him down to the sea.

Once the rowboat hit the silver waves, he untied the ropes and pushed his rising anger into each stroke of the oars. He wasn't doing anything wrong. He and Celyna had their arrangement long before North even existed. A mutually beneficial agreement that in no way involved the female that he'd stolen away to open his portal. He refused to give in to the urge to look back to see if she was still watching. An ache ran along his jaw from how hard he clenched it.

After dragging the boat to shore, Tik-Tok took a steadying breath and shoved all thoughts of the silver-haired female from his mind before marching up to the glass house.

Celyna was sprawled on her back in the sand outside the

door, naked, eyes closed. The sun glistened along the planes of her lithe body, her large breasts begging to be touched. "You really *did* come earlier," she said with a small curl of her lips.

It took Tik-Tok a moment to remember what she meant. *Ah.* That was right—she'd told him to come earlier next time and he'd forgotten. He laughed. "I didn't want to miss out again."

"Or you hoped to get an extra vision out of me now that you have the female." Celyna beckoned him closer with the curl of a finger. "Luckily, you've caught me in a mood."

"A mood?" he asked, sauntering nearer.

"*Mmm.*" She slid her fingers up her sides, arching her back in a stretch, before running them back down the center of her chest.

Tik-Tok took in her hardened nipples, the heavy rise and fall of her chest, and the slickness coating her inner thighs. A *mood*, if he ever saw one. His cock rose to the occasion and he licked his lips. "Am I interrupting?"

"If that's what you wish to call it." Her black eyes opened and the force of her lust washed over him. "Come to me, pirate. Let's see what the fates have to tell you today."

Tik-Tok didn't need to be told twice. She was giving him *exactly* what he wanted—in more ways than one. As he stepped up to the sea witch, she spread her legs wide. He dropped to his knees between them and leaned over her body, a hand on either side of her head.

She flicked her tongue across the seam of his lips and gripped his jacket, tugging him down onto her fully. He opened his mouth, allowing her access and taking the opening she gave. Soft moans of anticipation rose from her as he met her tongue, thrust for thrust, pulling a groan from him.

Beneath him, Celyna circled her hips, grinding her core against his length. He responded by sitting up to shuck off his clothes. If he didn't get inside her now, he might not last long enough to make her come. Not when he'd been dying to bury himself in someone else for weeks now. Someone who had been pressed against him last night in the most delicious form of torture. His jacket hit the sand and he pulled the white tunic over his head. The scent of sweet vanilla struck his nose.

And he froze.

It smelled like North. His cock throbbed, his pants straining to contain him. Celyna was exquisite and skilled, but North … was different. And he wanted it to be *her* beneath him now. Her and no one else.

"Fuck," he groaned. "I can't do this."

Celyna ran a hand down his bare chest before squeezing him through his pants. He shook with desire, wanting desperately to unleash himself. But not with Celyna. "You most certainly can."

"Celyna…" he said with a hint of warning.

But she was already untying his pants and pulling him free. Her hand wrapped around his length, stroking in a variation of long, hard pulls and soft caresses, precisely as he liked. His head fell back at the sensation. Maybe he *could*. The vision she could give him would be worth the guilt, after all.

When his eyes fluttered shut, an image of North sleeping in his bed flashed across his eyelids. The way her hair cascaded over his pillow, the soft breaths escaping her rosy lips, and the gentle sweep of her long lashes. How vulnerable she had appeared, hands tucked beneath her chin. Trusting him explicitly as she slept. He jerked back out of Celyna's touch. "I can't," he insisted, tucking himself away.

"You got what you wanted," the sea witch seethed, suddenly on her feet. "She's the key to your portal. Nothing more."

Tik-Tok pulled his shirt back on. "She *is* more."

"Oh?" Celyna walked, hips swaying, toward the ocean. "Perhaps I should make sure she knows her place."

"Don't." Tik-Tok's vision blurred with rage. "Don't go anywhere near her."

She stepped into the sea and grinned.

"Stop fucking with me, witch!" He snagged his tunic off the sand and stepped toward her.

But she only grinned wider before swimming directly for *The Temptress*.

"Celyna," he yelled. *Shit.* There was no telling what she would say to North, what lies she would spew. He raced back to his boat, shoving it into the water. His hands shook as he rowed faster than he'd ever rowed before. "If you touch her, I'll fucking kill you! *Celyna!*"

CHAPTER FOURTEEN

NORTH

The sea witch? North couldn't keep the shocked expression from her face as she watched Tik-Tok row toward an aquamarine sandy shore. He'd detoured the ship to have sex with a female? Did this sea witch care that he'd been sleeping beside North in his bed? Why was *she* worried about it? Because… Because…

A body pressed up beside her, pulling North from her thoughts. "He goes to visit Celyna every year," Echo said. "They both get what they want when he sees her, but we were here right before he went to the Emerald City. It's too soon to be back…"

Both get what they want? North pushed away the images that slid forth of Tik-Tok bare-chested and unlacing his pants. "He can take a whole troop of faeries to his bed if he wants. I don't care what he does."

Echo arched a red brow.

"I don't." Her voice came out a bit higher than she would have liked. *Gods.*

"The captain's never been interested in anyone outside of the bedroom. But if anyone were to hook him, it could quite possibly be you." Echo grinned. But before North could reply, the siren continued, "I've got some crates to prepare downstairs with the others for when we next make landfall. Go relax for a while, then we can train more later."

"All right." North gripped her axe as Echo headed toward the open door leading down to where the valuables and alcohol were kept.

She wished she had another bottle of spirits—only this time she wouldn't drink the whole thing at once. *Bah*. She avoided the urge to go and ask Echo for one. North didn't feel like heading down to her room, so she padded to the back of the ship and plopped down behind several large barrels.

North glanced down at the weapon in her hand, rotating it around and around, then stopped on the engraved star. Not *just* a beautiful axe, but a thoughtful gift. When Tik-Tok had given it to her, her chest had fluttered. Something about the gift, that mark—she thought there'd been an implication behind it. Like perhaps he was starting to see her not only as a means to open his portal, but, maybe, as a friend. Even when Tik-Tok had first called her his star, it hadn't annoyed her like everything else about him had. She supposed it was because no one had ever given her a nickname before, and she knew, in the mortal world, that the North Star could guide anyone home.

With a sigh, she set the axe aside and unbraided her hair. It was either that or chuck the weapon into the sea at the thought of Tik-Tok and the sea witch. Him sinking into her, her clenching his back as he brought her to bliss.

Closing her eyes, North listened to the waves and hoped their rhythmic lapping would help unlock the possible magic within her. Wave after wave collided against the hull, and she let her veins hum along with the melody. She tried to focus, dipping in to the mental exercises that Tik-Tok had shown her so she could attempt to unlock her supposed power. *Breathe in… Breathe out…*

She didn't know how much time had passed when a soft female voice whispered her name, "North, come here."

Her lids jerked open, but there wasn't anyone around. Had she imagined it? The voice had been so quiet, as if the wind had sent it up to her.

"North." Her name came again, a gentle alluring murmur.

Jolting up from her position, North peered over the edge of

the handrail, and her eyes connected with two dark orbs that seemed to glimmer within an oval face. Long green hair floated around a blue-scaled neck and shoulders.

She couldn't break away from the female's gaze, didn't want to. It reminded North of something, someone… But she couldn't recall whom.

You're going to complete a task for me. The shapely dark blue lips on the female's mouth didn't move as she spoke, but North could hear every word inside her head.

Magic tugged at her tongue, pulling an answer out. "Yes."

I know in your heart what you want. You want Tik-Tok, don't you?

"Yes," she whispered.

Why don't you take him? Show him your deepest desire.

A playful grin spread across the female's lips as she ducked beneath the surface of the water.

"North!" a voice boomed. She angled her gaze to find Tik-Tok rowing fiercely in her direction. "Get away from her!"

"Tik-Tok?" North asked, her brows lowering. A throbbing ache pulsed through her head and she rubbed at her temples.

She snatched her axe from the deck and hurried to the middle of the ship as Tik-Tok climbed up the rope ladder. He flung himself over the handrail and hurried over to her, grasping her face between his hands.

"What did she do to you?" he demanded, ragged breaths escaping his lips.

"Who?" North wrinkled her nose, not understanding what he seemed so frantic about.

"Celyna. The sea witch," he rushed out, releasing North and looking out at the crashing waves. "You were speaking with her."

North frowned. What was wrong with him? "I didn't see anyone."

"Fuck." He slammed his fist against the rail. "She can be a devious bitch when she wants to."

North took a deep swallow and settled her gaze on his rumpled state. The ties at his pants were loose, his tunic backward, his jacket missing.

"I suppose you got what you needed from her, though?"

Tik-Tok drew her to his chest, his eyes focused on hers again. "She's in a … *mood*, and there's no talking sense into her until morning. You'll have to come with me tomorrow so she can remove whatever fucking spell she cast on you."

North rubbed her head, trying to see if she could somehow bring the memory forth. But she couldn't, and Tik-Tok appeared to be telling the truth, judging by the anger rolling off of him. "I'm fine."

"This is my fault. Come with me." He grabbed her by the hand and tugged her in the direction of his room. It was hard for her smaller legs to keep up with his long stride, but she managed it. Opening the door, he brought her inside.

"Why are you acting like this?" North asked, setting down her axe on the floor and taking a seat on the edge of his desk. "Even if she tried to cast a spell, I don't think it worked, because I feel fine."

"That's the thing with her spells. She doesn't cast them often, but when she does, you won't know. Celyna can take your memories and you wouldn't miss them, or she might've told you to drown yourself later tonight."

Could that have happened? And if she had, would North be able to fight the temptation to do whatever the sea witch had commanded? "Perhaps she only wanted you to think she'd done something, and she really didn't."

"She did. I know her." He gritted his teeth as he paced back and forth across the floor.

She'd never seen him so discomposed. "Why would she want to cast a spell on me anyway? I haven't even met her."

Tik-Tok stopped and lifted his head to look at her. "Because I didn't fuck her."

North's brows lifted. He hadn't tumbled her… Why not?

"She gets her visions when she orgasms," Tik-Tok continued. "I needed her prophecy, to know where exactly the portal would open, or, if she couldn't tell me that, how to avoid an old enemy. For some reason, I couldn't…" He trailed off but didn't shy away from her wide-open stare.

"Why not?" Her tongue felt thick in her mouth as she asked the two simple words.

"I … I don't know, North. I don't fucking know. Ever since you…"

"Ever since I what?" she whispered.

He sank down onto the chair in front of the desk and stared up at the ceiling before looking back at her. "I'm in control, North. Me. Not you."

"You're not making any sense."

"I fuck." His hand struck his chest. "I don't do more than that with *anyone.*"

North's gaze locked onto his red irises, his powerful expression, and something softer that possibly lay beneath. An urge pulled at her, one nearly identical to what she'd felt last night. She hadn't wanted to acknowledge it then, but now…

Sliding herself from the desk, North stepped toward him, *wanting to*, but it also felt as though an invisible hand nudged her forward.

Tik-Tok didn't say a word, only parted his lips when she spread her legs on either side of his thighs—her skirt riding up above her knees—straddling him in the chair. She leaned nearer, so near. "Why is that all you do?"

His throat bobbed as he ran his metal hand over her hair, entwining his fingers with her silver waves. He drew her head closer until her mouth was dangerously close to touching his. "Because the only one to own me, is *me.*"

And then she closed the distance, her lips on his, kissing him. He didn't hesitate, and their movements were almost savage. She liked it. Liked how he kissed her. North softly bit his lower lip, and she could feel him harden against her core. And she liked that too, how it made her center ache for more. She'd never had someone's length pressed against her in this way.

In one swift movement, Tik-Tok lifted her off him, and she thought he was going to push her away. But instead, he turned her around in his lap so her back was flush with his strong chest, his sandalwood scent enveloping her.

"Tell me how you like it," he whispered in her ear as he swept her hair away, giving him access to her neck. "Tell me what pleases you the most."

"This," she whispered, arching her back and rolling her hips against him.

His hands came to her thighs and opened her legs wider before trailing his fingers up to the exposed flesh of her stomach—the digits of his right hand were cool—the left, warm, both equally intoxicating. He ventured to the top button of her bodice and, with practiced movements, unbuttoned them one by one until they were all undone. Tik-Tok didn't remove the fabric as his hands glided up her flesh, lightly over her scar, to cup her breasts. They fit perfectly in his palms, his fingers expertly pinching and rubbing at her nipples. Breaths uneven, North arched her back even more. His mouth landed on her neck, his lips kissing, his tongue flicking.

There was no suppressing her moan any longer and it escaped through her lips.

"So responsive." Tik-Tok flicked that glorious tongue of his up her neck once more. "What else do you like, my star?"

Bold. Bolder. North interlocked her fingers through his and slid their hands together down between her breasts, to her navel, then slipped them beneath her hitched skirt and between her thighs. She wanted his touch, wanted to know what it felt like to have his warm digits inside her.

She released his hand, allowing his fingers to descend farther down on their own. And he did exactly that.

"You're so wet," he rasped, his digits dancing against her. "For me?"

"Yes." Her voice came out raspier than she'd ever heard it.

She rolled her hips again, and he let out a low growl.

"Keep doing that," he demanded. The palm of his hand circled her clit, stroking, and rubbing as he dipped a finger inside her, then another.

The things he did to her were so wickedly delicious that she burned for all of it. A groan escaped him when she ground against him harder, and she could have sworn his length swelled even more. North leaned back into him and wrapped her arm around his neck. He worked her breasts and center with his practiced hands, while his lips and tongue did magical things behind her ear.

Then something ravenous washed over her, and holy gods, it was wonderfully consuming. As though the sea was surrounding her, the waves crashing, water rising, a purple rush of color collided through her. North gasped as her body shook from the brilliant pleasure.

"That's it," Tik-Tok purred, his fingers not slowing for a moment.

The violet kept blossoming behind her eyes and, even after her body stopped shaking, the color lingered.

"Do it again," North demanded.

With an approving growl, Tik-Tok flipped her around to face him and his lips crashed to hers. Their kissing grew frantic, desperate, their tongues worshiping one another, doing what her body longed to do. He yanked down his pants, then hiked up her skirt to her waist, so she could tear her undergarments down. Then there was nothing between them as she rested against him once more. His hardness was like velvet in between her folds.

"Go slow," she said, lifting herself to give him entrance. "I haven't done this before."

Tik-Tok froze. "You what?" He stared at her as though maybe he'd heard her wrong.

His horrified expression made her want to take off running, yet that invisible hand urged her to continue talking. "Don't worry. Keep going."

Tik-Tok lifted North off him so fast that she wobbled on her feet. He pushed up from the chair and gripped his hair. "That fucking bitch. I know exactly what she did."

"What?" North cocked her head, not wanting to talk anymore. She yearned to have him pressed up to her again.

He stepped back when she reached out to touch him. "She

thought that once I found out you hadn't fucked anyone before, I would return to her. I don't take innocent females to my bed."

North's heart pounded furiously. She knew she should have been embarrassed, but the nudge kept driving her forward. "It's okay. We can continue."

"You're only saying that because of what *she* did." Tik-Tok's jaw tightened. He inched toward her, buttoning her bodice back up with clinical movements.

She swallowed, trying to clear her head. But after tasting him, touching him, she only felt the desire within her.

"We're not waiting until morning—we're going to Celyna now. Come on." He grasped her hand and tugged her out of his room.

"What's wrong?" Echo called, dragging a large bucket across the deck with Dax beside her, carrying thick, heavy rope.

"Celyna spelled North because I didn't fuck her," Tik-Tok spat. "I need you to come with me. You're close to her kind."

"Dax, I may need you," Echo said.

"For what?" He lifted a brow.

"You'll see."

North's clothing felt too tight, and she *needed* to go back into the room with Tik-Tok. But she followed him down the ladder to the rowboat anyway. She was about to settle beside him when he twisted her around to sit across from him. Dax plopped down next to Tik-Tok and Echo's warm hand wrapped around North.

"How far did you go?" Echo asked as Tik-Tok started to furiously row across the gentle waves. "Did you two…"

"No." But the urge was growing stronger, *tightening*—she was aching to have him inside her, even if it was right here in this boat with Echo and Dax watching them.

"Don't look at him." Echo grabbed North's chin between her fingers and turned her head so their gazes met. "I don't want to sing to you, but if you can't control yourself, I'll have to." She turned to Tik-Tok. "And quit growling. Even your voice makes her want to fuck you more."

"It wasn't like this at first." Tik-Tok said. "I didn't realize…"

North tried to stand, to go to Tik-Tok, but Echo held her back.

The siren's nose twitched, seeming to scent the air. "With each passing minute, I can smell the desire in you getting stronger. Close your eyes," Echo instructed her. "Take deep breaths."

North shut her lids while her chest heaved, but within the darkness, all she could think about were Tik-Tok's fingers, his mouth, his length. Echo kept telling her to breathe, and it somehow grounded her enough not to lunge across the rowboat for him.

"Celyna! Get over here!" Tik-Tok roared.

North opened her eyes and her gaze met a naked blue female with scales along her flesh, standing at the edge of the water. Long green hair, black eyes, beautiful. A storm of jealousy plowed through North—she'd never seen this female before, but knew it was the sea witch.

"I was only giving you what you wanted, pirate." Celyna stepped into the water, making her way closer to their boat. "And here you are, as I knew you would be."

"Take the spell off her," Echo said, her voice deadly. "Or I'll bring my mother into this."

"Oh, Siren Princess, I meant no harm." Celyna shrugged. "And why bring your mother into this when we both despise her?"

"Remove the fucking spell," Tik-Tok seethed, his fists tightening at his sides.

Celyna smirked. "You need a vision—so that means I need you."

"It doesn't have to be Tik-Tok," Echo said. "Dax is more than willing to fulfill your fantasy."

Celyna peered at Dax, who seemed poised to leap from the boat toward her the moment she agreed. Licking her bottom lip, the sea witch nodded. "I suppose he'll do." Her eyes gleamed as they trained on North's, and a voice whispered in her skull. *I release you.*

A veil seemed to lift from North and she hunched over, gasping for breath. She remembered Celyna at the ship, then everything that had followed. Her eyes slowly lifted to Tik-Tok's, but she couldn't read his expression. She jerked her gaze away, recalling everything they'd done, him touching her, ravishing her, her liking it too much. How she still liked it. Would even do it again. But he was disgusted by her, that she was *innocent*... Her cheeks grew blazing hot.

A purple flame lit within her, as it had when he'd brought her over the edge, writhing in bliss. That color.

"I feel it," North whispered, her entire being filling with wonder. "I feel my magic."

CHAPTER FIFTEEN

TIK-TOK

North felt her magic. *She felt it.* Tik-Tok's heart nearly pounded out of his chest as he rowed back to *The Temptress*, leaving Dax on the island with Celyna. He'd begun to wonder if North would ever access her latent power or if they would be stuck sailing the seas forever. Waiting. Hoping for something that would never happen.

Echo and North spoke in rushed voices, but his pulse was pounding too loudly in his ears to make out the words. They appeared excited—all smiles and hand gestures. He should be excited too. But he wasn't—he didn't dare let himself hope too much. What if it was something else? Another one of Celyna's tricks. Or... Or fucking *gas* that she mistook as the rumble of magic.

Shit. No. It was definitely magic. The citrusy scent of it was almost too faint to recognize, but it was there, tinging the air.

"Climb the ladder," he told North. Once she was halfway up, he began to follow, stopping after a few rungs to look back at Echo. "Take the boat back and wait for Dax."

Echo wordlessly grabbed the oars and pushed the rowboat away from the wooden hull.

"You've got this," he encouraged North when she fumbled

near the railing. "Swing your leg over."

She listened, disappearing onto the deck, and a moment later he joined her. Respen, Cyrx, and a handful of brownies stared at them in obvious confusion. *Nosy bastards.* Tik-Tok took North's hand and rushed across the deck to his quarters, ignoring the stares.

Once inside, he slammed the door. "Show me," he demanded.

"*Show you?*" she said, trying to catch her breath between words. "How am I supposed to show you a feeling?"

Right. She felt it, but that didn't mean she could *use* it. He tried to even his breaths, calm himself, but he'd waited so long… To have the magic he needed be so close and not be able to access it…

"Are you okay?" North asked.

He met her stare, reading the nervousness there, and unclenched his jaw. "Are *you?*" He looked her up and down, appraising. It hadn't been long enough for the scent of her bliss to dissipate completely from the room. His heart thumped as it reached his nose, creating a direct path to his throbbing groin. *Bad Tik-Tok,* he chided himself. This wasn't the time to get distracted. He rubbed the pad of his thumb along his bottom lip. "Any lingering urges from Celyna's spell?"

North blushed. "No."

Tik-Tok's eye twitched with annoyance. *Calm down.* It wasn't her fault he'd pissed off the sea witch. If anything, what had happened between them was *his* fault. He should've realized North wouldn't have come all over his fingers and begged for more without external help, even if she had planned to seduce him. There was a difference between luring someone in for personal gain and luring them in due to genuine desire. Today had been the latter. So Celyna *knew* North was untouched and that he would never stick his cock in her once he found out.

"Your magic," he said in a tight voice, pushing away the memory of how good it felt to have her on his lap. The heat. How wet she'd been. Each little noise she made when he touched her. He cracked his knuckles. "What does it feel like?"

"It feels…" She paused, brows lowered as she seemed to ponder how to put it into words. "It feels like the sea itself is inside me, like the waves are a part of me. Both calm and thrashing. It's different than anything I've ever experienced."

Tik-Tok paced back and forth a few times before perching on the edge of his bed, leaving a large space between them. "And what brought the sensation to the surface?"

She shifted uncomfortably on her feet. "Is that important?"

"Of course." He set his elbows on his knees and leaned forward, looking up at her from beneath his lashes. "If you know how to tap into that feeling, we can work on manifesting it into something useful."

"Like opening a portal?"

He grinned. "Like opening a portal."

"Can I have a minute?" She rubbed at her chest. "To see if I can find it again?"

Tik-Tok watched her intently as she focused internally. The small line of concern that appeared on her forehead made him want to run a finger over it, to smooth it out. Her silver hair was windblown, strands sticking to her cheeks, and the buttons of her bodice were fastened unevenly—his fault. He hadn't wanted to lower his gaze as he closed the fabric over her supple breasts. His palms tingled as if begging for another chance to hold them. *Stop.*

But it was too late—his skin warmed with desire, the sand inside his own shirt suddenly itchy against his too-sensitive skin. He stood, crossing to his chest of drawers, while pulling his shirt over his head. The sand hidden inside the material rained to the floor. Dropping the soiled shirt, he opened the top drawer and dug through his clothes for a fresh one.

Cool fingers traced down his back. Down one of the more prominent scars. And Tik-Tok froze. "You're supposed to be testing your magic," he grumbled, shifting away from the touch. "Not seducing your captain."

"You're not my captain," North whispered. "What happened

to you?”

“What does it look like?” He yanked on a black tunic, hiding the marks given to him by the King of Ev. Of the thousands of lashes he’d received, only a dozen had scarred, compliments of healing potions. But there was a reason these remained. They had been deep, bloody, and gotten infected. He hated that North had seen them—that he’d been too preoccupied with thoughts of her to remember to keep his back turned, like the other night when she’d seen him without his shirt. Facing her now, he kept his gaze on her chin so he didn’t need to see the pity likely swirling in her eyes. “Figure anything out yet?”

“Yes.” She stepped closer, hand hovering near her mouth, and stared at his chest. “What happened to your back, Tik-Tok?”

He grunted in frustration. Even the densest fae would recognize lash marks and dare not ask about them. Yet he spoke, regardless of how much it bothered him. “I was the ward of the King of Ev for a few years before becoming a pirate. Being young and alone, I was an easy outlet for his frustrations.” The faint echo of a cracking whip sounded in his head and he tensed. “Happy now?”

“No,” she breathed. “Why would I be happy about that?”

Because she’d gotten her answer. “Stop changing the subject. Your magic—”

“Let’s make a deal,” she said quickly. “If you tell me why you want to open the portal, I’ll tell you a theory about my magic.”

“Aren’t you the conniving one, my star?” He smirked and stepped back, finding a seat on the edge of his mattress again. Only Respen knew his full past, and that was only because they’d both found the bottom of too many bottles one night. There was nothing she could do with the information to damage his reputation or put him in danger—no upstanding fae thought highly of him anyway and *he* was the one to be feared. He didn’t want to divulge his secrets nor relive his pain. He would though—if it meant unlocking North’s power. Even if he had to force it out. “Sit.”

North padded to the bed and took the empty space beside

him. The faint scent of her from his bed didn't compare to the source. Her nearness left him drunk on it.

"There are chairs," he said, throwing his hand out toward the three seats around his desk.

"Do you think that's safer?" she asked, crossing her arms. "If I remember correctly, we slept uneventfully together in the bed, but your chair—"

"All right, all right," he said, wincing. *Stars above*. Did she have to remind him? Twice in one day, he'd gotten worked up, only to have his cock soften, unsatisfied. The ache in his balls grew heavier by the second. "Point taken."

"So…" she prodded.

"Why do I want to open the portal?" He twisted toward her, taking her chin between his thumb and forefinger so she had to look him in the eye. With a deep breath, he answered, "I need to kill my father."

Her lips parted on a gasp.

Tik-Tok chuckled ruefully. "Not what you expected?"

"You… But…"

He snorted, releasing her chin. Of course she couldn't comprehend patricide—Tin had wasted no time swinging his axe in her defense. "Not all fathers are as protective as yours."

"*Kill* him, though? Is that necessary?"

"What does it matter to you?" he asked, genuinely curious. "You don't know him or what he's done. Why do you care if he lives or dies?"

North shifted, squeezing the fabric of her skirt. "You're right—I don't know him. But to go through all of this? You cut off your own arm and took me from my family to murder one male?"

A dry laugh escaped Tik-Tok's throat. Yes—he'd cut off his arm. He'd stolen North. He'd betrayed Captain Salt, the asshole of a fae who'd saved him as an adolescent, taken him from a lifetime of slavery to the brutal King of Ev. And he'd done *more*. He *would do* more to make sure his father suffered an excruciating death. Tik-Tok was going to rip the bastard's limbs off, one by one. He would cauterize each stub to keep his father from bleeding out before he was finished. Then he'd carve his chest open and snap his ribs apart. Feed his intestines to wild beasts. Peel his skin from his body as he begged for mercy. *And then* Tik-Tok would deal the final blow.

"My father…" He eyed the cupboard holding his personal supply of spirits and sighed. It had been a long time since he'd talked about this with anyone, and when he was finished, there was no doubt he would need to drown away the pain. "To call him a fucking asshole is an understatement. My father *and* my mother, actually. They were horrendous parents to me and my three siblings. Constantly berating and beating us. My oldest sister escaped through marriage when I was three and my older brother took a job in another town when I was four, which left me and my younger sister to deal with them on our own. If only they had stayed away…"

He closed his eyes, rubbing the lids in an attempt to erase the images of his siblings *before*… Of them alive. Laughing. Protecting him and his little sister from their parents' fury. And then, there was *after*. An ending saturated in blood.

"My oldest sister announced her pregnancy the last time she came home," he said quietly. "She would've made a wonderful mother, given the chance."

"What happened to her?" North put a hand on his knee in what had to be an attempt at comfort. All it did was make his pulse race.

"My parents killed her," he said in a hoarse voice. "And my brother. And my little sister. And … me…" He glanced sideways to gauge North's expression. Her wide eyes were glazed with a mixture of shock and horror. His lips curled into a rueful smile. "Obviously I was harder to kill than they expected, even at thirteen years old."

"But … *why?*" she asked gently. "Why would they murder their own children?"

"Power." He held up his left hand and let a small spark of red smoke twine around his fingers. "They used a dark spell to steal everything from my siblings then severed their spinal cords, but they couldn't pry my magic out no matter how hard they tried. In fact, their attempt only made more manifest."

He closed his fist around the swirling red magic, extinguishing it. His useless power to scent magic had suddenly been joined by the ability to turn living beings to stone. Then the more volatile ability to crush the hardest of rocks with a mere thought. The new power had exploded from him, fierce and untamed, doing for him what he'd always wanted to do. *Crushing, maiming, in order to free himself.*

He smirked maliciously at the memory. "And I used it to crush every bone in my mother's body. A slow, agonizing death. Instead of helping her, my cowardly father ran off with my brother's portal magic."

"And disappeared through the portal?" North guessed.

Tik-Tok nodded once. "The world on the other side lacks magic, according to the tales told in Ev, and my parents wanted to become gods. My father, I assume, succeeded."

North was quiet for so long that, if her hand didn't still rest on his knee, he would've thought she'd left. He flopped back on the bed, staring at the wooden beams overhead. Anger stirred inside him, clawing, biting, frantic to find an escape. He wanted his father *dead.* Wanted *vengeance.*

"Captain Salt isn't exactly what you'd consider *good,* but he was different toward me. He became something like a father after he snuck me out of Ev. He taught me to fight and, because I saw him doing so many wrong things, I learned to always do the *right* thing." He looked down at his metal arm and felt the scab over his guilty conscience loosen. The right thing *wasn't* to hold a mutiny against Salt. Was Salt the best male? Hell no. But Salt was the best male he'd had in his life while growing up. Perhaps, that one time, he should've simply acquired his own pirate ship another way. Abandoned Salt instead of actively betraying him.

North shifted onto her knees on the mattress and leaned forward, blocking his view of the ceiling. "I don't know why I *felt* my magic, but I know what else I *felt* at the time. Maybe … maybe if we recreate that, it will work again. I want to help you. You should have told me this earlier so I understood."

Tik-Tok's eyes snapped to her face, his gold hand fisting the blankets. Was she seriously going to resume her plan of seduction? *Now?* After what had happened because of Celyna. "North…"

When he didn't continue, she leaned closer, breath shallow. "What?"

He suppressed a groan. Taking an innocent into his bed had always been a hard line for him—the females got attached and he didn't need that kind of trouble. "You need to give yourself to someone better than me. Someone capable of doing more than fucking."

"There are other things we can do," she whispered. "Things we've already done."

Blood surged to his cock. *Yes,* he wanted to tell her. He wanted to have his fingers in her again, have her touch him in places she hadn't explored yet. His hard length pressed painfully against his pants and he groaned in his head. It wouldn't take long. Minutes, if that.

But, as much as he wanted to take her up on the offer of *other things*, he wouldn't. Not if it was simply meant to draw her power out. He'd had enough exchanging of sexual favors for magic with Celyna. North meant more to him than that. He stopped breathing as that realization struck him. *Oh, fuck no.* That was a reality he refused to entertain.

If North needed … *something* … to help her release her potential, she would have to use her own hands. Or another crew member. Dax would most certainly be willing, but then Tik-Tok would be forced to toss him overboard.

He gave her a tight smile. "As much as I want to kill my father, I won't use your body like that. There are other ways to achieve my goal—and for you to find yourself. I'm willing to wait a little longer to do this with my morals intact. What's left of them anyway."

She tilted her head, a tinge of sadness in her gaze. "It doesn't have to be about my magic or the portal. It could be … fun."

"Fun," he echoed and lunged up, pressing his lips to hers in a quick, desperate kiss. Then he stood, pulling her with him, and crossed the room. "Forgive me, my star. But I can't." He swung the door open and gave her a gentle nudge. "Go to your room and practice feeling your magic some more, all right?"

North opened her mouth to say something, but he didn't wait to hear if it was an agreement or a refusal. In a moment of desperation to be alone with his feelings—both mental and physical—he slammed the door in her face. He only made it as far as his desk before unbuckling his pants—an illusory image of North on her knees before him—and gripping himself with a low, desperate groan.

CHAPTER SIXTEEN

NORTH

North paced back and forth across her room, her arms folded at her chest. She'd been doing it for a while now, trying to draw out that vivid violet magic. Nothing. Not a spark, not a flame, not a single bit of smoke.

But it *was there*.

She thought about the spell the sea witch had cast upon her, and she should have been livid, but she wasn't. Everything she'd done, she'd secretly yearned to do. Wishing her magic came to her as easy as it did to Celyna, she tried again. Nothing.

"Gods, come on," North growled with frustration.

Perhaps it was because she was too wound-up from her earlier conversation with Tik-Tok. There had been so much bottled up inside that male—more than she could have dreamed. The wounds on his back, his parents, the King of Ev... She could tell he hadn't wanted to confess to her any of it, but he'd still confided his past to her. His revelations had unlocked another part within her that had nothing to do with magic. *Feelings*.

And then she'd offered herself so she could find her magic again and help him succeed in his vengeance, even though it wasn't hers to seek. Maybe it was because of what her own family had faced in their past. Tik-Tok's father could've become like the

Wizard to another world and brought it to ruins, like Oz had.

Tik-Tok had denied tumbling her, so she'd offered to do other things that could lead to pleasure. She'd wanted him to feel the gratification she had earlier in the day, to return the favor. Instead, he'd slammed the door in her face.

"Bah!" she shouted to herself and threw a pretend axe at the wall. It hit right where she wanted it to. If only it had been real.

Her door swung open and she jerked her head up. She hadn't expected Echo, but was glad to see her, nonetheless.

"I wanted to check on you," the siren said, climbing down the ladder.

"I'm fine, *Princess*." North grinned and sat on the bed.

"Mmm." Echo plopped down beside her. "I stripped myself of that title after my mother fled our underwater village instead of helping to defend against the invading forces. But it needed to be used today to help a friend." She gave North a small smile.

Friends. That was what they'd become. North swallowed, wondering what kind of life the rest of the crew members had faced. She'd had a great one growing up, and her chest tightened over how the small arguments with her parents now seemed minuscule. "I'm sorry."

"I'm better off staying away from her. However, I don't think you're truly *fine*, and I don't think the captain is either. He's holed himself up in his room and didn't answer when I tried to tell him Dax was back. Celyna had a vision that he needs to speak to the captain about. She also wishes to see Dax from now on."

North puckered her lips. "How does Dax feel about that?"

"He said he's more than willing to do his duty." Echo rolled her eyes. "But Dax would hump a tree if it could get him off."

She chuckled softly, unable to stop the image of Dax doing just that from flashing inside her head.

"So, what's really wrong? Is it about what the sea witch made you almost do?"

With a sigh, North shook her head. "The opposite."

Echo perked up, her smile growing wide. "Go on."

"I wanted to…" She took a deep breath, her cheeks heating.

"I told Tik-Tok that I felt my magic after he … after I…"

Echo blinked. "Orgasmed?"

"No—more like the rush of feelings that come along with that. Feelings for him. I offered to sleep with him, but he doesn't tumble innocents."

The siren's brows lifted all the way up her forehead. "You haven't before?"

"Nope." She wasn't going to go into the story about how she'd saved herself for Birch because that aspect of her life didn't matter anymore. It was strange how quickly things could become clear, how everything could be so unexpected yet feel like the right path.

"Oh…" Echo stared up at the ceiling. "I'm still surprised he didn't take you up on that offer. We all want the portal open, but no one as much as him." Her gaze settled on North's. "I can't believe you haven't. Perhaps it was because I was sixteen when I took my first lover. But I started drowning fae from the moment I could speak."

Echo must have noticed North's horrified expression because she continued, "That was another life, though. It's my nature, what we sirens are born to do, but I didn't want that life anymore. That's why I joined this crew."

"I'm glad you did, Echo." North smiled. "Because I wouldn't have met you otherwise."

Echo let out a low whistle. "Oh, you never know. You could have visited the sea one day and stumbled upon me. Perhaps even been scared at first and held up your axe. You're strong, even if you don't look it."

"It's my size, isn't it?" North chuckled.

Echo smirked and stood from the bed, pulling North up by her wrist. "Come on. Let's go take out some aggression on deck with the weapons. What do you say?"

At that moment, swinging a real axe would be much better than throwing a pretend one. "Sure."

North followed Echo up the ladder. A few of the brownies were doing their usual cleaning duties or taking watch up in the sails while Kaliko and Cyrx stood at the helm. There wasn't any sign of Tik-Tok, Dax, or Respen. At the middle of the ship, near the rail, rested her old axe and a sword, as though Echo had already known North needed this.

As she scooped up the axe, a tinge of disappointment hit her that it wasn't the one Tik-Tok had given her. But she'd left it in his room. After he'd slammed the door in her face, she wasn't going to go to him—he'd have to eventually come to her, if he decided to see her at all. She'd done enough, offered enough, had been willing to give him *everything*.

Echo brought up her glistening sword and North swung her axe against the silver blade, the loud clang echoing across the ship. The ringing in her ears and the vibration in her arms felt good. Echo thrust her sword forward and North easily blocked it.

"Perfect," Echo said.

"Meet me after you finish. I have something for you," Respen called to Echo with a smirk as he made an appearance, carrying a large sack toward the storage space below deck.

"You'll have to wait a while." Echo shrugged, her eyes dancing mischievously.

"I'd wait an eternity for you." He blew her a kiss and disappeared down the stairs.

Echo swung her sword and North whirled out of the way.

"How did you two get together anyway?" North asked, lifting her axe higher.

"Respen tried to woo me for months and I refused his gifts, his conversations, all of it, but then one day, he didn't try anymore. It hit me then that I liked him. If he'd kept trying, I don't think I would have ever changed my mind."

North had never been wooed in her life, and if it had been someone like Respen, she would have probably given in on the first day. She was about to say so but caught sight of something black high up in the sky, drawing closer.

Echo followed North's gaze and craned her neck all the way back. "What the fuck is a bird doing way out here?"

North inhaled sharply as the bird soared nearer. She knew that crow!

Grandfather.

Relief flooded her—this was the proof she needed that her family was truly no longer stone. Dropping the axe with a loud thump, North ran to the end of the ship and waved her hands in the air. "Over here!" she shouted so he could see her.

Her grandfather swooped down and landed on the deck beside her. Black smoke enveloped him and a few feathers floated to the ground as he transformed into his fae form, wearing a dark tunic and pants, and equally dark feathers braided within his hair.

"Who are you?" Echo asked, bringing up her sword. "Step away from her."

Crow released his blades from beneath his bracer, the tips extending over the back of his fingers like talons. "No. *You* step away from my granddaughter, siren."

"What the fuck is this?" Tik-Tok boomed as he made an appearance. He must have heard her loud shouting. "Go home, pheasant. Like I told the queen, I'll bring her back safely once she opens the portal."

"You've had her long enough." Crow glared. "She's coming with me."

"Oh really?" Tik-Tok drawled. "Do you plan to carry her back to the Emerald City in your tiny claws? Or perhaps I should turn you into stone instead?" He cocked his head and raised a hand.

"Wait!" North cried before he could change Crow into an ornament. "Let me discuss things with my grandfather alone. Please. I'm not leaving."

Tik-Tok ran a palm across his jaw and flicked his gaze to Echo, then nodded. "Find me when you're finished," he said to North and motioned for Echo to follow him.

"North." Crow turned to her, retracting his blades, relief written all over his face. "We've been sweeping the seas to find you. Are you all right? No one's hurt you, have they?"

She shook her head. There was no point telling him about being stabbed by Rizmaela. The top of her dress was, thankfully, covering her scar. She was healed and the dwarf was dead, so it would only worry him more than he already was. And it would only make matters worse if she'd brought up being spelled by the sea witch.

"Thank goodness." He exhaled. "I have a plan to bring you home, but I'll have to leave you here to get reinforcements."

Home. But … she couldn't, even if Tik-Tok would allow it. "Grandfather, I want to stay. I know you're not going to understand, but I have my reasons. I haven't been mistreated."

Crow pursed his lips. "Your father will never agree to that."

"He'll have to understand." North folded her arms. "I'm not a youngling anymore and I've found that I do indeed have magic." He didn't need to know that she couldn't wield it yet.

"It's true, then?" Crow asked. "You're able to open portals like your father?"

"I think I can, but I need to stay to find out."

"Reva will have my beak for this," he grumbled.

"Does this mean you're going to let me stay? Grandmother and Father will understand. You and Mother will see that they do, like always." North's mother had once left her mortal home to come to Oz—she would understand more than anyone.

Crow tightened his fists, a low groan coming from his throat, as though he were warring with himself. "You've been old enough to make your own choices for several years."

"I love you." North threw her arms around her grandfather and held him tight, breathing in his calming, woodsy scent.

Crow took a step away from her and lifted a brow as he scanned her clothing. "When you come back, you might want to wear something different. Your father would shit a brick if he saw you in this."

Her smile grew wider. "He'll have to understand this too."

"You give him too much credit." Crow chuckled, then sobered. "I can stay here, if you need me to."

He'd already faced too much in his past, and she needed the

chance to grow on her own. "No, go home. Let them know how much I love them." North took a few more steps back because if she hugged him again, she wouldn't let him leave.

"I love you. I've always believed in you." A cloud of dark smoke formed for a brief moment before her grandfather's bird form darted up into the sky with a loud caw.

She watched him as he flew farther and farther away, becoming the smallest of specks, and then he was gone.

Tears fell from North's eyes. She wiped them away and exhaled a puff of air, determined to see this through. Resting her arms over the handrail, she closed her eyes, concentrating. That bright violet was right there, within her reach. She conjured an image of a hand inside her and slowly crawled the fingers forward, trying not to scare the magic away. The closer she inched, the harder it was to keep herself from lunging for that vivid purple sphere, but she forced herself to wait. And then, when she was a hairsbreadth away again, she grabbed it, latched on, and tugged. Her eyes flew open as the burst of power flowed through her.

The silver sea rippled, the waves thrashed, until finally, the water parted, creating what looked to be a whirlpool. The liquid slammed shut, the violent waves calming.

A giddy laugh escaped her as she slapped her palms against the handrail. "Gods, I did it!" she shouted. She would do it again, too.

CHAPTER SEVENTEEN

TIK-TOK

According to Dax, the vision Celyna had told him was of utmost importance. Tik-Tok believed him, and yet … he'd left North alone with Crow. *The* Crow. Slayer of Locasta. Ruler of Northern Oz. Her grandfather. Sure, he had jested about Crow carrying North away, but if anyone could—it was him.

Dax spoke, repeating the sea witch's words, but Tik-Tok struggled to focus. His mind was full of images of North being whisked away. Hidden from him. Why hadn't he been more specific in his deal with Ozma? He scowled. Would he have a right to take North a second time? Was it breaking the deal if someone rescued her *before* the portal opened?

"Captain," Echo said in a harsh voice. "Are you listening?"

He jerked upright in his desk chair. "Of course I am."

"Then repeat what I said," Dax challenged, crossing his arms with a scowl.

"Shouldn't you be more relaxed after fucking Celyna?" he snapped, angry to be caught pre-occupied with thoughts of North.

Dax threw his hands up in the air. "Shouldn't you be more *concerned* with the fact that North could get lost—or worse—if she opens the portal for you?"

"I—" *Wait. What?* Tik-Tok inched to the edge of his chair

and put his palms on the desk to steady himself. "Why didn't you tell me this sooner?"

"You wouldn't answer your door," he said in a flat voice.

It was a valid point… He'd only left his quarters when Crow showed up because he smelled the male's magic on the air and heard the commotion on deck. "Repeat what Celyna told you."

"North will open the portal here," he said, tapping at the map spread between them of the Northern Sea. "But there are different possible outcomes. In one, you get your vengeance and return relatively unscathed. In another, when North opens the portal, it sucks her inside and she'll be lost forever. And, if the portal closes once we pass through, none of us will return to the Fae Lands."

His breath caught. Lose North? No—that couldn't happen. He had given his word to return her home, and he didn't renege on his word. "So, we'll make sure it's the first outcome."

"That's the problem," Echo said. "She couldn't see the event that decides which outcome will become reality."

With shallow breaths, he stood, staring at Echo, then Dax. "What are you doing here, then? Get back to the beach and *make* her see it."

"Trust me, I tried. Apparently, *it doesn't work like that*," he said, imitating Celyna's voice. "That's why she only saw you once a year. Decisions had to be made outside of your goal before she could tell you, definitively, what to do next."

That made sense. A lot of sense, if he was being honest. But they would simply have to stay docked right where they were until Celyna *could* see the correct path. *There.* That was a decision.

"What are you going to do?" Echo asked.

She refused to meet his eyes—likely because she was worried that Tik-Tok's desire to open the portal would matter more than North. He wished it did. That would make his life much easier.

"I don't know," he admitted. But first, he needed to make sure North was still on his ship. "I have to talk to North. Alone."

Tik-Tok stood, flew around his desk, and rushed onto the deck. Echo and Dax could leave his quarters behind him. He didn't care if North was finished talking with Crow yet—he should never have allowed them time alone to plot an escape. No matter what he decided, he needed North there. With him.

Scanning the deck, Tik-Tok found no sign of Crow in either of his forms. His heart gave a small, panicked spasm as he searched for North. He wasn't prepared for the sweeping relief of finding her at the rail. The pink skirt hugged her ass where she bent slightly, leaning forward onto her elbows. Jerking himself off hadn't been nearly satisfying enough.

Approaching her slowly, he spoke in a wary voice. "Where's your grandfather?"

"Gone." She tilted her head to look at him when he joined her at the edge of the ship. "I told him I wanted to help you."

She ... what? "Why?" he blurted.

"Because I do."

"And Crow *agreed* to that?" The skepticism in his tone was clear, even to him.

She shrugged. "He didn't like the idea, but I'm grown. You should be happy he was the one who came instead of my father or grandmother."

"I don't doubt that."

North bit her lip, trying hard not to smile. "I did it," she blurted.

"Did what?"

"Used my magic!" She was practically bouncing with excitement. "I made a small whirlpool. It didn't last long, but it's something. I'm sure I can do it again." She spun toward the water. "Watch."

"Wait." Tik-Tok desperately wanted her power unlocked, but did it have to be right now, when he had learned only minutes ago that it could lead to her utter downfall? He sighed and nodded toward his quarters. "Will you come with me? We need to talk about something."

North lifted a brow. "Are you *asking* me?"

"I can demand it, if you prefer," he said, smirking.

Tik-Tok didn't wait for her to reply before heading back to

his quarters, and the soft pad of her feet followed at his back. He made sure Dax and Echo had left with a quick glance, then shut them inside, alone.

"Thanks to Celyna's vision, we know exactly where the portal should open." He crossed to the cupboard and took out two glasses along with a bottle of his finest rum.

"That's a good thing, isn't it?" North asked as he poured them each a drink.

"On one hand, yes. I get my vengeance and we all go on our merry way." He tipped back his drink, swallowing, and turned to her with the other in his hand. Before he could extend it to her as he'd intended, he downed it on an impulse, slamming the empty glass on the table beside the first. "On the other hand, if fate goes against us, there's a chance you get sucked into the portal and meet whatever that world has in store."

North stared at him, mouth hanging open. "I don't understand. The only way you'll get to your father is if I…"

"No. They are two very different potential outcomes. In one, we all survive."

North swallowed hard. "So either we all win, we get trapped, or … I die?"

"Celyna didn't say you *died*, necessarily." He grabbed the bottle from the desk and took a swig straight from the source. "Only that you were sucked through and lost."

North opened and closed her mouth a handful of times, forehead creased, eyes glittering with worry. Finally, she met his gaze. "I don't want to get lost anywhere."

"I don't want that either." Tik-Tok slumped so that he sat on the edge of his desk. His whole life had been spent trying to catch and kill a monster. And now that victory was in front of him— *right in front of him*—he wasn't sure he should risk it. Was killing his father worth losing North? For all he knew, his father had already been murdered in the other world and his entire mission was in vain. But he refused to consider that possibility. "Celyna also told Dax that if the portal closes once we go through, none of us will return. That means you would have to stay nearby. We don't know how your magic works yet and we can't risk putting distance between you and the portal." He released a humorless laugh and drank again. "The more I consider it, the more I think maybe I should stop. Let the past go."

"No." North dashed to his side and pulled the rum from his hand, placing it back in the cupboard. "After everything you've told me, I'm invested."

He snorted. "*Invested?* You're willing to die for my revenge?"

"That's only one scenario, isn't it? Everything could work out," she said carefully. "Also, you said I would be lost, not dead."

"North, no." He hung his head. *Fuck*. How could he let her risk her life in exchange for the chance to end his father's? But … how could he not? They would simply have to put off the portal until Celyna could see how to do it safely. After waiting for decades, what was another year? Ironic decision, considering he'd been ready to do anything to make it even a single day sooner. He looked over North, eyes slowly scanning from her feet up to meet her gaze, and resigned himself to the delay. The risk to her life wasn't worth it. "I'm sorry for slamming the door in your face earlier."

North feigned a gasp. "Am I hearing things? It sounded like you apologized, but that can't be—"

Tik-Tok silenced her with his lips. The kiss was so sudden that she froze beneath his touch. Just as he was about to pull away, to apologize again, she moved against him.

He was in awe of the softness of her lips, how perfectly they slanted over his. His kiss was demanding and rough, her answer gentle and pliant. She tasted like fruit sweetened by salt—cherries, and the sea. He cupped her cheeks, held her in place, as her hands fisted in his tunic. The first sweep of her tongue nearly undid him. Groaning, he slipped his own out to meet hers. Brushing and twisting together in an intoxicating dance, each passing moment of it was too much and not enough. He wanted more. Wanted to taste her everywhere.

No. Damn it—no.

Forcing himself to break their kiss, Tik-Tok rested his forehead on hers, still holding her face. "You make me feel things I don't want to feel," he whispered. "How did you get so far under my skin, my star?"

North used his shirt to tug him nearer. Her breasts pressed against his chest, each heavy breath she took going straight to his cock. *Respectable pirate, respectable pirate, respectable pirate*, he chanted silently to himself. When a soft, impatient sound came from her, the mantra completely shattered.

Respectable, my ass.

"Kiss me again." North leaned up on her toes, bringing their faces closer together. Her breath skated across his lips, drawing him in as if she were the siren on board his ship.

Tik-Tok flicked his tongue out, tasting her. "If I kiss you again, I'm not sure I'll be able to control myself. And I don't—"

"It's not like I've never touched a cock before."

"You…" He lifted his forehead to better see her expression. The prettiest shade of pink colored her cheeks, her lips plump and red because of him. "I thought you've never been with a male before."

"I haven't," she admitted.

Tik-Tok studied her, his head tilted to the side, and warred with himself over saying *fuck it*. He wanted to bend her over his desk. Take what she'd offered on multiple occasions. Rip the fabric from her and replace it with his hands. His tongue. His body.

An intense throb in his cock made him shift. *Fuck.* There was no denying this—denying what was between them. His fingertips slipped from where they tangled in her hair and trailed gently down the sides of her neck. In a strained voice, he asked, "How far *have* you gone with someone?"

"I've kissed." North licked her lips, staring at his. "And I've been touched."

"I meant before me," he clarified. "Before I brought you on my ship, how far had you gone?" Trailing one hand down to caress her breast over her clothes, he brushed a thumb over her hardened nipple. "Was I the first to feel these?"

North pushed her chest into his touch. "Yes."

He held back a groan and skimmed his free hand down her chest, over her stomach, to lightly graze her mound. "And this?" He knew the answer—if no one had fondled her chest, they most certainly hadn't explored her tight channel—but he wanted to hear her say it.

"Only you," she breathed.

He moved both hands to grip her hips. "Then, tell me, what bastard let you touch his cock without making sure you were also satisfied? Was it the male you found after Birch rejected you?"

"It wasn't like that." She spoke quickly, her hands flattening over his abs. "I wanted to forget about Birch, so I snuck to a gathering in the woods and found a male. We kissed and I … took him from his trousers, but then I stopped it."

Jealousy nibbled at Tik-Tok's insides. The thought of her delicate hands gripping another fae's length… A small, possessive growl rumbled in his throat. "Will you stop me?"

"I thought you didn't touch innocents."

"It would be a night of firsts for us both." He smirked. It was too hard to deny the attraction sizzling between them anymore. "But only if you're sure you want *everything* from me."

"I'm sure," she said eagerly.

Tik-Tok gripped her chin with his gold hand and forced her to meet his blazing stare. "You need to be *sure*."

"I am," she promised. And he saw the truth of it glistening in her eyes.

Was he really going to do this? Break his rule. Take the one female that could, if she wished it, destroy everything he had worked for. He was willing to give her a year to ensure Celyna had a definitive vision before deciding whether he should give up on his vengeance. A lot could happen in a year… But he was sure of one thing—one huge, terrifying thing: North meant something to him. More than any other fae ever had.

"If I do anything you don't like, or if you want to stop, you need to tell me immediately," he told her, tightening his grip on her chin to make sure she understood he was serious.

"I will." North looked up at him from beneath her lashes. "First, I want to return the favor from last time."

Last time. When he made her come all over his fingers.

If she kept looking at him like that, he would come in his pants. Closing his eyes, he kissed her deeply, delving between her lips with his tongue, crushing her mouth to his. Then he brushed his lips across her cheek to her ear. "Get on your knees for me."

North's breath caught and she sunk down in front of him, eyes locked on his.

He forced himself to tear his gaze away. If he did look—did see her in front of him like that with her wide brown eyes and just-kissed lips—he was certain things would take an embarrassing turn. His seed would end up across her face before she even touched him.

The moment he unlaced his pants, his hard length sprung free. North's sharp inhale made him pause and wait. He was larger than most and, for someone who had only briefly encountered a cock, it had to be intimidating. But, instead, she reached up tentatively and wrapped her fingers around his shaft.

"Oh shit," he hissed, hips jerking. Had the simple touch of another's hand ever felt so good? "Wait." He covered her hand with his. "I want your mouth."

"I … don't know how," she said softly.

Slowly, he moved her hand up and down as he spoke. "Open your mouth and cover your teeth with your lips." When she did, he slid her hand down to his base. "Now close your mouth around the tip."

White light flashed across his vision when the warmth of her mouth touched the head of his cock. Precum leaked from him as he resumed moving her hand.

"Use your tongue," he rasped. In answer, it ran across the ridge and he fought the urge to fist her hair and shove his way into the back of her throat. There would be time for that if she wished—after she was used to taking him like this. Releasing her hand now that he'd established a slow rhythm, he tilted his head back and groaned. "Just like that."

North worked him with clumsy strokes and repetitive swipes of her tongue, but it was absolute bliss. Every tiny twitch of her fingers had him on the very edge, the buildup of heat from her mouth making him feel as if he were on fire. Because it was *her* that was doing it. And she was fucking perfect. A tingle started in his balls and he backed out of her grip before he could come. There were too many things he wanted to do first.

She wiped her lips with the back of her hand. "What—"

"My turn." In one fluid movement, he had her off her knees and spread across his desk— maps be damned. Kneeling between her thighs, he shoved the fabric of her skirt up to her waist and slowly slid the undergarments away. The sight of her, of the fluid covering her entrance, nearly sent him over the edge. "So ready for me," he said with a grin.

Leaning up on her elbows, she looked down at him, panting with lust-glazed eyes. "What are you doing?"

"Do you want to stop?" he asked. He would. It would be monumentally fucking difficult, but he would. When she shook her head, his grin widened.

Tik-Tok maintained eye contact this time as he leaned forward and flicked his tongue over her clit. North's head flew back on a moan, giving him all the encouragement he needed. With his tongue, he circled her bundle of nerves. He gently pressed his gold palm against her abdomen, keeping her in place, while his other hand found the slick entrance.

Using two fingers, he worked her with languid strokes, curling and twisting his digits until she grabbed the edges of his desk to steady herself. Thirty seconds more was all it took for her walls to clench tightly around him. The entire crew must have heard her cry out as she came, and a part of him enjoyed the idea. North was his.

"Gods," she said between gasps for air. "That was…"

Tik-Tok stood, licking her sweetness from his fingers as she watched. His cock was painfully hard now. From where he stood between her knees, it was so near her entrance that it wouldn't take much effort for him to rub the head in her wetness. The last bit of North's innocence … protected by half a step.

Damn. Fucking close. So fucking close.

"Don't stop," North said. She must have noticed his hesitation as he fisted himself and stared. His free hand gripped her bare thigh.

"Not here," he forced himself to say. Pulling her toward him, he lifted her against him, her legs immediately circling his waist, and he carried her across the room. "The bed." North shivered in what he read as anticipation. But what if it wasn't? His mind was too fucked up to tell the difference. Gently, he set her down on the edge of the mattress. "There's no going back once it's done. We can do *something else*," he said in a questioning voice, repeating her earlier offer to him.

North's reply was a playful smile. With quick fingers, she unbuttoned her bodice and tossed the material to the floor, then she peeled off her skirt and kicked it away. Tik-Tok drank in her completely naked form on his blankets. The soft curves. The lean muscles. Pebbled nipples on firm breasts, the light pink scar between them. The glistening reminder of her orgasm coating her inner thighs. *Shit.* He was done for.

North scooted backward, laying down. "Are you coming?"

About to—in more ways than one.

He prowled toward her, placing one knee on the mattress, and leaned over her. "You're *sure?*" he asked in a tight voice.

"I swear, if you ask me that again, I may have to get my axe." She grinned, gripping the hem of his shirt, and slid it over his head.

Tik-Tok settled over her then, nestled between her thighs, his cock resting against her lower belly. And he kissed her. Slowly this time. Softly. Even though his body demanded he *take her now.* "It might hurt," he whispered. The thought of hurting her was enough to stamp down his primal urges. "I'll be gentle, but…"

"It's okay." North brushed away a loose piece of his dark hair from where it clung to his lashes. "I trust you."

She trusted him? A new kind of peace settled over him. He'd

been trusted by crewmates before, but North was different. She had come to him with hate, and now… Now it was different. Tik-Tok buried his face in the crook of her neck, kissing and nipping, as he continued to hold his weight off her. She trailed her fingers down each individual scar on his back.

Then he lined himself up with her core.

The first press inside her warmth made him fist the blankets. When he'd gained an inch, North inhaled sharply. He paused, shaking with the exertion, and covered her mouth with his own. His tongue nudged hers, mimicking the slide of his cock into her.

He took his time sinking into her, letting her adjust to his size before going a little farther. North's groans vibrated against his mouth where he kissed her, pulling a heady growl from him. If it weren't for her nails digging into his lower back and the way she urged him to move when she was ready, he would've risked her axe to his throat to make sure she was still all right.

Finally, after what felt like hours, Tik-Tok was fully coupled with North. The rumble that escaped him came from somewhere deep inside. Their breaths mingled, heavy, as the kiss continued. This was usually when he thrust hard and fast, fucking a female into oblivion, but, instead, he shifted slightly. Another time he would show her hard and fast—but not now.

"Tik-Tok," North mumbled against his lips. "I want to feel all of you."

He swallowed hard. "Are you—"

North bit his lower lip hard enough to silence him. "Stop asking that and *move*."

He chuckled, pressing another lingering kiss to her lips, before setting his forehead on the pillow. His gold hand cupped North's breast, eliciting a pleased gasp from her. Rolling his hips as gently as he could, he pulled back until the tip of his cock was the only thing left inside her. And glided back in. Laboriously, exquisitely unhurried.

North wrapped her legs around him. "Again. Faster."

Who was he to deny her? He began a steady rhythm, faster, but still tender. The tingle returned to his balls as they tightened, nearing release. But she still hadn't come again. He slid a hand between their sweat-slick bodies and rubbed tiny, quick circles over her clit.

"*Oh.*" Her back arched, her breath quickening.

Tik-Tok smiled against her neck. The way she responded to him, the sounds she made, it was a perfect symphony. All leading to a remarkable finish. His thrusts became irregular with more power behind each one, but North didn't seem to mind. In fact, her walls fluttered. She gripped the sheets tightly, her chest pressed hard against his, and her hips shifted upward to meet each thrust.

"Come for me," he urged. *Begged.*

A satisfied scream tore from her as she clenched around his cock, nails biting into his skin.

"Oh fuck!" he roared as his own pleasure barreled through him. His cock jerked with each powerful release. "Fuck," he repeated on a harsh exhale.

He'd never come that hard in his life.

CHAPTER EIGHTEEN

NORTH

North's chest heaved as she stared into Tik-Tok's scarlet irises, no longer the color of blood, but beautiful as the deepest red rose. Her thoughts were scattered while she continued to stare up at him. She'd known the act of tumbling another must be at least somewhat decent—otherwise, why would so many fae do it? But, *gods*, she couldn't string words together to describe it, or all the emotions flowing through her.

Tik-Tok furrowed his brow as he studied her. "Are you—"

"My axe is still in here if you finish that sentence. I'm wonderful." She chuckled, cradling his warm cheek. "Are *you* okay?"

"I'm … I don't know what I am, my star. But I *do* know I want to keep you in my bed forever." He settled beside her, his breaths heavy.

With a smile, she grabbed his wrist and rolled to her side, then draped his arm around her.

"What are we doing now?" he purred in her ear, his chest and body aligning perfectly with her backside. "I'm happy to give you seconds, but I'll need a moment."

"Cuddling." She glanced over at him and arched a brow. "Do you not do this?"

"No."

So he would only tumble females, then leave. Something about being an exception to this made her heart swell.

"Well, you do now," North said with a smile.

"Whatever you want." He pressed his lips to her jaw.

"Even the portal? What if opening it is what I want?" She had to ask—she was going to convince him to go. After everything he had faced, he deserved to avenge his family.

"We're not going yet." His tone was an end-all to the question, but it wasn't to her.

"Tik-Tok," she started. "Will you at least get the crew to take us there and help me practice my magic in the morning? That's all I'm asking, for now—to go to the location and check it out. If you don't agree, I won't stop asking you." But once they were there, she was going to open that portal, regardless if he said no. If others in another world were at risk, then why procrastinate?

Even though she wanted to open the portal, that didn't mean she wasn't nervous. It wasn't only the possibility of death that had her on edge, but the unknown waiting on the other side of the portal and potentially getting lost there, never finding her way back. It wasn't even a living enemy she was facing, like her family had in their past adventures. It was a hole in the sea—just a tear in the fabric of reality. Would it be easier, or far worse? Yet, she'd chosen, and there was no turning back. It was the right decision, even if he didn't realize it yet.

Tik-Tok sighed. "I suppose I can do that." He eyed her suspiciously. "Just practice. We should arrive by midday tomorrow if I tell Respen to hoist the sails soon."

She smiled and turned to face the wall. Tik-Tok had at least given in on something. "Shouldn't you go tell him, then?"

"Later." His teeth grazed her neck, then nipped at her ear. "I like where I'm at right now."

Behind her, North felt him harden. "Already?" she asked with a laugh.

"If you want my cock inside you again, then you need to say it," he cooed, his voice demanding.

She did want it … very much. "I want your cock inside me."

"I like how you say *cock*." Tik-Tok kissed her right below the jaw again. "It rolls off your tongue quite nicely."

She turned to face him, capturing his mouth with hers. His lips moved in a sensual manner, his tongue slowly flicking. He cupped her breast as he buried himself inside her in one stroke, filling her once more.

"Try again," Tik-Tok instructed. "Focus."

North tightened her grip on his metal hand as she looked out at the sea. She'd been outdoors with him for only a little while, but her magic didn't seem to want to come out and play again.

Closing her eyes, she thought about her night before with Tik-Tok, the rush of elated emotions she'd felt. North relaxed for a moment before opening her lids. The violet magic within her swirled, and she reached inside herself to grasp it. Her hand passed through it. Taking a deep, steadying breath, she tried again and latched onto the magic tightly, holding firm.

She studied a small wave, and stretched out to it with a stream of purple. Her body quivered with exertion as she tried to stabilize it. At last, the wave stopped mid-motion, frozen. Her heart kicked up at the sight and she grinned.

"Good," Tik-Tok said. "Now split it in half."

"Easy for you to say," North muttered.

Brushing against the magic holding the wave, she concentrated and watched as her power divided into two tendrils with fingers peaking from their ends. Before she could pull the wave apart, it flattened back into the sea with a crash.

North growled in frustration.

"Keep your shoulders loosened. Try to relax your body," Tik-Tok said, releasing her hand. "Perhaps I can help with that." He walked behind her and swiped her hair over her other shoulder.

His lips came to her neck, and he kissed up her jaw, his hands trailing down her waist to her thighs.

Her stomach tightened for a reason other than the magic. "That *isn't* helping."

He chuckled in her ear. "Try now. Then after, spin the water."

She peered out at the waves as his arms folded around her and he set his chin on her shoulder. With a deep breath, she pushed out two violet tendrils and watched them drift forward, halting a wave. Jaw clenched, she dug the magic's fingers in and ripped it in half. Her heart practically skipped a beat as she pushed the two tendrils back together. Dipping the magic below the sea's surface, she worked the liquid, spinning it around and around. She was doing it!

Tik-Tok whirled her to look at him with a smile on his face, her magic snapping back inside herself. "Perfect, North." His lips came to hers in a single, blissful kiss.

She itched to try more, so she took her gaze to the sea once again and started to churn the water. Then she clenched a wave, yanked on it, making it increase in size. She could feel the entire ocean tuning into her magic's call. It wasn't only a small area of water she could control, but the entire sea if she wished.

North wasn't sure how much time had passed as she practiced again and again. Her mouth was parched when she finally decided to stop, her body aching. Kaliko had brought them water earlier, and she walked with Tik-Tok to the pole where their drinks had been left. Lifting her glass, she chugged the water down as Dax approached.

"Captain, Respen and I need to discuss some things with you," Dax said, raking a hand through his rumpled blond hair.

Tik-Tok gave him a brief nod and turned to North. "I'll meet with you later."

North set down her empty glass and went to scoop up her axe to go and take a bath, when Echo came up beside her.

"Someone reeks of sex," the siren drawled as she drew her sword from its sheath.

North peered down at her feet and blushed before making eye contact.

"Don't look so embarrassed. I have to bathe soon myself, but first this." Echo swung her sword forward and North lifted her axe, blocking it. "Excellent."

The sparring with Echo was another way for her to distract herself from what was to come, so she decided to linger on deck a little longer.

She and Echo exchanged blows with their weapons for another hour before they were both drenched with sweat and decided to go down and bathe. Dax had heated the water so it was extra warm, as though he knew her muscles ached. And it wasn't just the ones sore from the training, but from Tik-Tok pressing inside of her. The second time he'd had his way with her, their tumbling had lasted even longer, as if he'd wanted it to go on for an eternity. She hadn't wanted it to end either.

After bathing and throwing on a silky deep blue dress, North went to the deck and sat alone for a while, eating jerky and a dried plum.

A shadow fell over her, and she glanced up to find Tik-Tok peering down at her with a smirk. "Avoiding me?"

"No. I was thinking." She shrugged, rolling the plum in her hand. But she had been—she hadn't wanted him to realize how antsy she'd become about the portal. Her lack of eye contact and twitchy fingers were bound to give her away.

Tik-Tok lowered himself beside her and plucked the fruit from her palm, then sank his teeth into it.

"Hey, that's mine." North took it back from him.

"We share." His grin grew wider while he chewed.

Rolling her eyes, she tossed it to him. Her stomach was starting to feel queasy, knowing they were approaching the portal's location.

Tik-Tok continued to munch on the plum. One of his legs was straightened, the other bent, with his arm lazily dangling off it, and his head leaned back against the wall of the ship. He appeared composed, as if it were just another day sailing across the sea.

"We're not far from the portal," Tik-Tok finally said. "I'm considering turning the ship around before you do anything we'll both regret." His relaxed composure started to unravel as he eyed her. He knew her plan…

"Why haven't you turned it already, then?" North replied, holding his stare.

"I should." He pursed his lips. "I should take you home right now."

"But you won't."

"Not unless you say so."

"I won't. I'm doing it. Once I figure out how to open the portal, I'll keep it open once we pass through—for however long I have to." She clasped his hand and inched closer to him. "Are you worried about facing your father?"

"No. Not in the slightest." He furrowed his brow, his grip on her hand tightening. "I'm more worried about you disappearing into the fucking portal."

She was too, but she was still going to face it. "There's no changing fate, and I'll try my hardest to make everything go smoothly. Besides, you'll make sure this other world doesn't end up the way Oz was before I was born." If opening the portal didn't go their way, it would be one life sacrificed to save everything that lay in the world beyond. But if she wasn't close enough to keep the portal open, it would mean Tik-Tok and the rest of the crew could be trapped.

"Celyna saw different outcomes, but I'm only willing to accept one." It took a moment for him to speak again, as though he was having an internal struggle with himself. In one swift motion, he scooped her off the floor and settled her in his lap so they were face to face as she straddled him. Her eyes widened and she glanced behind her to see if anyone was watching.

His fingers caught her chin and turned her face toward him, their gazes trained on one another. "It doesn't matter who watches," he said. "This moment is between us." Tik-Tok's mouth claimed hers, his lips moving in a soft caress. He pulled back from the kiss and hugged her to his chest, his calming scent enveloping her. "Fight like hell, my star. Fight to stay with me when we get there. That's all I want. All you have to do."

Tears pricked at her eyes as she folded her arms around him, gripping him so tight that she thought she might be hurting him. She loosened her hold on him a smidge while resting her head on his shoulder. There were so many words she could say, but this said it all, was more than enough.

A throat cleared behind them. When neither moved, it sounded again.

"Not now, Respen," Tik-Tok muttered.

"We're here, Captain," Echo said.

They had arrived. Echo and Respen stood beside each other while a few crew members were scattered across the ship. North released Tik-Tok and pushed up out of his lap. He peeled himself from the wall and rose beside her.

"North's going to open the portal." Tik-Tok peered out at the sea, and from his face she couldn't tell he was worried in the slightest, although she knew he was.

A brownie wearing a green smock freed the anchor into the sea with a loud splash.

Respen stepped up to North and placed his hands on her shoulders. "Whatever happens, you're one of the crew. Echo and I will be by your side the entire time."

Tears streamed down her cheeks and she swiped them away. "Let's begin."

"There's no rush," Tik-Tok said, his lips pursed.

"No use in waiting either." North moved out from Respen's grip and turned toward the water. She placed her palms against the handrail.

Tik-Tok came up behind North, his body caging her in as he set his hands beside hers. Perhaps he thought it would prevent North from being torn away. And maybe it would.

"Keep your eyes open the entire time," Echo told North, coming up on her right while Respen took the left. "There might be another way back if you're looking for it, if you do get lost.

Don't give me that look, Captain. I'm only saying this in case something *does* happen. So she'll be prepared."

"I'll keep them open," North whispered, clenching the rail. "I'm ready."

"If you need to stop," Tik-Tok said, "then you stop. Don't force yourself to keep going. Listen to what your body needs and don't overexert yourself."

She nodded and looked at each of their faces—faces that had become familiar. These were her friends, and she wanted to do it for all of them.

Exhaling, North settled her gaze on the silver waves, their gradual movements. Her violet magic stirred, as if it could feel the portal already. With invisible fingers, she pushed down inside herself to the swirling pool of purple and snatched it. The power unfurled from her body like a tree blooming with new flowers. As it spun from her and stretched out to the sea, her body shook slightly. Tik-Tok inched closer to her, his chest brushing against her back, keeping her grounded.

The violet tendrils touched down on the surface of the water, and the waves' light movements kicked up, becoming stronger, forceful, thrashing. The sky above them darkened, thunder booming. Was her magic doing that too?

She kept her eyes trained on the water, squinting at the waves. The magic formed into its smoky hands, their fingers digging into the liquid, then peeled it slowly back. A jagged line opened so deep that there was no seeing an end. Her magic vibrated, erratic. The waves crashed together, the ocean's surface whole like before. Her heart pounded harder and beads of sweat dripped down her face. She didn't know if she could truly do this. But she remembered her earlier training with Tik-Tok—she hadn't gotten it the first time then, either.

North shook her head, finding focus once more as she plucked out the magic from within herself. She kept her eyes wide open this time too, and the waves rose as she pushed her magic out in their direction, their swells growing taller. The ship jostled.

Her body shook harder when her magic dug into the water again. It was as if she might be torn in two.

Tik-Tok's arm left the rail and wrapped around her waist, holding her in place, grounding her. It gave her a new drive as she concentrated, pushing her power forward. A dip in the silver water formed and liquid around that center started spinning in a circular motion. The slow movements churned, growing faster and faster until the sight before her blurred.

North felt herself being pulled away from Tik-Tok and toward that silver shimmer. Her feet rose of their own accord so she was on her toes, her hair lifting around her head, the waves sounding like the world was cracking in half. Tik-Tok's grip tightened as her heart accelerated, pounding against her rib cage.

She didn't know which path was currently being chosen for her, but she kept going anyway, holding onto the magic so tightly that she knew, if her invisible hands could bleed, they would.

With an ear-piercing scream that burned her throat and rattled her chest, she thrust out all the magic she could at the churning center, only this time, more controlled. A heavy, all-consuming force slammed her backward across the ship, colliding with the floor on top of Tik-Tok.

"North!" Tik-Tok lifted her in his lap.

"Are you all right?" Echo asked, crouching beside them.

Everything spun and her body was limp. The magic had reeled itself back inside her, and she was too exhausted to even speak, let alone try to open the portal again.

"She did it," Respen breathed, rushing to them with his eyebrows up his forehead.

North must have had energy left after all because she leapt away from Tik-Tok and darted for the handrail. Below, the spinning circle was no longer silver, but glowing bright violet.

"I *did* do it." She smiled, her voice coming out faint. North's body drooped to the side and Tik-Tok caught her.

CHAPTER NINETEEN

TIK-TOK

The moment North collapsed in Tik-Tok's arms, a loud *boom* echoed in his ears. Not from the newly opened portal, but from behind them. He knelt and curled his body over North's as the ship jerked sideways. The explosion blocked out the sound of choppy water slapping the ship's hull, and a rain barrel crashed against the railing, splintering apart.

"Incoming!" Respen yelled from somewhere close by. "Get down!"

Oh, shit. Tik-Tok clutched North harder against him, holding so tight she would likely have bruises. But no fucking way was she going to be knocked overboard and dragged helplessly into the spinning vortex—to be lost through the portal like Celyna warned. *No fucking way.* He stormed toward his quarters despite the violent rocking of *The Temptress* and threw open the door. Stumbling around the now-crooked desk, he hurried to lay North on the bed. If there was another attack, she probably wouldn't stay there, but he'd rather she fell to the hard floor than into the sea. Swiping his sword from where it had landed near his desk, Tik-Tok rushed to join his crew. He hated leaving North alone, but he couldn't hide inside while his crew fought for their lives.

"Who the fuck is attacking us?" he asked, joining Echo at the main mast as the brownies scurried below deck.

Another ship, wholly undetected before the first explosion, with huge white sails, plowed through the water, straight for them. White light flashed, and another boom sounded. Tik-Tok grabbed onto one of the ropes to keep from falling as the bright magic hit the side of the ship.

"Not sure, Captain," Echo said after the violent swaying of the ship had ceased.

"Dax!"

"Up here, Captain," he called from the crow's nest above.

Tik-Tok squinted at the enemy ship. "Send wind to keep them from getting closer." He scanned his crew. "Echo," he ordered in an even tone, turning toward her, "steer the ship away from the portal before we're accidentally knocked through it." She bolted toward the wheel to do as instructed, and Respen replaced her at Tik-Tok's side in a flicker of magic. Before he could speak, Tik-Tok commanded, "go see who we're dealing with."

Respen was gone and back in less than a minute, eyes wide with worry over whatever he saw on the enemy ship. "It's Salt. He's got three elementals with him—two water and one wind."

Motherfucker. How were they supposed to withstand that kind of power? Dax blowing them in the other direction was like a bird trying to fly against a hurricane. If Rizmaela hadn't stabbed North, this wouldn't be happening now. Tik-Tok would've gotten his cloaking device in Merryland, and his old captain would never have known that *The Temptress* sailed through his territory. *Gods damned dwarf.*

"What are we doing?" Respen asked.

What are we doing? They were absolutely fucked. What *could* they do? For all Tik-Tok's arrogance, he was still a single—albeit powerful—male. He could turn Salt and his crew to stone, but they had to be close enough first. From this distance, there was no stopping the powerful blasts of magic.

"Parlay," Tik-Tok said with a grimace. After he killed his father, after North was safely home, he and Salt could fight to the death. But now, too much was left undone and unsaid. Not to mention the portal swirling far too close to the ship for his liking. They needed a parlay—a meeting where both parties negotiated under the understanding that neither were harmed. "Tell him we need to parlay. Bring him here."

Respen vanished again, traveling to Salt's ship to follow his captain's orders.

"Dax," Tik-Tok called. One elemental against another was fair, but not one against three. Dax may need to use his wind to get them out of there if the parlay went poorly. "Save your strength."

Gnawing on his bottom lip, Tik-Tok watched Salt's ship inch closer and closer. The blasts of magic had temporarily ceased, but a hum remained in his ears. Each second that ticked by only served to speed his pulse a little more. Respen wasn't there to chat—only grab Salt and return. Anything more would put him in danger.

Respen reappeared, and, beside him, the male who'd saved Tik-Tok from the King of Ev. It was strange seeing him again after so long. Oddly nostalgic. Bitter. The fae reminded Tik-Tok of too many things: his whippings, his betrayal, and his father. Or, what his father *could've* been if he wasn't a deranged murderer.

Captain Salt swung a fist toward Respen's face, but the blue-haired fae dodged the blow, shoving away. Salt's short white hair showcased a handful of jagged scars along his scalp and the tip of one of his ears was missing. His gray eyes held none of the affection they'd once had for Tik-Tok. Instead, they swirled with the force of a thousand storms.

"Long time, no see," Tik-Tok drawled. "Bit of a dramatic reunion though, don't you think?"

"I didn't agree to parlay," he snarled.

Tik-Tok shrugged. Respen had undoubtedly made sure Salt's crew knew that was the reason he took their captain. They wouldn't attack when Salt was on board *The Temptress*, regardless, because it would put him at risk. "You don't have to agree."

"Ungrateful bastard!" Salt stormed forward, hands balled

tight. He was nearly as tall as Tik-Tok but broader with a patchy beard. "Out of pity, I snuck you out of the palace in Ev, raised you like my own son, made you my first-mate, and how did you repay me? *Mutiny.*"

All of it was true. He'd even felt guilty for a while about betraying Salt and stealing his ship to seek revenge. Then the captain had begun hunting Tik-Tok across the Nonestic Ocean. Completely understandable, of course. If anyone understood the need for vengeance, it was Tik-Tok, but he couldn't feel bad for someone who wanted him dead—the circumstances were irrelevant. If he had wanted Salt dead, he would've killed him during the mutiny, but that was never the goal.

Until now.

"Parlay," Tik-Tok reminded him as Salt lifted his fist.

"Fuck you and your parlay." Salt bared his teeth, swinging his fist down across Tik-Tok's face. Knuckles cracked against his cheekbone.

Tik-Tok spat blood onto the deck, his cheek stinging like a motherfucker, and slowly turned his gaze to his old captain. *A punch to the face?* He felt slightly offended that Salt hadn't done something more damaging. Pack a bit of magic into the fist, at least. "Feel better?" he sneered.

Salt lunged at Tik-Tok but a strong wind blasted him sideways. He landed flat on his back beside the rail.

From above, Dax called, "Parlay, ya old coot."

Tik-Tok snorted in amusement and stalked toward the prone male. He crouched beside him and lifted a brow. "I have one deal to offer. Take it or leave it."

"Leave it," Salt growled, sitting up.

"You haven't even heard the terms." His smile was cold as ice. "There's an open sea portal on the other side of *my* ship. We're going through it and you're not going to stop us. In exchange, when we return, I'll agree to fight you to the death. Get this whole sordid thing over with once and for all."

"A portal?" Salt barked, the sound ending on a disbelieving laugh. Then, when he met Tik-Tok's steady gaze, he sobered.

"You don't have an elemental on board causing the whirlpool?"

He gave a small, mirthless chuckle. "I betrayed you, Salt, but did I ever lie to you?"

Salt spat in his face. "No deal."

Tik-Tok stood, forcing his rage down, and wiped the saliva from his cheek. He hadn't come so far—betrayed Salt at Celyna's bidding to gain a ship and a reputation—to fail now. Calling on his magic, Tik-Tok pursed his lips and pushed the rough-edged power outward. Gray immediately crept over Salt's sun-darkened skin, locking bones in place, solidifying organs. He gasped, the sound a mix of shock and fear, and the stone froze his old captain's expression in place. Eyes narrowed, nose wrinkled in disgust, revealing anger that Salt's voice hadn't.

Ah, hell. Salt couldn't attack him now, but if Respen returned him as a statue, the crew would blow *The Temptress* into a million slivers. If they dropped him overboard, he would eventually return to flesh and bone when Tik-Tok was far enough away for the magic to fade … and then he would drown before ever seeing the sun again. There was bad blood between the two fae, but not even Salt deserved that torment. The entire feud was Tik-Tok's fault, so the least he could do was give the male a clean death.

"Take him back," he told Respen, flicking a hand at the stone fae.

Respen didn't hesitate to obey, but there was a distinct line of confusion between his brows. His confusion was fine. It was his silent trust in Tik-Tok that sent a twinge of gratitude through his chest. Moving behind Salt, Respen grabbed his stone shoulders and used his magic to whirl them both away.

The moment they disappeared, Tik-Tok looked to Dax. At some point, while the two captains spoke, he had climbed down from the crow's nest. Tik-Tok's shoulders slumped slightly. "They'll sink us for this," he said matter-of-factly.

"Then why take him back?"

Tik-Tok groaned, unsure if it had been the right thing to do. "Because if he doesn't return, or if we start sailing away with him still on board, his crew will catch up. They won't dare follow us through the portal—Salt's too superstitious about them. Let's hope seeing him that way startles the crew enough to make them turn around completely." The wind stirred and Respen reappeared, alone. *Shit.* That was fast—not that his first-mate would've stuck around for the fallout after dropping a stone Salt at their feet. "Sail into the portal. *Now.*"

Everyone on deck fell deathly silent. Dax, staring at Tik-Tok as if he'd misheard, Respen opening and shutting his mouth, and Echo and Cyrx frozen in shock where they stood at the helm. Another blast of white light lit the air, then a *boom* sounded, and a brutal crash of magic hit the side of Tik-Tok's ship. The waves lifted the vessel on sudden swells, shaking it like a youngling's rattle. Wood creaked beneath the sea's force and Dax was flung into Respen, taking them both to the ground.

"The portal!" Tik-Tok shouted. "Go!"

Echo spun the wheel so fast that when Dax blew wind into the sails, the ship jerked to the side. Tik-Tok gripped a rope circling the mast, keeping himself steady, at the same time a small shriek came from his quarters.

Fuck. North was awake. If she came out now, there was every chance she would fall into the portal—alone and without a ship to keep her from drowning. Celyna hadn't been specific enough about how North would be lost. The simple act of opening it could've pulled her in when the magic had lifted her from the ground, or was it something afterward that sent her tumbling through?

The knob turned slowly. Tik-Tok lurched forward, struggling to remain upright and shoved the door inward.

North stumbled back into the cabin wall, pale and wide-eyed. "What's going on out there?"

"We're going through the portal," he said, slamming the door behind him. "Salt found us … if we don't go, he'll sink *The Temptress* and everyone on it."

"I can control the water if you need my help against him," she said, holding onto the heavy furniture as it began to slide across the room.

"I don't care if you can break the ocean in half." He felt around the door in search of the handle. "Stay here, no matter what you hear."

North's head whipped toward him. "I can help."

"If you leave this room, North, I swear—" He found the handle, opened the door and slipped sideways through it, pausing before the last step. "I'm sorry, but I told you there's only one outcome I'm willing to accept."

He shut the door with a thunk and held on another moment as the ship rocked, tilting precariously on its side. His boots slipped out from under him, sending him skidding across the deck. Echo caught his metal arm through the spokes of the wheel before he could careen into the water.

"Brace yourselves!" Cyrx bellowed.

As if it would make a difference. Tik-Tok gripped the wheel, nodding his thanks to Echo, and held on tight as the ship entered the edge of the spiraling water.

The water grabbed onto the hull, whipping the ship into its rapid revolution. Spinning, spinning, spinning, drawing them closer to the center at an alarming rate. Sea water sprayed the deck, soaking them all. Wood creaked and groaned. The portal hummed louder and louder until it roared. The sound of perfect chaos.

And there was no escaping it.

CHAPTER TWENTY

NORTH

North stood inside Tik-Tok's room, gripping the edge of his desk as the boat jostled side to side from the choppy waters. She wanted to go outside and slap him across the face for telling her to stay here. Though she understood why he had. If North chose to, she could easily walk out of the room, but she wouldn't risk something happening to her—for his sake. There'd been fear in his eyes, an emotion that had reflected her own. If the portal separated her from the crew, how would Tik-Tok get the ship back, if she wasn't there to control it? She'd made a promise to remain, and she wouldn't break it until they sailed through the gateway and returned safe.

The boat jerked forward, and she felt it skim the waves as it rocked harder. North didn't huddle in fear. Instead, she held Tik-Tok's desk harder and kept her eyes wide open, preparing herself for the unknown.

Tik-Tok had mentioned Salt when he'd rushed into his quarters to check on her after she'd woken. Salt must have found them while she'd been unconscious from overusing her magic. Yet the portal had stayed open, still connected to her. If she hadn't been so useless, she could have been out there on deck, helping to protect the crew from Tik-Tok's enemy. It was a male he'd betrayed, but she was on Tik-Tok's side regardless.

North's magic pulsed inside her veins, her heart thrumming in sync with it. Her power expanded inside her, and she felt the portal, alive and looming, growing nearer, even though she couldn't see the Nonestic Ocean as they crossed the barrier. Every fiber, every nerve, twitched while the ship sailed through the maelstrom, rattling, vibrating, as if the wood might crack in half.

North's hair rose again around her head, her feet lifting up to her toes, the sound of waves thrashing pounding in her ears. She couldn't tell if the cacophony was from outside the ship or inside her own head. Glass shattered, furniture scraped the floor, and her entire body vibrated.

As if the ocean itself had frozen within her, the movements ceased, her silver hair pooled back around her shoulders. She released her death-grip on the desk. Everything was still and quiet.

They'd gone through the gateway, and she was still here, in one piece. The portal stayed open, churning in a steady circular motion. She could feel her tenuous connection to the magic that kept it in existence. If she wanted it to close, all she needed to do was shut off the violet magic. But she left it on, and she would let that light continue to shine bright until they were ready to go home.

North sucked in a sharp breath as she peered around—fragments of broken glass were sprawled across the floor near the cabinets, Tik-Tok's bed was now near the middle of his room, and papers from his desk had scattered everywhere. She rushed to the door and flung it open at the same time Tik-Tok seemed to be reaching for the handle from the outside.

His wild gaze locked on hers. "You're safe."

"I think so." Her eyes widened when she took in the dark gray sky filled with black clouds. A putrid smell hit her senses, like rotting meat. She cupped her nose and mouth with her hand. "What is this place?"

"My father's home." He motioned at the air. "It fits him

rather well."

North brushed past Tik-Tok on the slick, debris-free deck, and made her way to the handrail.

Her lips parted as she peered down at the water. The sea was so blue it was almost black. The liquid rippled—small bubbles popped at the surface, oozing a deep brown. North was certain the foul odor was from the sea itself, which appeared to be a thicker consistency than water.

As she looked out farther, the dingy green shore stretched across the horizon. A dark forest filled the land, and black smoke curled up from the tops of the tall trees. She squinted to see if she could see anything between the slits of the trunks, but the ship was too far from shore.

Tik-Tok's boots sounded behind her. He pressed up beside her, letting one arm dangle over the rail as he clutched his compass in the other. Holding it out, he watched as the arrow spun and spun, never slowing, until it did, right at the shore before spinning once more. "Now that we're here, I don't want to waste any time finding my father. It's dangerous to stay too long."

"I wish I could go with you." She stared out at the portal, still swirling a few yards away, its purple light shimmering. Within the dark water, it appeared like a beacon, waiting for fae to be drawn in. The sea witch had told Tik-Tok that if the portal didn't remain open, they would never return to Oz, and that thought made North's heart beat harder—she didn't want to let Tik-Tok and the crew—*her* crew—down. She took a deep swallow, steeling herself.

"No, you don't." Tik-Tok clenched his jaw. "My father ruined my life. I know I've made vile choices in my past to seek revenge, but I can't apologize for it."

"Even for taking me from the Emerald City?" North arched a brow.

"Especially that." He smirked.

North's cheeks heated. But a part of her felt awful for it because the fae of Oz had all been worried, searching for her. At least Crow would have told them to halt the search after he'd spoken to her. Perhaps sometimes it was all right to be selfish, though.

"What about Salt? Are you worried about him?"

"Don't worry about him." Tik-Tok sighed. "As soon as we go back through the portal, he'll be there, waiting. I may need you to use the ocean against him, so we can make a clean break."

"I can do that." North smiled at the thought of being useful instead of sitting back and doing nothing. As she realized what Tik-Tok would be doing next, a scowl formed on her face. "You're not going alone, are you?"

"I am." He nodded toward the ropes holding the rowboat.

A squelching sound came from somewhere within the sea's depths, and she suppressed a shudder at what might be lurking below the surface. He couldn't take the small boat without knowing what lay hidden in the murky waters. It could be nothing, but it could also be *something*.

"You're not rowing," North said, her voice serious, leaving no room for argument. "Take Respen. He can whirl you to the shore and then to your father. It's faster than walking the entire world to find him."

Tik-Tok chuckled. "I didn't know you were captain of this ship."

"I know you don't want to risk anyone," North started. "But if you need an escape, Respen can easily bring you back here, then we can sail through the portal. Please."

He clucked his tongue. "Fine. I'll take Respen, but no one else."

North nodded. Her heart pounded through her rib cage at the thought of him leaving. It truly hit her then, what Tik-Tok's father had done to his family. Years had passed since he'd seen the male, and no matter the powers that Tik-Tok held, his father's could be greater. Tik-Tok could die… But North would never tell him to stay, not after they'd gotten this far. He would face his own enemy, the way North's own family had.

"Before I find Respen, come with me. We have ten minutes

to spare." He grabbed her hand and pulled her toward his room, his pace quickening. She frowned as she kept up with his long strides. What was so important that he couldn't tell her right then?

He opened the door and kicked it shut behind them.

"Tik-Tok, what—"

Spinning around to face her, he slammed his mouth to hers, silencing her with a kiss. Tik-Tok backed her up against the wall, and she let out a small squeak before kissing him in return. He hoisted her up and wrapped her legs around his waist as his mouth coasted over her lips, tasting, taking. She could feel his hard length pressing against her core.

"I know this is wildly inappropriate given the circumstances, but there are so many things I want to say before I leave. There isn't time though. There's only this, my North Star." His voice came out raspy, thick, as he rubbed himself against her. A whimper escaped her lips as sensations pulsed through her from each grind of his hips.

When he'd called her his North Star, a different kind of warmth spread through her. She couldn't find the right words to give him in return, so she caught his bottom lip between her teeth and sucked on it, then lifted her dress to give him access.

She rested her forehead against his as he unlaced his pants and freed himself. Tik-Tok lowered her a fraction so she could feel him against her once more. With those wicked fingers of his, he pushed her undergarments to the side, not even taking the time to remove them. He then slid inside her with one perfect stroke, making them both groan in pleasure while he filled her. Her hands tightened in his hair as she took in a deep breath.

"You feel so fucking good," Tik-Tok purred, thrusting his hips forward, her back striking the wall.

He increased his pace, rattling her entire body with rapture. She was pretty certain they were shaking the entire boat, but she couldn't be embarrassed about this, this wildness, this animalistic side of him, of her, of them together. She'd loved when he'd taken her sweetly, loved it even more in this moment when he was pounding into her with ferocity. That pleasureful feeling was inching closer and closer and *closer*, each of his movements fueling her into oblivion. Everything within her shattered when he brought her over the edge, her head falling backward as she whispered his name. The orgasm had been so overpowering that she didn't even have the strength to shout it.

Both their chests heaved as she brought her head back down, their gazes connected.

"I need to go," he murmured.

"Don't make his death an easy one." She kissed his lips, hoping this wasn't their last goodbye. "He doesn't deserve it."

Tik-Tok lowered her to the floor and she straightened her dress as he tucked himself back inside his pants. He opened the door and led her out to the deck, neither saying a word to each other about what had happened between them. But from his deep breaths, she knew he was still reeling from the aftereffects, same as she was.

They made their way back to the crew, who were all huddled in a discussion.

"Respen," Tik-Tok said, "I'd like you to come with me. Can you bring us to shore so we don't have to worry about a boat?"

"Yes, Captain." Respen nodded. It was only briefly, but North could see the flicker of worry in Echo's eyes. Perhaps North shouldn't have suggested he take Respen, but anyone else wouldn't be as safe or as fast. This way, they could easily get away from lurking danger.

Tik-Tok instructed Dax and Cyrx to sail the ship and leave this world without them if they had to. North wouldn't let them leave without Tik-Tok or Respen if it came down to that, and she didn't think Echo would either.

Tik-Tok turned to North, his expression unreadable. "No goodbyes." He tucked a tendril of hair behind her ear, then walked away from her, toward Respen. The first mate placed his hands on Tik-Tok's shoulders. A cool wind kicked up and a yellow light gleamed, then they were both gone.

Echo jogged to the end of the ship and North followed,

meeting her at the handrail. On the shore, in the distance, stood two figures she could barely make out.

"No goodbyes," North said softly as she watched them disappear inside the forest, the black smoke continuing to rise into the sky.

"Are you all right?" North asked when she noticed Echo was still watching the empty shore.

Echo pursed her lips, her arms folded over her stomach. "With this life, you have to be. But that doesn't mean your heart still won't ache at times."

North's chest tightened. What if they didn't come back? How long would she and the crew have to wait here? North knew Echo would try going after them if it took too long, and she would too. But if North left the ship, she would risk the portal closing. For now, she had to drown the worry and focus on her own task.

"I'm going to grab you some water and fruit. You need to keep your strength up." Echo pushed off from the handrail and headed toward the door.

North didn't think she would be able to eat anything without throwing it back up. She was too full of knots. A swishing sound came from the direction of the portal and North jerked her head up. The magic within her shifted as if something heavy were moving through her.

Not her…

The *portal.*

She gasped and her heart thundered when a massive ship with large white sails rose out from the flashing portal. The ship was completely dry as the portal churned it in a backward motion. The gateway slowed, then the ship stilled, pushing off from the entrance, and headed toward them.

CHAPTER TWENTY-ONE

TIK-TOK

From the innermost city of Oz to the furthest corner of the Nonestic Ocean, the darkest thing Tik-Tok had encountered was that of a beating heart. Not all hearts, of course, but that didn't change the truth. Nothing was blacker than the evil residing inside a fae. And this place … it was a black heart given freedom from its chest.

Alive. Corrupt. The air carrying an ominous vibration.

It sent a shiver down Tik-Tok's spine as he and Respen walked farther into the strange land. The anticipation was almost too much for him to handle—being there, where his father was, after all these years of searching, made him want to crawl from his skin. Celyna's visions led him here and, back on the ship, his compass had pointed in this direction—he knew his father was alive. The phantom pain of broken ribs and dislocated shoulders assaulted him. His stomach twisted as if anticipating a *special* tart baked by his mother and force-fed by his father. The poison she'd used wasn't strong enough to kill them, but enough to make him and his siblings violently ill for days. Swallowing hard, he focused on how sweet his revenge would be.

The world looked like Oz when a raging storm approached, darkening the skies. Towering trees with needle-like branches gave way to steam rising from soil and a village nestled into the bottom of a ravine. It had only taken a short walk to find this place. They were barely past the trees, which led Tik-Tok to believe it was a fishing village. Some sort of port town, perhaps. This close to the sea, it was the most logical conclusion.

Soft white lights glowed inside the large homes—or what he *assumed* were homes. Sloping roofs topped the two-story dwellings, and fences, far too short to do more than decorate the grass, surrounded them. The structures were arranged in squares of four with gravel paths running between each. Beneath their feet, the dirt path turned to ground-up rock.

"Do you think the creatures living here are friendly?" Respen asked.

Tik-Tok shrugged and flipped open the magic compass in his palm. "I think I don't give a fuck."

The needle of the compass whizzed in clockwise circles before slowing, pointing directly ahead, only to whip back around to point behind them. Toward *The Temptress*. Where North waited. He hated leaving her—leaving all of them—when everything about this world was a mystery. There was no telling what may happen while they were tracking down his father.

Tik-Tok shook the nagging thoughts away and focused on his father again, urging the compass to direct him toward *that* desire instead. It moved, almost reluctantly, back toward the homes.

Respen removed a long, narrow blade from inside his boot. "Just in case," he said, surveying the quiet village streets.

With a grunt of agreement, Tik-Tok pulled his sword out, but held it in a relaxed position, its tip pointed at the ground. There was no sense in provoking the locals. If there were any *to* provoke. "Everyone seems to be inside," he mused.

A young female stepped from between two buildings as if his words had summoned the nearest resident. Her eyes landed first on Respen, then Tik-Tok. She froze, her face draining of color, even under the gray light, and a bucket of water fell from her hands with a loud *sploosh*. The following seconds melted together as they all held their breath, each waiting for the other to move. Her dark hair was drawn back, giving prominence to angled features, and overly large, orb-like eyes. If it wasn't for her rounded ears, he might've mistaken her for some sort of fae. Black fabric wrapped around her neck, twisting down her abdomen where it tied at her waist, hanging around her legs in loose, flowing panels.

Then she screamed. A high-pitched, frenzied cry.

Respen was behind her in a snap, cupping a hand over her mouth. "Shh," he urged. Her response was, naturally, to flail in an attempt to escape his grasp. "We aren't going to hurt you."

Fuck. She was making too much noise. They didn't need her family or friends coming to investigate, only to find two strangers accosting her. "Stop it," Tik-Tok demanded quietly, stepping forward. He would've turned her to stone, but she might have useful information. "I don't have time for your antics."

Tears gathered in her eyes, spilling out in inky streams. A defeated whimper left her, and Respen eased away. "P-p-please, Your Exalted Eminence," she begged between tiny hiccups. "I didn't realize you had recovered a-and you frightened me, is all."

What the fuck is she talking about? Tik-Tok frowned. "Well, that's one way to greet me. Much preferrable than *Your Mediocre Majesty.*"

"A Paltry Prince, if I've ever seen one," Respen quipped.

The woman looked between them, chest rising and falling in rapid breaths, and cried harder. *The fuck?* "You didn't hurt her, did you?" Tik-Tok whispered to his first mate.

"Of course not." Respen cocked his head, watching her curiously, and stuffed his blade back into his boot. "We mean no harm."

Her gaze dropped. "No one was aware of your visit, but if you'll give me a moment, I'll make sure everything is prepared the way you like it."

"I'm *extremely* confused," Tik-Tok admitted with a small smirk. "But since you're so eager to accommodate, I'm looking for my father." Not that he expected the first town they happened upon to be the *right* one, but perhaps she could offer a hint at the fae's whereabouts.

"Lizbet, what's taking so long?" A younger girl, no more than ten—if the beings there aged the same as fae—scampered down the street and latched onto the terrified female's hand. "You've been out here for—"

Lizbet drew the girl tight, shifting to hide her behind her skirts. "*Please*," she pleaded. "Let her go back inside. I'll do anything you ask."

The two pirates exchanged a quick, bewildered look, then Tik-Tok furrowed his brows. "I don't give a rat's ass what she does—or you for that matter." Assuming she didn't attack them, but that seemed extremely unlikely. "Unless you feel like obliging me with a bit of information."

"Go," Lizbet urged the younger girl. "Hurry. Tell Father that Glarondal is here and to ready the finest sacrifices."

Tik-Tok felt the blood drain from his face. *Glarondal.* His father. They thought *he* was his father. He bared his teeth, eyes narrowing. "I am *not* that piece of shit fae."

The female slapped a hand over her mouth. "Blasphemy!"

"Blasphemy?" Tik-Tok snarled. "Who the fuck do you think Glarondal is? A *god*?"

Shifting backward, feet dragging in the gravel, she eyed them both through a suspicious squint. Using quick movements, she covered her chest with both palms and brought them outward in a wide arc as if performing some sort of ritual. "Glarondal is *the only* god and may he strike you down for your insults."

Respen snorted. "Weren't you terrified a moment ago?"

"Come now," Tik-Tok drawled to his first-mate. "Fear and worship often go hand-in-hand."

The girl made the same motion over and over with increasing speed, mumbling words too low for them to make out. Each time she repeated the movements, Tik-Tok's chest tightened in anger. Blindingly violent wrath.

"Enough," he snapped. Whipping out his compass, he checked the face. This time the needle was steadfast, leading deeper into the village. He was in *no* mood to traipse through the entire fucking world searching for his father. For all he knew, they were on opposite sides of this universe.

"You okay?" Respen asked as Tik-Tok stormed away from the praying girl.

"Wonderful," he snarled. There was nothing quite like finding out you looked like the fucker who murdered your family. Except, perhaps, being mistaken for him. And that he was worshiped as a god.

"Let's make this quicker," Respen said, gripping Tik-Tok's shoulder. The world went fuzzy, whizzing by, until it suddenly stopped. Respen had whirled them out of the village and into a field with deep green, ankle-high grass. Large creatures stood on four legs. Light gray scales covered their gangly legs and long snouts, and black fur sprouted from their bulbous bodies. "Any closer?" he asked.

Tik-Tok glanced at the compass. It still pointed ahead, only slightly to the left. He tilted the tool to show Respen, who still had a grip on his shoulder. Again, they traveled with Respen's magic, stopping only to check the compass. Again and again. Appearing in glittering cities and bogs and outside of steam-powered factories.

Until finally, in the middle of a massive mountain range, surrounded by stony cliffs and climbing vines, the needle glowed gold. Sleet pounded down at an angle as Tik-Tok and Respen walked cautiously to the mouth of a dark cave. Water dripped somewhere inside, splashing softly against the stone ground. A wet cough accompanied it before trailing off into a wheeze. Tik-Tok slowed his steps, holding his sword at the ready.

Something was in there. His father, according to the compass, but perhaps he wasn't alone. Glarondal used to talk about this place—how it was ripe for his intentions. Others had visited long ago, returning with tales passed down through generations—tales about how it lacked magic completely. Even the mortal world where Thelia came from had traces of it, but this place had *nothing*. When Tik-Tok's brother realized he had the extremely rare power to open sea portals, his father had pounced. No one since Tik-Tok's brother had held the ability to open portals in the sea, not until North.

So, unless his father had brought any fae with him—and Tik-Tok was sure he wouldn't have risked any potential power struggle—it wasn't much of a threat. Especially with a cough like that.

"You don't have to come with me," he offered Respen.

He shrugged. "I'd rather watch him die, if it's all the same to you."

Tik-Tok grinned and took an orb from inside his jacket pocket to cast a small amount of light. It created shadows along the walls where jagged rocks reached out and up like spindly fingers. Water trickled from the ceiling, following the path worn by years of erosion, though in other places, it dripped straight down into hollowed pockets on the ground. Easing around sharp spikes, the two pirates descended farther and farther with light footsteps, and the darkness swallowed them from behind.

If it weren't for another round of hacking, Tik-Tok would've thought his compass was broken. Respen paused suddenly and nodded to the side. Tik-Tok cocked his head to listen and scowled. The sound was coming … from inside the wall.

Magic. It had to be. Tik-Tok reached out with his golden hand and brushed it across the rock. The wall gave beneath his touch, springing back like the top of Cook's warm pastries. He narrowed his eyes, scanned the wall, and sniffed the air. Traces of sweet berries, warm sunlight, and burnt wood mingled together.

"Fae magic," he concluded.

"Do you know how to get through?" Respen asked.

Tik-Tok's lips curled into a wiry smile and he lifted his sword. It was fae magic, but weak. Brittle. Otherwise, it wouldn't have given beneath his hand, and the sound of coughing would've been contained. With a quick bash of his sword's hilt, Tik-Tok smashed through the barrier. It fell silently, the illusion toppling like a stack of blocks, before disintegrating on the ground.

Inside was a large, squared-off cave full of gold furnishings. Most prominent was a throne-like chair, wide enough for two to sit in comfortably, with etched patterns across the back. An elaborate bedframe with rich brocade blankets and pillows sat in a corner, and a floating chandelier glowed brightly with attached orbs like the one Tik-Tok held. Even the wooden dining set sported shimmering leaves, and the rug was woven with golden fibers. A feast spanned the table, extravagant enough for the Queen of Oz herself.

And yet … everything was covered in dust and mildew. The food was blackened with age.

"What are you doing here?" wheezed a male, hidden somewhere in front of them.

Tik-Tok sniffed the air again, trying to scent the magic, but it *all* smelled of his father. He would never forget the bitter flavor of his magic—the way it oozed around him during every beating, the way it had nearly suffocated him during their final interaction—the day Glarondal and his wife had murdered their children.

Snarling, Tik-Tok stuffed his orb back into his pocket, keeping both hands free. "Venture a guess," he suggested.

Respen shifted uncomfortably beside him, but Tik-Tok refused to show the bastard an ounce of discomfort. If whatever shield he used was as weak as the barrier, it wouldn't last long.

"Your magic glows bright," the voice said, crackling. "Strong magic. I've seen that color before."

"Have you now?" Tik-Tok said through clenched teeth.

A body suddenly flickered into existence, slumped in the throne. The elegantly wrought chair with its fine designs held the vilest of beings. Glarondal's hair hung in thin, black clumps, patches of his head bald and bleeding. Brown spots dotted his dry, waxy skin. The rusty brown of his eyes was hidden beneath a blue film, and a large sore grew on the corner of his mouth. The body Tik-Tok had once feared beyond all things was now hunched, fingers bent at wrong angles, limbs little more than bone.

How? Fae didn't age like this. They stopped showing their years once maturity was reached, and only began again when they were in their final century or so. Even then, it was never like this. Never so … mortal.

"How did you come to my kingdom, fae? Is there another who can open the portal?" He coughed and blood spurted from his lips. A darker, dried crimson covered the white tunic he wore. "If there is, bring him to me and I will reward you handsomely."

"I will bring you no one," Tik-Tok said without an ounce of leeway. *No one,* but especially not North. He walked slowly into the room, skimming his golden hand over the backs of the dining chairs. "After all the trouble it took to get here, I'm surprised you would want another portal."

"This place will drain the magic from you," Glarondal spat. "So gradually that you won't notice until it's too late. You can't stay—take me back with you."

Tik-Tok smirked. Seeing his father this way, hearing the desperation in his voice, was the sweetest gift. Even sweeter than his mother's dying screams had been. "Oh, I have no intention of staying."

Glarondal pushed up on the arms of his chair in an attempt to stand, but fell back in his seat. "We should leave for the Fae Lands immediately."

"What will you do there?" Tik-Tok grimaced at the small white worms slithering through a bowl of fruit. "Will you rejoin your family?" He wasn't sure why he asked, but he was curious. Not of his plans, but if he had an ounce of remorse in his abhorrent body.

"My family was murdered by my son," he wheezed. "Hateful youngling."

Tik-Tok froze. *What the* fuck? Was he serious? All thoughts became suspended as he stared down the worthless male. Even emotions failed him. For a single moment, he felt nothing—not anger, not fear, not glee or disgust.

Then it all came rushing back tenfold.

His eldest sister, cradling her stomach, protecting the life inside, even as their mother dragged the very essence from her body. His older brother, leaping in to save her. Their father meeting him, midair, with his sword, spilling his brother's guts. The screeching cries of Tik-Tok's younger sister as Glarondal stalked toward her with blood dripping from the blade. How he'd severed each of their spinal cords to make sure they stayed dead. And the way it felt to be held immobile by magic, watching, *knowing* he would be next…

Tik-Tok lunged forward and, in the span of a breath, he held his sword against his father's throat. "*I* killed them, Father?" he seethed. Glarondal's mouth dropped open in shock. "I seem to remember it differently. Please, do tell me what happened."

"Tik-Tok." He drew a loud, gasping breath. "You've come for me."

He pressed his blade a little deeper and a line of red trickled down Glarondal's veined skin. "I've come to *kill* you, you wretched blackguard. For *decades*, I've hunted for someone to open the portal. I made sacrifice after sacrifice to be here so I could chop you into tiny pieces and feed you to the sea. Even then, that wouldn't be enough to pay back all you did to me and my siblings."

"You can't kill me." Glarondal laughed, but it quickly turned into a cough. Tik-Tok eased the sword away so the bastard wouldn't kill himself and rob him of his vengeance. "I'm a *god*."

Respen laughed from across the room, but quickly shut his mouth when Tik-Tok shot him a glare. "Sorry, Captain. It's just…" He gave Glarondal a scathing look.

"Captain?" Glarondal said, and latched onto Tik-Tok's sleeve. "Who would follow a vermin like you?"

"Who would worship a piece of shit like *you*?" Respen shot back.

A spark of magic suddenly zapped Tik-Tok's golden arm, tingling, and he yanked it away from his father. "Did you try to steal my magic?" he spoke quietly. Too quietly. Making it louder than the blasts from Salt's ship.

"What happened to your arm?" Glarondal croaked, rubbing

his hand as if it stung.

It probably did—his arm repelled any magic, including having it stolen, and his father had been foolish enough to try while touching it. Only one other had attempted it before, and the dryad had quickly become engulfed in flames, all from one small spark of protection. Tik-Tok leered down at his father. "I don't think I'll kill you after all," he said slowly. "I think there's a better end for you."

"Wh—"

Tik-Tok motioned Respen over with a nod. "Take us back to the first village."

"Aye, Captain." Respen lifted a brow and gripped Tik-Tok's shoulder. "Hold onto him."

Tik-Tok grabbed the dying male by the throat, eliciting a panicked gasp, and Respen's power dragged them from the cave, directly back to the crossroad where they'd stood only an hour ago.

Dropping his father, Tik-Tok strode up to the house that the young girl had exited earlier. He squared his shoulders and pounded on the door. Eagerness built in him as he waited for someone to answer. All this time, he'd wanted to savor his revenge, and this was how it needed to happen.

A portly being swung the door open and gasped. He was square-jawed and hairless—at least what wasn't hidden beneath loose black robes that covered him from neck to ankle. "Your Exalted Eminence," he said with a bow. The confusion on his face was hard to miss. His daughter had likely told him how *blasphemous* he'd been before, striking doubt into the whole family. "It's an honor. My daughters told me you'd arrived, so we prepared—"

"Enough." Tik-Tok closed his eyes for a moment before he lost control of his temper and punched the innocent man. "Bring your family outside to bear witness."

Tik-Tok whirled around and went back to Respen's side. Glarondal wheezed on the gravel, frantically searching for something, though surely, he couldn't see more than shadow with the blue cataracts coating his eyes.

"What are you planning?" Respen asked with a curious tilt of his head.

"I'm becoming a god," Tik-Tok replied with a disgusted grin. When he turned again, the two girls from earlier stood behind the patriarch, along with two older women, a young boy, and an elderly man. They strongly resembled each other in the face— dark eyes, darker hair, slightly upturned noses—but it was as if every day they lived had visibly aged them. The wide-eyed, younger children cowering behind the grown beings were the exception, but likely not for long.

"You've worshipped a false god all these years." Tik-Tok's voice boomed, and he loathed pretending to be the cruel god that his father had created. "This … creature…"—he shot a glance at his cowering father—"has taken my likeness as his own and fooled you all."

"What are you doing?" Glarondal snapped, pushing to his knees. "Don't listen to him. He's a great deceiver!"

Tik-Tok forced himself not to scoff and instead met each of the locals' gazes. "Would a god decay as such?" He swept a hand out. "Deal with him as you would deal with any *deceiver*. Punish him well or I will turn my wrath to your world."

"Liar," the young girl from before shouted.

Though the old woman pushed her further behind the group, he saw the defiance burning in her youthful eyes. "Am I?" Tik-Tok asked. "Shall I prove it?"

Before any of them could tell him no, he shoved the roughest of his magic outward. It hit the patriarch straight in the chest, sliding over his body, turning it to stone. The girl who'd called him a liar screamed so loudly that his ears rang, and the oldest woman fainted, collapsing onto the graveled street.

"Perhaps I will leave him here as a reminder," he mused.

"No," Lizbet whispered, stepping away from the group, repeating the ridiculous hand movements *again*. "We believe you. Please, Your Exha—"

"Shh," he hissed, a finger to his lips. Then he released his power from the man so he could return to his true form.

Respen shook with silent laughter when Tik-Tok grabbed his forearm.

"Not a fucking word," he said under his breath.

The entire family, unconscious woman aside, replicated the Lizbet's motions. Hands pressed to their chests, arms sweeping out, words mumbled with reverence. And they weren't the only ones. Other doors opened, more families coming into the streets.

Hell fucking no. Tik-Tok tightened his grip on Respen. "Let's get back to the ship."

"You don't want to stay and watch?" his first mate asked.

"No." This wasn't the revenge he'd envisioned, but his father was going to die slowly, painfully, desperate and alone. Truly alone. Those terrorized into worshiping him would take their own revenge for the awful things he'd surely done.

And Glarondal would leave this world—*all* worlds—hated. Despised. Powerless.

No. It wasn't what Tik-Tok had dreamed of. Not what his siblings with their kind hearts and fiercer love would have wanted. There was no battle to be won or bloody vengeance to exact on their behalf. Glarondal was already too far gone for that. But this … this was better. Tik-Tok smiled down at the male as he crawled toward his boots.

"Goodbye, *Father*," he whispered blithely as Respen's magic swept him back to *The Temptress*. To his home and to his future. *North.*

CHAPTER TWENTY-TWO

NORTH

"The bastard followed us!" Dax shouted, racing toward the middle of the ship and snatching North's weapons from the floor.

North whipped her head up, her gaze landing on the ship that had sailed through the portal. Once fully in the new world, the ship fought its way clear of the vortex and barreled straight for them. Its large white sails cracked like thunder with the wind, and its glossy wood coloring reflected from an obscured sun. This ship was as grand as Tik-Tok's, towering and looming. Several fae stood on deck, but she couldn't see their faces clearly. Her hands shook and her heartbeat increased. Tik-Tok was gone, and she wasn't sure what was happening. But she needed to retrieve her axe from Dax.

"Not again!" Echo growled withdrawing her sword as she stomped across the deck. She turned to the brownies who were hurrying into place, their expressions determined. "Remain here to defend your captain's ship—your home—if need be."

They nodded and stood in a huddle, most holding broomsticks and makeshift weapons.

Dax jogged to North with her axes in his hands, his nostrils flaring. "You're probably going to need them both."

As she reached to take the weapons from him, a familiar boom roared, making her jump. It was the same sound that had woken her after she'd passed out. A bright white light soared toward them, disrupting her vision. Magic struck the boat, slamming her body into the handrail. A sharp pain throbbed at her hip and a squeak escaped her lips.

"Is this Salt?" North asked, her heart thudding rapidly.

Dax yanked her down beneath the handrail so they were protected by the ship's barrier. He set her axes in her lap. "Yes. Tik-Tok turned Salt into stone during a parlay so the crew is probably pissed."

"What?" North's brows rose up her forehead. Did this all happen when she'd been unconscious? "Tik-Tok didn't think to mention these details to me before he left?"

"No one thought Salt's crew would follow us through the portal."

Another hard blow struck the ship as if a giant godly hand whacked it. The impact lurched North forward, rattling her entire body.

Dax stood, facing Salt's ship with his hands held in front of him, ready to use his elemental power.

North pushed up from the floor, her lips parting when she focused on Salt's ship. It was practically beside Tik-Tok's now and it would only take a quick row for Salt's crew to board *The Temptress*.

A light breeze drifted off Dax's palms, ruffling his hair. His wind took no time to pick up, quickening its speed. North gripped the handrail, her locks whipping around her face, *The Temptress's* black sails flapping harder. With a single shove, Dax thrust his power across the water toward Salt's ship. Two of the masts cracked in half. They fell to the deck, splintering wood and breaking the pristine railing with a deafening smack.

Two males sprinted to the front of the ship, their faces contorted in rage. They stopped near the broken handrail and settled their gazes on Dax, Echo, and North. One, a male with stark white hair and a patchy beard covering the lower half of his face, wore bronze cuffs on each arm. The other fae was a tall, slender elf with golden hair and black tattoos covering all of his exposed flesh.

"Where's your fucking captain?" the white-haired male seethed from his ship.

"You shouldn't be here, Salt," Echo shouted, her hand slapping against the rail. "If you proceed any farther, you will all die."

Salt bared his teeth. "It's you and your crew who will die, whore."

North's blood boiled in her veins, her eyes narrowing at the male. Tik-Tok may have betrayed Salt, but what had Echo ever done to him? Nothing. No one else on this crew had either— they weren't the original crew who'd betrayed him. She had to do *something*.

Focus. Focus. Focus on Salt. Your target.

Lifting her old axe, North kept her gaze locked on the male's face. She pulled her arm back, then hurled her weapon forward. It flew through the air, swishing and slicing, and planted itself with a hard strike in the face of the golden-haired elf. Right in between the eyes. Blood spilled down the elf's face as the force sent him careening backward, his body flopping to the deck, undoubtedly dead.

"Gods." North blew out a hard breath. She'd missed her intended target, but regardless, it was the first time she'd killed. She felt … sick. Even if it had been Salt that she'd hit, she would have felt the same.

"You took down their strongest fae." Dax slapped her on the back. "That bastard was always an asshole."

"You bitch!" Salt roared, his piercing gaze targeting North. "You'll be the first to die."

"She's trying to board the ship!" Cyrx pounded across the deck and rushed near the end of the ship. A female maenad leapt from Salt's side onto Tik-Tok's deck, landing perfectly on both hooves. Her antlers bobbed as she ripped her sword free of its sheath, but Cyrx was fast as he ducked from the blade and tore her head off her body. Blood oozed from the wounds and North watched, wide-eyed, as Cyrx threw the head and body overboard. The water splashed below.

"You're going to pay for that!" Salt bellowed.

"With the elf dead, I could blow the ship back through the portal to Oz, but they would be able to cross again." Dax shook his head and glanced at Echo. "Echo. I think you need to end this. None of them know what you are, what you can do."

A deep line settled between the siren's brows as if she were warring with herself. Perhaps even thinking about her past, when she'd brought males to their knees and killed them. Then she nodded. "Let's get this over with." Echo tilted her head to the side and popped her neck. "Salt first."

North held up her axe, the one with the star engraved from Tik-Tok. She wanted to have it ready in case she needed to protect her friend.

"I suppose you wish I were your whore, don't you?" Echo shouted to Salt, grinning.

"How about this?" Salt called back, his gaze locking onto Echo's. "You suck my cock as soon as I'm finished sinking your ship."

Echo opened her mouth, not to speak, but to let a song pour forth from her lips. The entire world seemed to freeze. Everyone. Even North. A light melody, full of magic and tales, darkness and light, alluring and deadly, like nothing North had ever heard before. A true siren princess of the sea. North was captivated, wanted to dance and spin in it. She wanted to live in the song.

Salt's eyes appeared glazed, his expression neutral, his movements stiff as he drew his sword from the sheath at his hip. His arm didn't shake when his own blade pressed against his throat, nor did he blink when it glided across his flesh. Bright scarlet poured down his neck, and he didn't release so much as a gasp or parting of lips before his body folded and collapsed to the deck with a thud.

Three of Salt's goblins ran toward their captain's body, taking in his still form. Their heads jerked toward where Echo was standing, and they withdrew their swords.

"I'm going to them before they have a chance to come here," Echo said.

Before North could free herself of the siren's spell and stop her, Echo leapt from the ship and landed in front of Salt's crew.

North leaned on the handrail as Echo's song came again, holding her in place. The low aria unfurled from Echo, growing higher and higher in pitch. North watched as she moved toward the three males, singing, persuading, taunting. The three goblins lifted their blades to their throats as Salt had done. Three bloody red smiles appeared on their flesh.

A deafening squelch rose from the ocean's depths, interfering with Echo's song. The familiar noise that North had heard earlier when she'd been out here with Tik-Tok grew louder and louder until it was a crescendo of its own. The sea shook, the ship quaked. Something from below was rousing, but North couldn't see anything within the water. Her heart beat so hard that it was about to burst from her chest. Echo's song had ended and North exchanged a glance with Dax, who seemed to emerge from his own spell.

With a resounding watery explosion, a creature shot up from the sea's surface. Water rained down on North while she watched in horror as it threw back, not one, but two heads, revealing razor-sharp teeth as it let out a powerful roar. The blast made her ears ring, and she cupped one while clenching the axe in her other hand.

Ghastly twin heads, with coal-colored orbs peering out from its sockets, hung from the creature's long, thin neck. Sharp, scaly thorns covered every inch of its massive alabaster body. Pointed teeth the size of North lined its open mouth. Two arms on each side of its body ended with curling claws, and a tail lined with spikes extended from beneath the water.

A dagger flew from someone on Salt's ship, the tip of its blade bouncing off of the creature's thick flesh. The beast released a shrill screech and smacked its long tail against the ship with a loud *thwack*. North jerked up her weapon, trying to figure out what to do. Her axe wouldn't make a dent in that thing, but perhaps she could do something with the water.

"They're only riling it up," Dax said, his arms falling to his sides. He glanced at her and shook his head. "Don't use your magic yet."

The creature wrapped its tail around the enemy ship, tightening. With a boisterous creak and groan, the beast dragged the entire vessel beneath the thick, churning water. The sails seemed to give a farewell wave before the ship was fully pulled under. Bubbles rose to the surface, and the water slowed, perfectly still, as if an entire ship hadn't been hauled away by a massive beast.

What if the creature decided to take down *The Temptress* next? North scanned the ship for Echo. But she wasn't there. Had she not leapt back?

"Echo!" North shouted down to the water, searching frantically. There was no sign of red hair anywhere. Only the dark water and the violet whirlpool.

"There!" Dax shouted. North followed his gaze and found where he was looking as a head pushed up from the sea.

Another creature jutted out from the water, smooth and slender like an eel, with hungry green eyes. It dove back beneath the murky liquid, and in seconds, Echo was pulled under. The water was so dark, but North could have sworn it became darker ... *blood*.

"Gods!" North didn't think—she gripped her axe and leapt over the side of the ship. Her heart lodged in her throat as her body smacked into the freezing water, a sharp pain shooting up her spine.

She opened her eyes and a slight stinging sensation pierced them. Everything surrounding her was black. She kicked her legs and swam upward through the thick liquid that weighed her down. When she broke the surface, another form shot up. The eel-like creature hissed and flicked his black forked tongue, tiny spikes covering the tissue. With a single swipe, she tore the axe across its body. Dark scarlet bubbled from the wound.

Another head broke through the water, and North was about to swing her weapon again, when she recognized the short red hair.

"Echo." North sighed, lowering the axe.

"Go!" She shoved North toward where Dax dangled a roped for them to grab.

North clasped the rope—it burned her hands as she climbed up. Her teeth chattered and the putrid odor of the sea clung to her.

"You shouldn't have risked your life like that!" Dax spat, grabbing her by the back of her dress and dragging her on deck. "Captain is going to be pissed."

"He'll have to deal with it," North said, her chest heaving.

Echo came up next and dropped to the floor on all fours. Dax knelt beside her and placed his palm to her shoulder.

Bright red blood dripped on deck, mixing with the water pooling beneath the siren. North gasped as she realized it came from Echo's abdomen. "You're bleeding!"

"It's fine." She sat back, her knees planted against the wood, and pressed a hand to her stomach wounds. "They'll be fine too."

North furrowed her brow. Echo must have been delirious.

Dax took in a sharp breath. "Respen doesn't know, does he? And you risked your life like that?"

"Know what?" North asked.

Crimson seeped in between Echo's fingers. "I'm with child."

CHAPTER TWENTY-THREE

TIK-TOK

After leaving Tik-Tok's father to his ill fate, Respen's magic dropped them onto *The Temptress* to a flurry of brownies, armed with brooms and mops, rushing toward the edge of the ship as it rocked violently back and forth. Dax and Cyrx knelt over someone at the center of the deck. They spoke in harsh whispers, expressions hard. Crimson blood coated the rail, more of it running in rivulets across the wooden planks.

Tik-Tok's heart stopped.

North.

Where was North? He took a single step forward and caught sight of Echo's pale face. The relief that it wasn't North was short lived as the realization hit—Echo was badly injured. If not dead already.

Cyrx lifted his head, dark eyes wild, and caught sight of Tik-Tok and Respen. "Captain! Thank the mother!"

Respen shoved his way through the brownies and slid to his knees. "Echo!"

"Shit," Dax said under his breath. He glanced at Respen, still leaning over her body, and met his gaze. "I can't fix this."

Tik-Tok's chest grew tight, each inhale a struggle, and his feet refused to move. He'd seen his siblings die up close—he couldn't watch his friend potentially do the same. "What happened?"

"Got everything!" North shouted from the stairwell.

His head snapped toward the sound of her voice. North burst from the door leading below deck and stumbled across the rocking ship with an armful of towels. Blood stained her skirts and exposed forearms. When her gaze locked with Tik-Tok's, she gasped. "Thank the gods you're back."

"What happened?" he asked again in a rough voice.

North ignored him, going instead toward the form between Dax and Cyrx, and dropped to her knees. Dax scrambled backward, his entire front soaked in blood, so she could apply pressure to the wound with a cloth.

"Echo!" The rawness in Respen's voice rattled Tik-Tok to his very core.

"I'm sorry, Res," Dax said in a gravelly voice. "I don't know what else to do."

North lifted her stare from the stained towel in her hands. "She's with child."

A desperate wail left Respen. The hair on Tik-Tok's arm stood on end. Echo was with child? With a wound like that… His stomach twisted.

"You have to risk taking her to land," Cyrx told him.

And it was a risk. Respen's power could potentially make her wound worse, but it wouldn't improve by waiting until the ship arrived at a port. How skilled were the healers here? Without magic… Tik-Tok didn't move. Couldn't move. Echo was bleeding out. There was too much blood for her to survive whatever injury she'd suffered. He swallowed hard and turned his gaze to North.

As if sensing his stare, she looked up. Her eyes were dilated, and dried tears stained her cheeks, with more threatening to fall. "Salt followed us through the portal, but something destroyed his ship."

If Tik-Tok thought, even for a moment, that Salt would've followed through the portal, he never would've left. The ass was somehow both fearless and superstitious. Crossing into other worlds would *anger the gods*, or so he'd claimed. He swallowed hard.

"Destroyed by what?" he asked.

"Whatever is in the water. It attacked, and Echo dove in to save us and…" The ship gave another violent jerk. "We have to go back to Oz before it sinks us."

The first squelching sounded. *Fuck.* He ran to the helm and grabbed the spokes of the wheel. "Dax, wind!"

A large gust slammed into the sails, jerking the ship forward, toward the swirling vortex of the portal. The masts creaked against the force, the sails snapping as the wind caught at different angles. The spinning water swept them up, dragged them closer, swallowed them whole. Tik-Tok's stomach lurched with the rapid movement despite the years he'd spent on the water. Cyrx had braced Respen and Echo, keeping them from sliding across the slippery deck, while Dax held onto a mast and North caught herself on a rope. Kaliko and dozens of brownies skidded across the deck, some bouncing off the railing before sliding the other way as the ship twisted in the current.

"Hold onto something!" But the roar of the portal drowned out Tik-Tok's shout.

A moment later, the portal spat them back out. With a blue sky overhead, glittering silver waves below, and a gentle sea breeze, they were home. It was over in a single breath, but left Tik-Tok winded and disoriented. Once he regained his senses, a quick headcount told him that three brownies were missing. "Fae overboard!" he yelled, abandoning the helm. Dax continued with his wind, blowing them away from the portal, while Cyrx sprinted to the side of the ship, looking for their lost crewmembers.

"They're gone, Captain," Cyrx called. "No sign of them anywhere."

Of course they were—the portal was still wide open. There was no way the brownies could swim against the current. A heavy pang hit his chest as he realized Cyrx was right—they were *gone.*

But if he let himself dwell, let himself mourn their loss… *No.* He had to focus. Other lives still depended on him.

Jolting to North, he hauled her up from the deck by her upper arms. "Close the portal." There was no warmth in his voice, though he hadn't intended to sound so callous. He had to act like *Captain* Tik-Tok now, not their friend. Had to take charge and leave no room for questions about his orders. That's what kept things running smoothly in a crisis. He whirled away from North to return to the helm. With a quick glance at his compass, its needle pointing him in the direction of the nearest land, he spun the wheel to the left. "More wind!"

Dax rotated his hands through the air, churning the breeze into something stronger, and used it to fill the sails, sending *The Temptress* soaring over the silver sea. Behind them, there was no trace of the portal.

"I'm taking her to the Isle of Phreex," Respen yelled, his voice cracking with fear as he scooped Echo off the floor. Blood dripped freely from her abdomen, joining the pool already on the deck. "They can help her there."

Tik-Tok checked his compass again, adjusting slightly in favor of the right isle. "We'll meet you there as soon as we can," he promised.

Then Echo and Respen disappeared as he whirled her toward a healer.

"North," Tik-Tok called. She stumbled to his side, wiping her hands down her ruined dress. "What happened while I was tracking down my father?"

"I told you. Salt followed—"

"No." He inhaled deeply, readying himself. "Spare me no details."

The Isle of Phreex was a paradise—all sandy beaches and lush meadows with a picturesque mountain range—but the inhabitants were another story. The kinglet was an arrogant prick and the females loved luring males in, hypnotizing them until they went mad. There was also a large steam machine with one wheel that rolled around the island, crushing buildings and terrorizing fae. Then there were the different groups of cutthroats, like the Brotherhood of Failings, who wouldn't hesitate to snatch newcomers.

Respen used to *be* a member of the Brotherhood. The eight—now seven—males were outcasts who'd found somewhere to fit in. With each other, they had a family and a home, but they remained the bane of the island. What unsupervised younglings wouldn't cause trouble? The brothers simply never grew out of their mischievous ways. All except one.

Tik-Tok had met Respen by chance. A dice game in a tavern, the stakes, a challenge meant to be nothing but good fun. When Tik-Tok won, he had dared Respen to do something exclusively for his own happiness. Something Tik-Tok figured was open-ended enough not to piss off the Brotherhood so he could restock his ship and get the fuck out of there.

But he'd decided to join Tik-Tok's crew instead.

Respen assured Tik-Tok they would still treat him like family. *The Temptress* hadn't sailed back to the isle to test that theory, however, since it wasn't worth the trouble.

Tik-Tok stood beside North at the ship's railing, watching fishermen go about their business as if a pirate ship hadn't cast their pier in shadow. Their cargo of sea life was only a cover for something more nefarious—trafficking fae or stolen goods, perhaps even dealing with dark magic. Tik-Tok knew fellow pirates when he saw them. Their confident strides, the not-so-casual way they avoided fae who belonged to a different ship, and the gentle way they set down certain crates. No one took that much care with *shelled nuts*, if the stamps on the boxes were to be believed.

But somewhere beyond the pier, amid the uneven, chaotic rows of thatched buildings leading up to the three-tiered palace, was Echo. Fighting for her life, and that of her child, with Respen by her side.

"She'll be okay." Tik-Tok spoke to himself as much as he spoke to North. "Respen has an extremely skilled healer in his circle."

"Shouldn't we go into town instead of waiting here?" North asked.

Tik-Tok shook his head. "Respen's friends blame me for his leaving. While they can forgive him because he's family, I'm a *good-for-nothing pirate*." He forced a small smile and winked. It was better to stay on the ship and avoid any potential disasters. "Dax will bring us news when he has it."

North nodded, keeping her gaze outward. "And you?"

"What about me?" He leaned his elbows onto the rail, stretching forward to peer at the water lapping against the side of the ship. It needed repairs after Salt's attacks and the journey through the portal, but not here. The damage was small enough, thanks to the magic wards he'd commissioned years ago, that it could wait until they reached a safer port.

"Are you okay? You haven't said a word about what happened in the other world." She paused and his silence filled the air between them. "I told you everything, but you didn't even mention to me that you'd turned Salt to stone."

"Bastard deserved it," he murmured. "Attacking my ship like that." Tik-Tok couldn't bring himself to give a fuck that his old captain was dead.

North lightly set her hand on his forearm. "You're avoiding the question."

"I'm fine, my star." *A lie.* Soon, she would be gone from him too, and it might be the thing that finally broke him. After losing so much, emptiness consumed him, and North was his only flicker of hope. He would need to extinguish any trace of it now before that spark spread. If he didn't, if he let it grow, the pain of losing her would destroy him. "My siblings are avenged, and my father lives no more."

"You killed him?" She squeezed his arm a bit.

Tik-Tok shifted his eyes to meet her inquisitive gaze. "You could say that."

"Wh—"

He leaned in and placed a chaste kiss to her lips. A *final* kiss. "I don't want to talk about death now. Not while Echo is fighting against it and I've lost three of my crew on the way back through the portal."

"We can talk about it another time." North looked up at him when he remained silent.

"Someday," he agreed, and his heart weighed heavily in his chest. The time he and North had together was almost over. Her family expected her to return home—*she* expected it. He'd given his word. "If the wind ever blows us into each other's path again, I will tell you."

North's face paled, her grip tightening. "What do you mean?"

"As soon as Echo's well enough, you're going home like I promised." He pushed up and away from the railing. "I need to rest. Wake me if Dax returns with news."

Without waiting for North's opinion on the matter, he walked away. Each step took more strength than he felt he had. What he truly wanted was to bring North along with him, settle into his bed with her nestled beside him, and sleep, long and hard. His life's mission was complete, but instead of feeling vindicated, a … hollowness filled him. Numb. And the only thing he could imagine replacing the new emptiness with was North.

But he didn't want to be selfish. Even though he'd never cared about that before.

Unlike Tik-Tok, North had a family who loved her and wanted nothing more than her safe return. And she loved them too. Far more than she could ever care for someone like him. What could he offer her—or any other female, for that matter? Life on a ship wasn't meant for everyone. It was more than that, though. A male needed a purpose, no matter how small, and his purpose was finished. How could he drag North aimlessly around with him as he searched for a new one?

Kicking the door to his quarters shut with his heel, Tik-Tok shed his filthy coat and muddy boots. He should've taken a bath in his private tub, but he was too tired. Too … *nothing.* The desire to be clean paled in comparison to his *need* to sleep.

He flopped on his bed and rolled to face the wall. Instead of holding North like he wanted, he tucked the pillow that smelled of sweet vanilla, of *her*, beneath his chin and closed his eyes.

Today, his father got what he deserved. But three brownies and Echo got something they *didn't.*

Tik-Tok had won. He'd also lost.

And soon, he would lose more.

CHAPTER TWENTY-FOUR

NORTH

The next three days seemed unending—they connected and spanned an eternity. North tried to sleep, but every time she did, the sight of blood from Echo's stomach filled her mind, causing her to jerk awake.

Kaliko and a few of the other brownies had already scrubbed the deck, but North stood at the handrail, studying the now-empty spot. She had tried to visit Echo, but Dax refused to take her to see the siren.

Her gaze flicked back to Tik-Tok. He stood near the end of the ship, alone, his arms dangling over the rail.

Dax brought a pear to his mouth and came up beside her. "You keep staring at the captain."

North had tried speaking with Tik-Tok, but he'd been distant, different. He gave one-word answers and chose to eat alone in his quarters. She wasn't angry about it—she didn't know how she felt. Whatever emotions spun through her were her own issues to deal with, so she gave him the space he seemed to need.

"You should go talk to him," Dax suggested as Tik-Tok tilted his head in their direction.

"I've tried." She turned away from him and studied the opposite side of the empty ship.

"His loss." He shrugged as he chewed.

"I'm surprised you haven't ventured off to enjoy Phreex."

"This is the one place where my cock shall remain in my pants."

North had heard the story about a clan of females there who would lure strangers to their bed, and in return, the males would end up chopping off parts of themselves to feed to them.

"Don't talk to her about your cock," a deep voice drawled from behind her. She hadn't heard Tik-Tok saunter up.

Dax smirked and pushed off from the rail, leaving Tik-Tok and North in silence.

"So…" she said, toeing the floor, trying to figure out what to ask first as she gazed at his beautiful face. But he was staring past her at the sails. "Gods, why won't you at least look at me?"

"North, you—"

A shuffling of feet sounded behind her, and she whirled around to find Respen coming onto the ship. He looked as though he hadn't slept in days. His blue hair was rumpled, purple bags rested beneath his eyes, and even his normally straight body hunched forward.

"They're both going to be all right." Respen sighed, and there was such relief in those words. "She's asking for you, North."

Tik-Tok gave a slight nod. "Don't let her walk through town. It's too dangerous, and they don't want me there. Bring her back once she's finished so I can speak with her before you take her home."

"Yes, Captain."

"And, Respen? I think it goes without saying, but anything you or Echo needs is yours." Tik-Tok turned and headed back toward the front of the ship.

Respen studied him as though he wanted to say something else. Instead, he placed his hands on North's shoulders and blew out a breath. "I wouldn't let you walk through town either."

Based on the rumors, she wouldn't want to anyway. "I'm perfectly fine with that." As soon as she closed her eyes, the rush of falling blasted through her, her stomach dipping, but only for a few seconds this time.

North opened her eyes. She stood outside a small silver and gold cottage made entirely of metal. Large boulders hovered off the ground and leafy trees brushed the sky overhead. She glanced over her shoulder and gasped. They were on a mountainside, at the edge of a cliff—a woozy feeling shot through her as she peered down, finding the base of the mountain terribly far away. Huts and cottages were sprinkled all over the town, and in the center was a massive palace, each of its three tiers a different shade of gold. The hues flickered underneath the sun, making the palace shine like it was enveloped in fairy dust.

Respen knocked on the door, and a gnome with white locks of hair to his waist and a scruffy beard the same length, answered. The gnome came to about North's belly button, and deep wrinkles etched his flesh.

"Lou, I brought someone to see Echo." Respen ducked while stepping inside.

Lou eyed her with suspicion as she lowered her head and followed behind Respen. Herbs and something musty enveloped North as she pushed into the simple sitting room. She straightened and the ceiling brushed her head. A rocking chair stood in the corner with a fur blanket sprawled across its back. Misshapen glass bottles filled with colorful tinctures were scattered across a nearby table.

"This way." Respen remained hunched as he guided her toward an open door.

Echo lay on the floor atop a pallet of stacked wool blankets. An empty bed, too small for anyone besides the gnome, took up one of the corners. Echo's head turned to face them, and a weak smile spread across her lips. Sweat drenched her red hair and beads of perspiration lined her forehead. The siren appeared feeble, but she was anything but that.

"I'll give you two some time alone," Respen said softly. "Let me know if either one of you needs anything."

"Eat something," Echo told him.

"For you, I will." He held Echo's gaze until disappearing from their view.

The siren focused on North and her smile remained. "Don't even ask how I am. I feel as though I've been stabbed in the stomach."

"I wouldn't dream of asking you that." North smiled back and knelt beside her friend. "Why didn't you tell anyone about the child?"

Echo took several breaths before answering. "I didn't want to be treated as though I were fragile."

"You aren't." North grasped her friend's hand and gently squeezed it.

Echo bit her lip, tears filling her eyes. "I secretly feared they would have left me behind. That Respen wouldn't have wanted me any longer."

"Of course he would still want you!"

"I've never had anyone like him before. He's happy. Scared, but happy." Echo paused. "Once I'm healed, we're planning to return to the island near my old home. I can't risk the child's life again by living on a pirate ship. It doesn't mean we'll never come aboard *The Temptress*, though."

"I'm going home after this, too," North whispered, twisting her hands. "I won't be on the ship when you do return."

A crease formed between the siren's brows. "Do you want to stay?"

"He hasn't asked me." North was told she would go home once she'd opened the portal for Tik-Tok. But a part of her thought, after everything, that he possibly would've wanted her to remain.

"You can always ask him." Echo grinned. "Remember, he hasn't done this sort of thing before."

"Perhaps." If she asked him if she could stay, then he might feel pressured into saying yes, and she wouldn't linger unless he truly wanted her to. North knew her family wanted her home, but she wasn't entirely sure what she yearned for anymore.

North continued to chat with Echo about the siren's future for a while longer until her friend's lids closed and her breathing became even. Trying not to disturb her, North slowly rose from the floor and met Respen back in the sitting room. He leaned against the wall in a crouched position, fiddling around with Lou's tinctures. The gnome paced at a shelf, rearranging tattered books by color.

Respen set down the glass vials and pushed himself up to stand. "Ready?"

"Yes." She smiled. "Thank you for bringing me to see her."

"No." He placed his hands at her shoulders. "Thank you for saving her. She told me what you did by distracting the creature and killing it."

"I would have done it for any of you."

"I know," he said, a warm smile tugging at his lips. "Ready?"

North nodded and closed her eyes, sucking in a sharp breath as he whirled them back to the ship. When she opened her lids again, Respen had brought them to the front of the ship where Tik-Tok stood, facing them.

"Let me know when she's ready," Respen said, taking his hands from her shoulders before walking toward the middle of the deck.

"You're not going to take me home?" North's gaze flicked to Tik-Tok's, her voice coming out more desperate than she would have liked. But she assumed he was at least traveling with her to the Emerald City.

"I feel bad enough asking Respen to take you, and he's too exhausted to take us both. Besides, something tells me your family wouldn't enjoy seeing my face again." Tik-Tok picked up her luggage beside him and handed it to her, along with her axe in a strap. She attached the weapon to her back as he pushed his hand into his pocket and drew out something red and shiny. A stone heart. Tik-Tok dropped the object into the center of her palm. "Return this to Ozma. Tell her I didn't need this after all."

She stared down at the stone, knowing what it was because her grandmother had one that was exactly the same. It was a stone which could prevent curses. Reva had used hers for protection while helping to defeat the previous Northern Witch, Locasta.

He took a step back and spun to leave.

North's eyes widened and confusion jolted through her. "That's it?" she called.

"Have a safe journey home," he added without glancing over his shoulder.

Tears didn't come. She didn't feel hurt or sad, only *angry* over the most dismal farewell she'd ever had. Fury stormed through her veins. The magic within her touched down on the waves, making them rise in anger too, until they sprayed over the edges of the ship to the deck. "I hate you!" she yelled. It was pitiful. She should have cursed at him, but that was the most she could force out.

Tik-Tok stilled and glanced over his shoulder. "Back to that, are we? Good." His red irises shifted away from her as he resumed walking.

Her jaw clenched. "You're a coward." With a scowl, she turned to face the water, the waves choppy but slowing. She hadn't suffered in her past like he had, but, had their roles been reversed, she still would have given him more words, more emotion, more of a goodbye.

The sound of heavy boots thudded across the deck, and a growl escaped Tik-Tok as he spun her around. His face was inches from hers, his crimson eyes blazing, his expression as angry as hers had been. "I may be a selfish bastard, but I'm not a coward." He gripped the nape of North's neck and crashed his mouth to hers. His lips fit perfectly with hers, then he parted them with his tongue and pushed it inside, kissing her senseless.

When he pulled back, the anger was no longer on his face, and in its place was something else she couldn't read. He reached into his other pocket this time and fished his compass out. With gentle fingers, he opened her hand and placed the object on her palm, then he tenderly wrapped her digits around the cold metal. "It's yours. Go home. Think about it. If you fail to see sense and want to find me, use the compass."

She sucked in a deep breath, her eyes wide as she stared at his beloved object. "Tik-Tok..."

"Don't argue with your captain." With the finality of his words, he walked off again. And this time, she didn't stop him as he went inside his room. He didn't ask her to stay—he'd left her a choice instead.

"Well, that was interesting." Respen cleared his throat as he came up beside her. "Do you need more time?"

North studied Tik-Tok's closed door, then looked down at the compass. She opened her luggage and placed the two objects he'd given her inside. "I'm ready."

Respen nodded and grasped her arms. When she closed her eyes, nausea bubbled through her entire body with the longer journey, and the falling seemed to last and last until everything was still.

As she opened her eyes, bright green shone around her. The flickering emerald brick road, the glistening shops, the sparkling palace.

At the Emerald City Palace gates, every guard's stare locked on her and Respen. Her hands shook as she threw her arms around the pirate in a quick hug before releasing him. "Go!"

With a smile goodbye, he vanished just as an arrow whizzed past her to where he'd stood, flying through empty space.

"North!" a familiar voice shouted. *Birch.*

She turned to him as he lowered his bow. "I'm fine. You're still here?"

Birch wore his chestnut-colored uniform, his hair ragged as he pulled her into a tight hug. "We all are. Once Crow came back with news of finding you, we decided to wait for your return." He hugged her tighter. "I wish I could have done more at the celebration. I wish I had known Tik-Tok was coming."

"It's fine." North hugged him back, and none of the old feelings she had for him surfaced. She was simply relieved to see her friend. "No harm was done to me." At least not from Tik-Tok or any of his crew besides Rizmaela.

"Let's get inside so everyone can finally be calm. Your father and grandmother have been impossible to live with since you were taken. Even after Crow returned with word, the two of them have continued to rant."

North knew they both would've struggled with her decision to stay on *The Temptress*. With a sigh, she walked beside Birch past the floral gardens and into the palace. The entrance was mostly quiet except for a few servants cleaning the high-backed velvet chairs. They all looked at her and gasped, halting their movements as she proceeded past them into the throne room.

It was strange seeing the bare area now, when the last time it had been full of celebrating fae, frozen as statues after Tik-Tok had turned them to stone.

"Wait here while I get your parents," Birch said.

Ozma and Jack shot through the open doors before he could take a single step. Brielle was nestled close to Ozma's chest, her eyes shut as she slept.

"North, I'm so sorry. I had wondered if you were the one Tik-Tok wanted, but then you never manifested magic. So I was sure you were safe," Ozma rushed out, gently passing Brielle to Jack. She grabbed North and drew her to her chest. "Crow told us everything … that you wanted to stay."

North nodded. "It's all right, Ozma. If anything, I have you to thank because I was able to discover my magic. As for Tik-Tok, he isn't a villain. He went through the portal to save another world." She wouldn't confess all his reasonings to her family because those were his stories to tell. North knelt and opened her luggage to retrieve the red stone, then stood and handed the object to Ozma. "He wanted you to have this back."

Ozma's lips parted as she took the stone from North. Jack frowned, like he didn't believe Tik-Tok would do a good deed for no reason.

More hurried footsteps echoed throughout the throne room as her mother and father burst in with Birch. Thelia's chest heaved as she crushed North into a fierce hug, and her swollen belly pressed against North's.

"I knew you would be all right." She stepped back and tucked a lock of silver hair behind North's ear. "My strong, brave daughter."

Tin folded his arms around her next. "I've been worried out of my mind."

"I'm fine, Father." She squeezed him in return. "You don't have to worry so much."

Tin cocked his head, eyeing her, as if he knew something, could read all that had happened within her. Before he could say anything else, her grandparents rushed into the room with rumpled hair, untucked shirts…

Gods. She could feel her cheeks heating at what her return had so obviously interrupted.

"I can't *believe* you sent Crow home after he located you." Reva narrowed her eyes and crossed her arms.

"I had to find myself." North shrugged.

Her grandmother's gaze softened. "We all have to do that from time to time."

"Did Tik-Tok turn you to stone at all?" Jack asked.

After his question, more fired off in all directions about Tik-Tok—she had to explain over and over that he had treated her well and not once had he turned her into his personal ornament.

Birch must have noticed her drooping frame because he grabbed her arm and pulled her toward the door. "I think North wants to lie down for a little while."

"I needed that," she whispered so only he could hear.

"I could tell." He chuckled.

"I'll take her from here, Birch," Thelia said, wrapping her arm around North's shoulders. She led her out of the room and up the long emerald stairs.

North stayed quiet while her thoughts churned inside her head. Stay home? Or return?

"Are you really all right? Is there anything I can do?" Thelia asked as she opened the door to the room where North had been staying at the Emerald City Palace.

"I … I miss him already." She'd hugged so many people today, but she needed her mother. Her arms enveloped her and she cried, ugly, wretched tears.

And she told her mother *everything.*

That night, North warred with herself. Her mother had understood everything she'd confessed. After all, Thelia had left her mortal world and stayed in Oz with a male who everyone had once feared. And no matter what North chose, her mother would support her.

North lay in bed, rotating Tik-Tok's compass in her hand. She didn't know what to do, but it wasn't as if she could never return home if she chose to go back to Tik-Tok. There was one person she didn't want to hurt, who might not understand.

A knock came at her door, and she sat up in bed. "Come in."

As if he'd heard North's thoughts, Tin walked through the door, a scowl on his face.

"What did the bastard do to you?" her father demanded, taking a seat at the edge of her bed, the mattress dipping below his towering frame.

"Nothing." North rested her back against the headboard.

"You're different. I could see it as soon as you arrived."

She flicked her gaze toward the window. "I miss the sea is all."

"Be honest with me." His tone was serious, leaving no room for argument. He was good at reading anyone, but especially her.

Blowing out a breath, she turned to face him. "I miss him. I miss Tik-Tok."

He pressed his hands against his head before bringing them down to his knees. "I fucking knew it. I knew that look on your face. The sadness. The longing. Is it a spell? Please tell me it is, and we can get someone to remove it." It wasn't anger she saw in her father's expression, but worry, so much worry.

North pressed a hand to her chest, where her scar rested beneath the fabric of her nightgown. She'd thought about telling her father what had happened with Rizmaela, but she couldn't let him hold onto any more guilt. He knew what he'd done in his past, and this would only make him believe that it was his fault she'd been stabbed. She wouldn't hurt him like that. While she might not be able to hide the scar forever, he didn't need to know about it tonight or tomorrow.

"It's not a spell." She sighed. "He didn't even ask me to stay. He told me to go home and decide if I wanted to come back to him. But if I do go back, I don't want you to hate me."

Tin stared at her for a long moment, an eternity longer than any she'd ever faced. "North." He broke the silence and scooted closer. "I was one of the most hated males in Oz. Do you think your mother gave a fuck about who would hate her if she were with me?"

"No…" Crow hadn't stood in his daughter's way when she'd chosen to be with Tin.

"While I want you to remain nearby for the rest of my life, it doesn't mean you have to. Regardless of what you choose, you will always be my daughter." He held up a finger. "But if you do choose him, I will end his life if he treats you wrong. The bastard already pissed me the fuck off when he turned me to stone."

Tears fell down her cheeks and she launched her arms around him. "I love you, Father." She remembered how he would carry her on his shoulders when she was a child, throw her into the air, swing their axes together in sync, and had even let her slip flowers into his hair. "I thought you would hate me."

"That's an impossible feat."

CHAPTER TWENTY-FIVE

TIK-TOK

Large white sea birds cawed overhead as Tik-Tok busied himself with swabbing the deck. He'd fought off the brownies for the chore, just as he'd peeled vegetables for Cook earlier. Anything to occupy his time now that he'd gotten his revenge. Perhaps he needed to visit Celyna so Dax could fuck her and get him some insight into what to do next.

"Captain?" Dax approached with light steps and a wary expression. "We're heading into town. Are you sure you don't want to come along?"

Tik-Tok gripped his mop tighter. If he left the ship to venture onto the Land of Ix, he would get drunk at any number of taverns and then, when thoughts of North returned to plague him, his mood would *truly* sour. "No. Go enjoy yourselves—you deserve it."

Dax hesitated for a moment. "Cook left you a plate in the kitchen if you get hungry later."

"I'm not a child," he snapped, then winced, hating himself for being such an ass. It didn't stop him from tacking on a grumbled, "I can feed myself."

With a stiff nod, Dax walked backward to where the rest of the crew waited. "We'll return after the performance."

Quavo, a renowned minstrel, was visiting the Land of Ix, but it didn't interest Tik-Tok in the slightest. It was good for the crew, though. Not only had everyone suffered recently, but Tik-Tok wasn't the most pleasant fae to be around since North had left three weeks ago. Part of him wished he'd never sent her home, but another, more rational, part knew that it was the right thing to do.

Fuck being right.

As the crew filed down the pier and into the city, Tik-Tok's heart lurched. *Alone,* it seemed to say. When was the last time he'd had *The Temptress* all to himself? Had he ever? He wasn't entirely sure he liked how lifeless the ship felt without them. The yawning emptiness inside him widened a fraction, making him bone-weary. A nap would soothe the ache...

Another fucking nap. He wasn't *that* gods damn old.

Instead, he shoved the mop into the bucket of now-muddy water and tilted his face up toward the sun. The warmth of its light barely registered as he closed his eyes and sighed. What was North doing now? Did she also stand beneath the sun, or was she holed up inside a palace doing ... whatever it was she did before he came along? He should've asked her—found out what her days were like. It was too late now. She was home with her family, where she belonged.

Damn. This was disgraceful. He was a grown-ass male, not a sappy youngling, and he had to snap out of it. With a low groan, he rubbed his temples. But, combined with his new aimlessness, the sting of North's absence refused to fade. "What the fuck is wrong with me?"

Maybe he *should* join the others in town. Order Cyrx or Dax to keep him far from any sort of ale. The minstrel might even be as talented as the rumors say, which could lighten his spirits. The performance was hours away, though, which left too much free time on his hands. Time he could spend drowning his ... *feelings.* He scowled. If his cock worked anymore, he would even consider sticking it in the nearest willing female, but North seemed to control that from afar.

Bending, he dragged the bucket to the far side of the ship and hefted it up to the railing. Brown, soapy water sloshed out when he tipped it on its side, sending the liquid straight into the silver sea. A squeal sounded as it splashed against something solid below, and he leaned forward to see what it came from.

Gliding across the gentle waves was a small rowboat covered in soapy water and …

North. The soapy water had just missed her, hitting the front end of the boat instead.

Tik-Tok's chest expanded at the sight of her rowing the last few feet toward the hull. Dressed in a casual, deep green gown, she slid the oars gracefully through the calm water. The sun glinted off her silver hair, making it appear as if she glowed. He blinked a few times, sure that he was imagining things. But she was still there. Still rowing.

"North?" he called out. Was it really her? Why would she leave her family again so soon? Not that it mattered. She was *here*—exactly where he wanted her.

"Hold on," she called back, her cheeks flushed. "This kind of thing always works better in my novels."

A small, amused smile tugged at his lips, and he leaned forward, dangling his arms over the rail. "What is it you're trying to do, my star?"

"Rowing."

"Is there a reason for it?" There was a perfectly good pier she could've walked down to reach *The Temptress*.

"I was trying to be *romantic*," she said with a glare. "Throw me the ladder."

Tik-Tok simply watched her little boat bob along the silver swells. If he left to get the rope ladder, if he took his eyes off her for even a single moment, he worried she might magically disappear. And then what?

Then I would find her and bring her back again.

He shut the idea down immediately, determined to let her make her own choices, and reluctantly stepped away from the rail. It took mere seconds to grab the ladder, hook one end to the rail, and release it. The rope hit the side of the ship with a heavy *thwack*. He chanced a look down again and North began her ascent.

She's really here.

Something nudged at the emptiness inside him. Heat. A pulse. Sparks that weren't quite magic but might as well have been. Every second he waited for her to reach the top of the ladder was torture. He beamed down at her as she climbed. "Seems like you've made a decision."

"Stupid dress," she muttered to herself, ignoring his comment.

As soon as her hands curled over the top of the railing, Tik-Tok grabbed her under the arms and hoisted her over the edge. Chest heaving, she blew a strand of hair from her face and smoothed down the front of the dress. The fabric was covered in small, embossed flowers and gold ribbons crossed through eyelets, holding the panels of her bodice tightly together. Finally, she stopped fussing and met his gaze. "Hi," she said quietly.

"Hi," he replied.

She smiled, holding up his old compass. "I found you."

"I see that." He swallowed hard. "Why, exactly?"

The smile faded, replaced with uncertainty. "You don't seem happy to see me."

"Why are you here?" he asked, voice cracking. He knew, deep down, she'd come back to him, but there was still a new, uncertain feeling inside him. Only hearing her *say* it would alleviate the twisting nerves.

She tilted her head, examining him, and he was suddenly very aware of his appearance. Rumpled clothes, hair tied into a messy knot at his nape, stubble on his cheeks. It was a fucking miracle he'd bothered to bathe that morning.

"I want to stay with you." North bit her bottom lip and looked at him from beneath her lashes. "I came back to be with *you* … if you'll have me."

Fuck. Me. He would do anything to have her. To keep her. She was his North Star, his new purpose, and he would be damned if he let her slip through his fingers again.

Tik-Tok moved to her then, his lips capturing hers. His kiss was desperate and rough, his fingers tangling in her hair. With one swipe of his tongue, he parted her lips, and she let him in. A sigh escaped him as he tasted her sweetness. He felt himself come alive against her mouth as he took from her and gave everything he had in return.

She'd come back *for him*.

Her fingers tugged up the hem of his shirt and he broke away only long enough to pull it over his head. The sensation of her fingers trailing down his chest, over his abdomen, toward the tie on his pants, had him groaning with anticipation. His cock pressed painfully against the fabric, and he tightened his grip on her hair. With his other hand, he pressed against her lower back until she was flush against him.

The feel of her body, even through all the layers, made him moan into her mouth. "North," he breathed.

"I know. I need you too."

Tik-Tok groaned and backed her up against the outer wall of his quarters. With deft fingers, he began untying the front of her bodice. Each tug loosened it a bit more, exposing smooth skin beneath. The curves of her breasts peeked through the ribbons, teasing him. He cupped one of them over the fabric and slipped his thumb inside, running the pad down the small crease of her cleavage. Goosebumps rose on her skin in response, and he licked his lips.

"Wait," she breathed, her eyes widening. "They'll see us."

"Everyone's gone into town." After everything they'd done together, she was still so innocent. It made him impossibly hard knowing he was the only one who had seen her writhe in pleasure—pleasure *he* gave. "They won't be back for hours."

With a final tug on the ribbons, the bodice gaped open, revealing her breasts. The hard, pink tips pressed over the fabric like an offering. His cock throbbed at the sight, his tongue yearning to trail across each slope of her body. Sliding his hand inside her top, he gave the soft flesh a gentle squeeze.

She sighed and arched into his touch. He grinned at her, eyes sparkling, as he sucked a stiff nipple into his mouth, rolling the other between his fingers. North grabbed his head, holding him there as she rolled her hips into his.

"Patience," he murmured, though he was hanging on to his by a thread.

North slipped the tips of her fingers into the band of his pants and tugged him against her. "Gods, you make it hard."

Tik-Tok licked his lips and stared at her, seeing his own lust mirrored in her eyes. A sinful smirk played on his lips as he slowly—so *painfully slowly*—slipped her skirts up around her waist. His breath hitched when he found her bare beneath. "How presumptuous," he teased.

"You forget I rowed here, and it was hot." North panted.

"Uh-huh." He pressed his lips to hers again, breathing in her sweet scent, as he opened his pants to give her full access. When her fingers wrapped around his length, he inhaled sharply, leaning into her further. "Fuck," he said, tearing himself away from her lips. Locking one of her legs around his waist, he lined himself up with her entrance. "Hold on to me."

The moment her hands wrapped around the back of his neck, Tik-Tok pressed inside her warmth. His body quivered with the strength it took to hold back. He wanted more. Harder. Faster. Wanted to *claim* her as his.

"Do you know why I came back here?" she breathed into his ear.

"To be pleasured by me?" he said in a strained voice, thrusting languidly.

North huffed. "No..."

"No," he agreed. "You came back because you love me."

Her eyes locked onto his. "Yes, and I would row back to you again if I had to."

His hips moved faster at her admittance, breaking free of his careful control. "I love you too, my star. More than anything that this world or any other has to offer," he told her. He never thought he would love anyone. Not after his siblings died. But then he found *her.*

One hand gripped North's ass, pulling her forward to meet his every thrust. He reached between her legs, stroking her where she needed it.

"Gods, keep doing that." She leaned into his touch, taking all she needed. As he removed his hand, her heel pressed into his lower back, urging him to let go.

Tik-Tok leaned in to nip at her ear. "Whatever you need." His resistance snapped. He buried his cock as deep as it would go. Again and again and again until North threw her head back, panting his name in a way that showed she cherished him. He gave a low growl as his release followed quickly, but they remained there, chests heaving, for what felt like ages.

"Do you have your axe?" Tik-Tok asked when he finally remembered how to speak.

North raised a brow. "It's in my luggage, which I left in the rowboat. Why?"

Tik-Tok smirked. "I wanted to make sure before I asked if you were okay."

North shimmied a bit until he released her leg and she stood on both feet again. Stretching onto her toes, she gave him a lingering kiss. "You're lucky I'm too exhausted to retrieve it." A huge grin spread across her perfect face.

Tik-Tok leaned his forehead against hers and closed his eyes. "I missed you."

"I'm sorry it took so long to come back." She cupped one side of his face and ran her thumb over his cheekbone. "It turns out that traveling on land without Respen takes forever."

He chuckled. "Why do you think I have a ship?"

She spun and took a few steps away. "You know, after all that rowing, I'm second-guessing my fondness for traveling on ships too."

"*Try* leaving again," he warned playfully, tugging her back to him.

North laughed as she faced him. "I want you." She snuggled in closer, laying her head on his bare chest. "And I want the sea."

Tik-Tok wrapped his arms around her, holding her resolutely. *North* was his family now—not the ship, nor the sea, but her. Contentment washed over him for the first time in his life as he hugged her close. "Then you shall have it."

EPILOGUE

NORTH

TWO MONTHS LATER

"O w!" North squeaked.

"Fuck!" Tik-Tok scooped her off the floor and placed her on the edge of his bed. "This isn't going to work."

"It will if you *practice*." North rolled her eyes as he removed her boot and inspected her foot. "It's fine. It's the tenth time you've done it, so I'm used to it by now."

"The only dancing I want to do involves far less clothing." His lids were hooded as he peered up at her from beneath his thick lashes. "Are you sure I have to behave myself until we return?"

North laughed and leaned forward, cupping his face with her hands. He tilted his head back and closed his eyes as she ran her fingers through his hair before she pressed her forehead to his. Since she'd returned, he continued to challenge her, woo her, love her. And she loved him, more than she could have imagined. He'd wanted to learn more about her life before she came aboard *The Temptress,* so they'd shared their lives and stories while he'd taught her how to steer the ship, raise the sails.

"Keep touching me like that and I can't guarantee you'll look this pristine when we dock," he purred.

Her hair was pinned into two buns atop her head with a few loose tendrils hanging down the front. She wore a long, dark pink dress, its skirts pleated with silver jewels lining its length.

North itched to remove his tunic, his pants, until he was bare before her, but they would have to wait. "After the celebration." She didn't pull back, leaving her forehead kissing his. "Are you ready to properly meet my family?"

Tik-Tok arched a dark brow. "I'm thrilled."

Her grin grew wider. He was doing this for her and wouldn't dare step foot in the Land of Oz otherwise. Crow had sent word that there would be a celebration in the South with food and dancing in honor of North's new brother.

"Have you decided where we're going after we visit Echo and Respen?" Once they left her parents' territory, they would be headed there.

"First, I want to read the romance book that made you think rowing was romantic." Tik-Tok stood and picked up North from the bed. She wrapped her legs around his waist as he carried her over to his desk before he set her on the cool wood. He spread her legs apart and pushed closer to her warmth, causing her breath to catch. "Then I want to watch you peel off each piece of clothing." He kissed the corner of her mouth. "Very slowly." Another kiss to the other side. "I think you know what happens after that."

With a smirk, he leaned in, her body heating. Her heart thumped wildly, and she was about to give in to temptation when his hand brushed past her. A shuffling of papers sounded as he picked up a folded map from his desk. Taking a step back, he opened the map to a picture of all of the Fae Lands and took a seat beside her. Across the yellowed paper were numerous black circles within the seas.

He pointed at each one of the markings near the South. "These are the portals I've learned about over the years that lead to different worlds."

Tik-Tok motioned at the map with his chin for her to choose where she wanted to go. When she'd learned there were more portals she could potentially open and explore, she'd wanted to discover what else was out there. She studied each marking.

"How about this one?" She pointed at a dark circle directly in the middle of the sea.

"As long as it isn't infested with bloodthirsty fiends, then your wish is my command, my star." He paused. "Before we go to your parents, I have one more thing to show you." A crease formed between her brows as he clasped her hand and drew her out the door of their room to the deck. "What? I'm full of surprises."

"Sometimes," North drawled, taking in the salty scent of the air, "those surprises involve long training sessions."

"You did tell me you wanted to learn how to aim." He grinned. "You'll get there eventually."

She hadn't gotten any better, but she would never stop trying. The extra time spent with him was worth it.

Tik-Tok stopped in front of the handrail and drew off his glove. His golden appendage flickered beneath the suns' rays. He peeled off the magic ring he'd placed on her finger once before.

"Give me your hand." Tik-Tok cocked his head, the edges of his lips tugging upward.

North held out her hand and he slowly slid the ring onto her middle finger. She watched as the band changed from silver to the purest of golds.

"There," he said, locking his gaze on hers. "In case you ever need it, while my heart still beats, you have my magic."

"What if I want to share my magic with you instead?" She peered up at him, blinking, her chest feeling fuller than it ever had.

Tik-Tok stood behind her and entwined their fingers, his nose nuzzling her neck. "You already have."

THERE'S NO PLACE
LIKE OZ

Did you enjoy Faeries of Oz?

Authors always appreciate reviews, whether long or short.

After Oz are you read to enter Wonderland? Check out Rav, the Vampires in Wonderland prequel!

You think you know Wonderland. But you don't.

Imogen, the Queen of Hearts, is known for taking the hearts of those who betray her, including her servants. Her king, Rav, ventures to the mortal world to lure in new prey to replace their dwindling help. One bite, one simple exchange of her blood is all it will take for a mortal to become one of them. And this time, Rav chooses a girl named Alice.

ALSO FROM CANDACE ROBINSON

Wicked Souls Duology
Vault of Glass
Bride of Glass

Marked by Magic Duology
The Bone Valley
Merciless Stars

Cruel Curses Trilogy
Clouded By Envy
Veiled By Desire
Shadowed By Despair

Untamed Darkness Series
Dearest Clementine: Dark and Romantic Monstrous Tales
These Vicious Thorns: Tales of the Lovely Grim
Savage Delights: Two Dark Tales

Cursed Hearts Duology
Lyrics & Curses
Music & Mirrors

And Then There Was Silence
Her Cruel Dahlias
Hearts Are Like Balloons
Between the Quiet

ALSO FROM AMBER R. DUELL

The Dark Dreamer Trilogy
Dream Keeper
Dark Consort
Night Warden

Forgotten Gods
Fragile Chaos

When Stars Are Bright
The Prince's Wing

Vampires in Wonderland
Rav (Short Story Prequel)
Maddie
Chess
Knave

Once Upon A Wicked Villain Series
Spindle of Sin
Forest of Carnage

Faeries of Oz Series
Lion (Short Story Prequel)
Tin
Crow
Ozma
Tik-Tok

Acknowledgments

Thank you, dear readers, for sticking with us through the series! We'd like to thank our families and friends for supporting us. To Amber H. and Elle, thank you two for everything you do! And to the amazing people who helped us with this story—Tracy, Vic, Jenny, Jerica, Lindsay, Ann, and Gladys.

I hoped you enjoyed our fae version or Oz. These characters will remain with us forever. And if you have a favorite character, we'd love to know who it is!

About the Authors

Candace Robinson spends her days consumed by words and hoping to one day find her own DeLorean time machine. Her life consists of avoiding migraines, admiring Bonsai trees, watching classic movies, and living with her husband and daughter in Texas—where it can be forty degrees one day and eighty the next.

Amber R. Duell was born and raised in a small town in Central New York. While it will always be home, she's constantly moving with her husband and two sons as a military wife. She does her best writing in the middle of the night, surviving the daylight hours with massive amounts of caffeine.

www.ingramcontent.com/pod-product-compliance
Lightning Source LLC
Chambersburg PA
CBHW061846310726
48972CB00004B/910